DEVIL'S TOR

by

David Lindsay

I0742955

Published by Bookship, 2018, 2023.
First published by G. P. Putnam's Sons, 1932.

ISBN 978-1-9996269-3-8

Cover © Murray Ewing 2018, incorporating images from Wikimedia Commons and Pixaby.com.

This novel is a work of fiction. The names, characters, incidents and locations portrayed in the story are entirely imaginary. Any resemblance to actual persons, living or dead, or events, organisations, companies and other bodies, is coincidental.

Devil's Tor

BOOKSHIP

Publisher's Note

Devil's Tor was first published in 1932, and some of the views it presents are a product of its time. This novel is being made available by the publishers because of its interest to readers of David Lindsay's work. Its publication does not represent an endorsement by the publisher of the views or ideas the author and his characters present.

Contents

I

The Thunderstorm

No sooner had they quitted the sunken lane, with its high banks and overshadowing trees, and entered upon the long stretch of open road, bordered at first by walls of piled stones, but soon running unconfined for mile upon mile across the rising moor, than the full menace of the advancing storm struck them. The young girl Ingrid Fleming turned her head towards her male companion with an inquiring look, as by a sort of sympathy they came to a dubious standstill.

"What shall we do? Go back?"

The man gazed doubtfully upwards and around, at the same time pulling off his cap to pass a hand over his heated forehead. It was a swelteringly hot evening in early August. Ingrid noted his high, bald, domelike temples with that almost imperceptible little frown of calm displeasure which his aspect always seemed to summon to the upper part of her face. Something in the colouring and person of this new-found cousin of hers secretly antagonised her; the ensemble of his thin intellectual features, his tropical bronze, his long, drooping red moustaches, the fierce blue eyes. It was not that he was ugly, for she even rather scorned beauty in a man, but their blood, their race, was somehow antipathetic. She, though English born, of English parents, was accustomed to insist in her mind on the distant Norse descent which she fancied was her peculiar personal heritage, whereas Hugh Drapier, like his father before him, an outsider to the family, was obviously a Gael, a Highland Scot, whose nameless ancestors had been unbreeched savages when Kolbiorn the Marshal, from whom the Colbornes (her own kin) derived, was already subduing peoples and framing laws under the great King Olaf Trygvesson, nearly a thousand years ago. The pedigree was in black and white, and undisputed. Thus their cousinship was nil in actuality, and if she genuinely wanted to admire his choice of a wild adventurous life, and to respect his modest reticence in talking about it, this instinctive repugnance to his breed invariably interposed itself. He had only been with them a week, but she already longed for him to go away again, and leave them to their unconstrained routine. At least he had paid her no attentions; for that she was thankful. In fact, this was the very first walk they had had together, nor would she have come even now had he not expressed a wish to be shown Devil's Tor.

"I certainly think we're in for it if we keep on," was his hesitating reply to her question.

"Then we'll turn?"

"We may as well. Your mother——"

"I'm thinking of you. I go out in all sorts of weather, and personally am just as ready to go on as back."

"We can always go there another time."

"As you please."

"I think we'll funk it. Not much sense in getting ourselves wet through for nothing, apart from the thunder and lightning."

The girl gave a twisted little smile. "If you're studying my poor clothes, I assure you they've already been through many a drenching. Yours appear fairly seasoned. But if you're alarmed at the prospect of thunder, I'll do whatever you wish."

"Presumably we could find shelter on the Tor itself?"

"Of a kind, I suppose."

"How far is it now?"

"About twenty-five minutes."

"We might chance it."

"Very well," said Ingrid.

She was simply and gracefully dressed all in white, in an old jumper frock, with hard-wearing stockings, low-heeled shoes, and a small hat, close-fitting to her head of fine flaxen half-long hair. Her slender ungloved right hand carried a man's ash stick. Her indifference to clothes, with that complete apathy as to Hugh's approval of her person, had permitted her to slip into her everyday tramping outfit without a moment's conscious hesitation; and her cousin noticed nothing, except that she looked very attractive.

Her form was long, slight and lissom, with straight slim legs.

Yet if she had nothing on to spoil, and on the other hand was quite unthrilled by this excursion with such a companion, the balance was still not so nicely suspended that she could ignore her own half-malicious pleasure at his decision. An unpleasant storm threatened, and somewhere near the surface of her mind hovered the vague cynical desire to pit her resolution against Hugh's, to make the test which would maintain the more coolness in a disagreeable emergency; he, a naturally excitable man, toughened and disciplined by his foreign experiences, or she, a mere shielded girl, handicapped in everything except her race. Really, however, it wasn't spitefulness, and she wished him no humiliation; he would of course smile at their thunder, as at the discomfort of a soaking. Perhaps then she merely wanted to prove to him that she could despise both, against his expectation— though that would be setting a value on his opinion, which she hoped she was equally despising. So it must be that the prospect of their serving as moving targets to unnerving vicious electric discharges on the open moor was tempting her subconscious imagination with the picture of a relief of reality from the irritating monotony and conventionality of his deadweight society. He might be roused to some kind of appearance of life; or, if he was not, she need not continue so aware of his proximity. Careless of analysing her soul more closely, she left it at that. Accordingly, after another brief extension of the pause of reluctance on Drapier's part, who guessed nothing of what was passing in the quaint kaleidoscope of his frigid young cousin's mind, they started to walk on again.

Overhead towering masses of black, purple, pink and orange cloud were thrown together confusedly, through the narrow rifts of which small patches of blue sky were visible. The sun was hidden, and only in the far distance was a section of the low-lying country glorified by its rays. In the south-east the sky was increasingly venomous in appearance. The upper clouds were travelling against the wind, and suddenly the first low, sustained growl broke the oppressive silence of the moorland. Some cattle, further down, had left off feeding, and were glancing around them apprehensively. The long panoramic line of tors behind had become black and bleak, like a silhouette against the livid sky.

"I expect some of the tropical lightning displays can be quite terrifying?" queried Ingrid presently, the spirit of speech moving her, as they strode along together. "That, and high mountains, I should love to see."

Instead of responding to her immediately, he took a moment to remark, as he had so often already remarked during his stay, the odd note of inaccessibility safeguarding her approaches to him. For it appeared to be for him alone. She could be warm enough to Uncle Magnus and entirely gracious and affectionate with her mother, but up went this automatic protective fence so soon as ever she needed to pass a word with himself. Was his visit annoying her? Or was it that she wasn't used to strange men and was shy in their company? That was hardly likely; she had a quiet self-possession that was surely incompatible with awkwardness, while her exceptional good looks must have brought her the sufficient experience. Was she piqued by what might pass for a certain boorishness in his manner towards her? He had never wittingly been rude. The vanity of a vain girl could not be tormenting her, for, if he had seen anything of her character at all, it was certainly too dignified and high-minded for that kind of vulgarity; besides, particular attentions could scarcely be expected of him, fifteen years stood between them, she was still a child and he already nearly a middle-aged man. So he concluded that it was just the reverse, and that she had set herself to *dis*courage anything in the nature of a too warm intimacy. She might be personally disliking him, or she might be fearful that he would snatch an ell for every inch offered. Whatever the source of her mysterious chilliness, it was sparing him much bother. His mood was all wrong for a sex *camaraderie*. His preoccupations were insistent, he was half in another world, he needed much private time, and he had also a special matter to attend to down here. The present stand-off relations were best for both. Neither had he ever had a great deal to do with women. This he knew about them, that feminine friendship was apt to be, not a stationary, but a progress-ive condition.

"Would you rather not talk?" asked the girl, with the merest glance at his profile, and he thought that either she was extremely simple or more than a little dry.

"I beg your pardon, I was lost. You were inquiring——?"

"You must have been in most countries of the world. Which would you say has the worst storms?"

"I don't know. In travelling much one rather takes leave of the comparative sense. The earth becomes more homogeneous. I've seen intensely vivid lightning in Europe, Asia, Africa and Amer-ica. Happen where it will, it's always a nasty phenomenon."

"Even in England."

"Surely, since persons continue to be killed by it here, as an annual toll to Nature."

"But you of course have no fear of it?"

"No, in a way. Well, I've so much fear, that if I were a savage instead of a civilised man, at this moment I'd cut for shelter as the safest and most sensible course."

"If you feel like that, we can still turn back."

Drapier smiled. "I'm the civilised man.

"And that's why," he proceeded, "I've small faith in half the tales of the ancient heroes and demi-gods. The nearer to the beginning of the human race, the more untutored the emotions. Don't we know that Hector, the bravest of the brave, was chased by Achilles three times round the walls of Troy?"

"He was an Oriental."

"No, nearer to the eolithic wild man of the woods. Why should he superfluously get himself cut down by a bigger champion when he had a pair of legs? My dear girl, courage is no more than another name for the fear of the mass of cultured opinion. People are fearful in the second degree; they're afraid of being thought afraid. Whether it represents a true advance of the moral soul, I know not."

"An advance of morality, undoubtedly. Only, morality in a sense is so poisonous, Hugh. It will allow no other fine things to grow under the shadow of its branches."

"What things?"

"Morality is the imposition of standards, the standards are necessarily those of the highest contemporary public opinion, and so everyone either sincerely conforms, or makes a show of conforming, or becomes an outcast. But that has not been the way of the great. They have chosen rather to conform to the greatest of their own souls. That is a tremendously different thing. A man that faces death, not because it is expected of him, but because he knows how to despise life—that is my idea of courage."

"And for a moral man that's impossible?"

"A moral man, I suppose, is thinking of the world all the time, while the natural laugher at death is holding the world very cheap. There have been whole races like it. You should read the Sagas."

"Well, we aren't without such men even to-day. Take your racing motorist and your long-distance aviator. No one will accuse them of holding life too dear."

Ingrid shook her head.

"No, you don't understand. You are talking of record-breaking and sports, but I'm talking of men who would despise that sort of thing equally, except perhaps as a useful exercise in hardihood."

"If you're referring to the Northmen, they had a pretty fair notion of honour."

"They honoured courage. The coward was held despicable, and was given the name, *nithing*. But the courage they honoured had nothing to do with the fear of opinion."

The girl's quiet intensity reduced Drapier to gravity and silence. After a few moments he sought to round off the debate by affirming simply:

"However it may be, we can't get back into the egg."

"No doubt I have been born in the wrong age," returned Ingrid. "Yet to be born out of one's right age gives another angle; and, I imagine, more depth."

"You are certainly a new kind of girl to me."

To that she made no answer; and already regretted having disclosed so much of her spirit to one not framed to comprehend it. So both now held their peace, and during the respite which followed they quitted the road for the moor.

Ascending the sharp slope obliquely in a westerly direction, they had the parched peaty soil under their feet. Ingrid found without difficulty the narrow track through the broom and heather she was looking for, and it was plain that she was a competent guide, though the height for which they were making still kept out of sight. Drapier's long sinewy legs measured the ground behind her like a pair of compasses, without effort. Busy with her thoughts, she had unconsciously put on speed, until her breathlessness forced her to slacken again.

The evening had grown darker, as though twilight were already falling, and at the very instant that she halted altogether, to recover herself while facing Hugh and taking a survey of the country behind, a flash of lightning stabbed the sky, perhaps a couple of miles away, over the hills to the south-east beyond the road they had left. After an interval, a long roll of thunder succeeded. The sky overhead seemed to gather together. Ingrid regarded her cousin with narrowed eyes, to ascertain how he reacted to the warning.

"There's something awfully mysterious and grand about approaching darkness," she half-soliloquised, when the sound had quite died down. "My favourite goddess in Greek mythology is Nyx—Night—the daughter of Chaos, and by that very relationship so much nearer to the terrible beginning of things than the bright Olympian deities. Had I been a wealthy Athenian woman in classical times, I'd have dedicated a magnificent temple to Nyx. And it should have had a score of great chambers leading from one into the other until the very heart was reached; and the outermost chamber should have been gloomy, and the next darker still, and so on until the absolute interior should have been pitchy night itself. And there, in that night, I would have sacrificed, without lamps, candles or torches."

Drapier's wonder at his cousin increased.

"You read a lot?" he asked.

"In the early fables. They are my Scripture."

"For their poetry?"

"No, they're so deep and full of symbolic meaning."

She went on. "I honestly can't warm to a single God; the conception seems to me so hollow. Perhaps it runs in the family. I was glancing through one of Uncle's books the other day, and came across a passage where he insists that the notion of a separate divinity for each phase of human experience, besides accounting for a host of contradictions in life that the Jews and Arabs discreetly shelved, has also an infinitely more respectable origin than that of a sole Creator, Despot and Judge, first making a world, then commanding it to be despised; first making men and women, then punishing them for their defects. The old conquering Aryans—the Greeks and the men of the North—arrived with their freedom-loving intellects at the gods. The pitiless, mercenary Semites, with their tribal instincts and subordination of every fine feeling to the passion for gain, temporal or eternal, they arrived at the one God, from whom all favours were to be expected, on the express condition of obedience. Then further on he expands the statement—but I'm boring you?"

"No, please finish."

Ingrid was vaguely annoyed and perplexed by her own unintended loquacity. She hardly ever unburdened her mind so freely, and especially to this man, of all persons, she would have believed it impossible. She hated to think that he might be regarding all her words as a display of learning. She must be fey. Indeed, underneath all, a very indistinct presentiment was troubling her that something might immediately be going to happen in her life, to interrupt the smooth uneventfulness of its course hitherto. Her voice therefore was lowered to a new tone of dullness and anxiety as she scamped the rest of what she had to say.

"He maintains that the mental tendency to reduce all the natural and supernatural particulars of the universe to a single Principle is identical with the tendency to *possess*. The mind is single, therefore whatever it is thoroughly to understand must be single too; but to understand and to possess are the same. So this double tendency is essentially appropriate to the Semitic genius.

Whereas a multiplicity of gods can *not* be understood or explained by the human intellect; consequently is never to be possessed, but must be freely and grandly accepted by the generous soul as a mighty overarching fact existing for its own sake, not for the sake of humanity. And all this was well-known to the Greeks, and the Aryan Brahmins, and the northern peoples of Europe. I'm afraid I can't fill in the idea any better than that. You should read Uncle Magnus for yourself."

"The theory seems rather to ignore Christianity, which, in the present state of the world, it isn't very easy to ignore. However, as you say, I must read his books some time."

"Though perhaps there would be little in them for you."

"I'm too fast stuck in the old views?"

"It is for you to say. But what I mean is that—well, probably climbing needle-rocks in the Himalayas, and crossing rotten bridges over foaming torrents, would be more in your line than pondering abstruse theological and metaphysical problems. I intend nothing unkind."

"I expect you're right, allowing for the exaggeration."

"Then why have you come home? What is there in England for a man like you?"

"One has to come home sometimes."

"I fail to see why, unless for business reasons. You've no ties here."

But Drapier, no longer replying, stood resting his hand heavily on the crook of his stick, squarely facing the direction of the storm, his whole attitude that of a simple, thoughtful, impressed man, in no haste to remove himself from the spectacle of awe and beauty, but also on that very account indisposed to proceed with a discussion of petty personal affairs. Ingrid nevertheless watched him curiously for a moment, as though she were not wholly satisfied with that fixity of absent regard as a substitute for speech.

"Shall we walk on?" she asked then, not choosing to press him, but feeling more and more sure that he must have brought down with him some disagreeable business that up to the present he had not found the courage to present.

"Yes, we had better."

As they resumed their advance, with Ingrid still in front, another flash crossed the sky, very much more vivid than the last had been, and the interval between it and the associated muffled crash of thunder was noticeably briefer. Drapier saw his cousin glance sideways down at her bare neck, as if doubtfully. He gnawed at the end of his moustache.

"I fear your mother will be feeling wretchedly uneasy about you, though."

"It won't look so bad from the windows of a house." She did not turn further round for that cool answer.

"What do you say, shall we scamper back?" he tempted her. "We may still have time before the worst comes on."

"We have less than a mile now, and shall probably get wet through either way."

"All right! though candidly I think we're behaving like a pair of lunatics. Just look at the sky behind you now!"

"I saw it before."

"As long as you acknowledge it for a caprice."

"It is only one of your Asiatic expeditions in miniature. You seek your dangers on the grand scale, I have to snatch mine when and how I can. Why should you grudge me reality for once?"

"Women have certainly changed. And I am sufficiently old-fashioned and out of the swim to be continually surprised by the fact. You must pardon me if I have seemed to wish to patronise you."

"I believe the present generation of girls is different. My own inspiration hardly comes from anything in the air of to-day. I detest sports, and haven't the least desire to ape men."

"What *are* your interests?"

Still without turning round to him, she gave a light shrug. "Walking, reading, and dreaming, I think."

"Yet you will marry."

"I may," she returned, half-smiling, though he could not see that, "but it will be a special sort of man."

"I wonder if you will allow me to inquire what sort?"

"Someone who can understand my queernesses, I suppose—and who has compensating queernesses of his own."

"Are you so queer?"

"My own impression is that I am little else than a bundle of intuitions, Hugh."

"Of what nature?"

"I am dreadfully passive. I fancy I may be mediumistic."

Why was he so anxious to keep the conversation turned upon herself? Somehow this walk had quite finally converted her to her mother's obsession that he was in financial difficulties, and had come to borrow a sum from Uncle Magnus. The latter, of course, was suspecting nothing; he disliked Hugh too much to take any notice of his embarrassment of manner. But the worry of the affair was miserably harassing her mother, while Ingrid herself was already growing steadily more indignant with Hugh for keeping them so on the rack. It was lamentable that he had not as much moral courage as physical. Now, having him alone to herself, away from everybody and all possible interruptions, she felt that she would like to encourage him to a confession; and perhaps, if the talk led anywhere near it, she would still venture it, though nothing of the sort had been in her mind even a short half-hour ago. Only, she could not *lead* the talk to it, for that was a manner of hypocrisy outside her range. She was too lacking in the arts of the world.

Then she found that she was doing it, independently of her volition, for, tired of having her own life challenged, she was now challenging his.

"And when will *you* marry, Hugh?"

"I? Never now. I've left it too long."

"Far older men than you get married. But perhaps you've an antipathy to women?"

"I don't know. I have sometimes thought that I have, but then again I have realised that it is not antipathy so much as ignorance. My mode of life has deprived me of the necessary experience of women. They put fear into me. I except your mother and yourself."

"I imagine we *are* your nearest?"

"Absolutely."

"Apart from marriage, women make very good friends, Hugh. Mother likes you. Why are you so reticent with her? She is sure you have something on your mind."

Drapier was silent and reflective for a moment or two, wrinkling his forehead.

"Did she say so?" he asked.

"I have no authority to speak on her behalf." Ingrid halted and faced round. "However, since I've begun the topic I may as well end it, so that it need never be referred to again between us. She is privately rather distressed about this visit of yours. She's afraid you are going to worry Uncle over some business proposal or other. The prospect is seriously disturbing her, because during the last year he has become very much frailer. The doctor has advised us both to spare him all we can. You do understand?"

"I suspected something of the kind. I am glad you told me— though, for your reassurance, I am definitely not down here on any financial business whatsoever."

"Then I'm glad I spoke, too. Mother will be immensely relieved."

"I'll have a chat with her."

Ingrid turned once more, and the advance proceeded. She fell into dubiousness. Why should he want to chat with her mother, when the bare statement to herself would have sufficed? Also the qualification "financial" was quite remarkable. It could mean only that he had other business to discuss, not concerning money. What could it possibly be? He had not been near them for twenty years, so why should he suddenly take it into his head to invade their Dartmoor privacy? . . .

A terrific blue fork lit up the sky, appearing almost immediately overhead, though the deafening peal of thunder that succeeded it was still tardy. A few heavy drops fell, but soon ceased, and Nature again seemed to wait. A little breeze sprang up, but the air remained disagreeably hot and close. The evening grew darker and darker. The long hillside they mounted offered not the least cover, and they instinctively hastened their footsteps.

"We shall see Devil's Tor across the valley a few yards further on," announced Ingrid, always in front.

"Whence its name, by the way?"

"The pile on top has a more or less definite resemblance to a diabolical face."

"It has no history?"

"I've never been able to discover that it has. Though in my own mind I'm sure it has had one, and perhaps a very extraordinary one."

"Why, what do you go upon?"

"Experiences valid for myself alone, Hugh. Fancies. I often come up here by myself, just for the sake of dreaming strange dreams."

"And what do such dreams tell you?"

"That the hill was known very anciently. First there must have been the Stone Age men, who perhaps offered magic sacrifices and worked wonders on it. Then there followed the Britons of the centuries immediately before Christ—peatmen, foresters, and the like—to whom the traditions of a haunting had been handed down, and who gave it the name of an evil spirit. And afterwards arrived the English-speaking Saxons, who inherited the traditions, but translated the name to that of the only evil spirit in their christianised cosmogony. Perhaps now you will begin to understand the queer extravagance of some of my intuitions."

"I find the imagination quite a reasonable one, if it goes no further."

"If I, a decently-educated girl of this sophisticated twentieth century, can sense uncanny presences on Devil's Tor, wouldn't it be far easier for the primitive moormen, having the sun and wind and stars in their bones, and their intelligences still uncorrupted by the ready-made wisdom of the books and the parrot-cries of the crowd? Maybe our inadequate modern occult faculties no more than represent some atrophied sixth sense, then rich and splendid. I mean, just as there have been mammoths, mastodons, megatheriums, so there may have been seers. And those seeing men must have had human predecessors as mentally remote from them as they themselves are from us. That kind of journey back staggers one."

"I don't scoff," said Drapier. "Indeed, I've spent too much of my life amongst mountains not to be well acquainted with their weird influence. It's one of the multitude of things a townsman remains ignorant of. I really think I do begin to approach you."

He had in mind how prolonged lingerings in solitary high places were wont to conjure up the phantom voices and sudden irrational panics. A nervous young girl would be peculiarly sensitive to the combination of loneliness, silence, wild Nature, skies, and altitude. Of course she would dream. The frame and content of her dreaming signified nothing. Only, she seemed to have a preference for this particular height for her rambles, and was that chance, or did it express a quality in the place? He was quite curious to see the Tor. She might even possess the second-sight, which was an authentic psychic gift. In the Scotch Highlands it still survived, while in the black-wintered, troll-ridden Norway of old it must have been so common as almost to pass notice. The whole family regarded Ingrid as the typical Norse Colborne.

The more she spoke with him, the more puzzling and interesting he was finding her, and that coldness he had fancied in her seemed already like a misunderstanding of half-acquaintance, she had so opened herself to him during the walk. Her conversation had the ideality and originality of a man's. There was something to give him pause in nearly every one of her utterances.

He admired the dignity of her light motions and the graceful sweep of her long slender limbs, as she went forward over the uneven ground. He also admired the fineness and colour, of palest gold, of the curling fall of her otherwise smooth hair, clinging to her nape to emphasise its purity of whiteness. In the remembered oval of her face the features for delicacy and length had surely attained the precise focus of beauty, between mere prettiness on the one hand and unpleasing strength on the other. Her long mouth was strange and lovely; it might be passionate, but he could not imagine her sexual. Her grey-blue eyes, in their perfect orbits, were the hardest of all to decipher. Superficially they struck one as tranquil, quiet and simple, but then something waiting in them began to appear, and at last one might suspect that they were essentially not in the present at all. They might be the eyes of a prophetess, going about her everyday jobs. It gave a marvellous latent power to the whole face.

And her true nature was so very much a paradox to him. Such a fair, clever and favoured young only daughter of a well-to-do household might far too easily be spoilt; and Ingrid appeared unspoilt. Her amiability at all times and unquestioning obedience to the practical suggestions of the others in the same house were even quite extraordinary for any girl. She also helped her mother in everything as a dutiful and feminine-souled home-staying daughter should. She did it all seemingly without effort or self-conflict, yet it could not be her character. Probably she was content to conserve her strength for the later bigger things of life; and perhaps that explained the quiet inward expectation of her eyes.

Biologically singular it was to note how she had reverted to the pure Nordic type, which had totally skipped her mother above her in the direct line; while Dick Fleming, the father, a capital good fellow, had been a true-blue Britisher. Ingrid's race was in her complexion, the fairest and most unblemished ever seen. Certainly the moist, cool, fragrant Dartmoor winds and mists must have been kind to it, still no mere Saxon blonde could have possessed such a skin even to start with. It was the legacy of long ages of snow and ice. She was twenty-two, and, chit-chat apart, must soon think seriously of marriage.

Helga, her mother, was his first-cousin. Her wedded life had been of the shortest, for Dick, her husband (a small, nimble, fresh-complexioned chap with a pointed little beard; Drapier had met him) had broken his neck in the hunting-field when Ingrid was still hardly out of her alphabet. Ever since, Helga had kept house for Magnus Colborne, her uncle and his, who presumably would leave mother and daughter all his worldly goods when he should depart. And he was already past seventy, and to all appearance going fast downhill. No doubt Helga had something of her own put by, but it was quite understandable why she should prefer a soft home with this temporary sacrifice of independence to a grind-along on insufficient means. Already she was the virtual mistress of the place. No one could grudge Helga Fleming the highest good fortune.

A sudden hail-shower began, slackened awhile, then without warning descended as a tropical sheet of hissing white rain, instantaneously drenching them through and through. Ingrid stopped, turned to laugh at Hugh, flung the wet from the locks over her ears, and, with a gay exclamation he failed to catch, started again to run up the hill, only a few yards of which could be seen in front of them. It was like the end of the world. To hasten their panic, a fierce blaze of violet light flashed out from the sky just above, illuminating the rain and the moor with its enduring flicker; then, before it ceased, there sounded a sharp, sickening, tearing noise, as of cloth being violently rent, followed immediately by a deafening and appalling crash which left them aghast. The rain affected them as if full of electricity, while Drapier fancied that he detected the smell of singeing. Perhaps a part of the turf had been struck and burned. When the downpour had moderated somewhat, a cool breeze seemed to spring up, but it was deceptive, the air continued as close and oppressive as before. The storm, far from having exhausted itself, had hardly yet begun.

For company's sake they now pressed forward side-by-side.

"We're not likely to get a nearer one than that," Drapier encouraged his cousin.

"Did it stop you too?"

"It was certainly a vivid moment."

"And I suppose you are going to overwhelm me for dragging you out here!"

"Not at all, for I was a party."

"No, you were complaisant, I was perverse, and some demon in me has led us both by the noses. However, why worry? We can't get any wetter, so let's take our ease now."

He accommodated himself to her reduced step, and almost at once Ingrid pointed her finger ahead.

"There's Devil's Tor."

II

Under the Devil's Head

The rain had nearly ceased, but the immense lowering black clouds above augured nothing good. The moor immediately around was intensely green and purple. On the left, across the valley, the hills rose dark and uncoloured, but with all their details very clear. Where they terminated, however (the end of a mighty buttress set in the lowland plain, sloping downwards to the sea), a magic picture was afforded of the soft distant landscape, all localised rain-showers and areas of shadow, wisps of moor-mist, and isolated shafts of sunlight emphasising the fields and woods from behind gold-rimmed cumulus vapour masses. The heart of the storm was crawling up ominously from the south-east, across the heights which recommenced still further to the left, directly behind them.

Just as Ingrid pointed and spoke, a dazzling fork suspended itself in mid-sky straight ahead, enduring without change like a phenomenon while they could count. Its lower extremity was behind a rocky peak of no great height, but so singular in shape and of such sinister unrelieved blackness that Drapier, as he sighted it, involuntarily came to a standstill.

The hill rose up sharply no more than a few hundred yards away, just round the shoulder of the slope they were traversing. It was a steep, imperfectly-symmetrical sugar-loaf, with a truncated top, carrying an upright granite mass that had become strangely weathered into the rude form of a human, or inhuman, head, supported by a narrower neck-stem. The rock, which had been

segmented presumably by exposure to the elements during countless ages, was about thirty feet high, and projected from the
perpendicular at a dangerous-looking angle. The overhanging side
was that which contained the so-styled Devil's face. Seen in
profile from where they stood, it appeared a true gargoyle. The
nose shot forward, the mouth was a deep black cleft between two
flat layers of granite, while the one cavernous eye visible was
represented by a circular hollow in the rock, showing where water
was accustomed to accumulate. It was a grinning and unpleasant
natural statue, carved by time and accident, which seemed all the
while to be meditating a plunge to earth.

Some seconds after the lightning had vanished, there came a
long crackling cannonade in the sky, ending in a loose and hollow
roar, as though a mighty load of solid matter were being discharged from above. Manifestly the storm was now all round
them. The rain commenced to descend again heavily.

"At least you've now seen it at its characteristic best," laughed
Ingrid, as they resumed the way. "That fork surely completed the
picture like a positive improvisation of genius. For five seconds it
was a real Witches' Heath—and now alas! never can it be the
same to me again. Hereafter it will always lack that never-to-be-
repeated *coup de théâtre!*"

Her cousin remarked how her spirits were risen with their
experience.

"But its name seems quite intelligible from the shape of that
pile, without adducing the more fantastic derivation," he suggested thoughtfully.

"I suppose so."

"But you stick to your intuition of a strangeness there?"

"I must."

"Of course you have run up against nothing tangible?"

"No, Hugh. It is all feelings." She was grave again. "No doubt
you will go on believing with all the rest that that monument is
natural, even after I have assured you that I'm sure it is artificial.
But it is my firm faith."

"Made by men?"

She replied by a nod, and he asked again:

"Has the point ever been discussed?"

"Not that I'm aware of. Why should it be, when there are scores of certainly natural similar formations all over Dartmoor?"

"Still unsupported intuition, or have you a reason for your belief?"

"I simply feel it is so."

"You suggest a tomb?" Drapier tugged at his moustache. They were now always walking side-by-side.

"Yes, a tomb."

"Since you have this conviction, and live more or less on the spot, can't you influence excavation?"

"I don't personally know any archaeologists, and should never dream of writing to the newspapers on any subject. Besides, who would pay any attention to a girl's fantasies?"

"Does the intuition go further?"

"Perhaps. But I don't think we'll speak of it any longer."

Then she turned to eye him attentively.

"Am I mistaken, Hugh, or is my innocent suggestion interesting you more than it should? What really put it in your head to insist on coming out here to Devil's Tor?"

He smiled evasively. "You're a dangerous person! You are looking for tombs in me now."

"Because I think you may be rather psychic too. And you may have heard something about the hill from somebody else. I am not imagining that that has brought you all the way down from London."

"It certainly hasn't; since, until the place was spoken of by your mother at dinner yesterday, I was quite unaware of its existence on the map. Hills are always very magnetic to me, this one happened to be named as within easy reach, I had the additional inducement of your proffered company, and so—here I am."

"Then this time I have made a bad guess."

"Perhaps you craved a spiritual associate."

"Oh, no, I am perfectly content to be lonely in my dreams."

"The snub is deserved. And in any case I am the worst of

companions in all departments of experience. Loneliness is my proper mantle throughout; not in dreams only."

"Because you're a man, and it is possible. A girl or woman only belongs half to herself. The other and larger half of her belongs to her circumstances."

"It is your sex's good-nature."

"Or weakness. We have too much tenderness of sympathy, even with people that we know are far from deserving it."

"Or else you would not be women; and that would be lamentable," he rejoined. "I fancy, though, that you will make an excellent wife."

"Why, Hugh?" She blushed a little, beneath the rain-drops standing on her face.

"You seem to have an ideal temperament for calm seas. Great tolerance, and very little rebelliousness."

"I don't know that I shall ever marry; but, if I do, I shall always insist on my husband's being his greatest, and he may find that the worst of all possible trials in a wife."

"Then you must be sure and make a happy choice."

Thus he had succeeded in covering over her questioning of his true motive in visiting Devil's Tor. Indeed, with the best intention in the world, he could not well have replied to her both truthfully and satisfactorily, for all was still dark even to himself. But Ingrid, on her part, was so far from the cynical habit that she could acknowledge her blunder and freely accept his version of the initiation of the jaunt without a reserved thought in the background of her mind. Her intuitions flattered no pride in her, and she recognised that some of them might be imperfectly captured. She believed him, and they continued walking on in easy companionship, but there was no more conversation between them for a while.

The evening grew so dusky that Drapier took out his watch to confirm the hour; but it was still barely half-past eight, by summer time. They had begun to descend towards the dip that lay between them and the Tor's base. Another brilliant flash was accompanied by an almost simultaneous crash of thunder, which seemed to shake the ground beneath them, the heavy rumble continuing to reverberate among the hills for at least half a minute. The rain again left off.

Ingrid glanced round at her cousin, with fearless candour in her eyes.

"I've been puzzling over that last remark of yours, Hugh. Was it meant dryly? Has mother been saying anything to you?"

He remembered what he had said.

"She only told me that you are *not* engaged, if you mean that. I want to pry into no secrets."

"Well, you are one of the family, and I should like you to be able to put right any floating rumours about me—not that I expect any outsider will ever mention me to you. There is an artist—Peter Copping—who comes to see us quite a lot when he's down here. As a matter of fact, he's due down from town to-morrow, and you may have the pleasure of meeting him. I want you *not* to couple his name with mine. It would offend him terribly. We are only quite good friends."

"The right of dictation is yours. And I shall be happy to meet him; but where is he putting up?"

"He occupies a studio-cottage of his own at the end of the village."

"You have no special taste for Art, however?" questioned Drapier, after a pause of meditation.

"He is friendly with us all. His father and Uncle were business partners."

"I shall look forward to seeing him," repeated her cousin courteously; and that interlude too was over. Their conversation seemed a succession of little back-doors. Ingrid flushed, as she hastened to change the subject.

"And what are your plans for after you have left us?"

"I shall get back to London."

"And then?"

"I can't tell. At present I'm hardly in a position to arrange for too long ahead."

She wondered why not.

"Presumably the *wanderlust* will still take you? You are just back from Tibet; where next?"

"Truly, I seem to care less for England each time I come back to it. The towns are abominably stuffy and over-thronged, while such scenery even as this can't hold a candle to the real open spaces of the globe."

"But you can keep away; and that is everything. I think I should regard you, for that one circumstance, as the very luckiest person of my acquaintance, except that for some reason or other you don't impress me as being frightfully happy with it all. Are you?"

"I have had pretty good luck so far; but happiness is always an ambiguous term. The merest trifle can destroy it, while a fortune may not bring it. It is surely best not to seek it at all."

She understood that he was unwilling to speak out, and so said no more.

They then crossed the tiny rivulet which, descending from the upper moors, marked the line of cleavage between the two hills; and at once started to climb the wet, rock-strewn lower slopes of Devil's Tor itself. The wilderness of loose boulders and stones, flung haphazard in every quarter, suggested strange prehistoric geological happenings on that lonely moorland rise. The black crag of the summit stood high above them, against an ugly lead-coloured background of sky. Its face was no longer recognisable, but the new towering elevation of the pile lent it a still more evil and menacing character. It looked as if it might fall and over-whelm them as soon as they should approach within practicable range.

Half-way up, the sky became of a terrifying blackness, and for the first time a scared expression stole into Ingrid's eyes, though by force of will her features remained calm and disdainful. A cataclysm seemed to impend.

"Come on!" exclaimed Drapier, grasping her arm with bony fingers. And he hurried her uphill, steering the way through the debris. As he did so, three flashes of horrible lightning glittered in the sky in different quarters, followed at once by a stunning explosion in mid-air which burst in upon their ears, but was almost too near to be heard as sound. The whole hill trembled. Rumbling thunder—either the diminished end of this explosion, or its echo among the crags and hollows, or independent peals further off—continued until they imagined that the storm was now to be incessant. It was neither day nor night, but a sort of ghastly dusk. The air remained hot and clammy. Suddenly what appeared to be a solid wall of rain, descending vertically from the sky, shut them in from the world as though they were in a water-prison. Drapier dragged his cousin up the last section of hill, until they were underneath the granite tor.

They had only just taken cover beneath the projecting face of the perilously-inclined pile, when an unexpected fierce squall drove the rain again full against them, compelling them to seek another refuge. There chanced to be a cavity at the back of the rock, away from the wind, big enough with a little squeezing and bending to shelter both from the worst of the weather. Ingrid dashed the water from her eyes, shook out her hair, and laughed, but was unable to find breath for a minute; so rapid had been their ascent and so brutal the assault of the cloud-burst.

"What an adventure!" she gasped, when she could.

"You won't soon come up here again in a thunderstorm."

"But I'm glad."

And upon the quieting of her organs after another space, she added, "I wouldn't have missed it, for now I understand how fury and malice are the expression of this Tor's deepest nature."

"Notwithstanding which, we had better not stay here longer than we can help. You look positively drowned. We shall have you laid up."

"I am hard enough."

They ceased talking to regard the entire sky in front of them being lit by a wavering blue glow, the effect of lightning above the low intervening clouds. The squall stopped as suddenly as it had come, and all the air was still, when a prolonged bass growl of thunder filled the silence like a solemn, supernatural voice. When they had heard it out, Ingrid commented soberly:

"That's the grandest music, after all."

"Yes, it speaks straight to the soul. But you—aren't you peculiarly responsive to the grand in music?"

"Have you discovered that, Hugh?"

"I took the great liberty of watching you the other evening, when your mother was playing the Waldstein."

"And——?"

"You seemed under an enchantment. I fancy you were not merely held, but seriously disturbed. Where were you?"

"In a strange sphere, unsuggested by the music, I expect. Music is never more than a releasing factor for me; and that is why I am cold to nine-tenths of music, for it doesn't release."

She proceeded:

"I can secure the same emancipation from things without music at all, much more slowly, but rather more retentively on that account; as up here—alone and at peace with everything actual. I've told you something about that. It must be the beginning of the sublime, though I've never been on this hill long enough to follow it up. Perhaps one would need to be solitary here for weeks, months or years. I wish I could learn the connection. I am certain of a tomb beneath us."

"Yet a fiend's presentment for a tombstone!"

"There might be good reasons, Hugh. Robbers of grave-treasure were to be supernaturally scared, or the tribe was under the protection of that demon-god, or the tower itself may be artificial, the portrait a later natural freak. You mustn't believe that I am trying to explain things. I should need to know the feelings and wisdom of a quite different race of beings. I'm not so unimaginative as that. . . ."

Her cousin nudged her elbow gently, pointing upwards to the sky. When she quickly followed the direction of his finger, her expression changed to tenseness, while she left her speech unfinished.

Under the closed canopy of black upper clouds, which completely shut off from them all direct light from overhead, a single large, flat, lurid patch of vapour, of an ugly pale yellow hue, travelled rather rapidly towards them, seeming to descend and uncoil as it did so, until it was barely the apparent height of a tall tree above their heads. It was but too patently the carrier of a deadly concentrated charge of electricity; the least external cause might easily suffice to liberate its freight. The ground atmosphere became a sharp and tingling medium. Drapier's skin crept, while the girl's limbs refused to support her, so that she sank backwards with her shoulders pressing into the rock. Both waited in silence for the inevitable discharge, devoutly hoping that the pinnacle itself, as the highest spot, would receive it.

As they still stared up in numb and helpless fascination, a knob of what looked like liquid blue flame visibly and quite slowly separated itself from the cloud, and, followed by a half-fiery trail, as in a pyrotechnic display, dropped slantwise towards the stack, which appeared to attract it.

"What can it be?" demanded Ingrid in a swift whisper.

"A fire-ball."

Simultaneously the electrical body, of whatever nature it was, reached the rock under which they sheltered, and began to wander lightly over its surface, much in the manner of a child's toy balloon moved by a current of air. It approached their refuge, and at one time was within two feet of Drapier's face, while he held his breath. Then it glided like an animate thing upwards out of sight, round the rock.

He forced the unprepared girl to her hands and knees, and dropped himself.

"Scuttle out of it as fast as you can!"

On the ground he gave her wrist a jerk forward to emphasise his meaning. But her wits were already nimble to grasp the necessity of what he commanded, and she put no surprised questions before commencing quickly to crawl beside him on all fours through the dripping turf, away from the pile. The danger must be real, she supposed, had she time to think about it; but all the experience was suddenly too dreamlike, and she was exerting her body, and Hugh, by her side, looked so absurd—she could not feel afraid. Even she half-expected with a pleasurable curiosity the explosion at any moment behind them.

A half-minute later Drapier felt one of his legs being thrown gently but irresistibly over the other, while his whole frame was forcibly impelled onwards along the ground with a slithering, twisting motion. The propulsion ceased, when he found himself lying impotently on his back at full length, shaken and stupid, but so far as he could judge unhurt. He had a confused notion of an earthquake. Rocks were falling somewhere, though the noise was so mingled with that of heavy thunder that it was impossible to distinguish which was which. He could see nothing of what was going on, by reason of the fierce sheets of hail that drove over the hill-top. The white pellets were cutting his face, and bouncing from the ground all around like peas.

III

Thor's Hammer

The sting of the hail coupled with fears for Ingrid's safety urged him quickly to sit up, in which posture, while sheltering his eyes with a hand, he looked with swift anxiety across to where she should be. She was lying at full length front-downwards only a few feet away; but at first he was unable to distinguish how matters had gone with her, by reason of the swishing white curtain between them. Mercifully, she was at least in her senses. Her head and shoulders were lifted from the ground by her pair of propping arms, while the neck was thrust back and twisted towards himself, obviously for the purpose of ascertaining *his* condition. He hoped that if she was not at once getting up, it simply meant that like himself she was still bewildered by shock.

The sound of falling rocks had stopped. The thunder all about the hill grumbled alone, a mystic bass to the hissing downpour and the whistle of the squalls. The place was wrapped in gloom. Half-visible through the vicious showers, the womanly indignity of his cousin's serpentine plight, with her wild wet clothes and hair, in that first quick photograph he had of her, did not at all strike him as a matter for laughter or compassion, but on the contrary showed itself as a glimpse of surprising beauty. She seemed in the aptness of her pose and state to the whizzing confusion and dark, lonely mountain-foulness of the evening almost like a female spirit in the moment of emerging from subterranean depths, and elevating her head in doing so to regard heedfully his intruding person.

The fancy died even while he was ignoring it, for just as he had willed to rise to the assistance of the distressed girl, she anticipated the movement by wriggling round on her own account to sit upright on the hail-white turf, and the spell was broken. He could not see her face's light quiver of pain resulting from the action. She was calm again at once, and in an easing of the rain their eyes met.

"Are you all right, Ingrid?" he called.

"Comparatively, I hope. But what really has happened?"

"The stack must be struck. Haven't you heard stones crashing?"

"Yes, I heard that."

"You're not damaged?"

She returned no reply, and, taking new alarm, he hurriedly picked himself up to attend her.

"What's the matter?" he asked again, standing over the girl.

"I seem to have twisted my ankle, but I hope it's nothing much."

"I sincerely trust not. We've three miles to go."

He dropped on to a knee beside her, and gently put away the hand with which she was gingerly exploring her injury.

"Is this the spot? Am I hurting you?"

"Only don't press."

He went on passing tender, skilful fingers around and across the area of trouble, until at last he could assure himself that the scare was groundless in so far as there was no dislocation.

"It should be only a small sprain. Try if you can stand up."

She obeyed. Bearing on his arm, she cautiously lowered her weight on to the ankle.

"I think I shall be able to limp home, but it's unfortunate it has happened so far out."

"You'll have to lean on me. We might as well be off at once, unless you'd like a few minutes more to get over it? The worst seems to be passed."

"Let's go."

Though the frozen hail had already degenerated to soft rain, the gusty pelts were still too rough to permit them to see away. Also a white mist was settling over the hill. The stack was invisible even at that short distance of their crawl. Curious to learn what exactly had happened to it, Ingrid took a more permanent hold on her cousin's arm, and urged him forward.

"Thanks for saving me, Hugh! Your quickness was wonderful."

"Our luck was wonderful."

"That too, of course."

Limping painfully, she took with him the first experimental steps towards their late refuge. But an anticipation of some odd difference in the limited view was possessing the two simultaneously, and before the perplexity of either could find words their feet, seemingly of their own will, first dragged, then stopped. Drapier, after a long spell of staring ahead, turned round to his cousin.

"You're realising that the whole thing has gone overboard, *en masse*?"

"Yes."

A still longer pause of silence and wonder followed.

"I might have known that all that noise could represent nothing else," said Drapier at last. "The din was hellish, and there was no other thing to blow down. We were absolutely favoured."

"It seems so incredible."

"Why, no. Very impressive to our puny senses, no doubt, as also the happiest of escapes, and something of a coincidence—I mean, our being on the Tor at the time. But perfectly explainable by dynamics and statics."

"This memorial hasn't meant to you what it has to me, Hugh."

She fell again into abstraction. Now, the wind abruptly dropping and the rain diminishing to a vertical spotting shower, they were better able to discern the completeness of the wreck. A single pair of entire massive granite blocks, with some far smaller fragments of others, lay quiescent just within the extreme verge of the hill, where its steepness began; and that was all that visibly remained of the Devil's head. The whole of the upper twenty-five or thirty feet of the stack, ponderous segments of rock of different sizes and shapes, had necessarily been hurled down the hillside, to crash in huge bounds to the valley or be precariously halted on the way. Older by far than the Pyramids, a slowly dipping landmark to innumerable generations of men, the pile had tumbled at last; and the witnesses of its ruin were the girl who knew and loved it so well, and a man who had journeyed from the far ends of the earth but just in time for the spectacle.

Of those two blocks in view, the larger, a flattish rectangular slab, must clearly have been the base of the whole erection. Its narrow edge was in line with the torn cavity in the soil left by its upheaval, and the measurements appeared identical. It lay bottom-upwards. A tall man could stretch himself across its width, while its length might be half as much again. The other block, which was the nearer to the edge of the hill, was a big irregular cube. It should have stood the next upon its companion in destruction, as the lowest section of the Devil's neck. The imbedded slab must have been wrenched from the ground by its leverage.

And the stack's site itself lay before the cousins hollow and violated. All that left it recognisable was its grim interruption of the natural turf and weathered sunken rock-knobs of the plateau, outlined on the side furthest from them by the low parapet of that slab which until a few minutes since had filled it throughout an age unthinkable. Drapier, twisting an end of his moustache, reflected how excavation work would now be easier, supposing that this girl on his arm wished still to insist on her theory of a tomb. Such a feature of the destruction seemed not to have occurred to her yet; nor did he desire to hurry her processes, for come to it she must in a few more moments, and till then he had thoughts of his own.

So they continued fast where they had halted, a short dozen paces from the nearer rim of the depression, both appearing intent on silently absorbing what was already won of the catastrophe, before caring to investigate the rest. The rain was gentler still, but the driving mists grew denser, and the natural dusk perceptibly advanced. Drapier's face had acquired an expression of sternness and anxiety. Ingrid seemed in a kind of passive trance.

Presently she said:

"It is not incredible, of course, for nothing is incredible that can happen. But it is strange. It is strange that I should have been talking to you about a tomb here only a very short time before the tomb is opened for us by a miraculous intervention. That is what I have been thinking about."

"I wondered if it was so."

"Now let us go on to see, then."

"So you receive it superstitiously?" he inquired, while they slowly advanced again.

"I know that in your heart you are not laughing at me for that, Hugh. I am not pretending to read your ideas, but I can see that you are taking a man's view of this affair."

"A man's view?"

"A serious view. For consider! How many hundreds or thousands of tons of solid rock have been thrown down?—and by one diminutive whirl of electricity. It is scarcely in nature; and I am up here when it happens, and you are up here too—in spite of your denials of knowledge of the hill, or interest in it. What have *you* been thinking about, Hugh?"

"Honestly, I never heard of the Tor before yesterday," he persisted.

Ingrid was troubled, but again might not contradict him in mind. The site of the destruction became once more veiled from them by the rolling white vapours that were the legacy of the storm, making of the hill-top a cauldron. Thunder still growled from the west, but there was now no lightning with it, and the rain had left off. The fair weather of weeks past seemed suddenly to have vanished, to make way for the more characteristic Dartmoor grey skies and mists. The breeze blew soft, moist, and at last cool, the moor all at once smelt sweet, inexhaustible supplies of damp-laden air must again be coming up from the Channel, ready for conversion to hill-vapour. The girl felt the familiar friendliness of it all, though her mood could not respond.

New to her disability and full of cares, she paused again before quite reaching the hollow, which at those few paces continued wholly curtained off. And at the identical instant her eyes, fastened straight ahead, became set and strange, for they had seen an extraordinary thing—or was the true explanation of her overtaking different?

During the rest of the evening and night she could never decide upon the character of that vision. It had come and gone with the swiftness of thought. Yet only its speed and its nature had been unreal, otherwise it had transcended everything that she understood by reality. Whether it were some intuition of hers taking visual shape, or absolute hallucination, or a hill-haunting, as a house might be haunted, or a personal apparition manifesting itself to her for a purpose, or a transformation by her faculties of some queer efflux from the Tor—she could not come to any peace or settlement about it.

Looking towards that cavity where the monument had stood, she thought she had seen—no, she *had* seen—a woman, or, to be more exact, the upper half of a woman, of marvellous height, since her unseen lower limbs must have stood in some depression still deeper than the evacuated bed, and her head was yet but little lower than Ingrid's own. She conceived that it had been a sudden rift in the white wreaths of fog which had opened and closed again that track of vision for her as far as the hollow, exhibiting the woman erect in its depth, facing her. And she had been clothed in dark-coloured clinging antique draperies, of no recognisable fashion, but the wonder had been her flesh—and her beauty altogether—the full beauty of a beautiful woman expressed in supernatural terms, which made something totally different of it. Her face, neck and arms alone had been bare, but the colour of these had resembled snow illuminated by moonlight, instead of the muddiness of human flesh. That face's beauty had been neither young nor old, living nor dead, but was set apart from all comparisons. It had been wise and tranquilly terrible, like a celestial's.

Then, before Ingrid's amazement had had time to turn to the bristling horror that is the body's blind, ungovernable defence against all that comes suddenly upon it from an alien world, the phantom had been blotted from her sight by the thickening of the mists once more. Thereupon it had been, while she trembled, staggering, too late, that the lightning vision so wondrously impressed upon her retina had begun quietly to separate itself into the pictorial details that afterwards she was to recall as the actual optical contact.

Drapier, always supporting her arm, had become aware of its stiffening, then glancing round at her eyes he had seen their odd rigidity as well. Afterwards came her slight trembling and swaying. Yet nothing unusual, nothing at all, was distinguishable through the drifts ahead. He hoped her nerves were not giving under the evening's strain.

"What's wrong, Ingrid?"

She felt that that image might at any instant reappear. Her instinct was that she must not betray it to him—it was for her alone. His question told that he had not seen it. And so she unlinked her arm, to be in solitary readiness for the renewed ordeal; but Drapier courteously would not restrain her, although he knew her helplessness. Her pride returned, she now declared to herself that she must under all circumstances exercise control, and took his arm again. But to answer his inquiry was indeed difficult.

"Did anything startle you?"

"I thought something was there, through a break in the mist," she explained, as evenly as she could.

"What kind of thing?"

"It could only have been fancy."

He accepted the statement. In fact, there was nothing else there that could have upset her.

"I ought to understand these alarms. Vapour at a certain altitude is a very living thing—and may, for instance, permanently stamp the soul of a whole people; such as the mountain Scottish. It's the constant anxiety of eye and ear not to be caught unawares. . . ."

He broke off. A new advance had at length brought them to the very edge of the wrecked bed, and Ingrid was plainly not listening to him; but in any case he must have ceased.

"And so there *is* a grave."

The words were hers, uttered in a quiet, sharp voice. Drapier looked on without reply.

The hollow, like the slab which had filled and fitted it, was an oblong. Its floor was no more than a couple of feet below the Tor's surface. In the middle of this floor was another smaller oblong; but it was of nothingness. Thus the true floor was but a narrow ledge or shelf running round the four sides of the bed, with a hole in the centre.

The granite of the ledge was jagged and unfinished. Its material was hidden by an accumulation of disintegrated dirt. The oblong hole inside was dark, but not of a uniform darkness. The length of the whole bed was from south to north, the upheaved slab was on its east side (the way they had come up), and the downlooking two were on its west. The hole was lighter at the south end, darker at the north. Drapier stepped down on to the ledge.

Yes, there could be no doubt about the artificial character of this inside oblong at his feet. It had been done by tools; primitive tools, of course, and the shelf's sharp edges had crumbled with age, but still the opening was human workmanship. The discernible actual stairs, however, leading down to the unseen depths put the fact beyond question. He saw two rude granite stair-treads, each with a drop of a yard from above, and below that the remaining third of the seven-foot length of the hole was occupied by blackness. The width of the treads was a yard, and the whole descent looked frightfully archaic. The black section indubitably represented the invisible continuation of the stairway previous to passing underground, beneath the north arch of the ledge. How far down into the belly of the hill it all led he was of course no antiquarian to conjecture.

What he could see of the granite walls was rough and bossy. It was impossible to conceive that prehistoric workmen with quite inadequate tools could so have carved a way down into the earth through solid rock. Nearly certainly, advantage must have been taken of some pre-existing natural fissure: wrought, it might be, in another geological age by earthquake. The fissure could have been trimmed to these steps without any great miracle. But in that case they must lead down to a cave, also natural, which would be the tomb.

He determined to make the descent; only not now. The air must first be suffered to purify itself a bit, and it was also unjustifiable to run risks, with Ingrid waiting for him above in her present lamed condition. He could come up alone before breakfast to-morrow, with a torch.

So, springing to the upper ground again, he said to his cousin, who never looked at him, even when he spoke:

"It certainly is a grave, and after this I shall respect your inspirations. But we had still better not stop now—you're wet through and hurt, it's growing dark, and your mother will be anxious. I'll explore it before breakfast in the morning, and report to you. No one can possibly anticipate us to-night."

She heard him with a part of her thoughts only, and returned no reply. She was meditating that the apparition had been standing in a deep hollow, for only the upper half of her form had shown above ground. The feet, therefore, must have been on yonder first stair-tread, far down—which would make her *so* tall. . . . And she must have been ascending, not descending, for she was to appear. . . . And thus this ancient stairway explained the vision, which must otherwise entirely have baffled her understanding; while the vision surely explained this stairway leading to a tomb she had always *felt*. It was the woman's tomb. It would need a being of such spiritual importance to radiate her influence through the ages. But were there women ever so near to heaven, and so inexpressibly lovely and awful? . . .

Drapier offered her his arm again.

"I don't wish to interrupt a flight, but it is getting late, and there's this painful trudge in front of us."

"Yes, we must go, Hugh."

She accepted the arm, and they started round the wreck towards the edge of the hill.

"I think I am now entitled to the whole of your intuition," said Drapier gravely. "I may be able to confirm its accuracy in the morning, but I should know what I am looking for."

"There is little else of it. Only I have always somehow felt that if there were a tomb here, it must be a woman's."

"Why?"

"I've always felt it."

Her thoughts were never away from that vision. It was the truth that her intuitions had always spoken of a woman's grave; and now this was she. She had been of high birth and power, to be buried here, under so grand a monument. A queen of those days. Although, indeed, she had been more like an angel or goddess— but perhaps that was the transfiguration of her death. . . . Was it foolish to fancy that she had willed to be received, upon her grave's reopening, by a girl of seriousness and noble birth? For men, even, that tomb might be sinister. The fiend's portrait would be the symbol of such an interdiction. Probably she ought not to allow Hugh to go down. . . .

From the hill's verge they saw other fragments of the shattering, but still most of the ruin was veiled from them by the clinging white mists and the deeper twilight of the valley. Drapier chose another way down, to give a wide berth to any temporarily-arrested boulders that might start again without warning. From a safe distance they glimpsed a few such. He took a mental note to advise the setting-up of a danger-board. Another proof that the stack had been artificial was that its component stones must have been cemented together. They were easily separable, yet, had they been quite loose, the top ones must have whizzed off without levering up the underneath.

A chill came on with the darkness, and Ingrid grew rapidly cold and dispirited. She seemed to herself to be turning her back upon a high-seat of grandeur, in order to re-seek dullness, meanness and commonplace. There was no more thunder, meaning that the spirit-world was no longer speaking to her. As they descended to the stream, the fog grew denser and wetting. It was a token that now the hideous prose of reality, no longer its sublime poetry and music, was to claim her. Her ankle, as often as she mismanaged it, was excruciating; her limping progress otherwise was fatiguing and absurd, and she had the dreadful consciousness all the time how she was over-burdening poor Hugh. So clearly the Tor was intended to be interdict for her as well. Yet but a short time ago she had had that sensation that something was immediately to happen in her life, and it had almost at once been followed by the preternatural unsealing of the tomb and the emerging of its ghost. She must endure yet a little while, and perhaps her reward of super-reality would come. She knew not what she expected. She was tired and wretched.

But when they reached the top of the opposite height, they stopped to rest, and could exchange words again. The mist was thinner here; looking back across to Devil's Tor, they saw its rocky base starting from the valley bed, but its crest continued vapour-wrapped, as though its degradation were to be concealed from view. Ingrid recollected the fork which had glittered behind it, it seemed no more than a few minutes since. It must really have been a portent of the destruction.

"Hugh, I feel that you should not attempt that tomb to-morrow," she said, endeavouring to put ordinariness into her voice. "It may be out of proportion. The problematical gain may not be worth the risk."

"Someone will go down if I don't, and you wouldn't have me funk what another man dares?"

Their way over the shoulder-traverse would now be downhill

and smoother, so that they could talk as they went. Ingrid accordingly urged his arm, and they moved on. The driving spray that more and more assimilated to fine rain, as they kept their faces towards the invisible houses and beginning lights, was soon to develop to the steady drizzle of the remainder of the walk. She answered him:

"Now we have changed arguments, for it is my turn to say that a thousand years ago neither you nor any other man would have dared. You would have understood that the monument was struck to nothingness by the hammer of Asa-Thor, hurled in wrath. That hammer was named Mjölnir, and was what we call lightning. So you wouldn't have dared to visit in idle curiosity a spot so banned by a god. And though we are truly in the twentieth century, it still may not be wise."

"Do you suggest a ban?"

"I feel that it may be unlucky."

He pondered her dissuasions, which, coming from nearly any other person of his acquaintance, would have sounded so lunatic, but she already stood out for him as unique in this proved foreknowledge of hers of at least some things to appear. She had predicted a tomb against all the wisdom of the archaeologists, she had almost as wonderfully twice approached his own secret association with the Tor, and that without curiosity or persistence, but, as it were, merely because her unconscious mind was troubled from time to time by some psychic emanation from his; and now she was warning him against the unluck for him of the place. He might not wholly believe her, he remained unterrified, yet it was impressive.

"Unlucky generally?" he asked. "For anyone?"

She turned half-round to him, with a weary look in her eyes.

"Hugh, there's something tragical about this evening's work, that is all I know. I think it will be imprudent in you to undertake any exploration to-morrow morning in the spirit of sightseeing. I don't think the pile was struck down for anything like that. I'd rather you left it."

"Somebody will go down," he repeated, "and I'm as appropriate as the next man. I've no responsibilities, and my job's done. Strained nerves apart, it's only a trip down a hole."

She saw that he was quietly obstinate to make the essay.

"Then have you an electric torch?" she inquired.

"Yes, I brought one down."

They reached the open road none too soon, for by then, though it should still have been daylight, the low clouds and now continuous downpour made all so dark that they could scarcely see before them, but the moor was full of traps. Ingrid weighed more and more heavily on her cousin's arm. She was fagged, soaked, miserable; she longed to be home. After the most protracted silence of all the evening, she violently shook off her apathy, to demand:

"I've told you far too many of my fancies, Hugh, while you have told me far too few of yours. You were so very thoughtful, looking at that ruin. Won't you confess what you were thinking?"

Drapier considered his response.

"The idea took me how the earth must have appeared untold aeons back, when still untenanted by even the lowest form of animated slime, but was composed exclusively of basalt continents, fishless seas, an unbreathable gassy air, and innumerable horrific active volcanoes spouting flames, lava and chemical ashes incessantly—and suchlike. It was an unforced and uninvited picture, that I have since been wondering at. . . . Another followed, as spontaneous. I imagined a vast clock of Time without beginning or end, and not circular but straight, the minute hand of which before my very eyes had just jerked viciously across another of its marked spaces, each space somehow representing ten thousand years. And it struck me how eternity was made up of an infinite line of such single minutes of ten thousand years; and how each contained the appearance and disappearance of empires, nations, even races.

"I was reminded of the time when, as a very small boy indeed, I was carried wrapped-up from one house to another at night-time, and shown the sky of glittering stars overhead. My mother, I remember, told me that there was no end to their number, but that one could go on counting them for ever. And the impossibility of grasping such a stupendous conception made a metaphysical impression upon me then that has remained ever since. Well, on the Tor I obtained the same thrill, only for time instead of space.

"I conclude that these two involuntary pictures, both having to do with ancientness, were in some manner imposed on me by an inherent antique character of the height. I think that that forcible bursting open of its interior may have released certain elements. You, I believe, may understand me better than most people. All hills and mountains are ancient. One hears of 'the everlasting hills,' and 'the eternal snows'; which are popularly supposed to be figures of poetry, but in fact the adjective represents a much more real and positive thing. We can't climb a few thousand feet without feeling the sense of enormous *age*; and actually the hills are survivals of a former state of the earth. The plains and valleys are a paste of cemented disintegrated particles, but the heights sticking up out of them—particularly if their rocks are igneous— are what they always have been since towards the laying down of the first foundations of the globe."

"You mentioned the release of certain elements, Hugh."

"I think that there may be the slow accumulation through the ages of a chemico-physical secretion, our invisible contact with the fine emanations from which may produce in us the mental atmosphere of an awful antiquity. I've experienced it on a hundred eminences; and since things, to be recognised, must be named, I have wished to give such a secretion the name of 'eld'. . . . However, either your Devil's Tor must possess the substance in double or triple measure, or else, as I say, the sudden exposure to the outer air of the contents of its interior has given my receptive answering faculty the augmented dose."

He added in a lower and different voice: "I am inclined to believe, though, that the Tor is in itself highly magnetic, both in a very intensified degree and in a very peculiar manner. I could hardly explain the reason for my faith, but it seems to me that it might even be attractive from a great distance."

But Ingrid was inquiring of herself whether this hypothetical 'eld' of Hugh's could at all account for her vision. She dismissed the notion. A mere stimulus could not have created anything half so wonderful. That stimulus might be valid for Hugh's own dreamings.

And in the new silence that ensued, her cramped fancies continued to cling to his case, from the sheer inability of her will to rouse itself to a change of subject. It dawned upon her that he must be a devitalised man. "His job was done"—those were his own words. He was so young still, yet seemed to be entirely without plans, and regarded himself as too far advanced in life for marriage. Then his manner: always low-pitched, taciturn, brooding, reserved. He couldn't be ill in body; just the reverse, he struck her as an amalgam of red iron blood and tireless muscle. But there must be some spiritual blight on him. . . .

What was he to discuss with her mother? It was not to be financial business—not *financial* business—but business of another kind, or he would not have come down to them. Perhaps he wanted to provide for their looking after his affairs, in case anything should happen to him. Yes, that must be the simple and innocent solution. He was contemplating the making of a will, and wished Uncle Magnus or her mother to act as executor.

Well, a man might make a will. Still, he had no known dependents, so why was he suddenly so providing for the contingency of his death? . . . *Death!* Was he imagining that he might die soon? Was that the depression, taciturnity and abstraction of his manner? He might have the presentiment. She, so full of intuitions as she was, was clearly not entitled to jeer at the intuitions of others. He might be feeling the foretaste of death within him. And at the thought the contact of his bony arm afflicted her for a single instant as though it were that of a skeleton, escorting her to her own prepared grave. She shook off the absurdity. . . .

And she dreaded this adventure of his next morning. Was that in connection with his premonition of death? If he were to be killed up there, the feelings of both of them would thus have proved true. Yet how could she tell him so? Very rightly he would deem such a picking of his soul an insolence, and she would only have added anger to his obstinacy. His now determined, dour silence was giving her no opening. She was so tired that she felt she must drop.

It was nearly eleven when the crunch of their steps on the gravel brought the girl's mother to the front-door for at least the fourth time that evening. She was as worried as possible. She knew where they had been going to, knew that they must have been caught on the open moor in the storm, and black night had descended long after they were due to return, still without a sign of them. The rest of the establishment were in bed. She detained her cousin, as he was slipping past her to go upstairs to his room.

"Won't you come down again, Hugh? I suppose you have some excuses to offer for this sort of conduct, and I'd like to know all about it. Get into dry things, and find your way to my room. There's a fire there."

She spoke with smiling reproach, but he knew that he could never be afraid of Helga.

"Thanks! I will."

And so he departed through the hall, leaving Ingrid to her mother.

IV

The Hemisphere

Whitestone was a long, low, white dwelling of two storeys, standing alone on a high-up part of the southern moor. More than a century old, its austerely simple stone front, interrupted by a porch having Tuscan pillars, was long since made charming to the eye by a careless profusion of climbing Gloire de Dijon roses and jasmine. A shorter wing in keeping, though later in date, flanked the west of the house, overlooking on that side the long downwards-sloping lawn that steepened at its foot to the valley separating the estate from the moors beyond. These were the moors stretching presently to the north of Devil's Tor.

The house's east peeped over a privet hedge at the lane that was its approach from north and south. Its south front faced an imposing sweep of main lawn, level and better kept than the other, behind which were flower-beds and dense shrubberies; with the fields at the rear of all. The utilitarian back of the house looked out on to a protective clump of ash and sycamore trees, that were very leafy and beautiful in the summer.

Ultimately the moors were all around the house, and slanted mostly down from it, but, standing as it did on a cultivable plateau, there were a good many crop-fields first on the south and east. Belhill village to the south-east began about half a mile away, the advanced cottages of which were the house's nearest neighbours. The lane passing Whitestone joined a quarter of a mile on the east-and-west highroad that proceeded through the village. The lane itself then continued downhill towards the Devil's Tor moors.

The house contained a few large handsome living-rooms on the front ground floor, some extra smaller rooms on the ground floor of the wing, and a number of bedrooms, also smaller and slightly old-fashioned, on the upper floor of both the front and the wing. These bedrooms possessed lovely near or distant moorland views; from the windows of those of the front a gleam was sometimes obtainable of the far-off silver Channel. All the rooms had a notable fragrance as of combined lavender and moor air. None of the house's residents used tobacco, while Helga Fleming possessed in wonderful degree that kind of womanly sensitiveness which cannot endure the least suspicion of domestic uncleanness. For her, that scent of lavender was no sweet disguise, but a symbol of feminine law and order.

She had very capably ruled the household for her uncle during the past fourteen years, having taken charge shortly after the death of her husband, in the days immediately preceding the war. Magnus Colborne himself had bought the freehold of the estate twenty-five years since, through the agency of Copping senior, the then thriving Tavistock estate auctioneer, now dead. The negotiation had started the later close personal intimacy between the two men, based partly on a parity of age and fortune, partly on a common overlapping of intellectual tastes, and partly on the requisitions of their ensuing business partnership, the ultimate and unforeseen fruit of which was the securing of the liberty of the upper moorland domicile to Peter, the younger of Copping's sons, the artist-tenant of the village studio whom Ingrid had (perhaps so superfluously) named to her cousin as the one man with whom she was not to be mentally coupled. Peter was mostly in London, but once or twice a year at least he was in the habit of spending some weeks at Belhill; and then he would always be in and out of the house of these great good friends of his. At White-stone he found many desirable things: tactful sympathy, intellectual interest, appreciation, stimulation, music, and spiritual splendour; but not all in the same person. He cared not to seem to force his visits to Dartmoor, yet to the pondering mind of Helga things were surely drawing rapidly to a head.

Drapier, even after a week's stay in the house, hardly knew which, of two or three lower rooms at its wing end, her private den was. But artificial light came shining through the crack of a door ajar at the end of the passage, so there he turned in; and found his assumption correct. Helga, indeed, was temporarily out of the room—no doubt she was still with Ingrid upstairs. A lighted lamp, however, stood on the table, the fire had been newly stoked, chairs were drawn up on either side of the hearth. He wondered if these deliberate preparations meant that she was to challenge him about the real purpose of his visit. Well, he was anticipating the challenge. Beside the lamp on the table he set, as a preliminary, the small tin box that he had brought down with him from his room.

For a minute longer he remained gazing incuriously about the room. The window curtains were drawn, and in the dead quiet of the house the periodic spattering of rain against the panes spoke of a night going from bad to worse. This femininely-appointed little chamber was nothing to him; in spirit he was scarcely there.

He came to a stand before an oil-painting—a girl's likeness—
hanging by the door. It had subconsciously drawn his eye on first
entering, and now he saw that the portrait was Ingrid's.

She was younger than now; perhaps seventeen or eighteen.
And her lovely yellow hair was long and undressed, flowing over
her shoulders, while she also appeared to be in some sort of
Eastern fancy costume. A long dark-red cloak hid most of a
simple yet foreign-looking blue dress reaching to her feet, as she
stood in the doorway of a hut, gazing out at the night; a raised
hand on the lintel. A yellow beam from a lamp not shown illuminated her profile. The hut was otherwise dark; and outside it was
blacker still, except for the last long faint line of what must have
been a red sunset, underneath the silver finger-nail of a moon.

Drapier mused upon the picture, finding it as beautiful as
oddly-conceived. Though the clue was wanting to the puzzle, it
was anyway evident that whoever had painted the work must
have seen fairly deeply into the possibilities of Ingrid's character.
The face was set in an expression almost too old for it. It was
calm, displeased, troubled, expectant; all at once. She was *waiting*
for somebody or something.

Helga came in while he was yet looking at it.

"It's Ingrid as the girl Madonna in her father's home, before
the arrival of her supernatural destiny. I more or less keep it here
to avoid the trouble of explaining this to visitors. Peter Copping, a
friend of ours, did it. He may be down before you go. He is a
great admirer of Ingrid's genius, and possibly understands her
better than any of us."

"She mentioned him. You say, her genius; what is her genius?"

Helga's smile seemed sad, as she gently led her cousin from
his stand before the painting to the remoter of the chairs by the
fire. She herself dropped into the other.

"I have to confess to being a little jealous of her, Hugh, and
that's why these unkind things sometimes escape me. You see, I
never enjoyed such adulations when I was a girl. No one ever
predicted a mystical career for me. I was just a simple young
woman, who was rather lucky to have secured a good husband.

The luck, however, was not to be!"

"There of course you don't do yourself justice, for you were always the young queen of your set. However, I do agree that your daughter may be something exceptional in the way of girls—and very proud of the fact you should feel, Helga. But what is her true bent?"

"She is very unlikely to do anything great or outstanding of herself, but she may be a source of inspiration to some man of parts. I hope she may be. She is the last hope of the Colbornes, at all events; for somehow one hardly identifies *you*, my dear."

She rose again, with a brighter smile. "But I am being frightfully inhospitable. What will you take?"

"Nothing at all, thanks."

"I know you are teetotal, but medicinally?"

"Really no, thanks. I am not in the ranks of the fanatics, but I've so often had to go long spells without either alcohol or tobacco, that now the resumption of the double-habit appears not worth while."

So Helga sat down again. She had not failed to notice the japanned box. Ingrid, also, had mentioned to her upstairs that Hugh was proposing a chat with her, probably on business, but not financial business. She knew that this box must be in connection with it. She was well trained to patience and civility, however, and would say nothing before he was ready. There was no fear of their *tête-à-tête* being interrupted.

He glanced more than once across at her, and thought how in spite of this long passage of years she was still the old Helga. He remembered that she must be forty-three or four; but her peculiar fascination for him had never been in her features or contours, but in that intimate tranquil searching of her green-hazel eyes, which was at once like a cool hand resting upon him and a mild electric stimulation of all his soul. Given a longer and more serene leisure, he might even still be in love with her, as when he had been a gawky boy, all red hair, freckles and joints, and she an already grown-up young reigning beauty of that vanished Sydenham society, consorting with responsible men on equal terms.

Truly the spell had begun to work again, he realised, only now the antidote was within his blood, and the entire surrender was happily no longer possible.

She had taken good care of her looks, too, and in her highly becoming evening frock of black and gold was remaining a most attractive woman, to be reckoned with. He supposed she must be vain. Possibly all women were—though he was unsure about Ingrid, who gave him the impression of caring nothing for dress and the artificialities of the toilet. Helga's aesthetically-arranged, stylish brown hair, with its golden lights, distinctly spoke of vanity: her hands also were white, and he imagined that her gown should be from an expensive shop. Yet all this was not a crime; while her calm, languid, intelligent features continued as thin and as lovely as ever. He could not escape from the idea that the vague constant shadow of a great disappointment was hanging over her life. Her smiles were so often melancholy, and into the searching of her eyes there seemed to have crept something wistful. Then she was as tall as her daughter, and still quite slender, which physical type and contradiction of her years likewise permitted the faint note of tragedy.

He conceived that repression over a long period had done its work. For the sake of this home, and the expected after-reward for her sacrifice, she had buried herself and her daughter in a half-dead house in the depths of the country, to tend a crabbed old misanthrope, who doubtless ruled out every sort of society; and the effect upon a cultured, lively mind, yearning for its proper atmosphere, must be immense. Her sudden reduction to a state of comparative poverty upon the hapless death of her husband Dick must also have shocked her tremendously; while now he recalled that her unfortunate mother's last illness a few years earlier had been of a particularly distressing nature. He could not even wonder that, with her high personal attractions, she had never married a second time. Uncle Magnus was reputedly so well-off that the temptation would need to have been very great. Now, however, she was probably suffering for her good sense and long views. In fact, a woman of her age, feeling all the time that romance is slipping faster and faster out of her existence, must be depressed (he ruminated) as often as she allowed her thoughts to take a flight from the things of every day.

Sitting there, opposite to her, he discovered in himself some difficulty in approaching the subject which doubtless both wanted. For a man did not plant a tin box in a room for no reason, and she must have seen it at once, and be continuing to see it all the time. He felt a fool to be seeming to ignore its presence for both of them, while going on lightly to talk of other things of no importance. It was sheer hypocrisy, of course. Nor was the business itself so hard to state; yet he could not introduce it. It was as if it were of weightier consequence than he knew. At least he was glad that Ingrid's words had dissuaded him from following his original counsel, of addressing the request to old Magnus Colborne. Helga was a woman and sympathetic, whereas the old man might barely have comprehended the service required. Though in the part of the business alone to be disclosed, heaven knew there was little enough to go wrong about. Drapier then felt he might be dreading the possible requiring of fuller explanations, which might open up very much more of his intimate personal concerns than he wanted.

He weakly compromised his hesitations by breaking the short silence to talk of Ingrid's hurt. But Helga, finding his inquiry perfectly natural and reasonable, reassured him without a special glance for the reluctance of his voice.

"It isn't much, we may be thankful. There's no acute pain, and hardly any inflammation, so I trust there will be no doctor's bill to pay on this occasion. But it might have been far more serious, and I'm really amazed at you, Hugh. Surely you must have appreciated the unnecessary risk you accepted in crossing the open moor in such a thunderstorm? Everybody saw it coming on."

"Yes, it was silly, and honestly I don't know why I did it. Ingrid seemed to want it; while I suppose it needs more experience than I possess to stand out against the whims of your sex."

Helga laughed, putting tapering finger-tips to press her cheek.

"So spoke Adam! However, I'm sure you won't ever repeat

the offence, so I shall say no more. You scared me dreadfully.”

“I am sorry.”

“And Devil’s Tor has lost its decoration?”

“Yes, it was struck.”

“Ingrid tells me you had the narrowest escape, both of you, and that it was your marvellous readiness that got you out of a real disaster. Having scolded you, now I want to thank you, Hugh, on her account and mine. If she had been up there alone——”

“It isn’t worth mentioning, Helga.”

She, however, directed towards him one of her lingering looks, that always had for him the queer double effect of breaking down the barrier between their two individualities, and setting up a more impassable one compounded of femininity and foreignness. He flushed beneath it, which seeing, she smiled, while proceeding to say:

“You can’t prevent my gratitude—and admiration. But now explain about this tomb that has come to light. It is one?”

“It has every appearance of one. There is what should be a stairway.”

“And you intend to investigate it in a few hours’ time, before breakfast?”

“Yes.”

“What boundless energy you have, Hugh!”

“Not at all. You know I like an early stroll. It’s a habit of mine when at home.”

“I hope it isn’t evil conscience?”

“No, it isn’t that. But on long caravan trips one has to make a start with saddling-up round about dawn, or one would never get away; so at home I wake up and tumble out automatically.”

“May you make an interesting find for your pains!”

“I know nothing about these things, but there is the antiquity and the adventure.”

His anxious eye chanced, in glancing past her, to rest again on Ingrid’s likeness.

“How extraordinarily she resembles your father, as I knew him, Helga!”

"Yes. We all think it so strange that the family in her case should have skipped the generation. There are the two types of Colborne; her type, the northern fair, blue-eyed, and Uncle's, the dark, heavy, financially-shrewd Dutch type. I belong to neither; I am not a true Colborne at all, but am purely and simply my mother's daughter. You were acquainted with her?"

"Of course."

"Of course you were. Then you know how in nearly every physical and mental respect I take after her. I suppose no mother and daughter ever were more alike. Because I am tall and slim, some people have chosen to find a likeness between me and Ingrid, but there is absolutely none. I'm a brunette, with a warm colourless skin, and more heart than head, I fear. Ingrid is my precise racial opposite. You also met my husband, her father; she got still less from him. And here she springs into bloom, the feminine replica of her maternal grandfather, as you have just pointed out. What is the law governing these concerns, Hugh?"

"I have no idea."

"He was a queer, reserved, self-centred man, my father. He shouldn't have married. Books and solitary sport were his two grand passions in life. Most summers he was away with rod and gun in Sweden, Finland, Lapland—always northern Europe. And, you know, he couldn't afford it. When he died, there was hardly anything to come to my mother. Fortunately for herself, she died soon afterwards, poor thing! She had a hard time in every way. Let us trust that Ingrid's being a girl will render her more human and compassionate than ever he was."

"Yet he was a *man*, Helga. Perhaps he was unfitted for married and family life; nevertheless he had great qualities. I recollect quite well how he always made his company look small. In another age, under other conditions, he might have found himself, only probably he was right out of sympathy with our commercial set of those days, and so got adrift. I used to admire him tremendously."

Helga smiled.

"It's nice to hear one's father praised. And he really wasn't to blame for his coldness. The rule in the family seems to be, one authentic fair-haired Colborne, and one only, to each generation; and he was it. Uncle Magnus and his sister, your mother, have belonged to the heavy dark-haired type; just like their father before them, old Harold Colborne, the ship-owner. *He* derived from his mother, the Dutch-woman. Well, imagine!—I don't know with how much of all this ancient history you are already acquainted—but of the whole of a quite large family of brothers and sisters, of whom this Harold Colborne was the eldest, not one possessed the Norse yellow hair, blue eyes and handsome features except one of the younger boys, who later characteristically got drowned in Iceland, when crossing a half-frozen stream. Shall I go on? Are you at all interested?"

"I am immensely interested."

"While in the generation before that, I've been told, old Harold Colborne's father, our great-grandfather, who was born in the year of the taking of the Bastille, presented the very image of a northern Viking as pictured in the books—the fair hair, fair skin, heavy fair moustaches, scowling blue eyes, prodigious stature, and all the rest in accordance. He could bend a horseshoe out of shape with his fingers, they say; and after the Peace of 1815 used to hunt bears in Russia, where he was actually killed by a falling pine in a forest. But who represents the type in the generation to which you and I belong, Hugh, I can't imagine. Clearly you don't, while poor Alan and Janet were just as good Drapiers as you." She referred to his brother and sister, both of whom had died years before, the boy Alan having been killed in France during the war.

Hugh twisted his moustache.

"I'm not so sure that it mayn't be I, in spite of the colouring. I seem to have obeyed the voice of the wild very much in the manner of those others, and from where else should I have got the obsession? My worthy old governor interested himself in nothing but the leaving a respectable fortune behind him, in genuine Pict fashion. Nor have I ever heard of other geographical adventurers in his stock. So it must be through my mother."

Involuntarily Helga glanced at the clock. It was midnight, and though there was still no need to hurry, she preferred now to let an unnecessary topic die a natural death, so that Hugh might come all the more quickly to his intended business.

"It's half our lifetime nearly since we met, Hugh," she remarked pensively after a pause, her hands being clasped over crossed knees. "It's a most sobering thought. What things we have both seen, done, and known in the meantime! Uncle must appear sadly changed to you. You haven't seen him since you were a lad?"

"Not for twenty years, to put a rough date to it. Of course he's changed, but then he's getting on."

"I want you to be as considerate to him as you can. I know he's generally grumpy, and only seems to wake up to say something caustic, but you must remember the infirmities of his age; and he has really been awfully sweet to me. He quite stepped into the breach when poor Dick died."

"I haven't so far intentionally been discourteous to him, Helga. I trust superfluous discourtesy isn't my nature. On the other hand, it's pretty obvious by now that my society affords him no excessive satisfaction; and as I, for my part, assuredly stand in no need of any strained agreeableness from him, we must probably for the short remaining period of my stay carry on as at present. Perhaps I should entertain a greater private respect for him if he hadn't gone into money-making. It rather blunts the edge of his philosophy for me."

"But money is so necessary. And he was thoroughly upset by the poor reception of intellectual works that had cost him years and years of thought. That estate agency business, too, it wasn't sought, but was practically thrust under his nose; and there has never been any question of surrendering his culture, which has always continued to exist side-by-side. I wish you had my faculty, my dear—to place yourself more in the skins of other people."

"You're a finely-tempered soul all round, Helga. Only don't expect persons without your natural advantages to be the same."

He got up, stretched his arms, with the affectation of a half-yawn, and looked down at her.

"You have guessed there is a particular matter I want to talk to you about?"

"What matter, Hugh?"

But the whole of his week-long timidities and caution had suddenly flown with these first ventured words of his, and now he seemed to experience a wonderful coolness and clearness of mental definition, which would enable him exactly to state his request without exciting his cousin's surprise, or extending the ground alone to be made known to her. And first he saw that he must bring up the affair of his estate.

"It is what I came down to Whitestone for. But up to to-day I've been meaning to speak to Uncle Magnus about it, and then, during a whole week, either he's been in the wrong mood or else I have. So I have decided to have it out with you instead. Ingrid warned me only this evening against worrying him. I'm glad, for with you of course I can talk very much more at ease, and you will have a quicker apprehension of the case; besides which, since you are to be my executrix—but that's a preliminary thing. . . ."

Helga was encountering him with a tranquillising upward regard.

"Won't you sit down again, Hugh?" He complied, and she added:

"I didn't know that you were appointing me your executrix."

"I took the liberty of naming you when I made a new will after the death of my sister. You and Ingrid then became my next-of-kin, and so I drew up the will in favour of you two. Under the circumstances, I took it for granted that you would undertake the executorship. If I never notified you at the time, it was because I wished not to raise possibly false expectations. I might be getting married—though that was always highly improbable. Now it's quite out of the question, and I can give you the straight assurance that you and your daughter are to inherit, in equal proportions. At present—supposing I were to die at once—you would get something like nineteen thousand pounds after payment of death duties; between you."

Helga, gazing at him oddly, sat amazed and silent. She had imagined that he was in money difficulties, and now he was all at once able to leave so much behind him! She was unaware of any immediate access of pleasure at the surprise. For one thing, it was little likely that she (being so much older than Hugh, and he so fit-looking) would ever outlive him. And, his own declaration notwithstanding, he might still find a wife. There were notoriously such swarms of marriage-seeking girls in India, where he so often was. She could not determine Ingrid's chances of inheritance.

He talked on.

"The estate's perfectly straightforward. It certainly doesn't represent a millionaire's fortune, still it should prove a useful little addition to what you may have already. It's the unconsumed portion of my father's hoard. All of it in good sound non-speculative stock, mostly trustee; with a few ready hundreds at Coutts', Charing Cross, and personal effects very much scattered over India, London and here, which it wouldn't be worth your while to worry much about. My solicitors hold the will; Marquis & Kent, Norfolk Street, Strand. They would act for you if you wished."

But Helga's continued dumbness and air of disturbed abstraction were chilling him, for he had expected at least some little show of gratification, whereas now he was being driven to conceive that she was only affronted. Possibly in his clumsy failure to provide that margin for the extra sensitiveness of women he had conveyed to her the idea that he was deliberately insulting their assumed position of dependence and poverty. If so, it was very silly of her, and he did not know how to put it right. He trusted that her own better sense would put if right for her and him in the next few moments.

"Marquis & Kent," he repeated, in a colder tone. "Shall I write it down for you?"

"No, I shall remember it, Hugh. But I am thinking how to thank you, this provision of yours is so awfully decent and considerate. In all human probability you will survive me, so I don't count, but I'm intensely touched by what you are doing for

Ingrid. Sometimes I positively can't face the thought that the poor child must one day fight the world alone."

"Let us hope that she'll be safely and happily married to a good fellow long before you depart."

"We'll speak of that another time, Hugh. You have earned the right to be our adviser now. But may I tell her this?"

"Why not? If you wish. I really only mentioned the business to pave a way to what follows. If you are ready—?"

Helga threw him a swift glance, which was not for his seeing.

"I am ready, of course. It has to do with that box, has it not?"

"Yes. Before I begin, however—you aren't offended over this matter of the will? You are not imagining that I have taken too much for granted?"

"Why should you think that, Hugh? I am only very, very grateful."

"You seemed perturbed."

"No, indeed. I think it is a perfectly beautiful action, since it is not to deprive any nearer person."

"No one else has a claim at all."

Her grown quiet warmth of manner now satisfied him that she had never felt affronted, but had only perhaps been overwhelmed by the unexpectedness of his news. He was even glad that she had taken it so. It showed dignity and the complete lack of greed, which he had always been certain of as her character. He could therefore proceed more easily.

"In my possession is a thing of value, Helga, which I am to exhibit to you in a minute or two, for identification purposes. Yes, it's in that box. And in connection with it I'm to ask you a favour—which I fancy you ought to be able to grant. But if you can't, then you will refuse it, and I shan't take offence as long as I know beforehand. The article in question strictly doesn't come under my estate—which is why I was first of all going to beg the request of Uncle Magnus, though not an executor. In other words, it's not my own property. I want it got back, after my death, into the hands of a couple of men who have the better claim to it; though in fact it's not theirs either. Now, Helga, I can't give you the address or addresses of these people, so the whole of your commission will be to hang on to the valuable until they personally apply for it, which may be to-morrow or in three, six or twelve months' time. Soon or late, they are pretty sure to apply for it; but should they fail to, I want it thrown out somewhere, where no one can ever get at it. Keep it by you, say, three years, not longer. That's a sketch of the service."

"It seems a not very onerous one, Hugh. I could easily do that."

"The thing in these days is usually in that tin box; otherwise loose in my pocket. The moment you hear of my death, I want you personally to run through my effects, and secure it. Nearly certainly I shan't ever be leaving England again."

"I will do that too. But why do you speak as if you were under capital sentence? Surely you are quite well?"

"I may die," he returned evasively, "so, as an obligation of honour, I am taking the necessary steps. I'll give you the names of the men, and I can also pass you a snapshot I took of them in Tibet, which is where I ran across them. That's all the rough idea, I think. And you will undertake the job?"

"Of course, Hugh."

"Thank you. It's a weight off my mind. Now I'll show you the curio, and you will memorise it for next time."

From his trouser pocket he took a bunch of keys, then, finding and separating nearly the smallest on the ring, he got up to insert it in the lock of the box on the table. Helga watched him strangely, without moving from her seat. She saw him remove what he wanted from the box, but could no more than distinguish that it was small before her hand was actually touching it. Silently he had given the object to her, and was standing by. It was like the half of a broken sea-shore black flint pebble. In circumference it was about the size of a crown-piece. The fractured interior surface appeared tough, smooth, horny and faceted. It conveyed no meaning to her.

"What is it then, Hugh?"

"Its value is traditional, and also natural. The first we needn't go into. Something of the second you can appreciate for yourself here and now, if you wish it. By holding it from the light, you will get the appearance, or illusion, of some sort of interior motion. Get well round from the lamp and the firelight, and stare down into the snapped face for a long minute. . . .”

Exceedingly puzzled, she obeyed his directions, turning her back to the room’s radiance, while encircling the steadied flint on her lap with a wall of additionally-darkening fingers. Then she frowned down at it, and in this way most of a minute passed in silence. Drapier had dropped into his chair again.

Before the whole minute was up she moved sharply, as if startled, but went on looking.

Something now was travelling perpetually across the face of the flint, from right to left, that resembled smoke. It was a kind of white vapour, now thick, now thin. Its form was ever-changing. Its drift across the flint was quite slow; and the smoke seemed to be in the flint, not on its surface. . . .

Next, after she had become more familiar with it, the tiny field of vision seemed mystically to have grown magnified, till she could fancy that she was peering down at an animated black night sky, over the face of which *clouds* were sailing. And sometimes this whole imaginable sky was filled by the mass of cloud-forms, while at other times they parted fantastically, in the manner of true clouds, to reveal deep rifts of blackness. And at still other times all was black sky, containing no more than a wisp here and there of nebulous vapour.

Of course it was less like the image of an overhead sky than the reflection of one, say, in the quiet illusory depths of some leaf-blackened roadside pool; but dwarfed in the process as well, as if an invisible reducing lens were in between. Yet unmistakably it remained a night sky; the blackness was not of the medium, or not alone of it. Surely what she had been beginning to imagine a glittering aberration of her sight could really be nothing else than infinitesimal star-points shining forth! . . .

A large foreign object came rudely between her eyes and their magic spectrum. She realised that it was Hugh’s hand. He was standing over her again, proposing to take back his little hemi-sphere—stupidly she heard his words.

"Better not spend too much time on it, Helga. You may get fascinated."

"And then?" Her unwonted note of exasperation surprised herself. She made no appeal for longer time, however, and without protest saw him restore the flint to its box.

"You are the last person I should wish to see in the grip of the abnormal," was his simply-uttered reply to her question. She was unable to resolve what significance there might be in it, but was still patient, while her momentary anger had vanished, for she knew that she must now hear more—that he was of his own free will about to tell her more.

"Are you in such a grip, Hugh?" she asked, with a quiet sim-plicity equal to his.

He faced her from his chair.

"I hadn't meant to confess that I am, but I suppose the fact will appear of itself from the rest of my explanation. An honest man can't turn thief without practical justification, and still remain normal, Helga. Well then, not to mince words, I *stole* this thing you have just seen. And why have I stolen it? Because it won't allow me to give it back to the thieves immediately before me in time. So that's what you too have to fear—that it won't let *you* give it up. But then there may be the devil to pay! And that is why I cut short your experimenting."

"But in that case it is very odd."

"Would to God I could find it in my heart to tell you half the oddness of it, Helga! It's fast leading me to believe that the uni-verse as a whole is very odd."

V

Lucius Cornelius Sulla

"And now that I've disclosed my right position, you may change your mind and not choose to associate yourself in any shape or form with an unclean transaction."

A look of sharp inquiry translated his suggestion to a question, but Helga neither availed herself of the offered loop-hole nor hastened to assure him of her magnanimity. For quite a time she held her peace, while trying to make clear to herself the meaning of the curious new swell of her feelings, which nevertheless could not only have begun to work within her that night. It was the culmination of a week's growing recognition of Hugh's strangeness of mood and manner. Something morbid, perhaps tragical, was advancing upon him—she definitely had the intuition of fate, and events yet to come. She earnestly wished to help him to fight his trouble, but had the further instinct that he would decline her assistance. She was especially anxious not to appear or be inquisitive; she must judge the whole from the part that he would elect to confess to her. She did not feel that it was to be anything vulgar, such as the fear of a criminal attack by those men he had robbed. His soul shone out to her as mournful, steadfast, remote. She had no idea what part that queer stone she had just had in her hand was playing in his concealed distress, nor how far its weirdness was influencing her own low fever of spirit, sitting here at past midnight with a man whose existence she had practically forgotten, whose thoughts were of death; and suddenly she determined to put the interrogation that she ought to have addressed to him before. And so, not having answered his inquiry, which perhaps she had received only as a form of self-condemnatory apology, she said:

"Hugh, that appearance in the pebble—what causes it? And what is the pebble itself?"

"Is your consent so conditional, Helga? Are you beginning

already to see difficulties and problems? I was hoping that as a woman, and my cousin, you would have the simple loyalty. As for the phenomenon, no one has ever expounded it to me, so I can't to you. The flint's tradition I merely know as having reference to the ancient worship of the 'Great Mother'."

"Then it is a sacred stone?"

"So I've understood. It has evidently been lodged for an incalculable number of years in a certain Lama monastery in Tibet, which is where that pair of fellows found it. But that would have nothing to do with the earlier tradition. The Lamas don't go in for goddess worship. It must have been reverenced by them on account of its mystical virtues."

"Where originally did it come from?"

"I wasn't told. Perhaps Asia Minor. Cybele was one of the many names of the 'Great Mother' in various lands, and her cult was rampant in Phrygia and all over the Near East. Other names were Rhea, mother of Zeus, in Greece, and Ops in Rome."

"But how was the stone associated with that worship?"

"I wasn't told," repeated Drapier.

"Why are you really so loath to give it up, Hugh?"

"Its examination leads one on and on. One always seems to be on the verge of an important discovery."

"Which never arrives, however?"

"It hasn't arrived yet for me."

"You believe it occult?"

"Yes, I do and must."

"Perhaps it is."

She thought awhile; then began again:

"These men looted it from the monastery?"

"I had better give you the story. I met them about the middle of May last, well inside Tibet, about twenty marches off the frontier passes, as they were going further into the country and I was coming out of it, towards Leh. They gave their names as Arsinal and Saltfleet. The meeting was purely a chance one. I had heard of Saltfleet as a Himalayan climber, but not of the other, and had never before clapped eyes on either of them. So we joined camps for one night only, and had a grand pow-wow over roast yak, biscuit and souchong. It was our first and last acquaintance. Next morning we went on our respective ways."

"At that meeting, I suppose, they announced to you their intention or design of stealing the sacred stone. Or how was it?"

"Yes, they said they were going after it. It seems that Arsinal is a specialising student of the Cybele cult, and had tracked the flint, or its reported existence, down to the monastery we are talking about. Saltfleet, I gathered, was helping him by his expert knowledge of the land and its commissariat problems."

"You are to show me their photograph?"

"Yes, soon. Well, they had perhaps a matter of eighty miles further to go to their destination. I left them to it. At three marches from the Ladak frontier—that is, at some time quite early in June—I was overtaken by a native runner from the pair. He reported that the Sahibs and their round dozen of followers were defending themselves, when he left them, against a mob of Tibetans, incited thereto by their sacerdotals; that there was no immediate risk of anything worse than an undignified and evil-smelling arrest, but that the older Sahib (which should be Arsinal) had given him food for ten days, and sent him off by another way under cover of darkness, with orders to follow and find the red-haired Englishman, and give him 'this token.' I grasped the situation easily enough, knew that they weren't wanting fighting help, but a confederate, and so, having scribbled off a note— 'Your news duly received'—which could compromise nobody, and sent it back by the Ladaki, I went on climbing peaceably out of the land."

"Would they have got that note?"

"He seemed a trusty fellow."

"Do you know if they are released yet?"

"Yes, they are. My agent has cabled me that the two were back in Srinagar, the Kashmir capital, as early as July 10th."

"Then what is your guess, Hugh? That they are so eager for the restitution of their prize that they will follow you all the way to England for it?"

"I've no doubt about it; since they went to the far greater pains of a very hard penetration of a forbidden country, to secure it in the first place. And Arsinal can't be that kind of man at all. He was distinctly of the delicate sedentary type."

"How soon could they be home?"

"They'll lose no time, Helga. On the day that fellow was sent off after me I calculate I was ten marches on from where we had parted. They might be nearly as much the other way; or say, eighteen days in all from me. Add anything up to a week for their confinement after the scuffle, and you get a probable three weeks for the interval between us at the frontier. Well, at Srinagar they were just *two* weeks after me. I passed through a fortnight previously. You mayn't appreciate what that week's difference implies in Tibet, but if the figure is accurate it means they must have killed the cattle. And I haven't the smallest doubt they'll do the equivalent of killing cattle all the way to the Thames docks and London."

"Could they trace you down here?"

"I had to leave my address at the hotel in town, for my correspondence to be forwarded."

"When is the earliest they could come?"

"I haven't studied the shipping. They might turn up at any moment."

"Hugh, what is to happen?"

"God knows! A row, certainly."

"You will refuse to give it up to them?"

"Yes."

"In the consciousness that this is pure madness and weakness, my dear?"

"Yes; in spite of every sane and moral consideration, I shall stick to it, Helga. That's a final rigid decision, not to be reasoned for or against, and you are not to try to dissuade me."

She did not try, but was silent. And Drapier, stealing a surreptitious glance at her face, was struck by its set sternness, showing how unpleasantly she was regarding his business. All her habitual unconscious little affectations of a charming woman

seemed suddenly to have become swept away by this new intense
seriousness of her naked spirit. It had the incidental effect of
making her ten times more beautiful to him. And the house continued like a tomb for quietness, while the rain pattered against
the panes. Helga herself, however, was meditating how, even
when the whole great world slept, as now, like some gigantic
weary monster, its blood still pulsed incessantly through its
arteries, and this blood was *time*. Every clock-tick through the
night was bringing every sleeper in the land an instant nearer to
tragedy and death. There was no such thing as a pause from life.
Fate worked on always, and they were the wise persons who, like
herself and Hugh, sat up to steel themselves against its approach.
It was the death of each at last that rendered it a tragedy. Not to
feel the constant terrifying advance of death upon one, was to
miss the true nature of existence; but it was *time* that brought it
on. A clock, such as that faintly ticking on the mantelpiece, was
the grisliest symbol of one's end. . . .

"Moreover," added Drapier a minute later, "I'm no authority
in the ethics of a case like this, but it seems to me that a distinction is drawable. A thief, stealing from other thieves, has surely
no right, even in honour, to restore the thing stolen to them; his
duty must be to restore it to the proper owner."

"To the monastery. But you are not proposing to do that, and
you have asked me to give it back to the—thieves."

"Very true. I was being Jesuitical. I mustn't lie as well as steal,
Helga; tempting and easy though it may be at the meeting to
come. They must at all events be confronted by the flat truth.
Well, I'll show you their likeness. . . ."

"I want to see it. But, Hugh—what will the international
consequences be of this robbery? Surely a complaint will be
lodged?"

"That may well be; but whether the 'pinching' of a twopenny
relic is a big enough affair for the Viceroy's *dossier* is another
thing. I can't hear any questions being asked in Parliament about
that. What the Tibetans may be able to do is make a fuss about the
infringement of their treaty with us. I don't at all imagine that

Messrs. Arsinal and Saltfleet had taken the necessary trouble to furnish themselves with a permit to enter the country. However, any such storm will descend upon their own heads only. I can't be convicted of cooperation on the bare word of a Ladaki. You certainly, under any circumstances, can't come to harm."

He found the unmounted print, and having barely glanced at it to refresh his memory, at once reached forward to pass it to Helga. She frowned as she mused down over it.

"Saltfleet, I suppose, is the taller of the two?"

"Yes, Arsinal is the baldish one."

The photograph, a happily-secured, excellently-printed quarter-plate snap (slightly crumpled, however, from its long lodgment in Drapier's flexible case) showed the two posed men, both seemingly in young middle life, standing side-by-side, hatless, smiling, and facing the camera. They wore what looked like goatskin short coats, with riding-breeches, puttees and huge fur gauntlets.

"I took it the morning we broke camp. Temperature, if I recall rightly, 22 Fahrenheit, with a bitter searching wind. . . . Does Saltfleet, the bigger chap, convey anything to you?—remind you of any known historical character? It's most unlikely. But have you ever visited the galleries of Rome?"

Helga quietly returned a negative answer. In fact, she had been abroad but little. Her husband had not cared for foreigners, while after his death she had mostly been chained to this one spot.

She continued regarding the photograph in her hand, as the illustration of Hugh's explanatory next words.

"In one of them is, or was, the presumed bust of Lucius Cornelius Sulla, the notorious Roman dictator—so maligned as he always has been. The handsomest type of military consular; every bone of his face patrician. Powerful neck, stern features, sunken cheeks, coarse, haughty, rather brutal lips, wide forehead, pride and daring written all over him. Evidently a tall, big, strong man. Now then, Helga, if the subscription of that exhibit read 'Saltfleet' instead of 'Sulla', I assure you in sober truth the likeness would be just as good. You don't see it of course in the grinning picture you're looking at; you would need the introduction to the man in the flesh. But then it's most astonishing."

"If I remember my Plutarch, surely Sulla was an absolute fiend?"

"He may have made him out to be, but I fancy it was Mommsen who exploded that conception of his character. He was a very unique and tremendous individual living in a peculiarly savage time, who, I don't say worked his way up, or hewed his way up, but almost *yawned* his way up from the extreme bottom of his noble class to unlimited sovereignty over the lives and fortunes of millions. To get the scale of such a man you have to contemplate his horde of bloody-minded, energetic, ambitious contemporaries, in what was probably the bloodiest, fiercest and corruptest chapter of the world's whole history.

"He won all his battles—by sheer ferocious determination, without pretence of *finesse*. He ruined all his personal enemies; except Sertorius, whom he couldn't get at. He made his name a byword of terror to the nations of the East, who were generally so uppish—as they are still, and eternally will be, let the pump-politicians note the fact! He grasped a position in the huge chaotic Roman Republic that had to be created by his own imagination— that is, he made himself, in a very dignified letter to the Senate, the first uncrowned Emperor, as Julius Caesar was the second, and Octavius only the first in name.

"And when no more heights remained to be scaled, when there was absolutely nothing else at home or abroad that he could conceive as worth the doing, then of his own free choice and being still in the height of his faculties he threw up everything, to step back and down into private citizenship. Is that the biography of a fiend, Helga?"

She still gazed at the print, held at arm's length, but now it was in a wide-eyed kind of magnetic dreaming.

"It's difficult to think of any actual man before us as being essentially bloodthirsty. You've detected a resemblance, but of course the differences must be much greater. He climbs mountains?"

"Yes, he has quite a big name for Himalayan ascents."

"Wouldn't that be an anomalous taste in a man having human passions and the political sense? How could he be a Sulla?" She seemed unable to withdraw her eyes from the snapshot. "Though he truly has a sort of imperious look—and personally I think I should prefer to shun an open breach with him. Tell me, Hugh— was it one of your motives in coming down here, to keep out of his way?"

"I trust I'm not a coward."

"Forgive me. I do believe you could hold your own against most men, but this one frightens me. What is his first name?"

"Henry. Henry Saltfleet, and Stephen Arsinal."

She turned to Arsinal in the print nearly with an effort, and her tone seemed to alter.

"How did *he* impress you?"

"Why, Helga, he is undoubtedly a man of very fine sensibility, and exceptional brain-power and education. In his quieter way he may be as masterful as the other; but the other is the more obviously striking."

"The affair is his, and so he has the voice?"

"Presumably. But Saltfleet appears entirely to have identified himself. There should be a pretty complete understanding between them."

Helga saw that Arsinal was shorter than his friend by half a head, and still seemed in no degree undersized. He looked spare, erect, and forty or so, his head being thrown back as in the exhaustion of mental effort, while the eyes were meditative and deep in their orbits. Accordingly, the conceded smile on his lips showed unnatural and masklike. Both he and Saltfleet were clean-shaved.

"You have to consider as well," said Drapier suddenly, on another train of thought, "that this prize of theirs was put into my hands under no contract. I never undertook to relieve them of it; and another man might have called their action in passing it to me under stress a piece of brazen impudence. As they were so callously prepared to compromise me—a perfect stranger to their affairs—with three sets of authorities, I mean Tibetan, British and Chinese, it seems to me I might justifiably retaliate by annexing the thing itself as my price.”

“No, you could have refused to take charge of it, but having once accepted the trust, your single possible course of honour is quite clear.”

He nodded; then took back the print that she was reaching out to him. He returned it to his pocket-case.

“You can see the stupidity of my obsession, Helga, when I am under the necessity of forging all these false excuses for my own conduct. You don’t believe them, and I don’t either, and I suppose the long and short of it is, I’m a worm. All the more reason for your not following suit. So I want you to give me your word that, imagining that this flint does come into your possession, you won’t ever play with it on your own account.”

“I don’t promise that, because I needn’t. I have other people to think of, and all my life I’ve taken long views. You perhaps can afford to indulge, Hugh, but I am a mother, and have a house to run.”

“And also you are not the kind of person to waste your time on insignificances. Therefore I may congratulate myself on having applied to you to carry out the posthumous restitution. The honour and the good sense will both be yours.”

“My dear, I know how you’re reflecting that women are the practical, unideal sex, but on this one occasion only I wish I could pass some of my unimaginativeness on to you. Can’t you see how you’re placing yourself in an utterly wrong position with these people? They’ll have the right to be as offensive to you as they please, if nothing worse; and all for what? That for a little while longer you may go on trying to satisfy a quite unimportant intellectual curiosity. Haven’t you really any sense of proportion, Hugh?”

“You don’t know all, Helga. I can’t tell you all. And it may be that in that very little while longer of yours, the case will have settled itself otherwise. Less may hang on my decision than you think.”

"That I don't know about, but listen, Hugh! You're to meet these men in a very short time, when either you'll return them their treasure or else you'll refuse to return it. Only an unforeseen fatal accident to you can prevent that. Then why this urgent visit to us, to arrange for its disposal in case of death? The chances of your death within the next week or month are surely too negligible to worry about. Your conscience must be peculiarly distressed if the wrong you are doing is appearing so terrible that you daren't and can't wait."

"I have a presentiment of death," responded Drapier gravely.

Helga was neither shocked nor surprised. She seemed to herself to have been expecting the statement; and now she began to understand why for a good many minutes past her thoughts had been morbid. It was telepathic suggestion. She couldn't doubt the truth of his assertion, it so explained his despondency and absence of manner ever since he had been with them. He needn't even be deluded, for she knew of these cases. Yet if he was to die so soon, it would be ghastly. No wonder he could shrug his shoulders at a petty act of dishonour—be illogically content to have it set right hereafter.

What if his possession of the stone had something to do with it! It was ancient, religious, weird; supposing a curse were interwoven into half its nature—the immaterial half! Such things also were.

The impossible grotesque shapes and prismatic colours filling her wide eyes from the half-burnt oak log of the fire, on its nest of black and glowing coals, rendered the lengthening silence of the room an unreal fantasy. She felt so dreamy and so wise, that the nameless overspreading fear of her heart was even pleasurable to her. It added a deep, dark tone, akin to sublimity, to this reactive mood of hers, which somehow was just failing to connect itself with actuality. It seemed to her that it would be time enough tomorrow—it was already "to-morrow," but she meant, in cold, clear daylight—to be practical, and truly apprehensive, and inventive.

Then she roused herself, and should have proceeded to argue

him out of his beguilement, but her automatic speech flowed with quiet earnestness in support of it.

"If you have a presentiment, I have good reasons not to be stupidly sceptical in these cases, Hugh. Dick, my husband, was a very much more worldly and happy-go-lucky individual than you, yet he was twice subjected. On both occasions the presage was followed by the event. The first time, certainly, hadn't to do with death, but it was just the same. On the last day before our very first meeting in life he was by himself at a hotel in Edinburgh; and afterwards he averred that a kind of preternatural restlessness, not unhappy, possessed him throughout that day, preventing him from doing anything. He was to leave directly after breakfast on the following day. But while in bed asleep the same night, he was visited by a female phantom, incomprehensibly tall and strange. She seemed to fill the whole doorway of his room, and to be persistently and smilingly thrusting him back, as often as he tried to leave it. The vision so remained with him on waking, that he stayed on at the hotel. And in the evening, I arrived."

"That was queer and most romantic, Helga, yet hardly in the same category."

"A future event was foreshadowed. Then just a year before Ingrid was born, Dick again oddly enough had occasion to travel to Scotland, but for the whole day beforehand, utterly unlike himself, fidgeted and could settle to nothing. An irrational gloom and sense of dread coloured every minute for him. He and I weren't in the habit of keeping things from each other, and when I challenged him at the time, he confessed it; so what I am now telling you is the literal fact. That same night again, in bed, he saw the identical phantom woman of his previous vision; and, as then, she filled the entire doorway of his room, refusing to let him pass out. Only on this occasion she wasn't smiling, but scowling. We debated in the morning whether he ought to take the journey north, and happily I persuaded him in the end to put it off. Less than twelve hours later the papers reported an appalling train crash in Yorkshire. It was the train he was to have gone by, Hugh. . . . Yet before his pitiful hunting fall, that killed him, he had no premonition whatsoever."

"We can't apply our little staff of reason to these transactions."

"I have tried to, by taking a very simple view; and still it explains nothing. Apparently Ingrid's existence was required; but once she had appeared in the world, fate had no further use for poor Dick, or interest in him, so that he was at liberty to go to destruction as soon and as inconspicuously as he pleased! That at least is the effect."

"It's beyond us."

Helga allowed her personal memories to subside; then asked:

"How long have you had this feeling, Hugh?"

"It has been swelling for some time. I may have recognised it as far back as Tibet, a couple of months ago."

"Mightn't it be just hypochondria?"

"I think not. I have the very definite flavour of death in my mouth. I seem not to be able to see an inch of the future, but there's a black curtain across my life."

"You are otherwise well?"

"Yes, I am very well. Only, this thing is to happen. . . . And since it would be grievous if it should happen down here, in the midst of you all, I'll now be off again; having done what I came to do. Perhaps to-morrow—the day after this one now beginning—would suit?"

"No, you can't hurry away like that, leaving me in suspense, Hugh. Stay on for a little. We'll talk again. . . . We must go to bed now; it's getting late."

She stood up, and looked across to him kindly and softly.

"It is a thousand pities you were never married, my dear! So many of these bogeys would be impossible with a wife."

"I was once in love with you, Helga."

"That must have been a long, long time ago. Now I am nearly an old woman."

"Your eyes could never grow old. They always seem to me to be looking out of your soul."

"My soul is old too. I am terribly old altogether. But I have Ingrid, and you haven't a son. I don't know that I regret very much of my life, except its tragedies. Can you say as much, my dear?"

"How do you keep your tranquillity? You must have a great peace inside you."

"It comes of a long subordination of one's will to the little duties of the day."

"Then that is what I have missed," said Drapier. "I've done almost everything I wanted to in the world, but, I fancy, very little that I haven't wanted to. It's easier for a woman, however."

"We haven't so much strength as you, to get in the way of a surrender, but otherwise nothing is easy for women, Hugh. We have no golden mountains before us, we feel when we ought to be thinking, we are all nerves, and our bodies are usually below par. We have to live up to traditions framed in the barbarous ages. You had better not die, my dear, or you may be born again a woman."

"The language of all of you is alike, Helga; but I can't believe that you would be a man if you could."

She no longer replied, but instead bent swiftly down to him as he continued sitting; and kissed his forehead. Then she stood erect again, and smiled, while he joined her on his feet.

"Thanks, Helga! Yet I also remember that so they kiss the brows of the dead."

"You are to live to see Ingrid married," was all her shocked answer.

When, however, he had gone out, leaving her still standing facing the door that had merely been pulled-to after him, her thoughts went quietly back of their own accord to that man whose reproduced features were quite like no one else's whom she had ever seen. His must be a very determined, powerful, dynamic nature. It was Saltfleet's face, of course, that she mentally contemplated. She could not help feeling—it was like some small, insistent, very deep-down and distant voice calling out to her from the profundities of her own soul—that he it was who was to bring Hugh to his fate. She wished she had begged to be allowed to retain that photograph.

If *he* came after Hugh to Whitestone, she should see him in the body. How ought she to treat him, when nothing had been planned, no attitude decided upon? The true stroke of genius would be for her to win such a man to compassionate and assist Hugh, in place of throwing down the gage. She did not know what weaknesses he had; perhaps none, for a woman. The other man would be like a fish, and hardly seemed to count, although probably the principal.

Couldn't she send Hugh away somewhere—to one of her friends, further away from town—till the business had blown over? Then Saltfleet would negotiate personally with her. But Hugh would have bound her beforehand, and still nothing would get settled. If in the meantime his presentiment came true. . . . but that would need to be an accident. What kind of accident? Why, anything. He might fall downstairs. At that, Helga recollected that he was intending to venture down those uncovered ancient stairs on Devil's Tor, in but a very few hours' time. If absolutely an accident was fated for him, where likelier than there? But she supposed it was his toughness and expertness and experience that prevented her from feeling the slightest genuine alarm regarding that excursion. No, Saltfleet was in some manner associated with Hugh's crisis to come, of that she was superstitiously convinced.

How could he, a modern Englishman, very possibly having a university education, be a Sulla, with the ferocity and perfect recklessness of one! No doubt it was partly because it was one o'clock in the morning that she was imagining absurd things. For all that, she wished she could have seen him before Hugh went back. Had she still any remains of her old power to fascinate? She hadn't seriously asked herself such a question for years, for nowadays few men came, and none preferred her to her daughter. Five-and-twenty years ago she had but to sit in a chair, and the men would arrive. . . .

She trod sadly to the mirror on the wall, and stayed in front of it for a long time, regarding her image, with only occasional changes of pose.

VI

The Three Strains

Drapier rose again soon after five, before it was quite light indoors, made a quick toilet, and let himself out of the house while no one else was yet stirring. Notwithstanding the preceding evening's fatigue and his late going to bed, he had hardly slept, so that for an interminable time he had watched with sick impatience the slow changing of his room from black to grey. When at last he might he had got up with that fagged relief that brings no contentment with it.

Insomnia had already begun to plague him in India before coming away; now, in England, the condition had grown so evil that his resting hours were a nightmare to be expected. Another man would have sought drugs for it, but to Drapier, who neither drank nor smoked, the idea never occurred. He had sustained plenty of hardships in his trekking life, whereas his purity of body was a very real asset to him.

So his account to Helga of his reason for early walking had not been strictly accurate, though it did in fact represent a supporting motive. He got up because he couldn't sleep; and he couldn't sleep because of his sensations of impending death. There was no element of fear in it. He knew how to lie on the broad of his back in bed, and stare death calmly in the face with open eyes, wondering queerly how that last moment would taste, seeking vainly to analyse his unanalysable feelings; never once yielding to any swift panic desire to be assured of long life. By day he attempted no remedy of forgetfulness in the social excitements. His instinct never informed him when the event might be anticipated.

A torch was in his pocket. He should easily be back for breakfast, and it was an unutterable relief to be abroad again. The tingling morning air cooled his cheeks and toned his lungs, oxygenating him to a new carelessness of acceptance of his rearing night. Being a doom, by no contrivance of his to be avoided, he found its advancing increase immaterial and empty of menace. He might even be fated *not* to return to breakfast, and still it should not particularly matter. This underground stairway to be explored might do his business, but Helga had been spoken to, those people were to get back their own, his last scrap of earthly anxiety was removed, and to-day was as good for the purpose of his death as to-morrow or next week. It should be near.

The steady night downpour had reduced the temperature by twenty degrees, recharged the atmosphere with its highest carrying capacity of ozone, and set it briskly moving; the breeze blew straight off the moors, sharp, wrapping, flogging, wonderfully fresh and sweet. The sun was not yet up; and would not show when it should be, perhaps in not many minutes now. It would come up behind that long low band of cloud across the east. And he was glad that his humour was to escape a gaudy spectacle. The stern, clear-cut purity of this half-stormy silver dawn was worth many coloured sunrises. All was black and white. The soaking rains had brought out a hundred soft pungent odours of the soil, of the trees and bushes. In the second half of the morning the depression might finally spin off and the sky clear, but till then occasional showers still threatened; which was why a mackintosh was across his arm. The suit he had worn to the Tor last evening was wet yet, so he wished to keep this he had on dry.

Poetic by blood, and made additionally susceptible by that long series of broken nights, he fell quickly into the lonely mood of wild musical melancholy bequeathed him by his ancestors of the red-deer hills and rushing torrents and phantom mists. It was a formless melancholy, delicately ennobling the preoccupations of his brain, rather than presenting anything of its own. At the most, he knew it, without also knowing what it desired; he could express to himself no particular of the vague yearning that was like a drawing of all his fibres towards this natural world around him, as the moisture of the soil is invisibly drawn to the skies.

The mood was familiar, and since he could not understand it, he had long ago invented a formula for it. The mysterious hour and dusk, the aloneness of his being, the dark friendly trees, the intimate wind, and breaking sky—it, as its equivalent of sombre enchantment experienced elsewhere on earth, he recognised to be the right element of his eternal part. Yet it was all no more than *hint*. It stood for nothing of itself, but was the faint imperfect copy of heaven; the proof being that, though it might call, it could not satisfy, but on the contrary produced in him such states as disturbance, sullenness, infinite longing, sadness, despair. Thus he was inevitably reminded by it of some grander world not present. His formula, therefore, was that the merely beautiful might suffice a soul, but that the sublime (which was the shadow of the beauty of another world) could never suffice, since with it came gropings that must amount to pain. . . .

He crossed the deserted tarred main road, and at once plunged downwards between the high banks of the lane's opposite continuation. It was the way he had come with Ingrid yesterday.

The misty trees overhead dripped regularly their surplus of saturation on to the skin of his face or neck, while under foot the liquid umber mud triumphed from ditch to ditch. After a last steepening and bending of the hill to the right, however, appeared the old long straight bottom stretch that introduced the open road across the moor. Here the walking proved drier, and yet there were still the high banks, and trees above them.

He wondered how all this cultivated part of Dartmoor would have looked, say, in Tertiary times, before the advent of man on the planet; before that uglifying master-brute had put a hand to his congenial and self-honoured labour of clearing lands of their established life. Savage and lovely beyond thought, no doubt. So what had been gained by the substitution? Additional sources of food supply for man himself and some dozen kinds of degenerated animals, his servants. For this, fair trees had been uprooted, strange, beautiful beasts and snakes of the wild exterminated, exquisite birds made rare or extinct, the inhabitants of the streams slaughtered and poisoned. Verily, a ruthless campaign!

And the effective result? Why, this foul trail of earth-viscera and metamorphosis wheresoever man passed. All over England

and Europe, and gradually all over the world, the houses, pavements, factories, mines, quarries, cuttings, bridges, railways, cars, engines and machinery, slag-heaps, gas-works, roads, stagnant canals, the grime of unreckonable chimneys, the grit and dust of a hell-maze of thoroughfares; and the slums, and backyards, and hidden corners of filth and shame. Or the cabbage-rows, and manure-heaps, sties, stables and pens—to demonstrate the superlative vulgarity of this scrambler for easy food, the human biped, whose stomach was paramount in the existence of a mystic universe.

It would be an excellent thing to die, and leave it all! . . . And under what law, other than *force majeure* (to propound the question in the parliament of all the creatures of God)—under what law had the so-styled lower life been dispossessed and destroyed, to make way for a single species? The ugliness of it might pass, if a merit could be shown for the wholesale annihilation. To allow the entrance into the world of idealism and spirituality, he supposed the cant answer would be. Then all that murdered life had the right to demand, where are those things? And the man and woman of to-day gave the reply by talking only of money, luxury, sport, amusement and sex. The Aryan Brahmins, the Stoics, the Christian saints and martyrs, the Puritans, the makers of noble music, the sublime philosophers—they had been the justification for the destruction; and they were departed, and others had not stepped into their shoes. That assassination of Nature, begun in the instinct of self-preservation, continued in blindness and barbarism, never at any time in history aware of its own iniquity, but presently, during a very few centuries out of long thousands of years, offering to the Creator an equivalent compensation in the shape of the worship of His invisible height—it was now being brought rapidly to its last horrible consummation, in its destruction as well of the whole of beauty; in the insane building by that single conquering species of an iron prison wherein it should spend the rest of its span combating its own denied instincts, that must forever break out into monstrous excrescences.

A most sinister state of affairs! How had it come to pass in this world, otherwise of flame, loveliness and passion?

The ultimate answer was refused. The cause in time of the crime and blunder of course started with the possession by man of a brain; and was ending with over-population. The infinitely greater weight of the mass nowadays was an irresistible force pulling men towards each other and away from the lonely Austere and Sublime. The other name of this gravitation was democracy; so that democracy was the grand evil. No one man could fight such a pull of a whole world, however much he might know it to be suicidal and terrible. Or if he enlisted assistance, he was but inviting a second small democracy. Men united only to discuss men and the affairs of men, whether these affairs were on earth or in Paradise. It was all as hopeless as the coming on of a cancer.

Yet if it was the ordained and necessary course of a world? For just as the thoughts, circumstances and environment of a child were mysterious and rich in beauty, while for the adult were only grim duties and responsibilities of lead, so it might be with the life of the species, and of the corresponding species of every life-bearing planet. First, Nature lived with and dimly apprehended through a veil of glory; the gods and goddesses, witches, elves and fairies. Then the transition; the Almighty and His saints, speaking the language of the Cross. And lastly the fully-emancip-ated intellect, finding itself amazed in a fearful life without per-sonal future, for which it had never asked.

Arsinal's "Great Mother"—she was Nature, when men had been children. She was dead. Men themselves had killed her. Or could she conceivably rise again, in the fashion of a dead god? . . .

His stepping off the open road on to the moor coincided with the bending of his thoughts to his own more insistent problems.

He had to consider what had happened to him since his talk with Helga last night. It was upon his first getting out of bed that the uneasy awareness had stirred in his brain of the very obscure and baffling existence of some link of true association between his various strains. Up to to-day he had never suspected them to be connected.

It was the more obtuse in him, since all three must have dated approximately from the same time, namely, from between Tibet and Simla, on this last trip. He could recollect the indistinct beginning of one only in Tibet; after Simla all three were in action. The Tibet strain was queer, the other two were quite unaccountable; they had sprung up in him like strange weeds in a protected flower-border.

The chief in rank was his premonition of death; but that was not the Tibet one. It was like a taste in the mouth, destroying all other tastes. Little by little it had sapped his love of life, till now he was not so sure that he would accept a longer career as a gift. It had introduced to his soul quietness, and easiness, and something of majesty; but not daunting or depression—he thought not depression. There were necessarily accompanying practical embarrassments, such as his new shunning of outside society, and his complete neglect of the future. But on the whole the taste was good. It was somehow both tranquillising and exciting. The tranquillity concerned his affairs, his worldly affairs, which by now seemed not to matter at all; but the excitement consisted in the adventure of it. It was like a preparation for a journey; anything might be going to happen to him. The principal evil of the business was that it left his present short remainder of life rather empty. He had too much time on his hands in which to hark back to the past, and repent the little use he had made of it.

For, dividing all human acts into the two classes, those having eternal meaning and those others having only temporary applicability to the things of earth, then, obviously, he had woefully squandered the best part of his days and chances. He had loved none, he had brought into the world no work of perpetual beauty, he had relieved few in distress, and that most scantily, he had done nothing for the spirits or bodies of men, for long years he had not communicated directly with heaven; but he had hugged his aesthetic misanthropy in burying himself in wild places; and would leave no monument behind him. Unless it were his grave-stone, on which should be carved the words:

Whatsoever this man hath done, do thou avoid.

Indeed his death mattered the less, because his life had been so trivial. Neither had it been ennobled by high deeds or love, nor darkened by suffering. A thousand million living persons knew the deeper experience.

His sense of being slowly enveloped by death was not a bodily taste. It was not a blight, or *malaise*, gradually destroying his hold on life, and so translating itself for his consciousness. It was not a supernatural voice or message. If it could be compared at all, it was like a coming, rather than a going. Something positive was approaching, and this something was his death, and it was already dark, and void, and of a peculiar bitterishness, and altogether indescribable; but it was not being a mere cessation of his known experiences. It was bringing a new knowledge. Sometimes his heart seemed to beat with a slow, heavy exhilaration, as if it was hearing music—solemn music, that his ears could not.

The second and earliest of his strains had to do with that flint he had shown Helga. It consisted in the always-increasing subjection of his imagination to what was surely the most amazing vision of natural beauty, reduced to the dimensions of art, that could at any time possibly have existed on earth. It amazed, because it was as living as a mirror reflecting real things, and yet the real things in its case were nowhere present. Provided the experiment were conducted in shadow, that night sky was just as visible by day; or those stars were just as needle-bright and shining when the true sky was thick with a mile of cloud. This he had discovered at a very initial stage. Since then, the little marvel had been in his hand a couple of hundred times perhaps, over a period of two months, so that his eye was sharpened to a much finer adjustment to the difficult details of its weird field. Great doggedness had been called for in the beginning. Barely enough advance had been yielded to encourage him to the persistence.

Bit by bit had he been forced to discard his successive hypotheses. It was not a right mirror, because, looking upwards from it, he failed to see its images in space. But neither was the appearance a false one, due to some smokelike motion within the body of the stone. The tiny star-points sprinkling the black rifts and spaces between the white clouds, they were congregated into constellations—constellations unknown to him; and these constellations *shifted*, not quickly like the clouds, but during weeks of patient observation. The progress was from left to right. The constellations disappearing altogether off the right-hand margin of the field never came back; those appearing on the left were new. So a real sky of stars would behave; so no interior animation of the stone could. Therefore he was seeing the image of stars existing somewhere. And yet they were not real, but must be mystical, because by ordinary physical eyesight they must be indistinguishable by reason of their minuteness. There might be a hundred or more of them, scattered over a ground of a couple of inches. No human eye could separate such a packing, and make out its configurations, unless it should see *differently*; and so the phenomenon was both real and unreal; in short, of a world, but not of this world.

Thus it was mirror, microscope and magic crystal, combined. And he had begun to chart that sky of stars from day to day, but doubted if the exact information so obtained would form a sufficient basis for calculation within his time. To map the *fourth*—or as they would say in these days, the *fifth dimension*—it was fantastic enough! Yet if the theory was glib, what other covered the thing at all? Such a sky must be near enough for sight, while actually it was not in sight; therefore he must be regarding a part of physical space in another way. To state one possibility out of hundreds, he might be looking behind him, instead of before him round the extension of a prodigious circle. The same star might be seen by the eye in those two different manners.

The flint itself might originally have dropped from the stars. There it might have been the product of an intelligence higher than any on earth, which had known how to construct such a celestial spy-glass. Some intuitive ancient on earth had recovered its properties, and had split it, to see inside. The other half had been lost; perhaps fifty thousand years since. This had travelled from temple to temple. Not inconceivably, it might have been so.

A second of his senses had co-operated. One day, chancing to hold the stone nearer to ear than eye, he had *heard* too. The throb of what might be music was sounding; but so faintly, he could hardly distinguish between it and the vast silence of the Himalayan amphitheatre enclosing him as a mighty crescent during their midday halt.

Afterwards his hearing, like his seeing, had adapted itself queerly to receive the elfin beating with a magnified distinctness, and then not quite the tune, almost the rhythm, came to him; perhaps from across space, the breadth of a universe away, the distance being mystically diminished. A strange half-caught pulse, quite beautiful in its suggestiveness. He had never been able, however, to better that achievement on that line. His brain, framed by Nature for practical use in a starved world, lacked delicacy for picking up any such unearthly musical message, if it were one.

The flint in those days only moved between his hand and his pocket. When the monotonous caravan duties of the daily trek were again concluded each evening, supper consumed, and the log and records written up, he would seclude himself in his personal tent, or if it were warm, windless and still light, wander off to the nearest convenient open solitude, away from the range of inquisitive native eyes, and there once more lose account of time in a fruitless wrestling with those shifting hieroglyphics of another sphere. The idea had occurred to him, he forgot at which one of such camps, that the thing might literally be a communication from some planet of another far-distant sun; which opened other possibilities. As the communication was to *two* of his senses, while the transmission to both was imperfect, might not it be that the message was intended for a third sense, unknown on earth, perhaps lying midway between sight and hearing, and so being distantly related to both? It was a thought that impressed him tremendously; for then a sensible writing by a spirit differing from all human spirits was displaying itself there before him, signalling matters which it might be highly essential for the world to know.

Uncomfortable had been his hesitations during those mountain days, as to whether or not he should wait for Arsinal on the border, to get the whole story from him, and probably learn something of the right manipulation of the flint. Yet already the determination was concreted in his mind not to give up again this prize, come into his hands by the wheel of fortune. So that meant that he would need to lie to Arsinal, declaring it to be mislaid or lost; for brass enough in his constitution to deny him the thing outright, he had not. And next the smell of death had begun to be in his nostrils, persuading him that he might be soon to die. Since all was so uncertain for him, it would be better for the present to lead the pair to suppose that he had merely gone on ahead without word, on a call of private business.

But the spell of the stone had grown and grown within his head, until now no threat or counter-temptation on earth would induce him to part with it, and he had at last that "brass enough" to face Arsinal, with the other at elbow, and simply notify to him the fact that this running-away of his was no piece of mere caddish indifference on his part, but a deliberate escape, covering a confiscation to be upheld.

Latest of all—between Leh and Simla, he thought it was—had appeared, in extremest subtlety, the third of his three strains, yet still only as a rudiment. It was the instinct or occult attraction that was not to cease its silent work until he should be standing on a Dartmoor height, in England, over he knew not how many thousand miles of sea and land; yet that height he had never heard of, while in England itself he had had no business. Nor could he at the present moment be certain that the attraction had run its course. He was being further drawn to the *interior* of Devil's Tor. There it might be intended he should find his own grave; and so this instinct and that other of approaching death would have coalesced and come to a common fulfilment.

But the instinct of death had known his other strain for its fellow in the affair's beginning; and this, as he had to-day begun to see, constituted the linking, or a linking, of all the three.

For once he had decided to keep his prize, and once his presentiment had become too strong to ignore, he had had these two motives for getting back to England; to put distance between himself and Arsinal, and to settle with his lawyers in London the posthumous restitution of the stone. Neither reason for going home was over-strong, since he might have written the lawyers, and escaped to any other country; however, he had booked a passage. And in the very act of paying for it, it had flashed into his head that ever since Simla at least he had definitely planned to travel straight through to England, so that this later revolving of other motives for the journey was supererogatory. But on what account he had so planned to come at once to England, he puzzled himself over repeatedly, but never could remember. It had worried him greatly, in a minor way.

Then, sailing from Bombay, he had arrived in London near the end of July; where three or four days had not passed before the same extraordinary mental freak overtook him. The weather in town during that week before last had been insufferably hot and close, there had been nothing to do, and the visit to the lawyers he had kept putting off; their trained questioning might elicit the theft, to his infinite humiliation. He had gone to a show or two, and been abominably bored. And so he had thought of his uncle and cousins in Devonshire. Helga was to be his executrix, and should be told of the will and its contents. Uncle Magnus might be the right person to address in the matter of Arsinal's treasure. There would at least be fresh air to breathe, and corners of the moor to escape to, away from people. He had not seen any of them since boyhood. He wondered how Helga would appear to him now; while her daughter too should be interesting—a grown-up, doubtless pretty girl. Accordingly he had written off, proposing a week's stay. And at the actual moment of posting the letter, he had realised—this time with a following shock that closely resembled fear—that it was on board ship, before his arrival in England at all, that the intention of inviting himself to Helga's had been fast fixed in his head. Yet, cudgel his brains as he might, he couldn't for the life of him recover under what circumstances he had come to the decision; what his special reasons had been, or what had started them.

So mysterious a second case of losing and regaining a practical design affecting his movements excited in him, the more he
thought about it, a rising though still sluggish curiosity concerning his whole present condition of soul, with its various quite
unassociated stresses. He told himself that he might be in an
abnormal state all round. But still his foretaste of death had
prevented him from really feeling anything of the natural alarm of
a man whose mind should begin to crack. He did nothing about it;
indeed, there was nothing to do. A doctor might certainly inform
him that he was mad—and how would that help?

Helga's reply had been friendly and pressing. During the first
few days of a pleasant enough stay, nothing more had happened
in the way of this sympathetic sounding of forgotten plans. But
then at lunch only the day before yesterday, the name of Devil's
Tor was for the first time in his life (so far as he was aware)
mentioned in his hearing. Helga, solicitous for his entertainment,
had introduced the hill as an excuse for an agreeable walk over
the moor; of no especial interest in itself. Ingrid had said nothing.
He had put a conventional question or two about it, and said in
the end quite carelessly that he might make the trip next day;
when of a sudden had come the same trick of astonishing
memory. Not only had he very certainly heard of Devil's Tor
before, but already, at some time since the beginning of his stay,
had he made it a settled thing that he was to go out there.

And now this was lunacy absolute. For how could he possibly
have intended any such excursion to an unknown spot? It looked
like imperfect control, or adhesiveness, or both jointly. A name
was suggested to him, a plan followed, and the two became stuck
together for him; then some fault of memory, always in the one
direction, antedated the first suggestion of the name, putting it
back half a week, a week or a month, as the case might be; and
still the plan went with it. The explanation was grotesque, but
might be correct. At least, there was no other at hand.

Lastly—a minute later at table—Helga had proposed to him
her daughter's company and guidance for the walk. Ingrid had
expressed her willingness; whereupon he, though still stunned by

this new prank of recollection, had returned his civil thanks and acceptance of the offer. But nearly simultaneously had he been struck by that final shock, which was like a reinforcing wave to the not yet subsided last. Ingrid's society as well had been provided for in that previous design of his! . . . So other persons too were to confirm and fall in with his forgotten plannings! Yet that would surely make it occult.

This, then, was the third and most recent of his strains. By now he seemed to guess that it was not insanity. With the dawn, its linking to the other two appeared a theory impossible to discard; nor could there be much doubt that it was his last night's talk with Helga that had wrought the development. He had told her so much that he had not meant to, and still he was feeling that he had told her nothing. What had he kept back of such supreme importance that it could be thought to constitute the whole difference between a confession and a non-confession? He had said nothing about this unconscious gradual drawing of the Tor. It was not that omission. It was the larger linking of all three of his prepossessions that had not been discussed with her, as he himself was unaware of it last night. Just because he knew this morning that there was something big that had not come up between them, his mind was sniffing this new scent of a connection. The notion itself had appeared in advance of any experimenting with it.

He *was* to die in these next few coming days, on Devil's Tor.

He stopped short where he was, on the moor. It had not been a voice in his ears, it was still but a silent thought, yet just as unmistakably was it an announcement. Before, it had been a mere idea, a question, a playing with possibility, but now it was a declaration from somewhere outside himself. He *was* to die on this height he was making for; though not necessarily as yet. And this should be his triple link that he was seeking.

He walked on again.

He had known that he was to die. He had begun to know that Devil's Tor had brought him step by step from India. Now quietly he was inspired that it was his possession of Arsinal's sacred stone that was at the root of all. If so, it should not be this morning, for he had left the stone at the house. But Ingrid's part?—for she too had been included in that magnetic pull; it had been in his unearthly consciousness that she was to accompany him.

But for her, he would have turned back home on account of the weather last evening. He could not say what difference that might have made.

Perhaps Devil's Tor long ages ago had been the original sanctuary of the stone. He who bore it, should be borne with it towards and to the Tor, by the latter's irresistible attraction. Perhaps it was to be redeposited in the dark recesses of that ancient tomb. Then he who served such a purpose might be to lose his life down there, that there might be no living witness of the transaction. . . .

He recalled those three flashes of ghastly lightning that had glittered round them on the Tor's slope yesterday. What if they had symbolised these three linkings of his strains a few hours later? Indeed, his soul was being lit by the awful violet glare of this sudden threefold enlightenment.

VII

In the Tomb

Without troubling himself to look for Ingrid's path of last evening, Drapier had struck off at an instinctive tangent up the long heave, confident in his sense of general direction. His shoes were already soaked by the wet of the moor. The dawn had nearly changed to day. There was no sun, but the eastern sky at his back was all pearl, rose and silver.

If that fragment of a stone was truly responsible for his gathered night of soul, which needed for its penetration these lightning-blazes of inspiration, surely there presented itself one very easy way of refinding his old happier state. He had but to make a parcel of the little talisman, and post it to his agent in Bombay for delivery to Arsinal, wheresoever he was to be found.

Thus its sinister spell would cease for him; Devil's Tor would no longer pull, death would no longer come grinning at him.

But he could not do it. The business had not clutched him for nothing; it was no accident that this magnetic death-hill lay within an hour's walk of a house to which he had the *entrée*. He was the wanted person for a commission, which therefore also included his individual case.

And supposing he elected to try to ignore the commission, still he knew that it was too late in the day to escape the stone's magic—its wonder, beauty, and message. It was impossible now for his imagination to shake itself free before the right nature of that enigmatic hieroglyphic sky should be better understood; its particular meaning read. On such a shifting tablet might be set down the symbolic representation of his own required work and fate. If it were meant that he should decipher the cryptogram, he must still live till then.

He wished he had it with him, to refresh his mind, staggering under these new insights and superstitions; scarce able to distinguish the one from the other. Of what use indeed to pay this second visit to the Tor without it? If it phenomenally needed to be lodged there by him, then he must still come up the third time, with it. Perhaps he was to prospect the tomb, in order not to have to waste time over preliminaries on that next occasion. He was ignorant of everything; could determine nothing. The flint assuredly had fetched him here from India, to die here; nearly all the rest was pure guesswork.

His mood had become peculiarly heightened, like that of a man going into action. He was glad that his worldly affairs were in good order and all behind him. The landscape was surprising him by its changedness; while his body seemed to him light and foreign, as though it were all at once no more than a mooring for his consciousness. So many endless wearisome years had he cleansed, adorned, fed and flattered it, as his supreme *raison d'être*, only to realise at last that it was spectral, doomed to vanish into thin air at this cock-crow of eternal life about to sound. Strictly true it was, and no fiction of the poets and mystics. And analogously, these grey slopes and rolling silver skies before him, they existed certainly, since they formed a direct material continuation of his own person, nor was their beauty to be denied; nevertheless in the twinkling of an eye they would pass into everlasting nothingness, so how should they not be a deceit of his senses?

His countless small cares, too—the anxieties, absorptions, willings, mean delights and meaner fears, of daily life, that so nearly exclusively employed a man during his mortal passage—somehow they had dropped from him like a foul skin, leaving him clean and innocent of mind, as though he had been a young child again, only now with no beginnings of the guilt of the world. As a child had not yet come to it, so he had done with it, that long middle hell of vanities, dreads and passions—that nightmare of the spirit's perpetual trembling on account of the false prizes and terrors of a very few years of existence inside an illusory body.

He understood. It was the high lesson of death, vouchsafed him by special favour while still undying. The lesson was that life was neither opportunity, nor education, nor growth, as the various orders of the foolish would have it, but a heady fever, the occasional grandeur flashing through the rare lucid intervals of which represented the soul's true condition.

Finding himself so near to the mood of death, he considered his courage; how he might expect to behave at the real last moment. Thereupon he seemed to understand that nothing earthly in the shape of attitudes was to serve his passage out; not courage, nor pride, nor apathy, nor theatricality, nor cynicism, nor superstitious asseveration, nor the hugging of a conscience; but that simplicity and humility must at the very end be exacted of him. He could not conceive what might come after. The world being all so false, he thought that there must be a true.

The scene around him grew ever smaller and more domestic. The cold, sweet, wet purity of the morning air, the living mists perpetually clothing and stripping again the streaming moorland, the sharp scents, identifiable or baffling, from the scrub, heath and tangle of his moving circle, the quitted road on his left winding its ascending way lower down along the side of the great shoulder he climbed diagonally, the soft and lovely cloud-ceiling shutting him in, the homeliness of all this solitude, in character so remote from comparison, from contrast even, with the bare, silent, awful solitude of death— the whole resembled to him in his present mood a toy world, charming but childish and unmeaning; exactly suited on that account to the requirements of his phantom bodily part, that also had no meaning. He couldn't with any magnanimity regret leaving it. As a biological product indeed he must do so, but as an immortal soul such a lingering back-gazing would be as mean as blind in him. For that real being was immediately to go on, first to the white, huge, mournful entrance-hall of another life incalculably vaster, since all the dead, of all time, had quitted the planet by its single door; and thence to that unthinkable archetypal universe which threw solidity and colours into the material world like its shadows, and instincts and passions like its faint distant voices. How could dwarfish man not be simple and humble when brought to the very threshold of such a heaven?

Drawing out his watch, Drapier learnt that it was still not six. Perhaps the day was quite come, but the low dark suspended clouds prolonged the illusion of dusk, while the sky held no tints except behind him, where he never saw them. A wet pellet or two stung his cheek, a sudden flurry of wind tried to whirl his cap off, and even as he rammed it more tightly on his head, the dark mass of Devil's Tor again stood up before him, nearly from the identical spot where last evening he and Ingrid had halted to behold it illustrated by that fearful blazing fork, that had been like the sword of an archangel. But when they had looked back to it from the same vantage on the homeward journey, the emasculated crest had been blotted out by the weather; and so it still was, for the jealousy of vapour wrapping the hill's top seemed not to have shifted throughout the night.

His mind moved over familiar ground, till it came to a new thought. He recalled Thor, and Ingrid's alarm at the idea of a descent. He continued to believe that he was perhaps wanted to return that occult stone to its former resting-place in the tomb he made for; though it could not be this time. His death might be at once to follow, nevertheless he knew no postponing desire. Then came his new thought. The stone being returned to the tomb, and he dead, what need was there for him to have troubled about that interview with Helga? For now she would only be perplexed in searching everywhere and never finding his treasure; and Arsinal in any case was not to get it back. Should this business so fall out! And so all last night's talk might well stand for nothing; in which event only another problem had started up—how was he to relieve Helga of the commission without either lies or a fresh confession? What to do about it, he could not determine; but this mental interruption had the instant effect of fetching back his entire spirit to the painful practical world, with which he had hoped to have done.

He pushed on in disquiet. This doubtless was the penalty for taking an active hand; for trying to steer destiny according to his contemptible human insights based on the codes and petty laws of society. He was to remain a thief even after his death, and nothing else had ever been intended. The penalty provided that his risen comprehension of death should be arrested and put back by this new invasion of the trivial. The lesson to learn therefrom was that as often as his will should become quick and inventive, so often must he begin again at the beginning of his peace.

Unconsciously despising the steepness of the hill at his feet, as well as to save a minute or two, he dropped straight down to the valley separating the two heights, then sprang across the stream, swollen after the rains, and started directly up the Tor's face. The way brought him through the main wreckage of the overthrown pile. Some of the great blocks surely *were* unsafe, so again he impressed it on his memory to get that public warning posted. He did not know if the Tor were at all frequented.

Nobody was aloft now at least, when he reached the top. All view off the hill was prevented by the mists. There was no excuse for delay in proceeding with his task, nor did he wish to delay it.

Those ancient stairs still showed greyly from the mysterious depths of their enclosing oblong hole. It was out of the question for others to have been up here before him so early in the morning, while last evening the night had been closing in on their departure, with the storm not yet quite ceased. So the adventure remained his, come what might of it.

Accordingly, bringing out and testing his torch, then refolding the loose mackintosh over his arm, he went on without more pause to lower himself to the first stair down of that queer nightmare passage, by the clumsy manoeuvre of squatting on the surface ledge and dropping his feet until they touched. When they were square on the rock, he switched on his light.

So this stairway was no illusion; and still he could continue dropping his legs to the second, and third, and fourth granite treads. At the fourth, however, a rocky roof was already above his head. After that, he counted all the steps.

Yet was he aware of no great interest in the descent; certainly of no excitement. He was in this place so quietly, so almost suddenly, that it was all being more like a dream to him; he was here because one minute always followed another, and a man's movements must be continuous. The introduction to the adventure had ended at last, so the adventure itself was commencing. He supposed that he was merely being absorbed into a hole by some fate that willed it. A mighty marvel even might be awaiting him, and yet there was this absence of curiosity from his soul. His death would be so infinitely mightier than all other possible marvels.

The walls became a rude spiral. They were of rough natural rock, chipped away in places to allow a wider passage. Of what substance could have been the tools of those ancient workmen, so to subdue hard granite? He thought of the Pyramids, the building of which also had been a miracle.

And while he continued without pause first to sit on his muscular haunches, then to dangle his feet to their next support, the light of his torch at each moment showed brighter, indicating thereby that the darkness was increasing. But the air never grew worse than cold, damp and earthy.

At the fifteenth drop he touched bottom. At that forty feet and more below ground he was shown the way now going forward without further perpendicular drop, though still falling sharply. What was before him, in effect, was a descending tunnel, the continuation of the curve of the staircase, so that his flash revealed only those few paces ahead. Already the circle might be complete and he be right underneath the upper hole again by which he had come down, as high as a house above him, as far off as another world.

Then, erecting himself for the last time to proceed onwards between these enclosing walls, that grew increasingly unreal, he found that his senses had begun to watch for the dangers that his mind despised, and that a supernatural awe was creeping over his temper which he had fancied to be steeled by that assurance of death. He supposed that the confinement of the place was recalling to him the forgotten fears of infancy; a psychologist doubtless could have explained it all. The walls sometimes were wide enough apart to have allowed room for two persons going abreast, and then they would come together again quite in the manner of an evil dream, putting him in the irrational apprehension that should the squeeze get much tighter he might become totally and inextricably jammed; and this indeed might be his doom. But ample air space was above his head.

And then again, after a hundred feet or so of this widening and reclosing in of the walls, upon turning a final acute bend of his dipping darkness he discovered himself beneath the effect of a natural archway, that imaginably might once have held a great door of wood; though the panels of such must needs have been fetched down separately from above; and had quite vanished. The arch, however, was only the emergence of the tunnel into a vast bell-shaped cavern, that was somehow strangely like a natural bubble in the solid granite of the hill.

He paused in the doorway, directing his flashlight over the walls and vault of the place, that were of craggy grey rock. The floor too, though it had come to a level at last, was all hollows and roughnesses. There could be but little human art in any of this.

The cavern was bare. If particular purpose it had ever served, it must have stood for ante-room to yonder seemingly more important interior recess that was scarcely distinguishable through an opposite archway. The line of these two doorways continued that of the last of the tunnel behind him, and ran across the greatest length of this outer cave. Moving on again, he was more than ever convinced that the entirety of the underground formation around him, with the tremendous crack of the stairway from the upper air, must have been wrought, before men were at all, by earth-shock.

But in the second archway he stopped again, gazing sternly forward, while playing his light over the dimensions, character and contents of this extreme vacuum of the hill, that should be the sepulchre itself. For with it the possibility of his further progress ceased; no sequel through another gap was revealed. And *there*, besides, should stand the granite corpse table.

He would not enter yet. This buried crypt was holy with antiquity and mystery and night, so that to take one undedicated step into it would be like profanation. The hard white modern glare from his torch was already a profanation, but look he must.

It was a hive-shaped cavern, smaller than the outer; all of the same grey bossy rock, that displayed no discernible trace of working. And still it was not positively small, for half a hundred men perhaps might have stood conveniently within its round. The great table which saved its emptiness could itself have carried a dead giant.

The immense single granite slab of the table was raised a yard up from the floor on six block-legs. The slab and the legs must have been hewn down here; they could never have been got through that passage. The table's length was sideways to him where he stood. It had the appearance of a kind of shelf running along the far grey wall of the cavern. There was nothing on it— neither bones, nor ornaments.

A granite pedestal, its top no more than a foot square, on one slenderer supporting leg, stood close to what should thus be the head of the big table; nearer to himself. Its use he could guess; on it had been set the meat and drink for the departed, to sustain her ghost during its long fearful journey into the land of night. . . . *Her*—for never was it possible for him to forget Ingrid's intuition, that this tomb was a woman's tomb. His mind was queerly settled that it must be so. Indeed it seemed to him that he was sensing it for himself—that his present halt was really due to some indistinct shrinking delicacy of his manhood, hesitating before the invasion of the last bed-chamber of a high-born wife or daughter of primitive times, defended throughout her life by her own savage purity; now defenceless. . . . Only, he had still been fetched here from across the seas. They could not say of him that he was here to spy and peep.

Her bones were long since crumbled, and their dust dispersed. The ancient dreaming that had dreamt this woman had wiped its tablets quite clean, so that not the cleverest brain of the coming future would be able from the tiniest bit of yellow cranium to reconstruct another cruder Helen or Cleopatra. Her jewels could scarcely similarly have melted with the ages, yet none such were visible. Perhaps there had been priestly trickery at the interment; or perhaps the times had been greedy and matter-of-fact: or her tribe had obeyed other superstitions. It was little likely to have been so advanced in culture as to prefer spiritual to bodily adornment as the chief treasure for its women.

And God knew what horrid rites of a cruel faith might have been enacted here! Conceivably an entire train of luckless female attendants had been clubbed, choked, or left entombed, to breathe out the last of their warm breath in the icy society of a mistress who was no more able to guide and protect them, but who had suddenly been made awful by the withdrawal of her flame. A dizzy, endless chain of blurred intervening lives, generations, centuries, was suggested.

Without warning the mental overtaking passed into a physical giddiness, obliging him to catch blindly for support at the archway upright at his elbow. As quickly he recovered and the stumble had been only momentary; but he was impressed that the imprisoned atmosphere, so deep down as it was, must be foul with its thousands of years of exhalations; and thought that he had dreamed here long enough. Now he had better be quick to see at closer quarters what else to see there was; then go at once. Unnerving was it merely to be standing rigid and hunterlike thus alone, exploring all with the suspicious eyes of a foe, listening to the beating of his own heart, and imagining throughout as a background the beginning appearance of spectral shapes, always just beyond the range of his circle of torchlight, that but served to make the contrasting blackness fitter for the breaking of such wraiths upon him. Fifty feet of granite roofed him in. No human soul was near the hill.

He moved forward into the death-chamber. The ensuing accident happened so swiftly that he never rightly understood what had caused it. He believed he had been directing his light and looking towards the pedestal, on which had been nothing at all, when possibly a trailing end of the mackintosh over his arm had caught under his foot, and tripped him. At least he did trip; and fell. But in falling, he had naturally tried to save himself by catching at the nearest solid thing, which in his case was the pedestal; and that had not quite stopped the fall, but had broken it, so that he had reached the ground indeed and was shaken and angry, but had not been so badly hurt as he otherwise might have been. Only the bulb of his electric torch had struck the granite floor, and was hopelessly shattered. Instantly he was plunged into night.

The torch in hitting the ground had escaped from his hand, so, staying down, he began to grope for it, but could not immediately find it. Then, as he proceeded to crawl here and there with lightly feeling fingers, they encountered something else small and hard on the rock floor, which was not the torch. Doubtless it was some tomb treasure that he had overlooked—it surely felt like a precious stone or talisman, half-round, half-flat. Out of the question it was to examine it there and then, so he slipped the thing into his coat pocket. A moment later the torch met his fingers.

He stupidly worked the switch up and down, but the smash had been effective. And so he got up again, bruised, wrathful, sightless, and having completely lost his bearings, though since there was but the one way out to above, he need not fear to miss it. He fancied he was by the arch once more—his hand could circle round an upright granite shaft. He had no matches.

Was he inside or outside the burial chamber? He might blindly have repassed through the gap. While he still stood feeling the wall behind him in hesitation, an optical phenomenon began, that quite nonplussed him, although it brought with it no new alarm.

The cavern's blackness was being replaced by a dusky grey, like that of earliest dawn. It revealed nothing, yet neither did it ever give way again to night; on the contrary it seemed if anything to grow brighter. Something apparently was affecting his optic nerves in the way of light, which was not light. There was nothing in this subterranean dungeon from which light could be derived. Cynically, he found it very appropriate to the whole general eccentricity of his being's conduct during this last time.

But then the grey steadily intensified to true light, until he could very dimly discern that he stood just inside the doorway of the extreme chamber, facing the corpse-table from his original post. It was yards away, yet loomed through the luminous grey a solid shape of black, scarcely separable from the other blackness of the wall behind it.

He forgot to breathe, for all at once it was seeming to him that some supernatural thing was about to happen.

He could have declared that a dark recumbent shape, a wrapped human form, was consolidating upon that ancient table of death. If a ghost indeed, it was of quite incomprehensible length.

Also there were associated mysteries. How came the table to look so much further off than he knew it to be in reality? And since there was nothing visible from which to gauge the human length of that phantom shape upon it, what could be his grounds for pronouncing it prodigious? The table itself was no measure, for both ends beyond the shape remained merged in the night of the wall at the back. Yet the impression of a marvellous stature persisted; and his sense of an unreal distance persisted. Thus he must be seeing this wonder with other eyes.

Definitely now the dead form assumed appearance. Its wrapping was a shroud, that yet left parts of the flesh revealed. The drapery continued as black as the table beneath, while the greyness of the intervening air became no brighter, but where there was flesh, it was shining faintly now like a silver moon; with the same white gleaming purity, though far more dimly. It was a woman.

She reposed on her side at full length, her back towards him. One entire arm, from shoulder to finger-tips, the neck, both feet and ankles, nothing else, glimmered there in that distance as if lighted from within; exactly like a lunar lamp shining through the gloom. So might show the after-glory of the dead physical case of a blessed saint.

He found in himself no hardihood to advance in order to view her face.

The stature was incredible, while everything besides that he could distinguish of her was sacred, proud and exquisite. The upper arm, dropped behind her towards the floor, with relaxed taper fingers suspended in air, resembled less a physiological member than a lovely fall of music. The feet were not rigidly set together as in the conventional preparation of the dead, but rested with lifelike naturalness the one above the other; the over one arched; its beautiful and undistorted toes slightly curling. She should be young. He could not question the nobility of her birth. . . . Yet was she not more of the nature of the angels?

The pale shine of her flesh dulled and faded. So slow was the vanishing, however, that his deep sense of that height of vividness could continue for long moments to reinforce the remaining vision before he grew aware of it. But then the phantasm went in again to nothingness the more swiftly for him; and in the shortest time was no longer there. The table too departed, with the repassage of the cavern's dusk to night. Absolute blackness reigned once more.

He stole bare-headed forth, as from the celebration of a sacrament. He now knew the archway to be at his back.

And as, with feeling outstretched hand and unseeing eyes, he trod unsteadily through the rugged outer cave and succeeding tunnel, he felt that he had laid down his citizenship of the world indeed. Such visitations were not vouchsafed to men having long lives before them.

It was the fourth and last of his strangenesses, and perhaps, when it was granted him to meditate upon it, it would explain the earlier three; and they, it. . . . Or perhaps he was to be told no more on this side of death. It was significant that her face had been hidden. The possibility of a repetition of the adventure did not as yet occur to him. Afterwards, however, it was too late.

Above, he consulted his watch, to find it not yet seven o'clock.

This upper scene of last evening's destruction recalled Ingrid to his mind. She would want to know what the tomb contained. Yes, she deserved to be informed, for her queer psychic gift. The uneasy presence of that queenly ghost had thrilled the fineness of her nature—but let her go down herself to see. Of the table perhaps he might speak. Of his accident with the torch, certainly; and that would cover all the imperfections of his explanation. He had nearly forgotten, as well, the treasure in his pocket. . . .

He drew it out. A shock of surprise left him staring at it stupidly, there in his palm.

It was Arsinal's flint—that which he had shown to Helga last night! Yet he had picked it up from the rocky floor in that darkness down below.

His mind travelled without delay to a common-sense explanation of this new mystery, so suddenly sprung upon him on the heels of all the rest; and found one that might pass. The coat he was wearing he had had on with Helga those few hours ago. He was under the strong impression that he had then replaced the stone in its box, but now that could not be so, and he must have slipped it into the side-pocket of this coat. Then when he had stumbled, twisted and come to earth down there just now, the object had jumped from his pocket, and he had refound it, imagining it to be a new find. But the fact could easily be tested when he should get home. If the box were empty, then of course it must have happened so. . . . But if his stone were in the box, this in his hand was its fellow and counterpart!

A train of mental consequences began to spring from both alternatives. If the stone were his own, it was not he that had brought it out to the Tor this morning, but it had brought itself; his accident below was the hand of fate; in retrieving the stone, he had frustrated that mystical purpose. Ought not he to go down again, and restore it to the tomb? . . . And then surely he would gain at last his release of death.

It did look so exactly like his own, that if in truth it were not his own, then it must surely be its other half. Thus the attraction across half the world would be explained. The attraction would be occult. The rejoining of the two halves of one original whole must be followed by an incalculable consequence. . . . It was quite too fantastic to be credited—and yet what could be thought impossible, after the great ghostly glory he had just witnessed?

When, in three-quarters of an hour, he should get back to his room, it would be shown him to which of these two weird lines of imagination he must devote the striving of his remaining understanding. Never had a dawn for him been richer in philosophy, miracle and utter bewilderment than this one. All life, and supersensual life, seemed fast closing in upon him; yet if it were destined that he was by his poverty of nature and world-insignificance to be but the blind instrument of activities lying outside himself, for that too he was prepared.

He returned the flint to his pocket.

So this ancient stairway, lying here at his feet, crowned by the moving white wreaths of the morning, remained open for the visiting of all the vulgar. Advertised conducted trips would appear outside the shop-fronts of the neighbouring towns! It was the ultimate desecration, which nothing that he could do might prevent. A charge of dynamite should wreck it, but how to set about that he knew not; and there was not time. Men, women and children should begin to flock up to-day.

A prolonged low roar of thunder penetrated to his inattentive consciousness—which was not thunder. It came from under the earth, and seemed especially to sound by way of the crack of the stairs. It was an ominous heavy, deep-down rumble, very much like the noise of an express train that should be rushing through a profound tunnel beneath the whole mass of Devil's Tor. He recognised it almost instantly for an earthquake.

Without any sort of alarm, but quietly and quickly, he transferred himself from the immediate vicinity of the stack's torn bed to some little distance away; then sat down on the ground, to await the ensuing physical shock. In England it could not be much.

Five seconds later the hill trembled, just as though heavy seas were bombarding its base, and next began to sway as if he were on the deck of a ship riding on a gentle swell. At so mild a case he smiled unconsciously. Then, however, to rebuke his sapience, came a sharp, vicious stomach-lifting wrench, that was like nothing else than some subterranean attempt to split the Tor. He was sent sprawling. A visible fissure in the earth north and south of the staircase aperture, extending it at both ends by yards long and inches wide, was celebrated by such a terrific din inside the bowels of the hill, that he could have imagined all the damned in hell to be in mutiny! . . .

He pulled himself to his feet, retreated further still from the seat of the shock, and again sought the ground.

The second wave came from the reverse direction. In place of worsening the fissure already broken, it again hurled its sides together, to form a new continuity of earth and rock. Nor had its violence ceased at that, for where originally, but those few minutes ago, there had been level ground, was now a raised ridge. The stairway itself seemed intact, as he could best make it out while once more rising to his height to look. He had been rolled over again, but not hurt. The shocks should be ended. Peace had returned to the Tor.

He moved over to the stairs, to satisfy himself that they were still serviceable. The first drop remained good; below that, all was so tightly jammed by the coming together of the granite walls, that not a mouse could have got through to underneath. Indeed it was impossible that there could still be a tomb to reach, for those caverns and their approach must surely have been flattened out of existence by a force that could clap together solid upper walls of rock like so much pulp. The interior shock would not be less, but greater. An engineer, with drills, explosive, and a gang of men, could never undertake the hopeless folly of a penetration along the line of the chimney. It was a marvellous interposition.

He deeply regretted having spoken to Helga last night. Arsinal and Saltfleet had long since, it seemed, passed below the horizon of all this affair. That vision of a dead one had been for him alone; the grave was sealed again for all eternity, and his experience was to be unshared, as unrepeated. He thought that no mortal woman could ever have been like that. The wise men of the Bible had spoken of angels. Helga was of the world, and he had surely sinned, although in ignorance, in confiding to her earthly intelligence a sacred thing. . . .

At eight o'clock, in his own room at Whitestone, he opened the box, and discovered it to be empty. So was it put beyond doubt in his mind that it was truly the treasure of the Tibetan monastery that he had recovered so queerly in the recesses of Devil's Tor. Thus either the stone had not been to be deposited there, or else he had thwarted its destiny. Now, therefore, he had very many things to think about.

VIII

The Unseen Working

Helga, in bed in that morning twilight, listened for the sound of the front-door's shutting behind Hugh; then, while its quiet slam was still in her ears, jumped softly to the floor, to confirm from the window his authentic departure. She watched his dark form skirting the front of the house to reach the lane gate. She also had not slept well. Saltfleet, and poor Hugh's presentiment, and his flight from India with those men in pursuit, and occasionally the will, had kept her tossing; but now she was only wondering if she might dare use her cousin's absence from the house to examine for a second time that extraordinary occult mineral specimen he had brought home with him. It had all at once begun to tease her imagination again, with the possible opportunity of handling it anew. It might be that its reputed fascination, leading as far as dishonesty and dishonour, always started in this way, yet at present she was unaware of any obsession in her mind. She believed it merely to be a very natural and harmless curiosity.

Unless he came back for anything, which was unlikely, he should be out of the way for quite two hours, and much less than that would serve her purpose. She need not be at all long over it. Then of course he might have the little wonder with him, or the box in which it was might be locked, and if she had a key to fit, it would be lucky, so that after all she might not have the decision; and there was small sense in disturbing herself with hesitations before the fact was ascertained. Merely to learn whether she could or could not do it, and without needing to decide before-hand whether she *would*, she might just step along to his room to find out if the object was there and accessible. . . . Yet on the other hand how upset Hugh would be, if he knew, by such an open disregarding of his express wish and warning!—how disgusted by her descending to such a thing behind his back! And yet again how *should* he ever get to know? The fact was, she was proposing no harm to either him or his property. He seemed to think it might hurt *her*. She did not see how one more brief sight of its queerness could hurt her, but if it did, surely wrong did not enter into it. . . .

Nevertheless that dread of his displeasure, and some stubborn persisting sense of the falsity of the action, and her pride of dignity as a lady and the mistress of the house in which he was a trusting guest, and also her half-conviction of the uselessness of the attempt—so many considerations outweighed the single instinctive desire; and she returned to bed.

For an hour and longer she lay in the unnameable state between waking and dozing, sometimes forgetting her half-will to have that monastery stone again in her hand, at other times revolving still, but very feebly, its supports and oppositions—long spells of drowsy whim and doubt, broken by occasional passing spasms of impulse nearly amounting to a realising leaping from bed once more. Then her customary time for rising approached, and nothing yet need be determined though she should anticipate it by a few minutes. Accordingly, getting into dressing-gown and slippers, she opened the door, to put out her head and listen—as she had listened that hour and a half ago, but this time for noises in the house. No one stirred, and there was a heavy silence.

Should she go forward?—for this chance would never come her way again. He could scarcely be back for half an hour yet. His room was only a few steps along the same passage. She ought not to be such a coward. And so she glided out, and found his door, and passed in.

The bed-clothes were all heaped together and dragging on the floor, from which she understood, with a sigh, how much worse his night had been than even hers. She began to search in turn the drawers of his chest.

The japanned tin box was rather wedged at the back of one of them, preventing her from getting at it without taking it out altogether. When she had it free in her hand, the lid lifted; Hugh hadn't locked it. That probably meant it was empty—but no, the stone like a broken flint was there. Illogically she blamed his remissness. He must have been over-perturbed on going to bed, as a result of their talk. It was silly in him to make such an ogress of her, she was very willing to fill the place of elder sister to him, if he would only whole-heartedly consent. Meanwhile, however, she must be on guard against the surprising of her by the others in the house; so it would be wisest to carry the box off to her own room, keeping her ear and a corner of her eye to the window, for

Hugh's return.

Thus she bore away her prize. But the door of her bedroom being locked behind her and the box set down ready to her hand on the dressing-table before the window, she stood for a moment longer to quell a rather pronounced hurrying of her heart, that annoyed her by its resemblance to the protest of a conscience. And when this moment too was passed, and now her thumb was actually once more on the box's lid, still another postponement arose. Indeed, the intervention was of the most singular and unexpected kind, for, quite unaccountably, the whole floor of the room shook violently, just as though a procession of heavily loaded motor-lorries were passing down their lane outside—only, worse than that, for the sustained tremor was being accompanied by the wholesale swinging of the picture frames against the walls, and the musical dancing of her pretty ewer inside its bowl on the wash-stand.

"Here we have an earthquake!" was her inward declaration, while she forgot the box, in trying to see all things in the room at once.

A yet ruder shock confirmed the sagacity of her guess, for it was succeeded with the briefest pause by a hubbub of clattering pans and the disastrous smashing of crockery, ascending evidently from the kitchen downstairs. She darted to the door, turned the key like lightning, flew out to the landing, and was about to call to the maids, but then, recollecting that if they had been up she must have heard them before, she decided to hasten down the stairs to investigate the mischief at first hand.

Ingrid as well limped from her room, to peer uncertainly over the banister. The noises had ceased, however, and there was no repetition of the shaking of the house, so she turned back to her mother's room, intending to acquaint her with the incident if she were asleep still, or discuss it with her if she were awake and already aware of it. But the room was vacated, and for a few seconds she continued standing hesitating by the door.

Her idly-wandering eye rested on the tin box lying on the dressing-table, which she failed to identify. It never occurred to her imagination that her mother could have a secret from her, so, less out of inquisitiveness than for the sake of occupying herself while waiting, she moved across the room; and, with that lowest possible degree of curiosity, opened the box to look wide-eyed in.

Wonderingly she took the fragment of apparently common flint in her hand, whereupon the cheap metal lid fell back with a clash. By so extraordinary a chain of small whims and accidents was it fated that Hugh Drapier's own proper treasure must be lost to him, and he not know it. For just as she edged to the window to get a better light for the stone, a crunching footstep on the gravel outside and below persuaded her to thrust her head out, the sash being already up, and lo! advancing upon the porch—Peter! . . . in knickerbocker tweeds and soft hat, a thin suit-case in his hand, his cheeks pale with the unnatural life of London; the inevitable cigarette glued to his lips. . . .

Heedlessly dropping the flint into her dressing-gown pocket, that she never used, and making of her ankle-sprain an occasion for the display of her spirit's superiority, she came away quickly from the window, to re-seek her own room. She would hail him from the window *there*. . . . She was exactly in time to intercept him before he reached the porch.

"Peter, look up!"

Very little taken aback, Copping cocked his eye aloft, located the familiar soft voice, and raised his free arm in salutation, but deferred returning the spoken greeting until he was right against the wall beneath her. Then but a quite small interval divided their two faces, his looking up, hers down. A third person might have thought it odd that neither smiled. Peter indeed was not of the smiling sort, but Ingrid seemed to herself to be full of the strangest emotions, that were not far removed from tears.

He was a rather slight, rather short young man, of cool carriage, with a sharp darkish face, decorated by a diminutive artist's beard, that seemed in curiously perfect keeping with his eyes. They were green-grey, contemplative, noticing, and habitually lit by a light that rebuked complacency and was not of the crowd. A man having such eyes should be upon a spiritual journey. The journey being necessarily in art in Copping's case, since art was his medium, he might well possess the fundamental requirement at least of genius, namely, the distrust of existing principles.

Ingrid had come to hate that term *genius*, so cheapened as it was by misapplication to the merely clever, but the soul behind Peter's eyes which suggested its application to him as well, this it was that she could very easily love. Neither was she particularly interested in painting, which for her possessed not the immensity of architecture, not the frozen purity of sculpture, and not the fluvial might and darkness of music, but seemed essentially based on the exact life-like imitation of existing limited forms; yet this his choice of a mode of expression could never pain or vex her. Her faith was that the supernatural fire was sufficient in itself, and that all these arts were merely its temporal pastime. The living soul surely was immortal, but its thrown-off works on earth must be very grand indeed to last a few thousands of years.

And Peter found her nature as full of nonsense, and as wonderful. For a girl, she was so abnormally idealistic and occupied with the myths of the past. These barbaric personifications of chaotic and cosmic nature, these nondescript shapes and half-meanings, these male and female gods, demi-gods, eponyms, heroes and monsters, of the ancient twilight world, they loaded her brains with uselessness, and falsified for her everything modern. Sometimes, even, he had fancied that it would be a tremendous step forward and new link between them, if he could surrender to her will in the matter by *painting* some of those antique allegories and reachings-out of the human heart. But it was impossible. He could never bring himself down to tell literary stories in paint. He was for years past experimenting with pure symbolism, as the always unattainable height of his art. He was a scornful and reticent exponent in words, so that Ingrid, made duller by her indifference, was hitherto still ignorant how paintwork could forsake the likeness of real things in order to show their soul. . . . It appeared not to matter. In unvarying fineness of temper and all that was most opposite to the frivolity, affectation and selfishness of the generality of the modern girls and women of his acquaintance, she shone a jewel. Nor in any case did the inspiration of his art need a second.

So this subtle and as yet undeclared sex affinity of theirs could quietly override the menace of a future intellectual discord. Nor would Copping, turned twenty-seven, haughty, dogged, and a rebel by nature, have permitted financial considerations to obstruct what he deemed his blessedness. His father had left him the equivalent of six hundred a year, which he lived easily within. The estate firm itself had gone to his less imaginative, more practical elder brother, who was a married man with children. Thus Peter had nothing additional to expect in that quarter, while his work was unlikely to sell for many a long year; nevertheless his certain six hundred remained. Then the temporary upset of his career—his engagement to a girl living in the provinces, the finding a house and furnishing it, the damnable wedding arrangements, the honeymoon, the sacrifice of all his working hours for God knew how long to a new bride, however fondly loved—and afterwards the children—and more children, and worries and distresses of all sorts—this mental nightmare, in certain moods, ready to hurl itself at his throat so soon as he should propose to Ingrid, and be accepted: neither was *it* the obstacle, or he must have felt shame. It was another reason that to the present had tied his tongue with her, though for a couple of years past now their intimacy seemed to have reached a stage when it could only miserably mark time or translate itself to the definite understanding.

Some mysterious painter's instinct, going upon a thousand caught glimpses of a peculiar calm foreign power and aristocracy of her mien, with lookings-away of her eye and strange intonations of her voice that had nothing to do with her other romantic idealism, for very much longer than those two years had been warning him that he must not be in haste to assume that she was entirely his; or, in the broader view, his at all. Her affection, and dearness, and simplicity, and nobleness, and human imperfections—they were his; but if she possessed a second soul, and that second soul were for another man not yet appeared, then rashness might be tragical. Was he unequipped to live with and satisfy that deeper self of hers? The question stated the problem inexactly. So far as he was concerned he had no apprehensions, but was prepared to attempt it. She might not even be aware of the existence within herself of another nature—she could not be, for already he had her love in all but words. This, however, made it but the more disquieting, as showing that she had as yet overcome nothing of it. The true and more bewildering problem was, was that other self representative of some motherhood instinct in her, urging her, against her own knowledge, towards a special physical type of man, that the right children of her destiny might be produced?

For long before she had ever begun to attract him by her sex, the same idea must unconsciously have furnished him with the subject for his portrait of her as the young Mary. That was five years ago. Even so far back, he meant, she must have struck him as being a girl who was not to wed whom she pleased, but the man alone who could give her what she required. The picture hadn't put happiness into her face; the look on it was of expectancy and dread, as well it might be. But it was the long persisting of the intuition, as evidenced by the date of that portrait, that served to prove the genuineness of its correspondence to a real character of Ingrid's. No mere fancy could have lasted those five years and more.

Not its endurance, however, but its psychological rank, mattered. And just because the insight belonged to the great general family of his artistic dumb recognitions, and beginnings of inspiration, and emotions at variance with present realities, and the indistinct rising and forming of new truths, he was not permitted to abandon it as a probable misreading of personal idiosyncrasies of no special importance, but on the contrary was compelled to pay it the high honour experience had long since taught him to pay to all these dim workings of his spirit. In his art they constituted the one thing of value, never disappointing him, though often surprising him by their metamorphosis; so in life, the identical groping and obscurity, and deep-down sense and certainty of having encountered the *real*, must needs give him the longest pause.

The hell was that he was debarred by decency from talking this thing out with Ingrid herself. He would surely pain and offend her thereby, and as surely she must attempt warmly to reassure him concerning her singleness of heart; and, unfortunately, it would not depend upon her sincerity, for her self-ignorance also must be allowed for. Thus it seemed that for an indefinite period they must go drifting hopelessly and helplessly on, while he, for his part, must confine himself to the churlish retardation of the steady natural swelling to sweetness and torment of their friendship. If he did speak, it would end all at a blow. He would weakly be persuaded that this his instinct, a thing belonging to the whole foundations of his manner of truth, was no more than a fantasy of his brain. And meanwhile his supposed cowardice must be appearing so inexplicable to her and her mother. His character as a man must be wholly misrepresenting itself.

Yet standing as he did for an advanced type of the twentieth century, the finest love of which has acquired compassion, protectiveness, sacrifice, delicacy of consideration, and such-like virtues, as a more than equivalent exchange for the lost hunger and half devilish passion of past ages; also comprehending as he did how the violent native cravings of humanity, being frustrated, inevitably breed degeneration and vice; he could not indeed find the necessary iron within him peremptorily to cut the acquaintance as improper, but still would not adopt the easy alternative of suddenly releasing his pent will to prefer his suit. Suffering, he was sure, she was. Their bond, in spite of his long absences, already had the unbreakable strength of an invisible magic haircable. It was not in the least strange that he could summon no smile to his face, while he stood there looking up at her.

A very trifling accident that morning had already brought it about that his troubles were to end.

Never before in his life had he seen Ingrid's serious and anxious long, pale features appear so strong and lovely. From such beauty he knew he could not by sheer force of will alone wrench his existence, but only if it were for her own sake; and that must be shown. Especially he loved her for this unsmiling welcome, which displayed the terms they were on, raising the intimacy at a stroke, in the way of faultless taste, from the traditions of the world they both knew to the skies. And the extraordinary importance to her of his coming declared itself in the searching of her eyes, that now were *like* the skies. It declared itself still more essentially in her being at this window at all. She had never looked abroad for him on any other of his early morning arrivals.

It was out of his power to go on longer treating her so shamefully. He must speak to her—not now, but to-day. One couldn't foresee everything, and it was a bare possibility that she might throw another light on what was agonising him. So he planned of a sudden. . . . But unless Ingrid had shown herself to him thus, the plan would not have been; and unless she had previously been handling Hugh's stone by her mother's window, she could not have seen him from it, to be in time to greet him. Neither afterwards guessed how precariously suspended on that slender thread of chance had been the closer intermingling of their two lives.

Peter found no word as yet to say, and therefore, pushing back the hair from her forehead, she addressed him again.

"I am so glad to see you, Peter! I suppose you have been travelling through the night and have made the *détour*, to declare your arrival, as usual?"

His silence and gravity had begun to appear unnatural to her, although she dared not recognise them in distinct thought. Increasingly during the last twelve months, the dread was frequent with her that one day in the near future their parting would be altogether. He would meet some girl in town, or get tired of their dullness down here, or make Continental plans—she neither knew nor seemed to care how it would be; it would be the fact itself that would rob her of—what? He had never said that there was anything between them. He had a perfect moral right to close down the Belhill studio if he pleased. He might be hesitating to announce it even at this minute. The moment would be cynically appropriate, for she felt that on no former visit of his would she have taken it so much to heart. A dark *something*, not yet a conception, was in her mind, that she particularly needed since yesterday to cling to every particle of the warmth and love in her life, if she would escape this great shadow . . . hanging over her. . . . And still the shadow was centred and had its doorway in her vision on Devil's Tor; and that mighty dead one had been supremely beautiful—supremely good. . . . She hoped that Peter was to announce no disaster, but talk to her of sane London matters, and his egoisms, and his eternal warfare with democracy in art.

He, however, was afterwards to talk of something else, and till then of nothing, or as little as he might in securing that interview without alarming her. He returned a preoccupied affirmative answer to her two or three questions in one. By the absent wandering of his eye past her, and the unfriendly dry carelessness of his tone, she became still more chilled. She would not lose her courage for that.

She told him of the earthquake only a few minutes since. His raised eyebrows responded that it was intelligence for him.

"When was this?" he asked.

"Just now, Peter."

"I saw some hedge sparrows rather agitated."

She went on to relate her adventure on the Tor with Hugh the evening before, and its consequence of the injury to her ankle. She concealed from him her supernatural overtaking, which could only puzzle him. She felt that, delicate instrument of sensation though he was, even above the vast majority of others, he was somehow too rudely constructed ever to have the least communication with a different existence, that should be the source of *ultra*-sensations in men and women. He was none the less dear to her because he should be lower and coarser-fibred in this one respect.

He seized upon her accident to try to rid himself at a blow of the sense of personal inferiority in her presence that had quietly settled upon him.

"It seems to have been a pretty mad affair!" he opined,

through a cloud of cigarette smoke. "I hope it doesn't mean you are laid up?"

"No, I can get about the house."

"I shall begin to believe you need someone to look after you. Who is this cousin of yours who treats girls in such a prehistoric style?"

Ingrid had not yet referred to a tomb, and was impressed by the coincidence of his adjective. Was it another omen and presage? She *knew* that something was advancing upon her. . . . Or was it merely the sick seizing by her mind of any word that could be twisted? Yes, it was just a meaningless coincidence.

"It was Devil's Tor that treated us both in prehistoric style. The stack, being blown down, has opened what we think a Stone Age staircase to below. Hugh should be on his way back from there again at this minute. He has gone to investigate. . . . I am sorry, Peter. It's Hugh Drapier, and by choice of career, he is a great Central Asian traveller."

"And may be showing off to smaller mortals, as I see it! Has he been staying with you long? You never mentioned him in your last."

"He's been here a week."

"How very nice for you," returned Peter, without enthusiasm. He flicked away the stub of his cigarette. He had better fix up that talk for later, and be off. . . . "It's notable, though, that none of you has ever named his name before in my presence; whereas, in general, these family shining lights are rather insisted upon. Why the reticence?"

"He is hardly ever in England, and we had almost forgotten his existence."

He met her eye.

"Well, I must get along to breakfast. But I may see you during the day? You have nothing on?"

"Won't you lunch with us, Peter?"

"I have to settle in. I'll look in to tea, if I may."

Now she was sure that he was purposely being cold. And because they had parted warm friends, and his occasional letters to her since had been cheerful and spontaneous, it could only signify that he had suddenly bad news to communicate, and was feeling ashamed of it. But why need he feel ashamed to hurt her in this way? It was to make her greedy and appropriative, which was unworthy of him. She had never wished to retain him against his will. She could not copy his manner, and so still answered him with the ancient calm simplicity that, unknown to herself, he always aesthetically admired more than the most vivacious or coolly cynical address of other women.

"We shall be alone. You won't mind meeting Hugh, will you? In spite of your insinuations, Peter, he is really the modestest man in the world in speaking of his own achievements. He is red-haired, and hardly good-looking, but very pondering. His father was Scotch."

"I want to see you actually alone, Ingrid . . . say, an hour before tea. Can that be managed?"

Again he was looking at her, but this time with a quick, nearly professional glance, as if to ascertain independently of her answer how his words were received. He caught the downbent gaze—stern, startled, troubled, inquiring, all together. Then he realised that she could only be attaching one meaning to his proposition, and yet, just because she was a woman, must feign ignorance. So already he had blundered badly.

Ingrid, however, believed that out of the courtesy of his nature he wished to acquaint her in this delicate way with his intention of closing the studio and their friendship. She honoured him for the considerateness; a blunter and more selfish man would probably have wanted to get it over at once, but so far-reaching a decision—for her, she knew not for him—at least deserved a special interview. She replied:

"Yes, I can be ready for you at three o'clock, if it is important."

"I think it important. There are some things I want to say that may very much concern both of us, but it isn't quite simple. So will you just not worry about it till then?"

"I must worry a little, I suppose. But I do know you wouldn't put such a formal request to me without a good reason, so I must bear any suspense."

"It's something that has been engaging me a good bit lately. I expect I've said too much or too little, and you *are* going to worry. May I speak more freely, by way of prelude only?"

"Surely we know each other by now, Peter!"

"I hope so. I *hope* so. . . . Then I am to have it out with you on the subject of our future relations—or would you say emphatically at once that there is to be no development of the present?"

Ingrid's face took on a tinge of added colour, but her voice remained as steady as before, though it was lower.

"Should we discuss this here, Peter?"

"I'm only trying to sketch out a reassurance for you, to tide you over the morning. It has to do with our future relations, but won't necessarily amount to the iniquity of a proposal."

"I ask only one question," said Ingrid. "Are you going away from us? The rest doesn't matter."

"But that matters?"

"Yes, I want you not to go away."

"Is that all you want?"

"Please, Peter! . . ."

"Forgive me—I know it isn't permissible till this afternoon. Well then, no; I've no present intention of giving up the cottage. I should be very sorry permanently to turn my back on purity, sincerity and unstimulated happiness. Almost the only thing to induce me to it would be the direct command from you."

"Nothing else matters," repeated Ingrid, while she felt that sudden relief arising from the removal of her long fears; and yet it was leaving some curious doubt and darkness behind. Perhaps it was that his words announced that their old was to give place to a new, and the moment for a new relation was inopportune. She hoped he would not to-day ask her to marry him. She could not prevent his doing so. . . . They had shared so many things, and were certainly the nearest of all to each other. There would be the fewest terrors for a girl in such a marriage. But yesterday that *spirit* had altered something in her life for her, and she needed time for the settling down in her soul of this strangeness.

Even five minutes ago, it seemed to her, her thoughts had been different. Then she had been welcoming his sanity, but now he was in danger of exclusion. Indeed, it was not what he had to say to her, but what she must not confess to him, that signified. A marriage—two as one; and a great sacredness—one alone, a second forbidden. The states were as irreconcilable as odd and even. . . . If he asked her, he would innocently be bringing a great mystification on himself, for she would have to postpone her answer, but she had never up to now tried to conceal her regard for him. He would even have the right to accuse her of dishonesty. But he had just said he was not to ask her, but only to speak of their future relations. What that could mean, she did not know. Perhaps he was to state a hypothetical case—*if* something or other happened, would she marry him? It would certainly make the postponing answer easier to frame. . . .

Peter queerly thanked her for her tranquillity of patience, then went off, leaving her looking after his first steps towards the gate. When, however, she turned round into the room, her mother was standing in the doorway. Could she have overheard their talk? She feared she had, and that she was to be questioned about her heart.

"It was Peter, mother."

Helga came into the room.

"I know. You are pleased, aren't you? I happened to be passing, and heard voices, but at first I thought it was Hugh, and then I recognised the drawl—forgive me!—and was in good time to catch his fixing up that meeting for this afternoon. Do you wish to speak of it or not, my dear?"

"I think I'd rather not. But don't go for a minute, mother. There was something I wanted to ask you. Hasn't there been an earthquake?"

"Yes, it broke some things in the kitchen."

"I hope nothing has happened to Hugh on the Tor."

Her mother regarded her curiously.

"That isn't one of your intuitions?"

"I don't know. . . . That's what I wanted to ask you. How is it I never have any with regard to Peter? He is surely a man one might have intuitions about? I can never seem to see or guess what he is to say, do, or think. I believed he was contemplating the giving up of his studio, but he says not."

"I could nearly have told you that," replied Helga, smiling. "And I suppose the reason he is so unexpected is that he is a genius. The surprises of genius are the one thing unfated. For all that, do you love him well enough to marry him?"

Now that the question had come, Ingrid found that it gave her no displeasure. Her calm sincere eyes met her mother's calm affectionate ones.

"Yes, I am sure I love him, but I would like a quite long time for self-examination. Did you overhear everything?"

"Not everything, but enough. You are probably in doubt what this afternoon's private interview stands for. Yet it is not in the least difficult. He considers you a high order of supernatural being, and would like to lay down his arms at your feet, but fears his own unworthiness. I am only joking a very little, my dear. Have you forgotten his picture of you?"

"What other destiny than marriage could I have, mother?"

"There are no more Pythonesses of Delphi. You were too slow in coming into the world."

"But how would you take it, mother?"

"I should never disapprove of Peter," returned Helga. "And the money side of it, of course, you would hate to say or hear anything about; but still, if he is not a rich man, you will get enough hereafter."

She kissed her daughter, and left the room, while Ingrid remained standing in its centre, an upright pillar endowed with a half-consciousness that was all thoughts endeavouring to shape themselves from feelings, and feelings equally endeavouring to find a vent in thoughts; but the feelings were many, and buried, and discordant, so that the thoughts were as worthless as vanishing.

While passing Ingrid's open door on her return to her room

from the kitchen below, Helga had been momentarily terrified by the sound of a man's voice talking to her daughter from outside the house, through the window. She thought it was Hugh come back; and his box was still on her dressing-table. Then both the familiar assurance of the voice and her daughter's special manner of responding, had quieted her as quickly again; she now understood it was Peter, on his way up home from the station—he often thus left word at the house in the early morning.

The alarm was enough, however. Hugh really was nearly due back, and she had no longer time nor inclination to risk that re-examination. So she had proceeded to her room, and, without so much as lifting the lid of the box again—since she knew that she had taken nothing out of it, and who should have tampered with it during her short absence?—had carried it off to Hugh's, where she had redeposited it in its old drawer. She was glad the sin had been prevented. It would have been a sin, though a very small one—not because logic said so, but because throughout she had been feeling so apprehensive and uncomfortable about it.

Afterwards she had gone back to Ingrid's room, to hear her account of Peter. It was then that she had heard his own account of himself, if a proposed meeting with a young girl to discuss relations meant what it should. She told herself in justification, that no mother could have acted differently, a daughter's happiness being at stake.

She still did not understand her own wishes or feelings in the matter. Distinctly it could not be called a surprise for anyone; almost it was an expected thing. Peter, besides, was a nice boy, a dear boy, with so many lovable qualities. Morally and physically he should be as sound as a bell, his one vice being over-smoking. For a supposed genius, he was wonderfully amenable and sane; and appeared to be personally popular everywhere. These were the things that counted. Ingrid would come into money by-and-by. . . . Could there be anything in poor Hugh's death-presentiment? It was odd that these thoughts of death and marriage should be going on in the world simultaneously all the time.

How extraordinarily proud, troubled and beautiful Ingrid had looked this morning! Helga had even forgotten to ask about her injury. Was this altogether Peter's doing? She had an uneasy inspiration that such a mood and beauty must be above his head. A grimmer, grander man would deserve them more. Her mind flew to Saltfleet's photograph—but heaven help the child if ever she were to marry a Saltfleet! Peter was sound, small, domestic and good, like a sweet apple. . . . He would be angry with her for that description of his character, but she must show her practical benevolence by throwing her weight into his scale. His cynicism would get worn off in married life. He could not love and live with Ingrid, and be cynical.

IX

The Glory

Seated at the Whitestone breakfast table, Ingrid and her mother each in her different way expected Hugh's report. His presence at her right hand was renewing Helga's seriousness from that late talk last night. She saw that he was dumb and grave. She feared that, whatever he might have succeeded in discovering on Devil's Tor, an excursion to a tomb must be affecting him painfully in his present morbid state. This condition of his must be handled with the utmost care and sympathetic tact. Ingrid was the more directly anxious. She was sure—she saw it in his every look, movement and constraint—that he had penetrated to the burial chamber itself. And it concerned only her; her mother and grand-uncle were outside the affair, and Hugh was her impersonal messenger. She knew that anything he told them now would have to be expanded and made significant in their later private discussion. Meanwhile Uncle Magnus must be apprised of the introductory circumstances, for he had been told nothing.

She outlined for him their last evening's adventure on the Tor, and he grunted his comprehension. His attitude would follow when he had determined it. Only mother and daughter already understood that any scene in which Hugh Drapier had a part was necessarily so far damned for the head of the house, who, from the very first hours of his nephew's stay, had conceived a sort of malignant antipathy to him, the social disguises of which were an ignoring silence and the curtest exchange of general talk. For instance, the rough-banter he reserved particularly for Peter, he could no more have directed to Hugh than he could have fallen on his neck.

But the true origin of this aversion none was ever to know save old Colborne himself. Hugh's father, the "accursed Scotchman"—fiery-haired, bald, tattooed with freckles, and all bones, like the son—had upon a time, during his wooing of Thore, Magnus's favourite younger sister, the uncouthness to refuse him a considerable service, that would have cost him little and was easily within his influence; and to insult him, into the bargain, by his manner of refusal. And Magnus upon the spot had vowed never to have further dealings with the man, or connection with him, or knowledge of him even—a determination ever after tolerably closely adhered to. Consequently, now after forty years, for the double of that happily-laid ghost to turn up unexpectedly in the person of the son, affected him as disagreeably as if the mellowing veil of intervening time had been torn rudely away, revealing the past again in all its uglinesses, crudities and vulgarities.

He was short, compact, thick-necked, with a clever energetic brown face full of wrinkles and generally much gashed in shaving clean. He reminded one of Schopenhauer's portrait as an old man. Like Schopenhauer, as well, he had attained the art of combining a high idealism and intellect with a practical selfish cunning that was hard beyond the common; and of doing it sincerely. That part of his father's wealth that had come to him, he had kept, and doubled. Accordingly his genius was misanthropic. He contended with men on their own ground, and reviewed them on his.

His bald dome of an imaginative thinker, with the bright, shrewd, unfriendly black eyes, caved by bristling brows, suggested that dangerous overseeing of the villainies and infirmities of mankind; and he had never married; and had written books that few had read and none had liked. The business of making money, which he regarded as inferior and an employment suitable to inferior minds only, he had afterwards turned out to be very good at. It gave him secret pleasure to prove thus that the same persons who possessed no brains to understand his philosophy with, were of very little account in anything. It was a sort of demonstration of the worth of his writings.

The women of his household knew his signs. The soft, quiet voices and ways of both pleased him well. Of Helga's judgment, tact and managing capacity, he had a very high opinion, though she had to read it between the lines. He had never once regretted having protected her. But if he could be fond of anyone, it was Ingrid. Sometimes it nearly came to an association between them. She realised, and he knew she realised, the essential dark grandeur and dignity of this lonely setting of his to death, and he loved her for not expressing the understanding in any of the fashions naturally adopted by women. He did not fear death, but had never advanced as far as the wisdom which can accept the pity of others without shame.

She had also interested herself in his system of thought, and occasionally he caught her reading in his chief work, on Racial Derivations. That might be a piece of hypocrisy in others, but this child had pride. And so he rarely teased her, and if he should, would always spare her pride. The unmistakable signs of her lineage further defended her—the long noble beauty of her mouth, the uninsultable abstraction of her northern eyes.

Now, having paved the way with him, she turned at last to Hugh across the table, who at the first word looked up, yet dully, with none of the animation of an adventure to relate. He had scarcely touched his food.

"Are you to tell us what happened, Hugh?—or would you rather leave it till afterwards?"

"No, you can hear now. The stairs continued down, and I got to the bottom, and into a cave having a stone table for the reception of the dead, but nothing else—only another small pedestal for the death-food. There were no remains, or treasure. I had an accident, and smashed my torch down there, having to grope my way out in the dark. . . . It proved lucky, for if I'd stopped underground only a few minutes longer, I must have been trapped. I was hardly out, when an earthquake wrecked the stairs."

Helga glanced at her daughter.

"Then that was ours. What time was it, Hugh?"

"About seven."

"We had it here too, though only slightly."

"It was severe enough on Devil's Tor. Imagine for yourself a long fissure in the granite closed as if the stuff were clay."

"Is the tomb destroyed?" asked Ingrid.

"It must be."

"Are you sure?—for it's important."

"Yes, I'm positive it is. The shock would be worse the lower it was, while the resistance of the bigger cavity would be less. Whether or no, there's no getting down to it."

"Not with appliances?"

"There's no longer a way."

"To be opened yesterday after an eternity, only to be closed again to-day!" Her voice was only a murmur, though she continued to eye him interrogatively. She fancied him uneasy.

"How's your ankle?" It seemed almost a defensive inquiry.

"Oh, it's nothing, Hugh. Were you down long?"

"I didn't time it. It impressed me as both long and short."

It dawned on Ingrid that he might have seen something there that he wished to keep back from the others, so, meaning to speak to him alone afterwards, she ceased her questioning. Her mother took up the tale.

"Surely the coincidence is very unique, Hugh? For a thunderbolt and an earthquake to be directed against the identical spot within twelve hours, and for the second happening to cancel the effect of the first! It's supernatural, nearly."

"Most odd, to say the least."

Helga began to fear from her uncle's silence that he was

finding their insistence on the topic burdensome. She addressed him in another voice.

"Peter is down, Uncle."

"Then we may expect some rational conversation again at last. Is he coming here to-day?"

"To tea, I think—Ingrid?"

"Yes."

Magnus Colborne viewed the mother over his lifted cup.

"I shall not be sorry for the diversion. He is a youngster I can get on well enough with—it interests me to see the flapping of his wings of talent, and to identify the sources of this talent, which are known to me; some of them at least. His father, my old partner, was extremely pertinacious, in accordance with which Peter will pursue a false idea in art to a mile past its confessed absurdity, rather than cut his loss in time. John Copping was likewise exceedingly prone to the holding of his own counsel, and in the son this comes out in the love of surprises—that some persons confound with genius." Helga glanced towards her daughter, but Ingrid appeared not to remember that part of their earlier talk in her room. Colborne was proceeding without a break.

"It is so far from necessarily being the coequal of genius, that it may even be called its counterfeit. An artist of the first order cares for nothing but to present the profound beauty of life. He may do it in such a manner as to surprise people, and that is genius; but to *wish* to surprise people, as an aim of art, that is a cheap-jack business, the sole excuse for which may be that nowadays artists generally do not know what they are doing or what they want. They have had it instilled into them that genius surprises; they themselves are geniuses; and therefore they must think out and prepare their surprises.

"In Peter Copping's case the thing is complicated by the virtues he derives from his mother, a woman of high principle, who died too young. I knew her. She herself had a double nature, and he has received from both sides. On the one hand, she had a rigid puritanism that set the *idea* for her high above all considerations of personal advantage—and this, in Peter, repeats itself in his impatience of popularity and determination to paint nothing that shall bring him in money. And on the other hand Sarah Copping, of all the women I have met in the course of a long lifetime, was the one possessing the deepest passion for pure beauty, in all its spheres. This passion, I am of opinion, Peter has inherited in full measure; and it should at last save him."

There was a slow reminiscent mournfulness in the old man's mention of John Copping's wife, that caused Helga to glance over to him strangely. He had hardly ever named her before, but if really he had had this wonderful admiration for her, it might throw a different light on his affairs. His rather incongruous business association with the husband would be explained better. Any special intimacy between the two—the wife and the part-ner—could have been only ideal, yet it cleared other things as well—his liking for Peter's company, his settling down in this part of the country at all . . . and something in his attitude towards Ingrid, which hitherto had always puzzled Helga, but now she suddenly realised that perhaps he had long since reserved her in his mind for Peter's wife, thus romantically consummating his own prevented attachment. The failure of his supposed misogyny surprised her less than she could have thought possible. She forgave the deceit, for the sake of the interest of his human weak-ness. She loved him more for having been able to love this wo-man; Helga had never met her, but she would choose a quiet occasion to ask Peter about her—she had been told that she was a lovely creature.

She asked herself why her uncle was going into this elaborate analysis of Peter's parts. Evidently it gave him pleasure to refer even in such an oblique way to the qualities of the mother; but there must be something else. He must feel himself to be weaken-ing, and must be intending to use Peter's present stay to promote his scheme of a match between the two young people. If so, this speech of his still proceeding should lead up to some handsome praise of Peter's gifts—it would be put to the proof at once. . . . It was all so very unlike her uncle's usual style. She feared it signified his approaching end. Thus two out of the four at this table were occupied with death, while *her* part everlastingly was that of onlooker and knower, and Ingrid sat there like some mysterious dawning young sun.

So many thoughts passed through her head so swiftly, that she was still in time to lose nothing of her uncle's concluding remarks.

"It should save him at last," he repeated, "though in the meantime he may have a weary dance to lead. For till now he possesses that blessed faith in his own nonsense, that historically has nearly always succeeded in imposing on the world. The world is very anxious for new beauties and truths; it loves excitement, but the old is dry and dull. So any apparent opposition that his work may meet will be but in the nature of an added incitement; and years may pass before he discovers for himself that in art manner matters nothing—that the underlying ancient eternal beauty alone matters, which he might have sought at first.

"He will come to it, because he is his mother's son. Only let him not imagine until it is shown that he has it in him to set up a landmark in art, for that belongs to but one man in a century, and it remains improbable that he is *it*.

"He should marry. A noble girl, of known race and character, would not hinder, but help him in his chosen career. She would anchor him, so that he would not always be running after undesirable other women, wasting both time and money in the process. She would be his perpetual model, in case he wishes to paint the mystic height of womanhood. She would shield him from many of the roughnesses of life, that irritate beyond endurance, and may eventually destroy so large a number of men whose idealising tendencies unfit them for contact with the vulgar. And she would even stimulate him, because a pure and good woman has virtues not to be found elsewhere; and though it would not always be fitting for a man to imitate these virtues, yet it must increase him to contemplate their existence, and little by little come to understand their true relation to the distinctive virtues of a man, that will spring up within himself from the knowledge."

His eye, as he ended, rested for a single instant on Ingrid, who had coloured faintly. Drapier intercepted the look. He thought it very transparent that these last words of old Colborne were being directed at the girl, who somehow had become drawn so much closer to himself since last evening. He did not know indeed if the singularly inept allusion to her case in general company was seriously displeasing her, but anyhow it was manifest that she could not openly notice it. So instinctively he shook off his abstraction, to come to her assistance.

"I saw his painting of *you*, Ingrid, last night; and found it extraordinarily impressive. Only his choice of a Scandinavian type for the Virgin—who surely was Jewish—struck me as a rather essential blunder. Of course he may have his own ideas on realism in art."

"I don't think such an inconsistency would bother him, Hugh. Also he seems to wish to believe that Christ was blue-eyed, belonging by descent to the North."

"What grounds can he have for supposing that?"

"Christ's nature was so exotic. He was loving, and simple, and natural."

"So you assent?"

"I've always thought that all good things have come from the North."

Her background of other reflection broke through to the front of speech, and she brought him back to Devil's Tor.

"That accident of yours with the torch, Hugh—how exactly did it happen?"

"I fancy my foot caught in a tail of the mackintosh over my arm; and I got a tumble."

"In the burial chamber itself?"

"Yes."

"Had anything startled you?"

"No."

She stole a last glance at him, but said no more. Magnus Colborne on the other hand was eyeing his nephew with an ominous ambiguous grin.

"You are sure, for instance," he demanded, "that it was no apparition you saw, or thought you saw, in that place which caused your mishap?"

Drapier shifted in his seat, to return him the shadow of a cold bow.

"I am quite sure, sir."

"You believe I am joking?"

"I can't tell that, sir. I merely know that, coming straight from such a tomb as I have done, I personally feel anything but in the mood for indulging in jokes about it."

The old man grabbed at his napkin which threatened to escape from his knees, and flapped it out angrily before restoring it to position.

"You younger people," he began in his deliberate, precise way, "imagine that the world belongs to you. But I have sometimes been beyond my own front gate, and you are to learn that but for a certain experience of mine on top of this same Devil's Tor some five-and-twenty years ago, not one of you probably would so much as ever have heard of its existence—certainly none of us here assembled would now be seated at this breakfast table. To that extent the fates of all three of you have depended upon an incident occurring to me when two were still in or hardly out of childhood and the third was unborn. So you may securely consider that the subject is the very last I would select as a mine for jests."

He fixed a look on Helga, who accordingly answered him.

"May we hear, Uncle?"

"You know something of my life previous to that time, but Hugh Drapier doubtless has never troubled to concern himself with it, so that I had better address my introduction to him—if you will not be bored?" he demanded of his nephew suddenly, and nearly savagely. Drapier, however, pushing back his plate with a movement of finality, nodded without reply, and gazed away.

"You're interested, Hugh?" intervened Helga. She feared that her uncle's open temperamental dislike of him would find food in this unfortunate appearance of negligence.

"Yes, if it relates to Devil's Tor itself, I would like to know."

Colborne's glare subsided. He ceased to look at Hugh, although it was to him that he now went on to speak.

"As an example, you should be ignorant that my taking up my residence in the south-west of England was quite by chance; or if you prefer it, by fate. I never had a sentimental predilection for Devonshire. I sought at the time a house to live in. Properties roughly answering my requirements were offered me in half a dozen counties, and Whitestone, on Dartmoor, was one.

"My father died when I was turned thirty. His shipping business passed to his widow—my mother and your grandmother—and yours, Helga. Until her death in turn three years later I continued to manage it for her, when it came to me in my own right, less certain deductions in favour of your respective parents. I disposed of it as quickly as so complicated and flourishing a going concern may be disposed of, without foolishly throwing it away; and went abroad.

"During the next five or six years I indulged my taste for the arts. I travelled; and may confidently affirm that within that period I visited every European gallery of note, every considerable medieval religious structure, all the more important Continental Roman remains, classical Greece in its entirety, the Egyptian temples over the navigable length of the Nile, and much of Asia Minor. Only Palestine I did not visit; for the aesthetic culture of the original Jews has always appeared to me both barbaric and frivolous. We know that the *best* of the race have scorned graven images.

"But one cannot be acted upon by the world forever, one must also act, so by the time I was forty, my head being already full of philosophical devils, I returned to England to relieve myself in some volumes. There is assumed to be an intelligent public that interests itself in cosmical problems. It seems, however, that it has failed hitherto to hear of my books; at least, it has not bought them. Understand well, I never was in need either of money from my writings or of literary glory; still, you may conceive the small inclination I felt to go on spending myself in a vacuum. As a second motive to once more changing my mode of life, I was by now surfeited with the eternal daily spectacle of mean modern city faces, the indices of meaner souls. The contrasted solitariness of a country existence sang its song of enchantment to me.

"There is no need to describe how I came to enter into partnership with John Copping, the Tavistock land agent, on whose list was Whitestone. Within his limits he was a very fine fellow, if no saint, and it suffices to say that we afterwards bought and sold residential estates and farm properties together. Yet let me assure you that, sharp and far-sighted though he was, he was never able to trip his colleague! His son, an idle scamp, is the youngster who is expected here this afternoon. I have already spoken of him sufficiently."

He glanced again half involuntarily at Ingrid, who, however, continued sitting in absent thought like a statue, her fingers propping her cheek.

"So that is my history," rounded off the old man, suddenly showing his yellowish teeth to Drapier in an ironic grimace, that as abruptly vanished. "But as to the incident on Devil's Tor, I do not profess to be a Psalmist, and you will doubtless consider my report inadequate."

"If, as I suppose, it is a case of wonder, sir, the shortest and baldest account should be the most effective of all."

"I am reassured! . . . You are to understand, then, that I had already on the spot decided *against* Whitestone, yet still stayed on at Plymouth pending an expected communication from other Shropshire agents, when, to pass the time of waiting somehow, I came up again to view the house. As recently as then there were no cars, or none for hire, while the trains were infrequent; so before returning I had yet a few hours on my hands, which I used in walking out to Devil's Tor. It was, I remember, a warm, grey day in June—fine, clear and windless. Lying at length on top of the hill, I dozed. And in this state I experienced what one perhaps would call a dream, but another a vision—I mean only that my condition was doubtful between sleeping and waking."

Drapier seemed somewhat paler than usual, as he interrupted him.

"You saw that same apparition, sir, you were asking me about?"

"I saw no ghost, or shape. What I did see was—the hill in *glory*. . . . You have no inkling of my meaning. However, as a traveller upon the grand scale, you have witnessed notable sun-risings among the Asiatic mountains and elsewhere?"

"I have so."

"And have been struck to silence and worship, supposing that you have the common feelings of a man. Then you will grasp better than your cousins the sort of spectacle I have it in my mind to convey; and what my corresponding sensations necessarily were. There was a very slow *crescendo* of rosy light, turning to gold, and later to a magnificent refulgence that was less like any passage of the solar rays through the terrestrial atmosphere than the radiance of heaven itself. It seemed to me that I was out-stretched on the ground, rather awkwardly raising myself on one arm—hardly for the purpose of *beholding* the phenomenon, for in fact there was nothing to interrupt the prospect of the eye; but rather to steep myself more entirely in its amazing beauty and invitation. I have said—or think I have—that the day was grey, without sun; the sun, in any case, does not rise at noon. The appearance therefore was phantasmal. If it were dream, I have known no such dream before or since. If vision, then I was in a holy place. Then, as well as afterwards, I believed that the splend-our was supernatural.

"I wished to buy the hill, but it was not for sale. Instead, I bought this house, as its available near neighbour. And still you will find it noteworthy that between that overtaking of mine on Devil's Tor and the present moment, I have chosen to pay it no second visit."

"I can understand it," said Drapier slowly.

"In what sense can you?"

"An impure man of the world might well hesitate to challenge the angelic."

"You call it that?"

"That, or illusion."

"It has not repeated itself in your case, however?"

"No."

Magnus Colborne was silent for a time, then proceeded:

"Or perhaps I have reflected in season that a man in middle life has better things to do than dream voluptuously on hill-tops. Be that as it may, you will have the fairness to acknowledge that I have probably given you a lesson in candour. For my eyes are still quick enough to observe that you are strangely perturbed since your return from the same height this morning; and that you have left your breakfast."

"I have really nothing more to tell you of my adventure, sir."

"Why aren't you eating, Hugh?" asked Helga.

"Perhaps I've gone too long without, and should have had a snack before leaving the house."

"You are feeling all right?"

"Oh, yes."

He turned to his uncle again, to stop the personal attack.

"I should mention, while I think of it, sir—some of those big blocks from last evening's ruin are halted more or less insecurely on the east side of the hill. It might be advisable to notify the responsible owner."

Colborne's bright eyes continued to fasten on him for a few seconds, before they removed sharply to the other end of the table, where Helga was.

"You hear that?"

"Yes."

"Go round yourself to Dunn, at the 'Bell,' after breakfast, and get him to telegraph Harkaway, of Chagford—at my expense, if he likes. I fancy it is still Harkaway who owns Devil's Tor; but Dunn will know. To the effect that the leaning pile on top was overthrown by lightning yesterday, and that some of the stones composing it are dangerously lodged on the hill slope, demanding a notice board. You said 'dangerously'?" he added to Drapier.

"I said 'insecurely'."

"I cannot see a distinction."

"Any mountaineer would understand the distinction, sir. A danger is said to exist where there is a very grave risk to life. With common precautions, there is no such risk here. It is the foolhardy folk who are not in the habit of using their eyes, that perhaps ought to be protected."

"You are charitable."

"I think a board should go up, if merely for the sake of conscience."

The old man scowled.

"I fear my conscience does not embrace fools. . . . Do nothing," he concluded to Helga.

An awkward silence descended upon the party, in the midst of which the master of the house abruptly pushed back his chair without excuse; and rose to leave the room.

Afterwards Ingrid and Hugh talked in the drawing-room. It was the stateliest apartment of the house. Its walls were hung with valuable paintings by Flemish masters, that a hundred years ago had come over from Haarlem as a part of the dowry of the Dutch bride of that Colborne who had bent the horseshoes. Their rich time-darkened beauty, their remains of a quiet reality more life-like than life itself, seemed to render these interiors and portraits very appropriate to the still intenseness of the conversation. Ingrid had shut the door, and they stood in the middle of the room, facing each other.

He knew why she had brought him there, but still would be unable to profane his vision of the tomb, by speaking of it. He was curious to hear what she, with her remarkable intuitional gift, would have to say about that other far-back vision on the Tor— old Colborne's. If all these occurrences were linked and fated, it surely pointed towards a climax of more importance than his own miserable death—yet how could she assist him, when he was to tell her nothing? She was not to know about the vision, nor the flint, nor the flint's history, nor his attraction here from India, nor his premonition of death. Then he expected her unprovided intuitions to explain everything—not to her own understanding indeed, but to his. Truly he was clutching at straws in thus gravely facing this young modern girl as though she were a sibyl of the antique world! No, he would simply answer her questions, and be off again.

While Ingrid, on her side, was already seeing that she could not in justice interrogate Hugh more intimately about his adventure—supposing he should not speak spontaneously—when she herself was prohibited by that secret silent command of her heart from relating her dreadful-lovely vision of last evening on the Tor. She remarked how his brooding taciturnity persisted, she was sure that he had concealed some very important feature of his penetration of the tomb, and yet her tongue was tied.

Had he encountered down there her *spirit*? . . . Was whatever he had seen or heard of urgency enough to explain the tomb's phenomenal opening?—of weight enough to allow immediately afterwards its quick closing again for ever? His manner permitted it. Yet if he was not to speak—if this secret, weird or immense, was to remain everlastingly locked up in his single human consciousness—then it must concern him alone. And certainly it was queer that he had arrived back from India just in time. But still her participation, and her sensations on the Tor for such a long time past, and her sense of something to happen to her . . . and, infinitely above all, that *spirit-woman*! . . . More things yet must be to take place. A great working was going on, independently of them all, so that it seemed to matter little what one said of it, or did. It was leisurely as well as swift. Uncle Magnus's experience had been before she was born.

She said queerly to Hugh, after a quite long silence:

"Of course you know that we are to talk about Devil's Tor. Events are moving rather fast. Since our getting back last night, there have been your earthquake, and Uncle Magnus's story, and anything you may be keeping back about your investigation of the burial chamber—three things. Only, I won't urge you about the last. You may have your reason for reticence."

"I was sufficiently pestered at the table just now. I can't add to the account I gave."

"Very well, Hugh—but you are willing to discuss the matter otherwise?"

"If it is perturbing you."

"It is all happening at a time when I especially want to be at peace. I've the strong feeling that I am personally concerned. In part you know what I mean, but there's something else as well that I haven't told you, and can't ever. Would you care to hear how the Tor is appearing to me? It is just like a volcano, suddenly active again after a very long period of supposed death. It might be a haunted hill merely—I mean, Uncle has had an experience there, and I—have always had my peculiar sensations and instincts, and you constitute a third, I am sure. But no simple haunting would bring down lightning to it, or raise an earthquake. It goes beyond. How far are you now sympathetic to such a feeling?"

"I have an open mind."

"Please understand I'm not trying to enter by a back door, but—assuming anything did happen to you this morning, it was *after* your accident with the torch?"

"I can only repeat that the accident was uncaused by any sudden start."

"So, if my feeling about you is right, you stumbled and broke the torch first. And in that case, surely it was *meant* you should be left in the dark. And it would go with the rest. . . . Now I want to ask you, Hugh. Between the opening and the destruction of the stairway, would be—how long? Less than a dozen hours. So during ten, twenty or fifty thousand years, the tomb has been available for exploration for just under twelve hours in all; with a miracle at either end. And you, out of the whole of the human race during all those thousands of years, have been down to it. Then what I have to ask you is, can you truthfully declare that your experience inside this tomb has been significant enough to justify the election and the supernatural machinery used towards it? Do you understand me?"

"I understand you perfectly. The answer is in the negative. I will tell you at once that I have come out of that place a changed man—nevertheless I can honestly see no good reason why mountains should move in order to transform my insignificant personality.”

“So that more yet is to come of it?”

“It seems out of the question, now that the place is apparently ruined beyond restoring; and still I won’t dogmatise, and it *may* be possible.”

“You made use of a strange word with Uncle. *Angelic*. Was it careless or deliberate?”

“It expressed my thought.”

“Then how do you regard his story?”

“That radiance of his must have been as the radiance of the angels, but its seat and centre must have been below ground, in the tomb itself.”

“And it too was for a purpose?” Ingrid asked.

“Yes, we may think that it was for the purpose of retaining him in the district. . . . You see that you have brought me so far without confession of mine. In fact, Devil’s Tor surely is alive and working to an end, or such coincidences are clustered round it as never were in the history of the world. I said my mind was open. I suppose I am as convinced as you are, Ingrid, that we are here suddenly in the presence of a great wonder. I know things that you don’t, but there is small sense in talking about it all. Your mother told me only last night how your own birth was superhumanly brought about and defended by your father’s dreamings of a woman of extraordinary height, who showed him his direction. I am not sure that this doesn’t belong to the same category as Uncle Magnus’s vision. If so, he was kept here because you were to live here, and know Devil’s Tor.”

“Thank you for telling me, Hugh. . . . You really brought nothing back with you to-day?”

“No, nothing.” For since his return to the house he had been certain that the stone he had picked up in the darkness of the cavern was genuinely his own. The empty box said so. And he thought it unprofitable to acquaint her with that story, that actually was so unassociated. It could only end in his repeating to her the whole of his last night's confession to her mother; but words were difficult to him this morning, nor was it necessary for her to know.

The girl's perplexed silence, however, as she continued to face him, raised in his mind something like an uneasy conscience. He sought for some other fact or circumstance that she might carry away with her, to turn her ideas to the future.

"It's on the cards," he said, twisting his moustache, "that a man may be coming down here to see me, who could perhaps throw new light on all this business. It would be a very indirect light, if any at all; but it might be completed by your intuitions. You could speak to him, at least, if he comes. He is studying the ancient cult of the 'Great Mother.' His name is Arsinal."

"When do you expect him, Hugh?"

"He may be here any day."

"Will you promise to make us known?" She refrained from pressing him for more information regarding this individual so unexpectedly appearing on the scene, for a curious reason of her own. It was that the conviction was already growing within her, that it was not to be by any act of willing or seeking that she was to find her solution of these bewilderments and awfulnesses. Supposing that she had truly been chosen for a part, it was her passive nature that had gained it for her. And therefore she would ask few questions of anybody, but for the future wait—and wait. . . .

"If I am here to do it, and circumstances allow, I will willingly introduce you," replied Hugh gravely.

"Won't you stay on till he comes?"

"It may not depend on me."

Ingrid had a sudden feeling that he meant that he might die before his friend arrived. She looked at him anxiously, but dared not interrogate him. The same telepathic thought had been with her last night, but then she had coupled it with his intended descent to the Devil's Tor tomb; and he had survived that.

She could not understand what any of these things meant, and without more conversation they left the room together.

X

Hill Shades

At the appointed hour that afternoon Ingrid, hatless and in a sleeveless frock of pale green, met Peter when he had just turned in at the lane gate to get to the house. He was neatly dressed in a grey town lounge suit, with a soft felt hat, as for a call of ceremony. Ingrid already knew that he would never do the socially wrong thing—that it was only intellectually that he was a scorner and independent; and still it vaguely displeased her to see him thus; she wished he could have left formality out of a meeting which surely merely concerned their two hearts. But they greeted each other in quiet friendliness, and Peter never replaced the hat he had removed, but in another moment cast it carelessly on to the porch seat as they passed by.

The day had turned to fine. Above it was all blue sky and white clouds, the sun kept coming and going; the breeze, more caressing than keen, brought the sweetness of the moor to them. The thirsty ground had sucked in last night's rainfall, leaving the grass underfoot dry again. They made for a well-known seat halfway down the sloping lawn on the west of the house. Ingrid was limping a little yet, but needed no support. She dreaded this conversation to come.

Nothing to the purpose, indeed, was said until they were settled down, with that lovely view before them of the narrow dipping valley at the lawn's end, and the slow ascending beyond it of the purple moor to its invisible top. Then, however, Peter lost no more time in reaching the subject that had fetched him to the house so early. For once he was not smoking.

"I conceive that if any two persons in the world can begin the discussion of a thorny theme without preliminary embarrassments, it is you and I," he started in his cool fashion, that some called conceit, and others an absence of warmth from his nature, but which Ingrid herself knew to be pride, and nervousness, and a real distinction of his mind, all together. And he went on, with scarcely ever the flicker of a glance at her, while she too gazed straight ahead.

"So we'll skip the prelude, and enter on the theme. It relates of course to the possibility and advisability of a marriage between us. I am very desirous of making clear to you at once that my doubts are not the usual ones of an over-modest worshipper. I do on occasion very nearly worship you, as a matter of fact, just as I am perfectly prepared to admit my general inferiority to you—but in the present instance the hesitations neither refer to my unworthiness, nor specifically to me at all, but to you. . . . For an offer of eternal life, I wouldn't give you an unsuccessful marriage, my dear. And the problem in my head is, have you—you yourself— any internal prompting that another type of man altogether would bring you greater blessedness? This is a question I want to put you before ever going on to inquire—the customary inquiry. . . . Perhaps I have muddled it for you. What is in my mind is, that your nature, consciously or unconsciously, may be requiring for its fulfilment another nature, stronger, and—haughtier, and more passionate, if you like—all in the sense of the world only. I may be these things in art. I am not asking about your affection, of which I'm sure—I am asking about your natural spiritual correspondence. I have this painful instinct that *our* sort of love is not to be enough for you . . . almost that you will need to *fear* your husband—if fear you can."

Ingrid had grown pale; yet without turning round she answered him calmly and immediately, if in her lowest voice.

"You know, Peter, I have not met anyone whom I could ever regard as I regard you."

"Thanks for that woman's reply. It remains a woman's reply, however—it confines itself to the personal fact. The question was as to your future unfolding. At present you are in a state of innocence—supreme temptation hasn't come your way."

"You think I need a man of the world for my husband?"

"Heaven defend you from such! But a man able to *daunt* the world—a man able to fight and defeat the world with its own practical weapons. Someone who can set you high. For you are this queer compound of the regal and the surrendering, and over and above all, the world can hardly, in any sense whatsoever, be a real place to you. That someone must see its reality for you as well. Both qualifications go beyond me. The whole of such activity as I possess goes into my work, while life is passionately true to me only so far as beauty can make it so. These are my intuitions, expanded. You are a girl living quietly at home, and I am a dabbler in paints; but whereas I shall go on being a dabbler in paints, you should have strong wings preparing—that conceivably may bear you a very long way off from me. Has nothing ever whispered in you, Ingrid?"

"I have never thought of a husband, apart from you, Peter."

"My dear! . . . Yet that is the very danger. If you had more of the egoism and vanity of the ordinary girl, you would by now have considered all men for their desirability or falling short. Also a woman's ignorance of the arts of attraction implies a corresponding ignorance in her of the attractive force of others. You're to go through life safe-guarded only by your own height—which may suffice in the cases of all men except one, who will sweep you off your feet by reason of your long accumulation of secret repressions. I don't wish to say disheartening things. Haven't you ever suspected anything of the strain in me?"

"I've known for a very long time past that something has been troubling you. Can it seem so real to you?"

"As real as whatever stops one's happiness."

"What can I say? No doubt more than a few of us have these affinities somewhere, if by luck we could meet them; but we never shall. How could it be possible in a world teeming with population and split into the tiniest circles of acquaintance? Tell me how to help you dismiss this misery, Peter."

"You have helped to rivet it, my dear—by denying *our* affinity."

"Is it essential that we should be the spiritual halves of each other? We can admire, and love, and honour one another without that, Peter—it's even a rule of life that it should be so. Life is an endless affair of makeshifts and compromises, and our spirit has been given to us for the very purpose of ennobling such a terribly human condition. You can't be supposing that in the event of a marriage between us, I could afterwards turn to another man?"

"Not in evil."

"Then I am weakly to allow myself to be wretched on account of an imagined missed joy? The whole world is hardly worth so much to me."

"Very true—you desire no joys. You are pursuing something else quite different, which presently your nature will tell you about. That is precisely my instinct."

"But, Peter—you have forced yourself at last to make this confession—with what motive? Why have you *wished* to speak? If you are truly so fearful of my later on meeting someone who will be nearer than you to me in soul, how can verbal denials of mine assist?"

"I believed that talking it out with you might be useful, my dear. I saw how my reserve ran the risk of being misunderstood; also I hoped against hope that you might show me my lunacy. But doubtless the chief reason of all for opening the subject was my appreciation of your gift and habit of deep feeling. So I want you now to consider, not your heart, but your whole being, in quietness. Inform me later—in a few days—that my apprehensions have just grounds, in so far as an essential part of you knows me not, but scorns me; and I will then go away again—in small gladness, as you may imagine, but at least on the long weary road to peace once more. So will you do this?"

Ingrid glanced oddly at him, but it was only for a moment. She was a longer time silent. It had come suddenly to her mind how Hugh that morning had mentioned a friend who was to visit him here. The mention had been in connection with Devil's Tor, and all at once everything concerned with the Tor was become significant. It was therefore fated that she was to know and somehow get involved with this stranger; whose name, she remembered, was Arsinal. And now Peter, for the first time in all their intimacy, was insisting on his instinct of a man, other than himself, in her life. What was she to reply to him? Was Peter too an instrument? Was their quiet love, on this very threshold of its acknowledgment, to be arrested? Presumably a professor—and Peter, whom she had known all her life. . . . No, she was incapable of thinking any more about anything whatever. These flashes of some great storm advancing upon her were paralysing her brain, and she could but hold on to her courage, as it were with both hands. She must be passive and stoical, yet Peter's love she would never renounce. She could promise him nothing in words until she knew what was wanted of her. That spirit-woman must be an announcing phantom of happenings immediately at hand. She *was* and they *were to be* . . . and how dull and shadowy seemed love itself, beside such a dreadful coming on of the invisible! All the ancient life of these parts might be heavily moving again, after some long dream of death. . . .

Peter, however, made uneasy at last by the continuance of her silence, turned cautiously to view her profile—long, fair and foreign as already he was aware its illusion was, with that absence of foreground. Her features were serene like a sphinx's, her eye was veiled by its sweeping lashes, but a line of pain seemed to cross her forehead. He could not understand her. She appeared always so simple, even to weakness, yet always behind it too was her immovable strength and strangeness, as though she were less a girl than a mythological interpreting daughter of compelling fate. With a new stab he once more knew that she was not his. She was that man's, who could approach her. Her affections and softnesses were her lowlands—*they* were his. . . . He looked away from her again, biting his lip.

"Perhaps I've picked a bad time for perplexing you, though," he said aloud. "You may have some other business to worry you, and so can't give this proper concentration. I could even hazard a guess at what it is."

She moved round, surprised.

"Something certainly is occupying a good deal of my mind just now, but you can scarcely have any knowledge of it, Peter."

"Yet I fancy it concerns Devil's Tor."

She waited for him to explain this mystery of his acquaintance with a matter that none but she and Hugh had discussed. But he must have seen Hugh during the day, and fallen into talk with him—though this too would be singular.

"Am I right?"

"Yes, though I can't imagine how you have discovered it," was her quiet answer. "Have you by any, chance met my cousin Hugh Drapier to-day, out of doors?"

"I believe so. You did describe him, only I couldn't have been listening very attentively. He's red-haired, lean, and tall?"

"Yes."

"I ran across such a man on Devil's Tor itself. I should explain that I went up there, on your story, to see the effect of lightning on rocks. I wasn't happy at home. However he and I had no conversation to the purpose, and my sense of your preoccupation springs from other sources."

"Tell me, Peter."

"Why, to put it shortly, the hill is bewitched, or else I am insane. I know you were up there yesterday in peculiar circumstances, I know your cousin has visited the place *twice* to-day; I found him in a trance; a prehistoric tomb has been opened and blocked again; and *you* are half in a dream all the time."

"But what do you mean by its being 'bewitched'?"

"I'll give the story another time. We have our business to settle first."

"But it is just this that is standing in the way, Peter—can't you understand that?"

"I thought so, but wanted to make sure. What do *you* know about the Tor that you haven't told me, Ingrid?"

"I've a thousand feelings, and hardly one clear idea. You have had the facts. There was an earthquake this morning. Uncle told us at breakfast of an extraordinary experience of his there many years ago. I long since had the intuition that there was a tomb under the leaning pile."

"I went up a little before noon. Do you believe in ghosts?"

"I must."

"Then you as well have probably seen something. But if you are still too impressed to speak of it, don't. I'll get on with my tale?"

"You are outdoing me in generosity, Peter, but I'd actually rather not say anything about my own case."

"I've never asked you for the keys of all your doors, my dear. And as to generosity, it's sometimes the height of generosity to let a poor man make a gift without return."

"You need no such counterpoise. And if ever I can tell you, I will, but till then I will tell no one else. Now what happened, Peter? Why do you talk of ghosts? How came my cousin to be in a trance? What was the order?"

"Recollect that I couldn't know him; yet I could have a shot at his identity, from the colour of his hair."

The tail of a great cloud that had hidden the sun grew attenuated and passed quite away. The quiet, quick rising to full golden sunlight, occurring at that moment of their conversation, seemed to Ingrid like a wonderful joy to come—yet Peter had said that she desired no joys. Then at once she was plunged into chill shade again by the unkind coming on of another mass of cloud, darker and greater still; and it was as if she were cruelly deprived once more of the promise of that joy, and of every joy in life. She believed this chance rising and sinking of sunshine in some strange way to present a picture of her fortunes. In less than twenty-four hours it had all become omens with her.

"He was sitting on a rock as I came up," Peter was continuing, "just inside the edge of the top of the hill, facing the site of the destruction and the direct road home.

"He sat all huddled up, with hunched shoulders and rigid, staring, sightless eyes—like the eyes of a man that has had a seizure. One hand was clenched over something on his knee. I knew at once it was some sort of a fit, and since there were none of the signs of paralysis, apoplexy or epilepsy, I concluded it to be catalepsy, a condition I know next to nothing about. It put me in a quandary. Ought I to rouse him, with the risk of giving his system a bad shock; or ought I to leave him to come round naturally, confining myself to helping him off the Tor afterwards? I decided it wasn't safe to interfere, although the situation remained distinctly unpleasant. And so I filled in the time of waiting with sauntering around, inspecting the ruin.

"The earthquake up there, which of course I hadn't heard of, has confused the whole area, so that there were fully as many puzzles for me as evidences of destructive lightning. However, I satisfied myself that there was no way down to any tomb, I saw and ruminated upon the two big blocks reposing on top, I peeped over the edge for the rest. I gazed at this and that, and kept returning to my red-haired man in a trance, who never stirred. Ten minutes or so may have passed in this mode.

"The sun was just breaking through for the second half of the day, and there was a fresh wind. As a matter of fact, I felt rather more alive and present in my senses than usual, when abruptly, without notice, the transition occurred. My eyes darkened, my limbs were all at once like lead, and I barely had time to avoid a fall by finding and sinking down on to another knob of rock close by the other man's—so that most of my back was to him, and my view was more directly over the valley one crosses coming up.

"It wasn't the same—that view. It had slipped into a different. And what for an instant I had thought to be a darkening of my eyesight, now by quick degrees established itself as a true darkening of the day—to, say, somewhat more than the brightness of full moonlight at its strongest. But the scene so lit was harder to realise. The familiar general features were retained, but the heights, proportions and aspects were all hopelessly wrong. For instance, the moor on the right had become an elevated plateau, while the shoulder over the valley towered above the Tor and me. Its face was no longer a grassy steep, but cliff. The foot-track you know, that brings one to the Tor, was scarcely represented by a tricky-looking precipice ledge, with a sheer drop. I got the impression that the valley was very much deeper, but its bottom was out of sight."

"And the Devil's head, Peter?"

"Was absent. It would have intercepted my view, which remained uninterrupted. . . . But I must explain about the quality of the light. Though so dark, it was definitely daylight, not moonlight. At the same time, it wasn't my eyes; they were catching all the light there was—and yet the day should be brighter than I saw it. I was seeing the *ghost* of a scene, in ghostly light. Can you understand, Ingrid?"

"I am trying to."

"Then, on the right-hand moor I spoke of, was a herd of monstrous brutes, that might have been elephants. . . ."

"But, Peter, did all this strike you as unreal—did you fancy yourself dreaming—or was it actual to you?"

"Both, in combination. It had everything of the consistency, detail and cold logic of a real experience—nothing of the fantastic foolishness and impossibility of a dream; and yet my memory was contradicting it for me. It was not the world I had lived in all my life. In that sense, it was dream-like. It was in the nature of a prodigy, without known parents, dropped from another planet on to this. But let me come to the extraordinary part of the story. . . . I saw coming round the bend of that ledge half-way down the face of the cliff across the valley, the head of a long *funeral procession*.

"It was in half-profile, as soon as the angle was turned. The distance away would be about the same as now—some hundreds of yards—far enough to make the persons of the procession, in that light, appear like goblins. . . ."

"*As now!* So you instinctively realised that that different landscape was the phantom of an earlier stage of the present one?"

"Yes—I knew I was seeing a phantom of the past, and why not? For if haunted houses can be, why not haunted landscapes as well? And if you object that the landscape was not only haunted, but metamorphosed, which doesn't happen to a haunted house, I reply that, given the necessary vividness of manifestation, it might happen to a haunted house too, and the rooms and furniture might be changed. In effect, my sensations, that endured as long as the phenomenon went forward, certified the supernatural character. A slight horror and quaking went on continuously in me to the end; meaning, first that my blood scented the presence of an alien world (dogs have the same instinct very powerfully developed, as in bristling and howling on account of the unseen) . . . and secondly, that my logical brain was raising no protest of the non-existence and impossibility of what I saw, as presumably it must have done had the thing been simple passing hallucination. It would have sought to rectify the illusion at once; and would have succeeded; but this vision and quaking went on."

"But would there be no term to such a haunting of a land-scape, Peter?"

"At least, before we can assign a term, we must know what is to wear out in the haunting. . . . Here there were elephants in England—or shall I say at once, *mammoths*? I have no science, but imagine that should give us very much more than ten thousand years, for example. So this particular haunting, if true, is proved to be practically unwearoutable. Shall I now resume?

"The funeral train—the persons composing it were half-bare savages, clad in a single animal skin apiece, with flowing manes over their shoulders; brandishing primitive weapons. Caesar's Britons must have scorned them for aborigines; and indeed, they were little more than apes. Their squat trunks, brief legs, gorilla-like arms, crouching balance, and tangle of unclipped hair, were absolutely in the character of apes. And they came along that cliff face in file, an endless string of them, all stamping and dancing outrageously, in true savage style. Only the covered death-hurdle—that made it a funeral for me—required a pair of supporters at either end, and they, in reason, could not dance. The outer two looked to me to be very precariously balanced over the edge of the ledge.

"All were just grey shapes. The colouring and sex were indistinguishable; except that they appeared as little like women as could be. Yet, dim as they were—perhaps additionally because of that dimness—their advance was singularly awful to my imagination. What must have been in my mind was that the path they were dancing along was the equivalent of the path *we* know, leading to the Tor. So they were making for Devil's Tor, and I was on it."

Ingrid touched his sleeve.

"Peter, were they going to bury their dead on Devil's Tor?"

"It was my instinct that they were."

"The monument of course would not be up till the grave was filled. So did you see a grave?"

"No, I neither saw nor looked for one."

"I would have looked for it—still, the entrance may have been temporarily covered. What have you to say about that dead one, Peter?"

"The bier was hidden by a hanging skin or cloth. Its length was unusual—abnormal, even—but whether the corpse was of a length corresponding, was not disclosed. I thought it might be. In fact, that prodigious drawn-out extension of the bier was the most dream-like feature of the whole business. The rest was spectral, but possible; this a fantasy."

"It necessarily was a bier?"

"Yes, all the signs were of a funeral."

"So there was nothing to show if it were a woman or a man?"

"The question to ask is, what would a dead person, taller than our tallest men, be doing amongst those thick-set gnomes? By the honours being paid, he should be some prisoner of war, treated during his lifetime like a god. A woman, on all those accounts, would be less likely."

Ingrid already knew his error, but was silent; and he proceeded:

"The six leading creatures were blowing into conches, that sounded across the valley like far-off French horns—most thin and weird; above a perpetual thunder of invisible waters. A long way down the grotesque snake-line of mourners came the quiet burden, out of it all—and it suggested to me, my dear, what I have just said: a captive of high race, civilisation and rank, fallen into the hands of those simians, and worshipped by them, but never let go during the term of his natural life."

"And then, Peter . . . ?"

"That was the whole. The present landscape began to reappear through the ancient, the stronger light melted it away to nothingness, and the sun came out. Very shaken and moved, I found myself still sitting on my stump of rock; with your cousin, just as helpless, behind me.

"In a minute or two I got up and went to him. Before long he came round, and when his first desperate daze was past, we exchanged a few words, but we neither of us told our experience. It was somehow not the thing. I had the feeling that we had seen different visions. . . . He informed me of the earthquake, said that there actually had been a tomb, and that he had been down to it earlier to-day; but gave me no details; and refused my company off the hill. So I left first."

His recital being ended, he put a cigarette between his lips and lit it, but Ingrid, sitting on, with hands clasped above her lap, incorporated in silence the story with her other bewilderments. She wondered how Peter could have beheld such a marvel but an hour or so ago, and come straight from it, to talk to her of marriage. He must be trying to hide his own shock, in his English way. Some men, the more deeply they were moved by a solemnity, the more taciturn were about it. Others might be responsive at the time to a supernatural happening, yet the impression might quickly wear off with them, their own affairs being always too insistent. Thus Uncle Magnus had never cared to visit Devil's Tor a second time. . . . Or, having fixed the appointment with her for this afternoon, Peter had felt morally bound to go through with it, though disinclined. She asked herself what Hugh could have seen simultaneously. His trance had begun sooner, finished later, and must have been heavier. But she knew he wouldn't speak about it. In Peter's words, "it was not the thing."

So Hugh *had* cared to visit the hill again. Twice to-day he had been up, and perhaps was there now for a third time—she had seen him disappear with his hat on directly after lunch. He was certainly psychic, as Peter couldn't be. Possibly art was a channel that drew off all one's sense of reality into representation, so that even a quite fearful ghostly experience might become for the artist softened and unreal. But this couldn't be their incompatibility that Peter had referred to.

She must go up again. To-day it was not possible; but perhaps to-morrow. She must doctor and rest her ankle in readiness. What was Peter now expecting her to say? . . . But he was resuming, turning to her through a wreath of smoke.

"Well, what do you make of it? Of course you accept the *bona fides* of the adventure? I did see these shapes and hear these sounds, exactly as I've reported; and I wasn't asleep and dreaming—you accept that?"

"I accept it all, just as you have told it to me."

"Nor have I distorted. Drapier has said nothing, though? Have you seen him since?"

"Yes, he was back to lunch, but said nothing; and ate nothing."

"I'm not surprised. I only sat down to mine because it was got ready. What did he find in the tomb?"

"Two stone tables, and nothing else."

"Enough to work him up, at the least, since we meet him on the hill a second time."

"Yes, I think he regards it seriously."

"A pity! These mediumistic trances, if they continue and he is going to keep on with them, look like leading him straight into nervous lunacy. His face was ghastly. Let those follow up the topsy-turvy affair whose professional work it is. . . . Anyway, I'm very glad your hurt prevents *you*."

"You aren't to follow it up then, Peter?"

He slowly expelled a cloud from his mouth before making reply.

"No, I'm not going to. I considered the point on my way back, and found there was nothing to gain by my going further into it.

"What has happened, I take it, is this. After a number of years a stack of rocks on one of the minor heights of Dartmoor has been blown down, and an ancient grave uncovered. A resulting strong physical effluence from that opening is being able to affect the physical brains of those standing near by in such a way as to reproduce, photographically and phonographically, former happenings on the spot. It is very curious, very interesting, and essentially a case for science. But it is not a case for art. At first I was tempted to believe it might be—that optically and philosophically I could get something from it. I still might, but the charge is too high. For just as I would not swallow cocaine or opium for the sake of enriching my general imagery, so, my dear girl, I will not play Tom-Tiddler's-ground with the world of spooks for the same purpose. Ghosts have never done the human race one atom of good. I should be excited, brought to a fever, poisoned for the milder stimulations—and left. . . . Accordingly, your cousin must do what he likes about it—though, if you're a helpful young woman, you'll pass him on my warning—I, for my part, propose to walk out after this first act. The play threatens to be too realistic and exacting. I hope on due reflection you'll do the same."

Ingrid returned him a quiet look.

"You see I am a prisoner. I quite approve your decision, and admire you for it, but don't let us speak of the matter any more. Thank you for telling me what you have."

"I am very willing to leave it. So let's get back to our proper business."

"Say exactly what you want me to do."

"I have said. For years I must have had this feeling about you, but now the march of our intimacy seems to have brought us to a point where it can't any longer be ignored, and I want to hear from you whether it is a possibly right or a definitely wrong feeling. . . . You were quite correct about its being unnecessary for us to be the complementary halves of each other. Obviously we have differences; and they don't matter, and are not at all the sort of thing I mean. What does matter, my dear, is whether a marriage to me would permit you your best and finest life. So I beg you to examine your sources—and believe me, the significance of it goes very much deeper down than any mere brave planning of good intentions. Everyone has two wills, an active and an instinctive, and woe betide the person who thinks to construct his or her life wholly according to the active! Though for another girl and another marriage it might be all right."

"How is my case different?"

"You know you care for none of the things that girls do care for. At present, in this household, you're as fast asleep as the Sleeping Beauty. You'll have to wake up some time—to what? Shall I be with you when you wake up?"

"I hear these words from no one but you, Peter."

"The question is, if they are true words."

"Can one ever do more with one's life than go on living from day to day, advancing, if one does advance, by choosing the good that offers, and rejecting the bad?"

"That cannot satisfy," said Peter.

"If I marry, I shall have children perhaps; and they may satisfy."

"Should they be worth the love and care."

"That's in the hands of no woman."

"Of no ordinary woman."

At this, Ingrid glanced suddenly round to him.

"Do you mean anything special by that, Peter? Have you been leading me up to talk of children?"

"No, I wasn't going to refer to it. I am not sure if it is immediately in my intuition, though, I think, necessarily implied. If a woman needs one man for a husband, and no other man, it seems to follow that Nature is speaking in her and that his completing qualities aren't for her alone. It's difficult for me to explain these matters without crossing the line, but you can't have forgotten the picture in your mother's room. I had the conception so long ago."

"Of a girl beginning to feel her instincts?"

"Do you imagine Christ's birth to have been miraculous? For if so, my argument drops to the ground. But if Mary bore her wonder-child from a mortal man, then wouldn't you say that Joseph was essential for her?"

"I am not Mary."

"Listen! A line of phenomenal women has always existed in the world, and it is not going to cease by reason of our modern vulgarities and mechanical improvements. So long as the world is to be saved by its great men, so long will those great men have fated mothers. By what signs may they be known, those fated mothers? Perhaps only he can recognise them, who is to be warned off. And perhaps you are such a fated mother, and I am to be warned off, and that is my intuition."

"This is madness."

Both stood up, facing each other. Peter had pitched away his cigarette a minute before.

"It may be that," he replied to her. "As I'm refraining from going heartily in to win you, probably my reasons should be fantastic to madness. Or else the madness of it may be only a point of view—that of the rule, denying sanity to the exception. The rule is that all the affairs of the world shall come under chance; which is an 'x' quantity, that may or may not be equivalent to long fate. The exception occurs when for once in a way this fate is seen actively displaying its hand, thus ruling out chance. Men, you see, have worked out their scheme on the hypothesis of chance; so must deny intention. But God is not an insurance actuary, and this terrific frame of flaming suns and their attendant whirling planets has not been put together from statistics and averages and probabilities. The miraculous human exception, over ages, will appear, and disappear, and reappear. It appears springing out of flesh-and-blood mothers, who have been known, spoken to, criticised by their sister-women, and familiarly met. Nevertheless they have been distinguished from other women by their *fatal* character. And, Ingrid, *you* have marks of distinction from the rest of girls and older women. Where is my madness if I see them somewhat more clearly than other people, and dimly apprehend what they may stand for? They discern a noble nature merely. I earnestly trust it may be no more; but have been told that you are too rare a girl not to represent a concrete purpose."

"You can stand up to me, Peter, and use this language, that all our acquaintances would laugh at, if they heard it!"

"I mightn't risk the enormity if I had not seen what I have to-day. What a pin-point of time we are on, and what does it matter, my dear, how we strip our souls to each other, with one eternity lying behind us and another in front! I'll speak it even more plainly. Very often you have seemed to me—and at times when I haven't wished it—like the future mother of another supernatural saviour of the race."

Ingrid was silenced. Pale and fascinated, she stood staring into his eyes, that were sorrowful; without meeting the spirit behind them. It was opened to her at last, with a withering clearness that was like a sudden day sprung from she knew not where, that this his instinct was being far too deeply and painfully felt by him to be wholly false. Perhaps he was understanding it wrongly, perhaps he was adding to it according to his general mental lines, or drawing conclusions suggested by his sex and jealous affections; but surely it was based on a true perception by him of *something* in her that was present, yet not in the forefront of her nature. . . . Another man, not Peter—and a supernatural child—and destiny! Was she dreaming, or had he just now said such words to her? For while he had spoken only of that other man, it had remained a fancy, just because it was not impossible; but now that he had dared as well to talk of a phenomenal birth, it was too dreadful to continue of the imagination alone, it all at once concerned her depths, and either she must descend to her depths to grapple with this monstrous impossibility, or else immediately, between herself and Peter's insane suggestion, she must put the shield of sober common thinking. Yet hadn't he explained that her children were not in his intuition, except by implication? Unhappily, that made no odds. The roots were struck in her own mind now, and it was not what he had said, but what her thoughts henceforward were not to escape from.

Yes, it was meant that this fearful growth should begin in her conscious soul, and he was but the instrument. Thus it was to-day that his speech must be given the necessary inflation by the remaining fever of his vision on Devil's Tor. And *she* had been prepared too for its reception by that lovely spirit yesterday.

She dared not begin to disentangle what was possible for her of his words from what must be a blasphemous offence against heaven. She dared not reject the one with the other. The message to her—not his tormented delivery of it—seemed sanctified by all these celestial and preternatural events and stories of four-and-twenty hours. By the response of her heart also, where a peculiarly desolating loneliness, such as she had never before experienced, was as if trying to suppress the gleams of a strange faint distant joy, that marvellously resembled reminiscence. . . .

That mystic funeral he had witnessed from the Tor, was *hers*. So she had truly lived and died, and had been a mortal woman, though now a spirit. So, again, she was not to be feared. But then she should have belonged to a people; and that nobler and statelier race than any since had historically inhabited the earth; and during savage times. Could she but see her once more! . . .

Peter remarked the ignored tears standing in her eyes, and, coming closer, put his arm across her shoulder.

"I've upset you, I'm afraid!"

"A little."

"What part troubles you?"

"I don't know. . . . That you should consider me a girl for whom happiness does not matter, perhaps."

"Had you set your heart on happiness, Ingrid?"

"No."

"Would you still risk marrying me?"

She did not answer him, so he went on:

"Shall I decide?"

"Yes."

"If I have interpreted my intuition aright, other things may be in store for you; but we can't wait for all our lives to see if I am right or wrong, so what I suggest is—let us enter into no formal contract, but, if nothing in the meantime has happened to prevent it, let us get married in twelve months; and that should give fate long enough to work its will in."

She buried her face in his arm which still caressed her shoulder; and this he took to mean assent. He kissed her white neck. Immediately he had done so, the contact seemed foreign to him, and he wondered at his own high daring.

They moved apart. Ingrid regarded him steadily, through her damp lashes.

"While as for notifying the arrangement," said Peter, "that shall be entirely as you wish, and either we can carry on, to all outward appearance, as now—that is, as very good friends, and no more—or you may, if you prefer it, inform your mother alone, or all the rest of the world besides, that there is this informal arrangement, which is not quite an engagement, but on the way to one. So say what you want."

She was still quiet for a few moments, but then replied:

"There seems no need for others to know it, but I had better tell my mother."

"At once?"

"Yes."

"Do so, then. . . . Are you angry with me?"

"No. Why should I be angry, when I am aware you have only spoken from love?"

"I may come and see you, and talk to you, as always?"

"Of course."

"What are you thinking of me at this minute?" asked Peter. They had not yet turned back to the house. "That I am a poltroon, for not daring to try to win you out of hand?"

"No."

"What then?"

"I was thinking how much grimmer a business art must be than I supposed, if it is built up of such renunciations."

"Is it good?"

"So good, that I shall probably now always look for traces of it in all the pictures I see—especially in yours."

"You've discovered a profounder truth than all the critics together," responded Peter.

They started slowly walking back, but had not gone more than a few yards when Ingrid faltered. She caught at Peter, and they stopped again.

"Peter, what you have done to me is that I'm feeling an unspeakable loneliness. You've made me feel as if I were eternally cut off. I need you. . . . Kiss me, dear!"

He pressed her lips with his.

"So here's another force we can't ignore!" she said, smiling queerly, when they were apart again. "If fate is dictatorial, possession is just as dogged. They also say it is nine points of the law."

"It is very true. And I should also have borne in mind another small truth still better known to me: that inspiration follows, not precedes, action."

"And now we are like children, who are happier in breaking their good resolutions than in keeping them."

"Do you say so, Ingrid?"

"It is not I that put up an obstacle."

"How is your loneliness?"

She appeared to reflect.

"I must always have been lonely—I *have* always been lonely . . . but now somehow it's less an ache, more an emotion, and I can't see how it is not to go on. You have thoroughly made me realise that I am alone in the world, Peter."

"Alone?"

"You mean, I have you. But don't you know what love does for loneliness? It drugs it for half the time; and for the other half our loneliness takes its revenge by adding to itself horrible dreads of loss, and agonising regrets for past insufficiencies and what might have been. I am not sure that a lonely person ought ever to love. Love is for the alike."

"And so you are to be driven to me by an unendurable condition?"

"No; but I don't know what I mean."

"You do love me?—as a girl loves a man?"

"Yes."

"Won't it help you, to have me to tell all these things to? Free confession rids us of the best part of the burden."

"Yes, it will help."

"And once married, you will have a thousand distractions.

Shall we shorten the time?”

“If you wish it.”

“I shall be down again in November, and then we will see.”

He embraced and kissed her, while she stood with closed eyes, unsmiling and unresisting.

She wondered what she was doing, playing at this game of love. Thunderstorms, earthquakes, tombs and apparitions were calling to her, her secret heart was full of awful whispers, she was marked out by all her characters to be a woman apart. Every ancient thing was in movement within her range. Hugh might be on Devil’s Tor again, tasting new wonders. And Peter was kissing her in childishness, as though the dam of his long hesitation had burst at last. From him she could endure it, for it was his right and nature, and she had but within these few minutes given herself to him; nevertheless her self seemed doubled. If such caresses were now to go on, would not she be guilty of a duplicity threatening to become permanent? For the one half of her was not in his arms, but in the more terrible real universe. Was this his own prediction for her? . . .

But when he released her, they walked back to the house, composing themselves to meet the others there.

And Ingrid found her opportunity before tea to acquaint her mother with as much of their talk and plannings as she thought necessary. Helga was glad.

XI

Peter’s Art

Drapier was not back to tea, which confirmed and completed his uncle’s good humour, already established by Peter’s presence. Ingrid was quiet and pale, though easy to speak with. Helga wished she could understand if this manner of her daughter’s meant happiness only, or happiness and something else. Peter’s face did not enlighten her. Its exaggeration of a nonchalance that was habitual to it might just as well stand for unmitigated satisfaction as for a deliberate concealment of something to be concealed. The feature of this affair about which she was vaguely uneasy was that the engagement was not to be a straightforward, declared one. Uncle Magnus, for instance, was not yet to know of it; and there was to be no ring. She hoped she was not so small-minded as to confound the token with the thing itself, but still she was acquainted with the world, and knew that behind an eccentricity too frequently lurked an unpleasantness. She must not be ungenerous to Peter before she had found out that the fault of sense and candour was his, and so her occasional glances to him continued to be entirely friendly and as eloquent as the situation permitted; yet she wondered—and thought of her accumulating years as she did so—if this beginning of an illogical censuring of his conduct might not represent the germ of that traditional dislike of mothers for the snatchers-away of their children. She did not wish to be so instinctive and unmodern; she would even rather distort her feelings to a perpetual particular regard for him. Now she would furnish him with an opportunity of shining before Ingrid, in discussing his art, and that should please them both, and be her best immediate gift.

The sunlight had departed for the day from the sombre Flemish pictures, that were like a nearly living gallery to the quartet in the room, but the rich colours of a part of one of the rugs on the oak floor gleamed softly as a beautiful fire in the end of an oblique ray. Peter was quite approachable. She had seen at once that he knew Ingrid had told her—she would say a few words to him by-and-by. Her uncle was sipping his tea in amiable aloofness. All there were too familiar with his custom of holding back from a general conversation until a favourable opening should permit his effective capture of it, to attempt to coax him too soon from this retirement. How oddly-constituted the gathering was, Helga thought. An old man, who had brought his vanity of a boy right through life with him; a young man, chiefly intent on the cynical disguising of his love, that was no disgrace to him; a girl, having just received a girl's greatest prize, sitting apart like the pale young heroine of a drama of sacrifice; she herself, being tactful and harmonising, probably not from any goodness of disposition at all, but because she loved the effeminate softness of concord. They all four were showing this front of deceit; so no doubt the tendency was universal, and deceit was a necessary defence of humanity. But that caused prying and inquisitiveness in others; and thus armour and arms were forged in the same shop. Since she had now to set Peter talking, she conceived that so queer a puzzle in philosophy was translatable into his language. She wanted to say something to him, not nothing, he was always so very contemptuous of emptiness.

He rarely cared to discuss art at all, she knew, but on the present special occasion it was to be inferred that he would welcome the relief. Doubtless he was in some sort of magic heaven, despite his coolness. So long as he was under constraint in this room, his whole being must be crying out for violent expression; Ingrid, sitting there in profile to him like a phantom, must be maddening him by her mere intangible spectacle; and art alone held the elements of recklessness and incoherence requisite to his discharge. Already his news and theirs had been exhausted. He had barely troubled to disguise his complete lack of interest in both. And Ingrid was as absent; she had said hardly anything since coming into the room.

So Helga, bending forward while putting on a little frown of intelligence, questioned Peter concerning the symbolism he was always after. She wished to hear whether, in trying to express the invisible by the visible, he was dissatisfied with the *sham* of outward things? . . . For instance, the human face—a woman's face. Its pensiveness, or vivacity, or *hauteur*, might be—probably was, the expression of an acted emotion; the emotion was genuine, as far as it went, but had been deliberately adopted by the woman's will as an easy pleasure; and was not her true soul, that could only be brought to her face under outward stress. Was it the business of Peter's symbolism to present that true soul—and by means of it, the human soul in general?

Pulling out the familiar leather case, he tapped and lit a cigarette.

"That is really very good, Mrs. Fleming," he replied, putting upon his tongue its accustomed bridle of light cynical detachment. "The one objection I can immediately find to it is that the soul, naturally, can express only a single emotion at any given moment of time, whereas no single emotion can present the whole soul. Or if you mean that the character of a soul is identical with its ruling emotion, then as that *ruling* emotion is more or less always present, it seems to require no outward stress to call it forth."

"The soul of a professional actor, for example—how would you paint that? His face is seldom an index, and we will suppose that his ruling passion is money."

"I shouldn't attempt to paint it, unless it had previously given me some very strong impression. In the first place, hadn't we better understand what we mean by 'soul'?"

"I mean of course the deepest and most important part of our personality."

"Then how can it be concerned with money?" demanded Peter bluntly. . . . "You see, my dear Mrs. Fleming, how necessary it is to start off with definitions. I have argued with a man for an hour, and found at the end that we had been losing our tempers over totally different things. There are any number of 'souls.' There is the immortal soul, and the soul that goes out at death, yet in the meantime is capable of feeling very fine emotions, and the soul by courtesy, like that of your actor-friend, and the soul of animals—you have seen into a dog's eyes? . . . and I don't know what else. Define! define! define!—that is my constant recommendation."

"Then let us leave the soul out of it, Peter; and tell me what I want to know. Do you crave to paint *insides*, because *outsides* are false?"

He sat back thoughtfully, watching the ascending of his smoke towards the ceiling.

"The postulate is debatable," he said after a moment or two.

"Outsides, perhaps, are not so false, only they happen pretty frequently to disagree with what they cover. Take the bodily inside and outside of a man. No two collections of things could be more unlike, yet why have we to assume that the viscera are a grim reality, while the eye's shining and the noble sweep of the forehead are an accepted delusion for the amenities of life? No, outsides should be true enough. Only, what every painter worth his salt is trying to present—probably without knowing it—is neither beauty, nor life, nor truth (charming words, all of them!) . . . but—I don't know what. . . ."

Old Colborne grinned into his lifted cup, while Helga waited, content at least that Peter was now in full stride. His pause was brief.

". . . But *the whole universe*—at one stroke. By means, necessarily, of *action*. That is symbolism in a nutshell. Nothing exists apart, but only the universe exists. Whatever individual person or thing I paint must stand, not for itself, but for the entire scheme. As to the machinery by which this is to be effected, that's another matter. I've done quite a lot of smoking and lying face-upwards on the sofa lately."

"A dangerous practice, Peter!"

"None knows it better than I. On the other hand, I don't call it to work, to stand before a canvas furiously tracing the wrong road. One of the most energetic men of my acquaintance does allegory after allegory, while I do nothing; and still I am advancing, and he is not. . . . Allegories! The symbol and the allegory. Yet there remain quite well-educated persons who definitely don't know one from the other. A symbol is a mystic sign of the Creator. An allegory is a wall decoration with a label attached; if you remove the label it is just as decorative, but less illuminating; and that means that its special interest is purely literary. Nearly all allegories treat pretty girls, and that gives the game away at once. But it is just the same if they treat factory-hands or square-legged young male spirits mounting the path to heaven. It's all either voluptuousness or flattery or deliberate mystification. It explains nothing of the universe. . . . A picture should be *passionate*," he added.

Helga asked him to explain that.

"A picture can't help being quiet," replied Peter, "but underneath that quietness should be visible the mighty workings of the spirit; and that is passion. . . . For now consider, say, the stupendous feelings caused in us by gazing upwards at a dizzy cathedral vault; or consider our wild unrest before such a play as *Macbeth*; or the terrific rocking of our faculties when seized by such a piece of music as the beginning movement of the Ninth Symphony. Can pictorial stillness—that resembles a sort of glaze or enamel for the preservation of the painter's ideas—can it, in itself and for itself, aspire to the same class of importance as that cathedral vault, that play, and that symphony movement?

"Take these Netherland paintings on the walls." He gestured towards them, and threw a glance at the master of the house, but at once returned to Helga. "I'm a guest here, so mustn't criticise the appointments, yet in what single feature can a single one of these pictures compare with the symphonies and quartets of Beethoven, or the tragedies of Sophocles, Ford, or Shakespeare? You may see for yourself that what they are going for is the beauty of serenity. Serenity is the peculiar character of paintwork, by reason of its being stationary and unmoving and at the same time not *immediately* impressive like architecture; therefore that kind of beauty is the easiest kind for any picture. Our nerves are first soothed, then lulled, then numbed; the mere physical operation gives us pleasure, while there is just enough intellectual interest and aesthetic mastery to keep us dreaming instead of sleeping.

"A stroll through any gallery tells this story. We stand in front of some reputed first-magnitude picture not very well known to us, for the purpose of studying it; and the more completely we enter into its spirit—the more we find ourselves in the process of rising admiration—so also the more steadily tranquillised we become. The picture's idea has to struggle into us through a heavy soporose atmosphere of peace and rest. It's like being unmanned by the slow penetration of our veins and organs by some sweetly-poisonous Oriental syrup. This is first of all what the painter of living things has to contend against. The tranquility is wrong, if only because it presents an illusion."

"These are new opinions, aren't they, Peter?" asked Helga.

"They're *my* views. I say, an illusion is presented, because as a matter of fact Nature doesn't know tranquillity. Shall I illustrate? Imagine, then, a ruined classical temple of white limestone, standing up on the crest of a bare grass hill, against a sky of faultless blue. Here is *apparent* serenity in perfection, and it's the fault of your lack of sensibility if the tears don't spring to your eyes at the continued spectacle—though I fancy I'm speaking now of other and moister times. However, with or without tears, you would be worked up to emotional agitation by a *fraud*. The structure, in short, will be in violent action. All its constituents are straining towards the mass of the earth, towards each other, and towards their own interiors. And so with pictures. A picture's subject must be one of rest, because the representation of a move-ment never ending and never developing must be ridiculous. But if such rest is made absolute and self-sufficient, as in the Dutch paintings, then you get your illusion. To counteract the rest and so avoid the illusion, one needs the deeper internal movement. To discover what that movement shall be, is the business of symbol-ism."

"Doesn't our imagination supply the movement, Peter? A tall, solitary tree, growing in a meadow—someone paints *it*, and all that we see on the canvas is the stiff hieroglyph of a tree, unmov-ing in the wind, scentless, without ancientness, and smaller than ourselves. It is certainly not the tree. But our imagination supplies whatever is lacking to the image, and lo and behold! it *is* the tree."

"There are paintings of trees and paintings of trees. The ima-gination, as you remark, is very accommodating, and most paint-ings of trees do in fact remind us of pleasant times in the country, if we wish to be so reminded. Only symbolism doesn't wish to fill the equivalent of a snapshot album. A symbolic picture is not to be less, but more important than the beholder. It is to grip him roughly, and not send him to sleep or set him dreaming of happier days, but transform his life for him. The contemplation of a right symbolic picture should be like a visit to church in a spirit of piety.”

“Then you propose to confine yourself to religious subjects?”

“No. Behind the representation of a tree even, one might present the everlasting Spirit.”

“You would say that God is the soul of everything?”

“I have that faith.”

“And this is the aspect of the individual you would wish to bring to your pictures?”

“Yes. We are all, not self-existing, but symbols of the divine. Hence the name, Symbolism.”

“But how to start painting the divine, you don’t as yet know?”

“Anyway, it is the problem I am hammering at.”

“Peter, what is wrong with the method of the early Italian masters? Why seek a fantastic solution, when their quite simple one was so very good?”

“Some of the Italian primitives did in fact make an approach to symbolism, but it was only an approach. A very few angels and Madonnas *were* feebly suggestive of heaven. We have to do better than that if we’re to stir people to their depths, instead of winning their gracious approval of our efforts. I’m at present experimenting with the light of the human eye. That may be the solution— not so fantastic! I am not going for pictorial puzzles, or strange mystic alphabets; I’m not to furnish a separate clue with my work; it has to speak for itself—represent as well as present. The eye is the one part of the physique that is a window, not a wall. The light passes in, and the light passes out. If we want to see another world, it must be by way of the eye. So far I’ve got.”

“A tree has no eye.”

“Now we’re getting into deep waters, and had better stop.”

“But has it?”

“A tree, I presume, has no existence, as we know its existence, until we’ve created it with *our* eye. Let us create it differently, that’s all. Let us pass a different sort of light through our eye, resting on where the real tree should be."

"Do you mean that the artist must change his nature and become spiritual, when the things he sees will also become spiritual?"

"Oh, dear no! Anyone may quite well go on loving good cheer and soft lying, without in the least detracting from his ability to behold the symbol where another man beholds merely a fact. In general, the school of philistine thought that hopelessly confounds the use of life with its artistic presentation has done more to bring affairs to a dead level than all the freaks together. Persons are not to be made virtuous by my pictures. I am not a parson in paint. I don't care whether the public is moral or immoral, nor much whether it is theistic or atheistic—I simply want people to understand by means of my pictures that this world they are in isn't at all what it seems to them, but something infinitely more significant."

"It's difficult. Have you anything to show me round at the studio?"

"Nothing I'd care to be seen."

Helga suddenly gave it up. She wondered why she was asking Peter all these questions, and why he was troubling to answer them at such patient length, when both knew, and knew that the other knew, that the true centre of their interest in this room was sitting there alive, breathing, but pale, dumb, and motionless; like a clock mysteriously ticking beneath a continuous loud clamour of talk. Ingrid had not contributed one word. Helga was disturbed. Was she vexed on an earlier account, or was it a real indifference about Peter's artistic future? She must be vexed. It was barely a week since the topic of his work had come up between them, when Ingrid had half-complained to her that she still actually knew nothing, *nothing*, about his last plannings, yet supposed it was unnecessary. So her silence now could not mean that she didn't care. They must have been pulling different ways in that arranging interview in the garden. The event certified that they had compromised the point of dispute, yet evidently her daughter had been upset by his opposition, or it had begun to rankle in her mind since; or she was reconsidering a part of what they had agreed to.

Why was he not wanting the regular engagement? What was he waiting for?—what was he expecting in a few months' time that he hadn't got now? Certainly Ingrid had told her that she would have preferred an interval for self-examination, but somehow it struck her that a determined man would have got his way on the double question of definiteness and date. Since he hadn't insisted, it was more likely that he had suggested the form of their understanding, and she had reluctantly consented, and was now realising at leisure the offence of his grounds.

And it was disconcerting to become suddenly sensible how vague and dark his circumstances remained, even after the long years of their intimacy. Perhaps it was nobody's fault. She and Ingrid were hardly ever in town; it afforded neither any pleasure to go alone, but Uncle Magnus mustn't be deserted by both together. It might be a couple of years since her daughter had paid a brief visit to the Chelsea studio, and then she had been introduced to no one, and appeared to have seen only sketches which conveyed nothing to her. But he seemed to be neither exhibiting nor selling his work; nor even finishing anything. At twenty-seven he still hadn't begun to be known. He was certainly clever—but how clever? Giving him every credit for the magnificence of his ideas and ideals, more things than that went towards the making of a first-class painter. He never lately showed them anything, so how could they judge? His host of friends, some very high up in the arts, was no guarantee of a professional standing. He was young, unattached, handsome, quick-tongued, free with his money—how should he not be popular? Especially with women. . . . Especially with women. No, no! There could be no earthly sense in his unnecessarily tying himself to her daughter if he had other involvements. He was too cool-headed to be a fool with women. . . .

The silence prolonged itself without any in the room seeming to find it embarrassing or strange. Old Colborne drank his tea at intervals, and looked at nobody. Peter smoked on, gazing out of the window. Helga's eyes were resting pensively on her daughter, who, at a little way off, appeared unconscious of the regard. She thought her face looked thinner and her eyes tired, with a darkness beneath them. Was she merely feeling physically indisposed? Yet surely she would make some effort, and she was not so much as noticing Peter's existence in the room. It couldn't be a quarrel, for they had not been together since Ingrid had told her the news.

Where was Hugh all this time? She had a feeling that if he were to enter at that moment, Ingrid's manner would change, and she would take a part in the ensuing general conversation. She had been so civil to Hugh at both breakfast and lunch, although she knew she rather disliked him; while to Peter, to whom she had just engaged herself, she could find no word to say.

Then came that quiet explanation for Helga, to which all these tentative thoughts and discardings must have been leading up. This distraction of her daughter's was unconcerned with Peter altogether; it could have its origin only in her last evening's adventure on Devil's Tor. . . . Yes, the terrible storm, and their narrow escape from disaster, with her hurt, the discovery of a passage to an ancient tomb, and her painful, exhausting limp home in wet clothes through the rain—it had begun a work upon her imagination and nerves, that Hugh's account of his exploration had intensified, and Uncle Magnus's weird anecdote had carried into the realm of the occult. She was only a child. The organisation of a delicate girl was so easily upset. And that was why she had been interested in all that Hugh had had to say, and was showing no interest whatever in Peter's aspirations. He had been unlucky enough to hit on a bad time, that was all.

But was it poor Hugh's fate, then, always to be this involuntary obstacle to the pleasures of others? Having been nearly forcibly thrust between those men and their prize, now he was similarly finding himself set up between a young girl and her lover. So not only was Peter exonerated, it was even a piece of happiness for Ingrid that it was to-day he had turned up, if only to relieve her of half her sudden new obsession, by bringing back the rest of her mind to nature. Yet it seemed so incredible that this peaceful afternoon room, in which the sunlight still lingered, should be a scene of invisible forces that had to do with such things as death, and tragedy, and the supernatural. . . . What did she mean? The immediate memory of her own thought startled her. Hugh wasn't here, with his morbid presentiments, and for everyone else the future was to be ordinary. For a moment, however, it had been just as if the whole atmosphere of the day were charged with the dread of approaching woes for them all! . . .

She rose to pour out another cup for her uncle; and as she handed it to him, saw from his signs that he was to deliver himself at last, which gave her a sense of dropping back upon a solid support. He was viewing Peter with one of his dubious smiles, that somehow always had the effect of expressing both friendly raillery and a whip held in reserve; but Peter, who knew him well, had already turned to him in whimsical expectancy. Ingrid never changed her position.

While Helga was sitting down again, old Colborne began to the guest quietly enough:

"In art, as in life generally, there are some who employ costly and elaborate apparatus for the catching of sprats, and others who elect to angle with a slender rod for whales. The first-named, however superior they may be in sense and easy talent, will still by reason of their menial lack of ambition get nowhere; since he who thinks commonly must remain common to the last of his days, whereas of the passion for exploits only can anything be made. The second-named, despite their certain folly in so absurdly miscalculating the displacement of their haul, are yet the ones whom a rational man will desire to serve, if serve either he must. Vices of character are irreparable, but the judgment may at last be made a useful instrument by the repeated hard knocks of experience—by the lessons of other people's experience, if the subject be wise to attend in time.

"You, I conceive, are angling for a whale. You wish to paint such pictures as have never yet been painted.

"I shall still pursue the figure a little. You have sighted your spouting monster, and you have put out to sea in chase, but, as I fancy, you have neglected to take with you in your boat the supply of harpoons and length of stout line necessary to the killing and capture of so vast a floating mountain of blubber. It is not the audacity of your ambition that I desire to reprove, it is the inadequacy of the equipment with which you are to set upon the adventure.

"To kill a whale in art, you must continue to use the methods that always have been used in the killing of whales. These are, hard work, distinction of vision, the perfect mastery of your materials by constant practice, austerity of mind, following upon austerity of life, and the never-ceasing examination—in the spirit of love, not criticism—of the best work of the best of your predecessors. I do not pretend that such a list of essential factors to success is exhaustive, but, so far as it goes, it is indispensable, and I advise you to copy down its items in your notebook as soon as you get home. Above all, you must paint, paint, paint, and go on painting; and not spend any part of your time in lying upon couches, allowing all your ideas to run together in a mush.

"If it is written in the book of fate that you are to be a master of paint, these things will help you to it. If it is not so written, no amount of sterile thinking can do anything for you. For the rest, since you have set your heart upon the paintings that shall symbolise the universe, I recommend to you the symbol, of all symbols, which is the most vivid, the most passionate, and the most universal—the presentation of the Madonna.

"We know that you have already made a beginning with this subject. You need never come to an end with it, for its treatment is inexhaustible. You may, if you so wish it, go on painting Madonnas all your life—descend to posterity as the painter of Madonnas—there will always be something new for you to say, in each successive version. The symbol is vivid, because the human sympathies of all of us are immediately aroused, before the question of artistic merit comes up at all, by the mere representation of a beautiful young woman, nursing her infant. It is passionate, because of the semi-divinity of this beautiful young mother, and the entire divinity of her infant. And it is universal, because more than a mother is represented, more even than motherhood is represented; the whole female nature and spirit of this our world are represented."

Helga regarded him in a quietly-musing surprise. Her uncle was showing himself in an altogether new aspect to-day. At breakfast there had escaped from him his silent former devotion to another man's wife; and now he was going on to emphasise the significance of womanhood in general. All her existence seemed becoming unreal to her. Hugh talked of death, Uncle Magnus praised women, Peter and her daughter were engaged and not engaged; everything was as if moving towards that change . . . and she was understanding what had mystified her just now, how all the atmosphere seemed *charged*—it was because all the three persons with her in the room were behaving unusually, and be-hind it all was her last night's conversation with Hugh, which she had not forgotten and never could forget; and because at any time, even at this very moment, a footstep might be heard on the gravel of the drive outside and one of the maids might appear, announ-cing either or both of those two men from Tibet, whose coming was to be like a signal of the new swift crystallisation of Hugh's affairs. . . . Surely they were all "fey," including herself! Never in her life, but once, had she felt so nervously, irrationally appre-hensive. When Dick had had his second visitation, her anxious dread, without known cause other than that superstitious assent, had been just the same—or not quite the same; she had been able to apply that, but this was inapplicable to any definitely-impend-ing event.

She heard Peter's interruption of her uncle's momentarily-ceased monologue.

"I'll say this for your method, sir—that it is calculated to produce excellent *craftsmen*. The question that arises in my mind is—since we are to speak of the Virgin Mary . . . would Mary, by the simple process of working hard at her pots and pans, have produced the Redeemer? Every creative artist is, or should be, a sort of Virgin. He is to be informed by the Holy Ghost, keep himself unspotted by men, and conceive miraculously. . . . The rest of your counsel, though, is very good. I always have approved the Mother of God as affording in her person a symbol of the highest stamp."

"I am obliged to you for the explanation of much that I see around me," returned old Colborne sarcastically. "So many schools and coteries of painting to-day obviously have no parentage in the known world, that I have hitherto been nonplussed. Henceforth I shall understand that they have been directly fathered by the Holy Spirit!"

Peter viewed the red tip of the cigarette between his fingers.

"Did I stop you, sir? I am sorry, if so."

"I was to go on to speak of the singular advantage this subject of the Mother enjoys over the whole of the rest of Christian art. Angels, saints, martyrs, the Father, the adult Saviour—all have been painted; and not one has had much more than the force in representation to recall the associated myth. Only the Virgin-Mother, whether alone or with her Babe, has force to move us directly. Yet, far from being possessed of a higher spiritual rank than the majority of those others, in her lifetime she was principally characterised by her entire lack of spiritual will and effort. She is almost the most inconspicuous leading figure in the Gospel. The saints and apostles were consumed by the intense flame of their passion for the Almighty and His Son, the original disciples were forward in their earnestness and loyal love and following; only Mary remains an unknown person for us—as it were, a blank shape in a picture otherwise coloured and finished. Had she been another living flame, we should have heard of it. Or had she possessed the spirituality of a naive and simple temper, we should have heard of that. In truth, she had not the enthusiasm of those others, and so far was their inferior. Her personal qualities may have been higher. Only a lioness bears a lion-cub. The story does not tell us, for the story is concerned merely with the affairs of the Son.

"Nevertheless—I say it again—in representation the Virgin-Mother has force, as those others have not, to work directly upon our souls; and this because the human instinct is more powerful far than the human reason. While the latter (for the white-skinned race) has finally settled down to its two male Gods, the one for its metaphysic, the other for its practical living—I mean, Jehovah and Christ; while this has happened for the reason, the profounder intuitive craving of the heart has never ceased to be aware that the whole of this, the only universe we know, sustained as it necessarily is by its infinite number of single acts of generation, is in essence *female*.

"Accordingly, the source of this universe is logically to be sought in a female Archetype—not in an eternal Father, but in an eternal Mother. For, subversive of all our modern ideas though such a notion may be, the male function, the half of sex, the fount of all adventure and bed of all intellectual grandeur on the sphere, may still be nothing less nor more than parasitic and secondary— parasitic, because for its life it depends upon the female function; without women, it is evident, there could be no men; and secondary, because it has appeared later in the biological history of the world, and to that extent is superfluous and minor. I do not say that the female function has not been modified as well by the accidental sprouting of such an excrescence from its original unity. Manifestly it has been so. It used to be believed that the Pacific Ocean was the mighty hole left by the flying-off from the earth's surface at a tangent of the moon. Such a gap may have been left in the original femaleness before sex, by the flying-off of males. I cannot begin to discuss that here. It is a stupid condition of our life on earth that we are placed by chance at birth in one or other of the two sexes, and I hereafter must behave without candour to those who have been placed in the opposite. A state that demands of us a constant circumspection, and concealment, and picking and choosing of our words, cannot be a natural state.

"Nevertheless sex may appear a natural state in brutes, that do not resort to these disguises. That happens because human beings, of all creation, alone have succeeded in recovering a measure of the sacredness of the primal state, before sex.

"They have not done so through their bodily instincts, or brutes would have done the same. Neither have they done so through their reason, or we should not, in this most reasonable of all human centuries, be still glorifying and deifying the male in Nature, at the expense both of that primal female and its derived sexual feminine. But human beings have recovered so much as they have recovered of the primal state, through another and more ancient faculty, that perhaps is neither instinct nor reason, but lies infinitely beneath and behind and above both. Since brutes have it not, it has had to be recovered. I have also, a minute ago, named it as a human instinct, although it is so much profounder than all our other instincts. That was to distinguish it from reason, with which it has still less to do. Because it is real, and not feigned, it is always with us, and we cannot escape from it; but because it is other than reason, it does not speak the same language as reason; we feel it, but never know it, and may seldom know that we feel it. It is the *night* of our bustling *day* of the intellect. How then have we been so happy as to have recovered it? The brutes have not done so. The needs of civilisation have imposed on us a certain self-control in matters of sex. Our sex instincts have so far been limited and curtailed. This process has enabled us to clear away so much of the lumber of our later nature, as to reveal for us once more the large underlying fact that before *sex*, there was *motherhood*.

"You may, unless your nature be utterly corrupt, discover it for yourself in any walk across these moors of ours. The clouds, the hills, the solitude and loveliness of all, must inevitably suggest to you that Nature is female, not male. Nature, accordingly, has always been given that sex. The reason for it is obvious, and not to be disputed. Yet this female Nature will not go on to suggest to you—unless, I repeat, you are entirely corrupt—the effeminacies and frivolities of women. It is too grand, too pure, and too serious. The scene before you, therefore, will be female, without also being sexed.

"The wiser ancient world understood such matters better than we. We find the Great Mother publicly worshipped, under many names, in many lands." . . .

XII

At the Gate

Helga and her daughter both glanced involuntarily towards their uncle, for Hugh too had named to each this name of the Great Mother, that was so nearly unknown to both. For Helga indeed it remained one of those queer turnings-up for a second time of an unfamiliar word or allusion just encountered, that did so often happen in life and for which there was no satisfactory explanation; and she at once passed it over. Ingrid, however, knew that it was no coincidence. This whole conversation also had been destined, and now *twice* that name had been uttered to her. So it was to be remembered! . . . Through the madness of all, a sort of shape was surely consolidating. . . .

"Besides which," old Colborne went on without pause, "the deteriorated remains of her worship have survived the purer faith, even up to Christian times, in the more individual rites of such female characterisations as Demeter, Aphrodite, Isis, Ishtar, and others, each of which divinities in her day has certainly received the sacrifices and prayers of many millions of human creatures. These prayers and offerings have been put up, not as to a protectress, but as to a heavenly mother.

"You will point to the male counterparts of those goddesses, in order to challenge my hypothesis of a deeper instinct. War and conquest, however, are still to the male, and it is reasonable to conceive how your active chiefs and warriors should choose to address their supplications for strength in the field and success in the forcible acquisition of towns and lands to those deities possessed of a nature corresponding. Thus Jehovah, Zeus, Thor, have been invented, as the head's crude counterblast to the softer faith; while the first-named, as I before remarked, remains to this day, and has His temples in every town and larger village in Europe. Christ, again, is the sop that has been thrown to the primal instinct. He is more womanly than manly. His worship is already declining, for it appears that the sop has not been sufficient. He is womanly, but He is not a Mother.

"One Christian church only, I infer, retains its numbers, and that is the Roman. That may be due to its wise worship of the Virgin. The Virgin is more ancient in the human soul than either of her fellow-Gods. She is as merciful as the Father is just, and as compassionate as the Son is exacting. She is less shocked by the sin than tender with the sinner—one in distress may implore her as his own mother. Who would not rather weep at her skirts than prepare himself by a painful contrition and amendment of manners to go before an offended male Judge, who first of all will insist on the rigid letter of His commandments?

"The Virgin-Mother is explanatory of the world, as the others are not—for nothing is explained by the dogmatic assertion that God made the world, but to reach an explanation we have to look about us with our eyes, and see what can have been and what cannot have been, in the beginning. A horse will not engender sheep, neither will the heat of the sun form ice-fields. From an Eternal-Womanly must have sprung—women themselves and all their especial concerns, such as children, romance, marriage, the home, civilised society with its according manners, and, as the unconscious end and aim of all, the continuance of the race. But beyond this, the entire general character of the world also is female. In Nature are no straight lines, but only curves, and it is not accidental. Whatever on earth is of softness, sweetness, fineness, fairness, delicacy, aerial lightness, has derived from a feminine, not a masculine, source. The pleasing forms and colours of the painting art, the thrilling sensuous progression of musical tones, the haunting chains of poetry—they too are feminine. The very spirit that incites to the arts is feminine. You are tormented by an internal agitation to throw a part of yourself into the world in beauty; and so far you belong to the race of mothers. Subtract women, babes, beauty, love, Nature, civilisation, the arts, from life; what is there left? A workshop and a battle-field. Those other concerns may be representative of the nature of a perfect Being; but work is representative of imperfection, as war is representative of hatefulness and want. And so your perfect Being—should you desire a monotheistic interpretation of the world—must needs be female.

"Mary, then, despite her subordinate rank in the Roman worship, is actually supreme; and she, whether under that name of Mary or under one or another of her hundred preceding names since the creation of the human intelligence—she, I say, has always been supreme. The *Ewigweibliche*[1]—it matters not that her name in Crete has been the Mother of the Gods, in Phrygia Cybele, in Egypt Isis, in Greece Demeter or Aphrodite, in the North Frigga—it has never ceased to be understood by the senses of man, following upon his partial emancipation from the naked passions of sex, that this *Ewigweibliche* is immediately responsible for the construction of this the physical, mental, moral and spiritual universe through which we painfully wander, as in a dream.

"Mary is but the latest of her names. *Her* myth is familiar to one and all. Happily, little is known of her, so that we may fill in the gaps of her character and story from our own resources. She joins the infinite and the finite, she is at once a person and a principle. What may lie beyond that principle is not for our humanity. We are in a world, the whole significance of which is womanly. We are born of a woman, woman's blood is in us, we sever ourselves from the womanly at the high cost of becoming brutal, or denatured, or grey, dry and old before our time—our moments of greatest rapture, as well, are on account of a woman, and when we die, it is not bearded faces that we desire to see around our bed. The world belongs to women; not to us.

"So that, since you feel drawn towards the symbolic for your work, I warmly recommend to you the painting of this theme of the Madonna, and no other. Other themes can but offer you indirectly what she offers directly. You wish to present through your subject, not itself, but the soul of the universe taking this particular form. A tree, or a temple, must show it with difficulty, a contemporary woman's portrait with more difficulty, for now the

1. "Eternal Feminine".

associations of modern social life are to be withdrawn. But in the Madonna you have the existing convention, that people already understand, and on which you may immediately work. And having so skilfully at the outset avoided the Scylla of naturalism, you will now have but to elude with equal adroitness the Charybdis of medieval catholicism. Your Madonna is no longer to be the mother of the Church, her associates are no more to be John, and Catherine, and Simon Peter, and the angels; but she is to be the mother of Christ alone; and that Christ-child also must be a symbol."

"Of what, sir?" asked Peter.

"It cannot have escaped you that the world, notwithstanding its historically having been saved by the Son of Mary, is still in a deplorable way. It is due perhaps to causes with which religion has nothing to do. Starving men have other things to think of than their salvation, dissolute society women are scarcely to be blamed that they find no thrill in the rewards of the heaven of cobblers and psalm-singers, business men cannot be expected to credit the seriousness of the doctrine that property won by hard and honest work must be given away with both hands if the soul is not to be eternally damned. This means that persons will still go their way, in spite of the coming of Christ upon earth close upon two thousand years ago.

"The true Christ, therefore, is yet to arrive. The symbol of the Christ-child expresses not a fact, but a hope. Men, you see, are not only men, they are also and essentially *spirits*. The world is not their right place. Few recognise this, save in hours of vision or despair, for at other times the many has its work to do, whether such work be of necessity or pleasure. Yet men are spirits. Their desires are, if not illimitable, at least limited only by their ability to gratify them in a limited world and society. Their intellects range beyond their personal needs. Their passions may introduce serious harm to the organs of the body, or quite destroy the brain as a useful instrument, by their intensity. Accordingly, in their unconscious depths, men are unhappy in the world, which is not their place, and which confines them. In those depths, they crave that return to their proper conditions of existence, to which the name *salvation* his been given. The personal Saviour is the symbol of such a salvation—such a return.

"I will not now go with you into the matter of the association between these two symbols: that of the Mother and that of the Son. It would occupy too much of my time, and your patience. You must, if at all interested, ponder these things for yourself, on the basis of what I have already said. I shall content myself with remarking that the popular example of this association given in the New Testament is by no means the first of its kind within the records of the human race—that therefore the *double*-symbol as well would seem to be a demand of our deeper nature. The Egyptian Isis, to adduce but one single other instance, was honoured and worshipped by the same instinct that long afterwards honoured and worshipped the Catholic Mary; and both divinities have brought gods into the world. Between the functions of Horus and Jesus, there are some likenesses."

Having said his say, old Colborne abruptly turned his eyes from the visitor, and got up to depart. But as he passed by Ingrid's seat, he paused to rest a kindly though heavy hand on her shoulder, while she looked up in half-wonder.

"Always remember this, however, my dear," he said, in a tone of gentleness that was nearly startling, coming as it did as an entire transition from his manner to Peter that moment before, "—to difficult natures, difficult times! . . . Only do not attempt to see and decide everything at once, and I dare say you will do well enough. . . ."

He left the room, while Peter, smoking on in thoughtful silence, believed that his words had been an expression of his shrewd perception of something in the air between himself and the girl addressed; an expression as well of his benevolent neutrality in the case, which was all that could be reasonably desired. For old people hated changes, and no doubt her leaving home would make a break. But Helga, being remindful still of Peter's lovely mother, who had died too soon, thought that the strange admonition had been her uncle's encouragement of Ingrid's over-diffident heart in a time of stress, as he was not failing to see it—since of his eyesight there was never any question. He saw this marriage approaching of itself, and wanted it, and wished Ingrid to know that her secret was no secret. She was to take her time, consulting only her own desires, in the assurance that she would be causing him at least no pain, but even pleasure. She well remembered too his remarks at breakfast about a wife for Peter. He had talked so much to-day altogether—and now was urging on this match. She feared some change was coming.

"To difficult natures, difficult times! . . . ." Ingrid thought that this must mean, not Peter alone, but all her confusions. Supposing he were the wisest of all, and knew things about Devil's Tor that no one else had any idea of? He knew so much that others didn't. He knew about the Great Mother, and her strange re-incarnation in Mary. And Peter had painted her own portrait as Mary—and a man was coming to see Hugh who was a student of the cult of the Great Mother. . . . And this man, perhaps, was coming especially to visit Devil's Tor. No, Hugh hadn't suggested that—but otherwise why need he be at the pains to journey down to Devonshire, when Hugh would be going back to London in a few days? . . . The Tor could be—couldn't it?—without any straining of conceivableness, a site of the worship of the Great Mother, under one of her many names. . . . And that one of her names, that one of her mortal persons, had died in the neighbourhood long ages ago, and been buried there, for Hugh had been within the tomb, and Peter, with his own eyes, had seen the funeral *cortège*; and she, with *her* own eyes, had seen the risen dead.

And so, silently forced by this great outflow of will from that awful gap on Devil's Tor, Peter had been unavailingly reluctant to treat of his art, but must come to the topic of symbols, and Uncle Magnus must be brought further to the symbol of the Madonna. For the dead one of the Tor—the blessed one—she too had been a Madonna. . . .

With her eyes, she had seen one of Mary's nature, and not less than Mary. . . . And none of these thoughts, being once thought, could ever be discarded or diminished. But all the things of these present hours were slowly and terribly gathering together, like the rearing of a mighty sea-wave. . . . There was also a question—an important question, she had wanted to put to Peter about his art; but now was not the time, and she had forgotten what it was. . . .

No one made allusion to anything that had passed within the room, but in a minute or two Helga got up also. She looked at Peter, bringing a smile to her face.

"Ingrid has told me what you and she have decided, and I am very happy. I won't ever bother you about the progress of the arrangement, but do want you to count me as, next to Ingrid, your very best friend. And if at any time you should have worries and perplexities that have to be talked over with someone, bring them to me first of all."

He had risen for the speech, but contented himself with thanking her simply and gravely, in the fewest number of words.

"You'll stop to dinner?" inquired Helga.

He hesitated, glancing towards Ingrid, who, however, slowly rising from her chair in deep abstraction, seemed not to have heard her mother's question. So, guessing her wish to be alone with her fancies that evening, he would not make himself absurd and her uncomfortable by passing on the interrogation to her for her spoken "yes" or "no."

"We are rather anxious," he said, "not to indulge in anything of the nature of a celebration at present, and perhaps therefore the opposite extreme is indicated. If you don't mind, I'll spend this evening quietly at home."

"What do you say, Ingrid?"

She roused herself to answer her mother impassively:

"I think so, mother. Hugh will be here, and if Peter stays, things will come out, and the others will congratulate us, and wine will be drunk—and it will be hateful!"

"I'll be off now," said Peter.

Helga thought such a coolness between them singular, but would not urge the point against both their wills. The three went out into the hall together, where Peter said good-bye to his hostess, and sought his hat. Ingrid offered to accompany him to the gate.

"You're regretting nothing?" he asked her, when they were out-of-doors.

She replied to her understanding of his meaning.

"No. . . . No, but I was thinking how—unnatural—the conversation has been. . . . And there was something I wanted to question you about, but it has gone from me."

"About what?"

"It was while you and Uncle were talking of art, and it had to do with your overtaking this morning on the Tor."

Peter shot her a smile of wistful reproach.

"Always the Tor! Which, being interpreted, meaneth, never *me*!"

"It's only to-day, Peter—and the fault is partly yours, for telling me your story. To-day you'll forgive me for being upset and not myself."

"If it's only to-day."

He kissed her; and again she was limp, obedient, and unresponding. He was uncertain whether such a kiss were not sweeter than one invited. It somehow tasted more of her womanhood, less of her soul; but the latter overawed him, whereas her unmixed sex excited his, and with that sense of male possession his egoism as a man could return. . . . Yet afterwards he wondered if this were not the proof that in marriage they must meet on the lower level, ignoring each other's snows. . . .

At the gate they lingered again; but in a few minutes more were disturbed by the coming into sight of a man round the bend of the lane, from the direction of the crossroads. It was Drapier, returning from his walk; but neither wished to meet him.

"Is *that* your cousin?" demanded Peter.

"Yes."

"Then he was the man I ran across."

They hadn't yet been seen, so turned back into a shrubbery at the side of the house. Soon Drapier came up, when from their place of concealment they could observe him better. He halted just beyond the gate to gaze down at something in his hand, which was hidden from them. His downbent eyes frowned. Ingrid suddenly felt her heart beating faster and harder. The vision of Hugh brought back to her at once everything that she had been doing her best not to think about. He was like a living personification of all these slow forces moving against her.

Then both she and Peter perceived that the gate, and the lane, and the field past it, and Hugh Drapier himself, had vanished, while the brightness of the afternoon was dispelled by an usurping extraordinary misty gloom, that more resembled night, though things were visible through it. There were thick mighty forest-trees, and a hut of wattle, and a man, or ape, standing outside its doorless opening, directly facing them, leaning on a club. His prodigious chest was covered with lone black hairs, while his mouth of a brute was drawn open to show all its terrifying teeth, and the small eyes seemed to flash rage and malice towards them through the dusk. . . .

It had only lasted a second or two, and the day was back, and Hugh was still there past the gate, which he was in the act of swinging open, while his other hand, that had held something, was now in his trouser-pocket. The watching two turned from him to glance quickly at one another, and then knew by sympathy, without the necessity for words, that they had seen alike. Each recognised in the other's eye that unmistakable light of a great awe and confounding of reason. Peter drew the girl further into the thicket, out of sight of the gate and Drapier.

As he lit a cigarette, she noticed that his fingers slightly trembled, but otherwise his coolness would have seemed unhuman nearly.

"So once again . . . !" he said, keeping his eyes steadily on her face, though she would not meet them. "And this time the diabolism of the business is fairly manifest; your cousin being self-convicted. Let's get it right, however. You saw what I did? The day went, and a brute came?"

"What was it, Peter?" Her voice was as low as possible.

"More ancient history, without a doubt. And may I go on to suggest that in former times Drapier would have been burnt at the stake for a wizard of the blackest dye?”

“How can he be responsible?” The dropped last word was like a whispered effort. It was also a defence of her cousin, which Peter’s sharpness instinctively caught at.

“Responsible! So you do consent to the iniquity of . . . these ghastly reproductions of things dead and gone? I am very glad. But he is certainly responsible, on more than one or two accounts. This phantom ape was own brother to my spectres of the funeral train. Both times Drapier is present. Both times his hand is gripping some small article unseen. Either he is engaged in regarding it, or evidently he has been regarding it up to the moment of being overcome by a vision. . . . It must be a kind of talisman—which explains nothing at all. The whole point is, should he be allowed to wander about the countryside, subjecting innocent outsiders to these specimens of the black art? You had better have it out with him to-day.”

“It sounds true as you say it, Peter, yet it can’t be the whole truth.”

“I don’t assert it. I am not concerned with the whole truth. I am merely looking at the public nuisance of it; and if you like, the moral heinousness of playing with mysteries shocking to the nature of everyday persons. . . . Or would you rather I spoke to him?”

“No, that’s impossible!” she returned quickly. She appeared to reflect; then added:

“For you must be candid, and we both know that you are indignant on another account altogether. It would be unjust to Hugh to——”

“I know what you want to say. I’m angry because I come down from town to find you in a sorry state, and any dog will do to use a stick on! The first part is very true, at least. And just because you are in that sorry state, whosoever and whatsoever serves to keep you in it is for me a definitely sinister influence, to be brought up sharply. So if you won’t, I will, challenge the man.”

“It would do no good. This assumed talisman of his—I’ve no

idea what it can be, but anyhow, it isn't an essential. It is some psychic aid. It may help, but its absence can't hinder—that I *know*. . . . And your two experiences now. I must tell you that by comparison they have been so insignificant as almost to seem *thrown-off*. I don't even know that Hugh is very much better informed than you. He must still be experimenting."

"Then am I to understand that you have seen something even more wonderful?"

Ingrid was silent for a time, but then replied quietly, without any sort of emphasis or dramatic impressiveness:

"Yes, more wonderful by far."

"Yesterday? On Devil's Tor?"

"Yes."

"My visit has certainly been ill-timed! . . . And I am not worthy of being permitted to hear?"

"Please don't want it, Peter. I haven't told even Hugh."

"*Even* Hugh! . . ."

"It has nothing to do with intimacy. He is occult, and you are not. But I haven't told even him. And you know you engaged not to require from me the keys of all my locked rooms."

"Unless you're to hide yourself in them, away from me."

"It won't last long."

"How long?"

"How can I say, when I am as much a shuttle as anybody?"

"But what do you imagine is happening?"

"I think there is a psychical storm gathering, and its centre is Devil's Tor; that is all my intelligence tells me."

"Storms are destructive," said Peter, biting his nail.

"And so this may be."

"Destructive of what?"

She was again silent, until with a particular insistence he repeated the question. Then she answered:

"Of nothing little, I should judge! . . . Though the little may well be involved with the big. Perhaps, incidentally, this home is to be broken and its members will be scattered to the four winds—and that is why Hugh is back from India at this juncture, and you down from London. . . ."

An unpleasant fancy entered Peter's head without warning or welcome.

"Your cousin—this man Hugh Drapier—isn't he very much older than you?" he asked.

"He's thirty-seven."

"And you are twenty-two—a big difference! You're cousins besides. I suggest no harm, but he's not in the way of appealing to your imagination?"

Under the earnestness of his gaze, Ingrid flushed.

"That might be almost an insult, Peter dear."

"I hope not. I mean nothing conscious—but if it were only a growing pleasure in his society . . ."

"I have no special pleasure in his society. If you knew him, you would know that he is altogether misanthropic. Have I, then, to begin defending my conduct so early?"

"Forgive me!—no. . . ."

He saw that the unworthy suspicion was incapable even of stating excuses for itself, and wondered how he could have held it for a single instant. Perhaps her offendedness was only passing and in another minute she would have forgotten it, and still the incident was disturbingly symptomatic. Was this sort of thing to happen again and again after marriage? Was it an escape in any blind direction of his instinct of another man? . . . He glanced at her again, to discern that she had already forgotten—that once more her thoughts were far away. His pride came back. His work at the studio was waiting for him, and it was time to be off.

"I'm to see you here to-morrow?" he inquired, with the least of surliness in his voice.

But when he had received her quiet reassurance that she wished it, and had gone away at last, Ingrid, staring absently over the gate at where but a moment ago he had been, recalled suddenly without effort the question she had wanted to put to him about his art; though now it mattered less.

It had sprung up in her mind, not very definitely, while he had been declaring that a tree had no existence for the artist except that created by his eye; that his eye had power to create it differently; that, in order to do so, it must pass a different sort of light through itself to where the tree should be. She had simultaneously been dreaming of his vision on the Tor, and his statements had suggested this fantastic explanation of what he had seen. She had wished to ask him whether such a different light, making a new creation of whatsoever the eye should be looking at, could not be received by telepathy from another person standing by—received by the brain, and so passed to and through the eye?

For Hugh had been there with him, in a trance, and it was surely most reasonable to conceive that Peter's overtaking was somehow on account of that? . . . However, it had been a confused, not a clear, thought, and she had had no leisure to follow it up then, but afterwards it had sunk quite to the bottom.

To question him about it mattered less now, for since then they had both been amazed by this other half-lifting of a veil, and accordingly she *knew* her fancy to be true. And now, too, she had gone on to grasp something else, impossible to discuss with Peter. What he had seen twice, and she with him once, was not what Hugh had seen at all. He had seen—*her*, whom she had beheld yesterday. . . .

It must be so, because her light alone would have power so to fill the eye as to flood the brain within with the life necessary to the direct passing of its images. Still, in the passing, something would be lost—some part of the light would get through to the second mind, some other part would be arrested. The personal image of that dead one had been stopped, but her ancient mortal circumstances had got through to be shown. . . .

That she had died, however, and been buried on a hill, concerned her divinity not at all; for other gods as well had died. And this mystery, perhaps, was a part of godhood, since gods and men were not of one nature.

Then, suddenly, all her muscles tightened with the vehement intensity of her longing for the next day to be already here, and she realised (as if a second person in her were looking at a first) what hopes she was setting on that promised meeting with Hugh's

friend, the knower of the primal cult of the Great Mother—who
was to throw light on so many things for her! . . . To-morrow? No
one had told her, to-morrow—or any time; or definitely, at all.
And yet she was sure that he would appear to-morrow—or that
something not less important would happen. . . .

On retiring to bed early the same night, Drapier once more took
from his pocket the flint he had picked up in the underground
death-chamber. Twice since then, and a third time for a shadowy
moment, had he seen the vision of the dead. On the chief occasion
she had stood erect, as coming out of her tomb, confronting him;
but not looking at him, and motionless. Upon recovering his
consciousness from that trance, an unknown man had challenged
him on the Tor; but had had the decency not to put embarrassing
questions, and they had soon parted, Hugh hoped for ever in this
world. But from all these recurring visitations, he apprehended
that his end was near. It mattered nothing that they had been
brought about through the medium of a material stone, if it, as he
supposed, had supernaturally been given to him for the purpose.

He stared abstractedly at the flint, then closed his hand on it
again, to recall that miracle of her likeness, and nature, and
coming. . . .

Her face had so transcended womanly beauty—yet upon its
own road—that she was not even to be thought of as belonging to
the world; nor had any living woman ever been as tall. If her eyes
had rested on him, he must probably have died at once. . . .

He placed the flint on top of the chest of drawers, quietly
undressed, then, having blown out the candle and thrown up the
window-blind, found his bed. . . . Exhausted though he was by
another day's nervous rack, sleep still refused to come.

Again and again he beheld the weird ancient stairs going
down, the pitchy passage and caverns, the table of death, and
always following, the dim silvery image of the dead woman,
awful and beautiful as Nyx herself—swiftly changing to erectness
and unnatural stature in the upper air. An earth-quake rocked the
bed he lay on. Strange globes of fearful electricity flitted about

the room. . . . Or now he was walking through the snows and rocks of the Himalayas, and voices were calling to him from behind that he was immediately to die. Then the day vanished, and he was underneath a black night-sky of torn clouds and mystic constellations. . . . He never knew which part was dream, and which, sick waking fancy. At some time after midnight, he fell, worn out at last, into dreamless sleep.

How much later it was he could not tell, but he thought his eyes reopened to remark a bright mist in the act of ascending from the flint on the chest of drawers. . . . It rose and spread like a coloured gas dissipating in the air, till the upper half of the room was phosphorescent. Then, almost fiercely, it concentrated over his bed, seeming to draw down all the light from above, so that the whole chamber was black once more, save that luminous patch. Its lustre became the face, bosom and arms of a woman—but she was a spirit. . . . Then she disappeared suddenly, and the room was all dark again. . . .

An ineffable peace entered his soul. Surely she had seemed to bend over him, as though to smooth his brow—but that touch must have been his last knowledge of the world. And because he had known the same instinct during the day, he was assured that it had been *she.* . . .

He rose. Experiencing that immeasurable calm, he went to the window and there stood gazing up to the stars, which were as jewels in the sky—blue, yellow, ruddy, flashing white.

So often had she appeared to him. Doubtless it was his recompense for this sacrifice of his life. Somehow, his journey from India had served; now he was to be discarded. Since boyhood he had walked in innocence—he conceived not what other worth was in him, so to be chosen for the purposes of the High. Nor was it wise to attempt an understanding of such matters. With human wits only was he equipped, whereas elsewhere not only thoughts and willings, but the very meaning and basic nature of life should be different. . . .

He continued standing before the window until the first lightening of the sky announced another day.

XIII

Henry Saltfleet

In the middle of the morning of the next day, which was Thursday, Helga while engaged in writing letters in her room was interrupted by a housemaid, who handed her a card.

"A gentleman to see Mr. Drapier, madam."

"He is out, isn't he?"

"Yes, madam. He went out immediately after breakfast."

Meanwhile Helga had hurriedly glanced at the pasteboard in her hand, and was coldly shocked by the printed name thereon. It read, HENRY SALTFLEET. . . . She had really not expected that they would be after poor Hugh so soon; or that it would be *he*. . . .

She stood in long hesitation, then instructed the girl to inform the visitor that she would see him, and to show him into the drawing-room.

No, she would not change her dress for this man. She was quite presentable, and would not have him believe that she had changed on his account. She was in a dark, well-shaped house-frock, without ornaments, except her rings. So, after another long pause of thought, she merely rearranged her hair before the glass; and at once went out.

The caller stood in the middle of the room to which he had been ushered, erect and expectant, facing the door. He was big of build, clothed on reticent lines in well-cut, well-worn tweeds, and was unmistakably a gentleman, which his photograph had not certainly established. His grave countenance displayed a naturally florid skin, browned by travel. The forehead was noticeably wide, the features were strong, masculine, severe, the grey eyes direct and uncompromising. He was clean-shaved, and the set of his mouth fascinated Helga instantly by its expressive virility. She seemed not to have known before how a man's mouth could be at once so grim and beautiful. . . . No doubt it arose from the striving with realities—the realities of Nature. Instead of figures, markets, competitors, and labour troubles; things like precipices, storms and floods! . . . He looked so altogether different from other men. There was this open-air formidableness in his still, tranquil, menacing manner of holding himself. His composure, his bottled vigour—he seemed much maturer than his apparent thirty-four or five. He must be well-used to depend on himself in all circumstances, and force a way through. Who were his people? He should belong to a very good circle—at least, must have much money, so to be able to turn his back on trade and the professions, in order to indulge this hobby of expensive mountaineering.

During the electric seconds that elapsed between her coming into the room and Saltfleet's tardy first speech (for he, on his side, seemed soberly to be reviewing her as a new factor in the situation, before confiding to her any part of his business) such was the character of the thoughts that sped through Helga's head, leaving behind them a mere broad wake of blurred feeling, the main constituents of which were astonishment, attraction, and fear. Now, indeed, that it had come to the actual impossible moment, she had no idea in the world what she was to say to him, or how she was to say it. Should she help him to meet Hugh, or should she do what she could to stop their meeting? Where had he now arrived from? Was he putting up in the village or neighbourhood, or had he a waiting car?

She could suggest his writing, only a postponement would be so unsatisfactory, so futile. Before coming in to him at all, she ought to have prepared herself better. First, of course, she must know what attitude he was taking—but that too was only to put it off for a minute. These men were not importuning Hugh for a joke. They wanted what they did want very badly indeed. Really, all she had to decide—quickly—was whether she would be acting in Hugh's own best interests in hinting to this person standing up in front of her that there was likely to be a hitch in his business— or whether, rather, she ought not to fend him off merely for a time, until she could prepare Hugh for his inevitable second call. Everything was so exactly balanced in her mind, that she seemed to have no volition at all. . . .

In broad daylight, and standing face-to-face with him, she no longer possessed the folly to dream of captivating this man. . . .

Then she noticed his hands. They were unusually long, and muscular and nervous, but very quietly held. Yet he should be of an impatient temperament; and so their stillness implied the unceasing *will* to stillness, demanding in him an equally constant presence of mind. Such active natures she could respect.

And while his opening tones, very gratefully to her (for she had dreaded she knew not what brusqueness), were courteous and conversational, nearly the first uttered word did in fact display to her the controlled impatience of his temper.

"I must ask your pardon for troubling you," was what he said, while she remained standing a little way from him, just inside the room, "—especially so early in the day; but actually I came to see Mr. Drapier, and your servant has informed me that he is out. May I inquire the most promising time for getting him?"

Despite her persistent inward intimidation, Helga was still the mistress of her manner, and could return him one of her tranquil gazes.

"Yes, I am told he is out. I am his cousin, Mrs. Fleming, and will gladly give him a message, if you care to suggest anything. Are you staying near here?"

"I am at the 'Bell,' for the time being. Please tell him merely that I have called—and perhaps it would simplify matters if he could give me a look up on his return. I will wait in. He won't be out all day?"

"He should not be. I could possibly find out more definitely from my daughter."

"Don't bother. If you know of nothing, he will probably be back. So will you be so good as to pass him that message?"

"With pleasure."

But then, as he was moving, she felt that to let him go so, without the least effort on her part to use this happy chance of his visit during Hugh's absence, was sheer cowardice; and she added quickly, to detain him while she could still find eleventh-hour inspiration:

"He is expecting you, I know."

Saltfleet stopped short, in a kind of surprise.

"He is expecting *me*?"

"You or Mr. . . . Arsinal. He thought you might call on him here."

"So you are in his confidence in this business?"

"I understand it concerns something he holds in trust for you."

"You know what it is?"

"Yes."

"Then perhaps you can tell me—Drapier was called home suddenly, I take it?"

"Yes," she replied again, more faintly.

"Well, every man is entitled to put his own affairs first. But I trust he still has the thing?"

"Yes, he still has it."

"And—you may think it an extraordinary question to ask, but really he has treated us rather mysteriously . . . there is to be no trouble over our getting it back at once?"

"Won't you sit?"

Saltfleet complied a little reluctantly, while Helga took a stiff and nervous place on the edge of the couch facing him. The door was shut. His interrogation, which she might have expected and which she herself had brought on by admitting her acquaintance with the affair, was confusing her utterly—she must keep him there, and turn the blow, and temporise, her instinct was. For if she returned him a lie, or professed ignorance, that would not be serving Hugh, but if she told him the truth straight out, it would be too lowering. Hugh was her cousin, and his shame was her shame. She began to be angry with him for having put her in such a degrading position.

Could she without singularity invite Mr. Saltfleet to dine with them this evening, to meet Hugh? Yes, she did not think he ought to find the proposition strange, and it would be bringing the two together more amicably. Things could be discussed at ease; she could be present. The only strangeness would consist in this person's being introduced to the family circle. Yet no; he was just a friend of Hugh's, whom he had met abroad. Meanwhile she could have it out seriously with Hugh. His attitude seemed quite intenable and wicked to her, now that the right claimant had turned up in flesh and blood. True, they had stolen it themselves; but somehow theirs was not a theft, and somehow Hugh's would be. . . .

"I hope this does *not* point to a difficulty?" inquired Saltfleet bluntly, interrupting her vacillations. "You say you know what the article is—a fragment of stone, with a tradition attached. He still holds it. Then nothing is to interfere with his returning it?"

"Mr. Saltfleet, my trouble is that, though I do know something about the matter, I have not been authorised to speak. Who is the principal, you or Mr. Arsinal? Or are you jointly concerned?"

"Arsinal is the principal."

"Where is he now?"

"At Oxford; consulting some documents at the Bodleian. I am deputising."

"As one friend for another, no doubt?"

"Well, I have never taken pay from any man yet."

"The concern is purely antiquarian? Not financial?"

"The stone has no money value that I am aware of. . . . I'll explain my part in the transaction, if that is worrying you. I am not in any way interested in archaeology personally, but chanced to run across Arsinal in Crete a year or so ago, where we struck up an intimacy; and when he had occasion for this trip to Tibet, I put my experience of the country at his disposal, in exchange for the amusement of the adventure. It was at my suggestion that our prize was passed to Drapier for holding during an awkward time; accordingly I am responsible for its recovery. It is to recover it, that I have called here this morning."

"But weren't you rash to entrust it to a stranger?"

"We had little choice."

"Still, you would have done better to bear in mind that the nature of a romantic enterprise is to run eccentrically to the very end. You should have taken nothing for granted; and now, really, I must give it as my opinion that in case of any obstruction, at least half the fault has been your own."

Helga had no idea why after all she was taking it upon herself to prepare him for Hugh's ugly stroke to come. She thought that she had decided to speak to Hugh first. There was no sense in getting this man angry beforehand; he would not want his property any the less because she could show them to have acted imprudently. . . . Either it was that his dominating personality was obliging her to declare the whole truth . . . or else surely there must be some fatality about it, that was working by means of a second will within her, over which she had no control. . . .

He was staring at her for her remark, but she still had time to feel that it must be so—that the automatism of her tongue owed itself to a deeper necessity which was not appearing. What actually was at the bottom of the feeling, she seemed to be aware, was that as he sat there opposite to her—a perfect representative of the great outside world, his manners were so correct, distant and alien—he was creating for himself in her mind a distinct atmosphere—of . . . of being here to change things, for everyone. Hugh, of course, primarily; but somehow the household was never to go back to its old tranquil peace, which it had known before Hugh's coming. . . . It was another angle of her tea-time presentiment yesterday, of a general advancing evil. The caller was focussing it in his own person, and so, since a man was less than fate, it could not seem so dreadful; but this, perhaps, was why she could make no stand of circumspection against him. . . .

"Pray, what obstruction do you refer to?" he demanded, after what could be nothing but an ominous interval; and yet his voice was no more than a little sharpened.

"The word escaped me, I fear. No doubt, I had better leave you to talk to Hugh Drapier himself."

"I would like to know at once, if you can any way get over your difficulty of being without authorisation. I fancy I am entitled to hear if the affair is in order."

"But that is just what I can't tell you, Mr. Saltfleet. Supposing I see Hugh before you do, I am going to speak to him again about—your call here. Until then, however, I candidly do not know what his last intentions are to be. . . . It must sound alarming to you, and I was silly to say what I did. I can only offer you the hint. You and your friend appear to have made a very troublesome and out-of-the-way journey for the sole purpose of purloining this stone. Well then, seeing that it is worth so much to yourselves, why should not it be coveted equally by some other man? And if it were, wouldn't it be perfectly easy and natural for such a man to say to himself, 'It's no more theirs than mine'?"

Her heart was hurrying, and she dared no longer look at him, though fearfully conscious of his wide eyes. Too well she realised that now there could be no recalling of her speech, but that she had definitely committed herself, and Hugh also. How was he to take it? Had she merely done what had to be, or might she indeed with far more wisdom have held her peace? . . .

"The appeal is not to nature, but to honour," Saltfleet answered her, bending forward in his seat. "I can't understand, moreover, why Drapier should *want* to possess it. In any case, we could not allow it, or listen to any proposals towards it."

"Since, however, we have gone so far, I would like to hear what your attitude—and Mr. Arsinal's—would be to, let me say, an offer on his part."

"I believe it will be best to assume only friendly relations for the present. I repeat, it is an affair of honour; and your cousin impressed me immediately as being a man of honour."

Helga felt herself to be painfully feeble and daunted in the face of his rising indignation. In her daze, she fell back upon meannesses of logic which were the last she could ever have wished to use.

"You keep insisting on the word *honour*, Mr. Saltfleet; but is it really legitimate in any discussion of the case?"

"You mean, we stole the thing first, and therefore have no status. But that action concerns *our* consciences only. Drapier's obligation is to us."

"His previous consent was neither sought nor given."

"The question of honour would not touch his consent."

"Surely it must! . . . Imagine a pickpocket rushing by you in the street, followed by a hot pursuit, and slipping a gold watch into your hand. . . ."

"I should pass it to the first policeman; but that Drapier hasn't done. Nor are we pickpockets. When we shear a sheep, we don't call the confiscation of wool a robbery; and with no greater accuracy can you style it that, when a high-minded English scientist of international standing takes for his own service a financially-valueless object from a dying heathen temple in an unpopulated land, where for long years it has been lodged absolutely neglected. Drapier himself, I am convinced, would be the last man on earth to entertain any pettifogging scruples about it. He is familiar with the monks of Tibet, and he has met Arsinal. He knew what we were going after, and manifested no righteous horror at all. Permit me to say, Mrs. Fleming, that I can't in the least grasp what you are driving at with these contentions. If they are to excuse your cousin's repudiation of his plain duty, I would rather have it out with the man himself."

"I think you must. But will you let me apologise for that last illustration? It was discourteous, and I shouldn't have used it. . . ."

"It was unapt," said Saltfleet indifferently.

He returned immediately to the practical arrangement.

"Then with regard to meeting Drapier, I believe—in view of this new turn you have considerably more than hinted at, which I confess I don't at all comprehend . . . I believe it will be advisable not to rely on his caring to give me a look-up at the inn; I had better call here again later. I assume it hasn't arrived at the pitch of his wishing to avoid me? So will you suggest a time, and notify him as soon as he gets back?"

"He would certainly be in this evening. . . . You might like to take dinner with us, and talk to him after?" She smiled anxiously, consulting his face with a rapid glance. "If you are to be marooned in the village for any length of time, waiting for him, the 'Bell' is rather a dreary place, and you may be glad of a little diversion."

"It's extremely kind. I trust to get him much earlier than that, however; and, if possible, to be away this afternoon."

Helga was sure that it was as he said, not that he was despising her hospitality, and so she felt that she could press the invitation without loss of dignity. She must press it. Something was telling her that should these two meet by themselves during the day, Hugh would come to serious grief. She had to catch him directly he returned to the house, and use all her persuasions to induce him to give up this thing he had no right to want to keep. If he consented to, the trouble would be at an end. If he refused, or remained undecided, she must anyway get him to stop at home for the rest of the day. If Saltfleet ran up against him anywhere out-of-doors, as was otherwise extremely likely, there would be an infinitely worse scene between them; in fact it would be as bad as possible. Until it was all somehow arranged, she could not trust them alone together. . . . *Arranged!*—How could it be arranged, except by Hugh's unconditional surrender? But what would the other do? Helga already seemed to know that her second will, which she was so powerless to command, was intending to provoke Saltfleet, just in order to discover how far his threats would carry him. She was sick with dread for the impulse that was to make her so insanely brazen. . . .

Postponing the moment—for at least that was within her ability—she said:

"I think I would not be in such a hurry, Mr. Saltfleet. It is disagreeable that you should have to stay on, through no fault of your own; but still, I would like to get this settled amicably. Let me speak to him first. Will it be inconveniencing you terribly to put it off till this evening?"

"No. I am only anxious to know where I stand. You are to urge him to fulfil his obligation?"

"Yes, I want him to."

"Haven't you done so already?—since, evidently, you must have discussed it with him."

"I was rather taken by surprise, and it seemed not particularly pressing; but now that it *is* pressing, I shall certainly strengthen my arguments."

"You should. But yet there is one point I fail to understand. You have only just now been finding all sorts of reasons for his *not* restoring our property. . . ."

"Those reasons did not represent my opinion," she replied, with a true simplicity, that succeeded in convincing him. He judged, accordingly, that they had merely been testings to elicit from him the degree of emphasis of their claim.

So thoughtfully, after another moment, he said, "Very well, since I wish to get this affair fixed in any way that is the best, if we don't meet first I will leave it as you propose."

"You will dine with us?"

"Thank you."

"At seven—just as you are. We shall only be a small family party."

He half-bowed, from his seat.

Helga smiled uneasily. "Apart from this bother, you and Hugh Drapier must have many gaps to fill in. Did your fight develop into a serious affair?"

"No, it was never more than a feint, to keep the beggars employed until the spoil should be well on its way to Drapier. Afterwards Arsinal would not hear of the real thing, so we let ourselves be taken, stripped and searched; and before the brutes dismissed us again, they took care to secure the full sentimental value of their fetish, expressed in the terms of nine-tenths of our goods and ponies."

"Then how did you contrive to get back so soon?"

Saltfleet laughed.

"We adopted Napoleon's method, after Moscow. Arsinal and I came on ahead light, leaving the caravan to crawl home how it could. But as the men were to receive triple pay at Srinagar, they could not complain."

"You personally would perhaps have preferred to cut a way through?"

"I am not a very patient man."

"No, that I am sure you are not!" thought Helga.

Now he was immediately to go, and if she was to make trial of his true temper and ascertain how they proposed to manage in the event of a rebuff, it must be at once. . . .

"This curio, Mr. Saltfleet"—she discovered the words issuing from her mouth, seemingly almost without breath—"I can't help noticing that you have been very careful to say nothing about itself. Has it a quality, or why does your friend set such an extreme value on it?"

"To answer you, I fear I could only repeat what he has passed to me in strict confidence."

"I am persuaded it has a quality, then. And, unfortunately my cousin Hugh is just the person to have stumbled upon it, and be affected. You were quite right to describe him as being essentially a man of honour. In all normal circumstances, he would make large personal sacrifices before he would consent to fail in his duties. But he is Celtic and psychic, as well."

"That is interesting, but hardly has to do with us."

"I am going to be candid. Your stone, I happen to know, is appealing to him in the most extraordinary fashion. Is there any chance at all of his being permitted to keep it, for a consideration, of course?"

"It is absolutely out of discussion. Do you mean a money consideration?"

"I cannot suggest what else," answered Helga.

"The offer is yours—not his?"

"The inquiry is mine."

"Then, in you, Mrs. Fleming, it may be excusable, as I conceive you are only anxious to serve him and to get this matter put out of the way. But I think I should make it plain to you, before we go further, that here it is not a case of comparing one man's interest in a certain thing with another man's. Arsinal is the stone's rightful proprietor in a sense that your cousin could never attain to were he to live with it for another fifty years. Arsinal has taken vast pains over a very extended period to track the thing down to the native religious house where finally we unearthed it—pains of a heartbreaking study of ancient Hellenic and Eastern records, scattered over three continents; and pains of practical detective work, rendered possible by his acquaintance with half a score of specialised sciences, and twice as many peoples and tongues. So, to undeceive you at once regarding Drapier's prospects of being permitted to retain what already he has retained too long, even for an absurdly large cheque in return—they are utterly *nil*; and, as I said before, we could not tolerate so much as a broaching of the matter."

"I am sorry."

"It is not an affair of money. It is the crowning of an Idea, to which Arsinal has devoted all his life. The single excuse your cousin can possibly furnish for his delay in surrendering what is not his, is that he may be failing fully to appreciate the urgency of the expedition he found us on. Yet—not to drag in myself, being a man generally on some hazardous trip or other—he must surely have realised that a person obviously so physically frail as my associate does not go out of his way to penetrate almost the most difficult country of all Asia, for the sake of acquiring an object which afterwards he is to be willing to throw away for a few guineas, or a few hundreds of guineas. So now, on Drapier's behalf, to offer us money—*money*—forgive me if I discard courtesy in declaring the proposition to be something very like *impudence*! . . . If he were called home so unexpectedly, he should have left the thing in India under seal for us. But to run off in the way he did, leaving no message and no address, and on the top of it to request to be allowed to retain it for his own insignificant enjoyment . . ."

"Mr. Saltfleet!—stop, please! . . ."

A sort of low bellowing note had changed his voice, producing in her the strangest agitation, of sympathetic emotion, and aesthetic pleasure, and shock, and fear. It was nearly reminiscent of the first hollow opening of the full roar of a lion, and her intelligent feeling was that she must stop him in time. She apprehended she knew not what savage explosion of unrestrained ire. . . . So Hugh was right, and it might well be Sulla or another fearful ancient dictator and imperator thus confronting her with eyes of distended menace. He had risen.

Retaining with a conscious effort her own seat, she gave him a long, calm and friendly look, and he said no more. When, after a pause, she begged him to resume his place, he did that too. . . .

This anger, besides, was a virtue in him, since it was for a friend. . . . She suddenly and without a reason remembered her daughter; then, having remembered her, was glad that she was not here, to be subjected to her own womanly reactions. . . . That was absurdity; but she ought, for Hugh's sake, to dismiss the man quickly. He might come back at any moment—they might encounter here or in the lane, before anything had been prepared. . . .

But still she had to hear his extreme threats: and surely he could state them without a repetition of that beginning outburst. She must know them, so that Hugh might know them too. She must also know them for her own reassurance. Persons of Saltfleet's social class or Arsinal's professional standing could not conceivably dream of imitating the methods of American underworld criminals; but neither had they any recourse in law. . . .

In this way her singular secret will, that was independent of her upper sense, was captured by her everlasting desire for mental security. She would consent in mind to no action of hers that she could not understand, and so must invent these motives for her own predetermined conduct. Another eye in her saw that Hugh's persuasion or her reassurance was of the smallest moment in the case, and that it was for a different invisible result that she was, on her own seeking, to be put in fear by a most fearful man. . . .

"There is no need," she said, "to use such a very big club to destroy an inquiry so simple and humble as mine! You won't hear of it; and that is enough. But if I am to speak to Hugh, I ought to be informed. I hope he will be reasonable. If, unhappily, he is not, however . . . ?"

"Having entertained no suspicion of the facts, naturally, we have not considered the contingency."

"Please consider it now. I am not raising new objections, but, for instance, it seems quite clear that you could not prosecute your claim through the Courts."

"Should there be trouble, Arsinal must be fetched down. . . . Nevertheless, Mrs. Fleming, I would point out that this talk is very much in the dark. You are hinting, and hinting, and will tell me nothing definite of what Drapier has said to you; yet either you should make the plain statement, or else you should leave it alone. It is rather too much to expect, that we should present an ultimatum upon the mere vague insinuation. I can only say at once that we shall on no account allow your cousin to keep a thing which Arsinal regards as so infinitely important. . . ."

He stopped abruptly, to glance round. The door-handle had been turned from outside in the quick, casual way of a person entering a room supposed to be unoccupied, and now the door itself was in the moment of being swung open. As well as he, Helga, without needing to turn her head, beheld the apparition of her daughter arrested on the threshold; tall, pale, grave, striking and beautiful, in a dark dress. But then, at the spectacle of her mother and a strange man talking together privately, the girl would have retired again quietly from the room. . . .

"Come in, Ingrid!"

She accordingly advanced a pace or two further, with a slow, wondering self-possession, while intently viewing Saltfleet, who rose. Her queer thought was that it was Hugh's friend, Mr. Arsinal—only it was not in the least like her preconception of him. Helga also got up, to introduce the two; and then Ingrid knew her mistake, and was almost equally disappointed and relieved. Saltfleet's person impressed her a little disagreeably. She found him rather improperly big; his eyes too staring. She looked away from him.

The interruption troubled Helga, not because it was one, but because, somehow, the bare acquaintance of this man seemed not quite right for her child. She was vexed that she had detained her so impulsively—though, of course, if he was to dine with them, they would have to meet. Then, nearly instantly, she had the insight that this irrational dislike of their encountering was but the measure of her own secret dread of him. The dread had only occasionally risen to anything like acuteness during their interview, but now she realised that it had nevertheless been constant in her; that she had generally had to suppress it by her manner of determined urbanity. . . . He was become Hugh's enemy, she supposed, and that was at the root. And still the impropriety of his even resting his eyes on her daughter continued to oppress and puzzle her. . . .

Invent a conversation she must, now that they were together in silence, and so she questioned her about Hugh's movements; yet a little negatively, Ingrid thought, as though she wanted her to know nothing.

"He is out walking," she had to reply.

"May I ask if you are aware in which direction?" said Saltfleet. And Ingrid understood, from the compelling force and steadiness of his gaze, that she would be unable to refuse the truth to him at least.

"I expect in the direction of Devil's Tor."

"Is that far out?"

"It's about three miles from here."

"And you fancy he would be there at this time?"

"There, or coming back from there."

"Should I easily strike him, if I went after him?"

"On another day you should have no difficulty, but to-day is foggy."

"But there is only the one direct road?"

"Until you reach the open moor."

Helga felt very sick and chill. All her careful planning, therefore, for Hugh's safety and well-being was to be swept away by this incomprehensible certainty of Ingrid's that he had walked out there and nowhere else. And the *rencontre* on the moor would be calamitous. Whether on or near the Tor, there they would be totally remote from people and houses; imprisoned by the fog. She intervened hurriedly, addressing her daughter.

"Is it reasonable to dispatch Mr. Saltfleet on such an exceedingly doubtful quest? Hugh may not even be in that direction at all."

"He was constantly there yesterday."

"What is the attraction?" smiled Saltfleet.

"There was a shattering of rocks by lightning the day before last, the exposing of a prehistoric tomb in consequence, and yesterday again an earthquake, bringing about the destruction of the same tomb."

"That certainly sounds sufficiently interesting. I think I'll follow him up, then. How does one get to it?"

Ingrid described for him the route from the cross-roads, which he must have passed already in getting to the house. He thanked her; then returned to the mother.

"And the location of what we have been talking about—do you know where he has it?"

"I don't." Her reply was truthful, and yet she coloured. Saltfleet, perhaps remarking the colour, urged her.

"Not at all? Whether here or in London?"

But Ingrid, watching in surprise her mother's half-embarrassment, obtained from it her earliest faint intimation of a mystery relating to the visitor. . . . Hugh and he must have met abroad; the one was as weather-beaten and tough-looking as the other. And Hugh seemingly held something that this man wanted, only what it was, or to whom it belonged, was not clear. It was why her mother should be endeavouring to keep back a part of her information from the caller, that began to perplex her.

"Yes, I do know so much," Helga answered to his last interrogation. "He has it down here. But whether it is with him, or in its case in this house . . ."

"A box he keeps it in?"

"Yes."

Saltfleet, in the thought of both women, smiled rather significantly.

"It would simplify matters if we met out-of-doors, and he proved to have it on him. I wonder if you could ascertain at once?"

"It would necessitate my going through his private belongings, a thing I hardly care to do."

"I can't ask it of you."

Quickly succeeding her first mystification, a quiet shock passed through Ingrid of remembrance and enlightenment, that was like the promise of another door, a new direction, for the escape of all her pent thoughts. The box her mother spoke of, surely it could only be the tin one she had handled on her dressing-table before breakfast yesterday morning, just as Peter was approaching the house! So that what this Mr. Saltfleet was inquiring about was what she had taken from the box when her mother was still out of the room, and slipped unthinkingly into her dressing-gown pocket, as she had hurried off to her own room to greet Peter. There it must have stayed ever since, and it was peculiar that neither Hugh nor her mother appeared to be aware of the abstraction. Unless her mother's uneasy manner a moment ago meant that she had discovered the loss, but had not found the courage to confess it to Hugh. For why should the box have stood on her dressing-table precisely while he was out of the house on a long excursion? She must have taken advantage of his absence to borrow it from his room. Ingrid knew that they had sat up late talking, the night before. It might, in part, have been about this. . . .

Or else her mother's embarrassment was owing to her knowledge of some unpleasantness coming to Hugh from this Mr. Saltfleet. . . .

It was unusual that *two* acquaintances should want to look him up during so short a holiday-visit. Wouldn't it be on the same business? One person could have come instead of the other. An association of three men, originating abroad . . . seeming to have for its object the quite ordinary-looking piece of stone she had misappropriated in innocence. So was it in dispute? Was her mother trying to put off this big, ruthless-faced inquirer? Ingrid was afraid, in that case, that she herself had frivolously played straight into his hands. . . .

What could be such a fragment of stone? She was nervously impatient to get upstairs to her dressing-gown, in order to make sure that it was still there, and to inspect it again more particularly. For instance, could it be a specimen piece of ore from some rich mine they had struck in eastern Asia, and was it to make their fortunes? Her mother perhaps would tell her afterwards—though the possession of a mere specimen could hardly be a matter for a quarrel, the location of the mine itself being known to them all . . . And she did not think it was that. This person, standing ponderingly before her, evidently still debating in his mind whether it was worth his while to pursue Hugh Drapier in the fog—he had neither the greed nor the financial sharpness in his face that would speak of the chase after riches; while the other, Mr. Arsinal, Hugh had only mentioned in connection with his study of the ancient worship of the Great Mother. . . .

Then again, why was it just here that they were all assembling? For Mr. Arsinal might yet be to arrive. This locality was the nearest to Devil's Tor, which was in the hour of throwing out its wonders. And there, long ago, one had been buried who in her lifetime and after might well have passed for divine. Hugh, it seemed, had not known the Tor; but Arsinal might know it; and this disputed stone, a token of the Mother-Goddess, might somehow belong to and be to illustrate the Tor. . . .

The man in the room—she could not place him at all in such a business. There was no reverence of ancient things in his aspect, he could not possibly be a student of the old; yet neither, obviously, was he a mere messenger or subordinate. He must assuredly be the chief, or a chief, in any business he engaged in.

Just because he appeared so very much of the outside world, and was not to be conceived of as being in the slightest degree interested in occult concerns, or as having any other purpose for his visit than a practical one, nowise seeming to touch any of these progressive strangenesses—just because of this, Ingrid was unable to discard as ridiculous the fancy that he too might be involved. For since his active will must still be blind and unconscious about any such fated part for him, that would be the sign.

But of his mode of life she was quite ignorant, except that it was manifest he was used to exposure, and roughness, and perhaps danger. She regarded his coming here at all as very strange, very ominous; and from now onwards began to wonder painfully in what manner he was to be employed.

XIV

Hugh's Return

Thicker white mists rolled past the windows, and Ingrid kept picturing Devil's Tor on such a morning; and Hugh was there. She did not know why she was feeling so fearful on his account. It was as if a voice were saying within her that he was in grave distress on the hill. . . .

So quickly did the idea mount to conviction, that it occurred to her if the others too could be receiving the message, that they were thus quiet and waiting. But a rapid inquiring glance at their faces told her nothing.

Yet during a whole minute perhaps all the three, herself included, had been standing there, dumb, uneasy, and pursuing their own thoughts; so that an outsider might have imagined them less a group of conversing persons than a strange spirit triangle performing some silent rite in the darkened room. Now she doubted whether Saltfleet ever had been rehearsing his plans since his last speech; the expression of his face, when she had stolen her glance at it, had somehow been less practically considering, more troubled. The trouble in it might be because of an evil sensation concerning Hugh—surely, there was no reason why such a communication should not be made to more than one! . . . But he looked the unlikeliest man for it. . . .

The toneless ticking of the mantelpiece clock, which measured the stillness of the room, was just as full of dark meaning to her in her present disquiet. It, certainly, was not speaking of Hugh, and yet this dead silence, permitting its ticking to be heard, was fated; and so it *was* speaking of Hugh. Similarly, might not Saltfleet's pause from speech, that was the reverse of the same fatality, be both due to some ordinary working of his brain, and, unknown to himself, connected with Hugh? The first words to break the silence should be significant. . . .

She could not speak again uninvited, but she longed for him to return to the present and definitely decide to go up to Hugh at once. She would have guided him, had not her ankle been still so useless. Peter was not here, to send to the Tor; but in any case she would feel safer and happier if this man went. Energy, hard resolution, sufficiency, command, were impressed on all his features; no better support in a physical emergency could be procured. If only he would be off quickly! . . .

It was Ingrid herself, however, that was the cause of her mother's contribution to the general silence. For in the unnatural morning dusk of the room the girl's face loomed palely, like some young prophetess's, and, with its fair long-featured beauty, passiveness, yet illusion of a kind of perplexed pain in the away-slanting eyes, intensifying nearly to anguish, was presenting a spectacle not easy to understand, that Helga *knew* the caller was quietly absorbing all the while, even though his regard was never directly upon her child. His quiescence, indeed, could not be ignored, it was grown so absolute. The situation might be thought to be fast becoming peculiar.

Helga was holding her own peace, in part certainly because she wished to hint to her daughter to go again, but principally because she wanted time to feel whether this faint initiation of a new fear stood for something in itself, or whether it were an outflowing from her whole instinctive shrinking from Saltfleet. It seemed to her essential that she should know that. For if it was from general instinct, then so too might be her nameless dread in Hugh's case.

His final threats, which she was still to learn, would show whether she had been unjust and unreasonable, or he was universally abominable; since if he could meditate lawless violence in one set of circumstances, his soul altogether must be of a hateful stamp. . . . But the worst of all was that she could see how extremely attractive he might be to certain women. Ingrid scarcely yet seemed to her to be grown up, and yet in all things, except actual experience of the world, she was really exceptionally mature; and her intelligence was of the finest. . . .

It was so absurdly impossible, and still so near; as a person might feel secure from death on a thin sheet of swaying ice. For instance, he was already to dine with them. That first invitation would dictate a second, and a third. He could deliberately protract his business with Hugh, and ingratiate himself generally with the Whitestone establishment. He should have very fascinating manners when unarmed. . . .

Next, she took it all back; and in one complex surge of feeling was bewildered and distressed by her crudity in sinking so facilely to the common modes of thought of her sex, and still was the more frightened of the man because this latest inchoate alarm was shown to be without any but the flimsiest foundation. For it was all based on a silence of a few moments and a fortuitous contiguity in space; but the truth was, he did not look in the least like a person who would dally with women, nor was Ingrid a girl to cast away her dignity for the sake of a strange man. Then the silly apprehension, unpleasant enough for the few moments it had lasted, must actually have originated in her unconscious appraisal of his general character. He was to be, for her, one who might attempt or do anything. And yet why should she be crediting him with such a capacity for evil? He should at all events be a sincere and honest gentleman, obeying the canons of his education. Surely, he would just as little dream of violence towards Hugh. . . . And again, because both these fears were shown to be extravagant and irrational, while her fear of his *nature* was to persist even after their dismissal, so she discovered herself the more superstitiously repelled by him, more and more repelled and attracted by him. In what did the secret of his dangerousness consist?—would the time and occasion be hers to ascertain this? He would be gone within five minutes, but she must see him again. . . .

Then she suddenly wondered if he were married. . . .

Saltfleet, in fact, rather shunned the society of women, and, at thirty-six, was not married. With no active principle of aversion from the sex, he still told himself that the ways, tastes, desires, interests, instincts, and whole attitude to life, of women must perforce be so at variance with his own as a man, that any union of sentiment would entail the largest sacrifices on one side or the other; but, since no woman on earth probably could discard her sensuous, picturesque, and snobbish nature, it would nearly certainly be he that must conform. Against this, was the condition of his existing at all on the planet as a male; he recognised his liability at any time to a sexual storm, sweeping him off his feet. As one more interruption of the deadly monotony of life, it would be welcome when it came, but he trusted to steer clear of insanity in his choice of the woman so to overwhelm him. Beauty he shrugged at, delicacy, refinement and culture were things of course, a sharp or sullen temper would be fatal; otherwise, he insisted only on *character*. He wished a companionship of contempt for the small and insipid in the world. Such a wife should not be practically unrealisable; yet the years glided by, and the women thrown to him by chance were all flawed. He was content to have the hardest things said about him. . . .

Helga accordingly was right in imagining his present silent preoccupation with her daughter, but wrong in attributing it to the beginning of an admiration. The unusualness of the girl's beauty alone would have made him a little subdued and thoughtful— particularly that queer, almost metaphysical light of her eyes, that was new to him in a woman, and should point to the possession of a singular soul. Nevertheless, though he was to meet her again more intimately, it seemed, had that been all it would have gone no further than such a careless impersonal appreciation of a young daughter in a strange house, very much his junior.

His business was with Drapier. He had been told where he was, he had made the necessary arrangements for getting hold of him, so there was really no more to detain him on the spot; but now this girl had suddenly introduced herself in the affair, and the more he thought of it, the more it appeared to him as if it might matter.

Her evident pride and distance of spirit, with her anxious air, cold address, and unconcealed progressive bewilderment—for one thing, she could not have all her mother's facts, she was in darkness about some part of the transaction, yet she was just as obviously interested, and a light was dawning on her, that he felt might be a new light for him as well. He believed it would be worth his while to spin out the interim, if it was to occupy not more than a minute or so. In herself, it was the transparent truth-weighing of her eyes and manner that had the effect of suggesting to him that she should be, not the centre, but the *height* of this household. She should have so great an influence. . . .

And in Drapier's conduct, all was by no means yet clear. There was a mystery afoot between him and his cousin, this Mrs. Fleming, of which he, Saltfleet, had heard possibly half the account, and the girl in the room another part. . . . Well! if he had no luck during the day, he would accept that invitation to dinner, and see the girl again, and try to get her story quietly. He already trusted her to tell him no lies, hold nothing back that was not confidential.

He could find no way of obtaining a private talk with her until then. . . .

Helga comprehended at last that he was not to resume and end his business, nor her daughter to take her departure, until she herself should give the signal. She was convinced that Ingrid was sensing a strangeness in the matter, and was lingering in the room, not from any active inquisitiveness, but instinctively, to learn more of it. It was so unlike her to fail in tact. However, she must be dismissed—and next, Saltfleet—for Hugh might soon be back, and they were not to meet. She could acquaint Ingrid with the simple outline of the story—and how he was to dine with them . . . and then perhaps the child would help her to dissuade him from pursuing Hugh on the moor; so superfluously, from his point of view, so dreadfully, from hers.

She caught at Ingrid's arm, to say:

"You must know, dear, Hugh made the acquaintance of Mr. Saltfleet and a friend in Tibet, only a little while before his return; and there they entrusted to him for safe-keeping a certain valuable. Now Mr. Saltfleet is here to reclaim it. . . . He is putting up at the 'Bell,' and has consented to take dinner with us this evening, to meet Hugh. So the sensible view seems to be that it is perfectly unnecessary to go after him in this fog, when in any event they will be seeing one another in a few hours more. An out-of-the-way spot like Devil's Tor will be exceedingly hard to locate by a stranger to the district, on such a day. Isn't it so?"

Ingrid returned her mother a perturbed look. That some of her fancies had thus hit the mark gave her no pleasure; she was conscious only of her unquiet heart because of Hugh, while, as a background, dully wondering what her mother wanted, that she should be so reluctant to let this man seek him on the Tor.

"If Mr. Saltfleet has travelled in Tibet," she answered spiritlessly, "I should think he ought to have no difficulty in finding Devil's Tor at least."

Then, to the surprise of both the others, she turned with an unexpected swift impulsiveness to Saltfleet himself.

"Since I am consulted, I wish you *would* try to get in touch with Hugh Drapier."

"You have something for him?" he suggested, puzzled.

"No; but there is a disagreeable idea in my head that all isn't well with him."

Saltfleet viewed her.

"May I ask if it has any foundation?"

"No. . . . But twice already he has been nearly killed on the same Tor, in two days."

"A sinister spot! I presume, by the lightning and earthquake you before mentioned?"

"Yes."

"Then that has probably affected your imagination, and it is an example of unconscious superstition. However, I shall be happy to end your anxiety if I can, and I will be off in another minute."

Though he had never smiled, his mouth gave Ingrid the same impression as smiling, and some quick access of dislike and pride impelled her not to wait here for his departure, but to make her own excuses forthwith. So, with a simple word of thanks to him for his promised service, and another of apology for her intrusion, she left the room.

The two remaining facing each other alone were silent again for a moment. Then Saltfleet said:

"I fancy I can't be wrong in thinking that you are rather definitely against my pursuing Drapier this morning, and your motive, I conceive, is that you want to get in your first word with him—which, on your private information, of which I know nothing, may be a quite sensible and wise precaution. Now that I have pledged myself to your daughter, I must go. But, as you point out, it is very possible that I may miss him; so, in case you do secure your talk in advance, I beg you to make the situation entirely clear to him.

"I am aware we cannot proceed by law. Arsinal must decide how we are to proceed. But Drapier cannot be so eccentric as to be incapable of receiving a serious warning, and accordingly I do warn him here and now, through you, Mrs. Fleming, that we did not undertake that trip to Tibet merely that he might add to his personal museum an object to which he may have taken an unprogressive fancy. . . . Please assure him as forcibly as you know how, that we shall incur new risks and further disagreeables, rather than resign in so cowardly a way a thing that by the laws of acquisition and priority belongs to us, and by that of honour definitely does *not* belong to him. I have quite identified myself with Arsinal in this business. I will take from Drapier neither the open cynical flouting of our just claim, nor a postponement on any account whatsoever. We shall listen to no proposals."

Helga had grown very pale.

"A quarrel won't help you, Mr. Saltfleet."

"The dispute in words will not help us, I admit. . . . So now we are back to where I shied before! Very well! We mean this—I am speaking for Arsinal too. If pushed, we shall not hesitate to resort to action to get back our property."

"You mean violence?"

"It sounds unreal; and in fact I am aware that we are here in England, the great stronghold of legal security. But we are vastly concerned, so that, short of utter lunacy of operation, we shall actually stick at *nothing*. . . . I repeat Arsinal will range himself beside me in this. He is a man who will always sacrifice to principle; while I can be exceedingly hard when exasperated. Drapier will be unwise to put these assertions to the test."

"I certainly hope the need will not arise," rejoined Helga coldly, "for this I know of Hugh Drapier, that he comes of a very hard stock himself, and is the last man to be frightened from a course by threats. I think I won't do you the disservice to pass on any such message. If he's merely being restrained by personal regard for you both, the open breach will give him exactly what he needs. As to a risk, I don't doubt he will be very well able to take care of himself."

"I can't insist that you shall serve as intermediary; so I shall try to see him myself."

"And I cannot prevent that. Yet promise me, Mr. Saltfleet, that in case you do meet outside this house before I have spoken to him, there will not be anything—fatal to the later understanding."

"You mean, an assault! But the unqualified promise is rather difficult. I am ready enough to undertake that in the event of a clear-cut disagreement between us, the principle I shall act on will be the simple recovery of our article, with the least expenditure of time and temper. I am equally ready to assure you that I am really too little concerned with your cousin personally to bear him any grudge for the attempted embezzlement, beyond the heat necessarily generated in the act of prevention. . . . Pray understand that I am nowise trying to intimidate you—especially as, according to your own account, he is not the sort of man to be so coerced. I am simply informing him, through you, that we are determined, by fair means or foul, to get back the prize we won in Tibet."

"Tell me straight out—supposing that you do meet him alone, and he confesses to having it on him, or you strongly suspect it . . ."

Saltfleet moved impatiently.

"The precise shape of an affair depends on so many factors. If he carried the stone, it stands to sense it would be my best opportunity to get it from him. If he refused it, I should doubtless become annoyed. Farther than that, it would hardly be possible to predict."

"He is not a weakling."

"I cannot see how this conversation is to help any longer, Mrs. Fleming."

And as she stared at him without reply in timid mournfulness, he proceeded, while slowly starting for the door:

"You have said yourself that we cannot invoke the law. You have said that he is not to be moved by threat. If he disregards his honour, how can we appeal to that? What other course is open to us than force?—unless we are to employ cunning, to which I at least don't care to descend. Nor would *you* wish us to burgle this house, for example?"

"You can hardly be serious in that."

"Then be pleased to clear your mind, and ask yourself in quietness what Drapier has left us to do except the other!"

Helga returned from escorting him to the porch door, but not to go back into the drawing-room. Instead, she sought her own chamber. Standing there without plan or purpose, nearly insensible of her environment, she seemed for the first few moments only to be recovering her composure, that Saltfleet's call had quite driven to the winds.

She continued unsure, even, if he was still to dine with them that evening. She did not know whether he was a friend or an enemy. His last spoken words at the door had been to name a time in the afternoon for his return to the house in case he should miss Hugh during the morning. So, before making different arrangements, she had better wait till Hugh came in. It depended, supposing they shouldn't meet at all during the day, on whether Saltfleet would consider the harsh emphasis of his language towards the last to have cancelled their preceding more courteous understanding. Yet if nothing had happened before the evening, she would have to assume that his acceptance stood. That was one thing settled. . . .

Her condition of mind was peculiar. Still more curiously, it recalled occasional mental overtakings in the past that really had been due to quite a different order of causation. Especially after some beautiful and emotional day from home, or it might be only a few hours in the society of a rich nature, or simply upon returning to her people from some holiday remarkable for joy and incident, she had felt as a spiritual atmosphere, and marvelled at, this same disappearance from her life of what, but so lately, had seemed to show itself its climax and mystical explanation, with the silent succeeding of an emptiness that allowed her to feel her soul at last. Truly it was not emptiness at all, but a fullness so abundant that she could never be sure if the aftermath were not greater than the harvest.

And now that Saltfleet had removed his quite vivifying personality, which so long as he was still with her had produced such a welter of disorderly fancies in her head, she was aware for one time more of that quiet and sudden plunge of her soul into a vacuum, that resembled an interregnum of beauty between the ending of a wonderful dream and the cold taking up of the duties of the day.

She judged the force of his nature by the standard of this effect upon her. Her fears were not departed with his going, but, with the ceasing of the channels of new shock and ugliness, their image was softened to something of the enchanting unreality of a reflection in dark water. Against the dread of his surprising Hugh on the foggy moor, against her hopelessness for the whole misery into which Hugh had dragged his life by this ignominious obsession, against her newly sprung up, incomprehensible, rejected yet obstinately lingering delusion of a menace to Ingrid's peace from Saltfleet, was surely to be set the enhancement of her existence by this accidental encounter with an individual so unlike all others living; whose type, if type he had, must be sought among the furious world-shakers of twenty centuries ago! . . .

Thank God! it could be no sudden infatuation, evidencing a ghastly need of her physical constitution. She *knew* she could not love so quickly, or without her heart. And she was withered, far too old for another affair—certainly far too old for him . . . as he was far too tremendous a person for her! She could mean no more than that merely to be acquainted with such a man must be regarded as a singular privilege in the life of any woman. Yet in what was his uniqueness really consisting? She had been intimate before this with other strong, clever, wilful men. But they must have been, by contrast with Saltfleet—she searched for the distinguishing difference . . . *cautious*, was it?—*law-abiding?* . . . Yes, perhaps. They had been bold with restrictions. They had been harnessed to the laws framed by other men still; and so the world of the strong and audacious went on, each shouldering his way along *permitted* paths . . . but this man, careless of any path. He should truly be a Himalayan! . . .

Her troubled eye fell strangely upon her daughter, standing in the doorway. Why had she followed her here, and what was she to announce? Sometimes indeed Ingrid would pay her these friendly purposeless visits, when nothing in particular would pass between them, and time would seem to have no value; but her present appearance could not be of that kind, she looked too pale and constrained. And while one hand proceeded slowly to push the door behind her to its latch, the other, Helga noticed, was clenched, which somehow seemed to indicate an excessive agitation. It might still be her weird sense of a mishap to Hugh. What really should there be in that? She hoped it was not a true presentiment, of a horror coming! . . . No, no! it was to talk of Saltfleet—and she, as well, needed to talk of him with her daughter—needed to have it put beyond doubt that he had made no sort of impression upon her. . . . But then again, she might have come about Peter. . . .

Ingrid sat down without a word, and Helga busying herself with idly rearranging some papers on the bureau, for some moments each appeared to ignore the other's presence. Then the girl shot her mother a long glance, with lifted brows.

"Were you expecting him to call?" she asked, as if casually; but Helga believed that it was to introduce what else she had to say. She turned quietly round from the bureau.

"Mr. Saltfleet? Hugh has been not quite expecting him, I think."

"His friend that you mentioned, is his name Arsinal?"

"Yes. Hugh has told you something about it, then?"

"That he was expecting a visit from a Mr. Arsinal."

"This one came instead. The other is at Oxford."

"Is he coming later?"

"I don't know."

There was a pause.

"Mother, I want you to tell me what that thing is you said he called to recover from Hugh." She added, in her mother's silence of surprise: "I have a reason."

"What reason?"

"Can't you tell me first? Surely you aren't afraid of my indiscretion!"

"It is Hugh's secret, my dear."

"Isn't it what you were discussing together two nights ago, when all the house was asleep?"

"That can have no bearing."

"Well, then, I must think it is this. . . ."

Ingrid unclenched her upturned hand, displaying the flint she had taken from the box on her mother's dressing-table the morning before. . . . But Helga first beheld it stupidly, then took it into her own fingers in slow amazement. She turned it round and round.

"Will you explain where you got it from?"

"From your bedroom yesterday morning, when you were out of it. I was looking at it, but was called away suddenly at the very same moment, so I dropped it into my dressing-gown pocket, where it has remained ever since. But is it what Mr. Saltfleet came for?"

"Let me understand," said her mother. "Did you take this out of a tin box standing on my dressing-table?"

"Yes. You see, I had no idea it was a secret."

Helga's face had become flushed, but only slightly, while the frown that brought her eyes together as she still viewed the stone in her hand seemed neither of anger nor of personal anxiety. Ingrid, watching, felt that she had dealt her a blow indeed, but not one principally affecting her pride, so it must be nearly altogether on Hugh's account. . . . That was to say, her mother knew that Hugh, having missed the stone, had been obliged to avoid these men coming after him; but now he need no longer do so. And wouldn't that explain her attempts to dissuade Saltfleet from going up to the Tor? . . . Yet this, if true at all, could but represent the outermost aspect of a far deeper mystery. For her mother was standing there before her surely too stunned for such a mishap, while the whole case was so plainly of fate, which never took away only to restore. . . .

Helga, in effect, had not the egoism to dwell upon the consequences to herself of this calamity, so long as its import in Hugh's business remained to be grasped. Her embarrassment, certainly, she saw was to be very inevitable, very humiliating. For whether or not Hugh had yet discovered his loss unfortunately made no difference; she must return the stone into his own hands, with the full story of how it came to be taken from his room and from its box, since were she simply to replace it in that box in his drawer, saying nothing, it might result in his challenging her with the temporary abstraction, in case he *had* discovered it to be missing in the meantime. But then she must either confess the truth too late, to her utter shame, or stoutly maintain the lie, to her more inward mortification and confusion. . . . All this she perfectly understood at once, and yet was barely thinking about.

She was wondering if it were not a working of Providence that the object should go wandering just when it was being demanded by those men. Otherwise, Hugh (but then he must be missing it. Why hadn't he questioned her?) might have had it in the pocket of the clothes he was wearing this morning; and admitted as much to Saltfleet; and . . . that perhaps was not to be. . . . What ought now to be done? It was truly in the class of miracles. . . .

"*Is* it what you were talking about?" repeated Ingrid, in a quiet voice of patient persistence.

"Yes, my dear, it is."

"Then I picked a very unlucky day for meddling with it!"

"I don't know. It is a whole chain of blunders, accidents, coincidences. It is the oddest affair altogether. Yours has certainly been a link, but no more than one."

"You had no suspicion it was missing from its box?"

"No, I never looked again."

"What is its use, or value?"

"It is a sacred stone looted from a Lama monastery in Tibet."

"By those two?"

"Yes."

Ingrid took back the stone from her mother's lax fingers.

"It might just as well be a piece of common beach flint."

"No, I know it is more than that, even in itself. But I must ask you not to begin studying it too curiously. Hugh wouldn't wish it."

"Mayn't I question Hugh about it?"

"No, it doesn't concern you at all, and he would probably be very angry at your having even stumbled on its existence. He's distracted by other things, too, and far from well. So don't provoke him."

She added, as something which would have to be told her daughter some time:

"As he happens to be treating us very generously, we ought at least to respect his moods. He is to leave us all his money, which will amount to a very considerable sum."

"And that has been his business down here?"

"I have no doubt it was one of his reasons for coming to us."

"He has asked you to serve as executrix, and you were to dispose of this stone, in case he died before they arrived?"

Helga sat down slowly, while looking at her daughter with a sort of fear.

"Yes. . . . You are very sharp-witted, Ingrid. But you must not say a word to Hugh, or he will fly to the conclusion that I have betrayed his confidence."

"I don't want his money, mother. You don't, either. Why is he all at once imagining his death?"

"It is not necessarily morbidness. He is Scotch, and looks ahead."

"I wish my own present feelings would allow me to agree with you. . . . Let us leave it! . . . So, having been shown it once, you borrowed it a second time while he was out? And now you don't know whether he has discovered its absence from the box, or not. . . . You seemed so anxious just now, mother, that Mr. Saltfleet shouldn't follow him to the Tor, and I thought at first it was because you had both missed this thing I had taken away by accident, and you were afraid of trouble between them on account of its loss. But as you *haven't* missed it, perhaps Hugh is to dispute its ownership, and he has told you so?"

"I cannot say anything."

"And yet he has no antiquarian tastes, nor goes in for travellers' collections, that I have heard of. And if it is to go back to the others at last . . . surely, mother, this stone must be a very extraordinary specimen, to so attract an outsider?"

"You will end by deducing it all, while I can deny or confirm nothing. Since you are so intent, you had *better* speak to Hugh. His property must be returned to him when he comes in, when you can be with me, to explain your share in the mischance. Then you can, if you wish, proceed to torment him with your questions; though I am sure he will think, even if he does not say it aloud, that it is none of it any business of yours, and that you are certainly not his cousin for the purpose of prying into his personal secrets."

Neither disclaiming nor defending her curiosity, Ingrid sat on in troubled silence. If this then, she reflected, was the matter that had brought Hugh down to Devonshire, it could not also be anything to do with Devil's Tor. And still Arsinal, the wise one of the three, might have had some unseen hand in directing him here . . . or was it quite impossible? Yet Hugh had spontaneously mentioned Arsinal to her, as a man who might perhaps be able to explain something of this living awfulness of blackness and brightness advancing upon them all. . . . What the stone's character was, that she must first of all hear from Hugh when he returned . . . if he should return very soon, in safety. . . .

"It isn't prying, mother," she said at last. "Let Hugh establish that it's his secret, and I will gladly leave it alone. This bit of stone in my hand, I can almost feel it speaking to me; and do you know what it is saying? That it belongs, not to Hugh, and not to those men, and not to Tibet, or anywhere else; but to Devil's Tor. . . . That astonishes you, but I can tell you another thing. It's just as if you were all trying to turn me off a road that a very deep instinct teaches me is the right one. . . ."

"It has been an unsettling week," replied Helga, "but we must keep sane views before us. We know that this stone was in the house while Hugh was paying his visit to the tomb on the Tor. We know that he brought it with him from Tibet, where it must have been for a very long time. We also know that the tomb on Devil's Tor has been sealed by its monument for thousands of years."

"You have all the unanswerable reasons, and I have only my poor feeling, yet it assures me that either there is the connection already, or else there will be one. . . ."

She dropped a subject that could merely end in misunderstanding, suspicion and heat, in order to inquire:

"What is Mr. Saltfleet's profession, mother?"

"Hugh simply informed me that he has climbed in the Himalayas."

"Yes, he looks like it. Surely it must be characteristic, too, that he should choose the highest mountains of the world to conquer. I can well imagine that a man of his stamp would fly at the biggest game."

"It is the modern subjection to the idea of size. Big ships, big buildings, big spectacles, big mountains . . ."

"That unfairness can't represent your true opinion of him. I am sure he is not vulgar."

Helga viewed her daughter narrowly.

"You liked him?"

"I never thought. I didn't try to fit him in."

"I was wondering how he would appear to you. . . . For my part, he rather frightened me."

"I know he did."

"Then I hope he did not see it too. But I kept feeling that he was to bring me no very good luck by-and-by. Can you help me to understand?"

"You mean, through Hugh, mother?"

"That I can't tell."

"It would be remarkable otherwise."

"It would be an evil miracle." Helga spoke in a singular tone of restraint.

"Yet his coming here at all like this is nearly the beginning of one . . . and everything in these last hours seems to be holding more than a single meaning, so why may not his call while Hugh was out?"

"I am sorriest for Peter."

"Because I neglect him? But I don't wish him to be concerned with these matters."

"Nor he, you, I suspect, dear."

Ingrid said nothing, and she went on:

"I'm sorry for Peter, because he has so mistimed his arrival that the entire centre of the stage down here is already filled with other persons and excitements. And though of course I am delighted to meet Hugh again after all these years, still I could very well wish he had put off his visit till his affairs were smoothed out."

The girl's fingers slowly closed over the flint in her hand.

"But, mother, those occurrences on the Tor—you know they could not have happened at any other time, or in any other way. Hugh has been a necessary spectator; perhaps a necessary actor. Where is the sense in regretting a fated thing?"

"A much more emphatic fate than that couldn't prevent my wanting your happiness, dear."

"It is the ancient theme of tragedies, I suppose. Fate against love. Though it seems almost nobler to be a selfless instrument of fate. Anything of the will is surely mean and worldly, mother."

"Not mother-love."

"Perhaps not that. But otherwise, fate is so grand; and then we are not to be merely pawns, but we are to suffer. But that may be the reverse of the medal. On the one side, a destined new shape for the world; on the other, our individual suffering. . . . What makes me think suffering so terribly important is that it seems to be almost the only universal state. All men and women, the whole of the animal and insect worlds, and no doubt plants as well—all suffer. Doesn't it look as if the entire scheme of things were a mighty—*agonization*—towards some undreamt-of magnificence of change? . . . What do you think about these matters, mother?"

"It is many years now, my dear, since I have realised our true helplessness in the ordering of our own lives. At first the recognition saddened and depressed me, but afterwards I found compensation. Humility makes for clearer vision, and I hope the habit of little acts of kindness is at least as useful in the world as the constant pushing towards money and distinction."

"Are you happy?"

"Yes, I may call myself happy," replied her mother. "But not in a self-deceived way, like that of so many middle-aged women I know. They—some of them—unsuperstitiously dare to *boast* of their settlement and contentment; but I have had such fearful blows in the past, I can never forget the real insecurity even of our apparently soundest calm. . . . Human life, dear, is just like the sea—I know how trite the comparison is! But one hour everything is so blue, beautiful and serene, while the next, still without a cloud in the sky, it begins to roll inshore with great thuds; and then we remember the monster it always is. Were any bad thing to happen to you, for example—as I pray God none ever will!—my present subdued enjoyment of existence would instantaneously vanish as though it had never been, and yet amazement would hardly be joined to it; for I have experienced in the roughest school how such cruelties are nearly to be anticipated from time to time."

"Yes, mother. And mightn't you add, for your consolation, that the happy persons are necessarily the despised in the sight of heaven?—seeing that they alone are not shouldering their share of the burden. . . ."

Ingrid's thoughts, however, were never away from her preoccupation. Throughout the talk she had been anxious lest Saltfleet, after her leaving them, had been over-persuaded by her mother, or had changed his mind of his own accord, about following Hugh to the Tor; but she had hesitated to put the plain question, for fear of reopening a discussion of her undiscussible sense of evil. Now she could endure her suspense no longer.

"Mr. Saltfleet has gone after Hugh?" she asked, in a new, more present voice.

"So far as I know. I wish you had not enabled him."

"I think you have misread his nature. He is unlikely ever to do anything but what is right, and what else can we want? I am glad he has gone up, and hope they come back together. . . . And, mother—when Hugh does get back, may I see him alone, to return him this thing of his, and explain for both of us just what has happened?"

Helga was unwilling and displeased. It was some moments before she answered.

"There are two or three things against it, my dear. It will be making me ridiculous. And he will understand that I have been talking to you, in opposition to his express wish. And I think you have gone far enough into all this business already—now you must really have a little pity on Peter!"

"I promise that if you leave it to me, he will find it far less strange."

"How can that be?"

"I shall put it in so much less practical a way, perhaps he will pass over the liberty taken altogether."

"What has already happened between you, that you should have the confidence?"

"Since the destruction, we've rather met. Before, I believed we were hopelessly opposite, but now I am coming to regard him as the one other of all our family to possess the gift of . . . seeing through time and space, if you like, mother! . . ."

"And these are the matters you discuss when by yourselves? Then I am all the more glad his stay isn't to be a long one. . . . So did he tell you what else he saw in the tomb?"

"No, he wouldn't."

"So your conversations are general?"

"They are particular, so far as Devil's Tor can make them so."

"You are filling each other's heads, no doubt; and perhaps under the special circumstances it may be pardonable. . . . You may have your way for this last time, then. But, after this morning, I want you to promise me . . ."

A subdued knocking on the outside panel of the door caused both women to look round to it. The door gently opened, and Peter's countenance showed. Helga discontinued her speech. She rose, and Ingrid followed her, hiding the flint in her dress.

Peter came into the room. His face looked rather bilious and forbidding, as from a sleepless night, but he summoned a fleeting smile to it, while the others greeted him quietly, with half-inquiring eyes. But then to Ingrid Peter returned a longer regard of sincerely earnest interrogation. A night and so much of the morning had elapsed since their ambiguous parting, during which time all his tormented revolvings of what that last mood of hers had stood for, what it should or might become if only he allowed her a sufficient interval, had long since churned themselves into a paste of inconsistence. . . . The abstraction of her eyes, however, and the faint long lines on her brow, could have made him believe the lapse between the two meetings much less. It was nearly the identical image he had taken home with him, and nothing had changed. . . .

He shrugged, smiled coldly again, and lit a cigarette.

"I am just back from the station," he explained, now eyeing Helga. "I had to go for a parcel—which wasn't there. On my way out, at the cross-roads, I came face-to-face with a man issuing from your lane. Who is he? I expect he was from here."

"We have had a caller, Peter," replied Helga. "What was he like?"

"He was like a celebrity—which is why I am asking about him. A big, noticeable chap, with a weathered skin and a remark- ably alert manner of carrying himself. I bet he's somebody. A friend of your cousin's, at a hazard!"

"You're quite right. It's a Mr. Saltfleet, and he knew Hugh Drapier abroad. You haven't met Hugh yet, I think?"

"I saw him out-of-doors," said Peter shortly. "Frankly, and meaning no discourtesy, I am more interested in this other. Is he a frequenter of the wilds too?"

"He is a Himalayan climber."

"Ah! Then I do know his name. And is he returning here ever? If so, I think I should rather like to encounter him."

"Dine with us this evening, in that case."

"May I? I shall be very happy, and it seems my inquiry was apt. . . . Some persons, you know, Mrs. Fleming, affect you like a great work of art. They may even repel your private taste, and nevertheless you instantly feel all sorts of future consequences flowing from them."

Both Helga and her daughter turned sharper eyes on him.

"What consequences, Peter?" asked the former.

"I said I was curious about him because he looked in the way of being a celebrity. These conversational short cuts are so easy. My curiosity was actually raised, and is still running high, because of my wonderfully strong sense, half an hour ago, of futurity in connection with the man. You meet one person in the street, and seem to know his face very well, but can't place him; he belongs to the past. You meet another whom you are sure you have never met before in your life; and he belongs to the present. Then you meet a third, whom also you have never met before, yet who definitely and vividly belongs to your life notwithstanding, even though his type is antipathetic to yours and you are probably never to see him again. I say he is of the future. He corresponds to some invisible ideal in you, and *it* is bound to turn up again. The consequences you ask about, they are the affecting of your life by this ultimate turning up. The process has begun on this first sight of your man. . . . It is something like that. . . . Or my insight is a shade subtler and more unpleasant than that, but I'll say no more in present company. When I have met him in a room, and seen some of his face's expressions, and heard him speak, then it will be time enough to sharpen the analysis to a fine point."

They were standing thus. Helga and Peter both had their backs more or less to the shut long west windows of the room, that should have revealed the sloping lawn, with the moor beyond the valley, but now had merely the travelling mists for peep-show; while Ingrid alone directly faced the same windows. All at once she saw Hugh outside on the walk, staring into the room, his face nearly against a pane. She thought how ill, white, and peculiar he seemed. She could not understand why he should have come round by the far side of the house.

He vanished almost on her first glimpse; nor could she understand, either, in what fashion he had effected his departure from her line of vision. An extreme uneasiness urged her to intercept him instantly, before he should take refuge in his room upstairs.

"Hugh is back, mother!" she announced quietly; then added to Peter:

"If you will excuse me, there is something rather important that he has to know. I won't be long."

He nodded carelessly, and sat down to go on smoking, while Helga, unable to conceal her nervousness, gazed with half-frightened eyes after her departing daughter, whom, however, she made no effort to detain.

But upstairs, though Ingrid lingered on the landing for five whole minutes, and then five minutes more, outside the partly open door of his empty room, Hugh never came. A sickening supernatural awe settled on her spirits. . . .

She could not wait there for ever, nor did she choose to take his stone downstairs again. Accordingly, she sought her own room, to secrete it temporarily under some clothes in a drawer. . . . With the final contact of her relinquishing fingers with the flint, a furious uproar, as of violently rushing waters, stunned her hearing. She expected to swoon, so shocking, crashing and present was the volume of noise. Then it gave place again to the silence of the house, and was no more than a stupefying and inexplicable memory. . . .

She endeavoured to convince herself that it had been internal.

But it had too suddenly come and gone, while never before in her life had she experienced the beginning of so fearful a sensation. . . .

Sinking to the edge of the bed, she whitened her knuckles by the tight clenching of her fists, in the effort immediately to steady herself before venturing downstairs to face her mother and Peter again.

XV

Knossos

From the cross-roads Saltfleet plunged, without any slackening of his quick stride, down the misty lane that Ingrid had said would bring him to Devil's Tor.

His indignation with Drapier was governed, yet steadily mounting. His cousin, Mrs. Fleming, couldn't have spoken without knowledge, and it was manifest that Arsinal's stone was not to be passed back except under some pressure. It was rather necessary to keep distinct Drapier's motive in so trying to cheat them out of their property and the course to follow in recovering it. The first was only of psychological interest; the other scarcely needed rehearsal. He had simply to make the direct categorical demand, and see that he was not fobbed off. The single sincere member of this set seemed to be the daughter. She might help.

But at least the thing had come through all right, and was safe. Drapier couldn't now pretend otherwise, since his cousin had admitted it, and this was a tremendous simplification, in case of a row.

As for the psychology, in the first place it was sure that Drapier couldn't know what this article he was proposing to retain stood for. For no living soul had possessed the compound of expert learning, sagacity, imagination, and pre-acquaintance with the key idea, requisite to the deciphering of that clay-tablet inscription from Knossos, in Crete, until Arsinal had arrived, three years back, to spell it slowly out in silence, and communicate its message to no professional *savant* of them all. He, Saltfleet, himself had been the sole depositary of its purport, just because he was totally unconcerned with antiquity, and, of all the ancient languages, knew only Latin. Accordingly, Drapier by no possibility could be aware of the hinted past and future of that record; nor, if he were, could he conceive a connection between such a reference and the stone in his hands. Quite other researches and expeditions had supplied Arsinal with the clues to that identification.

No doubt, the thing's value for Drapier lay in the fact that others had made a trip to the ends of the earth to obtain it, and that it had been found resting in a holy place. Proprietorship, the mania for collections, and superstition, were three of the commonest weaknesses of the human mind, and sat down very amicably side-by-side. If a more particular motive was needed, Mrs. Fleming had styled him "psychic" and "Celtic." The return over the Himalayan barrier might easily enough have given him a few narrow shaves, and he might have appointed this his mascot. Nothing in the man's dreamy gravity and reticence carried to excess, which had made of him so wretched a companion during their few hours in camp together, contradicted such an infantile fantasticness. In fact, it nearly demanded lunacy to account for this preposterous flight across half the world, just in order to retain possession of a bit of fractured flint, which he knew nothing about, and for which he could have no earthly use. Saltfleet had no great faith in his sudden call to England. The so-urgent business seemed at present to be taking the form of enjoying solitary walks over a not very exciting patch of low moor, and relaxing in the society of secluded gentlewomen!

None the less, the hitch might be awkward. In that case, Arsinal might be the better man to deal with it at once; his quiet persuasiveness would keep down the heat always liable with weak persons to turn indecision to decision. But he was too usefully employed at Oxford. A wire to him would mean a set-back, obliging him to drop his threads of the second stage of the business, in order to re-pick up those of the first, that he believed to be done with. Then, too, anything like an admission of inability was odious to Saltfleet, while so far it really amounted only to a contingency; this Mrs. Fleming was a quite unknown character, who might well have added to her information from officiousness or a natural proneness to exaggerate. Or should Drapier actually prove difficult, Arsinal's habitual cautiousness might have just the contrary effect of fortifying the fellow's resolution, by crippling his own more forcible representations. So no telegram should be dispatched by him until at least he had secured this preliminary interview with their man, and learnt just what he intended. . . .

There was nothing for him to see but the road underfoot, the grey wet shapes of the trees on either hand, and the moving fog, that grew denser as he proceeded. He was on the straight stretch leading to the moor itself. So far the way was plain, and these meditations, somewhat superfluous as they were, yet helped to while away the monotony of the blind walk, being as appropriate as any other occupation of his brain.

He loosely reviewed the whole intimacy, which, three years old, though with a great intervening gap of more than two of them, had still not lost for him its singular fascination, the magic note of which had been struck during their first fateful week together in Crete.

The famous Minoan excavations, reformative of the world's immemorial notions concerning the classical Greeks and the origins of their culture, were then yet in strong blast. The marvellous palace of Minos, claimed by some to be the temple of the Mother-Goddess herself, continued slowly to yield up the stupendous drainage and architectural feats of its construction; smaller finds continued to delight and amaze by their beauty; and history, all the time, was being rewritten. This was at Knossos, near the "wine-dark" sea running past the north coast of the island, and not far from the mass of Ida, on whose slopes legend asserted that Zeus, king of gods, was reared by his still more awful, because ancienter, mother Rhea.

Arsinal, on the strength of his known standing in archaeology and its kindred sciences, had contrived to get himself retained as volunteer assistant without pay on the working staff of the British excavating party. Occasionally he varied his locality by crossing the island to Phaestos or some other equally rich field of discoveries, but mostly he stopped at the headquarters of Knossos.

Saltfleet at about the same time was in Athens, where he had been trying to track down his whelp of a legitimate younger brother, the head of the family, the Marquis of Kirton. He seemed to have been circulating among his private set that he had the intention, or a "dashed good mind," or something of the sort, to "stop his allowance"—of course, a libel dictated by accumulated spite. In his life Saltfleet had never had a penny of allowance from him, or a penny of money from any of his decadent brood of law-recognised half-brothers and sisters. They hated him too cordially; and if ever there had been a passage of coin between them, its natural flow would have been in the reverse direction. His late father and theirs, the tenth Marquis, had left *him* most of the movable estate. To the degenerate Charles he had passed down only what it had not been in his power to withhold, namely, the northern house and land, with the title; to the rest of the scissors-jawed, puling crowd born in wedlock, pittances just big enough to keep them idle and well-dressed.

And also Saltfleet had inherited the whole fortune of his highborn Prussian mother; distinguished, aesthetic and temperamental as few but German women of rank can be, but bitterly impatient of control and convention as well, as the severe Potsdam staff-officer, her husband, had discovered to his cost in the days before the war. The Marquis was too great a personage to be reached, so, in honourable fashion, the other had put a bullet through his own brain.

Considerably moved, for he was large-hearted enough, though reckless in all things, the Marquis had then conveyed his mistress to Brazil, where they lived together for a year or two until the affair should have died down. But it was she who, from an exaggerated fastidiousness of pride, consistently declined to marry him, thinking that it would then be said of her that she had killed her husband to obtain that elevation of degree. So in Brazil Saltfleet had been born, and a summer later his mother had sickened of a fever, and passed away quite suddenly. Of course, he could remember nothing of her.

His father had brought him to England to his own mother, the old Marchioness, a grim, intrepid, opinion-scorning lady of sixty, who lived for twenty years longer, but in the end left her natural grandson nothing of her wealth, declaring that what he had already was quite sufficient for a "bastard." Nevertheless she was fond of the boy, for his promise, to the extent of soon assuming the entire responsibility for his upbringing. She had even permitted him to use the family name—before marriage, she had been the Honourable Eva Saltfleet. Her race was prouder than her husband's, if not risen so high, for whereas before the creation of the marquisate in 1745 the roots of those Desboroughs of Kirton receded quickly through knights and esquires to the unknown darkness of all common ancestry, her own paternal line ran down over lofty piers of celebrated medieval personages as far as Robert Guiscard, the Norman adventurer, and *his* stock.

Saltfleet, accordingly, was in Athens, for the purpose of looking up his half-brother and, should the fact be as reported to him, giving him a quiet thrashing for his lies. But Charles had gone on to Venice in a friend's yacht, and Saltfleet did not care to follow him in that geographical direction, so shrugged his shoulder and let the affair drop. A near approach to the big cities of western Europe always rather disgusted him. The business of all those swarming, crawling day-labourers was not his, nor his theirs.

Before he moved east again, however, closer to the great Asian mountains that were his eternal loadstone, a mental phenomenon overtook him that was like nothing he had ever experienced, and still it was more singular than alarming. It was a warm evening at the end of May, and he was smoking an after-dinner cigar on the outside balcony of his hotel, in company with a few groups of other people, yet very much alone, when suddenly without cause the name CRETE flashed through his head, just as distinctly as though his mouth had uttered it. Then he asked himself, hardly understanding his own question, how it would be if he took a look at Crete, seeing that he had never been there, that it was said to be very interesting, and that it was quite easy to reach from this particular capital? The suggestion was already a desire to be on the island. What had started the name and the impulse, he never knew; he had not been hearing or reading anything about the place. He decided within the minute that nothing stood in the way of packing his traps and being off to Candia by the first available transport.

Afterwards he fancied that the decision was scarcely come to when a great rushing shadow swept across his eyes, too suddenly and swiftly to grasp, and yet the impression remained with him that it had been a *woman's* shape—or rather, a shape suggestive of the female, since it had been so vast, dark, and instantly swallowed up, that it never could have had time to look like an actual woman's.

The half-vision puzzled, yet failed to disquiet him. His health was excellent, his eyesight normal, and his nerves even robust. He had always conceded that the universe was a very queer place, full of unlighted holes and corners; so that this might quite well be a new wonder. As the invitation to Crete and the following hallucination had been so *nearly* simultaneous, evidently they were to be connected—in which case it extremely resembled a supernatural summons to the island. The notion pleased him.

After finishing his cigar quietly, he rose to get his hat, then stepped forth from the hotel for a car to Piraeus.

A trading schooner, the ultimate expression of dirt and unsailorly disorder, was to leave for Crete, *via* the Islands, at eight next morning. He was directed to the Levantine master at a neighbouring tavern by a knot of the Dago crew, found him there, an alcoholic-looking ruffian, having a countenance as craven and abject as cunning, and, plying him with a few drinks, finally succeeded in obtaining a passage in his disreputable tub for something less than the first-class fare for the distance in any liner. The cheat he ignored by virtue of his grown antipathy to the fashionable hotel life of those elaborate steamships. He preferred travelling *en prince* with human scum to associating on enforced level terms with the dragged-up western mob having money in pocket.

Landed at Candia, after a surfeit of oily diet and discomfort of the sea, he soon learnt that all the talk there was of Knossos and the antique marvels of the island still daily being unearthed. Already Crete was a little Egypt, it seemed; only hitherto it had been insufficiently advertised. Money was wanted. Next day he went to Knossos, which was but a few miles inland, and there met Arsinal.

There had been no rushing towards one another of attuned natures, but the development of an intimacy had been rather slower than might have been expected in so friendly, isolated and purposeful a camp, by reason of the two circumstances that Saltfleet himself was always as a haughty cliff overseeing the flats of the human race, and that Arsinal, a reserved, unassuming, yet oddly noticeable man, was too engrossed by his work and musings to pay at the beginning any special attention to the big tourist of curiosity taking a view of their hive. But Saltfleet, making Candia his headquarters, after the second day amongst those ant-like toilers, had begun to mark out his quarry. The rest appeared so universally interested in their treasure-hunt, as though they had been boy scouts playing with the utmost serious-ness a game of make-believe—always cheerful, industrious, welcoming with an equal welcome whatsoever might turn up— whereas Arsinal, by contrast, came to strike him as being upon the spot for a specific purpose, distinct from the long ideal of those others of recovering piecemeal in order to reconstruct a buried civilisation. That they were skilled, patient, persistent beings, knowing their trade, Saltfleet was prepared to acknow-ledge. Arsinal, however, had that different mien of one not bur-rowing at large, but meditatively watching and waiting for the emergence of some expected particular thing; which necessarily invested him for his silent witness with the moral advantage always, if irrationally, associated with the pursuit of personal aims.

He discreetly interrogated the entirely courteous and affable
acting-director of operations, and from him learnt that the individual of his notice was regarded quite as a free-lance, with
liberty of coming and going, as of taking as much or as little hand
in the excavations as he pleased, subject, of course, to the usual
reticences outside. Such privileges could not decently be withheld. He was one of the big men of archaeology; with the standard that belonged to that rank. He was there (he fancied) for a
particular detail of information, which, however, remained his
own secret. There was no question of his being an unauthorised
reporter for the Press or the societies. So far as the acting-director
knew, Arsinal had never written a public paragraph, or read a
paper, in his life. Personally he was not very well acquainted with
the man. Saltfleet gathered that his informant's attitude was one
of slightly peevish toleration.

He came to speech with Arsinal himself for the first time on
the third evening after his arrival. The active disinterring of the
past had sufficiently interested him to make him decide to stay on
so long. His mountaineering name was his passport to the acting
chief, who, indeed, seemed to feel a pleasure in explaining things
to him. Arsinal, on the evening in question, was standing in the
dusk, contemplating the now obscured valley at the foot of Knossos, from the height above the latter; and there the visitor to the
camp had chanced to mount to him, certainly with no expectation
or wish of encountering him. But naturally words must pass. After
the first involuntary movements of rather vexed surprise on both
their parts—for the evening was very fair and apt for solitude—
they had perforce to exchange nods, whereupon a spell of stiff
silence ensued; when Arsinal, still under reluctance, and with that
strange absent half-yearning look that made him frequently seem
either a saint or an innocent, inquired:

"You are really entering into all this?"

"In a very qualified way, and with a pretty complete ignorance!" returned Saltfleet, smiling. "The excellent Professor has
done what he can to put matters in a nutshell for me, but I fear I
am still quite hazy about his famous three divisions, and three

sub-divisions of each, of Minoan history. The scheme is rather too incredibly mathematical for my practical knowledge of how human affairs go. . . . And then, to accept his word for these nine periods, I am exceedingly at sea concerning the contemporary outside world for each. You assume fourteen hundred years for the whole Minoan empire. That gives you a century and a half for each period. During the entire time, Crete must have run up against Egypt, Babylon, Troy, Athens, Israel, the Hittites, the Phœnicians, the Philistines. Now, to me it is all a welter. I have no dates. . . . I mean this. To comprehend the globe at any given age, we first have to regard its skeleton, its broad outline, the nations pre-eminent, their political aims and interactions. Without all that, we cannot descend to individuals. Well, it is precisely all that, that your chief is very vague about. His nine periods seem to be based on the exceedingly precarious evidence of pots and vases. A future expert may arise to declare that on the contrary such-and-such is the case. So that, altogether, it is too theoretical for a plain person such as I."

Arsinal smiled in turn.

"An archaeologist goes forward on his hands and knees, you must realise. The history is being pieced together too, though slowly." He gestured with a hand towards the nearly invisible palace beneath. "And it is always the glory of these people that they are enthusiastic to spend themselves for the most doubtful chance of any important step forward at all. Here, in Crete, for instance, probably the whole of the historical record was delivered to parchment or wax, which would have been destroyed by fire at the great final downfall of the empire, at the hands of barbarous northern invaders. What record does survive, in the form of inscriptions on clay, is believed to consist merely of civic inventories, etc. The inscriptions are not yet read; but should that prove to be so, put yourself in our position, Mr. Saltfleet."

"Pardon me, but I fancy you aren't quite in the same gallery!"

"How do you mean?"

"You have impressed me as being a trifle less keen than the others here, that is all."

"Perhaps less generally keen."

Saltfleet's eye fixed him through the dusk.

"More expectant, at a venture."

"Of what?"

"My dear man, how do I know? . . . Presumably, of something being unearthed which is to confirm some notion of yours."

"But so are they all expectant. Expectancy is the soul and life of the working archaeologist."

"If you will have it so, it is no business of mine," said Saltfleet.

"Still, I mustn't be uncandid, and I think I understand the sort of distinction you point at. *Their* hopes are free, mine confined; they want anything, I want something—you mean that? It is not untrue. You know, of course, what Knossos, as the Minoan capital, stands for?"

"I've no clear information."

"For the cult of the Great Mother. . . . The island was a principal seat of her worship. Well then, as a man whose whole responsible life has been devoted to the preparation for the study of that cult, surely it is most natural that I should occasionally have been drawn hither to learn what is going on in the way of new discoveries? Only, the structure, drains, profane pottery, and so forth, of this palace and its compeers elsewhere on the island, do not happen to be in my line; and that must have been responsible for your perplexity on seeing me frequently stand hungry and idle in the midst of a banquet."

Saltfleet bowed.

"And so the case is explained. It remains only for me to apologise for my inquisitiveness."

"I hope you will not. Indeed, I feel honoured by the notice of so distinguished a———" He hesitated for the word.

"Risker of his neck!" laughed the big man. "However, you seem to be more distinguished than I, and the pleasure and honour are mine. Will you have a cigar?"

Arsinal refused civilly, whereupon the other selected one himself from the opened case, and bit and lighted it. The aromatic smoke rose straight up in the still air. The ever-darkening evening was lovely. Stars were creeping into the sky. Neither speaker was in haste to descend from the utter peace of that eminence.

"Then what induced you to take up your particular study in the first instance, Mr. Arsinal?"

The archaeologist straightened his shoulders, and put back his head wearily. The absence of a hat discovered his partial baldness. Otherwise he was dark-haired, shaven, pale and worn-looking, and every third minute drew himself up from his accustomed stoop with that nervous action of squaring his shoulder-blades. Saltfleet gave him a seniority of a few fears over himself; he should be forty or so. He was on the tall side of middle height, thin, obviously delicate, yet gave the impression of having a whole reservoir of moral stamina always at command to supply his deficiencies of physique. It suggested a powerful engine in a frail frame.

It suggested as well, to Saltfleet, a force of will derived from singleness, purity, faith, that should have more in common with the soul of the medieval saints and martyrs than with the meaner drive that devotes a modern scientist to his science. It was some kind of spirituality. The pained abstraction of his dark-irised, exhausted eyes seemed to proclaim him as belonging to the small eternal band of lonely thinkers, as incapable of communicating their insights before ripened by the years as of co-operating with fellow-workers in the same field, the cause being identical in both cases—the retreat of a noble sleepless spirit to the inner realities of the intellect, that no companion may enter. . . . Saltfleet began to be greatly attracted by him. He judged him unmarried.

Arsinal, too, became partly shaken out of his meditations, that had endured beneath the chat, to note more attentively the insistent personality of this large-framed stranger from the outer world. For Saltfleet was not an individual easy to ignore. The direct vigour of honesty at the back of the electric masterfulness and hardness of his address was very effectual in putting those he talked with on their mettle, as being challenged by a nature essentially at war with feebleness, therefore quick to detect it.

Defended from any such sense of inferiority by his multitude of intellectual problems always urgent for solution, Arsinal nevertheless had to know the shock of contact like the rest, and was roused accordingly. He had heard the man's interesting exploits referred to in camp, his stature and bearing were compelling, and, if he manifestly could not pretend to even the rudiments of archaeological lore, that coming of his to the island a couple of days since was at least in the nature of a courtesy that affected them all. He could not well refuse to be a host of such a guest. Why, indeed, he should be visiting Knossos, to prowl aimlessly about a work of which he was unfitted to understand the first thing, was a puzzle in mental stimuli.

For quite another reason, he was moved to accept this acquaintance not of his seeking. His programmes generally were very much ahead, and all at once it had occurred to him that, could an agreement be struck, Saltfleet might later be extremely useful to him. He must have practical knowledge of the countries north of the Himalayas, as of the special needs and difficulties of travel in them. His help might save Arsinal a load of trouble if and when his half-purposed journey to Tibet should come off. It might be twelve or eighteen months yet, or never. Other clues in the nearer East were first to be taken up, which might obviate the necessity for this hardest trip of all. And so he repressed the excluding answer almost on his tongue to Saltfleet's last question, to substitute one more amicable, if still reticent.

"The study of the ancient conception and worship of the Great Mother? The goal has been before me for very many years—since my school days, in fact."

"Surely a quaint ambition for a schoolboy!"

"Need it surprise? For if we could see into the heads of all schoolboys, we should gain many a strange sight. There and nowhere else, Mr. Saltfleet, is the grand mine of all the enthusiasms that presently are to move and transform the sluggish world. Perhaps no more than one in ten thousand may struggle through to maturity, but would not it be lamentable on that account to jeer at and discourage the whole display of fantasy? One might even assert, remembering the pressing need of high imagination in life, that its promotion should be made a principal point of education. More than a few English public schools, I fear, would require to change their methods."

"What gives a boy his twist?"

"In each of us, you know, there is a marriage of inherited characters, with resulting children, in the shape of new characters. And sometimes these new characters may swell smoothly and regularly from the germ; which is the way of genius. But at other times they may lie dormant and unsuspected for quite a number of years, until suddenly released by some fate of outside accident. And that, it has seemed to me, has always been the way of the world's outstanding saints and religious reformers. Paul was an instance."

"Which method has been yours, may I ask?"

"The second. . . . When a lad of sixteen, I experienced a night-vision, which left an ineffaceable stamp on my mind."

"May it be communicated?"

"I have never thought that I could tell anyone."

"Then don't break your rule for me," returned Saltfleet good-naturedly. . . . "Though, indeed, I am no scoffer at such things. Especially it would be inconsistent in me since a little psychic adventure I had in Athens just before coming here. It fetched me here, in fact. I heard something like a voice, and saw something like a shape—so here I am, awaiting my next instructions!"

Arsinal viewed him keenly.

"Yet one would scarcely connect you with such a habit of superstition."

"Nor is it a habit. Only, the single word, CRETE, came into my head, as if a command; and was succeeded by a sort of flashing shadow in front of my eyes, that seemed as though it might be a woman's."

"A woman's?"

"Yes. Though, if you can understand the distinction, I caught nothing in the way of skirts or smooth features. It was something big, formless, swift, and yet feminine—nearer than that I can't give it. . . . And it has been my first case of the kind. But what becomes of our boasted sense and solidity of nature, Mr. Arsinal, when one faint wave from a phantom world can upset all the plans of an otherwise rational man, to send him on a purposeless overseas excursion of a hundred leagues!"

"Unhappily, I don't know you, to be able to judge what such an incident might stand for. Yet there is this singularity about it. For me, Crete is so linked to the ancient cult of the Goddess, that I can but regard it as extraordinary in the extreme that its name, sounding in your ears, should have been accompanied or followed by a *womanly* phantasm for your eyes. The association truly has hitherto been unknown to you?"

"In my disgraceful ignorance, till coming on this visit I have only thought of the island in connection with such scholastic wearinesses as Minos and Rhadamanthus, Daedalus and Icarus, the Labyrinth and the Minotaur, Theseus and Ariadne. The maiden Ariadne, I will swear, is nowise responsible for the generating of my apparition."

A minute passed, while Arsinal stood uneasy and thoughtful.

"Perhaps I could now relate my own story, Mr. Saltfleet. Perhaps we really are to be acquainted. You won't let it go further, of course. . . . The thing happened to me in the early hours of a winter morning, in bed. I woke up to behold a tall, draped figure, female and angelic, standing by the bedside, looking, not down, but across me. . . . That conveys nothing of my necessary sensations. How could I describe her, indeed? She seemed not a created being, but a principle, or essence. . . . But when I awoke from *that* awakening—to common life again—I believed that I should know for all my lifetime what a *goddess* might appear to the sight. . . . I searched in every suitable book at my command for mention of the grandest female divinities of antiquity. Too quickly I found that the light Greeks were not the people. And so my work took shape."

"An old-time monk would rather have fastened on one of the saints, or the blessed Virgin herself."

"But mistakenly, so clearly increate was this Being."

There was another long silence, after which Saltfleet commented:

"The pedestal was sublime, if only you have found an adequate statue to erect on it. You can hardly soberly be proposing in these sceptical days to refound a dead female worship. Jeanne d'Arc had a realm to deliver, but realms are no longer delivered so, even if England needed your patriotic services. Without desiring to play the cynic, Mr. Arsinal, I can't see that the adding of a few more tomes to the world's learned library is any such illustrious matter, to demand a special visitation by heaven itself."

"Actually you are right, and my work is a blind work. I don't know where it will lead to. Only, I have written no tomes, and am not contemplating the writing of any. . . . However, there is still this point. For a man who is neither prophet, nor reformer, nor deliverer, it may be a sufficiently worthy labour to rescue from the defiling dust a divine shape of antiquity, though it be not of marble or bronze. In this simple service may rest an importance that none of us alive is to comprehend."

"It may be so, and I wish you the active protection and furtherance of your Goddess in the pursuit. But after Knossos——?"

"My movements will largely depend. For the moment I am essaying what my friends here consider a hopeless task, namely, the deciphering of the Minoan clay-tablet inscriptions without the aid of a bilingual writing. I must not call them uninventive, and yet that is what it may amount to. Still, there is a sort of instinct in these things—one has it, and another has it not. I wish to fancy that I am approaching the solution. How long are you staying, Mr. Saltfleet?"

The other gave a shrug.

"I don't know."

"Unless you have engagements, I would have liked you to stop on for a couple of days longer, by which time I might have had something to report."

"I'm agreeable."

"Please say not a word to anyone about my hope of a speedy success. The world is very interested in these inscriptions, the first interpreting of them will create an enormous excitement in the right quarters, and even popularly; but I am not yet sure that I shall attach my name to that first interpreting."

"You mean, you will suppress your discovery?"

"At present I wish only to retain in my power the doing so if I please."

"Very well. You may rely on my silence."

Arsinal smiled, which queerly beautified his face.

"Your call to Crete was perhaps to me, Mr. Saltfleet. I have already the suggestion to make to you that possibly there may be a joint expedition before us, in another region of the earth altogether. This you may choose to regard as an impertinence, yet I trust you won't. I have in distant contemplation . . . a *hunt*—not of animals . . . in Tibet. You know Tibet?"

"In part."

"It may not come to anything. If it did, it would not be for a year at least. So it is early days to broach the subject of expenses, for instance; but they would of course fall to me. Then you will proceed to inquire where your advantage lies in the proposition, and sincerely, I can't satisfy you. Nor may I appeal to your generosity or sporting spirit, since we are barely acquainted. . . ."

"An archaeological hunt?" asked Saltfleet bluntly.

"Yes. . . . I am not requiring a decision here and now, but only a slight indication of how such a proposal would strike you when the time draws nearer. I will be quite frank. I am no very attractive companion for any man, but, on the other hand, I have few cranks and am comparatively easy to get on with. I know how to respect the moods of other people, I can hold my tongue on occasion, and my temper is fairly equable."

Saltfleet studied his cigar.

"If I were free when you wanted me, I don't know that I should have any objection."

"Thank you!"

"I ask no details, though the connection between Crete and Tibet is rather obscure. Also, any part of the globe I can see at any time for myself, while the question of expenses doesn't enter into it at all. I should put up my share. So it reduces itself to the pleasure of the companionship. Without offence be it said, there are one or two things about you I rather like, Mr. Arsinal. You have long aims, and a full measure of individualism, with very excellent information on a number of first-class topics, I should say; and above all, the aristocratic temper, that detests publicity. I don't think I should be at all bored by a month or so of your society. Nor do I suppose that you would be bored by any society. You appear to possess the shutting-out capacity in supremeness."

"I believe that we should not bore each other," said Arsinal smilingly.

"But as to how you are to get me when wanted—I rarely have addresses. So much we shall have to leave to luck. I am oftener east of the Caspian than elsewhere, and that is nearly all I can tell you."

After a short, unimportant rounding-off talk, they had separated for the night. But a couple of afternoons later Arsinal had stopped his new friend as he strolled idly across the great Central Court of the palace.

"It has come with a suddenness I hardly expected when I last spoke to you," he announced, with eyes that could not conceal their unwonted sparkle. "You are still interested, I take it?"

"Yes."

Saltfleet understood at once that he had gained the clue to the Minoan inscriptions. He had also the *savoir-faire* to grasp that their present stand in the burning sunlight of the open excavations was as unsuitable as could be for the divulgence of a professional secret of such importance, though no other ear might be within a score of yards. He added quietly, therefore:

"Where shall we talk?"

"It is scarcely a conspiracy—it is merely a withholding. Yet these confabulations in public may give rise to . . . a suspicion of the fact. So I suggest the same spot as before, at the same time, this evening. It will not interfere with arrangements?"

"No, it will do very well."

"A clay was very kindly lent to me for study. It is marked with

the double axes, that have been generally supposed to be a symbol of the Goddess—which is why I fixed upon this particular
tablet, of many. It may turn out to be the only significant one of
them all. I need not ask if you have spoken to anybody?"

"I passed you my word."

"I know. I merely wish to say that the interdict still holds. This
clay happens to have a very strong message—but for the right
person alone. To broadcast it would be something extremely like
desecration. Sooner or later, of course, the inscriptions will be
independently read; but I am anxious that this one shall never be
read. Perhaps I shall take an opportunity to destroy it."

Saltfleet took a single glance at the speaker's eyes, and saw
the strange light in them. He nodded.

"I am glad you have the spirit. Anything which is to deprive
the crowd will always be approved by me."

"It is how I have understood you from the first."

"Since the world has thrown overboard its religious employ-
ments, it has far too much time on its hands. Again, since aristocratic sentiment is dead, it makes a very undignified use of that
time. This cheap mania for nervous thrills, which is the same
thing as the excitement of bodily danger, without the mortal
risk—it is what has come to take the place of the fear of God and
the scorn of amazement. You can't cure the propensity at this
stage of civilisation, you can only help to disappoint it on occasion. . . . I myself am not *of* the public, though *in* it. But if you
prefer to make no exception even in my case, I beg you not to
consider yourself bound by your request to me to stay on. Perhaps
I should have done so anyway, and the time I have spent here has
by no means been wasted."

"That I am glad of. But no, I do wish to make an exception of
you. My opinion of you is already formed, Mr. Saltfleet, and you
are different from the rest. . . . So I may rely on seeing you up
above, this evening?"

"I will be there."

Again, then, they had parted.

XVI

The Meeting

Saltfleet's interest in Arsinal had deepened as a result of that second short conference. It put him in a new light, that disclosed a hitherto unsuspected moral rigidness. His preparedness to smother, if necessary, one of the world's learned monuments in obedience to a higher law which would be vilified by all, entailing as it did a deliberate breach of trust and a violation of common honesty, seemed to throw the purely intellectual side of his character into stronger relief; and yet this intellectual side alone surely represented a tremendous nature.

Again the friendly chief of operations had consented to expand upon the subject of his wholly distinguished, if somewhat unwanted, volunteer helper, whose expertness in their common trade, indeed, might be just a shade too remote, too self-centred—*claustral*, perhaps, was the word—to render him of that use to them which his presence there had almost given them the right to expect. Without much pressure, he completed a rapid sketch of Arsinal's precise place in the realm of working archaeology.

He was skilled in the remains of the three or four Stone Ages, possessed an enviable knowledge of the pre-classical antiquities of the Near East, had (he believed) investigated as far afield as the Euphrates, India and Ceylon, was a leading authority on the ever-mysterious Etruscan culture, appeared to have dipped pretty deeply into Philology (implying, of course, an adequate acquaintance with a host of ancient and current linguistic formations and vocabularies), had handled and measured doubtless many hundreds of crania in his time—for what all that was worth . . . and, to state it briefly, should be all the more efficient in his own peculiar *métier* of exhuming, by reason of his multifariousness, for which not every spade-worker had leisure.

No, he could not be physically strong, but then, even for a delicate man, there were always ways and means of conserving one's health and economising one's vigour. Social engagements and town pleasures were answerable for a large wastage of energy in too many folk who should be sticking to their jobs. Then the law of accretion was very kind—the habit of amassing scientific facts induced the facility. So there was much that was admirable, but no miracle, in the position which this young man of forty-one or two had made for himself. The position was definite, though so far he might have no honours. For that matter, what sensible person cared two straws about honours or degrees? As for his ultimate ambition or ambitions, that appeared to be very much his own secret. It was quite on the cards that he held a monumental work up his sleeve—if so, it would certainly find its professional public. Married? He fancied not. Married men, in this branch of science, usually had their wives hovering somewhere on the horizon. . . .

But it was less the mass of exact knowledge thus patiently accumulated that humbled Saltfleet in mind, than the sublime doggedness with which Arsinal had inch by inch attacked and mastered that half-a-world of wisdom, merely in order to reach his mystical goal at last. Such an enterprise surpassed almost anything he had ever heard of in the way of special preparation. Without sympathy from a living soul, moreover, he could bear the deadweight of this secret aim in silence, while continuing more finely human and simple than other *savants* having nothing but straight careers to occupy them. His avoidance of the distinctions that should have come his way was probably symptomatic. He would naturally refuse even this kind of payment for labours that had never been undertaken from a social motive.

Accordingly, Saltfleet sought his rendezvous with curiously anticipative feelings, and began to see it taking shape that no more surprising experience on the island than this communion with a most exceptional man was destined to follow his occult seizure in Athens. He thought of that oddly precipitate offer of a joint trip to Tibet, and was now more anxious to learn its object. But of the message of the Minoan inscription he thought less. It was the man's grip and resolution that interested him; his superstition seemed even slightly insane. The disinterring of a far-back and forgotten female worship gave him no thrill, and it was still inconceivable what Arsinal proposed to do with his restored Goddess, when she should be in the full panoply of her coloured robes, observances, and metaphysics, in the modern upper world. The doing was more respectable than the to-be-done. There was a sort of effeminacy in the obsession, too, for a man. And still this softness, by adding one more plane to his strange variety of nature, did but increase the fascination of the whole problem. . . .

Arsinal was waiting for him. His manner was as nearly impatient as perhaps it ever could be, and salutes had barely been exchanged before he dived into the deep of his business.

"Here I have written down the English of my clay-writing," he announced, displaying a sheet of paper. "It is considerably paraphrased, since the Minoan construction is unwieldy; but I have forced nothing, and, I hope, have omitted nothing of the essential sense. . . . I will preface the reading of it by a single word of explanation, Mr. Saltfleet. I told you that this tablet is marked with the symbolic double axes of the Mother. Well then, I theorise that the double axe, or *Labrus* (from which, incidentally, no doubt has come the name, Labyrinth), besides inviting the Goddess and warning off profaneness, may be the conventional representation of the fractured halves of the stone you are to hear of. Meteoric stones, as a matter of fact, unworked to any use, have sometimes been found in association with rude figurines of the Mother. The connection is real, and therefore I opine that the double axe as well may be a sign of the descent from heaven. Should it prove not to be so, it will not matter, and yet I am hoping that my instinct has not misled me in this thing. . . . Now let us start. Perhaps my writing will be more legible to myself. . . ."

Accordingly, after the shortest pause for voice-clearing, Arsinal went on to read aloud from his paper, while the other, pulling thoughtfully at a newly-lighted cigar, listened in silent erectness.

"The scribe, obviously, is some temple-priest of the Goddess. He writes:

'That which came from the stars, and is full of words of its home. That which unwillingly flees from its bride in the west. That which has ever brought fulfilment and ill-hap to him who has borne it. That which the seer has said shall know no change until that it has united another man and another woman, of whom shall be born a son greater than they, greater than all mankind, who shall be the saviour. It alone of all the temple treasures has known the Mother. But a son of the Hatti, robbing the treasury by stealth and wickedness, carried it into the east, and Psor, a secretary, followed him, and slew him, but it is lost.'"

Arsinal ceased reading, to refold and put away the sheet. He glanced at Saltfleet interrogatively.

"I think the purport is fairly plain? No stone is actually mentioned, yet what but a meteorite could have come from above? And 'its bride in the west'—to what can that refer but the removed half of a fractured whole?"

"A meteorite with mystical properties."

"Dare we, with our limitations, deny the possibility of such? . . . Then, 'a son of the Hatti'—that is, a Hittite. So that our half-stone was taken into Asia Minor, where I have next to seek its traces. All this, you must be told, is not entirely new ground to me. The importance of the inscription, for me, lies in its prophecy, which *is* a statement more definite than any I have yet encountered.

"It is exceedingly queer how this fancy of a stone in connection with the Mother has always played its part. Zeus, in the Cretan legend, would have been swallowed by his father, Kronos—as the preceding five of his brothers and sisters had been swallowed—had not his mother, Rhea, the Great Mother of the ancients, substituted a stone, which was swallowed instead. When he grew up, Zeus recovered the stone from the belly of Kronos, and deposed him from his rank of chief of the gods. The stone was afterwards worshipped, where it stood, near the temple of Delphi. . . . Again, during the war with Hannibal, the Romans fetched with great pomp from Pessinus, in Galatia, the stone that was called the Mother of the Gods, causing it to be escorted from Ostia to the city by young Scipio, at the head of a body of respectable matrons. . . . In the Scoto-Irish legend, too, the Cailleach, or Old Wife, the mother of men and demons, changes herself into a grey stone overlooking the waters. In India, the goddess Durga is represented by a stone, to which animals are sacrificed. . . . And in the story of Deukalion and Pyrrha, the pair, being divinely commanded to cover their heads and throw the bones of their mother behind them in order to repopulate the earth, after the destructive nine-days' flood sent by the wrath of Zeus, interpret the command as meaning the stones of the soil, which accordingly they cast; and from Deukalion's spring up men, and from Pyrrha's, women. . . .

"So many quite unrelated variations on an original theme not given, Mr. Saltfleet, do at least establish one significant fact—that this connection between a goddess and a stone, probably meteoric, must date back in conception to exceedingly early times. In the rough rendering I have just given you of my own inscription, the phrase runs: 'It alone of all the temple treasures has known the Mother.' If such a temple treasure originally came from the west, where its 'bride', or equivalent fragment, was, then a Stone Age happening would seem to be indicated, for whether the inscription in question were graved in 2000 or 1500 B.C., the only still earlier western peoples to whom the statement could apply must have been the men of the caves and flint quarries. . . . And now you will begin to understand better the definite nature of my researches. I am not chasing a dream, but an event of the world. This phenomenal stone of the goddess has truly existed, may be still in existence, and may retain its magic and wonder. I am seeking it."

"But isn't it remarkable that the story has failed to come through in its purity? A first-rate miracle should surely stick in the memory of the human race."

"So have an infinite number of the world's truest and mightiest ideas failed to come through. Indeed, a certain coarse sand of robustness appears to be requisite, if an idea, or an ideal, is to come through. The jewels of eternity must be imbedded in a sort of grossness, if they are to live a thousand years on earth. Often and often have I thought that the world's greatest names do not represent the world's greatest achievements. . . . Because, for instance, the Mother has not survived, that is not to say that during a very extended period she did not set the rule to whole nations of earnest-minded men and women. But then came the fatal day—as always it comes—when spiritually-inferior persons appropriated the externals of culture, and scornfully refused the rest. The statues of the mysterious Queen of Heaven were overturned, and the Olympians came in, in a sunrise of blood."

"Is this history?"

"Yes, it is history. There was the Dark Age after the downfall of Rome; but there was also the Dark Age dating from the destruction of this palace of Knossos. . . . It should have been as splendid, and as horrible, as the combustion of dead suns in collision, with the slow, tortured emergence from their gases and elements of another luminary, more fiercely glorious than either of the old. It should have been, I supposed, as brimful of human brutality, cruelty, shocking anguish and hellishness of every kind, as all the succeeding centuries—twice as many—lumped, until the coming of that second Dark Age introducing medieval Europe. And yet both have been periods of regeneration. From the earlier shaped itself the Greek and Roman world; from the later, our modern group of Western nations."

He went on:

"Perhaps, *pace* the public optimists of the newspaper press, still one more Dark Age is nearly due. I don't know what you are in politics or outlook. It does seem to me that mankind is once again becoming brown and monkey-like, childish, malicious, chattering, and unspiritual, after having twice been raised to a height by the invading hordes of yellow-haired giants from the north. The Goths, Vandals, Franks, Saxons, were one such flood, the Achaeans and Dorians another. Achilles was as yellow-haired and blue-eyed as Hengist. I myself am dark, so have no bias in dwelling on this extraordinary ennobling quality in savages outwardly merely bloody-minded and greedy. . . . And it goes deeper. For it is usual to speak of the vigour of those northern invaders—as if the men they displaced were effete. The subdued peoples, in a number of cases at least, were entirely vigorous in the arts and sciences, in practical constructional work, in law-making, and civic pursuits generally; only they were unwarlike. And still, but for those successive bands of furious blue-eyed potential lords, and kings, and feudal landowners, the temples of Greece and the Gothic cathedrals could never have arisen. A spiritual germ was under all that horror of throat-cutting and ravishing.

"No otherwise, Mr. Saltfleet, may our modern culture, surpassing though we think it, stand in invisible need of impregnation by yet new yellow-haired barbarians, could they anywhere be found. Strange fresh churches to the All-High, not inferior in sublimity to those of the grand classical and Gothic religious architects, would certainly spring up. . . . There might be losses too." He sighed. . . . "In Knossos here, for example, it was little that men were killed a few years before their natural term by the shipborne Achaeans from the mainland, that wives and daughters were carried shrieking off to shame and slavery, or that the palace was left to be licked to its bones by the monstrous flames; but that an ancient faith of very singular beauty and truth should be so thoroughly extirpated, that in its peculiar home and sanctuary nearly the sole explicit record of its existence should be represented by this scrap of paper in my pocket—*that* is the tragedy!"

"I think you are a poet, Mr. Arsinal."

"No, no! . . . For a poet *wills* to feel, while my feelings are painful and extorted. I am an overstrained and not strong man. I have undertaken the ploughing of a field perhaps past my strength. . . . I seek a primeval Golden Age, that possibly has never been. It begins to appear that *always* have existed these persons of mundane mind and communal tendencies in charge of the affairs of the day. It discourages me. . . . I have not wished to believe that this ancient earth has always been governed by the unimaginative-sane of the human race, knowing just what they wanted, wanting nothing impossible of attainment, steadily going forward to get it, constructing indifferently aqueducts, castles, pots, glass beads, dresses, edicts, with the greatest talent and energy . . . true instinctives, impelled by much the same processes as ants, bees and spiders. I have wished to believe that the vulgar noon was preceded by a wild dawn. . . . Further, I have wished to think that the inherited memory of that dawn afflicts the souls of more of us than outward signs suggest. I have wished to think that it may be responsible for much so-called *failure*.

"But I don't feel myself competent to decide who in this world is a failure, and who a success. I will even say that the validity of such a classifying of the moral judgment is inadmissible, since, religiously speaking, a man can neither succeed nor fail; he can, I suppose, only approach to or recede from the Godhead. But that must mean that the values of the world are wrong. We are like domestic fowls, picking up crumbs amid glorious scenery. In that sense, the fowl that picks up the largest number of crumbs may be called the most successful.

"So, this standpoint of mine being taken as the foundation, Mr. Saltfleet, can you suggest to me a more profitable work—I won't say, a more socially-useful, or a more charitable, work—than the one I am engaged upon, namely, the restoration, if it be possible, of a deity who in many respects already appears holier and milder than anything before Christ—I won't hesitate to add, than Christ himself? For the Mother, I am aware, has by no means always been conceived as such a type of everything that is loveliest in womanhood, but the terror of her power has sometimes predominated in savage intelligences, and she has even been made to be an obscene lover of blood and devourer of children. A creed, however, must be judged by its highest, not its lowest, and what I myself have seen in a vision has taught me for all time how the finest and noblest of mankind may anciently have represented her. I ask again, then. It isn't for me to recast a religion, but even were my quest purely egoistic, should I in your opinion be more importantly employed, for instance, in running a factory or newspaper, or voting after my leader in Parliament?"

"Instead of answering the unanswerable, may I rather put a question of my own?"

"Do so."

"Knossos, I understand you, was destroyed by the wild ancestors, just arrived from the north, of the classical Greeks, who were a blue-eyed and fair-haired race. Its religion of the Mother-Goddess was destroyed with it, though it may have survived elsewhere. But then, how came it that the best of human stocks failed to adopt this best of human worships, so ready to their hand? Or am I inquiring something stupid?"

"A pirate, holding in his hand a sword dripping blood, is scarcely in a condition to be converted to any creed; but afterwards was too late. In Asia the worship of the Mother degenerated rapidly to orgies unworthy of fighting-men, and had it not been so, the Greeks themselves too quickly went to pieces in a climate unsuited to northerners."

"You have a fancy that it may be in Tibet—your stone?"

"It is one of half-a-dozen places that I have my eye upon."

"But for the other places you don't need my company?"

Saltfleet subconsciously made of the reply to this query a test. Should Arsinal agree to have him for these unnecessary trips as well, or should he make false excuses for not wanting him, he felt that somehow he would still be disappointed in the man. His conception of his character at the present stage of their acquaintance was that under all circumstances he would pursue the unhesitating straight line to his ends, regardless of opposing claims, whether of friendship, or honour, or social duty. Apart from such a backbone of strength, Saltfleet did not particularly wish to know him. And therefore he found himself hoping for the rebuff, and was more than content with its actual uncompromising emphasis.

"I invited you to Tibet," said Arsinal, "because you know the country, and I don't. But the other visits are to be to districts of the Asiatic Near East with which I am possibly even more intimate than yourself. I have been there often enough, and am acquainted with the language, the people, and the travelling facilities. I am to investigate in the ancient Phrygia, Galatia, Lydia, and Caria. Your society, I tell you at once, Mr. Saltfleet, would be a pleasure, but also a nuisance. When I am upon a clue, I am frequently unapproachable. And so we will leave it at that."

Saltfleet shrugged a shoulder through the darkness, and smiled.

"As you like. You are leaving here immediately, I take it?"

"There is now no more for me to do here, and I shall be off to-morrow."

"Then I too. . . . But tell me. Your stone—will you recognise it when you see it? Do you know its appearance at all?"

"I am not sufficiently advanced to have met with any description of it; and yet it should contain its own evidences of authenticity. I have no alarms on that account."

"And having found it . . . ?"

"If, as I assume, it is the half of a broken whole, I should next have to seek its fellow."

"In the west?"

"Yes."

"You will need to be immortal, pretty well!" laughed Saltfleet. "Decidedly, I chose an easier job than yours, in climbing mountains!"

"Since you introduce that, may I hazard that you have not yet found your true work, Mr. Saltfleet?"

"Indeed!"

"Go on scaling heights, and imbibing purity; but still, you cannot be in the world for that. I have a trick of faces. This is not impertinence? . . . You should be a leader of men, rather. Do you know your stock?"

"As well as another. I have a good bit of your admirable northern blood in me, from both sides—though where to lay my hand on an unemployed swarm of yellow-haired savages waiting for direction, I can't quite tell!"

"No, I am not so mad as that," returned Arsinal, with a whimsical smile. "I only mean, it is remarkable how your personality has impressed me in our two or three talks. To no other person have I ever opened myself so freely. I have heard it said that with each two conversing individuals there is a superior and an inferior; but this surely cannot apply to us. I have the reposeful attitude to you as to a beautiful equal."

"We are both rather proud, I judge," had been Saltfleet's comment on that, "so if this coming-together of ours has really been destined, it was perhaps a *sine qua non* it should start from equality. There are only two virtues that I make a point of practising. One is disinterestedness, and the other is magnanimity. They are half-brothers. If you have them too, we may go through without quarrelling."

"In any case, we shall not quarrel," had said the other, closing the conversation, "for I shall always be too employed, and you, unless I am hopelessly out in my reading of your lines, too disdainful of the customary bones of contention." . . .

Saltfleet entered upon the moor, and ceased his reminiscences. Hardly anything was to be seen; merely the rocks, turf, gorse, ferns and heather within a circle of a few yards, all appearing grey and wet. The fog had become very thick. He turned up his coat-collar, while reflecting unpleasantly that from now onwards his chances of striking Drapier were extremely small.

At some time after twelve he reached the shoulder of the hill that faced the invisible Tor. Sensing that his destination lay beyond the dip at his feet, he began the descent, regardless of the slope's small slippery perils. At the bottom he crossed the stream, and at once met the beginning of the rockier steep, which could but be Devil's Tor itself. Without pause he went up, but never arrived at the top.

That girl's mention of a shattering of rocks had stayed in his mind, and, looming through the fog that here was nearly solid, there came to him, one after the other, two giant blocks which, as he passed by, he could distinguish were newly poised. It was the confirmation for him that he was on the right hill. Then, however, a third stone monster increased to darkness and definition—and something in connection with it moved him suddenly to run up towards what he saw. Underneath the granite mass appeared spread out the froglike figure of a lying man. . . .

The man's face was to the ground, and he was fairly

pinned . . . probably dead. . . . The colour of his hair was red. So had been Drapier's—it must be he. His form was quite still and stiff; the face entirely hidden.

Saltfleet stood by, reflecting how to dislodge the block without causing further hurt: though, indeed, the tragedy obviously was consummated. The only way was to shove it off the victim's back forcibly, further downhill. . . .

It needed less exertion than he had supposed. The great rock thudded away through the fog, out of sight, towards the valley. He gently lifted the head a few inches in order to identify the face. Yes, it was Drapier's—but its colour was grey, and the eyes were glazed in death. The expression was not terrified, but stern. . . . Saltfleet then tested the heart, though only as a matter of form. There was no whisper of a beat. The dead man had spilt little blood.

He stood up, to rehearse what now he had to do. The first thing, of course, was for the body to be fetched down—but he thought not to the house. There was that young Miss Fleming there, and her mother. Dunn, of the "Bell," must suggest a place; and attend to the whole business. The news need not be broken to the women till he was brought down and things were decently fixed. . . .

While he continued meditatively to eye the tragical form at his feet, he came to regard it as queer that the right hand should be clenched. It entered his consciousness that the action was unnatural. A man struck from behind, and falling forward, should have the instinct to *open* his fingers. . . . His perplexity became a curiosity to learn if the fist were empty or held something. . . .

Afterwards, however, he could not determine whether his identification of the thing recovered had been preceded by an inspiration of the fact, or had been completely unexpected on his first glimpse behind those prised-open fingers. It was Arsinal's stone. Only once before had he held it in his hand, but, finding it where he now did, there could be no mistake about it. Standing up again, he gazed at it on his own open palm for several blank seconds, and thought it the most astonishing solution of his difficulty. . . .

He slipped it into his pocket. There was nothing more to do on the spot.

He covered the dead man's head; then, having glanced at his watch, set off quickly down the hillside, to get back to the village.

XVII

Ordeal

It was after one o'clock when Saltfleet passed through the hotel entrance of the "Bell," and sought Dunn in his office.

The proprietor was a man turned fifty, short, pale, smooth-skinned and bearded, with shrewd brown eyes that still required no glasses. He was one of those safe, judicious persons to be found in rural communities, whose respectability, financial standing and personal weight, joined to a lifelong intimacy with local affairs and histories, render them, even apart from public office, the headmen of their district, naturally to be consulted in cases demanding a knowledge of procedure or the quick obtaining of special assistance. Saltfleet, on his first arrival that morning, had instantly recognised the type—the competent intelligence of the man, with its inevitable limitations, and his willingness to shoulder whatever practical responsibility should confront him in the course of the day's work. He approved his quietly respectful caution of address, judged his resources to be sufficient, and so, from the first minute of that detestable hillside find, had determined to surrender all the consequent morbid arrangements to his hands.

Now, by an impatient gesture, he stopped the attempted offer of service to refreshment, straightway to launch his news.

"Dunn, there has been a bad accident on Devil's Tor. I mentioned I was going round to Whitestone, to find a Mr. Drapier. You didn't seem to know him personally."

"No, sir, I don't. Dear me! what's happened?"

"I was sent on after him to Devil's Tor, from the house. You are probably aware the place was struck by lightning a couple of nights ago, and some rocks were dislodged. Well, one of them, temporarily perched midway down the slope, started for the rest of the journey this morning, catching Drapier very nastily. . . . There is nothing to be done—he's dead. But how can he be brought down?"

Dunn's pale face, in his disinterested agitation, grew yet paler. He was already standing, pen in hand.

"This is very terrible news, sir. Are you sure . . ."

"Unhappily, yes. It was a beast of a boulder, and caught him squarely from behind."

"Have they been told at the house?"

"No, I came straight here. No one has been told."

"Then you want me to see to it, sir?"

"If you will."

"I'll get on to it at once. There will be a hurdle wanted, and four men. A lorry can take them as far as the road goes. I'll 'phone the doctor, and the police, besides. You won't go away, sir?"

"No. And as I suspect I shall have to give evidence at the inquest, perhaps I'd better fix up a couple of rooms here at once—a bedroom and private sitting-room. . . . Then, another thing before you vanish, Dunn! Drapier—where do you propose to bring him to?"

The proprietor's face fell into guarded hesitation.

"You suggest, sir. . ."

"That there will be neither advantage of convenience nor humanity in imposing this additional excruciation on his friends."

"I see your point, sir, of course." . . . Dunn rubbed his cheek in perplexity.

"You probably have some suitable outbuilding. If they dispute your charge afterwards, refer it to me."

"No, it's not that at all, but my trade. And they mayn't wish it, at the house."

"There will be ample time to countermand the arrangement if it isn't desired. I think it will be desired."

"You are to break the news to them yourself, sir, as the friend of Mr. Drapier?"

"Yes, I'll do that."

"Then you won't go up again with the men?"

"I don't want to. The spot should be findable without me. It's half-way up this side of the Tor, where all the boulders have tumbled."

"The district coroner might be over on Saturday—the day after to-morrow. The inquests are mostly held at the Institute here."

"Very well. I am staying. And the other accommodation?"

"Well, sir, I won't absolutely say it can't be managed, if you are convinced . . ."

"I'm convinced that it will be an act of Christian charity, Dunn."

"I would certainly like to spare the ladies and the old gentleman all I can, sir. Then we will leave it like that. . . . I must be off at once. You too, I suppose?"

"Soon. Let them get their lunch over in peace."

"Follow me upstairs, then, sir, and I'll show you your rooms before I go. Or a small tonic to steady you, first!"

"Send me up a bottle of any whisky, with a siphon."

The sitting-room was a rather cheerless apartment on the first floor, overlooking the village street. Saltfleet identified it at once as his prison of unutterable boredom for the next couple of days. He wondered if he should send for Arsinal, to hear by word of mouth his account of their extraordinary escape from an unexpected bog; but would not trust the public wires from a place about to be so suddenly full of ears, eyes, and tongues, and believed that later in the day he might be able to slip down to Plymouth for an hour, and dispatch his news from there. He drank some whisky, looked repeatedly at his watch, once or twice drew out for inspection the stone he had recovered from the dead man's hand, and at last, for sheer want of occupation, went to his other room to lay out the few necessaries he had brought down in case of detention.

At two o'clock Dunn was still not returned to report. Saltfleet hastily swallowed some more whisky, put on his hat, and left the room and the hotel. The life of the street was quiet and normal. Intelligence of the tragedy could not as yet be generally abroad.

It simplified matters that the same servant opened the door to him as last time. Without delay she brought him to the room where he had been before. In less than a minute the mistress of the house came in to him.

Her manner was of controlled agitation, and her eyes fastened themselves on his face searchingly and anxiously. Ingrid's apparition had been strange and ghastly, while Hugh had not returned to lunch. Peter was no more than fifteen minutes out of the house; by Ingrid's urgent request, to seek him on the moor as far as Devil's Tor. Now he, Saltfleet, was back so unexpectedly, and it could surely only mean that he had bad news of Hugh! . . .

Something stony and inaccessible in the caller's look sent her heart down in the certainty that he was here as an evil guest.

"Have you seen Hugh?" she asked, in a hissing whisper, that sounded unreal to herself.

Saltfleet glanced at the door, to make sure it was shut.

"Please sit down!" But Helga continued standing.

"What's the matter?"

"I am sorry to have to report that Drapier has met with an accident on Devil's Tor."

An involuntary cry escaped from her. "Oh dear! . . . Then it has happened! . . . What——"

"You will be better sitting."

"No, no!—I am not to be foolish. But please tell me quickly! . . ."

"I got to the hill, and half-way up it. It was very obscured by fog. Apparently, one of the loose blocks thrown down the other day started moving again, and caught him from behind unawares."

Helga put a hand on her heart.

"He is dead?"

"I fear so," was his low answer.

"He is *certainly* dead?"

Saltfleet bowed. She turned away, and covered her face with her two hands, but not to weep. Then, when she came back, its expression was markedly harder and sharper for him.

"Who has been told? Has a doctor certified death?"

"One should be on his way up there now from the village. I have handed everything over to Dunn, of the 'Bell.'"

"He was *so* when you got there?"

"Yes; I found him lying."

"Still living?"

"No, life was gone already—I should say, not many minutes before."

"Was the death from injury, or shock?"

"He was badly hurt. On the other hand, I would imagine his heart was sound enough."

"Would it have been instantaneous?"

"I cannot quite decide that, but his sufferings must at least have been very short."

"What is the nature of the injury?"

"The spine, and no doubt some of the internal organs."

"Was no one else up there?"

"No; I should have been the first and only one to discover him."

"Your evidence, of course, will be required at the inquest."

"Of course," said Saltfleet. "And I have already made arrangements to stop at the 'Bell,' in order to be in readiness. . . . For the rest, Mrs. Fleming, I am entirely at your service, in case you wish to send for me at any time. I have taken it on myself to have Drapier temporarily lodged at an annex of the 'Bell.' I fancied you would wish it. You need not discuss that now with me, but as soon as Dunn is free, I shall send him round to you."

"If you please. It is quite essential that I should have an immediate talk with him."

The flint was not mentioned between them. Saltfleet, in the assurance that it was already securely in his possession, had nothing more to gain by declaring the fact, whereas the moment was inappropriate; but Helga could not trust herself to address this suddenly fearful man except shortly, to learn from him what she had to learn, and then at once dismiss him.

All her efforts were towards maintaining her outward composure. She felt as if the flesh of her face were being flayed from her soul, leaving her appalling, wicked, indefensible thoughts exposed to the cold glare of his eye. . . . Hugh's presentiment of death, Ingrid's vision of his ghostly return, her own unreasoning fear of this man from the first, they were all parts of one supernatural predetermined event; and *therefore* her thoughts were justified; and the times would correspond so terribly. It would be about forty minutes, or little less, from Saltfleet's leaving the house to her daughter's vision; his legs were long, and the distance was three miles. She dared not, while he was still in the room, go on blindly wrestling with these diabolical imaginations. She must push them away from her wholly, wholly! . . .

And always the same things were to happen to her in her life. Like a very far-off scene, but oh! so vividly dark and clear, was that time when, still with years and years before her, one had come to break the news to her of poor Dick's hunting crash; and now this was the same. . . . But that had left her poor, and this, rich. So grimly ironical was fortune! She did not want his money, and Ingrid had been right to say so. . . .

Why wasn't Saltfleet demanding his property? It must be always in his head, and now that there was to be no more obstruction . . . could the deliberate refraining be from delicacy? —or was he fearing to put it to the test, fearing to be confronted? . . . And she—if she could have spoken of it now, still Ingrid held the stone, and she too must first be prepared. Surely, she would not break in on them in the room, as she had done before. He must go—yes, he must go! . . .

"Then there is nothing more that I can do for you till then?" asked Saltfleet gravely. He sensed her new antipathy to him, and could even suspect its monstrous cause, but at such a time a woman's head would naturally be flooded with wildness and confusion, that must presently subside; and the facts were on their way. He was sorrier for her distress than indignant with her folly.

"No, nothing," was her faint answer. But the faintness was still hard, while her eyes continued to wander, with a hunted look, everywhere except to his person. "I will say what else I have to say to Mr. Dunn. Will you please ask him to see me personally? My uncle is old, and I do not wish him to be troubled. . . . There is only one more thing I would like to know, before you go. You say this dreadful accident has happened on Devil's Tor. How can you be so sure?"

"I am going in part upon your daughter's instruction to me of the way, and in part upon the number of recently-lodged rocks down the hillside."

She detained him no longer. But on his way back to the inn, Saltfleet conceived an inspiration concerning Drapier's unnaturally-closed fist. Had he been examining Arsinal's flint while slowly descending the hill, his palm would have been open; while his preoccupation would also have made him unaware of the great block bounding towards him from the rear, until there was no more time to get clear. Then, at the instant before the fatal impact, Drapier's unreflecting instinct would have been to secure his treasure by closing his fingers over it.

A fascinating talisman, since he was unable to leave it even when walking on the moor! And his determination to try to keep it for himself; and Arsinal's more considered valuation of it. God knew *he* had spent enough of his life and money to get it. The inherent enchantment must be there, so to magnetise two adult men, unconnected, of quite different natures and avocations. Arsinal must have heard of its strangeness beforehand; he would not have excited himself thus over a mere souvenir of a dead creed. . . . Then if others could discover its magic, why not himself? At the "Bell" he would have more than enough leisure. . . .

But at Whitestone, alone in the refuge of her own room, Helga was wrestling with her womanishness, that she was apprised once more by this blow was always to rise against her fancied strength of character and calmness in the hour of black crisis. She only of those in the house knew of this awful shell about to explode within it; while up on the moor Hugh was lying crushed, bloody, neglected . . . and the room's walls seemed to crush her too! . . . She had hated that Saltfleet should be with her, and facing her, but now that he was gone she realised the support of his vigour. He had at least been a man, while she was the weakest of weak women. Now she must begin her loathsome peregrination of the house, or some second blundering messenger from the callous practical world would anticipate her. . . .

As she still attempted to drag her feet from the room, Ingrid entered to her; and appeared, by an indefinable change in her face, to be preinformed of the tragedy. She regarded her mother in silence, and Helga could not speak.

"Mr. Saltfleet has been here again," the girl at last said, "and he must have brought bad news of Hugh with him. I can see that he has. Won't you tell me, mother?"

"Yes!" . . . Helga mastered her sensation of choking, and proceeded: "Yes, my dear—he has brought bad news; and your apparition was a true one. . . ."

"Hugh has died!"

"He has met with a fatal accident on Devil's Tor."

The girl embraced and kissed her mother. There was no more said for a minute.

"He was killed by a rolling boulder," began Helga again then. "One of those that composed the overthrown stack. His death was either instantaneous, or nearly so. Mr. Saltfleet claims to have arrived on the scene soon after. . . . He was the first to find Hugh."

"*Claims*, mother!" The two were apart again.

"There must be an inquest, and he is staying on at the 'Bell,' to attend it. It will all come out then. . . . A party is on its way to the Tor. Poor Hugh will be taken to the 'Bell'."

"Is that right?"

"We must give the first consideration to Uncle Magnus. And I must break the news to him now. . . ."

"Mother . . ."

"Yes, dear?"

"You must not go by the clock. You must not think horrible things. . . ."

"I am not thinking them—I am trying not to think them."

"You mustn't. There would be no sense."

"I shall send Hugh's stone round to him this evening, and then I wish never to see or have anything to do with him again."

Ingrid could not yet realise the stroke, its shock was too numbing. She wanted Peter to come back quickly. He must already know; he must have met *them*. She wanted to get hold of Mr. Saltfleet. She felt that a vast piled lake of consequences was being dammed within her head by her present ice-barrage of paralysed thought. She had the instinct to escape suddenly—out-of-doors, or to her bedroom. . . .

"What can I do, mother?"

"You? You can do nothing. You had better wait for Peter. He should be back soon, with the confirmation . . . and I am also expecting Mr. Dunn. You might watch for him, and see that he does not get to your uncle first. I am going to your uncle now. I wish Mr. Dunn shown into this room."

Old Colborne received the bolt more composedly than Helga had dared to expect. He asked few questions, made little comment, and even screwed his features to the shadow of a sardonic contempt, though this, she knew, could not be his feeling, but a disguise. He seemed content that his nephew was not to be brought back to the house. It was only as, relieved in heart, she was quitting him again, that he prevented her with a dour half-grin.

"The danger-notice was needed after all, it appears! It would not, however, have saved your cousin, who suggested it and was therefore alive to the risk. One concludes that he was dreaming; and the Drapiers have always had that vein of absent-mindedness, which has still consorted well enough with their holdfast temper. But I am not to disparage a man of my own blood, lying unburied. I wish to say this only. Your cousin I have never liked. I had excellent cause intensely to detest his father while he lived, and I have strained not one point, but many, to receive the son in this house at all. He constantly angered me. So I shall observe the customary decencies, Helga, since I can do no less; but I shall not pretend to grieve at heart, and in this respect I beg of you others to spare me. Being women, you will or will not put on mourning garments for him, as the fashion of the time dictates and I cannot—I ask you, however, to let everything else in the house go on as usual.

"I shall be too soon dead myself. There is little enough in death, that we should make so lamentable a disaster of it. I am to understand that this is the third attempt on Hugh Drapier's life on Devil's Tor within the compass of a few days; successful at last. If you are superstitious, you will put the circumstance to its best use, and in fact I have already told you that the hill is not as other hills. But on that account to pronounce it a *doom*, is to assume a wisdom that we do not possess. Supposing that death be the best for us, as easily it may be, then this imagined deliberate aiming at your cousin may just as well represent his *reward*. He himself has been the fittest judge of whether he has kept alive the spark that can alone seem to go through to another life. The life of the self is for the self only. *It* must go out."

Far too distracted was Helga to follow him to such regions. She kept silence for a space; then found words to assure him quietly that the house's routine would continue as nearly as possible without change. But when for the second time she was on the point of leaving him, she remembered that there was still something he must know at once.

"I am not sure if Hugh told you, uncle, that his estate passes to Ingrid and myself. I am executrix. I wouldn't mention it at such a moment, except that there is the question of the arrangements, with which I now want you not to be bothered."

Her uncle stared at her; and the stare fell into a scowl.

"How much are you to get between you?"

"I have only his own rough estimate of nineteen thousand pounds."

"It will secure your independence."

"We don't want independence, uncle. Nothing is to be altered."

"I am very glad to hear it. Ingratitude is the commonest, but also the meanest, of vices. I have no doubt, however, that Ingrid will soon be thinking of her marriage."

"It seems fitting in this time of cruel trouble that I should hear your wishes about that, once for all. You know she is very fond of Peter."

"If she desires to marry Peter, I have only to say that I shall raise no obstacle. The youngsters may live here, if they please, in rooms of their own; or she may leave home when she likes. If they have still not enough money for an establishment, let Peter come to me, to talk it over."

"It can't be gone into now, uncle dear! . . ." She kissed his forehead. "I am expecting Mr. Dunn, and I must go."

"Send Dunn along before he leaves the house," replied her uncle. "I wish to speak to him too."

At half-past three Peter returned. He was breathless with fast walking, pale and agitated. He had been all the way to the Tor, having reached the scene of death upon the very heels of the village party headed by the doctor. Not waiting for their slower return, he had viewed the preliminary proceedings in dumbness, heard the doctor's pronouncement, and started back at once. He saw Ingrid the first, and a single glance by each at the other's face informed them that there was nothing to be told. She took him to her mother, who was again in her room.

Peter made his superfluous report, and accepted a whisky-and-soda. His upset condition was very natural, yet Ingrid felt a slight involuntary resentment and scorn on account of it. It was as if, in spite of his accepted high idealism and wildness of genius, he were being shocked from his manhood by this ugly interruption of the domestic course of things. Death, surely, was fearful enough; but not so fearful. For herself, it was the day's grim reality, scarcely its human tragedy, that already began to raise her bewildered spirits to grandeur and amazement. Hugh was dead; and now it was no longer a play or fantasy, but the true working of that which lay behind and moved the practical world. So her soul was confirmed. Its long littleness, perhaps, was being cast at last. . . .

The instinct was with her that she must now very soon be summoned to make her own sacrifice. Hugh's death stood for that. Together they had stood on the Tor but two evenings ago, and together the supernatural had spoken to them. She could never forget her vision on the Tor. Was she too to die? Her sensations should be different—far more complicated. Her death, she felt, would be too simple a solution. . . .

They were all sitting, and her mother was speaking of Hugh's stone, that Mr. Saltfleet had called for. She was addressing Peter.

"There is one thing you can do for me, Peter—or perhaps I had first better have both your opinions. The Mr. Saltfleet who was the earliest to find poor Hugh, and whom you were inquiring about this morning . . . I will tell you under what circumstances they met. When Hugh was in Tibet this spring, as he was coming out of the country again towards civilisation, his caravan encountered that of a pair of Englishmen, one of whom was Mr. Saltfleet; the other, a Mr. Arsinal. They were moving further into the land, with the definite idea of robbing a certain native monastery of a certain rarity. They parted; and when Hugh was close upon the frontier, he was overtaken by a runner from the two, who put in his hands the prize they had been going after. They had got it, but the theft had been discovered, and they were in imminent danger of being captured by an overwhelming body, so this was the expedient they adopted for its safeguarding.

"Accordingly, Hugh took charge; but in the meantime came to be attracted on his own account by the little treasure, and hastened back to England with it, to keep out of their way. In justice to him, I should explain, Peter, that the thing apparently has no money value. . . . Then, when he arrived down here, he confessed the whole imbroglio to *me*; and begged me, in the event of his near death, to restore the property to these men, on application.

"And I undertook to do so. But now, this morning, Mr. Saltfleet turned up here unexpectedly, to have it all out with Hugh, and Ingrid, knowing nothing, sent him after Hugh to Devil's Tor. . . ."

Peter glanced at her, to understand the abrupt stop.

"You mean, your cousin had no intention of giving it up, so a row was threatened?"

"Something unpleasant certainly was to have happened, had they met in life."

"This surely isn't a suggestion that there is more to it than has yet appeared?"

"No, Peter . . . I daren't. . . . But the service I was to ask of you was to go round to Mr. Saltfleet, at the 'Bell,' during the day, and hand him back the curiosity in question. It is a small fractured piece of stone like flint. It looks nothing at all—and yet is in such very great request. . . . However, since the serious doubt has occurred to me, you had better first state your opinion. Ought the whole matter to be brought up at the coroner's inquest? For, if so, it seems to me it may be my duty to retain the stone for the proceedings, and in view of any international complications afterwards."

"Give the story in the witness-box by all means, supposing you want to furnish all England and the world with a sensational titbit! Forbidden Tibet, and a raid on a Buddhist monastery, and a stone of unnatural potency, and a mysterious death on a foggy moor!—forgive me for smiling in such an hour, but the newspapers will thank you, Mrs. Fleming. Keep it severely back, if you are wise."

"You have considered that it may be in the coroner's sphere?"

"Only if this accident were suspected to be no accident. *Then* you might come forward with your motive."

"You wish to throw the responsibility on me, Peter!"

Peter studied his finger-nails.

"Not at all. I would say you are not concerned. And with regard to the detained prize, considering *you*'ve not stolen or profited by it, but are merely innocently carrying out instructions, I can't at all see why you shouldn't return it to the man within the next half-hour."

"What do you say, Ingrid?"

"Mother, you aren't yourself. The public must know about Hugh's fatal accident, since that is the law; but nothing of all the rest is in the least connected. If you give the story, it will mean you think it *is* connected. Then you must either express in plain words in a public court what you must be afraid at the present moment to express even to yourself in the most shrinking thoughts—or else you must stop short of that, and everyone will think and call you malicious."

"I have no doubt you are both quite right. Then you had better take it to him, Peter. Ingrid has it. . . . But not now. I shall want you this afternoon—you mustn't go away. . . . And I ask you both to forget what has been said here in this room this afternoon; even between yourselves. My justification has been double. My head is whirling all the time; and Mr. Saltfleet is . . . a terrible man. . . ."

"So you will be all the better quit of him," returned Peter.

"Though I could still pass it to my lawyers, for restitution to the rightful owners, through the Indian Government."

Ingrid laid a hand on her arm.

"Mother, if you are to refuse Hugh's wishes, you must provide yourself with a perfect reason."

"Why are you so anxious to get this thing returned, my dear?"

"Do I seem anxious? And yet I would rather keep it myself . . . or, failing that, negotiate with it for the coming here of Mr. Arsinal, to receive it in person. Hugh thought I might have the opportunity of meeting him, but now, unless we did this, I never shall. But it would not be honest—and another thing is, I feel we ought not to interfere."

"But why do you wish to meet him?"

"He may know something—perhaps not *about* Devil's Tor, but to throw another light on it. I think Hugh said distinctly that, only I can't recollect his exact words. . . . So if I seem anxious, mother, to get it restored to Mr. Saltfleet as soon as possible, it must be because I want to put myself right with my own motives. I want to feel that I am not exercising the smallest will. I wish I could explain, or you understand. . . . Then, too, I suppose I want to cut short your worry of indecision. There is really nothing for you to be undecided about. You treat him like a ghost. He frightens you, and therefore you leap to the conclusion that you, or someone belonging to you, is or may have been threatened, and all sorts of lurid and ghastly imaginings fill your brain. . . . So I am going round to him at the inn with Peter, and that, I hope, will prove to you that I, at all events, don't find him to be feared."

"No, you can't go!"

"I must. You are forcing me, mother. . . . And I also want to speak to Mr. Saltfleet."

"Why?" demanded Helga curiously.

Her daughter regarded her as from a distance.

"But do I want to speak to him? . . . I sensed a tomb on the Tor, I saw Hugh dead to-day . . . and I have seen something else that was not there . . . and now, I suppose, I don't need to speak to Mr. Saltfleet—I've nothing really to say to him . . . yet I've the feeling that such a conversation is necessitated; that something will spring out of it that is fated to come about. . . ."

"Is it conviction, or only fancy?" asked Peter.

"I can simply answer that it is troubling me, Peter."

"Has it to do with the man himself?"

"Strangely, it does seem to have; but my knowledge of all these events is so adding to it, that I hardly know what is pure intuition in it."

"Perhaps a feeling of my own in the case might help to define the sort of thing you are experiencing. But I'll hold my tongue now. We'll see him together to-day, and *afterwards* discuss it."

Helga hated her daughter's going round to see that man. She knew that, since she had set her mind on it, nothing now would prevent her accompanying Peter—only if she, Helga, herself were to go instead of him; or if a servant were sent with the flint and a letter. It was too important a treasure to risk returning by a maid. She herself, however, could never dare, or bear, to see him again. Peter must go; and therefore Ingrid. . . . Hugh's unreal face, that her daughter had seen at the window, must have been at the very moment of death; but the times were not certain, within ten minutes. Saltfleet might have reached the spot, as he claimed, minutes later. And neither, in such an hour of awfulness, would he spend admiration on Ingrid; who, besides, was to be escorted by him who should serve as her invisible shield. . . .

But soon Dunn was announced, and was shown in, decently dressed in dark clothes, having been passed in the passage by the younger two, going from the room; and Helga blessedly had no more time to think.

The landlord of the "Bell" remained in earnest conference with her for a quarter of an hour. Afterwards she rang for a maid, and directed her to request Mr. Colborne to attend her in her room as soon as possible. The old gentleman appeared immediately; and the talk was resumed, now between the three.

Towards five o'clock Dunn left the house again, in company with Colborne, and Peter as friendly support to the latter.

XVIII

At the Inn

At the "Bell," at some time after seven o'clock on the same evening, Saltfleet was sitting upstairs in his room, erect in a hard-seated chair with arms, his legs outstretched, his back turned to the window directly behind him, and his lips moving about the stump of a dead cigar. On a round table at his elbow stood an untasted and forgotten whisky-and-soda. The dense white outdoor fog darkened the apartment to twilight. His lowered eyes were fixed in a frown. In the sheltered palm of his hand, being thus further shaded from even such wretched light as stole round his intervening person from the old-fashioned lattices at his rear, reposed Drapier's flint, which now for the first time he could examine at long leisure. The examination had been proceeding for a great while.

In the stone's black pool he had already detected that introductory incessant passage of vapour forms, and his judgment was vacillating as to the actuality or imaginariness of these new infinitesimal pin-points of brightness behind them—he assumed, *behind* them, since (if there at all) they were perpetually disappearing and reappearing. . . . So fully was he absorbed in the weird regard, that only for one break in many minutes had he looked up, to refresh his eyes in blinking at the opposite wall, while recalling a hitherto uncomprehended phrase of Arsinal's free rendering of the Knossos inscription:

"That which came from the stars, and is full of words of its home. . . ."

And certainly it demanded no inordinate fancifulness to identify these white wreaths travelling across a dark field with the clouds of a night sky, or these doubtful dazzling specks with stars, making due allowance for the scale. . . . He could accept, at any rate, the answering of the thing in his hand to that ancient description as the sign of its genuineness, as far as its recovery from Drapier was concerned. And any prior uncertainty of Arsinal's should be removed too. It must be the stone he had gone after. Saltfleet was not sure if he had as yet quite convinced himself of its authenticity; he had had little time to study it. . . .

A knock came on the door, and the hotel waiter peeped in.

"Mr. Saltfleet, sir, a lady and gentleman downstairs to see you. . . . Miss Fleming, and Mr. Copping."

"Who is he? Miss Fleming I know." He slipped the flint into a side-pocket.

"He has a studio at the end of the village, sir. No doubt they've come about this shocking business."

"All right, show them up."

The whisky caught his notice. He drank it off; then, rising, flung the cigar stump into the grate.

Ingrid and Peter entered, their waterproofs glistening with fine moisture.

"Won't you take off your coats?" inquired Saltfleet. And he proceeded to bring forward chairs for them, while the waiter vanished, closing the door. But Peter curtly declined for both. He would have ignored the seats as well, had not Ingrid unconsciously frustrated his purpose, first by naming the two to each other, obliging them to exchange bows—but Peter's was scarcely more than an unwilling nod; and next by sitting down quietly on her own account as a thing of course, whereupon not to have followed suit would have looked more churlish in him than he cared to show himself. Saltfleet brought up a third chair, and sat down facing them.

With the least trace of nervousness, yet still intrepidly meeting his eyes, the girl entered upon the delivery of her errand.

"I hope you won't consider it a liberty we are taking in calling on you here, Mr. Saltfleet, but it has to do with what you were discussing with my mother on your first visit this morning—the valuable you were anxious to get back from Hugh Drapier. . . ."

"Ah, so it's about that! Pray continue."

"I have now called to settle the matter."

Saltfleet frankly was puzzled. The object was in his pocket, so how were they proposing to settle it, in the only way in which it was to be settled? . . . He could only suppose that they were to declare roundly that it wasn't among Drapier's effects, and therefore they couldn't produce it; and that this, unless it turned up later, was the end, so far as they were concerned.

"You can't lay your hands on it?" he suggested, with the dawn of a smile.

"Oh, yes; we have it."

He was nonplussed. For the girl's asseveration was both positive and quietly emphatic, while her eyes were telling the truth, yet this was necessarily the reverse of the truth.

"Do you know that you have it, Miss Fleming, or are you merely assuming so?"

"I have brought it with me, to give to you."

"I suspect, in that case, that we are talking of different things."

Ingrid opened her hand-bag. She fumbled in it, and her increasing annoyance at not immediately being able to find the stone brought another veiled smile, but now of bewilderment, to

Saltfleet's face, and a scowl of displeasure to Peter's. She suddenly ceased searching the bag, to stare across the room in the endeavour to recollect.

"I am very sorry, but I seem not to have brought it, after all."

"When did you last see it?"

"Not many minutes before I came away. I thought I had put it in my bag."

Soon she grew certain that it had been meant for her that she should not bring it. Such absence of mind was so unlike her habit. She had no apprehension that the stone was lost—it should be in a certain drawer in her room still.

"I fancy it won't matter," smiled Saltfleet. "In fact, the thing that I want happens to be in my possession already, by a strange turn of the wheel of chance; so yours must be something else."

"It is a small broken stone, looking like a piece of black flint."

"The description tallies. But you have seen it to-day—since . . . the tragedy?" His voice lowered for the last word.

"Yes, I have."

"I, too," said Peter.

"Then what yours can be, I don't know; but the object I came down here to get from Drapier is at this moment in my coat pocket, so necessarily yours can't be it."

"But you never saw Drapier alive!" objected Peter sharply.

Saltfleet had not meant to confess the post-mortem abstraction. He disdained the awkwardness of the story for himself, however; and this girl would expect the whole truth. He gave a shrug.

"No, I didn't see him alive. But it was in his hand when I found him; so, as the shortest way, I took it."

Ingrid leant forward in her chair.

"It was in Hugh's hand at the moment of his death?"

"Yes."

"Would not that be very singular?"

"Yet explainable, Miss Fleming. He was evidently lost to his surroundings in contemplating it, as he came down the hillside, and so the block could get him unawares."

"You say it is in your pocket. May I see it?"

"Well yes, I think you may see it."

He handed her the flint, and she turned it about in her fingers in the dim light. Her brow was creased, and her eyes looked troubled and confused. Peter got up to peer at it in silence.

She passed it back to Saltfleet.

"It seems marvellously like ours. I can't understand."

"If I may hazard a suggestion, one should be genuine and the other a dummy."

"But why. . ."

"Drapier may have prepared things for Arsinal."

"Perhaps it would not be hard to pick up such a near facsimile on any shore, but are you justified in speaking so ill of him, so soon?"

"It is the only explanation of the mystery I can offer."

"And since he was studying yours at death, yours must be the genuine?"

"For that reason, and for a still better, which I am hardly at liberty to pass on."

He bestowed a last look on the flint, before dropping it again into his pocket.

Ingrid became deeply abstracted.

"Certainly, there would be little sense in studying a counter-feit," she said next, in low tones. "Neither, seemingly, could he just have found it lying, since it is not a flint country. . . . And, Peter, *your* adventure in his company on the Tor yesterday—what his hand was closed over then must have been the same. And in the garden again yesterday afternoon. He has always been looking at it, while mine—ours—has been mislaid from him. . . . And yet another strangeness makes it just as certain that mine is just as little a sham."

"What strangeness?" asked Saltfleet.

"When it was in my hand this morning, I was nearly over-powered by the sound of rushing waters."

"Was the connection sure?"

"So I felt at the time."

"What that could be as emanating from a piece of stone, I have no idea."

"Nor I." But her eye met Peter's, and the minds of both flew back to his mystic overcoming on Devil's Tor. He too had heard a perpetual thunder of invisible waters—Ingrid recalled that these had been his very words. . . .

"If you are convinced that yours is the authentic," said Saltfleet, with a half-grim smile, "I am willing enough to take both. My friend and associate, Mr. Arsinal, will put the matter at rest within a few moments of seeing them."

"The true stone—whichever it is—is a symbol of the 'Great Mother,' is it not so?"

"It should be associated with her worship." He was a little surprised by her information, but Drapier must have spoken at large to these women.

"Has it also any connection—before these last few days—with Devil's Tor?"

"That I have never heard, and cannot say."

"I would have liked to meet Mr. Arsinal."

"What is your interest, Miss Fleming?"

"It would be hard to put into words."

"Should he come down here before I am gone, the introduction would be simple."

"Thank you! I will hold you to that."

Peter, with a movement of impatience, drew forth his case, and lit a cigarette. He returned the case to his pocket, without having proffered it to Saltfleet.

"Does Mr. Arsinal know this district?" asked Ingrid.

"I have no idea. I have really been very little with him, and that only abroad."

"Why did Hugh Drapier covet your stone?"

"An hour or so ago I would have replied again: 'I have no idea.' But when your names were announced just now, I was beginning to find out. It appears to have a peculiar property of fascination. . . . I must ask you not to question me about that, Miss Fleming. Undoubtedly, however, it was strengthening its hold on Drapier's imagination."

"Why has he been killed?"

"Yes, your evil presage came true."

"Was it the stone that attracted him here to Devil's Tor, to be killed?"

"That, indeed, may be a theory to appeal to Arsinal. Yet there are strong difficulties, and we must not take it too seriously. Actually, it may have been a factor in your cousin's death; but a small bit of mineral, I imagine, will not have force to draw down lightning, or cause an earthquake. It is his repeated escapes there that are troubling you, and demanding the explanation."

Ingrid smiled faintly.

"You think me absurd, no doubt!"

"I will be candid, Miss Fleming. You appear to have far too many fancies of all sorts, and perhaps do deserve to be chaffed out of some of them. Nevertheless, I am not the man to do it. I have an uneasy feeling that your nonsense may be groping for the right road, while my sense is clinging for all it is worth to the commonplace."

"You are aware of a mystery?"

"We must still be logical, however. And if, in fact, the stone has had to do with Drapier's death, why then, this in my pocket"—he brought it out again—"is what he was holding at his death; and therefore *must* be the genuine."

"Please let me see it a second time."

All was silent in the room as Ingrid once more reached out her fingers to take the flint, when, without expectation, and before she had securely got it, she was stunned by the same terrifying roar of waters as had crushed her senses earlier in the day while still touching its double. It annihilated her for the instant it lasted like the sudden thunderous passage past a quiet country station platform of a heavily-loaded high-speed express. The stone escaped her, falling to the floor. . . .

Saltfleet picked it up. He offered it to her again, never suspecting that her failure to hold it had been anything but a miscalculation of distance. But now, apparently, her thoughts were wandering, for she made no new attempt to take the stone from him. It was not very easy to distinguish the expression of her face through the dusk. He supposed that some other intervening idea had occurred to her, and, as he did not choose to wait upon her, returned the thing to his pocket. . . . To Ingrid, however, the recollection of that noise was already forming itself to the resemblance to swollen floods thundering down between confining cliffs, so that she could almost have imagined the wetting of her face by the far-flung spray. . . .

Peter was dissatisfied with the unnatural rigidity of her poise. He feared that she might all at once be feeling faint.

"Are you quite well, Ingrid?"

"Yes."

But his small, distant voice travelled into her consciousness, and she reawoke to her environment. And meanwhile Saltfleet, from something possessive in her escort's tone, and the personal anxiety expressed by the question itself, as also from their being here together at all, fancied that the two must be engaged. He was but slightly interested, yet misdoubted if her choice were a happy one. For this young man, perhaps, was neither a fool nor a weakling, though he was obviously rather pulled down by an indoor existence; but he should be more conceited than was good for the health of his soul, while it must be a bad sign for any girl associated with him that he could fall so readily into surliness. He presumed that he was on this visit unwillingly. In that case, a stronger character would have declined it altogether. But *she*, Saltfleet guessed, would not easily be gainsaid by man or woman, her mind being once resolved.

"How, then, are we to leave it?" he asked her.

Peter too, regarded her inquiringly; but when she failed immediately to reply, got up, and said himself, with an affected yawn:

"We must be off. Cutting out the fantastic of the discussion, Mr. Saltfleet, its net result, I conclude, is that each side sticks to its own, and that all parties are to be content."

"If Miss Fleming, for her mother, is content, I think I may say the same for my friend."

"Well, Ingrid? . . ."

The girl's pale features moved in hesitation.

"Before we decide, couldn't Mr. Arsinal be fetched?"

"What exactly is in your head, Miss Fleming?"

"There is an extraordinary chance that we have none of us considered. We can put it to the test without him, but afterwards the question of ownership would be much more difficult, supposing it is as I think. . . . Your stone has been broken, Mr. Saltfleet. The one we hold is, too. What if they *belonged*! . . ."

A silence followed, during which Ingrid rose, and then Saltfleet. He stood erect in reflection, passing a hand over his chin.

"You mean, of course, that we can fit the fractures, to ascertain. Yet I would still like to have your chain of reasoning. The one stone—the one in my pocket, I am sure—has come out of Tibet; where do you suggest yours—the other—has come from?"

"Ours came out of Tibet. Since Hugh Drapier showed it to my mother with his own hands, it has not been outside our house. . . . But he visited the prehistoric tomb on Devil's Tor yesterday morning, and . . . it is very remarkable—and scarcely believable—but there, and then, I think, he must have found the stone now in your pocket."

"He discovered nothing to you of such a find?"

"No; but I was sure, from his manner, that some adventure had met him down there, in those depths."

Now also she understood how it had come about that the flint which she herself had taken from his box had never been missed. He had picked the second up in the darkness of the underground chamber, and, when he had got home, the first being gone from its place, he had believed that this was it—that the stone he had picked up had unawares to himself been in his pocket and dropped out. . . . She could not doubt it. . . .

"Would Drapier know he had both?" asked Saltfleet.

"No, he didn't know it. The Tibetan one was mislaid, by a miraculous chance, and he must have mistaken the other for it."

"I hope you may be right. It will mean much to Arsinal. . . . So when could we test it?”

“It is getting late, and I am so very positive that they do belong, we can well wait till to-morrow.”

“Then I’ll send Arsinal a wire?”

“Just now, when I dropped your stone, it was because I heard the same waters again. That is my proof—convincing to me. . . . The telegraph office is closed by now. We can test it by ourselves to-morrow, but I think he should come soon.”

“It’s the queerest business! I can only say, Miss Fleming, that Arsinal has long since inferred the existence of such a second half to his stone; that he wants it very badly, and is at this moment engaged in the most elaborate preparations for its world-wide search. Imagine if your news will seem of importance to him! . . . Yet now tell me. Assuming your suggestion to be accurate—you have mentioned a difficulty of ownership. . . .”

“Yes. The one, we know, is his; but to the other, you yourself will admit he can have no sort of claim, except moral. But I, too, may have a moral claim to it. The one that was found in the tomb—if it was . . . that tomb, and the whole of Devil’s Tor, are more to me than to anybody. Then Mr. Arsinal must show me that his claim is the stronger and more righteous. Let him do that, and I promise he shall have it.”

“I only beg of you not to be uncharitable, for here is a man who has given all his years, energy and fortune to the recovery from the void of antiquity of these complemental halves. After immense labour he has located and gained the first. Now the second may marvellously have turned up. The whole research is based on a mystical enthusiasm, of which I have no right to speak further.”

Peter caught Ingrid’s arm.

“We must go. Your mother shouldn’t be left.”

“The discussion bores you, Mr. Copping?” suggested Saltfleet, smiling.

“I came here to accompany Miss Fleming, and at the request of Mrs. Fleming.”

Ingrid, however, addressed herself to Saltfleet as though the interruption had not occurred.

"You may, if you wish, give Mr. Arsinal this provisional assurance. The stone we have is his, and he must of course take it. The other, that you have just shown us, was on Hugh Drapier's person at his death, and so belongs neither to you nor to Mr. Arsinal, but to the estate; of which my mother is the executrix. If we can't come to any agreement, we must exchange them, and then each side will have its own property. But I'll ask my mother—and she will listen to me—I'll ask her to hold everything over till Mr. Arsinal can get down to discuss it in person. And if he can establish his claim, he shall then have both. But the claim must be *occult*. The mere fact that he has spent a number of years in trying to trace these counterparts, would not in itself be enough. If that were all, my right would be stronger than his."

"What would you wish to do with such a stone, for instance?"

"It is not a question of any activity of my will; and you could not understand. . . . These awful events have been filling all the week. Now poor Hugh is crushed, almost as if a hand had launched that rock against him. I have been concerned, I feel I am to be still more concerned. And if the stone in your pocket has truly been recovered from the recesses of the Tor, it is a part of everything."

"You would say that nothing has been accidental?"

"No; it is like something taking shape."

"To what end, Miss Fleming?"

"I cannot guess."

"But Arsinal, perhaps, will give a guess. I won't say, a true guess, for that would be a miracle indeed; but there is a very ancient prophecy in his possession, which, without too great a distortion, might be made to point towards these initiatory happenings. . . . Though here, certainly, I should feel disposed to part company with him at last."

"You see how necessary it is that he should come. And he *will* come. I know that—and yet there must be new surprises too. We are very little more than looking on . . . even poor Hugh."

"Then why have *I* been fetched down to join the spectators?"

"I feel it is not long to remain a mere spectacle. I am taking a most serious view of it all, Mr. Saltfleet. Surely to-day's work supports me! *You*—you are a man, you are a human being. You may be a stranger here, but as an individual living in the world like the rest of us, you may be to be made use of, I imagine!"

"I don't joke, but if a drama is unfolding, what part have you conceived for me?"

But Peter, flicking the ash off his cigarette, spoke before she could.

"May I suggest that we get back to earth?" And his brows lifted. "This kind of talk may do very well among ourselves, Ingrid, but after all (pardon me, sir!) we are in conference with an unknown quantity in a strange inn. For Dunn, for example, I have the utmost respect of a sort, yet the bare possibility of his getting wind of the seeming insanity of his betters starts, I must admit, a certain dismay in my mind."

"I assure you that I shall hold my tongue rigidly about everything," returned Saltfleet drily. "The more so, as I believe I permitted myself a somewhat censurable action up yonder." He gestured with his hand towards the window.

"I think so."

"You disapprove, Mr. Copping?"

"Why, yes, I do."

"In similar circumstances, you would have the moral strength to abstain from laying a finger on what you should conceive to be your own property?"

"It now proves not to be yours! In any case, I have long since made up my mind that I haven't time to dodge the law; so I always go strictly by it, merely not to be bothered."

"Am I dodging the law?"

"It has that colour. Having confiscated evidence, you will be compelled, won't you? to pick and choose from facts for your story at the inquest. I don't know what that is but dodging."

"Are you by chance insinuating that the inquest may resolve itself into other than a purely formal inquiry?"

"I simply say that the coroner should be in possession of *all* the circumstances; and you are suppressing one of them."

Saltfleet, moving his shoulder disdainfully, turned from him. Not, apparently, to intervene, but because her mind had been elsewhere and had now reached a thought to be expressed, Ingrid said to Peter, touching his sleeve:

"If Mr. Arsinal comes to-morrow, perhaps you will lend your studio?"

"Why?"

"I wish it to be among ourselves, and would rather not come here again."

"Your mother is not to participate?"

"I want to talk to Mr. Arsinal alone. I want you—and Mr. Saltfleet, if he wishes—to come; but not to interfere."

"You can have the studio."

"Then you will wire in the morning, and let us know what time he is to be expected?" She addressed Saltfleet.

"Very well."

"My mother is the principal in law, but she will hand over the right to deal with this matter to me."

"We shall prefer it, Miss Fleming. . . . While you, Mr. Copping, I trust, will maintain a more or less benevolent neutrality?"

"Oh, I am outside it all! I merely provide a room with four chairs."

Saltfleet laughed. He turned for the last time to Ingrid.

"And you would rather he were fetched *before* the testing of these two stones, to see if they belong?"

"I am sure that they are counterparts."

No more was said.

Saltfleet bowed the two out, feeling nothing but exasperation for this young Copping, but for the other—the tall and gracious girl, whose ever-growing personality was so unsuccessfully obscured for his last glimpse of her by the shapeless, glistening waterproof, that could not prevent her appearing in it like the feminine aristocrat that she was—for her, something much more nearly akin to reverence than to the mere homage of sex. Indeed, he had encountered no woman of her type before. . . . For it could not be common admiration with him. Her beauty was not what he was remembering. He had no exultation of vanity, and was not ransacking his mind for memories of her particular glances and speeches, that might be twisted to his favour. And still it was always in his mind that her womanhood *had* played a part in the deep impression made upon him. . . .

But after dinner, while he sat smoking in the same room, now in profoundest dusk, pursuing his examination of Drapier's flint, he looked up sharply, to fancy that the tall-backed oak chair with arms, set against the wall opposite, was being occupied by the seated form of a gigantic woman.

Her shape was defined by a sort of phosphorescence, issuing indifferently from her garments and unclothed flesh; but the face was shadowed, so as to be scarcely distinguishable from the darkness of the room. She seemed curiously attired in antique draperies. He recognised her at once for a ghost. And in her immobility was suggested to him an inexpressible menace, her bare arms resting in strength like those of an image on the wooden arms of the chair, while she stared at him from the invisibility of her face and eyes.

She vanished.

Saltfleet felt a peculiar sense of anger for his subjection to such a phenomenon. Lighting one of the candles in the room, he poured himself out some whisky. Then, having swallowed it in a few quick gulps, as one impatient to be off, he immediately afterwards quitted the apartment, to go to bed, notwithstanding the unusually early hour for him.

XIX

Arrival of Arsinal

Saltfleet descended to the coffee-room for breakfast next morning, to be confronted by the surprising vision of the very man he was to wire, who must have travelled down from Oxford by the night train, reaching Belhill on the first connection from Plymouth. Arsinal looked thoroughly pale and fagged, having shadowy patches of exhaustion under his eyes; but otherwise seemed to have found time to shave and tub, and was sitting alone in the room in dark indoor clothes, pensively reading the *Western Morning News* by the window. He sighted Saltfleet quickly, and got up with his habitual unpretending dignity.

They met.

"I wished not to hurry your movements, so refrained from sending my name up," explained Arsinal. "In fact, but for a strange chance in a thousand, I would not be here at all. I was pressed to dine last evening by one of the professors I know very well, who desired me to meet his wife, and though I had work enough to do, I could see no way out, so went. After dinner they put on the wireless for half an hour, and among the news items broadcast happened to be this sensational death of Drapier's on a Dartmoor tor. Accordingly, as soon as I could decently get away, I motored to Swindon, and there caught the night express going west. . . . I thought I should be on the spot, in case of any hitch. At the station below they directed me to this hotel as the leading establishment, so I tried for you here at a venture. Now tell me, Saltfleet—did you get to meet Drapier before his tragical death?"

"No. But I was the one to find him lying dead. And as, quite amazingly, his hand chanced to be clutching our article, I made no bones about it, but took it; and have it. It is upstairs."

A gleam of astonishment and satisfaction crossed Arsinal's face.

"That saves much trouble. . . . I am to breakfast with you, I believe. And afterwards we can adjourn to your room.”

“I have a sitting-room.”

“You can show it to me there. But why didn’t you wire me, Saltfleet? You knew my anxiety.”

“Things happened, and I left it too late; but this morning I was going to.”

“There is no complication?”

“There’s a development, but we had better leave it till after breakfast, with the other.”

“Nothing awkward, I trust?”

“With luck, just the reverse.”

“Then I cannot imagine,” said Arsinal.

“I can only set things before you in their right order, so pray have the patience. And while I think of it, I must send off a line. Your coming is expected, and I must notify that you are here.”

“I am still to be told nothing?”

“I can’t tell you piecemeal. We’re to attend a meeting during the day at the place in the village of a man called Copping. To him I am now to write.”

Seating himself before the writing-table, he penned swiftly:

“Dear Mr. Copping,

A. is already come, so will you fix up a time as soon as possible, and send me word?

Sincerely yours,
HENRY SALTFLEET.”

He left the room, still licking the envelope, and found Dunn, who passed the letter to a boy at once for delivery by hand. Within ten minutes more Peter received it. But Saltfleet, returning to his associate, found difficulty in coping with his bombardment of new questions of perplexity, based on a total ignorance of the surprise in store, that might not yet be sprung.

“Surely, Saltfleet, you have not declared this singular accidental recovery of the stone to anyone here?”

“Two—perhaps three—know of it; but they are safe.”

"Was it necessary?"

"It may prove very fortunate."

"Of course, no discussion is possible so long as I am kept in the dark. But how came you to be on that hill at all?"

"I was directed after him there, from the house. He has been staying with relations at the address we had. A Mrs. and Miss Fleming—mother and daughter; and some sort of invisible uncle. The Copping I have just written to is a friend of the family, living somewhere in the village itself. He and the daughter may be engaged. You are to see him and the girl later."

"Whom did you talk to at the house?"

"The mother. She hinted at an obstruction on Drapier's part, so I wasted no time, but went after him; and found him dead."

"But an obstruction! . . ."

"Your stone must have begun to fascinate him."

"One wonders how, Saltfleet. . . . Yet his strange behaviour has certainly pointed to an obsession. And your response to this hint from her, was it friendly, or did you permit yourself?"

"Perhaps I did, a very little. I had to make clear to her that we were in earnest."

"No threats?"

Saltfleet laughed. "None that should bring me to the dock!"

"You must know what I have in mind. You will have to give evidence at the inquest, will you not? Then, if there is to be the least ambiguity as to the meaning of your presence on that hill, you must necessarily be rather closely examined. And such a professional examination may just suffice to attract notice in high quarters; when the international trouble for us will begin. We cannot keep too quiet. Are you sure that you have gone about this business wisely, Saltfleet? You appear to have antagonised one, and to have put yourself within the hands of two or three others."

"A big cheque will cover a multitude of small deficits!" rejoined Saltfleet enigmatically. And Arsinal gave him a sharp look to discover his meaning; but simultaneously breakfast was served.

They moved to the table. No other guests were down so early; perhaps they were the hotel's only ones, and soon the waiter went from the room.

"You were to meet him personally," pursued Arsinal in his low, incisive voice. "Why need you have embarked on this affair at all with Mrs.—Fleming, I think you mentioned as the name?

"These blunders seem fated. If I hadn't done so, I could never have followed Drapier to Devil's Tor, and what was in his fist up there might have been thrown out and lost for ever."

"That, I see, may be very true."

"Another consequence has been my acquaintance with the daughter, initiating yours, for which you should presently thank me."

"Why so?"

"For one thing, she is a girl of great character and intelligence. But her, too, we must leave till afterwards. Are you at all intimate with this district, Arsinal?"

"No, I have never been here before."

"It was a question of hers."

Arsinal ended his pretence of eating. He sat back in silence, thoughtfully regarding his companion's face.

"Who is the legal executor, Saltfleet—do you know?"

"Mrs. Fleming is, so I understand."

"Where is Drapier housed?"

"He is lying in an annex here."

"And when will be the inquest?"

"Perhaps to-morrow."

When Saltfleet was ready, the two passed upstairs.

Arsinal stared quickly and hard at the flint the other had dropped into his hand. He sat down with it, twisted it about repeatedly, and then brought out a pocket-magnifier. Through this he narrowly examined every surface of the stone. And all the time, Saltfleet, standing by, saw that his expression was falling—from eager expectancy to interrogation, from interrogation to bewilderment, and from bewilderment to dismay, terminating with a sort of resigned scorn for what he held and at last mechanically set down on the table beside him, while returning the glass to his pocket.

He met Saltfleet's eye.

"It isn't mine."

"Then Miss Fleming's assertion was correct. But what makes you sure?"

In the shock and newness of his disappointment, Arsinal scarcely heard the words, to draw fresh hope from their tone and sense. He took the stone up again, but replaced it immediately, afterwards wiping his forehead with his handkerchief, and getting unsteadily to his feet. Straightening his back twice or thrice according to his habit, he finally reaffirmed in a quiet voice:

"You have recovered the wrong thing."

"Is it certain?"

"Yes. . . . Though you were not to know, and the mistake is pardonable. And so mine must still be among Drapier's effects, and I must get round there quickly."

"Will you indicate to me where the difference lies?"

"The differences are very marked. The shapes are unlike. If you would bisect a rather long hen's egg, mine would resemble its broad end, this its narrow." For the third time he took the stone in his hand. . . . "Then the fracture surface of mine has a convex tendency; this, you may see for yourself, is towards a concave. And the discoloration of the worn surface—here the pale predominates so very distinctly, whereas in mine there is little pale at all. The surfaces have been exposed to different actions. . . . Be quite sure that I was meticulously careful to stamp the smallest details of mine very thoroughly on my memory for future identification. The precaution was especially dictated by the circumstance that it was immediately to pass out of my hands again. You may really receive it from me, Saltfleet, that there can be no dispute on the point. There is a superficial resemblance—possibly too close to be accidental. Drapier must have procured this fragment for the purpose of deceiving me."

"So I thought. Only, it was the other that I believed to be the fraud. However, now that you have had a first look at it, all this is merely preliminary. Now I want you to study the fracture in darkness. . . . I will draw the curtains, while you might turn your back a shade more to the window. The idea is to cut off all the light from it you can. Stare steadily down on the broken surface for about two minutes. You didn't see this before?"

Arsinal threw him a swift glance.

"This has a property?"

"Unless my eyes have deceived me."

He pulled the curtains to meet. Outside was still the fog, and the light of the room was effectually obscured.

"Last night, for my sins, I had more than enough time for it!"

"Say what I must expect, Saltfleet."

"I want the independent confirmation."

And while Arsinal sat bent to his task of peering for he knew not what, the other stood over him, erect and looking away, his spirit composed to patience, as though he had been a tutor awaiting the laboured performance of some too-familiar crude exercise.

Thus the two minutes crawled by for him; yet long before then the compound of the archaeologist's trained quick perception and fine interpretative understanding had enabled him to discern as real, not optical merely, first the slow progress across the flint's face of the massing and scattering clouds, and next, beneath all that, those infinitely tiny sisters of stars, conveying no idea of magnitude, but merely of fixity and scintillation. . . . When, however, he had sufficiently satisfied himself of this first actual character of the vision, he would indulge his risen feelings no more as at that time, for now he knew that very urgent matters awaited him outside—of interrogation, discussion, and practical action.

He got up, and Saltfleet threw back the curtains.

"Is it good, Arsinal?"

"Yes. I got it."

"And do you still insist the thing is not yours?"

Arsinal slipped the stone into his pocket. Then he stood gripping the edge of the table, as if he needed its support.

"I think you must be anticipating my answer. You have tried me purposely—a little unkindly, perhaps, Saltfleet!"

"I wished it from your own lips. This, you would say, though not yours, is as good as yours?"

"You cannot be ignorant what it is you have put into my hands."

Saltfleet turned his back, to draw a cigar from his case, bite off its end, and eject it into the empty grate. He lit the cigar, afterwards facing Arsinal again.

"Miss Fleming is the one to be thanked," he said. "The inspiration has been hers."

"The counterpart—mine—is still at that house?"

"Yes."

"I would give much to learn how Drapier contrived to procure this as well."

"The supposition is that he picked it up in a prehistoric tomb on Devil's Tor—opened by the crashing of its covering pile during a thunderstorm on Tuesday of the present week, and re-closed, presumably for ever, by an earth shock on the following day. Yesterday Drapier met his fate, and still Friday is only beginning. If Miss Fleming is inclined to be superstitious about it all, it is little to be wondered at."

"But the finding it there is supposition only? It was not announced by Drapier?"

"No, but the girl—who, I think, is his cousin—has satisfied herself that it probably was so. The other was temporarily mislaid, and the theory is that he confounded this with that, and never knew he had two."

"However it may be, it is clearly destiny. . . . Is she aware of the inherent strangeness of these stones?"

"I fancy she has not seen what we have, but with both of them she has heard a loud sound of rushing waters."

"Rushing waters! . . . Yes, I begin to understand that I must meet her. And it was this that gave her the connection?"

"No doubt."

"And so she has handled both?"

"Yes, on different occasions. She came here last evening with Copping, to return me the stone they hold. Drapier left directions to that effect. But, imagining that I already had yours, I told them so.”

“It continues available?” demanded Arsinal quickly.

“To you? That is just what is to be settled at the meeting you are attending. They very rightly maintain that you cannot *claim* both. Nevertheless, if you can show Miss Fleming your superior interest, it will do.”

“It will not be hard—though it is a pity the need for this favour has arisen. It is a pity you could not somehow have secured both. Of course, you were not to have grasped the true facts of the case until too late. . . . Pray, Saltfleet, have the two been actually fitted?”

“No; theirs was left at home.”

“Yet they came to return it.”

“Miss Fleming forgot it.”

“Is she so casual?”

“This is a very abnormal time for her.”

“These coincident activities of Devil’s Tor?”

“Yes—and Drapier’s death under intense circumstances. I was actually with her yesterday, while he must have been still alive and well, when she manifested a rather strong anxiety concerning his safety. She urged me after him.”

“Then she should have the occult gift?”

“We may think so.”

“She has impressed you generally, Saltfleet?”

“She will impress you too.”

“It is she, not her mother, who will have the voice?”

“So she has said; and I believe her.”

“What is her age, that she should already possess such a remarkable force of character?”

“Quite young. Twenty-two or three.”

“And her appearance, Saltfleet?”

“She is beautiful.”

“Since it seems I’m to conciliate her, won’t you throw a little more light on her disposition and interests for me? What arguments should I use?”

"I can tell you at once. She requires you to show your superior *supernatural* right to the stone—that was in my pocket and now is in yours; though I would also mention, Arsinal, that I have not formally passed it to you. In case no agreement is struck, it goes back to them, in exchange for yours. . . . So if you can persuade her mystical fancy, you will get both. And my own view is that she is easily reasonable and persuadable, but no fool. She has, if I mistake not, a rather uncanny mental divining-rod for the ascertainment of the truth. Don't *add* to anything."

Arsinal meditated for several moments.

"My supernatural claim may be set forth thus," he said at last slowly. "I have not made you acquainted with the connecting circumstance before, but it is not now invented or exaggerated. Everything turns on just that encounter of ours with Drapier in Tibet. For it is he only who, having relations here, could have hit upon Devil's Tor, of all the heights of western Europe, almost by happy accident. And but for his running into us quite unexpectedly, he never would have left India so hurriedly, in order to escape our demand for the return of the flint entrusted to him; accordingly, he could not have reached this tomb in time to be at its brief opening. The hypothesis that it was found there—the counterpart flint—is her own, and therefore I shall not be called upon to labour it. You tell me the tomb is wrecked again, probably permanently. Therefore, if Drapier had not found the stone when he did, it must have remained buried throughout eternity; while I must have gone on burrowing painfully among the records and collections of the ancient world for the rest of my days.

"So our meeting in Tibet was from fate; and I have never yet told you in what manner it came about. Until now, its fateful character being unguessed by me, I have scarcely dwelt upon the extraordinariness of the intervention, even in my moments of idle dreaming. But just as you and I, Saltfleet, were thrown together by a psychic phenomenon, so Drapier and I were. . . . For, originally, it was my quite unwonted apathy and listlessness at Darjiling that arrested my penetration of Tibet by way of Nepal; and much later, after we were actually across the Ladak frontier and a considerable number of marches towards Alung, you remember, don't you? how in camp at Nyak-tso one evening we debated between two routes for the next day—the one easier, the other shorter—and at last agreed upon the longer and less difficult. But in the morning again, you will further recall, I insisted very emphatically on reversing the decision thus come to—to your expressed astonishment and not a little disgust, I fear. And had the original plan held, you know we must have missed Drapier, who proved to be within a couple of marches of us, approaching by the shorter route; whereas we were quite unaware of his presence in that part of the world at all, and indeed of his existence.

"Well, Saltfleet, would you care to hear what impelled me thus to change roads overnight? In a soul-startling dream, that was a vision, in the small hours, I saw a tall, shadowy, shrouded female form, standing somewhat removed outside our tent, having her back turned to me, and an arm outstretched before her, the hand's forefinger pointing away into the distance. The phantom was past human stature, but, apart from this, my trembling of horror certified to me that she was not of the world. And she pointed towards the spur crossed by the road we had agreed to reject.

"Hitherto I have not dared to entertain the theory that this apparition could be identical with the divine one of my boyhood. It was possible, yet there was no necessary association. I did not see her very distinctly—her back was turned, and she was also in shade. And still, you will consider that it is always a *female*—twice with me, and once with yourself. . . . This, Saltfleet, might nearly be my supernatural claim with Miss Fleming, should you find the story sufficiently credible. You could support its enclosing outline."

"Am I to say what I think, Arsinal?"

"Surely."

"Then the story is believable enough, and she may be perfectly prepared to concede your sincerity throughout, and all the same, the fate in it may not necessarily be appropriable by *you*."

Arsinal viewed his associate, with a slight wrinkling of his brow. Some indefinable new note of independence and challenge in Saltfleet's objection struck upon his ear like a very faint discord. And so finely organised was his sensitive system that its small disturbance immediately became a thought; and the thought was this Miss Fleming must already and so soon be obtruding an alien influence upon a man he had always deemed quite insusceptible. . . . It was absurd, however; and Saltfleet could be no more than stating a positive standpoint rather roughly.

"If not by me, by whom?" he asked.

"You had better confess to her your practical aim in this life-long pursuit of yours. You have never told me. A sequence of visions occurring to a person merely for his own purposes, she might not consider an outside title."

Arsinal flushed.

"You have for some time wished to have this out with me, I fancy. . . . And I appreciate your tact, Saltfleet, in leaving the question unasked for as long as it was essential for us to remain on terms together. Another man might perpetually have crucified me by attacks that I must have found impertinent; but I could not have invited your co-operation had I not felt you to be a gentleman. We should now be soon to part, and so you find that you may allow yourself at last. I still don't know if I can satisfy you."

"I have made no such request. We are discussing Miss Fleming's attitude."

"Then I apologise. . . . Nevertheless, she may not put it in just that form."

"I think she will. It is her whole case. She herself can find an interesting and instructive use for the stone in dispute. Are your aims more special?"

"It is hardly so vulgarly practical."

Arsinal began to pace the room in perturbed thought, his hands clasped behind his back. Then he came to a stand again before his friend.

"You are waiting, are you not? for an answer to your note sent round. When do you imagine this meeting will be?"

"Perhaps this morning, perhaps this afternoon."

"We appear to have only too much time on our hands, and I

am wondering if I could attempt a sketch. If I am to open myself to this girl, Saltfleet, our long association deserves that I should first be as candid with you. Then, without a certain disloyalty, you could scarcely refuse to throw in your weight. . . . Yet I must add how little I ever expected that such a bribe would be necessary. I am convinced by my feelings that some change has taken place inside you since we parted at Oxford. You are perhaps becoming tired of the whole business? A new person, a new point of view, has corrected your vision of it. It no longer seems of importance . . . or your sympathies are rather suddenly transferred? I feel the advance of this cloud over our excellent relations hitherto. Not to suggest anything feeble or banal, is it that girl? Has she presented a view of ownership that happens to have caught your imagination? Tell me!"

"Far from getting tired of the business, it is just beginning really to interest me, Arsinal. The girl—yes! she does represent a new feature. Is there a change in me? There may be. But it would not be a transference of sympathies, but a broadening. An affair appears to be going on. Drapier was three times aimed at."

"You seem all at once, so very strangely, to be regarding my peculiar work as no longer peculiarly mine—but almost anybody's."

"Why do you want it to be yours? I will even be rather blunt, and ask you, in what sense the *divine*—which is your incentive and your mark—in what sense it can *belong* to any man with arms and legs? Surely, it must be the possessor, not the possessed!"

Arsinal gazed at him in mournful steadiness. Afterwards, straightening his back, he sat down.

"Words, as you know, Saltfleet," he said quietly, "may have all truth, all reason, and all right, in them; and yet may be false. I must see Miss Fleming myself before I can determine the degree of her deflective influence, if any such there be. . . ."

But while Saltfleet, taking a second chair, returned the other only a front of stone and grimness, he was already conscious in his heart that their breach was opened, and might not again be mended. For now he understood that he was *scorning* Arsinal, who of a sudden had shown himself without generosity. Because of a mystical vision in early youth, he had struggled through life under an imaginary mantle of destiny, rather too heavy for him; and yet this delusion had enabled him to do great things. But all was based on greed and egoism. Plain enough was it that the destiny, should it, against his refusal, prepare to quit him, was still to be forced to ambition. He was but a human, moved by vanity.

To the account of his secret aims, that should be at once to follow, Saltfleet prepared himself to hearken with these uneasy expectations. He knew an increasingly settled contempt for the man, on account of this revealed half-hypocrisy of his entire career. He feared, at the same time, the application to real persons and events of the prophecy of Knossos, that might well be to find utterance by an incited tongue.

Perhaps he was a little ahead of Arsinal. He felt only that he would come to it, and must be allowed to talk, and develop all the dark convolutions of his soul but *then* must be stopped. . . . He had the intuition that to-day was to be no less extraordinary in his life than yesterday had been. . . .

XX

The Great Mother

Arsinal sighed, was silent for another moment, then said quite suddenly:

"I gave you the Knossos record. Later I had the somewhat remarkable luck to strike a fellow to it in the vicinity of the ancient Aphrodisias, in Caria, which repeats the prophetic part of the text just differently enough to throw a new illumination. The inscription is on a small silver figurine of the mother-goddess, which I have secured. I can repeat its purport from memory. The Mother, you must know, was worshipped in Caria as well."

And he quoted:

"'To one bed shall I bring another man and another woman, of whom shall be born a greater than they, greater than all mankind, who shall put wickedness under foot, and found my people.'

"Thus, Saltfleet, this miracle of new birth, which in the one prediction was to arise directly from an action of the temple stone, in the other is to be the intelligent personal work of the goddess. It is one more piece of confirmatory evidence of the close connection between the two. The goddess either, mystically, *is* the stone; or else is to work through it.

"I surmise that the broken sections of the original whole stone are to be rejoined before the fated marriage of the man and the woman can be consummated. One knows not the beginning of the myth, and therefore one cannot pronounce upon it. Should you desire to scoff, you have every justification. Nevertheless, there are certain appearing facts in the dark emergence of faith from the mists of the planet's prime, that do seem to bear out a history of which these prophecies may be the intuitive fruit.

"Both records were inscribed many hundreds of years before the birth of Christ. Ostensibly they have in no way influenced the Gospel story. Yet those thorough-going folk who style themselves Rationalists will inform you that the legend of a Virgin and holy Child has arisen, as if spontaneously, in many lands of both the old and the new worlds long anterior to Christian missionary activities. . . . They have, indeed, gone a step beyond. They have assigned a fixed astronomical date for the common original of those legends; calculated, if you please, on the rising of the sun in conjunction with the setting of the constellation Virgo, whose five principal stars are assumed to have suggested to primitive anthropomorphic imaginations the outstretching of the Virgin Mother towards her infant Sun-God!

"By such imbecilities do scientists, snatching a holiday from their science, make themselves ridiculous in the eyes of gods and men. For the individual stars, equally with the constellations, were to be given distinguishing names by the ancients, and, since they, the stars, were in themselves sublime, after whom or what should they be named but the sublime gods and archetypes? And should a poor likeness to a known shape, in these clusters of stars, suggest the appellation, would not it be adopted? But most are unhappy. To affirm that the men of old literally *saw* in the stars the god or mythical type whose name they were made to bear, this surely is the height and apex of learned childishness! . . .

"The Virgin myth truly has reappeared in many surprising forms and places throughout the world, but it never originated in a constellation. Most obviously, it is a statement of the extremely antique Mother worship, distorted in this way and in that. In the Palestine version, for instance, the goddess herself is even eliminated; the human mother is half-confounded with her, half-remains in her own rank and person; the father is so completely despised and ignored that he is denied the honour of begetting his own son; the son is made a god; the extramundane meteor, that is so important an element of the earlier tradition, becomes a bright announcing star. Such a crass perversion of every feature of the original might reduce even a cynic to astonishment, but that it is all very instructive. . . . I don't weary you, Saltfleet?"

"No. Pray go on."

"For so many kindred myths distributed over the globe indicate, of course, a common source; and this of Palestine is manifestly an orientalising—probably of a north-west European faith. Here are my supporting reasons. The social equality of a free people would fail to find its counterpart among the rigid castes of the East; accordingly, the mother of a fateful son, if of known lowly birth, must be ennobled by heaven. Being thus translated, she would come to usurp many of the functions of the goddess, and in time the memory of the independent existence of the latter would altogether disappear. The goddess was alone; therefore her successor is humanly unmated—a virgin. Her divinity, however—how could it be otherwise in the East?—is still below that of her infant, by reason of his sex.

"You will understand, Saltfleet, that I am not attempting anything so foolish as the destruction of the historical figure of Christ, with His inimitable character and teachings. Since something does not come out of nothing, such a personage, whether divine or human, has existed. I simply maintain that He has become attached to a pre-existing myth, with which He has no true connection. This myth, I say, doubtless sprang from the north-west of the world known to the ancients, so agreeable is its nature with what we are told of the peoples primitively occupying that cold and mystic region. For only among those peoples do we encounter the reverence of woman-kind which, despite Schopenhauer and his tribe, surely remains as the basis of the finest qualities in humanity. Nowhere else could the chaste worship of the Creatrix have originated than in the first home of those free Scandinavians whose blackest shame it was for a man to set finger in anger on a woman; or of those forest-dwelling Germans, who according to Tacitus, believed the females of their race to be divinely inspired with the spirit of prophecy. . . ."

"Knossos came later?" asked Saltfleet.

"Necessarily, if my theory be correct. Knossos was a lingering on the road to Asia and to degeneration. Crete, of which Knossos was the then capital, furnishes perhaps our earliest exact knowledge of the cult in working. In like manner the final wanton worship of Cybele throughout Phrygia and Asia Minor generally, that was a presentment of the faith's flaring up to death. It had passed slowly eastwards, from the deep-natured, deep-sighted men of the north, to brown-skinned priests and moralists, and so on to heavily-bejewelled, painted, perfumed women, with their appropriate male companions, dancing mad orgies. The passage east was coincident with the passage of the centuries. Were it ever needful to seek a cause for the decay and death of a creed or system, here the explanation would not be obscure. A creed removed from its land, climate, circumstances, and own people, is already becoming something else. In but few cases can the new soil be as favourable as the old for its increase to purity and splendour.

"Let the first nation beyond the racial boundary receive the light, the separating out of the faith's elements begins. Let the next nations receive it, there ensues the same perpetual modifying and rejecting, until the creed shall have become interwoven with the imperishable racial traits of the peoples receiving. . . . Regard the destiny of Christianity, Saltfleet. Recall the innumerable types that at one time or another have presented Christianity: the simple fishermen of Galilee, the early anchorites of the deserts, the Crusading holy knights, the fanatical inquisitors of Charles the Fifth and his monstrous son, the grim Calvinists of persecuted Scotland, the old-time English hunting parsons of the shires, the modern Laodiceans of our national hierarchy, watching in despair the approaching end of all faith—what, of the Christian elements, have had those types in common? One has insisted upon the torments of hell, another on celestial love, a third on a mystical Saviour, scarcely to be understood, a fourth on the metaphysics of original evil, a fifth on right living. . . . A branch that is little in one land and century may become everything in another; and in yet another may wither to nothingness. . . ."

"Proceed to the matter, Arsinal. We know that the New Testament creed is a compound, and that a heterogeneous mass is unstable."

"I am merely emphasising that the root of a faith is necessarily to be sought in its land of origin. Every divine entity harboured by the human mind has needed a special environment in order to take shape at all. The Prophet's Allah demanded the glaring deserts and nightly canopy of glittering stars of Arabia; Aphrodite demanded the violet seas and perfumed air of the Grecian Archipelago; Thor, the mighty storms, salt sea spray and sunless skies of the iron coasts of the north. In like manner, I tell you, Saltfleet, the Mother could only have created herself in the human intelligence in some physical region of gloom, silence, and impenetrable forest. . . .

"The Minoan clay tablet has informed us—though not in quite so many words—that our monastery stone came from the west. This may indicate the western Baltic lands, Norway, Britain, Gaul, the old Hercynian Forest of Germany; but I cannot think, Spain or Southern France. In all those northern districts the archaic yield is rich. Thus they were populated very far back. The blood-descendants of that northern stock not only built all the noblest religious edifices of Greece and Gothic Europe, but created the dream-like Hellenic mythology, its naiver Norse compeer, and the clouds, ghosts, fairies, and legendary heroes of the lochs and isles.

"The savage ancestors of such creators obviously had it in their breed to see past practical existence. I don't mean, in the Semitic sense of an ingrained realisation of their creaturely impotence, inducing a relation to the invisible as of duty to a master; nor in the Hindu sense of a bodily and mental weariness of the grind of life, logically conducting in due course to Nirvana; but in the Cimmerian sense of a profound mystical recognition of the actuality of another world of phantoms and spirits interrupting and permeating their own . . . which long afterwards, Saltfleet, has become metaphysics and music. Even the grander monuments of Egypt seem difficult to account for, considered as the handiwork of a sun-baked race. The dusk and quietude of supernatural northern forests, one could almost aver, are reproduced by those fearful columns of Karnak, those sepulchral recesses of the Pyramids. . . .

"Yet mere climate and land will avail nothing unless the inhabiting race be appropriate, and a man be born to it, and that man be confronted, blinded, staggered, by his Highest possible. For the first condition, I would like seriously to put it to you: whence came those blue-eyed, deep-thoughted, metaphysical giants into the world? The native stocks of Asia, Africa, America, the South Seas, the Mediterranean, have no more than animals that pigmentation or that curiosity concerning the unseen workings of the world. . . . Nowadays, indeed, all colours and all characters seem so blended in our populations, that a man may inherit from many sources, and be inscrutable to himself and others. . . ."

"And render the whole modern theory unworkable!" completed Saltfleet. "For instance, pure blonds are still frequent enough; whereas my experience is that they are usually of the sportsman type, and spiritually rather peculiarly phlegmatic."

"Rarely are we so fortunate in science as to find the truth on the surface. Here, in this circumstance of yours, Saltfleet, it may be very much as with the massive ruins still strewing the globe from the receded tides of northern conquest and sovereignty. The sublime philosophies of India represent the turned ebb of such a tide of blue-eyed warriors sweeping in from the west. The vigorous blood, used to cold temperatures, sickened and ceased under withering suns; but the philosophies remain. So with the Goths, Franks, Normans, Lombards, in southern and western Europe. While they were yet superior to their new circumstances, lofty cathedrals everywhere shot up to express a ghostly faith. But those races, too, have sunk from their first height, and sometimes the earlier brown-eyed have crept back to equality, through the greater stamina of their blood in countries physically suited, and sometimes the conquering race has flamed up within these last few hundreds of years, only immediately afterwards to die out; as in the Gothic Italy of the Renaissance, the Gothic Spain of the conquests of Granada and America. Then, as well innumerable intermarriages between the races have depressed the higher, and raised the lower.

"But the cathedrals still stand. And just such a monument in his own person is the blond of to-day. The blood of his forefathers has failed, leaving him colour, physical habit, stature, for vestiges. Why has it failed, Saltfleet? Because over too long a time it has not been renewed."

Saltfleet was silent, eyeing him sombrely, through the smoke of his cigar.

"To renew it—that northern blood—we should need to know more of its beginning," said Arsinal. "As a *lusus naturae*, a miracle for it may have to be presumed. Yet such a miracle as even science might allow."

"Would this be the Stone Age happening, that once you spoke to me about?"

"With that idea I have played. . . . Yes, many times have I played with it; but never quite seriously before to-day. Indeed, it would be very awful to contemplate, Saltfleet. For imagine!

Long, long ago a meteorite, of elements unknown to earth, would have shot to ground in the west; and somehow, with that descent, originated the worship of the Mother. . . . And since men cannot be wise from nothing, our two predictions, of Crete and Caria, have been a history, and also with the descent of the aerolith, a people has been founded; but I have told you but just now that the earliest worshippers of the Mother may most probably have been the first ancestors of the northern stocks. . . .

"Chiefly I have connected these events because a racial change of supreme importance has been adumbrated. No change grander than the creation of this highest and noblest of all human peoples hitherto can be conceived. Nor can I feel that a Messiah has been indicated by the son who was to be greater than all mankind and put wickedness under foot. Neither is that need for a Messiah agreeable with the spirit of the early northern faiths, nor, historically, has such an one ever come out of the north or west. . . .

"I grow confused with too many associated thoughts, and can but sketch one here and there. . . . How could a meteorite have induced a racial change? A chemical emanation from such, terrific as that from radium, but of a far different nature, may well have had force to raise that atomic storm within the flesh of a brown-eyed pair—a savage woman and her paramour, lying together—that even the sacred citadel should become pierced through and through. . . . Thus a new son would indeed be born! . . . I could not support its probability against the meanest physiologist, but neither could the most expert deny the possibility. Hardly do we yet know all the elements of earth; and the spectroscope has given us quite unknown ones among the stars. . . ."

"What *is* this phenomenon of the flint in your pocket, Arsinal? How caused?"

"I can't yet decide. . . . But perhaps the whole was shattered, after arrival, along the line of easiest frangibility, and the halves may be polar. This polarity may indicate a strong galvanic action for the whole. It is a thought I have had. I have no more doubt that it is meteoric. . . .

"Then, the peopling of half a world from a single pair, with whole tribes of individuals having revolutionary new characters . . . this might well come to pass, given the necessary might of the radiated particles, continuing to be inherited by common generation. It is little in history for a strong character to triumph during many hundreds of years. The world has seen the Hapsburg jaw and the Bourbon eye. So one single pair, both possessed of the new force, and completing each other, might found that dynasty of a million natural kings.

"But the 'wickedness' to be put under foot. This can but signify the subjugation of the inferior races practising barbarism and savagery. . . . Or should it be a longer prophecy, relating to all the world, what in effect would happen—has happened—is this. Those possessed of the new characters went on multiplying in the north until a sufficient time had elapsed to over-stock it with these yellow-haired; when the usual choice between famine and migration would present itself, and be decided in the usual way. In this manner the conquest of the rich, unwarlike 'wicked' lands would begin. . . .

"Strange, Saltfleet, if true, that the first man and father of such a stock should escape mention in the early chronicles! Yet is it true? Snorre Sturlason's Ynglinga Saga relates the conquest of the northern lands, including Sweden, by a chief named Odin, removing with his followers from the neighbourhood of the Black Sea. This was not long before Christ. Now such an event, with all its magical circumstances, is to-day no more credited than the founding of Rome by Romulus; and yet the invention has its value of another sort.

"The chief god of the north has always been Odin. Of the south-east of Europe, Zeus. These chief deities had precisely equal functions; neither was a tyrant, like the supreme gods of the orientals, but both were the just, and on the whole benevolent, fathers and elder brothers of gods and men. The name of the mother of Odin is known, but has no connection. That of the mother of Zeus was Rhea, the Great Mother. . . . And so, if the human founder and hero of the northern peoples were still called

Odin, the other circumstances of his recorded career being all dismissed, and his date being put back even into palaeolithic times, then one might begin to see why in the mythology of the other branch of those peoples, the Hellenic branch, his counterpart, Zeus, after his apotheosis should have been given this Mother-Goddess for maternal parent.

"For, be his name Zeus or Odin, he, no other, would be the first product of that marriage which, perhaps too imaginatively, I am wishing to associate with the fall to earth of an aerolite, that has always spoken of the Mother. Thus, figuratively at least, he would indeed be her son. . . . And in the higher arch of his skull would at last be space for that vision of transcendental glory, that after the lapse of generations might make of him a supernatural being, a *god*. . . ."

"That is for him, then!" said Saltfleet. "And for the goddess? . . ."

Arsinal got to his feet irresolutely, but did not move away.

"I have no theory for her. . . . Yet perhaps she might be attached, mystically, to the aerolite—as *eidolon* . . . its spirit, or apparition. . . . I cannot explain. . . ."

The other pitched what was left of his cigar into the fire-place.

"And you are to have the hardiness, believing, or even only half-believing, these things, or some of them . . . to fit the halves together?"

"I could not have pursued them all my life, to draw back now."

"You have formed no notion of what is likely to happen?"

"I am not mad, Saltfleet, although you may think me so. A very ancient prediction exists. To put its wisdom to the test, now that I may, is surely not equivalent to the confession of faith!"

"It speaks of a man and a woman."

"I know that it does."

"Then are you to arrange for the presence of such a couple at your experiment?"

"Why do you ask me this? . . ."

Arsinal had turned pale, and, understanding that he had

reached the limits of his complaisance, Saltfleet urged him no more. But after a long silence, there dropped from him:

"I have seen your *eidolon*, Arsinal."

"You have not told me that."

"In this very room. Sitting here in the dark last evening, with your stone in my hand, I saw a phantom, silent and erect in *that* chair." He pointed. "It was in the shape of an extraordinarily tall woman; only just visible, but not to be mistaken. This is not an invention; neither could I have imagined it."

"What passed, Saltfleet?"

"Nothing. She vanished, and I went to bed."

Arsinal looked down at him heedfully, but soon turned his back, and there followed a long silence.

It was interrupted by a knocking at the door. Saltfleet opened it to the waiter.

"Mr. Copping is below, sir."

The two in the room exchanged glances, and Saltfleet said:

"Ask him to come up."

Peter entered; and again he wore his rainproof, and it was damp. In jaunty sullenness and without a smile, he took the introduction to Arsinal, returning him the stiffest of half-bows. Then he put back the cigarette to his lips.

"Please take a seat!"

"I am not staying. . . . I've looked in only to say that I duly received your note, and posted straight across with it after breakfast to the house; where I've spoken with Mrs. Fleming, who is Drapier's executrix. Miss Fleming was out so soon, so we couldn't get her concurrence to the arrangement. But in any case it is to stand. . . . That meeting at my place is off, Mr. Saltfleet. Neither of you, gentlemen, is to meet, or try to meet, Miss Fleming for the purpose of discussing *anything*. Word of honour being passed to this effect, Mrs. Fleming will let you have both the stones in question, for your own, without payment or further condition."

"Have you the second with you?" asked Arsinal quickly.

"No, Miss Fleming has it somewhere. It will be sent round

during the day."

"Why are we not to meet her?"

"Her mother thinks she has had nearly enough," replied Peter drily. "She is on the hypersensitive side, and this business threatens to drag on indefinitely."

"What feature of the business is principally appealing to Miss Fleming?"

"I cannot discuss it with you."

"Cannot, or do not wish to?"

"I neither wish to, nor do I know her whole mind."

Saltfleet spoke. "And if we don't care to go behind Miss Fleming's back in cancelling the meeting, Mr. Copping?"

"You haven't cancelled it—we have cancelled it. And there is no need for you to worry about Miss Fleming. The situation will be explained to her on her return."

"I am rather thinking of my own name for reliability. Mr. Arsinal personally has given no undertaking, but I have, after a fashion."

"Then it is regrettable, but I cannot debate it. This is Mrs. Fleming's offer. As having, by law, the disposal of Drapier's property, it is for her to say what she will do with it; and she is prepared to let you take both these stones, on the express condition that you promise to refrain from further communicating with her daughter. The proviso cannot hurt you, it is quite unnecessary to regard it as an insult, and I have sufficiently made clear what it does mean."

"What is to be the alternative?"

"If you turn the offer down, it will be withdrawn; and then Mrs. Fleming may decide to put in a claim to the thing you took from Drapier on Devil's Tor, besides reserving to herself the right to deal with the other as her lawyers may advise."

Arsinal drew his friend apart into a corner, to whisper:

"We had better accept this, Saltfleet. I must give up meeting the girl, rather than such a last chance."

"Wait!" returned the other. "First let us see what is behind it all."

He disliked the *taste* of this hasty negotiation. Evidently, the mother and (he supposed) lover had taken unfair advantage of the child's temporary absence to try to rush through an arrangement that they knew she would prevent if possible. The reason for it might be what young Copping said, yet Saltfleet felt also that *he* was being aimed at. They should be afraid of him, in some vague way. Perhaps Mrs. Fleming, remembering his threats beforehand, was imagining follies; and had infected her son-in-law to be, whose behaviour otherwise, indeed, was unaccountable. He had been on the verge of rudeness throughout both interviews. His cold eye, when he thought Saltfleet not to be observing him, had rested on him far too often in an involuntary distaste, curiosity and perplexity. . . . He chose not to be so branded. Neither would he rob Miss Fleming of her opportunity to discuss the matters she wished to discuss. He preferred to play a little with Arsinal's chances. . . .

Escaping from him, he asked Peter:

"How long do you give us to decide?"

"I must know now."

"Pray let me return the answer, Arsinal. It is this, Mr. Copping. Whatever happens, you have to wait for Miss Fleming's coming back before you can fulfil your side of the contract. Then do you at the same time procure a couple of lines over her signature, to the effect that she is agreeable to the proposed course. That we will regard as sufficient in the matter of a discharge; and having it, we will proceed to leave Miss Fleming rigidly alone."

"Miss Fleming is in an excited condition, and her mother wishes not to leave anything to her decision."

"But then she may not give up the stone to you."

"She can scarcely oppose her mother's executorship."

"How soon is she expected back?"

"She may be back already."

"Please give Mrs. Fleming that answer. Mr. Arsinal, who has not the honour of her acquaintance, will be extremely happy to accept her offer of these token-stones, which are probably of value to himself alone, and which he has long been seeking. The condition accompanying the offer, both he and I will willingly adhere to, so far as we honourably may. I, however, have passed some kind of a promise to Miss Fleming, who, accordingly, must first release me. One or both of us will make a point of remaining in during the rest of the morning, to receive your further communication."

"This, you realise, may decide Mrs. Fleming to reconsider the offer?"

"Our request is so reasonable, that I am sure that Mrs. Fleming will not regard it as a ground for changing her mind."

"You may think so; but I not. Her sole motive in this is to spare her daughter, while you are demanding the reverse."

"On the contrary, I have too much regard for Miss Fleming to wish to go against her best interests."

"*That* her mother might consider nearly an impertinence!" growled the artist.

He turned his shoulder, stood undetermined for a moment, but then bowed, very casually and almost with a scowl, to Arsinal, ignored Saltfleet, and at once left the room. It was nearing eleven o'clock.

"Why did you do this thing, Saltfleet?" asked his associate, coming closer to him. "I too might have liked to talk to that girl, but surely not at such a price. What is in your mind?"

Saltfleet laughed.

"You had better not take them at their own serious valuation, or you may find yourself disappointed of your bone, like Æsop's dog. The affair is hers, not theirs. This is a conspiracy of two against—her higher soul, perhaps. Very little has been needed to make it a conspiracy of four; and yet we might not—all the four of us—have succeeded in vanquishing her. Such, Arsinal, is my opinion of Miss Fleming."

"Then what is next to happen?"

"We must not go upon what has been said just now, but upon what was said yesterday. I have no doubt she will still insist on her meeting; and not much doubt that she will refuse to make over your prize to her mother till she has discovered more about it.”

“Will she look in here?”

Saltfleet shook his head. “I’ve rather been wondering if she has gone out to Devil’s Tor.”

XXI

The Undeclared

Reaching Whitestone about ten o’clock, Peter had learnt at the door that Ingrid was already out. Her mother should be in her room. He went along, and was admitted.

It was a dark, foggy day, quite unlike August, yet Helga thought that her daughter had gone for a walk. Her ankle was much better. She was no doubt feeling the need to escape from the house’s atmosphere of depression.

A flush came unreasonably to Peter’s cheeks.

“Surely she hasn’t gone to Devil’s Tor?”

“It would be rather far for her,” replied Helga.

Nevertheless he was convinced that the guess was right. Only her ankle had stopped her from making the trip before, drawn by her superstitious inquisitiveness. But had her loyalty and affection been as strong as that fancifulness, she would have *required* him to accompany her, for such a walk, on such a morning. Instead, she had not so much as troubled to conceal that she wished to go without him. Her hurrying off so soon after breakfast could only mean that.

Helga saw what he felt.

“She didn’t say she was going there, Peter; but if she has, she probably didn’t care to run the gauntlet of the village street to beg your society. . . . Wait with me a little. Sit down.”

He did so reluctantly.

“I have to tell you of the arrangements,” said Helga, “so it’s as well you came. The inquest is to be held at the Institute here, at eleven, to-morrow. I would like you to be present.”

“Shall I call here, or meet you there?”

“Here, please. My uncle and I must attend, but Ingrid, of course, need not and won’t. Then there is the funeral. No postponement is likely, and so I have arranged for the interment to be at Plymouth, next Tuesday afternoon. We shall leave here at two o’clock. No one knew him, so there will be nobody except ourselves; and you must come.”

“I will, of course.”

“I think that is all. Shall I have coffee made?”

“I’ve only just breakfasted, thanks.”

He accepted and lit a cigarette from her offered box.

“What is troubling you, my dear?”

Peter had the impulse to show her Saltfleet’s note that he had brought round in his pocket, and to confess the plans of meeting which had been come to at the “Bell” last evening. His anger with Ingrid had fetched him so far; and still it was a treachery from which his honesty and sense of oneness with her recoiled. He held his peace, smoking and looking away.

“You are not really annoyed with Ingrid for not waiting in?”

“A little—not much.” . . . Then he found that his confession had already begun, and must have an even wider range than he had guessed.

“To be quite candid, less annoyed with her than rather unhappy about her present condition of soul.”

“What is wrong, Peter?”

“I have been down now some eight-and-forty hours. Have you observed any noticeable difference in her manner during that time?”

“She is well, Peter,” said Helga quickly.

“I don’t know. Perhaps she isn’t so well. . . . Do you remember, yesterday . . .” He stopped short.

“What was that?”

“In the morning, in this room. I had mentioned having run into a stranger at the cross-roads, who then turned out to be your friend Saltfleet. I made sundry remarks in his connection, and alluded to an intuition of mine, but refrained from illustrating it fully. Do you remember that?"

"Yes, I do. I understand you were reticent on account of Ingrid's being in the room. It concerned her?"

"Yes."

"But how could it concern her?"

"I will tell you. My intuition was—it is—that this Saltfleet might become a very strong attraction for your daughter. . . . Though not, perhaps, in the soft sense. In a sinister sense. . . . Just as a 'rogue' star might pull out of its course the outermost planet of the sun it properly belonged to."

Helga's eyes watched him actively and seriously.

"There would not be time for that to become a danger, Peter, for after to-morrow he is bound to go away."

"I know. But you are scarcely acquainted with the whole story, and he has made such very good foothold since his first appearance yesterday. How many times has she met him? Twice, I fancy. Well, at the 'Bell' yesterday, I assure you I was nearly *de trop*. They have this miserable business of Devil's Tor between them. These extraordinary counterpart wonder-stones, the series of catastrophes on the Tor, and quite a succession of other phenomena, not all of them even minor—cumulated, they are already setting her thoughts whirling in a sort of devil's dance . . . and now he has a trump-card ready, in the shape of his confederate, Arsinal—who has just arrived. . . . I *must* tell you, Mrs. Fleming. It is violating an understanding; but a meeting has been arranged—without you—for his coming. It's to be to-day, at my studio. She insists on a conversation with Arsinal. Saltfleet more than humoured her, and I, very weakly, gave my consent to it. Here is Saltfleet's note, just received."

He passed it to her, and she read, then slowly and musingly handed it back. Peter returned it to his pocket.

"I won't reproach you, Peter, if this was your only way of keeping on terms with her in an hour of wilfulness. But what does Ingrid want? What is she aiming at?"

"On the face, the meeting is to be for the purpose of thrashing out the ownership of these two stones. She tells Saltfleet that Arsinal can have one already; and the second, if he can show his occult right to it. *Occult* is the word she used."

"And what is underneath these surface arrangements?"

"Her psychic storm—that is gathering force, and is presently going to tear her to bits, if someone doesn't interfere. She can't rest. Off she has gone to the Tor this morning—I know it. And I would follow her there, if I didn't also know that my reception at her hands would be that of an interloper."

"But she hasn't gone with *him*."

"No, not with Saltfleet. . . . I want you to understand, Mrs. Fleming, that my intuition says nothing about an infatuation. . . . For years and years I have felt that there was always this danger of a particular type of man coming into her life, to draw her, not towards her happiness, but away from it. I must have felt that I should recognise the type when it should turn up. I got the recognition yesterday, when I first saw the man. . . ."

Helga gave him a queer long look.

"What is your true opinion of him, then, Peter?"

"I find him repellent; yet I will give you a fair answer to the question. With his darkness, and pride, and beauty—and a kind of hellish generosity in him, too—he might be able to exercise an enormous sway over the mind of an imaginative girl. And Ingrid has certainly never seen anybody like him before. There is nobody like him. But all this is only the romantic shadow of a great solid fact that resembles a lump of lead in my heart, and won't take shape. It is not what he might be to any girl, but what he *must* be to Ingrid. . . . I will talk of it no more."

"She has said nothing, Peter?"

"What could she say? What could she know? She is on a blindfold journey."

"I do not like him, either."

"And, in one way, you go further than I, for, in your secret soul, you accuse him of a very shocking crime—or you would, if such a charge could find roothold in your innocence of the bad world."

"No, no! . . ."

"Oh, I am not a fool! But he never did it. There would be no need for him to do it—neither is it in his nature. To *kill*, you must have the hating temperament; but that man is too satanically remote—too aloof. Trust me! Ingrid sees him the most clearly. For her, he is in most excellent contrast to all other men—only his danger for her she cannot see."

"Peter, I have never whispered that he could have——"

"And there is another point," he interrupted her. "I need not have brought him personally in at all, but your daughter's present excited state of mind might have been enough to show you the necessity for some prompt action. It would have been the easiest thing in the world to demonstrate to you, that as long as this business of the proprietorship of your cousin's stones drags on, her state will get, not better, but worse. Yet I *have* brought him in. Why? Because I want to pass the whole of my own serious uneasiness on to you, Mrs. Fleming; and not to have you believe it is a simple medical case of young-womanly nerves. But the trouble is, I can't prove any connection of sense or likelihood. You would have to be able to read my spirit, and that I can barely do myself. Here is a strange man, down for twenty-four hours; and here is your daughter, who has spoken civil words to him on a couple of brief necessary occasions. And I am assuring you, as a sober truth, that he constitutes a possible dark factor in her life, that may not be ignored. You have every right to laugh at me. I wonder at myself—I feel at this minute as remote from practical life as if I were not a member of society, but a disembodied ghost. But I have the ghastly *knowledge*. This Saltfleet, unless prevented, is to act as a disintegrant to our little circle."

"I know it too," said Helga quietly. She sat a little away, upright in her chair, with the back of her head thrust to rest against its top, while her eyes now seemed tired. . . . "You think you have seen into me, my dear, but either you couldn't be bothered, or—you *haven't*. I have been nearly as miserable over Ingrid as you."

He stared across. "But not, surely, on Saltfleet's account?"

"Yes, on his account. My feelings about him may not have the precise colour or the certainty of yours, but I hated to see them in the room together. And yesterday, when you both left me, to call on him, and I had to stay behind picturing the scene—I couldn't rest, I couldn't sit down. . . . It is very, very strange and uncanny, Peter, but you are perfectly right, and he is a man Ingrid has to fear—an unthinkable change *is* coming to this household, unless God averts it, by our endeavours or otherwise. . . . Yet that vaguer ground," she added wearily, "hardly belongs, and I don't know how it is. When you were here to tea two afternoons ago—your first day down—before ever Saltfleet was here in the place . . . I felt then that something was approaching us all."

"Like a disturbance, reaching our finer nerves first. Much would I give to be allowed to treat this ironically in my mind, Mrs. Fleming; but, in fact, there is nothing even silly in it. It is a question of equipment. It appears that you, as well as I, are equipped to receive fine messages, from God knows where. Some blight is darkening our little sky. We cannot discuss it, for we are ignorant of its origin, quarter, mode of attack, and exact peril; we can only take what practical steps are available to keep away unpromising and undesirable persons from outside."

"She is not a shallow or fickle girl, Peter."

"Now I must tell you that I don't know her. That second nature of hers is coming into the open at last, that all these years I have dreaded. If you mean, dishonour is not in her soul, no, it surely is not—yet of what consequence are honour and honesty in an affair of destiny? The truest heart will find a way; or a way will be found for it. A thing fated to happen employs itself only with the realities. . . . And shallow! Had she been shallower, she would have been more immune against a fellow like this. He is not to go for her vanity or voluptuousness. He is a great silent *magnet*."

"If it would help you to understand him, Hugh Drapier was very insistent that he resembles in person a certain celebrated bust of Cornelius Sulla, the Roman Dictator—I think he said, at Rome."

"That may be. So let us ensure that he does not dictate

here! . . ."

Peter got up. After smoking in abstraction for some moments, he proceeded:

"What *is* in our favour is that we can talk alone like this for once; and we had better turn it to profit. Ingrid may be back soon—and if she is, I shall probably forgive her so thoroughly, that she will get her own way towards perdition once more. I ask you to support me in burning our boats, while she is still away."

"How?" The question followed a slow, intent look.

"Thus," said Peter. "Saltfleet, you hope and assume, is to be off after to-morrow's inquest. Then let us see to it that he is. But until his friend Arsinal has both his prizes in his pocket, I doubt they will *not* be off. And yesterday afternoon you heard with your own ears how Ingrid was wanting and wanting her interview with this Arsinal—and how she was feeling herself drawn, too, to Saltfleet, *without* wanting it; without the ghost of any explainable motive, indeed. . . . So I've to reply to this note in my pocket, and if the meeting at my place is arranged and comes off, then, as certainly as one step down a flight of stairs is followed by others, supplementary conferences will be demanded by all the persons interested. They might remain on the spot for a week or fortnight, talking and talking with your daughter, even after she had promised them what they wanted. On what account? That isn't for me to say. But Arsinal, whom I understand to be the intellectual expert of the two, would doubtless furnish the sustaining means; while his big bodyguard, with the grey magician's eyes, would eternally sit there as a third, reducing her, minute by minute, to helplessness, discord and ruin. . . . Do you wish that?"

"Some excuse they must find for behaving so."

"It lies to their hand, in Devil's Tor. That could be Arsinal's study in these parts. It is a place of vast antiquity, and the centre of our many occult happenings. It would also serve marvellously well as a *rendezvous*; one is quite out of the way there, and not easily surprised."

"But you are speaking of Ingrid, Peter!"

"It is the worst of a business like hers, that, with the sincerest nature in the world, one is very soon up to the eyes in deceit. You cannot hide one feature, and bring another into undue prominence, without entering upon the whole work of art. She has already hidden this desired meeting from you; as I *know* that she is hiding things from me. . . . And so we must stop it all in time. These fellows must be given at once what they are after. By you—for you have the right and the power, and nobody else has any to interfere. Then to-morrow, the inquest being past, there can be no inducement whatsoever for them to stop longer in a place like Belhill, since the Tor, without its exponent, will not hold Arsinal's interest beyond, possibly, a single visit. . . . And Ingrid must begin her process of returning to her normal self."

"You suggest my re-offering them what she omitted taking round last evening?"

"Yes; finish the job."

"On what conditions?"

"Leave all to me. I shall stipulate—no meetings; and the whole acquaintance with your daughter to end."

"Won't that be insulting them?"

"No. I'll say, what is the truth, that you, her mother, are solicitous on account of her health."

"I can't see why they should not agree, Peter."

"Nor I. They're to keep what they've got as well, and the concession is really very thorough."

"But Ingrid . . . ?"

Peter was silent.

"Who is to bear that brunt, you or I?" asked Helga, watching him through half-closed lids.

"I will, since the advice is mine," he answered slowly at last.

"Will you dare to, Peter? You may lose her."

"I trust not. But I'd rather be dismissed than see her go on the rocks."

"I mean, the final responsibility of course is mine, Peter; and I have made no sort of promise. You had better not appear in this."

"No; if I have been crooked with her, she must know it. I am most anxious that she shall understand I am not at all worrying about my own welfare. What I have done and am doing, is for her."

"Then who is to ask her for the stone? For she has it still."

"Could you lay your hand on it?"

Helga smiled faintly, while she shook her head.

"I think I won't show so much fear of my own daughter."

"And she would rightly resent it—perhaps even more than the actual killing of her plans. We must spare her all we can, Mrs. Fleming. A proud soul, in the throes of an obsession, should hate merely to be watched; it wants a world of blindness and darkness. . . . But that we needn't discuss. Now I'll be off to the 'Bell', as your envoy, with the conditional offer; and inform our men that the negotiated article will follow during the morning or afternoon. When Ingrid comes in, whether I am back or not, you must see her first, tell her what has been done, and insist on the immediate return of the stone to you without debate. Don't be drawn into any argument, but insist on your office—and, if you like, on the impossibility of your going against Drapier's emphatic wishes. Speak to her, not as her mother, but as the person invested by law. . . . And *then* refer her to me. It is I who advised the cancelling of the meeting with Arsinal, though he is specially down. It is I who have fortified you in your executorship, though Ingrid, I well knew, had come to regard this affair as her own. It is I who am seeking to block for her all the avenues leading from a normal life, although for the moment such an escape appears to her the one thing worth while. She must abominate me for everything; and in the word 'treachery' she will find my conduct's ready-made description. Afterwards, however, I hope she will come to recognise that all has been but the moving of my great love for her. She is too just to suppose that I have been impelled by petty jealousy. Let her want meetings with any other man, and I will stand aside."

"I know that, Peter. Yet I'm afraid. . . . I'm afraid! . . . Why couldn't you put all this to her beforehand?"

"Because I am in the right, but the right cannot always, or even generally, make itself appear such to other persons. Unless the thing is fixed before she returns, her character is so entirely obedient to the intuitions of her brain, and the sub-intuitions of her heart, that she will almost surely elect to act without me, and without you; and meet these men alone in a place we may both of us regard as deplorable.”

“Are we doing the best, my dear? We are taking it so much for granted that our view of her attraction to these people must be the wise one. It is a step we can’t recall. Wouldn’t you allow her to state her own attitude first?”

“She has stated it. I know it well.”

“I have the horrid feeling that instead of closing a door, we shall be opening one. She may break with you quite, Peter; and that may be the beginning of the end of all our old happiness.”

“If it is doomed,” said Peter, shrugging.

“Have you no such misgiving?”

“Perhaps.”

“And you dare to offer her the affront?”

“There is a storm coming, and its centre *seems* to be that way—towards all that medley, supernatural or sinister, of Devil’s Tor, and Drapier’s counterpart stones, and our two birds of ill omen flapping their wings at the inn. The actual fork to strike us may descend from another quarter of the sky; but assuredly, while we retain our wits, we have to move from the *obvious* threat.”

Helga viewed him.

“Is it to be soon, Peter?”

“The tension seems to be fairly high inside all of us.”

“What does it mean?”

“Ask a wild beast, creeping for shelter in front of thunder, what its fears are. Neither do I know anything. I know that I am becoming irrational and wish to urge you to send Drapier’s accursed stone out of the house, before it has had time to work any more mischief.”

“My dear! How can you suppose—”

“The man who brought it here is lying dead, anyway.”

Helga stood facing him in silence.

“Are you serious in this?” she asked.

"I know nothing else of the one you have, but if they belong, it should be as damnable as the other, which they hold. I ran across Drapier on the Tor two days ago, and he was playing with it, and it showed me a landscape full of ghosts. . . . Some other time you shall hear about it. Yes, Ingrid knows. So I can quite understand the enormous craving of these two men to get such treasures into their keeping; and I say in full seriousness: 'Let them have the stones, *and* the devil that inhabits them, death-dealing or otherwise!'"

"You think that all these matters are evil, Peter?"

"An untimely death is evil, the abnormal is evil, morbid cravings are evil, a young girl's forgetting of her friends and turning to strangers, that is evil too."

"And your way is the only way?"

"I must have said enough now to show you your daughter's situation," replied Peter. "And if you still can't apprehend my stand in preferring her lasting prosperity to the easiness of pleasing her for an hour or a day, then I fear that more than one of us is fey."

She returned no answer in words, but a moment later the artist left the room, determined to act as though he were empowered with the full commission.

When he got back to the house with the account of his failure, Ingrid had still not returned. Helga heard him with a sort of listlessness.

"And so you might as well not have gone," was her subdued comment, "for, since it is to depend on her, she will not consent."

"She must be made to consent. You must exert your authority."

"I doubt I shall have none here."

She went on. "And now, Peter, you may see for yourself how hopeless it is ever to dream of opposing that man's will. I tried to keep him from following Hugh to the Tor; but he went. We have tried to keep him from Ingrid, and he has refused, and they will meet. But what does he want with her? Of what possible use can

330

her conversation be to these men? . . . Or does he despise *me* so thoroughly, that he will not accept the thing from my hand?"

"That is nonsense, for why should he despise you?"

"He knows I—fear him."

"Then you must tell Ingrid so, and perhaps she will not wish to see her mother scorned."

There was a pause.

"She is a long time out," said Helga. "I hope she has *not* gone to Devil's Tor. They may make their way up there, too."

The suggestion startled Peter, who, however, took a minute to consider it, and then quieted down.

"One, at least, is to remain in. It is very improbable that they will part company, and anyway there is little for Saltfleet up there, while the other would wait to be conducted. They may be interested later in the day."

She had not proposed that he should go in search of Ingrid, and somehow he felt the strongest disinclination to do so, which was not indolence, but something more psychological. His pride was silent, and his anger had died down—it was like some invisible wall of objection stretching right across his taking further action of any sort towards Ingrid's insulation from this business. He was conscious of a defeat, and was obstinate in his following apathy, but the apathy was also active; it was laid upon him like a paralysing hand, for a purpose. He was dimly aware that a result was to come from the visit he had just paid. He *had* acted sufficiently; and therefore must act no more, but wait.

He lit a new cigarette, and presently went out of the room, but not from the house. Helga was left alone, with her nameless agitation, that grew and grew.

XXII

The Star

The rising moor that was the way to Devil's Tor, as Saltfleet
traversed it at a long stride, was clothed in a fine, white, quiet
mist, from which furze bushes no more than a hundred feet
distant would loom slowly and mysteriously, without details or
other colour than that of darkness. There was no drift, and all
nature's essence seemed to be in the mounting damp ground
exhalations. Before dropping to the valley at the foot of the Tor,
he paused to light another cigar.

He had not deliberately planned this walk, but he had entered
upon it as if naturally, without pleasure, purpose, or thought of
consequence. Arsinal he had easily prevailed on to stay in; the
expected message from Whitestone might come at any time.

Then Saltfleet found himself continuing to stand arrested
where he had lit the cigar, smoking quietly, his eyes glancing
down and away at the grassy steep before him, as far as it remained unswallowed by the mist. The Tor was quite invisible.

What really could have happened to put him so suddenly out
of sympathy with a man he had liked from the first, whose interests he had made his own for months past? In a way, the answer should be simple; yet its very simplicity was dark. Till
yesterday Arsinal's annexation of the affair had gone unchal-
lenged. Now the business had spread, the girl Ingrid Fleming was
interested, he himself was not without a stake. He meant his
ghostly adventure at the inn last night. The woman's attire had
been primitive, her size preternatural. Drapier's flint had been in
his hand. What part of that experience had been Arsinal's?

His Athens overtaking, again. And the image in the stone
itself; and the girl's shock of rushing waters. . . . The extraordinary coincidence of his finding in Drapier's dead fist the counterpart of Arsinal's stone. And Drapier's repeated escapes from
death on Devil's Tor; his destruction at last. . . . Why must he

suppress reason, and be loyal to a crazed man? These phenomena, accidents and adventures had no necessary connection with Arsinal's case. A long business needed a succession of instruments, and the earliest in might be the first to go. . . .

A long mystery in time, and an extended one in space, for its springs had reached to Athens, Crete, Tibet; not to mention Arsinal's early home, wherever that had been. In its minor way, it was even like the slow, fateful unfolding of a world-event—such as the battle of Hastings. A number of ordained acts, crises, encounters, clashes, deaths, and chance happenings, over half a dozen lands, in five, ten or twenty years, had to interrupt the lives of a multitude of persons, many of them unassociated, before the single final impetus, to hurl England to its destruction, could be consciously launched by the hand of Norman William. . . . But in this smaller, domestic, supernatural piling of apparently unassociated accidents and incidents, the nature of the crash to come was still not indicated; and it could scarcely be the death of a nation.

Doubtless the ancients had enjoyed a much clearer vision of the reality and inexorability of fate. They did not, like the moderns, confound fate with their deities, but it was above them as another, more primal, universe. Thus one could not become familiar with fate—importune it with prayers—give it an image. Saltfleet presumed that men had come down to an Almighty God because they were no longer big enough to confront a Fate— without pity, mercy, or hope. The ancients had done that; and, for their courage, had received the gift of soberness and balance. Christians, Jews, Moslems, Hindus, Buddhists, were all dreamers. Only, to gain this cold, clear sense of proportion, the concept of Fate must be *stripped*; it must not be regarded as for the use of man. . . . The latest developed reaction to fate resembled nothing more than the chaos of the intellect. Coincidence, luck, miracle, fortune, protection, message—those were some of the names attached at random to such fragments of manifestation as occasionally smote a man in the face as he went about his work. Sophocles and Æschylus were the voices of a wiser, maturer race. . . .

He stared across to where the Tor should stand, and knew that some change altogether had come to him since the same time yesterday. He contrasted his present frame of mind with that on the identical spot when he had been on his way to seek Drapier. What were the positive differences of circumstance? Then he had believed Drapier alive, while now he lay grey and stiff in a dark room. Arsinal was unexpectedly down. The other half of his flint, the search for which would have been well-nigh desperate, had marvellously turned up of itself. He himself had become acquainted with a most unusual girl. Last night he had seen an authentic spirit. One or two other new nonentities were irritating him. The invisible height before him had grown definitely consecrated for his imagination by the solitary dying sighs of a victim. Arsinal had disclosed himself a little more. . . .

But it was not even the totality of these matters that could explain his mood. The spectacle of death was no novelty to him, the girl was not especially capturing his thoughts, his phantom was only being recalled now and again. Arsinal, actually, was fatiguing him. Tibet had faded into a rather disagreeable passage of his unwritten autobiography. There was some other cause for what he was feeling.

Purity and loneliness seemed increasingly to enwrap him while he stood here. If it was a waft from Devil's Tor, it would be strange; and still, that was the likeliest. The hill should be charmed. The powers of air and earth used it as a competing ground, fate employed its loose rocks to bowl men over, a magical stone had in and on it been found and re-found. If all the theories advanced to him were to be believed, its ruined tomb might quite easily be that of the founder of the higher human species. It might yet be haunted, and the haunter might at this moment be signalling the psychic waves that were reaching him as his purifying and quieting of temper. . . . But then, what would be the connection between such a haunting and the much more tremendous fate that could stretch over half the world and through a human generation, to bring so many factors to a hidden end together? . . .

He squared his shoulders and yawned, wondering why he was stopping like a statue to put questions unanswerable by himself, when doubtless that girl awaited him yonder through the fog, who should be the most sensitive of any to the influences underlying the facts, whose most extravagant fancies, it appeared, were securely founded upon another sort of truth, whose home district this was, and who had never yet been unwilling to speak. But had he truly come up in the hope of meeting her? In part, yes, without a doubt. But also he had had to see Devil's Tor again; he had felt, he still felt, that it held something for him. Yesterday he had not got as far as the top, he had not seen the blocked entrance to the tomb's passage. . . .

He started the descent to the valley.

Arsinal kept returning to and teasing his mind. He was vexed that he could come to no finality about that man. Their friendship could not be the same again, now that his secret egoism had discovered its appetite, but he had trusted to see but little more of him, and to ignore him while out of his presence. His sudden great weariness of him should have helped to that. This weariness was probably the back-springing of the bow from their unnatural tension of intimacy of months. Yet Arsinal throughout remained just underneath, or just within, his conscious mind, like an un-pleasantness . . . and now all at once, half-way down the hill, it occurred to him that the involuntary brooding must have been busier than his will. For, somehow, his disdain of the inn had swelled to anger—and that was why he had been unable to shut out thoughts of Arsinal. But that was also why it had started with disdain. The anger was not on account of any injury done to himself, or it would have flamed up immediately; it was an impersonal moral judgment and condemnation, by the tribunal of his heart, not his understanding, and its earliest effect had been the failure of his respect for his old associate, and the strong desire to cease the acquaintance.

Thus it concerned a third person, who should be injured or threatened by Arsinal, and who, perhaps, was ignorant of the fact, and stood defenceless. Such a third person was sufficiently named! The man himself had sneered at Ingrid Fleming's "deflective influence." It was none the less a sneer because cunningly disguised by the aspect of gravity and reproachful sorrow; despite the self-pity, the shaft had been shot. It had been intended to hurt. And for the shape of the sneer: the "influence" related to his, Saltfleet's, plastic weakness in the modelling hands of a girl, and might pass for silly; but the "deflective" was more illuminating. It revealed that an armed camp was already in being. All outside the camp was enemy ground, and so this girl was Arsinal's rival and antagonist before she had even raised a finger to obstruct his plans. But she was unprepared without knowing more about it to sacrifice her curiosity and sense of wonder to his, and this was her offence. Everyone was to bow down before the career he had chosen for himself out of spiritual voluptuousness.

The unfairness, the greed and colossal insensibility of it were what were angering him. . . . Yet this could be neither early enough, nor deep enough. For surely his new dislike of Arsinal must have begun to work before this morning. *Instinctively* he must have known what the man's attitude towards that girl was to be, and his following words and gibes had initiated nothing. So that Arsinal's malice sprang naturally out of his lifelong obsession, and had always been predictable. His spirit was grasping. That it grasped not at money, power, or the common honours of men, mattered nothing: the high soul was magnanimous and renouncing. But though this should be the source and beginning of it, it was not the worst of it. That he should be so callously ready to refuse the legitimate deep concern of a girl coming to the strangeness by another road, was bad enough—if he should be waiting to insult her as well, however! . . . And not insult her alone, but, it might too easily be, *harm* her! For it appeared that the joining of these two belonging stones was to be no jest, but a serious risk. Clearly were they bewitched. They showed queer skies of stars, and were accompanied by apparitions and supernatural noises, and had come from ancient places; prophecies were written around them. Their reuniting was a bold man's business. But there was no security that she, in whose possession the one of them was, would not be invited to challenge their nature and the tradition, in her own person. . . .

Supposing Arsinal hid beneath his mild exterior this icy heart of insanity, then Ingrid Fleming must never be in his company alone. . . .

He stopped again on the brink of the rain-swollen, discoloured brook, and saw it not, although he could still smoke composedly.

These painful fantasies, it was his final mental task before proceeding, were somehow to be reconciled with the fact of his new purified feelings in the unseen presence of the Tor he was immediately to attack. The only half-credited superstitious explanation of the latter, he would drop at once. In effect, his half-amused, half-reckless enthusiasm for Arsinal's chase across the globe had fallen away, that he might stand back, silent, heedful, and rather disturbed, before the spectacle of wonders greater than himself; and this was his sense of ennoblement, that now the solitude of the Devil's Tor approaches but emphasised. Such an ennoblement, unless quite transitory—which perhaps meant, if continued to be fed by fresh marvels—was like a view of a known scene from an upper stand; the details should dwindle, and a background appear and assume chief importance. Thus Arsinal, from having been the centre and whole of an affair, was now occupying his correct place as one among many. That he should still strive to be the whole was a contradiction of the new circumstances, as absurd as offensive. That he should drag others to subserve his imaginary lordship, might be of the nature of crazy Lucifer himself. Saltfleet's discontent with that proud angel had always been that his pride was vulgar and second-rate; he had not that quality of pride that could scorn his own ambitions, he was infinitely far from the scorn of self, and so, before and after his fall, remained a boy. Arsinal too, for all his sapient airs, continued a boy—but boys, Saltfleet also remembered, were hard, brutal and cruel.

He need not take emphatic action yet—nothing unpardonable had been done or said. No need to break with Arsinal until it was not any longer to be avoided; wherefrom, later, the satisfaction would be his that at no stage of the business had his feelings been out of control. But again he determined it: from now on, after this morning and while down here, he must watch Arsinal's every movement as he would watch the craft of a lunatic. . . .

Why then had he been at pains to reject young Copping's offer, seeing that its acceptance would have closed everything, and kept the girl at arm's-length during their one remaining day? He reconstructed his mental reactions to the proposal, and believed that he had a very little wished to chasten Arsinal by a postponement, that the honouring of his own word had had rather more to do with it, and that he had also wanted to serve Ingrid Fleming, as no one else seemed wishful to serve her, by procuring her the satisfaction of her desire to remain included in the unrolling of the great mystery behind these wonders. Yet after all these imperfect motives were allowed for, there should still be a residue.

He dimly conceived that a recognition in his head of her psychic predominance was constituting a background to everything. Matters, during all the present week, seemed to be touching *her*, not Arsinal; their best interpretation was to be looked for from her. Arsinal was being clogged by the past, but her unencumbered and delicately-sensitive perceptions were just the fitting instrument. . . . And the background of this background showed itself in strange gleams of insight: that, if she was to be the affair's chief interpreter, it was also because she was the *nearest* to it—because it was for her sake. . . . His refusal of Copping's offer had been a response necessitated. She was not to go out; therefore something, someone—he—was to keep her in. So he too was an unconscious subordinate. . . .

With a smile not quite cynical, but arising from the silent antithesis between his spirit of independence and his eternal self-disdaining, he jumped the stream, and at once commenced the climb beyond.

Soon he came upon the scene of Drapier's death.

The ground around was much trodden by iron-shod boots, but otherwise all was as it had been yesterday, nor was the day unlike.

Very metaphysical, accordingly, seemed to him the disappearance of that crushed form. . . . He never halted, but still pressed upwards, step by step putting the limit of his last ascension behind him.

At the very top the breeze was livelier, and the dense mists constantly went past him, as on a journey. He stood, cigar yet in mouth, just inside the edge of the hill's crest, looking quietly about him. Quite quickly, Ingrid Fleming's still, sitting form arrested his whole attention. She was on a stump of weathered rock, with her back to the sea of white that suggested and hid the open south lands. No one was with her. Her profile was towards him, but she was not very close, so that at first he found nothing unnatural in her poise. There was no need for her to have seen him yet.

He would not advance on her till he had taken in, from where he stood, the rest of his surroundings. He looked west, and the ragged evacuated site of the stack was shut off from him by a long, flat granite block, one of two within the shifting proscenium of his vision. It was plain what they were, and where the remains of the hole must be. . . .

His gaze returned to the girl, in her grey mackintosh. She had never moved, and at last it struck him that all could not be quite right with her. Surely it was with an abnormal fixity that she was staring at whatever was straight before her, which the intervening block prevented himself from seeing. Her face was dead-white, too, and like a mask for its changeless relaxed calm. Yet she could hardly be in a faint, since the mere retention of her seat would demand a muscular effort. It was very low to the ground. The knuckles of the hand of one hanging arm were actually touching; but the other hand was loosely closed on her lap. She sat slightly bent forward.

He took a few tentative steps towards her, and then realised that her state was one of trance, or something very like it. From inside her bent fingers he saw peeping forth a stone, that at once he knew could only be Arsinal's original treasure from Tibet, which they had never seen since. For this girl had had it in her possession, and what other stone should she be holding?—while Drapier, likewise, had been grasping its fellow at death . . . and not improbably he as well had been in a trance, so otherwise incomprehensibly to throw away his life. But this present spectacle was painful to watch, and rather terrible to understand. Some real or imagined apparition must be standing up there in front of her. It was as if he himself were again in contact with a spirit.

When she recovered, would she reveal to him the thing she had been seeing?—for ask her, he never would. He wished not even to seem to have been near her at any time . . . and so again he retreated. Now he sought that side of the slab which hitherto he had not seen. The broken entrance to the wrecked tomb should be there, and in its direction her set, questionless gaze rested. . . .

He saw a long fissure in the ground, running parallel with the length of the slab. It ended, just before his feet, in a broadening and deepening, that spoke of a staircase, but no longer was one. No technical gang could ever reopen it. It was hardly essential that it should be reopened, seeing that its ghostly inhabitants could still slip through! The neighbouring soil had been all tormented by the earthquake.

Very positively, it was uncanny, this spot and this experience in a fog. Right underneath his feet was the home of Arsinal's second stone, whither Drapier, his *accidental* acquaintance, had by a long chain of *accident* descended, not for that purpose, *accidentally* to bring it back to daylight after God knew how many tens of thousands of years. And almost immediately afterwards he had died. But now a haunting had begun, and that girl behind his back was a present victim. . . .

How long should her seizure persist? How much longer then would she need for restoration to her common senses, before he might considerately address her? For of this overtaking she must speak herself, if she desired, but certainly her mother's proposition must be made known to her, and Arsinal's arrival, and Copping's new attitude towards a meeting. So, if it were an hour, he must wait. He turned round to her once more, and saw no horror in her face. The trance must run its course.

He returned to the slab's east, and perched himself on its edge, dangling his legs, while keeping a light watch on the girl by periodically twisting his neck towards her. An instinct of delicacy denied his staring at her defencelessness for all the time. He faced the way by which he had come up, but the route was veiled. During some minutes he pulled grimly at his smoke, and eyed the procession of the mists; and tried to think of nothing. . . .

Soon, however, an unaccountable lethargy, foreign to his temperament and impossible to withstand, seized upon him with an abruptness that gave no time for measures against it. Nearly at once, it seemed, his eyes became glued, and his senses stupefied. The hand holding the cigar dropped relaxed towards the ground, though the cigar was still held. . . .

He roused himself violently to sit erect, but now was seeing differently. The stupor had passed as suddenly as it had come, he was wide awake again, yet this new alertness was applying to other things; he was in other surroundings, and being confronted by other images. It was night, not day, and the fogs were gone.

It was no kind of blindness, for the sky was really of night, and filled with magnificent stars. A perpetual noise of rushing waters came up from below, but the darkness prevented his seeing to the valley. Penetrating the sound, an intermittent bellowing excited his ears, as of angry bulls, perhaps off the Tor, but still not far away. The bellowing was fiercer and more menacing than the challenge of any savage cattle within his experience.

High in the sky, midway between zenith and south horizon, above and behind the girl's form, that still showed darkly, a gleaming blue star, curiously like a lamp for its brightness and steadiness, first drew his attention by its superiority of splendour over all the rest, then retained it by the fact of its motion. Rather languidly it was passing through its immediate neighbours. Thus it could be no fixed luminary, but must represent either a meteor or a mechanical flying light. The vile intrusion of a machine, however, in this mystic sky was unthinkable.

Next, the star augmented to such a glory of mild intensity, that the meteoric explanation also had to be dropped. No aerolite, trailing through the earth's atmosphere, was ever thus steadily increasing and sluggishly lovely.

It plainly descended, so that its first slowness must have been due to its prodigious height in the heavens. Now, faster and faster, it captured field after field of the sky, in a kind of parabolic curve that, being pursued, should bring it to strike the ground somewhere near this hill he was on . . . and yet he could not have calculated it so nicely; it must be intuition. Anything half so weird and wonderful he had never known. Its blue was no blue of earth; its sheer brilliance was as incomparable. . . .

Already it must be quite close down—perhaps but a few miles overhead from the Channel, falling north at this last of its terrific sky-swerve, to meet the night-like moor. . . . But very suddenly it vanished. His final impression was that it had rushed down that concluding steep of space with a fearful momentum.

The whizzing thud of an invisible body tore the air diagonally from above to downwards past the hill. It seemed to him that the noise was occult, so awful was it to his imagination and so alien to his understanding. It was not the awe of combined mass and force, for the lump must even have been quite small, nor was it the awe for an unusual lithic missile from the sky, since his mind was astronomical enough easily to incorporate a meteorite, but there had been something special in the sound; with no musical note, it had been of the nature of music; with no communication to his intelligence, it had been like the passage of a messenger. By now the body should have rooted itself in the valley bed. . . .

And with scarcely an intervening moment there ascended to him, as if from a considerable way off, a confused uproar that silenced the constant thunder of the waters, in the manner of a vast multitude of people, all bawling, wailing and shrieking at once. It was the most phantom-like and shocking yet. . . . But when the clamour, with its risings and fallings, had endured for what might be minutes, and never grew less agitating to his ears, the sound of a sullen, heavy, booming drum joined in, to master all those other noises, its single ominous strokes being dealt at brief and regular spaces. Afterwards the hubbub of voices died down, without entirely ceasing; but the drum persisted.

A little later again, a shrill horn screeched sharply above everything else, three separate times, like a call to assembly. The drumming stopped; the cries faded to silence. The sound of the rushing torrent once more reigned. . . .

An angry reddening of the night, from low down, perhaps from round an upper bend of the valley, told of a conflagration out of sight . . . and now he obtained his first view of the changed landscape. Instead of the quiet outline and smooth flank of the shoulder across the stream he had traversed in getting here, that at its highest should not have overtopped this other hill by a hundred feet, his eyes were quickly startled by the spectacle of vertical cliffs and naked crag masses, all lit by this fiery glare and flicker from an invisible blazing valley beacon, to tower indeterminate, rude, topless, towards and into the black sky of stars above. To come to the lowest stars, he must put his head back. He was against a mountain. . . .

A monstrous beast in silhouette, massive yet low like a rhinoceros, appeared in the moment of lifting itself over the Tor's edge, midway between himself and the dark shape of the girl, who, when he looked round to her, never moved. The brute displayed no hostility, but only the resolve to put height and distance behind it, in its unreasoning terror of the red shine of the valley. . . . And Saltfleet knew that the hyperphysical part of him that could communicate with these wonders and false threats was not the part which could come to harm on their account, and that neither could that entranced form come to harm. He had no impulse to rise to her assistance. . . .

Next, almost immediately after, she stirred on her seat, and while he was still turned, viewing her in half-expectancy, awaiting he could not have said what from her, the spectral night passed, without warning or sensation. . . .

He knew not how he was facing the valley again. He was perched on the slab yet, except that somehow his feet were touching ground, and through the old daylight he continued blinking at the silent white unrest that was all his view past the hill's top. The ceasing of the noise of the waters resembled a return from music to reality. The toneless quietude of this bright morning fog, after that other tortured red and black of a deceitful night, gave him the relief of having slipped out of a dream—and yet it had been none.

The cigar still burned between his fingers, and, putting it instinctively to his mouth, he wondered at the circumstance, and sat thinking. So those illusive happenings had actually occupied a far smaller space than had seemed, and *such* a liberty with time was dream-like. Again, when had he turned from the girl?—for at the very last moment he had been regarding her. His feet, also, had found the ground without his knowledge. All this was of a dream. . . .

He smoked and frowned through the drift. His face, square to the unseen height across the dip, kept its colour and stern composure, only his eyes were lighted by an unpleasant gleam that confessed his disturbance. In fact, he felt dazed, humiliated, and wholly confounded. No, it had not been a normal sinking of his senses into a dream, but they had been forced from outside into the likeness of one; and so, as he had known, it was not one. His brain had been forcibly compelled by something stronger than itself; and that was his humiliation. . . .

The girl should be upon the point of coming round too, but he would not apply to her, or even seek her again with his eyes, till he had independently reached some idea of what this thing stood for. . . .

It seemed to him important to establish that it had not been the failure of his higher centres through sleep or coma. He had seen those sights critically, he had heard those sounds, not emotionally, but coolly; the queernesses in both kinds had not been the fantastic leapings of a dream; they had been *possible*—in the fast setting of a rigid, necessary world; if not the common world, to which he had been born and was accustomed. Therefore the experience had been real. The time of the *ego* of his daily life had continued to run straight forward without a break, he had not been in a state of false exaltation, but had remained curious and attentive, and he hoped he had retained that decent hold on his will. . . . And as little could it be a vision as a dream, since, properly, the two states were identical. To distinguish between the two, it was but a question of the degree of external consciousness. In the dream the brain was exclusively occupied with its own riotous images; in the vision it in part created its own images and in part remained in touch with the true world. But these images had not been created, for the faculties which should create them had at the time been legitimately employed. The proof had been his *sang-froid*.

So, being objective, it had been real. Then different realities could co-exist, since the old reality of everyday life had been no more than overlaid. But if so, the co-existence could only take place in different situations of time or space. Here the scenery, as to its fundamentals, had been identical for both realities—they had occupied the same space, therefore. Their co-existence had necessarily taken place over the prolonged running line of time. He had just been in ancient history. This, too, he already knew, without the aid of logic. . . .

The hill was haunted, then, and he was not the first to know it. Drapier must have known it; the girl, perhaps now up and gazing at him, she undoubtedly had found it out. Its phantoms were real. They were contemporaneous with the beginning on earth of the undivided stone, long since broken to confusion. That stone had been the descending blue star; this he knew by intuition. Could he have seen down into the valley, it would have been given him to learn among what kind of people it had been received. When last had giant wild cattle and the rhinoceros roamed in Britain? Whatever was to be thought of Arsinal's character, the triumphs of his intellect were not fading—and he had also put forth that theory of the founding of the northern stocks. . . . The nearer the approach to the truth as well of his two recorded prophecies, the more pressing it became to exclude him. . . .

Yesterday's apparition, by comparison, had been simple both in space and time, and understandable. Then he had been experimenting with one of the two flints; just now this girl had had the other in her hand. Yet the richer and more wonderful of his experiences was the indirect telepathic one; evincing either that the two stones were of unequal potency, inherently or according to the degree of correspondence in the experimenter, or that the potency of either was increasable by some nature of this hill. . . . Each moment his ghost-woman of the inn and Arsinal's goddess seemed to draw closer together, as if at last to coalesce. . . .

He smiled. Thus these phenomena were to crack his brain as thoroughly as another had once for all cracked Arsinal's when still a boy! . . . But, truly, he cared not greatly to follow any of it up, even at so developed a stage. The invisible, it seemed, could be sufficiently sense-subverting, and *yet* might be less than the haughtiness of the soul. For another feather's weight in the balance, he would go off the hill now, at once, with no last look towards Ingrid Fleming, in the contemptuous determination to leave the rest of this business to those who should want it more. . . .

He could not do that. There was a thing he needed to discover. Well aware was he of this girl's deep serious interest in the sequence of riddles riding against them; but now he wished to ascertain additionally whether she, unlike Arsinal, could if necessary despise and disown her concern. He wished to test the purity of her spirit's gold. He thought that the desire was nothing personal, but that he was seeking a standard of judgment between the two. On himself, it appeared, depended the last destination of the stone the girl was holding. If she insisted upon busying herself with this matter, perhaps it could not be hers.

His faith was that the greedy, possessive, desiring *self* was ever ridiculous and punishable. His excess of pride, that otherwise so flatly contradicted the Christian humility, nevertheless, in practical effect, met it round the circle, for the object of his undying chief hatred of heart was precisely that meaner pride of the individual that constitutes the worldly nature. He believed that the splendour of the soul consisted in its generosity of cold blood—it must give, give, and give; but not in exaltation, or from love; only because the soul's grandeur lay in its nakedness. . . . Of no one else in the world so far had he had such hopes as of this girl.

He looked round, and she was in the same place, but on her feet, watching him. Her face was colourless, and set hard in a sort of suffering. He went over to her.

Their eyes alone spoke during the first moments. Then Ingrid said, but in an incredibly small voice:

"How long have you been up? I have just had the most terrible and blessed vision."

"I too have seen something I could not have thought possible. . . . I have not been here long. You were unconscious when I arrived."

"I don't wish to speak of what I have seen."

"Then let us not."

Neither, in that case, was it necessary that he should attempt the relation of his experience. He considered it certain that they had known different things. She had been staring towards the tomb, and the present pain in her eyes told of a *passion* endured. . . .

"Do you want to talk to me?" asked Ingrid. "Did you come up, expecting to find me here?"

"Yes. I was told you were not at your house, so guessed you might be on the Tor. But don't hurry. You are upset, and had better take a few minutes."

She sat down again on her rock, but Saltfleet noticed that she had put away the flint. After a pause, she looked up to him again.

"What is it?"

"It is a practical question of facts, decisions, ways and means. But are you sufficiently recovered?"

"Yes; I am going home directly."

"In the first place, Arsinal has arrived. I didn't send for him, but the news of your cousin's death had otherwise reached him."

She showed no eagerness, hardly any interest.

"Then he will see me?"

"That, unfortunately, will now depend on *your* management. . . . For I notified Mr. Copping immediately, and he has since called on us. Your mother is taking a hand. She has offered Arsinal both stones, on the condition that we do not attempt to meet you again. Arsinal was disposed to accept off-hand, but I felt that you should be told first. In the meantime, Mr. Copping appears to have withdrawn his consent to the use of his place for a talk between you and Arsinal."

"But I think I must talk to him." . . . Ingrid fell into a deep musing silence. She manifested so little disturbance, that Saltfleet remained uncertain if she had thoroughly apprehended his information.

"Our difficulty, of course, is that we can have no means of judging what exactly this offer of your mother's stands for. She is Drapier's executrix, we are told; but can you, and will you, veto it?"

"I will speak to my mother when I get back."

"For me, I am no longer Arsinal's agent, and so I am indifferent, but he, you will understand, regards his acquisition of these two flints as supremely important. He would rather have that talk with you than not; but above all he wishes not to bungle his securing the things. Your mother has made him the direct offer, while you, so far, have declined to."

"I understand his desire, and also my mother's. I can settle nothing here, but will speak to her at home."

"You have your stone with you?"

"Yes."

"And cannot refuse it to your mother, on demand?"

"By law, I cannot."

"I don't wish to pry behind the scenes, but what attitude will you probably take with her, and what is to be the likely upshot?"

"I shall tell her my wishes, and abide by her decision then."

The girl's apathy surprised Saltfleet more at every speech. He asked her bluntly:

"If you are really so unconcerned, why have you wanted this meeting with Arsinal, and why have you hesitated to let him have what he is as anxious as possible to get?"

"Does it matter?" came her reply. "All of us have wanted this or that. Hugh Drapier has wanted something, and Peter Copping, and Mr. Arsinal, and I, and even you. In the whole of this week's events down here, whose *wants* have mattered? To put it in another way, of the circumstances that *have* mattered, how many have been willed, or wanted, or dreamt of, beforehand? Can't you read the signs, Mr. Saltfleet?"

"Yet each of us must act. . . . You are probably a shade disheartened by this overcoming of yours. It will pass. Until it has passed, let me suggest a course for us all. You do wish to meet Arsinal?"

"If he is what I have imagined."

"Then, presumably, Mr. Copping must be repersuaded to let us have his house or studio. Do you feel that you can arrange that for later in the day?"

"I'll try. Or I will send word to you of another place."

"And the hour. This afternoon I may have to come out here again with Arsinal—he can hardly not want to see it before he leaves the district. But even so, we could still be home in time for an early meeting—say, at five, or five-thirty. The latter perhaps would be safer for us, and more convenient to you."

"At half-past five." Ingrid barely nodded.

"But I would ask a guarantee," proceeded Saltfleet. "In accepting and attending such an interview, we shall necessarily be seriously offending your mother—unless, indeed, you can procure her consent. But otherwise she will certainly consider it a rejection of her conditional offer of the stone; and will as certainly withdraw the offer. Arsinal then will have to rely upon your good offices; but at home you may meet with opposition. You will, I am sure, do what you can for us. Nevertheless, I think that the object of contention should be *lodged*—to prevent your mother's sudden confiscation of it. This is in the nature of a guarantee, and so I call it one."

"Lodged where?"

"One moment. I haven't finished, and there is another unpleasantness. I will be quite frank. The stone has to be somewhere. If, in coming to meet us, you leave it behind at home, there is the risk of its being appropriated in your absence. The danger may be of the slightest, yet in any case it will be enough thoroughly to upset Arsinal, who therefore is certain to insist on your not parting with the stone so long as the negotiations are on. On the other hand, should you keep it with you, more than one at the meeting might feel the strong temptation to suggest and urge the fitting together of the two counterparts there and then. . . . That I would resist to the last ounce of my strength, and still, fate being so very much to the fore in all these concerns, I might well be overruled. Consequently, it will be equally undesirable for you to leave the stone at home, and carry it. The one third plan is to deposit it."

"Why don't you want them fitted?"

"The operation will be too hazardous," replied Saltfleet shortly.

"But Mr. Arsinal, if he gets them both, will fit them, if only to certify that they belong."

"I know he will. He is a man, however, and is entitled to take the risk for himself."

"Have you heard of a risk?"

"I've either heard of one, or imagined one. That topic is extraneous, and need not be introduced. I have made you the request, Miss Fleming."

She was silent for a short while, looking at the ground. Then she said again, in a hesitating low voice:

"Why, then, don't you accept my mother's offer? That is the surest way for you."

"We could not, before I had spoken to you. But have we now your consent?"

"The stone is in my pocket, and you may take it away with you at once."

"Why have you changed your mind?"

"My mind is the same, but my will has left it, and it has collapsed. Those who have the will should be allowed to gratify it, while they may. Who can say how long it will be for? So really Mr. Arsinal may have the stone, since you assure me that my mother is agreeable."

"Then are you throwing it all over?"

Ingrid rose and confronted him.

"You have found me here, in this out-of-the-way place, in such distress, and can ask me a question like that! . . . Can you not conceive that the stage of mere curiosity may give way to something quite different and very much more awful? Mr. Arsinal is happy that he is still in the time of groping and searching—if groping and searching he is. I do not wish to disappoint him, and so he may have this stone, and you may take it to him."

"How far do these psychic phenomena depend upon the possession of either stone?"

"I don't know."

"And you are willing *not* to meet him?"

She stood thinking, with averted eyes.

"I am not sure if that will be permitted—my not meeting him. Probably he is a person I shall have to meet. . . . And you have mentioned a risk to me in the joining of the stones. That may be only a forbidding appearance—an unpleasant-looking door, through which some of us have to pass. What have you heard; or, I think you said, imagined?"

"I doubt if I can tell you."

But her strange pale beauty and half-supernatural gaze persuaded him in another moment that it was to no ordinary girl of the world that he was being invited to make this otherwise unpardonable statement; and also she should be warned in time.

"There is an ancient Cretan prophecy—and a second from another place—in connection with the reuniting of these stones. It is to bring about the marriage of a man and woman, and of them is to be born a regenerator of the human race. This is associated with the worship of the Great Mother. Arsinal is of opinion that the entire fair-haired northern stock was the creation of the undivided stone upon its first arrival on the planet. It should be meteoric."

"Is he wise, or mad?"

"He is extraordinarily gifted. Whether he is also mad, you must judge."

“Isn’t he an archaeologist?”

“Yes.”

“But he should be a mystic, too.”

“He is that, too,” said Saltfleet.

“So you caution me against this strange man’s choosing to fasten upon me, a woman, as the one indicated?”

“It would be most painful for all involved. Yet I cannot say that his insanity would go so far, and I merely wish to give the warning that it is a possibility; besides the positive psycho-chemical risk of the rejoining.”

“But simply to talk with him, I may meet him without embarrassment?”

“Mr. Copping and I would both be present.”

She sent him a queer flitting smile, which was no smile at all, but like a silent speech; and asked him afterwards:

“What do *you* think of this thing?”

“I think that in this quick-spreading growth of wondrous transactions, any new miracle may find room. Arsinal, as well, has hitherto been peculiarly lucky in his guesses—far-sighted, if you will. I myself have seen and heard plain impossibilities both on this hill just now and elsewhere, in more or less near relation. . . . So I would like to adopt the sane, cynical attitude towards the prediction, but cannot. That is what you asked?”

“Aren’t you altogether working against your friend’s interests? First you have refused my mother’s offer, and now you have not yet accepted mine, and you are raising the points of his sanity and propriety with me as if an intimate. Is it because you are coming to understand that these happenings cannot be for him alone?”

“It is so,” returned Saltfleet, surprised. “At the beginning of the acquaintance I admired the man tremendously, and still recognise that he possesses valuable qualities enough to endow a dozen others, but within these last twenty-four hours the damned spot of his nature seems to have appeared. I am finding him self-centred.” He viewed her more steadily. “You may or may not understand me, but without, on the contrary, *self-contempt*, nobody, man or woman, can rise past a certain determinate level of willing. . . ."

"Yes, I have sometimes struggled with that idea. One must be able to despise even one's own aims, or pay the penalty of everlasting pettiness. This man, perhaps, cannot separate the two things: the service of fate, and the service of the will."

"And you?"

"I am a girl, and the abandoning of my will is naturally easier for me by reason of many physical and social circumstances."

"I don't know if we are speaking the same language. However, you are personally as ready to give up all this business as go on with it?"

"I have no eagerness to go on with it."

"How did it start with you?"

"Devil's Tor has spoken to me for years."

"What has it said?"

"I have long felt that there was a woman's tomb here. For the rest, it has talked to me as music, and wild nature, and silent prayer, talk to one. . . ."

"But now you fear?"

"Yes," said Ingrid.

"What do you fear?"

"I have things to lose, in spite of all."

"You are engaged, perhaps?"

"It is not announced."

"To Copping?"

"Yes."

He ceased his questions. He felt no disappointment that his grown companionship of a sort with this girl should still thus be easily surpassed, but such a relation to so ordinary a man mystified him, the more that he had heard it so calmly from her own lips. It always had mystified him since he had first surmised it, but now the puzzle seemed to have become active. His problem of the outward walk was already resolved. This business was hers, not Arsinal's, because she, not he, was subdued, noble, unenthusiastic, selfless, in it. Her interests, therefore, not Arsinal's, he must push and guard. Now, however, it was actively complicated by her curious affection, hardly to be understood, for that unamiable, dry-tongued young artist, who should be temperamentally outside everything and must be obstructing her mood at each inch of the way. Thus, since Copping was her choice and presumably she loved him, *he* should be helping her in her storms and confusions; yet apparently they were only lovers for a quieter time. Was this quieter time—the promise of it—the deep inward ground of her wonderful passiveness, or did that arise from the acquiescence of an unusual nature in what might well seem inevitably advancing tragical events?

The question was brain-spun; not of his wisdom. For in his depths he *knew* that her noble quietness and standing-back were being produced in her by her consciousness of having been chosen, whether by the blindness or the caprice of fate, for a central *rôle* in this play of deaths, ghosts, and distant heavens. Tossed by her thousand dark feelings and scraps of feeling, never comprehended by herself, a girl wandering in a night whose quick increase might terrify a strong man, she assuredly could not in these last days and hours be remembering her engagement at all. It was her time of trial. She had no helpers, but her spirit was being left to follow its course. She remained outwardly tranquil, peaceable, approachable; she spoke no hard words of her friends; she shunned nothing, she sought nothing; yet confessed her fear. Admiration for her grew up rapidly in Saltfleet's mind. . . .

In the long silence, she became restless, and at last said, without looking at him:

"I must go home. Do you wish to take the stone?"

"Thank you, no," was his reply. "I think you should meet Arsinal, for the reason that he may be of assistance to you. But, if you find the suggestion not too strange and impossible, let us *cache* it somewhere on this Tor, where either can retrieve it at need."

"The only strangeness I find in it is that it should be proposed by *you*, who unluckily have succeeded in giving certain other people a different impression of you."

"I know; but we need not speak of them."

"We will hide it, then, and afterwards decide who is to have it. It had better be at the further end of the top. Here visitors are sure to come, and disturb things."

Accordingly, they moved off; but Ingrid had not taken many steps before the other noticed the slight limp.

"Have you hurt yourself?" he asked.

"In the thunderstorm that opened the tomb, three evenings ago, Hugh and I were caught by the end of an explosion, and my ankle was sprained; but it is nearly well again."

He pointed behind them. "*That*, of course, is the tomb entrance?" And when she had replied, "Yes," he went on to inquire:

"You yourself did not go down any part of the way?"

"No."

"You suppose that a woman was buried there?"

"Please do not speak of her," said Ingrid.

But Saltfleet, understanding that that had been her apparition, fell into silence and thoughtfulness. He would not now or at any other time press her for her vision, yet if she had seen a woman, he too had seen one; and how could they not be identical? And that ghost was thus shown to be from the hill's ancient tomb. . . . She should at least be told *his* vision of the morning, for that concerned her. She should know all. . . .

Beyond and below the western edge of the Tor's plateau, they found a rock that might be raised from its bed of turf. Here, while he poised the rock upon its angle, Ingrid put the flint, and then everything was replaced and made inconspicuous. No word was exchanged about the operation during or after it; only, before they came away, Saltfleet, indicating the fog-buried country to the west, asked what lay there.

She told him that the bare moor ran for miles, without roads, houses, or notable landmarks, but only rocks, streams, bogs and heather.

"What is this Tor's history?"

"It has none."

"But why its name?"

"Its stack, that was blown down the other evening, was shaped like a devil's face."

"Was it artificially carved so?"

"It is impossible to decide, but perhaps it was."

"I've been in many strange places in the world," said Saltfleet, "yet certainly in none so strange as this. It *has* had a very remarkable history, this hill—a part of which it was granted me to see, visibly, with my own eyes, those not many minutes ago. If you care to, we will sit down by the tomb before going back, and I will tell you about it."

Ingrid looked at him with troubled eyes.

"I shall like to hear, but can't return you story for story."

"You have said so already, and I don't ask it."

A few minutes later they sat together on the flat slab facing the valley, and Saltfleet was relating his experience. His account was in the fewest words, and he avoided all picturesqueness, sensation, and departure from the plain facts. It was soon finished. Ingrid's face appeared even whiter than before while she listened to him, but afterwards she made only one comment.

"That sound of waters, then, was what *I* have heard twice."

"So it has occurred to me as well," replied Saltfleet. "That is only one of the many queer features of the phenomenon. The queerest of all, possibly, is the causation of it. I had nothing occult in my hand or on my person, it was very evidently brought about by your proximity, in plain language, it was from the flint on your lap at the time—I saw it there—yet *my* vision has not been *yours*, nor anything like yours. I am to ask you no question. So in this thing, there is a primary and a derived. They differ; and necessarily the derived must be the weaker. You said that yours was terrible. . . . I am truly sorry for you."

Ingrid had the impulse to tell him, despite her choking inward bond of silence. She suddenly cast her mind back to—*Her* . . . and all things else, before and after, this man included, again grew mean and mortal in her sight. . . .

Upon entering her trance, she had seemed always to have been viewing fearfully that astral shape of preternatural height, standing away from but fronting her in the hole itself of the tomb. She had been wrapped in swathed draperies of an indescribable mode, of the hue of the dark granite beside her. Her appearing flesh had been like the moon. . . . Then her eyes had fallen upon Ingrid, and for an instant it had been as if she was to speak, but her lips never parted, and no sound came; only, she had signed. The sign—very slow, awful, and beyond meaning—had been the setting of a hand over her heart. . . .

Ingrid could not impart these things to the man before her. They had already talked too much together, and now she must leave him, or he must leave her. Instead, however, he went on to recount his earlier vision, of another kind, at the inn the evening before.

Words continued to fail her. She got up abruptly, to cover the awkwardness created by her inability, and stood looking away from him, while he regarded her with a glance sidelong and anxious.

"Now there is no more to say between us?" he asked.

"No," her tongue formed voicelessly.

"Then let us go. I will, if I may, bear you company as far as the top of the next hill, but we need not talk for the sake of talking, and after that I will beg permission to go on ahead. Both of us have enough to turn over in our private minds."

Ingrid assented—neither knew how, but not in speech—and they descended from the top of the Tor side-by-side.

XXIII

The Ancestors

After lunch the two men retired for speech to the upper private room, where Arsinal, contrary to his wont, sat smoking a cigarette nervously, and Saltfleet stood or moved about in undisguised restlessness. The gong had already sounded before the latter's return to the hotel. During lunch itself motoring parties had been present, so that as yet he had had no opportunity of recounting his morning's adventure. Coffee and brandy were now on a tray. Saltfleet was not smoking.

"Yes, Miss Fleming was up there," he repeated; for so much he had told the other at their first remeeting in the lounge, though no more. . . . He gazed through the window at the foggy street, and added:

"She was in a trance."

"A *trance*, Saltfleet!"

"Yes. . . . I presently followed suit."

Arsinal regarded his back in silent perplexity; then said:

"Is this a long story? Is it further to complicate the case, and must I stay here the night?"

"Perhaps. I cannot say. Pray have reasonable patience, and I will get the tale out." He turned round from the window, while continuing. . . . "I found her rigid and senseless; her eyes open, but blind. When she came to, some while afterwards, she informed me that she had had a vision. As she would not relate its particulars to me, I cannot relate them to you. Her flint, however, was at the time in her hand; and must have brought the state about."

Arsinal frowned. "And *your* trance, when was that?"

"It seemed to start a minute or so after I had sat down to wait for her waking up, and finished a little before hers; or nearly simultaneously."

"I shall have two or three questions to ask before you proceed. What, would you say, originated yours?"

"I understand it to have been an overflow from hers, by direct telepathy."

"And had yours as well the nucleus of a vision?"

"Yes."

"Can you say, or guess, if these two visions were identical?"

"They were definitely different."

"How do you know that, Saltfleet?"

"Because mine was largely dependent on the existing geography of the place, whereas we were looking different ways.

Then, by her later manner, she must have been through something personal and emotional—I judged so, at least—while mine was purely spectacular."

"You described to me a phenomenon in this room last night; your vision to-day has been nothing like that?"

"No, quite of another character."

"Then let me hear it."

"I propose not to tell it you, for a different reason."

Arsinal set down his cigarette-end impatiently.

"All this business is so bewildering in itself, Saltfleet, that I would beg you not to add."

"My idea is to simplify, by arriving at an unquestionable explanation. You shall decide. Here we have certain apparitions, caused by either of the stones, singly. Their vividness and wonder have been strongest on Devil's Tor. I suggest, therefore, that you and I repeat the experiment up there, with your flint, as soon as ever you are ready to move off. The hill is three miles out. But this test will be most certain, least open to adulteration by preconception, if you come to it unprepared. . . ."

"Don't go on. If I can see a thing for myself, I will wait. I shall be ready whenever you are. . . . So now let us finish the rest speedily. What else passed?—of the matter of the ownership, I mean. Was she in a state to conclude anything? Am I to meet her?"

"Of course, you haven't heard again from the house?"

"Not a word," said Arsinal.

"They could have nothing to say as yet. . . . Well then, I have kept open that meeting with her, provided she can at all manage it, for five-thirty this afternoon, at Copping's, or another place— she will let us know. Further, I requested a necessary guarantee, to which she consented without demur. Her stone, at this moment, is lying secreted in an unlikely spot on top of the Tor; thus, temporarily, is safe from the mother."

"That was well thought of, Saltfleet. You can show me the spot when we go up. I had better know it."

"It would be a breach, I fancy."

Arsinal bit his lip.

"I was not to understand that. However, it will not be brought away by the other side before a meeting?"

"I have asked no assurance."

"It was casual. . . . Yet I have but to persuade this girl that my claim is good, and then we may take it, regardless of her mother's attitude?"

"As things are, she is to talk to her mother, and abide by her decision."

"So that it is you, not I, who have probably dropped the bone for its reflection in the water!" Arsinal's tone was suddenly sharp, as he shot the other an unpleasant glance. "You have taken it on yourself to decline an offer that was all I needed, presumably just to keep alive your acquaintance with this young woman, who now proves herself to be quite ordinary. No doubt, she is sensible to obey her mother, and I have no quarrel with her, but it is a thousand pities that you could not have used your eyes to better advantage."

"She strikes you, from a distance, as ordinary? . . . No. A strong agitation and a wonderful personal passiveness in combination can never be ordinary. Her mood, too, has swung round since yesterday. Now she seems really so indifferent about the destination of her stone, that she could offer it to me rather wearily there and then, on my assurance that her mother was to let us have it."

"You dared not refuse such an invitation as well!"

"I felt no inclination to accept it. Her mother had promised the stone on a condition that I had already broken—only half innocently. Then, if I saw a child giving away a diamond ring, I would put a restraining hand on its arm; and so here. It perhaps *is* to be of later urgency to her—neither you nor I can tell. . . . Also I won't be outdone in generosity by anyone. . . . And still another consideration presented itself to my mind. . . ."

"What?"

"I've somehow come to regard it as necessary that you should meet her; but once both stones are in your holding, such a meeting becomes distinctly more disagreeable in promise."

"I cannot follow."

Saltfleet returned him stare for stare.

"Nor do I greatly care to be more explicit."

"Either you should leave superfluous riddles, or not speak at all."

"Then let us drop it."

There was a pause, during which Saltfleet examined a discoloured oil painting on the wall, while Arsinal sat frowning and vexed.

"It will be especially painful to me," he recommenced, "if your habitual character of directness is to be affected with the rest. It can do neither of us good for you to remain perversely silent on a topic of importance to both, such as I conclude this to be."

"The risk has been avoided, Arsinal, whereas our relations are quite raw enough. Lift no curtain!"

"Is it that you can be resuming a fantastic idea hinted at by you in our after-breakfast talk? Has it to do with those recorded prophecies?"

"Yes; since you will have it. Nor is *my* sanity in doubt, when I bring into the open the circumstance that these same prophecies have included the mention of a woman."

Arsinal's face had quickly flushed. The other came over to him, to pursue the altercation more quietly and effectively.

"And, no more to beat about the bush," he added, in his new lower voice, "Miss Fleming is a woman, while not another is within sight."

"I will not be angry, though you try me, Saltfleet. . . . This is what I shall reply to your atrocious innuendo. Honestly to employ a weapon of superstition, one must have the faith; you, however, have none, and therefore such a stab in the back of a friend must be from a motive of malice. You do not dread the contingency, but you have thought of it for your purpose, and will make use of it. . . . It is time, indeed, that I also should take up weapons and no longer fatuously rely on a harmony that has served its turn. Yes, you have with an extraordinary suddenness changed camps. You experience the pressing need to justify your action; every renegade has done so. I will not descend to inquire what you can have discovered in this girl, thus to surrender to her with such lightning speed. These follies doubtless are in nature. But to seek as well to inspire her with a preliminary evil judgment of a man she has yet to meet—that, assuredly, is the work of a despicable *thief*. . . . You will buy her with mysteries stolen from me. Deny if you can, that you have directly passed this abomination to her by word of mouth!"

"Its possibility I have imparted."

"By what right have you? Those records, you are perfectly aware, were not to be spoken of to *any*."

"There is always a higher law, that refused to be so confined. She was not to come to grief because of my honour."

"*You* have never feared it."

"Yes, a danger has existed."

"What danger? Let me hear."

"Why I need be your voice, I don't know," replied Saltfleet, shrugging. "However, since it will serve to define our relations for the short remaining future together . . . listen then, Arsinal! A rather peculiarly reserved and shrinking young girl is to be brought to a conference with a pair of strange adventurers—for that is our aspect, and, strip us of our petty achievements in life, that broadly is what we are. One of these persons, esteeming himself the principle, has in mind for the occasion an experiment with twin occult stones, each of which, singly, is dangerously endowed; God knows what the two together will be able to effect. This principal adventurer likewise needs for the experiment a man and a woman, for the stars in their courses, we will say, have told him so, and he may not disbelieve them, under penalty of disbelieving all his chosen career. . . . All these constituents, therefore, are assembled, and the potion is ready to be mixed. . . . Were she your own daughter, Arsinal, and were that godless adventurer and experimenter to be a total stranger to you, would you consent to the encounter?"

"But you have brought things together which don't belong. When I do get the stones, they must be fitted, and as we don't yet know that they *will* fit, this will naturally constitute an experiment, apart from any special result. I have not, however, said that they are to be fitted here. In the light of your story, the great magnet of Devil's Tor itself has begun to impress my imagination as the proper setting for this joining of the two half-liths. Neither have I proposed the attendance of Miss Fleming for the occasion. That has been *your* suggestion. If, as well, I must refer to those ancient predictions, the bringing together of a man and a woman is not stated as a contingent possibility but as a certainty; thus, if I do believe the prophecy, I must believe it *so*. Therefore, I need not take thought or action, but the thing will positively happen of itself. . . . I have forgotten what other arguments were in my head. But, by way of conclusion, let me invite you to answer this. You assert that your gross violation of confidence was in order to protect the girl. Wouldn't she have been still more certainly protected by your acceptance of the mother's offer, with its consequence of the annulling of this acquaintance altogether?"

"Yes; but that was impossible."

"Why so?"

"Because it was not to be. The fate of this business is to throw you together; and I know it, and she knows it, and you also know it. Had you not had such a sense, when young Copping called on us, you would positively not have stood by to see your plans wrecked. I am sorry to say it, but you are lying and lying, Arsinal, and *that* is why I am protecting her."

Arsinal's eyes shot fire, as he rose, only to sit down again. Yet he would not speak before his voice was controlled.

"It follows that, in your opinion, I am a dangerous madman?" he then quietly demanded.

"You are just such a madman as Peter. But he too, at a certain critical moment, had an eye on two worlds."

The other gave him an odd, sharp look, but afterwards sank into a prolonged silence, which became troubled. Last of all, he said, even more quietly than before:

"Yet I am not denying any Christ in repudiating your charge, born of enmity. It is *your* conduct, Saltfleet, which is under censure. Since quarrel we must, let us do so like rational men. I shall detail as calmly as may be the grounds of complaint I have against you; then, in hearing your defence, I shall understand at last where and when the rot has started.

"Since two nights ago, you have opposed me so persistently, that it can no longer be stupidity or accident. At your first coming here, instead of conciliating Drapier's relation, that Mrs. Fleming, who always bore the possibility of being very useful to us, you seem almost to have gone out of your way to fill her with suspicion and alarm. Later, you quite unnecessarily disclosed to more than one that you had taken a thing from Drapier's dead hand where you found him lying. To-day you have rejected—and it is the height of jesuitism to misconstrue my surprised assent at the moment as a sympathetic agreement . . . that same Mrs. Fleming's quite adequate offer, the best she or anyone could have made me; for the sake, obviously, of continuing your meetings with her daughter. However advantageous and agreeable these meetings may be to yourself, I cannot see that my participation in them is to be of extraordinary service to *me*, and yet it must be if my other loss is to be paid for. In the meantime you have babbled my secrets to the girl, presumably in order to keep her romantic interest alive. On Devil's Tor this morning, you might easily have exacted from her sworn promises and safeguards; instead of which, she is to refer all to her mother still. . . .

"Were you my servant, Saltfleet, I would dismiss you out of hand for such an unrelieved chain of perverse disservice. To cover all, you are pretending a ridiculous risk to the girl, which exists nowhere but in your dishonest imagination. You have broken faith to me, lied to me, deceived me, insulted me, both to my face and behind my back; and in no one instance have you advanced my interests as a loyal and upright friend should. What more can I say? . . ."

"Finish!"

"I have finished. Why have you treated me so? Have I in

anything changed towards you?"

Saltfleet grimaced.

"So I must put up a defence, and we are to stop here for ever! Well, shall it be sentimental or practical?—of the heart and conscience, or of facts? I prefer the latter. . . . I will take your charges one by one. Mrs. Fleming—unless I had been in the room sufficiently long to scare her, the daughter would not have come in, to tell me Drapier was on the Tor. There I found him killed, and took the flint. That was one service to you. It would have been thrown out and lost till the Day of Judgment.

"Secondly, supposing I had kept quiet about that theft, you certainly might have got both stones, but then you would never have learnt the place of origin of the one I took, for that arose out of the whole conversation in this room with Miss Fleming. You would never have come to know Devil's Tor as an essential factor; and this afternoon's trial, for instance, could not have been meditated. Here is a second service. . . . The turning down of the mother's offer, besides, directly took me to the Tor this morning, to see what I did. But for it, you would still never have guessed the full significance of the connection. . . . In addition and incidentally, I, your enemy and ill-wisher, have given you the spectacle inside the stone itself, the one in your pocket. I have given you my last night's phantom.

"Now I offer—indeed, force on you—the acquaintance of a very singular, psychically-gifted woman, who certainly knows more of all these matters than all the rest together. Are you to suppose that, for the first time, nothing is to come of *that*? It is the whole trend, that something unexpected and wonderful will come of it.

"But if you inquire the inward nature and meaning of such a looking-glass service of mine—moving one way and arriving always mysteriously the other—why, the simplest answer, it seems, will be to call it supernatural at once. . . . Let us postulate an active fate in the case, and let us see how such a fate must work. The flint is to be recovered from Drapier's hand by me, therefore I must go up to Devil's Tor. Only one person knows that

Drapier is there, therefore *she* must send me up. I shall not see her, to be sent up, unless I stop in her mother's room till a certain moment, and therefore my talk with the mother is otherwise superfluously prolonged. It will not be prolonged by me, nor by her unless something in my manner succeeds in impressing her, so I adopt a foolish and unlikely attitude. But I shall not adopt this attitude unless I am inwardly persuaded that it is the best and necessary. What silent monitor so persuades me? You may call it instinct, or you may call it intuition, but the fact is that it is to deal with outward things, not in any way for my own service, and therefore comes to me from without—though certainly *via* my deeper self.

"And so with all the rest. It is where you and I differ, Arsinal. Your subterranean self is never, with your permission, to derive its lights and fires from the *without*, never from the *abroad*, but only from the *down*, and *down*, and *down*. Then this self, as well as its infinite reservoir, can still remain your own property. But once the under-surface feeding channel proves to be, not a private pipe-line to the infinite, but something more in the nature of a pervious sponge or marsh, open to contributions from all sides, at all depths, then, if we still want a soul of our own, doubtless we must look for it elsewhere. I find no good reason to suppose that at *any* depth we cease to be members of a whole corporate system. It appears to me—I have studied it a good deal—that there is precisely one method of dissociating oneself from the system and being a single soul, and that is by sincerely declining to be concerned. The world is from God and I am from God, therefore the world and I are brothers, but if I can scorn my own creation, and all that springs out of it, then my principle of scorning is *before* God, since it judges and may not be judged, except by its peers, who are nowhere in God's world. . . .

"Because you are acquisitive and I am philosophical, we have never truly met, Arsinal. It seems an odd thing to say, having reference to our known characters and outward tendencies, and people would not understand the remark. But it probably explains our diverging at last—rather suddenly. A sign-post has presented itself round a corner of our joint road, pointing you one way, me another. Personal heat, under the circumstances, seems absurd; let those fall to high words and blows who fundamentally want the same things. You desire to appropriate this business of the flints and Devil's Tor, whereas I, seeing that I am in life and a created being—shamefully enough, perhaps, according to some of the philosophies . . . I am content that it shall use me, if it will; but also I am determined that your greater activity shall not rob or hurt third persons. I end on the note of warning."

He moved towards the door, intending to wash his hands, but Arsinal stopped him.

"Stay, Saltfleet! I haven't interrupted you, and now must just reply. . . . I have to say this. Let us both forget a great part of what has just passed. In any case we are now very soon to go out of each other's lives, so that, to borrow from music, the last few bars ought to return to the friendship of the whole thematic character. . . . Indeed, I was in danger of over-looking how excellently your very mistakes down here have served me. Fault upon fault you have piled, and added the semblance of treachery—I now say, its semblance only. Each time something utterly unlooked-for of good has come of it. I decline your philosophical challenge and refrain from harking back, but let us rather resort to the Englishman's traditional substitute for lengthy explanations, recollecting still that some person within us has met, approved and admired his fellow in the other, however antipodal in other respects we may have turned out to be. . . ."

From his chair he stretched out his hand, which Saltfleet, smiling cynically, grasped for an instant. Then Arsinal proceeded:

"Were it but to tide us over the period immediately ahead, we must keep on terms. And to what I am about to add, I want no answer, but only ask you to reflect on it when you shall have more leisure. You likened me to Peter in his most shameful moment. I hope I am like him, not in this, but altogether, *except* in this. Peter gave up all to follow Christ, and so have I given up all—for in the worldly sense, Saltfleet, I might have made very much more of my life, and perhaps might have been of greater use to the public. So I too have been stunned by an illumination, and afterwards have suffered my life to be ruled by blind faith, and have renounced, surrendered and known pain and contumely, not in pursuit of personal gain.

"Peter, moreover, had his Christ in the flesh; he had but to accompany and obey. My divine one is a phantom, very hard to seek. You won't think it sacrilegious if I elaborate for you the sequence of my—I don't say, faith, but will-to-faith; in the terms of the New Testament. My ineffable apparition when I was a boy, she was the Holy Ghost. Christ is not yet—first I must know Mary. You have said that I am Peter; and I am content. . . . It is not for me to fasten upon any earthly girl or woman for Mary, but can you not understand how, if these things are to be true, she is the doorway through which I must pass to the new life? For the rest, I cannot conceive what she should be in time and space; and now I offer to you, Saltfleet, *not* to meet this Miss Fleming, if you imagine that she is in any way to pull me down from my dreams."

"Perhaps I have wronged you," returned Saltfleet. "Your ambition is as difficult rightly to get hold of, as the virtue of your faith to determine, but you do seem more willing than I had supposed to take second rank in the business. . . . Best of all would be if you could make your mind up to stand back from doorways altogether."

"Then why do you wish me to meet her?"

"For her sake. The glimmer you can shed may be of the feeblest, but so far she is in total darkness. Nobody at all has helped her."

"To what?"

"To the way out of this sublime madhouse!" rejoined Saltfleet.

And while the other was still frowning on the words, he smiled over his shoulder, and left the room.

On the open moor Arsinal, after recurring long spells of moody silence, broken only occasionally by the briefest exchanges, said more quietly, more significantly, to his friend:

"I haven't yet had the connected narrative of Drapier's doings on Devil's Tor. Will you tell me what you know?"

As Saltfleet perfunctorily complied, Arsinal heard him with a close attention. He appeared absorbed for several minutes afterwards; when at last he commented:

"So, plainly, it is something other than a purposeless marching of chance, and this independently of the ghostly element. For consider, Saltfleet! There has been the man's flight from India, to reach this petty spot in England no more than a few days before the one hour in possibly six figures of years when the pile of rocks stopping a tomb was to be thrown down like a card house; and there has been his exacter timing of the day and hour of the disaster, enabling him to be on the scene over its actual occurrence; and, lastly, there has been his not less wonderfully exact timing of the moment of the following earthquake, that was to be his limit of allowance for investigation. These three timings, of which he could have planned nothing, are to me more astounding than the natural disasters themselves. The disasters *might* be coincidence, taken alone; the timings were clearly of an unconscious clock in Drapier. The clock has not been his own, for it never was to serve him, and immediately afterwards he is destroyed. So what compelled him to these comings and goings, at the same time furnishing him with other shallower motives that he might understand, was necessarily something outside himself; for the instincts are for our use, and the intuitions are but a stranger way of seeing things, they could not predict invisible heights and, later, miracles. That something outside himself, Saltfleet, has been an *intelligence*. Its wisdom, acting through its will, has been for Drapier, as for all of us, a *fate*."

"To that I agree."

"And this Devil's Tor, this insignificant eminence of a small moor like a thousand others, which the whole phalanx of European experts has never heard of—if it should proclaim itself in such a fashion the mystic, hoary, fateful cradle of the northern stocks, that would be the same strangeness presented on another plane.

"And from such a cradle the uneasy half-lith that we recovered

in Tibet, whose later *pied-à-terre* for a paltry few centuries was
Knossos—it started its memorable, unsung journey across two
continents of all kinds of men, supernaturally drifted by that
invisible current—the captive of a hundred shrines and altars, yet
escaping eastwards always; until the predestined hour should
arrive when two persons from the west, and a third as yet unknown to them, should assemble beyond the frontiers of civilisation, to carry it back to its interred fellow—or bride, as the prophecy has said. And upon the approach of the thing of magic, the
tomb has yielded up its dead. But what could be the meaning of
so seemingly unnecessary a journey to and from the east? A very
big gap of time was to be filled up, Saltfleet. During a hundred
thousand years, perhaps, the world was to become slowly prepared for that second bursting of a mysterious potency."

"Thus you accept Miss Fleming's supposition that Drapier
found the stone on Devil's Tor!"

"I have tested it in my mind. Drapier could at no time before
his death have had *both* flints in his possession, for curiosity, or
an inward stimulus far stronger than curiosity, must then have
induced him to join the two; and there would have been, to put it
at the lowest, amazing results, of which we have seen nothing. So
it has been during his stay in the locality that he found the second,
by which time the first was already out of his hands. He seems,
however, to have been drawn to this Tor again and again; little
doubt, it was his descent underground that began the attraction.
There he must have seen a sight not easily to be forgotten. But if,
as you assert, the tomb is certainly sealed, that spectacle would
not have been enough, for he is dead, and the spectacle vanished
with him like a bubble; and all these voyagings of minerals and
men have not been for *that*. In fact, the finding of the stone in the
tomb is necessary. Without it, everything falls apart again, half
the circumstances known to us remain isolated and unaccounted
for."

"I think with you."

"The overthrown stack—obviously of human construction,
since it covered a grave—was it fashioned like a devil, that the

hill should bear the name it does?”

“So I am told.”

“Taking into account its long standing in a damp climate, could that portraiture have been intended?”

“Who knows? It is not here as in Egypt.”

“But if it *were* a work of art, magic or sacred, it would nearly point towards a female interment. For the times were savage and the tribal superstitions impossibly other than crude. A dead male chief, dreaded in life for his strength and ruthlessness, would surely keep off grave-robbers by the terror of his ghost. The departed wife or paramour of such a chief must be defended in her last house. And so a malignant spirit-entity, to squat for all time upon her bones.”

“Miss Fleming arrived at the identical conclusion, I have no idea by what means.”

“Thus already the guess is probably right.”

“Does it go further?” asked Saltfleet.

“I will say the things that I think, but I will not grasp at air.”

“Then I shall put it. If gods historically have died and been buried in stone sepulchres, why not goddesses?”

Arsinal threw him a side-glance of quick anxiety.

“Why this, Saltfleet?”

“It as well serves to bring more facts into the synthesis, and give it more cement. My shade last night should have been taller than the very tall. You know whom *you*’ve been seeking.”

“You are in earnest?”

“I think that if a woman has been buried yonder, she has been unlike all other women.”

“Could this afternoon decide it?”

“I have a plan. May it be fruitful!”

Arsinal’s face became expressionless and dark. He dropped the subject of the tomb, but, after some more steps pushed in silence, asked:

“Are there any surviving local legends or superstitions relating to this hill? For frequently such go an immense way back, their present unlikely form, as in a well-known children’s game, is identifiable with a surprising original."

"I've heard of nothing," replied Saltfleet.

They reached the angle of the shoulder, and Devil's Tor came suddenly into their view, startling both men quietly, for its identity was unmistakable, yet the apparition was unexpected and neither had seen its shape before. Saltfleet dragged foot and halted, whereupon Arsinal's remaining doubt instantaneously dispersed; but it already was as if he had known the hill from some existing picture in his head—yet none had even lightly sketched it for him. He too stopped.

Balls and streaks of white mist still clung motionless to the Tor, but it was truly visible at last as far as its flat top. The air had little draught; the surrounding moors were in a gloomy haze, while the sky was dull and colourless. From a bright patch where the south-west sun should be, a fan of dark vertical and slanting shafts fell on a circumscribed area of the great falling sweep of land continuing past the distant open road down below, lifting the grey-green of the moor to a sort of pallid solar shine; but elsewhere one felt that the day had failed. Already it was between three and four o'clock.

"We may get a better view by keeping along," counselled Saltfleet. And soon, as he had supposed, they won a point from which the whole east face of the Tor, from stream bed, up through the witch-kitchen of cataclysmal ancient rocks ringing the inferior slopes, to shorn summit, was thrown up for them and defined in close detail, interrupted only by those few floating vapours.

Standing there, his arms tightly folded behind his straightened back, Arsinal inquired where Drapier had died, and then where the overthrown stack had stood. Not too quickly, Saltfleet indicated both spots in succession with a considering forefinger. Afterwards they relapsed into a silence of contemplation that prolonged itself to minutes. Twice now had the one man known unutterable experiences upon that grey enigma always newly starting up; but the other's imaginings, less personal, were on that account possibly the richer and deeper in the grandeur of a metaphysical antiquity. It was Saltfleet who first restlessly broke the spell.

"Who could have been those tomb-makers, Arsinal?"

The addressed one emerged unwillingly.

"If the half-stone were brought here from elsewhere, I cannot answer you, and an answer is unnecessary. But if this hill, as we must dare to think, has been the first seat and terrestrial home of the undivided lith, then an answer would be more possible, though difficult. It is not the technical books, however, which will teach us what we wish to know."

"I ask *you*."

Arsinal faced his companion with an uneasy and still absent eye.

"Yet if I am to attempt any sort of reply, I must first clear the way. The paleontological library, I say, is increasingly a welter of chaos. Petrified crania and bits of crania have been measured, physical characters of human and subhuman types have been compared and contrasted, the vocabularies of the seven or eight great Aryan stocks have been exhaustively examined for common roots, to arrive at the last common habitat. Superstitions, proverbs, religions, fairy stories, have all been put under blood-less analytical survey, to discover what men could have started them, in what regions of the globe, under what circumstances. Then caves, lakes, marshes, mounds, barrows, have been dredged and ransacked, flint implements innumerable studied under optical power, all the available remains of 'mammoth' art squeezed for their last drop of meaning. The beginnings of an-cient nations as recorded have been ruthlessly pulled to pieces, in order to be reconstructed *de novo*. . . . And, as the broad result of all, to-day there is a wider contrariety of learned opinion than ever before, as to what manner of man or manlike ape has autoch-thonally occupied each land—what simian features have been contemporaneous with what degree of emergence to intellectual-ity. Each new fragment of yellow skull, each new far-fetched lingual derivation, but draws us further into the intricacies of the labyrinth—which in the end may well prove to have neither centre nor exit for us. . . .

"We are at least assured that the so-called Nordic races have been, beyond all others, warlike and freedom-loving, the primitive Romans stern, severe and disciplined, the Achaeans brilliant, rational, aesthetic, the Celts poetically restless and mystical. All these have been blue-eyed peoples. It is no conjecture, but a necessity, that these blue-eyed peoples, appearing suddenly as strangers in a world of brown humanity, should be derived from one stock. The later branchings and differences are to be otherwise explained. It is *scarcely* a conjecture that the home of that single blue-eyed stock has been north-west Europe.

"The metamorphosis took place—I have spoken of it to you before. It took place amongst a certain brown race, because of its latent possibilities of advancement. The after branchings—as of Goth, German, Roman, Celt and Greek—were a consequence of the tremendous spirituality of the new characters, overflowing into a vital flood that would not for long ages be confined to any one racial channel. But the north-west European race, who were the fathers of all, may well have been more stable. Over a stretch of a thousand or fifteen hundred miles, perhaps, and during untold ages, such a race may have moved practically not at all, in the way of social or spiritual development. It waited. It should have been in Britain; Britain was still the connected extremity of the continent of Europe. The North Sea was still a river, of which the Rhine and the Thames were unequal tributaries.

"And that race should be identical with the earliest of the Eolithic cave-dwellers. They need not all have dwelt in caves, but the caves have endured, the forest huts of mud and wattle have vanished. An outpost of that great widespread European brown-eyed people may have become settled in this valley at our feet, in a time when it was supernatural and frightful with dark trees. . . ."

"And they would be the tomb-makers!" said Saltfleet.

"They have even been described. Yet few have noticed the accounts, for science has had its other more beloved fashions. The Icelandic sagas are full of such descriptions. . . . I don't know now if we shall ever enter into the discussion. Certainly there is no time now, at this minute. We have stayed here too long, Salt-fleet.”

“On the contrary, I regard it as so extraordinarily essential to get you proved right or wrong in *all*, that I’m prepared to stop here half an hour longer if necessary. For the same reason that I withheld my vision this morning from you, I want you, in advance of the next, to predict its elements by pure reason, logic, intuition—call it what you will. . . . For supposing you have this demoniacal nose for hidden things, the common measures of prevention may not be enough. . . .”

Arsinal turned a wrinkled glance on him.

“So that I could refuse to answer at all, and be well within my rights as a sensible man. But I shall neither blow up our quarrel again here, nor will I waste time over urging you forward before you are quite ready. Let us only finish quickly. . . .

“I said, the sagas. To persons acquainted with the sagas and reading with heedful mind, a singular racial circumstance everywhere outcrops in them. It is that throughout all these northern stories, the two distinct types of northern men persistently appear, frequently in the same generation of the same family. A single instance may stand for all. Skallagrim had two sons. Now Thorolf, the older of the pair, as a child ‘grew to be tall and was fair of countenance,’ while Egil, the younger, was ‘ill-favoured like his father, with black hair’—and as the passage has always struck me as important, I can conclude it verbatim:

“‘When but three years old he (Egil) was as tall and strong as other boys of six or seven. He was soon talkative and word-wise. Somewhat ill to manage was he when at play with other lads.’

“And Skallagrim himself resembled that son, whereas Thorolf the elder, the brother of Skallagrim and uncle of Thorolf the younger, entirely resembled that younger Thorolf in fairness and good looks and affability.

“That black, ill-featured type finds mention in a hundred chiefs, sea-rovers and *bondis* of the north. Doubtless it was as prevalent as the fair, golden, sun-like type, which yet was ever the more popular and remained the standard of perfection of the stock. Sigurd Fafnirsbane, Gunnar of Lithend, Kjartan Olafsson, were yellow-haired, blue-eyed, handsome, easy of speech and open of character, the favourites of all men, the beloved of all women. Skallagrim, Egil, Skarphedinn, Grettir, and numberless others, were either black or red-haired, ugly, quarrelsome, and often secret-natured. Sometimes they were credited with being descended from the stock of the 'hill-giants'. . . .

"But also this curious natural antithesis finds presentation in an essential and principal feature of the Norse cosmogony which hitherto has always baffled the commentators. In the last day the sons of Muspellheimr, that flaming world of the south, headed by Surtr—he who sits upon and guards its border, 'his sword out-shining the sun itself'—are to sally forth and destroy the gods and all mankind. These fiery golden beings, Saltfleet, may well stand for the archetype of the yellow-haired men of the north; and that last destruction of the old order should surely be the second coming of the power of the lith, raising those yellow-haired ones to new and sublimer and final splendours.

"Very awful and beautiful to me is this mysterious sudden shooting forth of the mythos into an inexplicable quarter, like a flashing of genius. Opposed to Muspellheimr is Niflheimr, the abode of freezing cold and gloom. The Edda says:

"'That part of Ginnungagap that lies towards the north was thus filled with heavy masses of gelid vapour and ice, and every-where within were whirlwinds and fleeting mists. But that part that lies towards the south was lighted by the sparks and flakes that flew into it from Muspellheimr.'

"Those sparks and flakes, may not we at once call them the meteors of the sky, and may not the already ignorant reference be to the forgotten tradition of the fall to earth of one aerolith in particular? . . . Niflheimr: that is, the dark primal world of savagery and gianthood. And the account proceeds. From the commingling of the fire generated by those sparks and that congealed vapour, arose to life the giant Ymir, with the cow Audhumla, who fed upon the salt and hoar frost of the stones round about and the milk of whose teats nourished Ymir. But from the stones thus licked by her sprang the father of Odin, endowed with beauty, agility and power. . . .

"Those licked stones, then, were the same dark half-giants of Niflheimr; and that cow was the allegorised figure of the Mother. The stones as well, however, were doubtless the fragments of the aerolith, shattered by its fall to ground, and here the myth must somehow have become corrupted. The father of Odin and his named wife (to omit an obviously falsely inserted generation) were the chosen individuals from a pre-existing barbarous tribal forest-folk. Odin himself was the resulting god-man.

"But one entity remains over—Ymir. He, the frost-giant, was not before the cow Audhumla, for her milk nourished him; yet his *mention* is before her, and so it is to be understood that their appearances in the world were simultaneous and inseparable. With Ymir, indeed, we find associated a whole new branch of naively grand fable, with which we have nothing to do, and which may probably represent another myth-system altogether, crudely welded to the first at a later date. His original shape and meaning, difficult to grasp, perhaps too soon became troublesome to immature intelligences untrained to abstractions, so that they fell to easier stories.

"I hazard that Ymir was united to that female visitant from another flaming sphere of pure spirit, as a sinister 'infra' force, for the automatic defence of her sacredness in a dismal blood-reeking underworld of crouching beasts and half-beasts. His strength and malignity were those of death itself. . . . Well may it be, Saltfleet, that this hill standing up against us was at one time 'Ymir's Tor.' His carven image was erected yonder to continue his office after the most fearful of all burials. Drapier has fallen to his wrath. . . .

"And now I shall answer your question, or attempt to do so, after so long a digression. 'Who were those tomb-makers?' They were the infinitely-distant progenitors of the ill-favoured, black-haired men of the sagas, the original stock of the European north-west, probably for the most part dwelling in rude hovels in the extensive dark, marshy forests of those days, who in after times became the fearsome giants of countless songs and stories. . . . For the bones of these so-numerous giants have till now not been recovered, and we are therefore to credit that this popular term 'giant' anciently described not the possessor of an exceptional stature, but of a wild bodily strength, rudeness and unsociableness beyond the later common. Never did the type disappear, but it came to mix its blood with that of its supernatural fair-haired conquerors, and so grew erect and alert, better-mannered, fonder of the light of day; yet always the fundamental distinction en-dured. . . . More than the other northerners, perhaps, the Celts may have retained their 'giant' characters. . . ."

Arsinal paused; whereupon Saltfleet asked him:

"But why should not that mystical translation to the highest have occurred among another race? Nor do I see any great wor-ship of womanhood in these people, to prepare them for the bowing down before a Great Mother. That, I well remember, was a point of yours."

"Consider, Saltfleet. Isn't the cultivated rose, by nearly univer-sal acclaim, the loveliest of flowers? Yet it is from the simple briar, that has no more beauty than the violet, primrose, bluebell, or a dozen other wayside blooms. Why then has the rose been victorious over all wild competitors? Because the briar always possessed the capability of holding in its sheath-to-come the multitudinous curving petals that constitute the glory of the garden rose. And equally, the grim-featured, black-haired savage of the ancient northern lands must have possessed potentially in his foreshadowed later brain the group of strange and noble characters whose interaction afterwards was bound to produce that *saltus* for mankind.

"Still you may object that other races have attained a compar-able height by simple evolution, without a break and without unearthly intervention; but I reply, no! the height has never been comparable. The Chinese and Japanese have given us decorative forms of art that could not rise to sublimity. A few peoples have built magically for sky and land, not for heaven. No dark-skinned race has yet achieved a philosophy; for the Upanishads of India are from the Aryans. The Jews and Arabs have willed, rather than meditated, their sullen monotheistic systems, and these systems have remained barbaric, of blood and towards blood.

"All has been communal, non-individual; only in the European north and west has the genius of the individual soul been possible. Therefore, that slumbering, half-frozen stock, dreaming uneasily during some thousands of generations before the coming of the grand translation—it alone, of all the human peoples, was undergoing the impress of outward circumstance which could at last break it up into persons. The long black winter nights, the frightful brute creation, hunting as well as hunted, the impassable forests filled with imagined shapes of awe and panic terror, the bogs, rains, damps, chills and fogs, making of life one long misery and struggle, the splitting of the race into the smallest groups, wherefrom speech remained uncommon, concerted action unknown, and loneliness the rule—all was towards the formation of minds brought permanently face-to-face with *reality* . . . not the reality of practical things, but that of the whole of cosmic existence. But for untold ages the misery was escapeless and men sought no escape; hearts were being silently hammered to the beginning of agonised wonder, and there was as yet no thought in the north, but only a damming of the future thought that was to break through like a mighty flood. . . . Compare this, for example, Saltfleet, with the easy, eloquent tears and breast-beatings of the primitives of the Old Testament, the vocal distresses on account of the loss of possessions, whether human or material; and you will discover why the one people should already have swelled to maturity and run its short course, before the other had succeeded in establishing its foundations of dark majesty and sovereignty over all the latter nations of the planet. . . .

"But as for the worship of womanhood, that must spring from monogamic love, among the smallest isolated tribes or families, constantly threatened by the overwhelming perils of a terrible natural world. For when men begin to band together, and feel themselves strong at last to roam from place to place, then their protection of their womenfolk may in part be left to the community; but until then each man must defend his own, and such defence, from love, becomes reverence. And he who will not defend his wife will have lost the half of his life."

Saltfleet viewed him steadily.

"Then could not that people have progressed to its ultimate height without the accident of a divine interposition?"

"All things, perhaps, are possible. I can but say that it has probably not done so. The man I have described, he might well ultimately have attained to the mastery of the world by his own nature and exertions; and still that would not have been enough. The questions of his labouring heart were to be answered as well. He was to be a *spirit*. . . . A supernatural gardener was necessary."

There was a moment's silence.

"What is the world for, Arsinal? What is to be its last and most blessed state?"

"The world, I conceive, is for the understanding of heaven," replied Arsinal. . . . "And men, it may be, will have understood heaven as soon as they shall have realised that not they alone are in pain and in development. . . . Men now are angry and perplexed because they deem that their Creator has gratuitously set them in an abode of torment; but if ever they come to the wisdom that the Creator too is in torment, that the torments of the created are likewise the anguish of the Creator—and all to some high end . . . then I conceive that the angelic state may well be within grasp, even by suffering man. . . ."

XXIV

Beside the Torrent

Saltfleet wished now to get down quickly to the valley, and

Arsinal was more than ready.

"Where is the trial to take place?" he asked.

"I propose that we follow the stream up round the bend, and see what it is like there."

"You want it to be in the valley, and not on the Tor?"

"Yes."

"And that will bring us north-east or north of the Tor?"

"Yes."

He led the way along the upper path they were on, and Arsinal followed in silence. But as the curve swept round, Devil's Tor began to change shape. Then it seemed as though they could have thrown a stone to it, the valley sides were so brought together in abruptness, while their own slope mounted higher and higher above the track. The open country slipped from sight, the scene grew very wild, dark and desolate, the darkness being due to the shadowing of the gap by the intervening bulk of the Tor. The grey grass and rocks of the latter's north face slanted down nearly precipitously; the cut between the hills came to resemble a dismal dike. The sky, in being diminished, looked duller. Seemingly not far off, still further up the valley, an invisible peewit sounded at intervals its queer mournful cry.

And Saltfleet reflected that yonder tract of great broken boulders continuing to circle the base of the Tor must probably represent an appalling landslide of primitive cliffs, anciently a part of the height they were traversing. . . . Only, in that case, the level of the watercourse must have been much deeper down, since it must needs, the valley, have received unreckonable millions of tons of rock as that sudden gift. Thus the test to come was made still more dreamlike, for it was to be from beside a stream that once had been a roaring cataract, perhaps a hundred feet or more below the present bed, and he was somehow also expecting to be beside such a cataract. How this could be he did not know.

Then the divided heights fell apart again, the floor of the valley rebroadened, and at once a rain-gully offered itself by which the men could conveniently clamber down. At the foot, Saltfleet leapt the water to Devil's Tor. He stopped where he had landed, waiting for Arsinal, who joined him and halted too.

"Is this the spot?"

"It will do," said Saltfleet.

He appeared to hesitate.

"We must settle how we are to manage, Arsinal. Miss Fleming, having her flint in her hand, saw something; I, sitting near, saw something else, as I think. Her apparition, assuming that it was brought about by her holding of the flint, should have been the principal, and yet mine was so remarkable that I would be well content to repeat and pursue it; which is why I have fixed on the valley. Against this is the possibility that in some mysterious fashion her vision may have included, while transcending, mine, though I can't believe it has been so. Then let me hear your wishes as to which of us shall hold the stone."

Arsinal turned away to consider the difficulty, straightening his shoulders while he did so. Then he came back.

"*I* will hold it. . . . The point, however, may be less material than you conceive. The phenomenon's character, which, according to your showing, should be correspondent to its degree of vividness, can still hardly depend upon the physical contact, which would be making it too mechanical a business. I should be sorry to imagine, for instance, that an unrelated person, holding one of the flints, could be shown more than an attuned instrument sitting by. It would be to destroy all the fate, all the meaning, of these happenings. . . . Nevertheless, to leave nothing to chance, since I *may* be wrong here, and seeing that the affair is in every sense, and first and last, mine, not yours, I must insist on the active part in this essay."

"I was nearly sure that you would claim it, and you must have your own way."

He looked at Arsinal. "Did you study the stone's image again this morning while I was out?"

"Yes, for a long time."

"It's a night sky, and they are true stars?"

"That must be," replied Arsinal.

"But what are those stars? Are they of our universe?"

"I don't know."

"Perhaps they are of no three-dimensional sky at all?"

"You would suggest . . ."

"Of a heavenly sky?"

Arsinal quietly wondered at the unwonted simplicity of tone of all these interrogations. It occurred to him as extraordinary that he could have been so intimately in Saltfleet's society during many months without ever having suspected the existence in him of this second, or indeed third, nature. Besides being a tempered man of the world, then, and so lately that man of irresponsible levity, he now could be as a child, asking his strange questions in limpid earnestness. . . . But still he felt that behind it all was the strength of contempt—that none but a true scorner could so dare to expose his innocence to the scoffing thoughts of another. And it seemed to Arsinal that the struggle between them, like a disease working underground, was suddenly renewed when he had believed it arrested, and that it had become deadlier and all at once was seriously threatening his designs, since Saltfleet too could thus adopt the manner of subdued selfless tranquillity, yet quiet groping, of one called to the service of the invisible. . . . It was as if he had conjured to his side and support a phantom attendant, who now refused to be dismissed, but who was growing and growing in presence, and significance, and equality, and even fearfulness. . . .

He could still answer, however, with a dignity of simplicity not less than that of the man who questioned him:

"Between heaven and earth there may be many skies, and this indeed may be one of them. But, rather, I would credit that it is a book which we are enabled to read only in translation. Our own stars are an alphabet of twenty-six letters, and all the words that we can form for our imperfect understanding must be composed of those twenty-six letters, or not at all. Such matters are not to be discussed, Saltfleet. The brain of man has been evolved to empower him to hold his own on earth. It is the rudest structure, and if I have said that the world is for the knowledge of heaven, I have certainly never meant that knowledge to come through intellectual sharpness. But let us now finish with talking, and get to work. . . ."

Saltfleet glanced about him, then mounted the slope of the Tor to a large discoloured boulder not more than a few yards above the level of the stream. He sat down facing the opposite height, which was north, and carelessly signalled to Arsinal to come up too. He complied. Perching himself on an adjacent stump of rock, he took out the flint from his pocket.

"Are you ready, Saltfleet, and shall we begin? What exactly am I to do?"

"I would grip it, in case it falls when you lose touch. . . . Then wait simply. We should not have long to wait. Say no more. . . ."

Saltfleet's last words were scarcely uttered when he saw between himself and the stream below, only some half-dozen paces down from where he sat, the vaporous shape of a woman of astonishing height, clad in seemingly ancient dark stone-coloured draperies that met the ground. She stood there like a pillar, without increasing or moving, facing him. Through her moonlike substance he could still behold the rising hill beyond the water, though very obscurely, as if gauze intervened—her attire, though it should seem opaque, was yet preventing no more than her flesh. He stumbled to his feet. Despite the circumstance that she was shown as lower down the Tor's slope than he, he felt shortened by her incomprehensible stature, as well as animalised by her ghostly grace. At the same time, an instinctive shuddering tried to wrest from his will the rule of his faculties.

He brutally stopped that. And when, with the same access of violence, he further dared to seek the phantom's eyes, in order to fight the whole awfulness at once, he became aware that by this act of boldness the luminosity of her skin was intensified for him and the substantiality of her dress increased, so that the hillside beyond was now nearly hidden by her.

Then he was meeting those eyes, and any antagonism he had expected proved imaginary, for a wonderful sense of peace and amity was flowing from the contact. Nevertheless, his bodily horror persisted, causing his state to be all confused and self-contradictory; he was at a loss how to adjust himself towards her. . . . But the first solution was that anger swelled up within him. He was disgusted with his own fear of another circumscribed individual, apparition though she might be, and his wrath was that she should be expecting to so daunt him. Yet the arisen heat never dispelled his other feeling of being in some manner united to a constant spring of friendly mildness. The two motions acted upon him together, so that his indignation could not remain such, but became metamorphosed to pride without hostility.

Her menace, he now felt, was not for *him*, not for his ancient, aristocratic, unkillable spirit, that was at least her equal, but for his animal blood, curdling at an unknown ghastliness; and *it* was but in him to be despised and commanded. No need to yield to anger because an illusory bugbear was terrifying his automatic part. Even, she might be standing here to prognosticate his death, as perhaps she had prognosticated Drapier's; and still there was no threat. His body had never been immortal. He was not to turn as pale as she because he was at once to die, the announcement was not to enrage him . . . nor did he require the alleviation of the mystic message of those mild, infinitely wise eyes, filling rather than encountering his. Such an encouragement was a misinterpretation of his temper, and so the communication between them was imperfect; this wraith stood not for an intelligent envoy of another world, but for a shape trying to impose its nature upon a man too austere. . . .

But next he seemed to understand that this exaggeration of his pride of self was no more than the easiest form of a new influx of life from her presence that was flooding all his being. His pride was his deepest and widest and most used channel, so it was the most notably filled. The influx of energy was preternatural, for neither did it hearten him, nor were his senses roused, but life, energy, it was, since with the passing instants he was conscious, not of the change itself, but of its effects. The entire level of his mind was uplifted, until his memory of the common things of existence was fainter and less; men, women, his mountain journeys, business, pleasure, sport, seemed to lose definition for him, just as familiar scenes to a man leaving them for a far distant place. And he identified the change with this ghostly statue before him, by reason of the fact that all his thoughts were coming to him from her by way of her eyes, whose colour and shape he never grasped, but only that those eyes resembled the debouching twin-ends of a living river from the invisible, springing across yards of air to enter himself. . . .

Soon he was believing that, besides being an entity, she was a personification of some task about to be demanded of him, some labour of Hercules that was nothing new, but always had been the reason for his birth and existence. Only, since the task had to be, she could not be announcing it; her apparition must be the actual initiation of its pains. She appeared as a woman, doubtless, that the horror might be softened for him. He conceived that there was no true relation between them. The womanly sweetness and grandeur contradicting and at the same time augmenting her awfulness, they were the *unseen* itself, there was no person here at all, but his eyes were inventing her shape. . . .

Then, precisely at the moment of her vanishing, overtook him the strangest experience of all his life hitherto. Her eyes, her whole face, made some swift movement of vital change, which, he had the positive assurance, should have taught him all the rest, but that he was just too slow to catch it. And yet the fault had not been his, since he was also certain that it was that very transformation that he had throughout been expecting.

He failed to see it, but still a part of its impression remained with him, to torture him for all that day, and longer. It had not been towards a further humanising of their impossible connection. The change had been to something of the nature of *savagery* and *absolutism*. . . . It could not be for his alarming, but for the arousing of his deepest earnestness. . . .

He retained his self-control, yet, after vainly seeking everywhere with his eyes for the phantom, it needed still a minute or two before he could grow used to the emptiness of the scene.

Simultaneously, Arsinal had dropped straight into night, as a stone to the ground.

A great rushing river tumbled and bounded past him like a beautiful monster, its flecks of wet startling his face, and its hoarse roar overpowering his hearing. He was in the company of others, on a broad strip of heath beginning from its very edge. Stunted unfamiliar trees grew scattered among the huge boulders that were the lowest of a mountain walling the waste on its landward side.

A mighty blaze of piled branches and logs in the middle space crimsoned the waves of the swollen black waters, and illuminated the rough precipices beyond, that went up out of sight into the night. Where men or trees or rocks were near enough to the fire to cast heavy shadows, these were perpetually changing grotesque shape and seeming to pursue each other. Arsinal himself was too far out to feel anything of the heat. In the upper sky were stars. The night air was windless, yet sharp.

Closer than the blaze to him, midway between it and the foot of the mountain, an irregular crescent of those man-like creatures was ranged before a bewildering spectacle, consisting in an upright shaft, nine or ten feet high, of dimly luminous white mist. The firelight should have overpowered it but for that shield of intervening beings; who perhaps were rather apes than men, with their anthropoid physique, brutish crouch (in some cases assisted by the actual resting of hairy fingers on the ground, while the knees could stay unbent), and then the unshaped body-skin or fur exposing all four limbs, and the bestial big-jowled physiognomies, catching the red in occasionally turning, that were neither bearded nor smooth, but displayed an outlandish hideousness of partial plucking of hairs in diverse styles of eccentricity. The hair of their heads, however, black or flaming, flowed in all cases past their shoulders, except that some, seeming to be women, had plaited theirs and adorned it with glittering ornaments. Otherwise, in that deep shade, he could not well distinguish between the sexes; a female bosom showed, or a face looked smooth, but all was indistinct and his eyes were seeking elsewhere. Male or female, each that he noticed wore heavy beads and armlets, and carried some sort of rude weapon.

The pillar of mist issued from a spherical knob of brighter light, motionless on the ground. Manifestly the phenomenon was a wonder and an excitement to that straining half-ring of witnesses, greedy, it appeared, to touch and seize, were it not for the strange danger. None conversed with neighbour; but, from time to time, one would twist his head round as if towards a certain black quarter of the red-lit mountain base, where probably it was pierced by some ravine or cavern. Accordingly, a person or an interruption should be expected from there.

Meanwhile the incarnadined inky torrent, riding everlastingly over that brief reach between a spectral unknown source and destination, not only continued to unman him by its incessant thunder, but so synchronised in its recurring spells of highest dreadfulness of approach with the trembling of the ground beneath his feet, that at each new oncoming he feared the entire tract must give. And yet he had no will to move back to more assured safety, his thoughts were so little upon himself.

Suddenly a monstrous undefined form leapt through the air from out of night, to crush with its sheer weight one of the creatures whose back was turned. The rest jumped round with quick cries and screams, lifting aloft their spears, axes and clubs, of wood and stone. The cruel face of a black leopard appeared for a single moment lighted by the crimson and yellow of the fire. In its mouth was the man's arm, completely torn off from the shoulder. A woman shrieked high above the clamour, darting towards the victim. But as he gyrated to the ground, where he stayed lying face-downwards, a newcomer rushed into the circle of light from the outer blackness.

His coarse jetty hair was as a mane on his shoulders, while his mournful exasperated face, that was beardless, might by day have been lemon-hued. He was oldish. His sunk cheeks, with the deep-graved lines between nose and mouth, and others crossing the width of his forehead, served to single him out from the rest present. Arsinal guessed that he was that tribe's chief. His mightier chest and limbs, and his quicker alertness, declared how that was possible; and perhaps it was he who had been awaited.

His shifty eyes fell upon the ravener as it was in the act of retreating with its booty. With an astonishing swiftness of resolution and agility, he sprang forward after it in a wild flying leap, to strike at the back of the beast's neck with the short stone-tipped spear in his hand, using both wrists to give the stab additional ferocity. The pard, that was as tall as an ass, faced round with a frightful snarl, but even so would not drop the prey. The man, flashing out the spear from that first wound, jabbed with it repeatedly in intensest savagery at the disgusting visage, all streaming blood from its jaws. Then, roaring with rage and agony, the leopard relinquished the arm at last, to hurl itself at its torturer.

The spear timber snapped near the head, and the weapon was useless. The man dodged, turned short after the brute from behind, and seized its upper and lower jaws with his two hands. There was a sharp sickening wrench, then the leopard collapsed, writhing, with a wail like that of a lost soul. But snatching a new spear from a follower, the victor never ceased stabbing and restabbing the jowl of the senseless beast until it was an indistinguishable pulp of blood and matter.

He staggered back to straightness, or what could pass for it, then stood with rising and falling breast, glaring around at the details of the scene. It was not permitted that he should see Arsinal. The woman who had shrieked was still bending over her mutilated one, silently watching the blood well from his shoulder, like wine from a stopperless bottle. The chief came across to regard the prostrate man gloomily for well-nigh a minute. At last he raised the borrowed spear. Its point descended hard and swift upon the upturned back, reaching through all to the ground. To Arsinal, however, that unreal murder of a phantom, after its sudden horror, could stand out as an act of savage mercy. . . .

Fouled with gore from head to foot, the chief impatiently cast away the spear, to move straight upon the mystic pillar of light, while those nearest him cowered aside to make space. For a great time he viewed this spectacle too in silence, and it was clear that his reasoning brain worked more laboriously than his active. Yet, in the end, it seemed that he would have taken a tentative step forward in the decision to approach still closer to the misty column, with its nucleus of white brilliance; his lifted foot, however, appeared to lose its instinct of planting, so that his body became wrenched, and he stumbled and over-balanced himself, tumbling to earth in a heap—it was difficult to see how it had happened. The gradually thickening moon of followers fell back. Faces were set in consternation and wonder, while the chief still made no effort to rise, though entirely sensible. The torrent drowned all human articulation.

And those other shapes of both sexes kept issuing from the night, paying their preliminary toll of amazement from the outskirts of the scene before timidly and clumsily stealing forward to take refuge with their assembled kind and extend the semicircle's horn nearest the mountain. The whole circle was never completed, doubtless because the facing of the fire's glow interfered with the vision of that pillar of paler light. As they came up singly, each creature gazed with furtive intentness at those forsaken bloody dead ones, that told their own tragedy, but none paused long before proceeding to the final spectacle unparalleled by any memory within their primitive skulls. Among the last of all came one, half girl, half woman, slighter, more graceful and younger-looking than the others of her sex, though still of uncouth type. The contrast Arsinal could not pursue, for her next actions gave him different thoughts.

With but a glance of shock and recognition at the lying dead, and an anguished silent parting of her lips, she had already hastened forward to the Chief's helpless form. He looked up towards her as she came. She bent her strength to lift him to his feet, and afterwards supported him standing; whereupon it was confirmed that he had been temporarily paralysed, but not hurt. When the fire for a moment lit both their faces, there was such a resemblance, that she might well be his daughter. They exchanged silent lip-speech, he, apparently, slowly and sullenly, she excitedly. He pointed in turn to the mountain, the leopard's carcase, the dead man, and the pillar of faint silver. Finally, he shook himself free of her, while she, in staring in a wonderstruck way at the thing in their midst, no longer attempted to hold him. The uproar of the waters stopped every barbarous sound that might be their language.

No more than three long paces separated her from the column, and with a shuffling suddenness she stepped them. She stooped low, lifted easily and harmlessly from the ground the spherical source of the brightness, then, rising again, examined what was in her hand. The perpendicular misty shaft remained where it had been, save that its lower end now rested on earth; so the two phenomena were truly not parts. And almost instantly the shaft grew to be defined into the apparition of a miraculously tall, moon-fleshed, draped woman, who was like an inner ghost within a scene already spectral. . . .

Arsinal re-collected his wits, to study the effect of this latest phantom upon those witnesses, but not one of all their awed and painfully labouring faces that he could discern showed signs of awareness of the transition. Their eyes seemed always to be upon what the girl held. Accordingly, the new hallucination could not be for them, but the second-sight required for its beholding was not yet prepared in their still animal brains.

Alone, the girl displayed the extreme agitation of such a vision, such a knowledge, for, throwing down her knob of light in terror, she cast herself after it prone upon the ground with arms outstretched before that strange spirit, as if worshipping her. . . .

The two men came together. Saltfleet was grim, and Arsinal pale. A space of silence passed, when Arsinal said quietly:

"We have both *seen*, I think."

The other assented by a collected but curiously moved look.

"You as little as myself will care to speak of it at once," Arsinal proceeded. "Such prodigies and portents are not for speech. Perhaps afterwards—long afterwards—we may tell each other. Now I only wish to say, for a purpose: I have just been translated to a very ancient time, Saltfleet, and have been witnessing events, by night. Has your experience been of that kind?"

"No."

"Has yours, then, been the direct overtaking, and mine the derived?"

"From your outline, yes."

"Then it is singular. Yet it was necessary that I should have seen what I did. . . . And I hazarded in advance that the actual contact should be immaterial; nevertheless there must be a law, and what is that law? . . . Need your *direct* have been of more importance than my *derived*? Might not it be like an unfolding, demanding distance—a longer road? . . ."

"No. A stroke needs no unfolding."

"You have been stricken, in a way that I have not?"

"Yes," answered Saltfleet. "I am altered."

"But in another sense than after your morning's adventure on this hill?"

"I could still find myself active and plan-making after that. Now . . ." He shrugged, and turned aside.

"Now you regard yourself as fated, Saltfleet?"

"Fated—yes."

"In what degree? To what end?"

"Not to any end of mine. . . . Drapier might have known about it too. I would talk to him if he were alive—but you . . ."

"I am still to experience this knowledge. How can I attain it quickly?"

"Probably not by premeditation. If you are to gain it, you will gain it."

"What of Miss Fleming?"

"What I know, she must know."

A pause followed.

"I am rather physically distressed from this shock," said Arsinal, "yet, if it were to do any good, I would not hesitate to repeat the experiment at once, elsewhere on the hill. Would you be prepared to join me, Saltfleet?"

"No, I'd rather not."

"Why?"

"I have seen nearly enough for one day."

"Perhaps you are right. But we are not to part company?"

"We will keep together till to-morrow."

"You may be the man, after all," Arsinal pondered slowly, "yet definitely that has been the very last thing in my mind."

Mingling with and augmented by his supernatural excitement, his perturbation on account of the secondary character of his entrancement found all the less resistance in his will, so that he feared to disclose more of it than was proper. During another silence, he felt the urgent need to move—to walk—to get away. He suggested to Saltfleet that before returning home they should mount to the Tor's top, that he might be shown the site of the tomb, and then, in descending again by the directer route, Drapier's death-place. This, accordingly, they did.

XXV

Helga's Share

Towards three o'clock of that afternoon, in the inconspicuous slow creeping to brightness of Helga's still sunless room, she sat facing her daughter, constantly scanning her with eyes that held perplexity, and something else besides, very difficult to define. It was neither submission to a fact, nor a sense of loss, nor the calm foreknowledge of an inevitable evil happening, but a union of the shades of all three, none of them as yet in substance. The whole indescribable expression gave her face a fine mysteriousness that, in this sought conversation, was like a very fitting thing. But Ingrid only once or twice resented her mother's gaze with a quick ascertaining glance, while always she leant back exhausted, frequently suffering her heavy lids to droop, above cheeks as white as paper. A window was open, letting in the soft sweetness of the day.

Peter was not there. Depressed and thoughtful from his vain

long waiting for Ingrid's return, he had at last gone home at past midday, and was not yet back. Then, an hour after his vanishing, she had appeared, limping from her overtasked ankle and with a drawn face set fast in the stoical endurance of weariness and her spirit's shock; and, upon her mother's hastening out to her from the lunch table, she had declined the meal, announcing her intention to pass straight upstairs to her room to lie down, but as some brief explanation of her long absence was unavoidable, she had, before turning her back, also informed her mother that she had been on Devil's Tor, where she had been joined by Mr. Saltfleet, with whom she had spoken. . . . Helga, stunned, had said little to that, but had begged the girl to see her in her own room in another hour, to discuss an urgent related matter. . . .

For the rest of her silent meal with old Colborne, and afterwards, she could not make up her mind if Saltfleet had *sought* her daughter on the Tor or if it had been a chance encounter. But then she came to comprehend that it made no difference; for what alone mattered was that their meeting there should have had this distressing effect on the child. As the hour of waiting drew to a close, however, Helga's sternness of determination to end it all began, she knew not how, to crack and give place to what in her heart had the similitude to golden sunshine. The question shaped itself from all sides for her, just like the gathering of an inspiration: whether love, truly to serve, must not get inside the soul of the one to be served?—whether from the safe platform of sense and rectitude, the arms of even a very great love could stretch as far as perversity? . . .

Because, supposing such a blind enchanting of her daughter as Peter felt, the roots of the morbid fascination must still be so young and weak, so unrecognised by Ingrid herself, that they should be easily detachable; but was it to detach them to stop the manifestation, leaving the instinct intact? Surely, the reverse method should be the wiser; that of bringing on the crisis, in order that it might pass almost before being realised, and never recur. The way of courage and love. For if Ingrid had this nature, later in life *she* might not be there to guide her through her dark valley, while now the audacity of a single day might purchase immunity for ever. And the perfect love could have an audacity that without it must seem and be quite reckless; for the character of perfect love was miraculous, the whole of heaven was behind one's feeble stroke, and in a thousand stories the Devil had recoiled before the sign of the cross. . . . And so it might be the wisest, as it would be the most daring, to bring them together, that Ingrid might become visibly aware of this sucking depth of her soul, that incautiously adventured threatened at some time to bring her to disaster; but to-day its blackness would be lighted for her by the love of a mother. . . .

The sun went in from her spirit, and the mood was lost, yet she remembered it, wondering. She wondered how she could have been so gripped by a silly impulse that suddenly was declaring itself worthless. Very clear was it to her, with the passing of her folly, that the one sensible way to stop an infatuation, developed or incipient, was to forbid its opportunities. Ingrid's further meetings with these adventurers being refused, and they sent off to-morrow with their prizes, no more mischief could be done. But Peter's must be supposed to be the hyperbolic language of a boy living essentially amongst images and distortions.

Thus she thought to have dismissed the mental episode for the aberration of a moment . . . when increasingly it impressed her how the emotion had not seemed to be hers at all, but rather a suggestion from outside—an inflaming of her softer nature . . . as though some unseen presence in the room had whispered words in her ear in the spirit of seducing. She was in that room, her own, expecting Ingrid. . . . And next, while shrugging at such a superstition, she conceived more soberly that the emotion it concerned might be belonging to the whole lowering sky and electric flashings of intuition and occult correspondence, that all the week had represented the house's atmosphere. So it would be connected with everything; and had a purpose and meaning, if the rest had.

From what extraordinary impact of another world came these quick stabbings of all their brains? Peter was seeing a second Ingrid, Ingrid was being flung towards a man with whom she had nothing to do, poor Hugh had seen his death advancing upon him; she herself was being remorselessly drawn out of her sane shallows by this long procession of labourings, abhorrences, solutions that told nothing—the tortured shaping in her intelligence of hints that individually she could neither understand nor hold. . . . And it was not this week that it had all begun, for Hugh's business had started much earlier; and so, too, were Peter's thoughts old; and Uncle Magnus's adventure years ago on Devil's Tor . . . and Dick's two visions, if they could be considered related. No, it was all like a cyclopean fateful shrinkage of time and space to the small concretion within one last short week of a single pair of persons. Or if it was not that, she knew not what it was.

Nor had she yet been told if Saltfleet were married.

But the trivialness of this last twist of her brain, hunting or hunted, surprised herself by its abrupt crude colour of the world; then brought humility. Thus, if the man should be eligible, she might still, in an improbable case, bestow her blessing!—or what else should her feminine inquisitiveness stand for? The mighty workings towards some end unknown of such a fearful subterranean seething of chaos were to depend for her puny sanction of a mother and law-servile woman on whether this thrown-up phantom, this Saltfleet, should possess the social right to lead her daughter in gala through the nave of Christian temple! . . . Yet God and His ordinances were very real. Surely, whatsoever contradicted them must be of another origin. . . .

When Ingrid had come in to her, however, she seemed to comprehend from the child's earliest look and first words that she must not attempt to dictate to her. Suffering and confused evidently she was, and still from behind her fog of distress gleamed steadily, if faintly, a strange high wisdom for the finding of her way through the future, that somehow must be as different from Helga's own futile essays to reduce all to common judgment, as sacred from profane, or as starlight from the groping light of a candle.

The perfect bloodlessness of the girl's rigid face was stressed by her black clothes that already she wore for Hugh. Helga as well was in mourning. And her awareness of these tributes to a death which by now had lost its first edge of tragic excitement, to become a perpetual dull shock and horror to her under-mind, was as a chain of heavy reality binding her to crawling life, that inexorably went forward and never repeated its quietudes. So the new state was arrived, and all her endeavours would be unable, by reason of this death alone, to reproduce their happiness of but a week ago, before the quick, odd, hurrying intrusion of men and wonders. She contrasted in her mind two supremely fair days, the one before, the other after, a tempest; and they would be unlike. Into the second would have crept an air washed of its voluptuousness, a chill, the constant reminder of something that had been and no longer was. Therefore she must not require of Ingrid to bring back single-handed what in the nature of things was forever gone from amongst them. If in twenty-four hours she had ceased to be a child, that too was understandable.

And Hugh's vanishing should surely also be a symbol. Death, generally, was abroad; for every great change was a sort of death, and now the household might be cracking. Peter's bristling will vainly fought this oncoming wedge of fate, trying as with wild fingers to prevent its ghostlier entrance, while she herself perhaps was but more philosophic because her personal knowledge of the inevitable in life had long since cowed her heart; but what if Ingrid's nobler occult vision should be compelling her, against her natural womanly shrinking from a dreadful adventure, to await in dauntless calmness that man's advances? . . . Then her consent would be the wisdom of the affair, their foolish fear and counterplotting the unwisdom, sprung from their more imperfect perception of these things . . . yet only supposing fate always to be bowed before; never to relent at the eleventh hour for the energy of desperation of its seeming victims, the energy too being fated; so that fate never could be read, till all was over. . . . But if Ingrid's nature was double, and its buried instincts on both sides were risen to anything like consciousness in their internecine war for sovereignty within her body, then the obvious shocking of that body was explained. She had been on the equivalent of a rack.

Under the quick torture she might even have swooned.

Her wisdom, however, shone on through the torpor that sank her there voiceless and dreaming; it was mystic in the trance-light of her slowly shifting eyes, to-day in this room more grey than blue, now downcast in frowning meditation, now fastened unpleasantly upon a far part of the floor, rarely raised to Helga's own eyes which never left them. Perhaps, even, the wisdom, the vision, was not caring to become interpreted, but was leaving the child's lower understanding idle. How, then, should she address it? Her first question must bring Ingrid back to the world, and the light would vanish. She would relate the skeleton of her adventure on the Tor, she would minimise her emotional state, and perhaps agree to any plan suggested or wish expressed; but Helga wanted to capture her daughter's soul entire. . . .

Or should she wait until time should have softened these hard contrasts and brought that whole soul to communication in the poetry of perspective remembrance? It was impossible. For there were things to know, and things to be settled, at once; besides which, Ingrid's return to her normal manner must be signalised— by what? So heavy a mood could not pass without a consequence. It might take the form of a reactive loathing of the contact that had had such power to desolate her; but, more probably, her rising from this depth must mean new vigour, new life. Precisely in the transition her instinct towards a strange passion might know its next wave of unearthly joy and irresponsible hardihood. . . . She could not tell. Like Peter, now she felt she knew her girl no longer.

Yet had that other queer heavenly influx of *love* endured, it was just such a renewal of life that she would have dared to want. For love spoke not to cowardice or the heart's retirement to old peace; but to its high tides. And the brave exchange would have illuminated all the case for them both; whereas merely to persuade her child to her duty might succeed in its immediate end, but because they would have talked upon a plane of prudence and coldness it must be an alienating conversation, and the sacrifice without horror, from decency, custom, lassitude alone, must unconsciously introduce to Ingrid's existence a new character of disillusion and renunciation, insidiously destroying her youth. . . .

Then Ingrid, scarcely looking at her mother, stopped her hesitations by quietly telling what had not yet been told. She said that Mr. Saltfleet had followed her to Devil's Tor by *intention*. He could not have known, and had not known, that she was to be there, but he had learnt that she was out, and had guessed that her uneasiness might be drawing her to see the hill again.

As Helga heard her, the new fact so little startled her, that she was sure she had expected nothing else throughout. And it was a corollary for her understanding, how his trouble taken on a doubtful chance represented the measure of his earnestness to meet her daughter once more, as the calculation itself should represent the measure of his mental energy. . . . So that now their earlier arrangement of the day was cancelled, and all choices were again open to her. The perfidy could not anger her, for it was too serious, too dynamic. Neither was she permitted to stand amazed before any brutality or insolence of such a person; but what seized the rule of her pale silence of many unquiet thoughts came to be her groping after some reasonable motive in him for so flying at a girl unknown to him only yesterday, whose pure sphere was grazing his terrible one on but the infinitesimal point of an accident. For Ingrid, at least—thank God!—had had no part in shaping this encounter beforehand . . . unless her demeanour lied. . . . No, she could be keeping nothing back of that; and Peter's canker of an ancient monstrous instinct within her, how could the ugliness so soon, indeed, have acquired a corporeal form, requiring to be served by deceits? Then Saltfleet's was all the sin . . . and yet, again, she could not conceive him sensual. . . .

A feeble gleam of afternoon sun threw some lines of the window-frame on a circumscribed patch of the opposite wall, and Helga, glancing at the contrast, remarked it. She meditated how, in the properest sense, every joy in life was like the slow-moving sunlight on a prison wall, half a warmth and blessedness, but half a defining of one's bars. Then since the true joy, the full blazing of the sun, was outside the prison, and this only its travelling mockery for those who should never quit these walls except by way of a coffin, what a pathetic madness it was to lament the inevitable passage and final disappearance of the gleams, as though they presented a retainable good! . . . The long peace of years of their family was to crumble at last, and the storm come. When it had hewed and slashed among them to satiety, for some—those that were left—would begin a new peace, slowly accumulating sweetness . . . and that, too, must be broken, to the music of weeping and execration: and such was life. The moving of pale sunlight along prison walls! . . .

She returned to Ingrid, to comment slowly, without effort controlling her manner to a clear-eyed, rather beautiful immobility that was not the proper garment of her perturbed soul, yet allowed enough of its bewilderment and foreboding to peep through to preclude a charge of art, while the ground of calmness was her remoteness from indignation or quick dismay:

"This action of his was singular, however. Since you spoke together, didn't he give you the news of his friend's arrival, and my offer to them? It was on the particular condition that they were to let you alone."

"Either he couldn't have promised that yet, or he had the right to recall the bargain, so far having had nothing from you."

"But Peter saw him and his friend, when they professed to be quite agreeable to what I proposed; with the small additional proviso that your consent in writing should be obtained, for the salving of Mr. Saltfleet's conscience. . . . Now I am to suppose that they were only keeping me amused, knowing that the arrangement would fail on just that point? It was Mr. Saltfleet's way of rebuking my interference in a business he has come to regard as yours?"

Ingrid said nothing, and her mother proceeded:

"It's so impossible, on this insolent—or at least mysterious— challenge, to understand any longer what really they want. I hope you're to tell me. For if it were no more than Hugh's duplicate treasure, that you hold, surely one means of procuring it is as good as another to them? . . . I can't even resent this affront until I

learn what it means. If it is only the stone, they may still have
that. And perhaps the mistake I made was in insisting on a condition, that that man has been finding offensive to you—in a spirit
of chivalry not less offensive to me. So you needn't write . . . in
fact, I imagine this personal meeting was instead . . . but Peter
shall see them again, and hand them the stone without conditions.
Perhaps I insulted you by that demand. Of course, *you* will pass
me your word not to go out of doors until they are safely away to-
morrow."

"He wants me to meet Mr. Arsinal. So far as I know, he is
neither being chivalrous, nor taking up any attitude towards
yourself."

"Isn't it an attitude to flout my offer?"

"No, he is too caught by realities to think of attitudes. He does
see that you may take it in the human way and withdraw the offer
out of pique, refusing them the stone altogether. He could not be
expected to fathom the essential good nature of a woman who has
chosen suddenly to cease his acquaintance. So that contingency,
certainly, he has provided for; but it is still scarcely an attitude."

"Then you had better tell me what passed between you, in
your own manner."

Ingrid dropped her lashes, frowned, and was quiet. She looked
up again to say:

"But you have something to tell me, too. Why have you been
in such an inordinate hurry over this transaction, mother? Wasn't
it Peter who suggested the use being made of my absence?"

A slight colour stole into her mother's face.

"He is not to deny it. He's very seriously concerned about you,
Ingrid, and his whole care is to get these men dismissed without
an instant's unnecessary delay. Don't censure Peter."

"You two had a long talk?"

"You enabled it. He came to see you with the news of Mr.
Arsinal's arrival; but you were out."

"And every accident is helping! . . . Yet at the inn last evening
he agreed to the principle of a meeting between Mr. Arsinal and
me."

"You haven't seen that man as well?" inquired Helga quickly.

"No, I have said I *am* to meet him."

"To discuss what? And why was it hidden from me yesterday, when you came back?"

"You would have forbidden it."

"But you are telling me now."

"Because now I am willing that you should forbid it. If Peter has faced about, so have I. . . . And I shall obey your will in the matter. . . . But the discussion *yesterday* was to have been about the moral ownership of Hugh's two stones. They are occult, you know; and to the right person, very precious. Mr. Arsinal, however, claims to be the principal on the other side."

"As you are not, on this side, Ingrid."

"No. But it was a case of information, and you would have arrived at a judgment on the wrong points."

"You cannot say that, my dear. I did not talk to Hugh about our one of them, at least, for nothing."

"I am saying only what was in my mind yesterday. Now you and Peter have decided the destination of both, to which I agree, and that practical part of the business is closed. If I still met Mr. Arsinal, it would be simply to exchange wisdom for wisdom. Only, it is futile. Something, not at all a joke, is coming on some of us in this house and district, and no doubt the best wisdom for Mr. Arsinal, as well as me, will be not to try to calculate the incalculable. Otherwise, our meeting could still be at Peter's—at half-past five this afternoon. I've to send word. If you dislike the idea, I will cancel it."

Helga was silent for a few moments; then said:

"The signs are for your having been distressed on Devil's Tor this morning; but of that you have spoken not a word. Mr. Saltfleet wants you to meet the other—why?"

"I forget, mother. I forget whether he even did want it. You couldn't guess the last indifference of both of us up there. I'd our stone with me, and when he informed me of your agreement, I offered it to him there and then, and he refused it."

"It isn't good."

"He gave a reason; but his true reason was his high-minded-
ness."

Her girl's obvious trust in the man intensified the pang for
Helga. It was as if she were presenting her innocence to a knife.
That Saltfleet, in scorn of her forbidding, should deliberately seek
out the child to molest her, was the more atrocious that he had not
known her above a day. That he should know where to find her,
added the terror as of an uncanny sixth sense in him, for the
service of all his evil designs. What he wanted, that this gift of
diabolical logical intuition would always procure for him. But
that also the cynicism should be his to refuse to take from Ingrid,
on some excuse she wouldn't repeat, it was doubtless so unintended for acceptance—to refuse to take from her the object, to
arrange for the getting of which was his sole justification for
being up there on the Tor with her at all, while contriving, as by a
few bold strokes of art, to persuade her that he was being moved
only by a reciprocating generosity not less than her own, but his
right secret motive being the furtherance of this unlikely and
difficult intimacy . . . such a feature of the morning's work
seemed nearly the most fiendlike of all to Helga; for it spoke of
his ice-cold scientific preliminary dissection of her daughter's
nature, with the resulting manipulative skill in its weaknesses.

And, to the painful throbbing of her heart, she felt that should
her ghastly suppressed instinct concerning poor Hugh's tragedy
ever elude her insufficient control and rise to the surface of
emotional acknowledgment during these frightful hours, the two
impossible abominations centring in that man come like an omen
into their district—they must unite . . . and show her the full
horror of crime, as she had never seen it before—*crime* itself, the
abstraction in measureless extent, the reality in life-intensity,
loathsomeness, insanity, cruelty, and sordidness. For the two,
being united in a single monster, would create another dimension
for crime. The flawed soul would perhaps no longer be shown as
following the line of his flaw, and so even to be compassionated
by the merciful; but would appear as drawing his colour and life
from a sustaining element, the great primordial sea of crime,

existing before all the worlds—a fantasy and delirium to the sane mind—the ocean of metamorphosis. . . .

She denied it again, and now it was faintly adumbrated to her sick mind that she was viewing but the exterior of Saltfleet and of his activities of a day, from an angle that necessarily gave falseness and subjectivity. Even this base pursuit of a confiding child, that she could alone dare to bring to thought, might be not from sin, but fate; an apparently evil thing, which, being as yet unexplainable, she was applying to its closest superficial resemblances in her experience of the world. . . . . Had she been there, invisible, with them on the hill, she would have known from his words; she could have judged; but Ingrid's innocence was to repeat nothing essential. . . .

Ingrid: she *could* not so far be consciously within his gravitation. Reserved of heart she was, proud of temper beneath her domestic obedience; femininely romantic of the imagination she had never been; while always the affair was but that day old. Yet if it were no more than the first unwilled sliding towards an edge . . . for *repelled* she plainly was not; and his eyes were strong, with the deepest brutal fires underlying their cold chaining, such eyes as could not appear but once or twice in a thousand years . . . the jutting up, too, of those archaic savage rocks through his composed princeliness of modern manner . . . too well might her child be already lingering in fancy to discover what kind of man he truly was. Overstrung to breaking she should be, on his account, or on account of all these circumstances of which he was an integrant part. Her yesterday's concealment of that arranged meeting with his associate, her rapid changes of mind, this present emotional exhaustion of body and brain, with her fugitive retreat to loneliness, her unkind avoidance of Peter . . . some crisis was upon her; and *him* only, of strangers, she had seen. Nor still had she explained her particular upset of the morning, the tokens of which upon her were so manifest.

Yes, within twenty-four hours she was ceasing to be her girl, and changing to some more ancient ancestral self, such as she, her mother, might never understand; but its externals—this new alien nature's—could scarcely be more than hard shell for a seed infinitely rich and tender, unable as yet to face the world's mocks, sneers and violations . . . she meant, such hints beneath Ingrid's apathy as these faint stirrings, like the half seen, half imagined troubling from below the surface of a drowsing lake: of haughtiness, sibylline vision, foreignness, power . . . they were not new, however, but very old, very intrinsic in her opening, wondering soul. . . .

Nevertheless, it was the slumbering of just such an other soul and nature that had always baffled the friendly understanding of her daughter's acquaintances; being like a problem set for their intuition. Something quietly dominant colouring her milder dignity had secluded and ennobled her since such things were possible to her years, causing her to be respected by the feared, feared by the amorous and flattering. It had shone steadily through her universal self-effacement and willingness to be thought nothing. It was not *only* an uninsisted-upon haughty background of power, but that should be nearly the least significant and the outermost of its connections with the world. Helga conceived the true central shining to be some vestige of a type forgotten before the appearance on earth of the first historians; existing, perhaps, in an age when the foundations of the grand religions were ready to be laid. . . . It now seemed to her that very little of this new wonder of her daughter's nature could ever have been unknown to her. Only, a stimulus of fear was all at once bringing it to her door, and she could not escape its recognition. . . .

So Saltfleet might be no seducer, but Ingrid, as blindly tentative as he, might be equally drifting towards him; and the opportunities, as always, were created by the destiny of such a mutual involuntary approach. She obeyed an instinct. Being a girl, however, unused to the defiance of her antecedents, now again she was shrinking back upon her conscience. Then the reaction could be temporary only. For the instincts dictated the joys, as roots the leaves and flowers; and both inevitably must come again. . . .

She could reply at last, and yet her own words, both during

and after utterance, displeased her as being false, and in the spirit of falsity. It was that she had no courage but desperately to grasp the wreckage of their old life. The insight was with her that it was somehow gone, that life; and still she must be this dastard and fool, with the child she had borne.

"Highmindedness! . . . It is a queer term to use. And surely you could never have remarked it in him unless he had wished you to—but that is just the sort of proof Peter will hate of the springing up of an improper intimacy. . . . It seems to display your offer of the stone and his refusal of it as a contest in sacrifice— and so each apparently has wanted to stand up to the other in a certain favourable light. . . . But I fear all the simplicity has been on your side, since, evidently, he was manoeuvring for new meetings. Had he accepted your invitation, the loss would have been his."

"Of him I know you have the worst opinion," said Ingrid.

"I am warning you. He arrived yesterday, and already you have seen and talked to him three times. If I don't forbid it, you are to see him again. Steadily throughout you are exploring each other's reserves, until it threatens to become an association. Well, do you want this association, Ingrid?"

"He will go to-morrow."

"I hope he may."

"Two out of those three talks I couldn't help, and it is for you to decide about another meeting."

"It is more for Peter. . . . But I fancy he won't care to give them both sides of the bargain, as they seem to be demanding. And *his* vexation should carry weight with you. *Him* you cannot accuse of having a determined prejudice."

"His instinct against Mr. Saltfleet is the same. It isn't hidden from me. . . . Only, there is the awful distinction between your two antipathies: Peter's must be purely personal . . . metaphysical—of the type . . . while unspeakable nightmares are in *your* mind, mother. . . ."

"I did not put them there. But he cannot have had the madness to——"

Ingrid cut short her words.

"Neither do you have the madness! Such an abomination must be kept out of discussion, for decency's sake. I am glancing at it merely to contrast Peter's sanity of aversion. . . . And how could *he*—your mental victim, nothing else—how could he forget his pride to notice such an unspoken wicked slander? But—I said it before—he sees you declining his further acquaintance . . . and so it is assuredly not *his* interests you are considering; but his friend goes with him. He doesn't choose that Mr. Arsinal shall suffer a deprivation because *he* has had the unluck to become monstrous to you. Therefore, he proposed a thing to me, which I consented to: and Hugh's stone has been temporarily left up there on Devil's Tor."

She added, while her mother fastened her with a curious humourless little smile:

"He was afraid—on Mr. Arsinal's account, not his own—that you might mark your displeasure for this morning's business by confiscating it . . . denying it to them, after all."

"It is to wait there for—what?"

"Until I shall have met Mr. Arsinal."

"And meanwhile they risk nothing, for presumably they can retrieve it at any time for themselves?"

"Since you are to let them have it without conditions, it cannot at all matter to you if they do."

"No; but I see little highmindedness in a refusal to accept as a gift what can always be taken as a prize of fortune."

"Because you cannot imagine his manner or the trend of our conversation, mother. I was not cheated. . . . Rather take another view of it. . . ."

Her mother eyed her, and her smile had faded. Ingrid went on:

"Something infallibly must come of this depositing—*something*. But the depositing itself has been brought about by Mr. Saltfleet's perception of your hostility . . . and you are hostile because of a terrible misconception of the possibilities of his character—some grotesque horror of him in you. Then the next course of events that will follow upon the stone's depositing and recovery, will have demanded your bad fancies as a necessary link in the chain. . . . A *link*, not a first cause; for the fancies could not have come out of the air. . . . And so I want to urge on you that the single events of this week may very seldom be standing for themselves; their meaning has usually been in something else to take place. Perhaps I express myself obscurely, but do you understand me?"

"Are you not inventing a psychic drama, my dear?"

"I almost wish it were invention . . . and yet I don't know. . . ."

"One tragedy and a number of strangenesses have happened all together, but that is very far from showing that there is a real connection."

Helga knew, however, that a drama was in progress, and that she was playing and to play a part in it. For all her revulsions, intuitions, unnameable fears, consequent soul-searchings and activities, were that part. And if, as Ingrid declared, such motions could become intelligible only in the light of events still to come, then of what rational avail was it to fight the preternatural tide, trying frantically to ignore and restore? . . .

Just as a violin, magically animated to conscious feeling, might be nothing but jarred by the vibrations set in motion by the drawing of the bow across its strings, knowing not the least suspicion of the music for the ears of human listeners, so *her* consciousness was being jarred and a progressing music might be elsewhere, the jarring representing but a mechanical sub-action having no sort of spiritual relation to that beauty hidden from her. . . .

So mystical it was. How could she not hope that she was being thus deceived by her plain understanding of experience, that was without the wings with which to rise to such a visionary vault? Ingrid, it might be, was upon the flight. . . . But the inept challenging of her conventional mind persisted, while the girl seemed less to attend to her mother's voice than to observe her eyes for these profounder dreams.

"A drama so truly weird to impossibility, for instance, Ingrid—it could be allowed only on the condition that not one of its scenes should prove superfluous . . . excrescent. But here you insist that a vast deal of machinery has been used to get poor Hugh's stone secreted on the top of Devil's Tor. Well, with or without my permission, these persons will certainly remove it for themselves, and wouldn't it have been just the same if they had honestly closed with my offer this morning? Any . . . shrinking of mine, from the contact of one of them, will have given them another walk, no more."

"Who can say that, mother? . . . For you were right: I *was* distressed up there. I came straight home from the distress, and this last of it showing in me still . . ." She broke off, to shrug. . . . "I only wish to suggest to your imagination that whoever fetches down the stone will have to go to the Tor for it."

She could not confide her ultimate secret, yet was painfully moved to prepare her mother for the swift, sudden calamity that now she no longer doubted was to overwhelm herself at least. . . . She thought, besides, to go towards liberating her mother's mind from its oppressions concerning a guiltless man. For the purpose, though half-unknowingly, she had throughout been adding so many rectifying touches to his portrait. Now she would risk expostulation and ignorant alarm in relating the fact—the bare fact without defiling particulars, she could no further—of his vision, and hers. It would show him with austerer preoccupations, inconsistent with ogrish crime . . . and might afford her mother, too, so intense a glimpse of the Tor's power and miracle, that she would realise at last how it was the centre of everything, in this muttering and already murderous storm . . . whose emblem had been that other physical storm, when she and Hugh had witnessed the destruction. Its breathlessness, as from the pressure of an incubus, was even now translated to horror in her mother's heart. Thus she might be brought to see that the horror was for service; as a self-subsisting thing, false. . . .

Ingrid's sunken state, manifest in the chiaroscuro of her utterances and filling her silences with inscrutability, were the latter not rather born of shapeless idea—it was only in part the healing lethargy of her emotional brain after its duel on Devil's Tor with that *projected passion*. In larger part it was the dimming for her of her surrounding day by the continued spectral shining of—*Her*, within. . . . Her thoughts were not delicate enough for the analysis. She was less remembering that palely-gleaming shape, shaming and dwarfing women, than being growingly agitated by its essential life, that for a moment or two had stood it as against the hill-top and the sky. . . . The shape had never known the world by slow degrees, it was not from parents; therefore it was somehow unreal, and, its first shock being past, could start to fade from her mind, like all visions. But that which it had *meant*—the words of heaven, of which that moony image had issued forth the hieroglyph—this interior awfulness was as a ferment to agitate her not less but more as the hours should one by one melt before the last emergence upon her of the grand solving. . . .

She did not know how she could both be quieted and healed by her lethargy and still, far underneath her nervous system, be ever more violently rocked as to her unwilling soul by this visible element of meaning and passion; she believed, nevertheless, that it was good. An evil potency would approach her through pleasure. . . .

Her mother she was aware of, sitting there against her, like another phantom. But Peter was become still more shadowy. Whenever he had been named, she was recalling him, not as a living lover, with whom she probably was to pass her years, but as a sort of appendage of her old life, either vanished or indefinitely suspended—he seemed insulated from her, without reference to time, by a transparent solid wall, through which they might no more than behold each other's uneasy motions. She could feel no resentment for his obstruction of her imagined will, for the reason, that she was as unable to pity him. She was not wronging him, he was not opposing her, but a shrouded formidableness was ploughing through them both; and all their old affection and later playing with love—it was suddenly fled, like the breaking up of a children's game before danger. . . .

Her mother had been viewing her face in quiet thoughtfulness. . . . Ingrid's distress, then, was acknowledged, and might be learnt for the asking. She feared to ask; and her composure was instead. For the hurried prevention of further confession by a diversion would be weakness, while she desired only to collect her courage by little and little for this hateful necessary interrogation. . . . Nevertheless, her calmness and long pausing produced, first of all, only the evasion.

"You will tell me of your trouble this morning when you are ready. I have been rather assuming that it was singly on Mr. Saltfleet's account. . . . He *is* attracted by you, is he not?"

Ingrid, however, returned her look with one as clear.

"You are certainly not understanding him, mother. Nor are you understanding me."

"Your dignity, I hope, is secure, and I am inquiring about him alone. Can you say that you have failed to notice admiration in his manner?"

"It would be as impossible as horrible."

"Why so? . . . These are hard, mature men—cunning, bold— the world would find a name for them. With all their plausibility, the outstanding fact in their known career remains that they have robbed a native temple of treasure. I am not satisfied that Mr. Saltfleet intends you any good. The other may be his fellow. Why would it be so impossible?—and why horrible? These quick admirations are in every rank of society."

"On Devil's Tor I saw . . . a *spirit* . . . and he, something else."

There was silence in the room for a short time.

"And this was your distress?" asked Helga, as though distastefully.

"Yes."

"Then not he at all?"

"He found me in it. You are not to suppose that either of us could have avoided it."

"What did he see?"

"A haunting of another kind."

Helga by now was very pale, though her composure seemed but to establish itself the more. She recalled Peter's "landscape full of ghosts"; and commented:

"This may be so, as Peter apparently has had a psychic experience on the same spot, that might be identical. . . . Yet it was before these prodigies that Mr. Saltfleet sought you out. His coming after you was not for them."

"The Tor drew him, mother. He had the instinct, and accounted for it to himself by the lucky hit of his imagination, that I might have walked out there and that was what he should be after. Do you want a proof? He broke his word to you, you think. But such a man as he—so strong and unfriendly—wouldn't normally change his mind just for the softness of talking to a girl or sparing her silly pride; and therefore he was behaving eccentrically. He *had* to go up there—perhaps it has turned out that he had to meet me up there. But he could have had no notion of what we were to do together . . . so it was the Tor that attracted him."

"What were you to do together, Ingrid?"

"Why, I have said. The stone was to be buried, and he was to have his vision."

"Couldn't he without you?"

"No, it depended on Hugh's stone I was carrying."

"No wonder if you are thinking strangely! . . . But these are distinct matters. I now understand how you should have come back looking like death, yet *his* conduct remains ambiguous still. In this way I put it to you, Ingrid. If he is so innocent of evil intentions, then what caused my heart to shrink yesterday morning, when he and you were talking together? Peter, who is only too easy with you, and diffident of his own claims, why is he so quite wrought up by his fears of that man on your account? He could not be jealous in a day, nor I apprehensive in five minutes. . . . You have too little general vanity, or might have noticed something. Granted he was otherwise subjected on the Tor, that does not prove him a monk."

"You wish, perhaps, to make me ashamed to be with him, mother? My humiliation will hardly do it. But these sensations of yours and Peter's, they are so very curious, surely they can't stand for a mere instinct of danger. It may be that you are both to forbid me his further society. Perhaps your forbidding is to be a necessary instrument to our meeting under conditions outside our contrivance—conditions themselves necessary. . . . Or your feelings may be for another purpose, but this as well. . . ."

"I shall not expect you to go to any clandestine meeting."

"I am going to obey you; only, possibly, we may both be commanded."

Helga looked down in silence, then gave her daughter a single quietly-stabbing glance, before again dropping her eyes. Her hesitation was a covered one.

"Another thing I should make clear to you, Ingrid, for the prevention of misunderstanding. I am referring now to Hugh's case. You believe I could drop my shocking doubts if I would . . . no doubt, you have decided that I am enjoying some sort of—morbid delight of self-torture, or what you will. The psychologists and pathologists would give you all the necessary support for your diagnosis of such a very common deceit of nature. Otherwise neither you nor Peter could comprehend why I am electing to be so venomous against—*him*—without proof; or you would add, probability. . . . Well, I will tell you, my dear, that I would sacrifice nearly all I own in the world to be allowed to put this hideousness from me. . . . To no one else could I confess it, but such is my opinion of the man, that if I could be clearly shown to be in the wrong about him . . . I think I would humbly thank heaven for the great mercy of his acquaintance, even though too late. . . .

"It can't be romanticism, for that, I know, is voluntary illusion—seeing things and people as we are well aware they are not. But my imagination can add nothing to *him*. Nor is he stern and forcible—possibly brutal, too—for any quiet feminine friendship, which is all I have left to offer. His only association with us—our sex—would almost necessarily take the form of the mastery and enjoyment of great beauty, without any of its exasperating caprices. I could have no nonsensical hopes in connection with this man younger than myself; I have nothing of what he wants . . . and yet, to me, my dear, he is suddenly making other men look like nothing. That, too, is why I feel you cannot be so uninfluenced by him as you pretend. Between a true indifference and a conscious attraction, that may stop at that and not become infatuation at all, there are a thousand climbing, winding paths— all of them lovely, no doubt—all strange and unreckonable at least . . . on one of which you may well be at this moment. . . . But what was I to say? . . .

"No; my more or less defined feeling towards him since yesterday afternoon isn't that morbid bone-sweet pathological thrill, too delicious to abandon—just as the pressing of a half-exposed nerve in the gums may be. Yet I know it is just as little my honest answering to a fact. . . . Can I *want* him to be such a man? I mean, is my fullest admiration of him to depend on his inexorability— his scorn of laws, rules and consequences? So that my insistence on . . . an atrocity . . . would be a sort of loyalty to a certain image set up within me. You may say that that is the same thing in other words. . . . Then it still isn't this. It is a fear lit from another fear, as a house from its blazing neighbour. I know the other was before it, though dim in consciousness. It may have wanted the thoughts to be thought with at the beginning; and still have been devouring my instincts, that merely afterwards explode through thoughts. That earlier fear, my dear, lighting the other . . . he was an eagle swooping for prey—*you*; though you will deny it . . . and therefore wouldn't stop before any crime, however dreamlike. . . . He is this man, or he is nothing that my apprehension regarding you has felt him; and Peter's insight. . . . That is what I had to tell you, and the apology for my unreason, as you see it. . . ."

"It must be so, then; and I won't attempt to persuade you any more," returned Ingrid simply. But her mother had not yet done.

"For if it were any other man, do you suppose, Ingrid, that I should not know what to do with this vicious dilemma? While there are officials remaining in the land, I would see the sensible solution easily enough. But it is because it can't constitute an accusation in itself, but could only open the door to another of no public concern, that my hands are tied. And it isn't as if it could serve poor Hugh. I have the faith, too, that all abominations—if this should be one—must bear their own punishment. . . .

"I may be mistaken, and it may be a straightforward doubt; but *you* have not thought so—you with your theory of a mystical dictation, to an end . . . and that theory is uncontradicted by what I have said of the catching fire of my fears, one from another. By your assent, you have seen at once that I have only uncovered a richer mystical foundation for your mystical erection. . . . But then, why is the one of my excruciations intensifying, and the other not growing less, if they have already done what they were to do—lodged that stone on Devil's Tor? Or when they have achieved some other practical purpose, do you soberly believe that these miseries of suspense will droop and die in me?"

"A river naturally flows into a sea, mother; and so I imagine your particular troubles will cease with all the rest."

"I haven't asked you about your apparitions: do you guess why?"

"You dread losing me," replied the girl, "and you must be fearful of hearing how it might come about."

"God forfend I should lose you, Ingrid! What do you mean?"

"I don't know. Not by death. . . . But if the old childish life were nearly over for me. . . ."

"Through *him*?"

"I don't know if through him. Who can say what else he is to do? Yesterday he seemed like a breath from the world, but since then nothing has happened without him. One can only read what is written, and guess that it may go on so."

Withdrawing her look from her daughter's face, Helga went to the window, where she remained standing, gazing out at the garden.

She felt a rising as of some dark solidity in her mind, like the emergence from its depths of a monstrous lacustrine messenger of woe, dividing and ousting the existing images of her lake of consciousness. She felt that the room behind her was uneasy with an odd gentle stirring, that was not of the air. Before Ingrid's coming in, there had been the same half-whispering in her ear— she knew not what it was, or what she was being hunted to; she immediately knew merely that something infinitely subtle and impalpable must for a long time past have been seeking to assail her, now in this way, now in that; now ceasing, now resuming . . . that its delicacy was as fine as the faintest movement to arouse the attention, but its tormenting as insistent as a continued uncertainty of any of the five senses. Yet while her heart beat heavily in a curious unspeakable anxiety, her face was finding no other expression to substitute for its calm; the eyes, enlarged in that unseeing out-of-doors contemplation, were only more troubled. . . .

The rising—risen—thing was the answering of her many questions about Ingrid in one surpassing answer. No, it was not an answer, but a confrontation: what stood up before her was as a vast block—permanent and wicked. It had seemed dark in the emerging land that was the night-world it sprang from. And its solidity was the impossibility of its now ever leaving her again; she could no more refuse it than—she could some ghastly blasted tree in her path, that should have separated all at once from the mist. . . . But this confronting truth and the room's invisible stir, they were together. And still she was ignorant what was being done to her. . . .

Ingrid's two natures—they were not natures, nor the halves of any single uniting thing within her; but separate persons. She could not have said why the distinction appeared to her such a chasm—so awful. . . . Her gradually grown up and familiar child, peaceably passing these quiet days with those she loved and who loved her, the house's life, purity and youth, soon to be married to a decent man . . . and now, suddenly, also a strange woman, casting this child of hers out from her seat, disdaining relations as yet with any but these haughty adventurers, that were come to quicken the last of her unsuspected long, slow, lip-white fierceness towards the light. . . . Not *her* daughter . . . but a daughter of the mystic icy North, knowing terrible imaginations and affinities, scorning sanity, an outlaw through the night, demanding for her share the grimnesses, twisted passions, witherings, lonelinesses, of the mortal passage. . . .

What she had never seen, but saw now, was that this strange

woman was a completed soul. . . . And so long she had been gathering her volcanic fires for the hour of explosive horror, when a new mountain was to be formed of her who had been *her* child. And such was Peter's foreknowledge; the warning glare, invisible to others, had caught his quick perceptions. Well he understood how a long-preparing disaster might spring like a beast at last without declaration. Shocked to tenseness by those sympathetic prodigies from the society-encircling blackness that was her element, up to the man Saltfleet's awaited apparition this woman armed to assassinate her daughter was directing her frown—doubtless, it was an ancient recognition. Peter said it but little differently. For once, his art's equipment was serving him. . . .

"You dread losing me . . . not by death" . . . thus Ingrid was as wise. . . . And this, too, had been that queer boldness of love, like an incitement, felt just before her daughter's entry. Her heart had been quickened by the room's living restlessness (but she had rejected the urging) that she might be furnished with power against the menaced change. She had refused it, and so this more hateful scourge at the window was instead. She was meant to act. Ingrid was being protected: *something* must be curiously watching them both even now, and all the time; but a human arm, a medium, was indispensable. . . .

Then she conceived it to be yet more critical. If for this once her child's wicked translation could be averted, it might be altogether. For how impossible it was that her life could hold two such men, two such trains of unearthly wonders and agonies. A mystery of that aspiring evil other woman's soul inside her daughter's shape might be that, being *once* denied its sovereignty in the upper world and thrust back to darkness, it might banish wholly, for ever, like a baffled ghost at cockcrow; killed by the effort to be born. . . .

Aware though she was, as in another brain, of the riot and fever of all these imaginings, so past anything outside her dreams, Helga attempted not to quit the amazement. Presently she must return to sobriety—mad she would then seem to herself to have been . . . so all the more necessary was it now to adventure—and adventure—for Ingrid's salvation. Here, in this fire of intoxication and torture, lay the clue—nowhere else. It was the meaning. . . .

One perception she kept trying to grasp—it was so fine, it escaped her every time. The room's unseen control, its character should be of softness, pity . . . belonging not to these other communications and compellings, but staying behind all else, as an atmosphere—a presence. . . . She kept half-feeling it; and as often as she did so, the involuntary following half-idea came into her head, that it was *womanly*. . . . At length, she could not consent that it was delusion. For each time it came, it was anew; some one string of her sensitiveness was being sounded; it was not memory. . . . She could have asseverated that a woman's person was somewhere invisible in the room; not Ingrid. . . .

So nervous became the fancy that, scarcely comprehending her own impulse, she turned sharply round from the window to view the room and what was in it; but only the girl was there, sitting in lassitude where she had been. . . .

Only Ingrid . . . yet what little colour still had been in her mother's face now fled, while her eyes became globes in a nailed stare. . . . Here was not Ingrid, but . . .

The features, indeed, were unchanged—youthful, fair, known, as before . . . but how came they to be so ancient, and far-off? It was a fearful phantom, displacing her daughter. Her beauty, as well, was shining and lamp-like . . . the gleaming surely stood for the overflowing of mighty springs; from no waters of the world. It was inward, yet symbolic too, like the posthumous token of a martyred saint. . . . The features themselves, however—their foreign womanish fairness of poise and flesh remained; was even more emphatic; but only as a base. They were miraculously shrunk together, as a very, very ancient face's should be . . . without wrinkles or decrepitude—with all the bloom of early womanhood—but so *wise*; and a million years old . . . a million miles away: the room was not vanished, yet seemed to have no dimensions, no measurements. . . . Her child—the basic child in this wonder—she was loose, watery, sensuous, meaningless, the contrast gave that impression, as she went on sitting there, like an image of a *camera obscura*, through and supporting the other fulfilling phantom; which was all secrets, yet brought no shuddering of evil. . . .

The illusion was swiftly gone. The re-transformation outstripped her eye, and she understood not how it had happened . . . only, nothing was more certain to her than what had just been there. So real it had been, that all other kinds of reality, beside it, were faint and approximative. . . . It had been like another plane added to ordinary reality, by . . . *deity*. An apotheosis. . . .

She refaced the window quickly, fearful that Ingrid would address words to her. . . .

Thus she had been so ignorant—perverse! Her child had never rightly been, but only as a shadow, climbing, climbing, up to an ancient substantial state—how could that which was not, be lost? The state climbed to was past, present, future, all together: therefore, nowhere in cramped earth-existence, but elsewhere—whither, now, all the things of the world must ultimately be moving. . . .

Time: its nature must be conceived before the beginning of the understanding of any of these mysteries. How a soul could be in two or more times, at once: how each time would thus be positively true for it; as a mere moment of all time, untrue. . . . But if the apparent passage of time were solely for rudimentary intelligences, framed by intention to take in but one thing at once! . . . Her brain swam and sickened with its efforts to change its laws. . . .

Certain only it already was that she dare not refuse Ingrid the continuance and last bitterness—even to tragedy—of this man's acquaintance—of these signals from another time; another vaster circle, outside and inclusive of the little dreaming fragmentary practical circle called real life. The explanation, perhaps, would come with the course . . . or perhaps the word, *explanation*, was a mode of the temporary human brain, rudely symbolising some higher mode of apprehension, that should partake as well of instinct, emotion, music. . . . But, then, what seemed here grief and intolerableness might there be even purest beauty—one loftier word in a loftier speech might have force so to translate it. . . . With Ingrid she must stand in her casting of childhood. This, once again, she remembered, had been her impulse of golden mother-love, so short a time ago. . . .

Her thoughts subsided more and more to her accustomed world—for which, indeed, she waited—but soon she comprehended that her determination was fast; to be subject, though she should stand there an hour, to no further weakening or change.

She approached her daughter, looking down on her. But Ingrid, perceiving in her face the end of their talk and the announcement of a decision that must be important, herself got up, to confront her wearily with hanging arms; yet, even so, her grace could not be lessened. Their eyes never steadily met.

Helga said:

"Yes, it is true: I haven't asked about your apparitions, because I was afraid. And now, when perhaps the courage has come, I feel that your account in words—supposing you could find the words . . . would be—inadequate. . . . But you haven't said if your opinion is that such marvels are repeatable. If they might be, I would wish to try and see them for myself. If some influence of the place is speaking to you, you are my child."

Ingrid inclined her head in silence, and her mother continued:

"Peter is troubled, so he should be with us . . . we three together. And we could be joined there by those men, to be given what they want. It can be a last settlement of everything."

"Only not to-day, mother."

"No, I wouldn't ask it of you to-day. To-morrow morning, however, is the inquest, and the afternoon will be unsuitable. It will be Saturday: others may be on the hill. But later in the evening. . . ."

"To-morrow evening."

"Then so we will leave it. Peter shall see them, when he returns here, with the proposal. Surely they'll wait till then, knowing that they are to be contented at last. Meanwhile you will keep the house; and not write them at all."

"If Peter will explain."

"He will explain. . . . And I must caution you, too. All this has grown up very fast and fantastically, Ingrid; but one must have seen it growing. Neither could I answer your uncle's questions, nor you, I fear. So beware of heedless references. Try to be yourself before him. Already he has taken your absence from the table at lunch rather ambiguously. He knows that you are unhappy since yesterday: that all can't be too well with you and Peter."

"Perhaps, therefore, he should be told . . . yet what is there tellable? If his mind is to be kept easy by my total silence, I can promise that."

"You couldn't, of course, embellish it with hypocrisy."

There was a pause.

"With this great shame of your soul concerning a man you have fastened upon, mother," said the girl, in a quiet tone, "how *dare* you meet him?"

But her mother not answering, she was moved to find her own reply to the imperfect expression of what had risen up in her heart.

"Isn't it that your will is ceasing, like mine? . . . There is *a third* in this room with us. We are not willing or daring anything; but being ordered. . . . You never meant, a short time ago, to let me go up there again. The plan is an unreasonable one, appearing reasonable for a moment; but when you have to tell Peter, you will be quite embarrassed by its lack of impartible sense. . . ."

"Is there *a third* in the room, Ingrid? Wouldn't you, otherwise, venture to meet him again—you either?"

"I have no feeling about him. Mr. Arsinal I would rather not meet there."

"Why?"

"He will join those two stones, unless prevented; and a fearful thing may happen."

"You ask me to drop the design?"

"No. So evidently it is not yours, but must be. . . . But I have also thought—your fear and horror of *him*—they may not be *only* to bring about this occasion. . . . They may be, as well, to emphasise and complete your loss of me . . . soon. I hardly know what I am saying. . . . If I am to go away anywhere, you are to be told it isn't accidental, but fundamental. I am not to be followed. You and Peter are the world's representatives for me . . . and so I am to be altogether outcast. . . . Words cannot say what I feel. . . ."

Helga viewed her with a mournful steadfastness, that was already like the sign of a renunciation.

"Do you tell me, Ingrid, that your two destinies—yours and this man's—are beginning to unite?"

"I cannot say," replied the girl quickly. "I do not know. . . . It is impossible; and possible, too. All things are possible. I wish this were impossible."

"You have gone too far to be silent now, however: so would it be through . . . *love?*"

Ingrid for a few moments regarded her mother like a white young seer.

"No, mother; never through love. Peter shall have so much consolation. That man and I have only at the very first met in the natural world. That was yesterday morning, when I came into the room where you were talking, and could glance at him impersonally, as a stranger. On the other occasions, I daresay we have had no very distinct impression even of each other's persons or faces: our talk has taken us far away from any interest in one another. . . . But you will insist on this easiest for a woman and a man! Are these events being easy? The lightning flashes, the thunder is rising, the wind is moaning—and you ask if a strange and unpardonable romance is on its way! . . . No; if our two destinies *are* to unite, we should rather be appalled by each other, than love. . . . What could bring two shrinking beings together? No motive of the world, mother. That is why already I hate his friend, whom I haven't seen. There is no human need for him to be on the Tor with us . . . and yet no doubt he will and must be. . . ."

Helga, however, was kept obstinate in the whole frame of her plan, by that singular fixation of her memory of Ingrid's phantom. Its first terror had begun to be effaced by the minutes, but another sort of permanence seemed to be beginning for it: now it was becoming like a fast and unassailable *truth* in her head, her heart.

The truth of what she knew she had seen was a touchstone . . . almost, whatever she had before that dividing moment in her life imagined of time and the world, was now to be deemed false, until proved not false; but these unearthlier instincts and irrational decisions belonged to another category; she dared not reject them; she dared not change them in one particular. . . .

She wished Ingrid to leave her, that she might think more quietly of all those matters, before Peter came.

But the girl, understanding from her mother's silence and looking-away, and the agitated twisting of her joined fingers, that she had no more immediately to say, turned slowly from her, and left the room.

XXVI

At the Studio

Peter's was the very last house of the straggled village, at its end farthest from Whitestone. It stood well back from the street, that was a road across the moor, down a nondescript hedged approach, half lane, half *cul-de-sac*, continuing, as it did, past the house's skirting fence as a mere overgrown foot-track to somewhere, seldom used. An allotment was on the dwelling's other side, dividing it from its next neighbour. Peter, when acquiring the property, had knocked two joined cottages into one, and thrown the four upper-storey rooms into a single studio with a roof-light. The retained original windows he had modernised. Inside and out, the place was simple, yet pleasing. Red tiles replaced the former dirty thatch, the walls were green-washed, the chimneys low and snug. What had been kitchen-gardens at the back now flourished as a wilderness of docks, nettles and grass; Peter took some pride in preferring it so.

At a little before seven Arsinal, having Saltfleet at his back, raised the Silenus-faced front door knocker, and gave with it a sharp quick loud half-dozen raps; then waited, without turning round again to the other. Both men were subdued and taciturn from their afternoon's adventure. The knocking had to be repeated; but then the door opened. Peter showed himself. He recognised his visitors, started with the surprise of complete unexpectation, and gave them a blank look. No one smiled.

"You here, gentlemen! I very little thought of such a move on your part. . . . But say if you wish to come in."

"Perhaps it will be better to talk in a room, unless we are in the way." Arsinal replied this.

"I'm alone. Please follow me upstairs."

They went up. Saltfleet, going last, refrained from shutting the front door after him; an omission he was afterwards to find queer; but at the moment, being on this visit almost from the scorn of his own will, which wanted it not, he seemed to himself only to think to make it quick and informal. Peter either noticed nothing, or let it pass.

The studio was as light and airy as it should be. Its north windows, facing the patch at the back, were open, the south ones, towards the street, closed and curtained. A divan at one end of the room's long length was opposite a standing easel and platform at the other, but the easel was bare, while the few unframed boards and canvases against a wall were turned to disappoint curiosity. Some chairs, a rug or so, a floor litter of prints, portfolios and sheets torn from magazines for some interest of illustration, and a glass-topped table smeared with working paints, nearly completed the furnishing of the den, whose empty grate was strewn with cigarette-ends. Peter lit another cigarette now, and pushed the box along the table in the direction of the callers, but the action was ignored.

"Sit down."

A silence followed, for Arsinal, believing that this young man, however unfriendly towards them and possibly rude by temperament he might be, would yet have guessed their errand, wished not to say the wrong thing in being too quick to speak; while Peter was obstinate in declining to help him . . . Saltfleet, a glint of his eye informed him, was not to talk till aroused, he sat there grim and quiet, the other was to be the interlocutor. . . . Yet another sort of contact should be acting through that silence. Indeed, each in the room felt the same background, that in this new talk they were not resuming where they had left off in the morning, but that the incidents and wonders of the day had changed something else besides the negotiable situation. Hardly *now* were they associates, even in a business quickly growing more bewitched for all; only, to each it was seeming as though the others too were oppressed and depressed by the same labourings as his own. A dark magic had stolen into the air. The debate about to be renewed must not only be at a later stage, but also in this stranger peace, that was no peace.

And still they persisted, and could not well lie down together—Peter's fear, and grief, and spite, Arsinal's secret incandescence, Saltfleet's scorn: accordingly could that other identity of undertow spell no harmony. Each was no more than understanding it as a fish might understand the common helplessness of it and its fellows within an invisible drag-net. . . .

Arsinal leant forward in his chair at last to Peter, who was alone on the divan, smoking restlessly.

"It is hard to know how much I need say to you, Mr. Copping; and, to tell the truth, we have been half-hoping *you* might have some communication for us in your pocket. . . . You prefer to reserve the direct answer to that. It is legitimate to ask, however, if you have now seen Miss Fleming?"

"I haven't."

"Nor been to the house since her return from Devil's Tor?"

"Yes, I spoke with her mother."

"But didn't Miss Fleming appear at all?"

"She was lying prostrated in her room," said Peter, with a dry bitterness. "A girl is not a man . . . though Mr. Saltfleet here may care nothing for the difference."

Saltfleet frowned. "I am sorry for the prostration, but am hardly responsible for it."

"Not immediately; but you are an increasing part of the whole responsible cause of her whole condition. We won't go into that."

"She was to notify us, one way or the other, about a meeting for to-day," said Arsinal. "But we have had nothing from her . . . and so, Mr. Saltfleet conceiving a very strong sense that a personal application at the house would be taken amiss, we have come to you, as the only other recourse within our means. I know that any such meeting was negatived earlier: Miss Fleming offered the hope, however, that her mother might reconsider it."

"Certainly you must be hard up for shifts, to come here! I thought I had made my attitude sufficiently clear this morning. A set interview between yourself and Miss Fleming is both unnecessary and improper, and therefore I don't approve of one, and won't lend myself to one. You are no friends of mine, gentlemen."

"A meeting is not indispensable, but I wish to learn where I stand."

"I warned you this morning, and you would not listen. You can't take and expect to be given as well."

"That is your view, then," said Arsinal more coldly. "Pray what is Mrs. Fleming's?"

"How do you know that I am still acting for her?"

"I don't, of course—yet it is scarcely possible that a difference of opinion between you has brought about such a breach that you are washing your hands of the matter. Rather, Mr. Copping—I am going upon a certain reluctance and reticence in your present manner . . . you may have been begged actually to communicate a message to us, and are still debating its advisability in your mind. . . ."

"You are acute. Doesn't it make me out rather weak, though?"

"I should need to know the circumstances. If you have a message, I can only suggest it will do little good to seek to suppress it."

"Perhaps. As a matter of fact, I was lying down, revolving it all, when your knock sounded. The message was a quite good guess of yours. Only, to whom should it be said to belong—to the sender, to the intended recipient, or to the agent? My sole pay for its delivery would consist in the spectacle of the consummation of a bad blunder, as I see it."

"I have but to wait on Mrs. Fleming, to get it from her own lips." He turned to Saltfleet. "I personally have mismanaged nothing with her, that she should refuse to see *me*."

"On this information, no . . . still, you'll have to go alone."

Peter gave an uneasy stretch. "I'll not put you to the trouble—having registered my protest. . . . But I'd better explain my own office first. I never blessed the proposition. Mrs. Fleming was so firmly insistent, however . . . so in another place altogether, if I could try to describe a mood in her that I haven't known before . . . that I might as well not have been occupying her time. In any case, whosoever the messenger, the decision is hers, no one else's. I gave the sort of promise to see you, just to get back here and reflect in quietness what it all stood for . . . and if you conceive, gentlemen, that I was thereby balking your business—you must . . . or you may choose to give me credit for a pause not of malice, and that, if I am at all acquainted with my own incentives, will be nearer the mark. Perhaps you will find a reason for flatly declining the scheme: then you will have me pulling *with* you. I take it, for instance, that you are extraordinarily in earnest in wanting what you do want, whereas this may be thought . . . *pageantry*. I don't assert that Mrs. Fleming is going for the pictorial effect, but it happens that I cannot visualise her plan without a picture—that I wish was *only* absurd. . . .

"The purport is, that the little property all this pother is about, left behind on Devil's Tor to-day—supposing that you haven't retrieved it already—shall be delivered to you two on the spot, by Mrs. Fleming herself, in her legal right, at nine to-morrow evening. Miss Fleming as well shall be there, to stop further difficulties from you on that score; and I, at my option, to see fair play—or anything . . . The proviso that you shan't attempt more communications with Miss Fleming is withdrawn, since you so obviously mean to please yourselves in the matter. She will just keep away from you, except on this single occasion in her mother's company; and *her* undertaking to the effect is regarded as security enough. . . . Then, once being given your thing, you shall make all reasonable speed to evacuate the district; and return no more. Thus a business exceedingly dubious and disagreeable, launched in a tragedy, will be dispatched for good and all. There should be a less elaborate means, in my view; but this is Mrs. Fleming's solution."

The callers exchanged looks.

"It cannot be this evening?" inquired Arsinal.

"No. Miss Fleming is unfit."

"What is her attitude towards the plan?"

"I learn that she is as indifferent to all programmes as a nearly complete physical collapse can make her."

Then Saltfleet spoke, glancing doubtfully away. "Only, there is never an end to it; and here we are being invited to wait for a ladder to a fruit within reach. The absurdity, as you call it, may pass, and the delay is of small account, but how came Mrs. Fleming by such an extravagance? I believe you that her daughter has had no hand in it. This stone is offered us unconditionally; yet we are not to be allowed to walk up there now and fetch it away."

"I hear you had your chance this morning."

"So I did, but then I wished to leave open Miss Fleming's talk with Arsinal."

"Don't you take your engagements rather lightly?"

"You know if there was one, Mr. Copping. In any event, on a bad road one cannot decide steps ahead."

"I can't acquiesce that you are under any moral obligation to choose Miss Fleming's next steps for her. She has surely well-wishers and advisers of her own. . . . Anyway, she doesn't now want a meeting to talk."

"But that is new." He shrugged, then rose to move to the window, and look out into the garden of weeds. Peter glanced malevolently after him.

Arsinal addressed him:

"Nevertheless, Mr. Saltfleet's question was the natural one to ask. Before replying to Mrs. Fleming's invitation—I don't know if the reply is to be transmitted through you . . . ?"

"I will tell her."

"... We must be made acquainted with the whole intention. As Mr. Saltfleet suggests, we have but to fetch the stone away. Has so very simple a procedure not occurred to Mrs. Fleming? or what else has she in mind?"

"Why, I think we are all to lose our wits, but the women first! ... Doubtless, it is largely a case of impulsion. I know of no reason ... but ghosts and influences are lively on the Tor, so she must see them too. ... One cannot even describe it as an indefensible whimsy."

"Then she has no pity on her daughter?"

"An apt question! ... Yet it must be exactly her alarm for her daughter that has driven her to this caprice ... seeking to probe a mischief rather too underground for normal eyesight."

"What do you fear from—such a caprice, Mr. Copping, that you should be so opposed to it, even to the extent of nearly suppressing the message? You called it just now, a 'bad blunder'."

"It is one, *thus*. Accidents, incidents, phenomena, disturbances spiritual and mental, in a series seemingly connected—in these past days they have been selecting certain persons among us for attack. Drapier was most venomously attacked, and killed. So here is to be no quarter given. I myself have been attacked, more mercifully; or slightingly. Mr. Saltfleet here has not come off scot-free. But the most frequent, and, short of death, the most vicious attacks hitherto have been directed against a girl, a child, delicate more than robust ... who sees no escape for herself, nor any around her who will consent to pocket their curiosity for the good of her soul's health. Now, in four-and-twenty-hours longer, she is cited to the seat and stronghold of these congregated phantoms, that know how to hurl the elements, and recreate the no longer possible, and bring back chaos to the world, and move whatsoever feet and hearts they desire ... for my speech rises to poetry, yet I defy you to indicate *one* exaggeration in this account of the Devil's Tor elf-hall. ... Here, then, at the week's very end and as a fitting climax to its five or six days' flaying of the fair skin of the world for that number of persons, the chief victim— also happening to be the most defenceless and innocent—is cited;

no doubt, to receive her final sentence and punishment, since much more her spirit cannot endure. . . . I cannot proceed in this vein; but ask yourself if *you* find the blunder to be other than a bad one! I will not suppose that you don't understand every word of what I have said."

Arsinal quietly called across to his associate at the window, who, at the first special sound of his voice, turned round.

"Saltfleet, are you willing to have our afternoon's business touched on?"

"Yes, if you wish."

"You used an expression—'ghosts and influences'—Mr. Copping. The 'ghosts' I perhaps could talk of too, but I have no clear notion whether, by 'influences,' you mean the intangible impressing of imaginations, or a second order of more definite phenomena: not ghosts, but not mere atmosphere either."

"You have been up, during the day?"

"Yes; with Mr. Saltfleet, this afternoon."

"You have brought nothing away? You have both been talking as if you hadn't; but that might be to prepare me. You are offering it as the simplest way out, so perhaps you have already done it? I shall be very glad if you have; but *if* you have, please don't waste my time, gentlemen."

"The deposit is still there, unless another has taken it."

"Then it is almost a pity that you should be so honest where honesty could well be dispensed with, not quite so honest in observing contracts. . . . The word, 'influences,' as applied to Devil's Tor, slipped out as a more or less comprehensive one. On the one hand, you have the hill's attraction: persons must foot it there, once, twice, and perpetually. On the other hand, there is its spell, acting on one person *through* another. I have no doubt it is so. Without such a magnetic aid, a day—a day and a half—would be all too short a time. . . ."

"Here is a riddle!" said Saltfleet, gruffly.

"It is my advantage, that I have to do with intelligent men."

"You take another, to use your excellent control of language to shave dangerous corners, Mr. Copping. I shall have to be more direct for us both. You charge me with improperly keeping alive Miss Fleming's interest in a forbidden case? What concern is it of mine to do so? And who is now to feed her interest? You, who have brought us this unholy arrangement for to-morrow? or I, who would elect to stand altogether out of it, were it not for other circumstances? . . . But you are doubly inexact; for supposing I had in any way been able to coerce Miss Fleming, and were still merely this Tor's instrument or machine, as you have just said, then where would be my iniquity? . . . In fact, in such a weird business, for which my life has afforded me no preparation whatever, the chances are that she would be far more a principal than I. I am little accustomed to be a vent for the malignity of strangers who have happened to find me and their trouble on the same spot. From Miss Fleming's mother I must endure it, no doubt; but you are a man, Mr. Copping, and my patience has generally been thin."

"You would stand out of to-morrow's settlement, but for other circumstances: then what are they?"

"When you know as much as I, we shall discuss it."

Peter, with an unwonted spot of red in his cheeks, relapsed to silent smoking; but Arsinal had glanced sharply at his alienated friend. He guessed the allusion, and thought to turn it.

"Indeed, a great deal of this electricity in all of us is arising from our talking in the dark. Let me set the example of openness, Mr. Copping, even though my confession be of matters such as have come to be treated too falsely and apologetically in our heavy working world. For, undoubtedly, the supernatural must be all around us and is true enough, were it not that for the most part it has fallen into wrong hands—into the hands of the gullers and the too-easily gulled. . . .

"On his return from your Tor this morning, Mr. Saltfleet told me of a psychic adventure he had had up there, in company with Miss Fleming. Your own words seem to imply that you have had the other side of the story from her mother. Whether it be so or not, I found myself sufficiently interested to wish to see something of this haunting with my eyes, so we went up together after lunch. . . . In a state of trance, I witnessed very strange things, from near the foot of the hill, just above the stream. The whole mass should therefore be subject to such manifestations. . . . I can't spend time now on describing the particulars of my vision, but I was carried back to immense antiquity; while Mr. Saltfleet saw something, not the same. I am telling it, to invite you to an equal candour. There is a process of wireless telegraphy called *syntonising*: the despatcher and receiver are tuned to the same wave-lengths. Let us employ that process here, Mr. Copping. Apart from what you may have learnt to-day, what, if anything, do you directly know of the Tor's wonders you have referred to so eloquently, so curiously as well? . . ."

"You may not have been the only ones privileged; but what then? Are we to shake hands, or be awarded medals?"

"Were you alone?"

"If you will insist on a particular occasion . . . whereas my relation to the Tor's activities is rather that of compound to compound . . . no, I was accompanied. It was before Drapier's catastrophe, and *he* was there. We weren't together."

"Perhaps one of the stones was in his hand?"

"So I think."

"And you saw—what?"

"I saw a Stone-Age funeral party."

"And Miss Fleming—what has *she* seen up there, to-day or at any other time?"

"I don't know."

Arsinal paused; then went on:

"Thank you for your sincerity . . . and simplicity. . . . Thus it is put beyond doubt that these hauntings are objective, not figments of the fancy. But also it is established that we may scarcely dare to set ourselves against them; and I think you do wrong, Mr. Copping, to allow a persistent defeating of your will in the matter to swell into ill-will against persons. At another time, I could tell you much else, to demonstrate to you how broad this great general movement of the invisible should be; then anger, I am sure, would depart from a mind of which it cannot be a habit. Mean-

while, what exactly is it that you are asking us to do? I shall say
without concealment that I can't afford to go on risking Mrs.
Fleming's displeasure. My sole aim in these negotiations is the
procuring of that stone. Put it in my hand to-day, and cancel the
Tor meeting to-morrow in any fashion you please; but the stone I
must have."

"Saltfleet knows where it is"—the dropping of the title for the
first time was noticeable—"let him go and bring it away, as
suggested. I will take any responsibility."

Saltfleet came back to them from the window, but did not sit
down.

"Being only a party to a trust, I cannot do that."

"Are you a married man?" Peter seemed to smile, but it was
rather a contortion of transition and unpleasantness.

"No. Why?"

"I am throwing myself on your charity, and would have ap-
pealed to the relation. Have mercy on this unfortunate girl. I
address *you*, because you are the recurrent and permanent block.
Don't go for the stone if it's against honour; but at least suggest
another means. Stop this wretched gathering, by . . . raising
objections—or accepting and failing to turn up in time . . . I don't
care how it is. Miss Fleming and I will see to it that you lose
nothing, gentlemen, by the underground frustration. I don't ask
you even to *offend* her mother: there is plenty of difference
between disappointing and slighting. . . ."

But Saltfleet remained cold.

"The nature of the transactable business up there would seem
not to require the attendance of Miss Fleming. That should be
your way out. It is of course your affair, not ours."

"She has promised her mother to go with her. That may be the
tap-root of the entire idea; and Mrs. Fleming, after all, may have
an excellent insight into the demands of the situation. She wants
to discover what this appalling tangle is, that is so rapidly paralysing her daughter's functions and making of her present hours an
unutterable misery; and so she is inspired to bring everything
together, in such a way as to leave nothing out—you two men,

and her daughter, and my humble self, and Devil's Tor, and Drapier's stone. From these psychic and psychological ingredients, she will attempt the construction of a diagnosis, that she hopes may suggest the remedy and bring the cure. . . . I do not agree with her that the best method of studying a serious disease is to heighten its ravages."

"You have the general intuition," said Saltfleet, "and, like all general intuitions, it is both true and false, right and wrong. Accordingly, there is this distinction between our two attitudes towards Miss Fleming's coming to a meeting on the proposed lines: you *feel* a danger to her, Mr. Copping; I nearly *know of* one. But the danger presenting itself in my mind is probably the one of all others you have never dreamt of. . . ."

He proceeded, while Peter fixed him with his steady greenish eyes of genius:

"The quite likely accident of another occult seizure on the Tor would assuredly be a painful enough shock to her system, already much shaken; but would not kill her, or more than slightly affect the future course of her life. Neither are *we* bandits, to terrify or distress her on another account. Her mother would be there; and you. The flint is to be surrendered to us, so that there could be no scene of violence on that score. These are all the common threats to Miss Fleming. They are negligible, as against the inconvenience of attempting to prevent her attendance: she has promised her mother, you say; I fancy her sense of the supernatural in these things will be a bar to the retractation of her promise on purely cautionary grounds. We must make up our minds, therefore, that she will accompany her mother to-morrow evening. Yet a peril for her does exist, that will render the action most inadvisable unless a safeguard can be found. And it can be found; but will depend upon the benevolence of an individual. . . ."

"Who?"

"Arsinal here. . . . Arsinal, I beg you to do one of these two things . . . or there are three. Either keep away from to-morrow's settlement and let me deputise for you; or let me receive the property from Mrs. Fleming's hands, and I will pass it to you afterwards; or, if you must be present and take it yourself, at least give your word of honour now that you will refrain from joining it to the other while on the hill—anyway, so long as Miss Fleming is within range; and the range, we know, is considerable. In courtesy, I include her mother; of course they will be together. When they shall be out of range, then you may fly to your experiment as fast as may be. . . . The delay, if it is only one, won't be inordinate. If it is also a balk—that, I fear, must be your own private chastening. . . ."

"The two stones, supposed to be fragments, will naturally tempt a fitting." Peter musingly examined the cigarette between his fingers. "And as each is strong-natured in itself, the united product may be even dangerous to handle. That is feasible. Yet a few points occur to me. Why is Mr. Arsinal imagined to be rash enough to wish to expose outsiders—and women—to a first trial of unknown forces? And, the whole supposition being rather far-fetched, why are you stressing it? . . . Also, why is Miss Fleming being singled out as the one with most to fear from such a trial? . . . Or is this all an oblique resumption of some directer discussion gone before?"

Arsinal looked ill, and was clenching and unclenching his hand repeatedly. Giving no time to his associate to answer the other's questions, he broke in quickly, though quietly:

"So now it has arrived at a public attack, Saltfleet! Yet, in our after-lunch talk together, didn't I offer *not* to meet, *not* to know, Miss Fleming?"

"Truth to tell, you did."

"Then was the talk for nothing? In silencing you, was I merely driving back malice into its hole?"

"Hardly malice. Our terms have always been too equal for that. An idea was nearer inception a few hours ago, and proportionally weaker. This assembly, that wasn't on the table then, has put stature and vigour into it. . . . It is not prepossessing, Arsinal!"

"The conceit is as fantastic as disloyal. What! I must submit ignominiously to be excluded or bound, when my honesty will be admitted? The logic is strange."

"Put that way; which I say is a wrong and crooked way. For you are professing an aim, a single aim, and your honesty depends on the truth of the profession. If you have some further aim that you wish to remain concealed, then you are so far dishonest—not for the concealment, to which you have the ordinary human right, but for the profession of a thing untrue. . . . Efface yourself at to-morrow's settlement, and we shall know you are sincere in wanting Drapier's stone and no more. But decline all my choices, wrap yourself in this cloak of darkness, and what can I suspect but something . . . degenerate underneath! . . ."

Arsinal got up. Peter, not to be left sitting alone, joined the two on the floor, flicking ash from his cigarette and keeping his eyes down.

"That is a word the applicability of which I shall later have to ask you to explain, Saltfleet. I don't know if you have an intention in angering me before Mr. Copping, but, supposing you have, it is now sufficiently done and I would beg you not to go on treading the border of past confidences. . . . What I must think is that, having hitherto been content to confine yourself to helping me in all this pursuit, now all at once something in it is *personally* interesting you; and you wish to procure for yourself independence of action. So you insult me, in order to obtain your release: but the witness of a stranger will render the insult sharper, besides preventing the friendly return to understanding. . . . I won't indulge in the cynicism, that such an attack on me before a third may have been in your thoughts since that last unsatisfactory patching-up. . . . Neither will I have the primitive vindictiveness to suggest to Mr. Copping just *what* may be interesting you since yesterday in this business. But, taking leave altogether to ignore your interposition, Saltfleet, the covert threat in which I shall know how to despise . . . here is my answer to Mrs. Fleming! The affair is mine, not Mr. Saltfleet's. We are to be considered dissociated: he desires it, and I am not unwilling. Therefore I ask you, Mr. Copping, to instruct her, and her daughter also, that he is no longer authorised to act for me or represent my views. . . . There is your own attitude, and I am sorry to have to refuse it, but my interests are vital. Mr. Saltfleet's alarm you yourself have styled 'far-fetched'—it is its nearly weakest description . . . your own fears for Miss Fleming can hardly materialise in a gathering of four or five on a definite business; yet you will also observe to her mother that I am by no means requiring her attendance; I shall take her consent to the transaction as given. . . . With these pre-liminaries, and in simple acceptance of Mrs. Fleming's arrange-ments, I shall be on Devil's Tor to-morrow evening, at nine, to receive the property."

Peter shrugged, and was silent. Saltfleet, who had been stand-ing very erect on his feet, looking half-haughtily away, listening, after an appreciable pause turned abruptly upon his old colleague.

"I am content. Nor is it necessary to inquire how, if Miss Fleming isn't to be there and I am to be excluded, you are to get your stone after all. For you are not an imbecile, Arsinal . . . and so perhaps you have a better knowledge that Miss Fleming *will* be there. . . ."

"The spot can be charted."

"Let it be. However, whether or no, I shall be there too, since I can't get to learn beforehand if she has stayed away. You claim no right to the private possession of the hill for your purposes?"

"What I can't understand and you haven't answered me," said Peter, addressing Saltfleet, "is why this tremendous solicitude of yours is on Miss Fleming's account alone."

"She is the younger and more influenceable of the two women to be exposed."

"Nothing else?"

"Ask Arsinal."

Peter turned in silent interrogation to the man named. A faint frowning struggle crossed his face, before he said:

"The verbal *riposte* would be easy. But what Saltfleet means is different. I don't wish to fence. He refers to an ancient prediction, in which he has no faith, and I . . ."

"And you . . . ?" Saltfleet spoke.

"I have no grounds for applying it to a young woman I have never met; and am not so applying it. Please say no more of it,

Mr. Copping."

The artist returned to Saltfleet. "You will be up, then. But tell me specifically what you are to do, in a party apparently not desiring your company."

"I shall be there to watch all; and, if needful, to take measures."

"Preventive measures?"

"You know the ultimate of arguments, Mr. Copping."

"And this is *your* message to Mrs. Fleming, that you want conveyed?"

"If you please."

"Certainly it may have the desired effect; and I thank you. . . . So, before clinching the arrangement, I shall need to go back for new directions, Mr. Arsinal."

"Permit me to come with you to the house . . . now."

Peter regarded him. Arsinal's face was paler than ever, but he had stilled its commotion, to a new calmness that seemed even unforced: it was a delicate repose almost, as if a remote inaccessible will far within was being unconcerned with his physical frame and its possible insultings and mischances. For an instant the artist became an artist again, in pondering the case of this strange beauty of quietness and resolution in a man who, nevertheless, by his eyes, might be crazy. . . . But once more he dropped his gaze, to shake his head and refuse him.

"You'd better not. Everyone there isn't initiated."

"Yet you go primed against me. Refined women are to be alarmed by this hint of reckless unprincipled men, fallen out on a point and probably to come to blows before them. Were Mrs. Fleming to envisage me, I fancy her alarm would change to a smile! . . . I could also perhaps persuade her that Mr. Saltfleet's true and ostensible motives for presenting himself on the Tor uninvited are different—that the true motive may have more of insolence, but certainly carries nothing that tact cannot deal with. And surely, it is an extravagant picture . . . of a couple of mature men of culture, not unknown in the world, engaged in a physical scuffle over a point of remote superstition! Neither can you have failed to note, Mr. Copping, that it is always within his power to stop the whole settlement, with its alleged dangers, by anticipating it in the manner you have suggested. But he is 'a party to a trust,' so cannot see his way to do that. The principle, no doubt, is sound, but what must we think of a peril to a lady, that is after all of less account than her imaginary disappointment or other emotion in a transaction which has already seen her indifference?"

"The first of this idea of picking up the stone was his, as a matter of fact," said Peter, glancing interrogatively at Saltfleet. The latter returned:

"But never as a practical proposal. I found it odd that Mrs. Fleming wasn't offering us the thing in the directest way."

"I believe, you are right: I apologise. Then the rest of your argument, Mr. Arsinal . . . ?"

"I wish you to convince Mrs. Fleming that the attendance of herself and her daughter on the hill to-morrow is most unlikely to be followed up by any unpleasantness whatsoever. If I don't put it stronger, it is because, as a scientific precisian, I am accustomed to find the exactest words the most forcible. Mr. Saltfleet, I think, has wanted to break with me, and so has insulted me. But over and above that, he must be wishing to wreck this final settlement to-morrow. It goes against some private plan he has laid down for himself. . . . It is a little more than hypothesis, unfortunately: the facts in support are too many. For he it is, Mr. Copping, who ever since yesterday, before my arrival, has sought occasions with Miss Fleming. I won't offend you by conceiving her manner of response: he may have succeeded in interesting and exciting her in this occult business, or she may at last be principally repelled by the persistency of his intrusions. To retain her, he has nearly from the first made use of my technical knowledge of some of the matters which may be supposed to impinge on her own intellectual, and even emotional, preoccupations. He has constantly urged upon us both the advantage, the necessity, of a meeting between us, to discuss the territory on either side of such a common border. Thereby, her release from us and our affairs has been from hour to hour put off. . . .

"On her account, too, it is—I shall say it openly—that he will neither prevent to-morrow's assembly on Devil's Tor by an action that will necessarily stop all further acquaintance, nor permit, if he can help it, that assembly, which equally is to bring everything to a short end . . . but he will spin out, and he will spin out! . . . I, the man of dark design, I have expressed my willingness indifferently to either course. . . . And then, must I speak besides of his rejection for both of us of the offer brought this morning? It was a good offer, and for the emphasis of its condition he had but himself to thank . . . so good an offer, that even he dared not return it directly on your hands; but first must superfluously qualify it, and then altogether outrage its terms. . . .

"And similarly, this second offer, that you yourself find only too just and generous on the part of a lady who might well have sent us to the devil, after our bad treatment of her . . . he means to outrage *it* as well. It seems that he proposes to do so by putting fear into Mrs. Fleming's heart: the fear of a scene of violence, the fear of an experiment that is not in the programme, only I will not be coerced in a case that is no one else's but mine. . . . Assure her therefore, Mr. Copping, that there will be no assault made by the far stronger of two men in the presence of a delicate-minded girl, who could never wish to have the continued acquaintance of such a pugilist and brigand. Assure her also that so far am I from intending her daughter that grotesquely-conceived occult or biochemical mischief, that I am even prepared not to *see* her— you shall blindfold me with my own handkerchief before her arrival. The proffer is not more ridiculous than the fear to be allayed by it. . . . I trust to your honesty not to pass on Mr. Saltfleet's baseless suggestion in order to procure the withdrawing of an arrangement you dislike, omitting to pass on these just as emphatic and much more reasoned considerations of mine. But a personal interview with Mrs. Fleming this evening would be the best."

Saltfleet smiled sourly.

"So many words, Mr. Copping, and still not that one little undertaking which would have obviated them all!" But Peter's attending stare was unsympathetic.

"I shall report everything, gentlemen. Altogether, the affair isn't growing more agreeable as one sees into it. Of course, the feature I strongly resent is this intolerable bandying of Miss Fleming's name. Neither is the one of you privileged by a chance, or stolen, meeting or so to seek to constitute himself her protector at another meeting she will attend under the conduct of her own people; nor is the other of you doing anything but insulting her by that laboured suggestion that she is being pursued for her acquaintance by a man she as good as doesn't know. I am the youngest and probably the least-travelled in this room, and yet I must surmise that you, gentlemen, have acquired less than I of the world's discretion. That, as it happens, I am to marry Miss Fleming, is not the point. A lady isn't to be so freely appropriated by strangers."

"For any excess, I apologise," said Saltfleet. . . . "However, you should be rather confounding the human and superhuman elements of the case, Mr. Copping. Let Arsinal make his own excuses: I don't wish her acquaintance, and that is enough said of that. I would see her well through a peculiar occasion if I could. You are shying somewhat suddenly; just now, I remember an appeal on her behalf!"

"To stop the meeting; not to rule it."

"And you thanked me for proposing to rule it too."

"If it were to stop it."

"I ask no better."

Peter lit a new cigarette, and for a time said no more. Then, while they all uneasily stood still within that small circle of the floor, looking different ways, he announced:

"Very well! I'll be off, to see if I can get the consent of Mrs. Fleming and her daughter to your fetching away the stone as soon as you like, so forestalling that meeting. You both wish it?"

Saltfleet assented.

"And you, Mr. Arsinal?"

"I've said so. For the stone I must have, at all hazards, but if a particular meeting of persons *can* be stopped, it is very evidently not fated."

"Fated! . . ." repeated Peter after him, in a musing undertone.

It was the last word of their talk, but none moved, and they remained standing there. It seemed as if, now that the Tor gathering was refused and this other simpler, less dramatic settlement substituted, the neglected supernatural in the case were starting to work again, like an unborn thing, within the recesses of them all. Peter, finding, nearly in amazement, that he alone had achieved the decision, giving it its permanent shape, was to doubt, with a doubt sinking to dismay, if objective horrors after all could be so easily penned; if destiny could be bent back without the worse disaster of irresistibility at last for the vain delay. He pictured, as it were in one complexity of image, Drapier lying in an open shell in a dark room, and those grey ghostly mourners dancing along a ledge, and the stack of great rocks in the act of being hurled headlong over the Tor's side in a grisly storm, and Ingrid and Saltfleet standing face-to-face, pale, eyeing each other peculiarly . . . and other things . . . and to all this, his own feeble, querulous, "No—no!" . . . So a creative artist might feel, who had cheapened his soul in the name of safety, turning his eyes from a vision of life coming in the form of madness. . . .

But Saltfleet was recalling for one time more those metamorphosing spirit-eyes of the afternoon, and knew inside himself the beginning of a sense of abashment for his cowardice in the face of a great adventure, as for his betrayal of the higher unaffected dauntlessness of a noble girl. . . . While Arsinal already seemed to become aware of his impurity of haste, greed, circumspection, that had shown him impotent in this short miraculous day of failure and twofold triumph. For once he had thought to have lost the flint, then, in a swoop, had swept down upon its brother and it; yet because his soul had somehow parted from its faith, these events had been merely luck for him, and more luck he had feared to risk, and so would possess that original and still-unsecured of the twin stones certainly. But had it *not* been luck for him, had it been unseen design and contrivance, the mighty tide-wave might yet have been advancing, not ceased. . . . As a contemptuous alms from these underlings and strangers, the stone might be given him this very day. It could not be the same, but something would have gone out of a transaction made safe and vulgar. . . . The retribution of the high—it should entail, perhaps, the slow climbing back to worth, during years. . . .

A noise sounded outside the room, and Peter, who alone might realise its strangeness at that hour, moved after another moment to the door, looking puzzled, and even alarmed.

XXVII

Intervention

Ingrid, white-faced, dressed all in black, frowning from her indecision, stood there on the tiny landing, one gloved hand still suspended towards the door latch that evidently, after doubt, she had been about to depress. As well as the immediate vision of Peter, her eye, in its instantaneous exploration of what it could take in of the room through the gap, saw enough of its standing occupants to know who they were. With dismay she realised what she had come to and was interrupting; yet the suspicion must have been the cause of her hesitation while the room was still ominously shut against her, if in silence. But Peter, thinking that that quick probable ascertaining of the identity of his visitors would be followed by a prompt retreat, put back his hand to close the door; and now they were alone and face-to-face.

"Mother sent me. She is rather anxious at your being so long gone. They were out?—and you left word that they were to come on here?"

Her dropped tones, nearly a whispering, were on account of those open-eared men just beyond the thin panels, yet also seemed like awe for the coincidence of their drifting together still again. Peter's sensitiveness understood it so. Without reflection almost, she must be including it mystically in her whole scheme of wonders; nor, doubtless, was she unjustified. Abandoning from lack of hardihood his first instinctive movement to grasp her arm, and contenting himself with continuing to eye her in a kind of mournful scrutiny of curiosity, he said:

"We'll talk afterwards. I want you now, if you will, to come in to them for a minute."

"Then is nothing to stand fixed, Peter?"

"Let me judge here. It's rather material you should meet them for this once."

He reopened the door, to follow close on the girl's reluctant and dreamlike entrance. Saltfleet first and then Arsinal bowed.

"Here is Miss Fleming herself," said Peter. There was no other introduction, but, after a quick glance at Arsinal, Ingrid took the chair offered her, while the firstcomers obeyed Peter's sign to reseat themselves. The artist remained standing. He went on to say:

"Mrs. Fleming has been getting uneasy, and her daughter has come to find out what is doing. It happens very well. Now, gentlemen, she can give you the desired assurance in the matter of fetching that stone away."

His spirit was shut again to unearthliness. These evil changes since overnight in Ingrid's physical condition were filling him with too much indignation. Simply as a man caring for a woman, he could not let it fester and spread—the nightmare attack on her sweetness . . . while the pair attending her were like ghouls seeking to drag her down. . . . But no one answered him immediately.

"I should be a little more explicit. Your mother's latest offer, Ingrid—we've all three just been discussing it; and have come to the unanimous opinion that it represents a needless delay. These gentlemen are promised the thing they want; it is at the present moment on top of Devil's Tor, where Mr. Saltfleet can put his hand on it; so that there can be no sense in keeping them waiting another day. Are you agreeable to their having it now? It's not too late to get it this evening."

It was the unanimity, however, of their dislike of a plan that she knew was not of her mother's human prudence, therefore doubtless must prevail in spite of all, which the light behind Ingrid's confusion seized for emphasis out of all the rest of Peter's words. She felt it singular that these three intelligences in the room, each otherwise willing and wishing differently, should so suddenly be united against a happening perhaps fore-ordained. The obscure bewilderment clothed itself in her murmured reply:

"Unanimous! . . ."

"Do you find that queer? Yet a meeting to-morrow is really in the interests of none here. The transfer needs no formalities. If you want to talk, you can do it now. What is the use of waiting?"

"If it is to be settled by judgment. . . . But what can I say, Peter? Do you wish to throw the responsibility on me? I have no standing to decide anything."

"We are not requiring it. Mr. Saltfleet, I understand, is only carrying his scruples as far as the obtaining of your word of personal willingness; while Mr. Arsinal has none at all. Before you reiterate, let me state it in the form I wish. Do you *forbid* their appropriating this stone when they please?"

"How can I forbid it?"

"Supposing Mr. Saltfleet fetches it down to-day, there will be no charge of dishonesty brought against him?"

"I begged him to take it this morning, but he wouldn't. I have, since, had a long talk with mother, and have promised to go to the Tor with her to-morrow. Now you are asking me to help to disappoint her. How can I do it, Peter? . . . I can only say that if Mr. Saltfleet does bring it away in the meantime, I don't know whose it is, so certainly can't charge him with dishonesty."

"Of course the dishonesty wouldn't refer to the point of ownership, but to his single appropriation of a thing left jointly."

"In any case I should not accuse Mr. Saltfleet of dishonesty."

Peter turned to Saltfleet.

"Is that good enough?"

"Yes, I think so, now that Miss Fleming has been made acquainted with the intention, and is not directly forbidding it."

"Your mother has no essential stake in that meeting."

"I don't know," said Ingrid.

"None that can weigh."

Arsinal, his fingers nervously intertwined over his crossed knee, was always musing on Ingrid's face, that gradually he found impenetrable and witch-like. It was different from what he had expected, and into his trouble of understanding crept something of dread. He began to be oppressed that between her essence and his there was already no comparison; that his work hitherto had been but journeyman's work, while she, without wisdom or ambition, might yet have it in her to be the finer, sharper instrument of. . . . *Her.* . . .

A woman, too, by virtue of her sex, was a vessel; a vessel was for filling. A man, perhaps, could not so entirely receive the grace of heaven. . . . And in her long, stern-featured loveliness speaking of the snows and dark nights of another world, he believed he discerned the prepared bed of a passionateness that should far exceed his own cool flaming, which now, in consequence, all at once started to seem to himself arid, exhausted, contriving. . . .

Nothing of this had he expected, yet something of it all he must have brought with him to their meeting. Surely he must have been convinced, nearly from Saltfleet's opening account of her exceptionalness, that in a most particular sense she was the local heart of his quest, so curiously come to fulfilment in the downhill of his life, after his thousand diggings, gropings, defeats and half-victories in all those foreign lands, upon an obscure ancient height of his own native island, of which she should be as the warder, or votaress. . . . Its warder and watcher—for him?—for his coming? . . .

Constantly he found himself obliged to stop his thoughts, flying off centrifugally from the case's centre of simple facts; yet was not such a tendency in itself the proof of the presence of an energy in him obedient to another mass? Arsinal was torn. He wished not to exceed his intellectual permission, but at the same time his blood was being subtly fired by this new recklessness of footholdless adventure that strove to incite him to actions in the dark. Again he wondered—now more consciously, more immediately, more *solidly*, it seemed—if his exaggerated cautiousness of moving one step and no further at a time could be consonant with that moment of translation which in the first instance, so long ago, had commanded him to these aims having no visible mark. He was not easily to forget Saltfleet's cruel likening of him to Peter in the palace of the high priest. This allowing a half-faith to rest in abeyance till some new incident should occur to reinforce it, was it then but a cowardice of his heart for the incalculable consequences of the full and final profession of allegiance to his secret ghost? Was he temperamentally incapable of moving limb against the all-compelling gravitation of human sanity, so running with his blood and grown together with his fibres that already he might no longer call himself an individual, but everlastingly must shrink from all the adverse whispers of opinion? . . .

For the sane life was all around him, and so strong! And yet not for nothing could it be that this girl was daunting him, beneath her weariness that sat upon her as a thing not her own, but still was most appropriate. The silent barrier between them was not for anything he had said, since he had not spoken. He was as sure that it was by no means Saltfleet's treachery that had erected it for him; neither womanly disdain nor rancour was being displayed, but only the simple ignoring of his company. Rather was it an antagonism of strange souls . . . as such, it should be the sign of her authenticity.

Small doubt there was that, in their manhood and womanhood, they were as opposite poles of the higher humanity: he intellectual and volitional, she, it was clear, subconscious, nervous and instinctive. Should, therefore, this first unplanned encounter be repeated and improved, not any pleasure of either in the other's type, not any harmony of spirit, not any automatism towards completion, would have effected it; but the pure fate of these concerns alone. And so the enticements of sex were being unrequired; for they were but a single substitutable tool of the celestial scheming, a scheming older than the most ancient tools to shape the world; and because the common passion was here to be set aside and scorned, therefore should the larger grandeur be presently made manifest. . . .

His face grew set in care while he considered hers. But she had never turned to him again after that opening look. She seemed quite unconscious of his unceasing quiet regard. . . .

"Then I shall go for it now," said Saltfleet. Noticeably, however, his voice was more reluctant and questioning, less decisive, than its wont. . . . "Yet whether it is to end the business, the providence of it knows, not I."

Ingrid asked him:

"Have you been up again?"

"Yes; this afternoon, with Mr. Arsinal. Do you see the signs?"

"It was your doubting of an end so easy. You should be finding it hard to think that any of us can keep off the Tor till a real end comes . . . not this forced end."

His eyes rested on her. "Mr. Copping, however, for example, keeps off."

"Yes, he does," agreed Ingrid, after a queer silence.

"I very well know how you would both explain such an exception."

"There is no mystery about it," said Peter. "I've work to do in the world; and it lies off the Tor. I hope I possess so much strength of mind as to set my solid goods before my excitements." But Ingrid knew that he spoke to her.

Saltfleet answered him:

"The best of *my* work is mostly behind me, I fear. It's inevitably so, from the nature of my profession—which some would think none at all. Anyway, I've all the more time for the attempted unravelling of this weird affair, that must be needing assistant souls."

"You have the freedom and the strength," returned the girl. "You may go up there again, again, and again; and still defy the bad enclosing the good."

"Who can say! Your unfortunate cousin was just as fit and free."

"He had a presentiment of death."

"You are to leave after the inquest," Peter reminded Saltfleet sharply. "Therefore all this talk of unlimited investigation, and the

personal assets necessary to it, is a sheer impertinence, if you will
pardon me."

"Very true. If we secure the stone to-day, we are to be off to-
morrow."

"Then what your other remark means, I do not know."

Giving a light shrug of helplessness, the other attempted no
explanation. Ingrid hesitated, while she turned nervous eyes
toward Arsinal.

"Mr. Arsinal. . . . I wish to ask you. . . . We are speaking of
Devil's Tor. A woman of singular height was anciently buried on
top, whose spirit still has power to become visible in the vicinity
of her tomb. I have seen her. Who was she?"

An instant look of reticence had come into his face, and his
answer was delayed.

"It was to inquire this that you wanted to meet me?"

"I don't know."

Only after another pause Arsinal replied to her question:

"She was not born—not born on earth . . . but descended from
space."

"Was she in the body, or always a phantom?"

"What is body? Who of us can assert that he or she is in the
body? . . . But also there may be degrees of corporality. According to the degree of one's grossness, one has or has not a body.
Neither, because a seeming body is buried in a tomb, is it necessarily there. The New Testament declares no otherwise."

"How are you sure of what you say?"

"I witnessed her first coming this afternoon, from below the
hill."

"In what shape was she?"

"In the beginning, as a pillar of light."

Ingrid closed her eyes as if to think—to shut out the company.
A quite long silence followed. Peter, smoking still, wandered to
the nearer of the two open windows, and gazed abroad. Then
Ingrid looked again at Arsinal, and asked him further:

"The Great Mother—I am told you have pursued her myth for
many years . . . also that she is somehow associated with these

stones, which is your interest in them. Had she never a personal name or history? Was so little known of her?"

"She had many names, and too full a history of ignorance and distorted tradition. An undoubted name of hers, badly come through, was Ourania . . . daughter of Ouranos, not Zeus; Plato's inadequate heavenly Aphrodite, distinct from the corrupt Aphrodite of fleshly love and beauty."

"She of the Tor . . ."

"Is still unrevealed."

"You can go away, and leave your work unfinished?"

Arsinal returned no reply.

"Is yours, then, merely a student's interest?" demanded Ingrid.

"No. It began with a revelation by night; and has not grown less through all the years."

"So wouldn't you adventure your life—or anything—to know her more directly?"

"Yes—anything." The emotion in his quiet, simple response was impressive, because obviously against his will. She read in his face that with her, perhaps, he would be more expansive, less afraid of the profanation of these mysteries, but for the presence of the others—of Saltfleet, for some strange rough contempt of different strength; of Peter, for his dry self-exclusion. She did not know how to help him.

"There is a prophecy as well?"

"Of that I would not wish to speak. I have found it preserved in Crete and Asia Minor."

"Dare you have faith in it?"

"I am ignorant how much you have heard; but indeed, it would need a great surrender of the common ways of thought; or a facile madness."

"You aren't mad?" None in the room found insolence or absurdity in her question. It seemed to have been introduced, and was unironically put. Arsinal appeared even to consider it before replying.

"I should not be mad. My related ideas should be sufficiently consecutive and logical; what is more to the purpose, they should be grounded. Such satisfaction as I derive from them is neither sterile nor degraded, as I must believe. These should be the assurances of a whole mind."

"So that your faith in the prophecy is such that you have at least had to . . . doubt yourself? The prophecy is of the transfiguring sort? . . . For the single stone, before its fracture, began a new race on earth; and the equal miracle is to follow from the reuniting of the halves. . . . A wonderful faith, I think, is necessary!"

Arsinal was pale, but collected.

"I shan't aspire to the founding of new races, if only men may be brought back to worship."

"To that you could aspire?"

"Yes. To the living worship of the highest."

"This phantom has been womanly. No shape of sex can present the highest."

"Our eyes cannot see the highest, but only the shapes which are towards the highest. The womanly may be most conspicuously such. . . . Just as human lips may possess a legion of varied smiles, ranging from heaven to the pit, so the womanly form may express any of an infinitude of essences lying between the two extremes of deity and beast. You say that you have *seen*—in seeing, have you not understood this directly?"

Ingrid bowed her head, while she murmured a reply that should be assentient. Saltfleet interposed:

"Neither may I play the sceptic. You can't pick and choose out of the plain statement of events to come, however; and it is definite about the founding of a people . . . a race, not a sect—I go by your own reading, Arsinal. Either you must have faith in the whole prophecy, or in none of it. But the practical prodigy nowadays is so grotesquely unthinkable, that merely to examine its possibility must be nearly lunacy. Men are to be brought back to worship. The old spirits and tempers of men are shrivelled— who except the troglodytes can worship to-day?—accordingly, the new type must be created . . . from a single pair, miraculously informed, I say it for you. And then? The very first purest children of that new type will find themselves already surrounded by a mechanised civilisation, the advantages of which cannot be renounced, so its corruptions likewise must endure. Such a civilisation of decay will resume its old evil work with the earliest visit of the doctor, the earliest paid caresses of the hired nurse. As surely as all waters fall at last into the sea, mankind is doomed to go on descending to the universal mess of vulgarity. No miracle can come before a primary natural operation. . . . These are some of the facts against your restoration of the divine on earth, Arsinal."

"The refuters have always refuted with their brains," rejoined the other, "but the believers have believed with their hearts and souls; therefore, many a thing declared impossible has come to pass. . . . The true intention of your speech is not hidden from me, however."

"You may tell it, if you know it."

"Ostensibly addressed to me, it has so evidently been for Miss Fleming's alarming. . . ." He was to have said more, but thought better of it. Saltfleet's lip faintly curled.

"Persuading her to keep out of eccentric company! I could have found directer arguments. No! it was merely that I fancied the conversation to be drifting from sincerity."

"I had already explained my attitude," Ingrid rather hurriedly said to Arsinal. "Mr. Saltfleet might have left the room for Devil's Tor without more words at all, and he knows I would not have stopped him."

"He might have done that. Nevertheless, his obstruction was for you and no one else."

"I cannot feel that it was."

"What then?"

She returned no answer. But though her lips were so strangely tranquil again after those last utterances, in her eyes lay an indescribable look of suspended communication, that Arsinal's fineness recognised. He allowed a moment to pass, then went on:

"I have indeed no right to question you about Mr. Saltfleet's motive in saying what he did, nor do I wish to discuss that prophetic record with you; but I suppose what I am really asking you is whether or not you concur in general in his view, that this whole business in all its branches, however extraordinary, however miraculous even, is still to be regarded as necessarily subject to the common known laws of the world?"

"But how can such a contradiction be?"

"So you can rise above that contention?"

"If it were not standing outside the laws we know, we should not be seeing it as a business; it would appear to us a mere fantasia of coincident arrivals, accidents, destructions, unloosed ghosts. . . . But because we are sure in our hearts of the connection, we have begun to understand—an *activity* . . . an activity too speaking not to be intelligent . . . an advancing of some dreadful fate on our group, I am certain. That is what I mean by a contradiction. In astronomy, a total eclipse of the sun can be accurately predicted, according to laws, hundreds of years ahead; but the annihilation of our sun by a dead star, there is no known law for that, and it can't be predicted, but it is fate. It has never happened yet, and so you cannot say what new overwhelming forces will be liberated, to mock the small astronomical brains of those asserting this and that of it. . . ."

"You are not afraid to employ so extravagant a figure?"

"No doubt I am becoming out of all proportion. . . . But Mr. Saltfleet's logic would be so very blind, if truly it were a product of his brain alone. . . ."

"Was it less blind because instinctive?" demanded Saltfleet.

Ingrid's eyes moved to him.

"Already your will was weakening, and you must have been fortifying it with those arguments aloud. I felt so. Your refusal of that prophecy, on the ground of the impossibility of its coming true in the modern world . . . how dull and mechanical, how altogether short of what I've seen and heard of you, it sounded! All your life, I suppose, you have been *pursuing* life—disdaining it for its insufficiency, despising other men for so easily, like animals, taking the world of existence for granted . . . attacking frightful and forbidding mountains out of sheer *ennui* . . . or raiding, without two thoughts, an evil temple for the wager of a little excitement and an unprofitable short triumph, against death or disgrace . . . and the mightiest, noblest feat of all, on an infinitely higher plane—*that* you can shrug your shoulder at for impossible! This is why I know it was no more than an obstinacy of your determined will, looking for supports . . . intended neither for Mr. Arsinal nor for me."

"You mean, I am at once wanting your mother's Devil's Tor meeting, and willing against it?"

"You know that if I had expected to find either of you here this evening, I should not have come. But if the coincidence were to stand out by itself as the one accident during the last days not strange, that would be the very strangest. So perhaps the call is to make a difference. You may all three be needing the meeting; and I may be here—not to change your minds for you, certainly, but to supply a diversion. . . ."

"What do you advise?" asked Saltfleet, plainly yet quietly.

"I can't advise you—except to listen attentively to yourself . . . though even that may be superfluous."

"You realise that my will can't be opposing your mother's plan without a motive?"

"It is to spare me."

"Mr. Copping has already resented my solicitude."

"Peter! . . ." He turned round at the low-voiced appeal, but only to prevent what else Ingrid had been to say.

"Do I receive a meed as well? Was *my* vote born of altruism, *contra* height? I take you to affirm that we are all in the same morass!"

At that she rose to take his hand with her fingers, and so remain standing. "Peter, don't be angry; because these matters are too awful. . . . My eyes are clearer than yours here. You are needing to-morrow more than anyone."

"Odd!"

"I say my eyes are clearer; yet you know it too. If there is to be any sort of ordeal for me, and you care for me, my emergence from it will be the illumination you dare not miss. . . ."

"You are emphatic."

"I am unhappy."

"Notwithstanding all which, I opine that the public debating of the case here, in this studio, is rather conspicuously undesirable."

He disengaged himself from her touch, and, tossing his unfinished cigarette behind him through the window, began to pace the room in undisguised perturbation. She was right! It was no true ending, that could recommence; it was no solving of a problem, to leave a ragged menace of indistinct advancing abysses. . . . Her reference to wills *versus* needs was correct also. In swimming, one had to forsake the solid bottom, to surrender oneself to the sea, composed of death; and so now. The bottom, in this affair, was the will's excellent sense; but the sea was all their needs, instincts, horrors. To declare such a sea could be left unswum, ignored the fact that they were in it. . . .

For Ingrid's powerlessness against this living mystical savagery clothed as enigma—an enigma sprung above ground during a few days, but whose roots went back whole years—to sit patient and motionless through the night of oppression in expectation of a delivering dawn at last, to conceive already that that night in its worst depth of storm and blackness was past, though the morn was not yet visibly appearing—such might be the mode of long optimism in the case of a beloved whose beauty of soul and body should be as her shield: practically, one knew that beyond a determined quantitative strain for each instance, cast iron snapped, trees became uprooted, men reverted, and women suddenly drooped and failed, as under a withering desert blast, to be thereafter like walking catafalques. . . . Unless there came at once such a quick cessation of this phenomenal tempest as would necessarily make the matters already befallen a travesty of fatality. . . . No! those years-long roots, this awful up-shooting stem of events risen before their very eyes, and *no flower*!—it was impossible. . . .

These marvels could still not be outside Nature. The fiends pre-eminent in cruelty of the incomprehensible Omnipotent, expressly loosed on earth to torture those humans set apart for surpassing nightmare punishment, they requisitely were of their employment most skilled in the craft of screw and rack, sensing diabolically the nerves of highest personal anguish in each victim. Thus a third time Ingrid was right! It was no cataclysmal accident of occult chemistry he had to fear for her, since any other would have served for that brief fate; but all her marks were for a tragic *life*. . . . Not the ordeal, but her emergence from it. The slow skin-casting agonies of a spiritual metamorphosis. . . . It was shown. Defensive plans were contrivable, but the day was not yet out; to-morrow was yet to come. Twenty-four hours further down in time—forever Saltfleet—the flints, the Tor—the joining, at every angle of the day, of another evil occult tributary to the already brimming waters! Such factors meant a long, not a short, fate. . . .

Drowning, and at last (her terror past) laughing, she would then be to carry with her for the rest of the mortal course—as it were some gallery, horrible to her own imagination, of all she had been and was no more—her memories sporadic and memories associated, her habits, tastes, distastes, limitations, and fixed person. For none of those could again be hers. The "I" they built up would be dead with her lost life; her new "I" would use them and hate them like the clothes of a stranger. . . .

He stopped again before her.

"I know very little of needing a meeting. Because my reasons for disliking the idea are only the best of an imperfect brain, must they therefore be unsound? Then where are the perfect brains, that we should carry on with reason in the world at all? A pure flame, you know, may come from dirty straw. . . . The need is problematic, but I assert the dislike is instinctive, natural, and valid. This even on your own argument. No matter whether what I apprehend from such a meeting be here or there, isn't the natural response to *any* fear—escape? . . .

"You yourself are assuming a beautiful impersonality," he added. "I can't remember, though, hearing anything from you of a surrender of preferences. It may simply be that you have the gambler's pride, refusing to act, demanding to be acted for. Forgive me if the reading is wrong, and the word over-hard! Anyway, you seem unconsciously to have loaded the dice against us for your mother. I count on you still, gentlemen. Before you came, Ingrid, we had decided against to-morrow, and since your entering the room the spirit of unsettlement is abroad once more. You will stand aside, but nevertheless wish things in a certain way. . . . So I think I have the right to ask you this. As all the rest of us are to find our true account on Devil's Tor to-morrow evening—I because I *need* the occasion, and Mr. Saltfleet because it is a fitting feat for him, and Mr. Arsinal because it will be a pity if he fails to lick the pot clean—and because, besides, some other spirit of night inside us all is putting forth a stretching arm towards the Tor, to bring us to it . . . in view of such considerations, are you, Ingrid, to find *your* account in and at the same rendezvous? Are you——"

"I don't wish to go," she interrupted him.

"You are frightened, or merely disinclined?"

"I am unwilling."

"But then, why have you been talking all the other way? We fixed a thing, and it is as if you have been trying to unfix it. How is it to stand at last?"

"I can't help you, Peter. . . . I've always regarded it as my personal hill, so many quiet hours, private moods, sensations I couldn't communicate, I've had there. Any business on it—even this—would seem like a defilement . . . the troop of twentieth-century persons over that grave! . . . Then nothing, perhaps, could reconsecrate it for me, unless another tragedy. . . . I have promised mother that if she goes, I will; it is in your power to anticipate her—that is your affair, and I can't decide it for you. It may not matter. . . . That great rock leaping down the hillside, it never stopped till it had caught Hugh. What is to stop this fate but—someone else of us? You are trying to escape it: do you know its path?"

Peter was silenced. After an instant Ingrid turned to Arsinal, who, while she addressed him, rose in courtesy. Then Saltfleet, the last to remain sitting, also got to his feet.

"Mr. Arsinal . . . that interred one of the Tor—she was buried, so must have *seemed* to live, perhaps many years . . . but these apparitions are only for a minute or so. . . ."

"I know. Yet the inconsistency could so obviously be accounted for. Not to speak of what might still happen, at least it could not *yet* have happened in our time. These phantoms could in no case be more than prelude. The stones remain apart. . . ."

He continued: "It may indeed be that the fitting them together would—will—effect nothing new; that the first state is irrecoverably lost. That we cannot tell; but there is this too. Even were the inconsistency one of equal conditions, it need still show no inferiority of psychic faculty in us; but the reverse. For the life, or seeming life, of that ghost on earth should have been in the nature of a visitation to thick skulls and animal blood, demanding the persistent presence, whereas we must be supposed to be towards the spiritual. For us, it may be, the endurance in our midst of such an entity would be disruptive of our but comparatively recently erected earthly reason, forcing our instinct towards the light into new channels no longer reason, therefore unfitted to our earthly case. Thus the minute or so should provide us with all we need and *can*. The brutish lives of those others were to be more heavily moulded."

Ingrid's eyes looked away out of her sheet-white face, wondering. After a pause, she asked:

"The worship of the Mother, has it been good?"

"That we may not doubt." His voice grew quieter still. "For how could it be other than good? The marvellous liberating joy of purity—bodily, mental, and of the soul—it must present an incentive to right living and the restraint of evil passions, not less effective than the fears of humanity under the conception of a rigorous eternal justice. Pride, hypocrisy, pharisaism, intolerance—even hatred and cruelty—may and do nest under the harder, harsher creed. Blood enough, at least, has flowed. Purity, however, is a tender growth; it cannot subsist amongst the luxuriant, vicious weeds of the soul, but the ground must be cleared for it. I think it cannot be squared with *any* vices. Then was it ever practised? I have no doubt that innumerable populations of men, women, children, have in their day bent the knee before the

Mother, discovering in Her the source of their best. She was easy to be thought real. She is in all Nature."

"Nature, below its tenderness, is terrible."

"Accordingly, the Mother also has been conceived as terrible. And still, the wild, hunting life of the woods, the devastating storm, the eldritch, mocking mountain voices, they have not contradicted purity. That has been reserved for the works of man; but the chief of his works is arbitrary law; and the chief of his laws is that which claims jurisdiction beyond the tomb. There can be *no* law beyond the tomb; there can only be reunion. Purity meanwhile, however, is a partial reunion. . . . Understand me, when I talk of purity. I don't mean a little matter, but *my* purity—the purity I have in mind—is distinguished and aloof . . . metaphysical, of the stars . . . of the big spaces. . . ."

"I do understand you."

"These are modern notions, you may object; they cannot have been in the past. At least, they can have been latent in the past. The noblest of those worshippers have not been concerned solely with propitiatory sacrifices. The history of the creed's fortunes shows no such chronicle as the Christian crusading wars, wars of conversion, sect wars, political wars, inquisitions, burnings, torturings, excommunications, confiscations, and the like . . . no such constant and inevitable process as the Christian public professions of faith, differences in faith, then argument, insistence, anger, blood, destruction . . . but the religion of the Mother has evidently gone for other tokens of reverence. She has not been tribal, but universal; so could not need the testimony of numbers. In purity—that purity reaching even to the stars—was no personal merit, equipping one to act as persecutor, warrior, and judge; but a state of soul—a state introductory of heaven, not with impunity to be exchanged. . . ."

"If Christ has been unable to purify human nature," said Peter, "I fail to see how a woman-god should do it."

Arsinal paused.

"Christ!—always Christ! . . . And therefore, being so perpetually invoked, should He be more ancient and rooted than the tale goes. In fact, so many faiths, schools, traditions, predictions, philosophies, and risen floods of thought and feeling, have gone towards His making, that ever is He likely to remain the world's grand anomaly; unless a finer enlightenment shall hereafter come to prevail. . . .

"But His best was already in the Mother—that we may say at once. . . . And a proof of the assertion will appeal to you, Mr. Copping, an artist: His face has never been portrayed, because it could not be. The attempted paintings of the adult Christ—they have not contented anyone: lachrymose, cadaverous, *undivine*, they have been on a parity with His whole impossibility. For two genders have had to be reconciled within His person; and each has had to be absolute: the man and male god, the law-dispenser, stern, rigid, awful; but also the womanly spring of that love, compassion and purity, that only in the female nature seem to be original; in males, derived—an act of will, an effort. . . . This we feel. And so I say that that special spirituality of Christ, deemed new, was not rightfully His—whosoever He may have been, whencesoever come . . . but was first of all, in far greater strength and brightness, in Her whom we call the ancient Mother. . . ."

While Peter stood looking at him in unpleasant pondering, an invisible flurry, not of the air but somehow in or through it, seemed to cross the studio, causing all the four there involuntarily to stir, and shift their eyes; but nothing was moving, or different. Peter's surprised first conception was that it had been a bird outside flying across the window. Arsinal glanced to the door. Saltfleet fingered his chin, and was silent . . . they were all silent, however. Was it that the impression for everyone was so insignificant, so transient and unconnected, that it was not found of sufficient moment to mention?—or was no one, perhaps, caring to start this new superfluous wonder? . . . Ingrid appeared to shrink within herself, not looking towards the others; seemingly, not choosing to be informed if that sense-deceit had been hers alone or general. She closed her eyes once, while a vertical cleft of pain divided her brows. . . .

The silence became accepted. Its excuse was the natural conclusion of Arsinal's topic, the interval for the subsidence of his interrupting idea, before they might return to a clearing discussion of what was to be done. But each was knowing the others' quietness for a respite. That agitating trifle, nearly too shadowy to be presented in words—its truer strangeness for all was only dawning with its recession in time. It did not stand alone, to be called a fanciful no-thing, but surely had its congeners among their few or many other phantoms and fearful messages. . . . That some of those had broken through to full consciousness, while this had no more than been the waving of a veil, took not from its awe—an awe built up, besides, of all the rest; but enhanced by this. The right awe (all received it, for it was instinctive) consisted not in the focused spectacle, but in what lay behind and was acting. Very enormous to their imaginations began to appear the night-world's force, thus able to bend and sway the solid crust of the empire of day, as it were unreal smoke or fog! . . .

XXVIII

The Drag-Net

Quickly Saltfleet's mind had reverted to his last night's visitant at the inn. This perhaps should be a repetition—failed, because of more unfavourable conditions for the appearance. There were conflicting wills in the room, a confusion of persons; and it was daylight still, instead of that deep suggestive dusk; and no one was handling the stone, but it was in Arsinal's pocket. . . .

Above the Tor's stream that short time since, again, the wraith had been most perfect, because at home. The three cases (if this were one) were as if representing its merging into pure meaning at one end of the scale, its merging into nonentity at the other end, and the spectral middle. The same operative will was trying to get through. Here, in this place, there should be a thicker crust to be pierced.

But *who* the wraith was, the other Tor visions showed: his own of the morning, and what he was able to understand of Arsinal's and Copping's. She was from the sky. Her phenomenal earth-existence had been thousands upon thousands of years back, when men were beast-fighting savages. Strange if she had not been as a goddess! In truth, she could never have been anything half so elementary; but was always the terminal shape of a super-natural stream issuing from another sort of reality. . . .

So this stream was now again striving to enter what he viewed as the room; perhaps mainly prohibited by Copping's antagonism. . . . Particularly he was bewildered—with the bewil-derment of a resolute man unused to the state, and impatient of it—by that swift, savage, fancied turning of the phantom's eyes and face, at the extreme last of his afternoon overtaking *yonder*; even while she had been in the silent act of emptying the land-scape of her significance; so quite incongruous it had seemed with all that had gone before. Savage, yet not hostile; but more in the nature of the fierce incitement of an essence grand and dis-dainful enough to include fierceness as well.

For there Arsinal was right. Every important passion or feeling of the world should be a derivative of a higher thing of the same kind in the supermundane whole. Love, pity, sacrifice, etc., were such derivatives; but whereas in a male saviour, a Christ, the fiercer temper must be put under before the milder could rule, a supernal female essence must be conceived to include within the confines of her nature wrath, cruelty, passion, love, sacrifice, at once. There was no right inconsistency in it. What necessarily became a vice when incorporated in the self of an individual woman, could well remain an energy and sublime scourge in that terrific Unself, the great chastening Mother of spirits, men, and all Nature. In this sense, the savageness of such an Entity *was* love.

If man were no more than mite, crawling on the surface of an astronomical ball, then the answer to fear should be prayer; to corruption, regeneration by the grace of heaven, by means of the symbols, types, and agents of heaven; to the passions, a spiritual emasculation, instructed by the example of the long line of Christian eunuchs. Should he recognise himself, however, for an original soul, doomed for a few fleeting years in all time—what time stood for—to suffer the million degradations of the corporal condition: then those answers to baseness were another baseness; he was on the wrong road. For the salvation of a personality was the accepting that personality as a thing undisputed. Ten thousand mystics, sages, metaphysicians, might so have accepted it, and still personality was not the soul, but merely a bundle of earth-characters, stamped with the stamp of alien possession.

The soul was the highest; nothing was higher; therefore, to whom should it pray? Being elemental and above corruption, how could it be regenerated? Being compound of sublime passion, how could a factitious peace of heart assist or represent it? . . .

Accordingly, he must first of all break from his ignorant preconceptions of the world: the Christian myth that, in the divine, love and mildness were synonyms; and the universal superstition that the soul's function was to serve, fear, and imitate the divine, its source and spring. Here, in this big confusion and wonder advancing on him, and not him alone, with giant strides, a *passion* should be to be faced by passion: an attempted coercing of his equal soul by a miraculous manifestation, apparently of the divine, was to be stripped of its rapture and amazement, and examined, so stripped, for its accredited passionate message of eternity, that alone his own inmost spirit could receive as an authentic sign between peers. . . .

Nevertheless, how to account for that spectral shape of a woman, who had descended from the heavens, lived, died, and been buried; and now, after whole ages, could show herself abroad again? Either her sex was illusion, or she was but a secondary agent. For creation truly held many a token of female origin, yet the male marks were on it too: grandeur, force, vigour, boldness, lordship. Thus already Arsinal was imperfectly informed. But if, in fact, this tomb spirit could somehow be presentative of the All before sex, what meant her constant sex for every witness? . . .

A dark wave of exploit suddenly crossed him as he apprehended what now he must do in order to reach the apparition's *penetralia*, to uncover its mystic heart and errand. He stood stopped before the outer gate. Some miserable flaw of his psycho-physical manhood was knowing the phenomenal contact under that female form; beyond must be surprises. By *beyond* he meant, along a certain road: that of the bringing together of the two flints, in the fittest place. Thus it was essential that Arsinal should conduct his trial, on Devil's Tor; in *his* company. The adventure might be accomplished within the hour. This, indeed, since Copping's proposal to them, both must have intended; but only now the wonder of the experiment was opened out. . . .

For, till it was achieved, he no doubt might procure new hauntings by the medium of either stone alone, but these could only continue the simple spectacle—deceitful, idle. Among the torn and thunderous titan-heights of Asia no man knew better than himself, never had he worshipped undangerously with his eyes but he had felt the ardour to follow audaciously with his body that might be destroyed or broken—perhaps deserved no greater dignity. The yearning was sublimity, but on the upper snows and crests themselves the sublimity had always vanished, to be replaced by freedom. So sublimity should not represent a natural state of the soul, but be, as it were, its homesickness. This he applied: and fancied that the reuniting of the stones might—but how, he knew not—be fated to bring him the same emancipation. . . .

Mentally he set the impress of his fingers upon it for a decision—well he could recognise his own irrevocable decisions, from their attendant dark glow of triumph, with the rapid clearance of his brain from its preliminary vexations, thought-litter, and suspense. When, however, his constant awareness of this one removed woman in the room amongst men caused him again to remember her case, unsettlement once more began. The plan, indeed, was to avoid her risk, and she might doubt its adequacy and fear its refusal of fate, yet was not to forbid it; but a disquietude of his conscience predicted that the weird drama was not to swerve so abruptly from her upon the word of human command.

For she chiefly should be involved in everything, while this was to dispossess her of her rank, for her safety or their haste of greed. But if their paths were thus made to diverge, who could say whether she or they would come earliest to the catastrophe! Who was equipped: he, that perhaps merely looked to the sensation; or she, that was oppressed by these accidents and presentiments as by a horror of real life? His eternal nonchalance was rebuked by the contrast.

Nothing in the world, he had thought, was serious enough for seriousness, were not laughter worse; but *her* seriousness could belong to the spheres. His chastisement at the hands of the offended Demiurge was that he might barely appreciate from her present instance how, in that unphilosophic grim heaviness of opinion called seriousness in general, which was humanity's response to its living forest of illusions, the function itself could be quite apart and separate from its misuse; how, if the latter were nearly the most pitiable of the reactions of the original universal spirit shattered into individuals, the former, the function apart from its objects, could be the whole grand weight, density, mass, of the same spirit considered in its originality. For all the past gleams of greatness in the world had been born, not of a light scorn and mocking, but of brooding—of a sort of sick despair at what a man had seen, and his will to change it, or rise above it.

So this girl in the room should be despairing, though her misery were personal. No orthodox feminine end was in sight for her from these crowding distresses, nor had she a man's compensating temper of adventure, or cold blood to turn a resolute back upon it all, or affinity of pre-existent occupation to draw a profit from it; but she must marshal her resources to dare the whole psychic onset in pain and stupefaction, being unconscious of any folly in her own conduct to explain so otherwise unprovoked a benighting of her wits—of her tranquil common mental processes of a woman . . . she, scarcely more than child, tortured and blessed by a special sensitiveness that surely ought to be reserved for the discovering of new chambers in the great house of mysterious spiritual beauty; and now, instead, was sustaining the hammer-like shocks of an affair of the open supernatural, that should be well-fitted to strike down the human equivalent of oxen. . . . Therefore she had the right to seriousness. Therefore he, who probably had none, was subaltern in the case; yet was impudently proposing to order it! . . .

No seriousness? None?—no kind? That was to traduce himself, however. Of the right seriousness he had enough. For there was exactly one seriousness, one grimness of response to reality, for an earthbound man; namely, that of the chains of the body. Very clearly it showed itself in the circumstance that all other matters in the world gave place to birth and death. In the appearing and vanishing of the spark of life lay the contrast with eternity for even the dullest eyes. And this deep cognition of his false mortal state and its transience, he was never, or rarely, without. His lightness was his scorn of the affairs of such a shadow-penitentiary. . . .

It seemed to him of extreme urgency to know what other claim than her serious interest in it this girl was making—not to the conduct of the business, for its conduct she was declining—but to its peculiar bearing upon her personal case . . . yet that, too, he had no recollection of her having ever declared in so many words . . . perhaps, therefore, a claim by her existed nowhere except in his own expectation. It was equal. Her seriousness of answer to these strangenesses amounted not to a claim; and she was willing, for instance, to surrender to Arsinal his second prize—willing now to stand altogether aside. Yet all of them with her in this room knew, *knew*, that whatever was happening to-day, yesterday, before that in the week, or, in connection, in the diffused past, was proving to point, and always must have pointed, to *her*—to Ingrid Fleming—as surely as the wavering needle of a compass pointed throughout its violent oscillations to a fixed midway mark that could only be north. Thus Drapier's tragic end might be a north-east pointing, Arsinal's triumph might be a north-west, but to her magnetic north the next incidents were always returning, from this side and from that.

How came he by the certainty? For with its origin clear he could better understand the rest—what type of fatal sequence this was that, in stark fact, could choose for victimisation an unassuming girl wishing only to lead her quiet life with a man of her own station eminently equipped to give her quietness; while he (Saltfleet), and others rather too eager to snatch whatever glory or thrill might be in the lively assault on the earthliness of them all, were contemptuously being thrust back into second rank—yes! even Drapier—Drapier, as personally insignificant to the business in death as in the last days of his lifetime. . . . So whence sprang his certainty?

Was it the answer, that it was not her trifling degree of pain, her mere confusion, to the present, that could have brought the insight—not that, but another feeling within him, of the class of a foreboding, that such pain and bewilderment presented merely the penumbra of a darker shadowing on the way? . . . that she stood here on this floor an *inevitable*—a wretch of Design—insulated already from her fellows by her prime-marking at the hands of the unseen? Could *this* be his assurance of her spiritual predominance in the advancing glare from another world? . . . It was so!—it was so! And how hideously mean and small appeared all at once his scheme to prevent her dignity under fate, by that appropriation of the final experiment with Arsinal alone! . . . Never in all his life had he experienced anything like the groundless conviction of this appalling feeling towards one who, after all, was known to him only by her beauty and distinction of mind, and passing distress. . . .

Continuing very erect, he clasped his forehead with a tightened hand, and turned from the others. And as he did so, occurred to him what a marvellous store of cryptic truth should lie in the beginning chapters of Genesis. The forbidden trees of Eden: wanting them, it must have been a mere pleasure-park; having them, it became the picture and symbol of the ghostly universe. Eve, not eating of the fruit, must have remained the simple insipid female of her species; but the serpent, who surely was God disguised, persuaded her to her fiercer, higher heart, when instantly her immortal soul could know both itself and the horror of her unreal body. . . . Nor was the recorded following action of herself and Adam in contradiction.

Whosoever, therefore, should invite—nay, tempt—a woman not less than Eve to taste of a fruit of equal significance with that of the tree of good and evil knowledge—that one should be the instrument of a very fated, very inherent work . . . inherent within the prime ancient foundations of the world; the fate merely being its apparently casual startling and insulting of sanity in due season.

Nearly an axiom it was, that the veto of human sanity in great supernatural concerns *should* be insulted. Looking past health and wholesomeness, which were but negatives, one had to suppose that the illusory bodily life offered not a single positive value that was worth the coveting, as against the dimmest hints and reminders of the spiritual. Earth's castles and palaces were too truly of thin air; a paltry hundred years at most would blow them all away for a man; and it were well rather to crack one's brains in refusing the magic sham in its hour of greatest cloud-strength, than preserve those brains entire by keeping within the sham's internal laws, that were as the intellectual frame and principle.

The laws were many, and so cunningly devised that only the wisest could know them for what they were, appearing as they did more like the necessary conditions of possibility than fantastic rules sprung, God knew where from! for man's obeying. They pronounced such things as, that all reality for the mind was ultimately derived from the sense of touch; that nothing could enter into experience save what was related to past experience, though but distantly; that the infinity of gaping little "I's" must show as masses and flat surfaces, and that the monstrous imaginary life of these variegated collections must govern the world; and a hundred other *non sequiturs* as instinctive.

But outside those laws for human sanity only—outside the whole witchcraft and imposition shaped by, yet hiding, them, as the flesh of a body its skeleton—should rest the true existence, evoking another correspondence that was neither sanity nor insanity, but more akin to the latter; without, however, the cracks and evils necessarily attendant on any failure, even of loyalty to a sham. A correspondence passed over by worldlings . . . better known to a small minority of mystics, saints, musicians, children. . . .

While Peter, and Arsinal too, starting from premises approximately identical, were arriving by quite other roads within sight of the same conclusion.

An instinct of alikeness had drawn Peter's mind back to those sense-enchantments of his first day down: the shadowy funeral train coming across the face of the height over against Devil's Tor, that had for its focus of unreality that covered bier of a length to confound his imagination; a few hours later, the second peeping of his perceptions through a gap of madness, there by the garden gate at Whitestone, confirmed by Ingrid's parallel seizure, her nearly-finished queer fish of a cousin being again present, as he had been the first time; so that the material object in his hand *both* times was of necessity the deceit's immediate cause.

This that had just happened, then—though what had happened? Nothing had happened. . . . But it could be a shaft from the same quiver—its failure to intensify to a living phantasm was explainable. Some discord of persons was neutralising the influence, or (guessing the stone to be probably in Arsinal's pocket) Drapier had been the better medium, or the direct contact of the hand was an essential factor. He also remembered how last evening at the inn the self-same stone had passed from Saltfleet to Ingrid without other queerness than the clairaudient shock for her alone. . . . So there was no doubt a law, but he was unacquainted with it. These confederates, too, had talked of having seen something on Devil's Tor since lunch; by the same stone's agency of course. Saltfleet and Ingrid had shared an earlier psychic incident up there in the morning. Indubitably it was the flint. Accordingly, it had just been trying to act on its own account, through cloth; through a man who was a bad conductor. . . .

But the proof that this last flickering for his eyes had not been fancy was that the others too had turned to it, and now were standing, as he conceived, subdued and privately puzzled. A repugnance stopped him from asking her, but Ingrid should have seen more than he. It could not affect the case's fearfulness, if his interpretation were true. That lay, not in any ghostly picture, but in the conception of the breaking-through of his sensuous defences; even though the swaying wall between two worlds had not this time passed silently over him like a wave, abandoning him amazed in another magic place. . . .

He was impressed by the very insubstantiality of his momentary displacement of vision. So might a permanent new life be imagined to begin: not by spectacles. He thought that if he should retain his senses in the hour of death, his physical environment must come to daze him in just such a manner. The supernaturally wise eyes of so many of the dying should be due, not, as popularly supposed, to the anticipatory sight of heaven, but to a subsidence of that confusion to acceptance at last. He seemed to be aware of something of the same wisdom—of the same acceptance—in his own present eyes. . . .

When, however, the character of this inexpressible glimpse of nothing was become a certainty to his understanding, he discovered that he was already upon a new grandeur, to concern his art. More than that of the inspiration he would not acknowledge, until it should have passed through the cooling chamber of his spirit.

Should it be an authentic lighting of his landscape, pride and loneliness, as ever, were in readiness to spring up: the inevitable escorts of his spiritual audacities. Ingrid herself would then not be suffered to intrude her paralysing gladness within a case which barely *he*, in all the immaculateness of solitude, could apprehend. . . .

For these befallen wonders were as curiously uplifting him through their quietness of mode, unquietness of significance, as if they had been monuments carved with unknown characters of a people vanished; monuments sullen and alien in the modern daylight, after a sepulchre of a hundred centuries. Even this last failed flitting was like such a monument: as calm, archæan, and exalting. But an especial flavour distinguished *it*. It should have been an antique appearance, yet actually had been void; accordingly its ancientness, empty of shaped phantoms, could swell his imaginative soul as a real thing, not false.

The single wonders were uplifting him, while all of them together, associated—that sequence was as though *speaking* to him; inciting his will; the half of his existence which was yet to be. The emotion and the passion were apart. For his will, it was no affair of reiterated dim shinings and interferences across time, initiated by some force strange to humanity conveniently to be called psychic; but the signals were like a message being spelt out letter by letter; all the letters different; for four, five, and six persons . . . perhaps a different message for each recipient.

His own message he could not share. It belonged to his personality. But when, after a great while, his personality should have absorbed and transformed it, *then* a whole world might share it; according to the fashion in which the great messages of beauty were shared—by means, in the first place, of chosen representatives; at last, of hollow fame. . . .

Images started to his mind. Just as the archaic atmosphere of the single happenings somehow seemed to resemble for him the deepening glow of a sky after sunset, so this incitement of his active will by the succession of happenings was, rather, reminiscent of a bursting dawn out of the entire midnight sweep of shades . . . that, here, were the vast shapelessness and lurking instincts of years. . . . West-east! And so the whole sublimity was outside the cardinal points, and something new! . . . Next, his achievements and essays in art hitherto—they suddenly appeared to him hardly more than as a tuning-up of his soul that was an instrument, in readiness for the first tap of a supernatural baton. . . .

His depths stirred, as a tree begins to stir after a long halcyon calm; but because between a man and his depths can come no companion, Peter's sense of utter loneliness grew apace as an icy sickness that was a note of his agitation's chord. Were he alone in the room with Ingrid, still he could not find words to tell her what was passing in his being.

In this future she could have no part. . . . So that when really they should be alone together in a few minutes more, she would understand from his confused explanation only that he considered his pleasure; that his grudging solicitude for her welfare throughout had been but egoism, in that he had always intended to follow up these matters for his own curiosity and intellectual increase, could he, with it, find a way of denying her . . . his motive, not care for her weakness, but jealousy—jealousy of her lead and greater employment; finer sensibility. . . .

How was it possible for him to impart the indescribable new faint trembling of the waters of his inspirational well, which was as if a creature were at length emerging that all his life had lain covert? It was impossible, because his loneliness was an inherent character of everything he was feeling.

The tea-time conversation at Whitestone two days ago had foreshadowed it. His own talk of symbolism in art, and symbols; followed by old Colborne's recommendation of the Madonna as the eternal and inexhaustible symbol. Here now looked to be such a symbol—such a living personification of the All, brought to his very doorstep! For that dead one of the Tor, of whom Ingrid and Arsinal had spoken—whose phantom bier he himself had seen— who doubtless, in some unheard-of way, was working through the entirety of these miracles: *she*, surely, might be the old man's Madonna; *his* sought symbol of the universal frame. But then, with his own eyes, he must behold her. . . .

It was his ascended sense that, knowing her with his eyes, he would thereafter be transfigured as to all his higher faculties. Truly, his existence on earth might be scorched and blessed by her spectacle as by the point of a sword out of heaven: his art, that was his existence, might unfold, to men's amazement, in sign upon sign! . . .

The machinery to the end was dictated, or found itself, so easy it was. On Devil's Tor had been that ghost's conjuration, with Drapier's flint must she have been conjured; but were the belonging stones to kiss there, she might well be brought back nearly to body . . . . Terrible promised to be such a moment. Saltfleet, with his mind's eye, saw it clearly; and had taken measures in time to prevent Ingrid's foolhardiness, whether of apathy, obedience, or superstition: but seemed to fear nothing for himself; and as soon as this queer meeting of starts and silences was over, he should be on his road to the experiment with Arsinal. For it was highly improbable that, the power being in their hand, they could resist the temptation. Then *he* could accompany them. . . .

And therefore he, Peter, while all these others had been surfeiting with marvels, had till now held back in coldness, being instinctively aware that the meaning for him was different and his hour not yet come. Curiosity, expectation, ecstasy, the dark fascination of the magic—the compound of all or some of those for them: but, for him, his *clue*. Was there no distinction? . . .

Yet, as he stole another look at Ingrid, his thoughts still proceeded upwards, as in a rising spiral; and now he remembered how, if there should be a different meaning for each partaker in these wonders, a different message for each recipient, his own meaning and message could not be all-important, but only momentous to himself. Thus everything became enlarged. Not his single personal stimulus, but a practical constraining of all their real lives, was this mystic succession involving so many; each in another way. Perhaps, like his own art, Arsinal's learning was to be brought to significance; and Saltfleet's idle grimnesses . . . and Ingrid's unknown and unformed cloud-swaddled primeval second heart! So he always confronted his intuition again, that refused to be forgotten. . . .

The Tor assembly scheme was wiser than any knew—for Ingrid's wisdom regarding it should be unconscious; largely so. The reason she assigned for his needing the meeting perplexed him. It was necessary that her soul should be illustrated by an ordeal; but now he seemed to be wishing the ordeal for her sake. Appalling to him must be such an apparition on Devil's Tor as could present the universal symbol for his art; yet since it was required to fulfil his profoundest spiritual movings of a lifetime, it must needs also possess a virtue far outranking the appallingness.

Should Ingrid be there too, as awful probably must be her adventure: then was she to miss the reward? . . .

He could go with these others without her; and obtain what he wanted—or fail to. She could be denied the trial still: the future happiness of both of them would approve. Neither, in the end, *was* it demanded of him to expose a dreadfulness in her nature that, this spell of chaos being past, might well remain as secret and harmless as the far more furious beast in nearly every man. But if it was to deprive her of an unguessed height of fortune! . . .

Rapidly now it grew upon him that the lightning perhaps about to descend through their four existences in the room could not be for them, but for itself. According to their shapes would it be shaped, and that was all: *they* were but roads. One of such roads—delicate, destructible, of greatest purpose to him—he had thought to stop. He had overlooked that, together with the peril and horror for her, he might thereby be preventing some extraordinary filling of her soul: some inflowing completion as electric in beauty as his intuited symbol that should stand both for the creative and the created Whole. . . .

Arsinal, at the outset, had glanced towards the door.

The mistake was intellectually corrected at once, for no one else was looking that way, and really he had seen nothing. But his mind, that was accustomed to examine the smallest oddnesses for their hint, went on automatically groping about that fancied striking of his eyes. It could have no bearing on things, yet the colourless subconscious teasing persisted; and so he stood there, silent and musing.

An idea broke suddenly from his pensiveness. Drapier's flint in his pocket must somehow have been responsible for . . . this rather more than imagined jolting of his sight, if it were so. . . .

The idea had come of itself. The flint had not in any way made itself remembered; it was passing no sensible weird current through him. . . . And the very spontaneity of the inspiration seemed to give it more weight. For had it been suggested by a sensation, he could have called the shadowy episode *preternatural*; but having been physically and mentally unsuggested, it should be, if anything, *supernatural*. The distinction was clear in his intelligence. The preternatural could be the name for any strong strange quality of the world; whereas the supernatural was essentially extramundane, extramural—something acting from outside the walls of humanity and humanity's molecular, atomic and ethereal *jinn* of ring or lamp.

Thus here could be one more psychic case.

His heart became uneasy, while he recalled his confounding at the foot of the Tor . . . and next, the overcomings of these other three in the room with him. Doubtless, either of the flints had always played its part.

Then they—the flints—besides being constantly joined to the appearance, must also represent its possibility. They were the cause of the appearance: though not the cause of what lay behind the appearance—the *noumenon*; the thing itself.

He must give his reasoning a sharper edge. These appearances, they were occult: for if they were not that, then they were of the class of hypnotic dreams; but a criterion in him pronounced them occult. And these mineral fragments, once a whole—they, it was certain, were from astronomical space. Internally, too, they spoke of a plane different. But the word *occult*, as he used it, signified the *acting directly* upon the spirit of an unknown force; the straight impinging on the spirit without the intermediary of materiality; and materiality, of necessity, included every physical activity the most refined, the most impalpable, even as far as telepathy, the dream life, and all the processes of the invisible excitants and incitants, bringing mood, state, emotive disposition—the whole tree of daily existence. The *occult* was everything beyond that; everything *not* that. A power, sign, or sense, communicated directly to the spirit; passed then by the spirit to the eyes or ears or touch; and by those senses back again to the lower understanding brain. . . .

Yet why *now*, if these appearances were occult, should they be needing the agency of material stones? For however weird and associated with weirdnesses might be the flints, they still possessed gravity, cohesion, reflected colour, and the like: basically they belonged to the material universe. . . . Or was such a base unreal? Were they too occult—over thousands of years? . . . Or half-occult! Something was present, but not the stones. Something was lying in another spatial dimension; something with extraordinary properties of mental compulsion: but the three dimensions of earth were too rudimentary to show it as it was, and so one could see no more than the broken halves of a worn pebble, and a sort of distant magic in them; and all the time might be looking at shadows, and touching emptiness. But those shadows and that emptiness would only be words of earth. The true substantiality should be there, to disclose itself as it might, in hieroglyphic meaning; in progressive action. . . .

Beneath this startling supposition, he doubted no longer if the astonishing of his sight, that had seemed to mark the beginning of their long silence, had been on account of what he had thought (and still could not but go on thinking) a *thing*—solid, resting lump-like in the pocket of his coat. That lump being an immaterial shadow, and that shadow being a strange force acting from another place, too surely would he be upon the very verge of the realm of all manner of subversions and phantasms. Like a great flood of . . . *fourthness*, a whole other world was being invited in this seeming room by the ghost he had ignorantly appropriated. Barely, the grossness of his body protected him. . . .

He calmed himself. So now the hour had arrived when his worth should be put to proof; when his ancient election by the divine should be justified. For his labour of many men in one throughout a number of years, his refusal of women and pleasures, his loyalty to the image of that immortal visitant by night: it all mounted not an inch towards the miracle of favour; the long debt was still unpaid. Sublimity could be repaid only with sublimity. Heavenly sublimity was like a violent rent in the noisome fogs of life, affording an unforgettable narrow blinding of heaven; but man's sublimity was not apart from tragedy and agony. *They* could repay his debt.

Thus quickly he was knowing what all his life he had chosen not to know; his vanity coming between. For in his born egoism, which he had allowed to grow up with him like a weed, he had never doubted but that he was fit to receive the messages and perform the will of the Unseen . . . he, without preparation by pain; untried; effeminate with contentment. The Unseen!—though he had seen it. He had seen that glimpse of it that should perhaps be the least possible. Never had it been repeated. He was to be visited by the godhead: no step of excruciation towards it had he designed at any time to take.

So small, mean and shrunken all at once he seemed to himself, that he pictured a devil, who should be purely intellectual—without vice, without cruelty, emotionless, set only and always upon his impersonal work: and if Heaven should appear to such a one, bidding him serve It, he too would obey, and doubt nothing of his qualifications! And the qualifications he would have; but they would be those of an implement; there would have been no favour, so there would be no debt. Was it really thus with himself? Then his labour was finished, since without the high wonder of it all he could not go on. . . .

That seen glimpse of the Unseen that had never been repeated!—but hadn't it been repeated this very day? . . . Yes; but as the *echo* of a sound; as the *picture* of a spirit. She had not come to him: he had seen Her from afar, come to others.

Perhaps the debt was still to be paid, by one terrible moment. He must not fail in it: he thought he would not. Supposing it to be so, what should be expected of him would not be, surely, the common fortitude and courage of a simple man, but . . . the tortured rising of every part of his nature, to meet . . . even bodily dissolution. Another had died yesterday.

For this, during so many years, he had hunted down his brace of phantom stones as though they had been solid; and one seemed to repose deceitfully in a pouch of his illusory earth-garments, the other was said to await him on an infinitesimal point of all imaginary space—out yonder on the Tor. But their phantomhood being known at last, all else was curiously changed to phantoms for him: the miraculous life had started.

And so it was true in its entirety—his whole quest, with every circumstance, the most insignificant as the most fantastic. Meaning and reality—emblematic reality—were throughout. Those prophecies of the ancient East could not be the one thing false. . . .

With a quick sigh, he looked round at Ingrid. She was not seeing him. . . . This deeply troubled girl!—she, too, was as if half destroyed, while her part continued as impenetrable as ever. Yet, humanly, her future was planned for her and unalterable: no place was in it for a strange man; by her existing affections she was defended against mystic capture. . . . He did not know that his features were rigid like a mask. . . .

Then for an instant two incompatible ideas seemed to merge in a new possibility . . . but no!—immediately again he saw the fancy to be fallacious. Never like the famous-infamous Delphic responses to puissant and moneyed inquirers could those predictions have been ambiguously phrased of set purpose. This sacredness could not pollute itself by that half-lying. A man and a woman were to be joined: therefore, before the prodigy they must be apart—strange to each other. Only by casuistry could the *fatum* be made to point to persons already affianced: who had needed for that degree of joining no interposition of ghostly flints. Indeed, his travail in the world had not been for Copping's sake! . . .

Oh, why must he follow in Saltfleet's wake by returning and returning to *her*! The district's landmarking hill, dedicated to a fiend, where manifestly now these wraith-stones were meant to re-meet after their doom of years perhaps as apparitional—it was accessible to all, and women were not rare. Neither, if she went, would it be alone—the single representative of her sex; but it would be in the company of her mother, who also was a woman.

Truly, it was an enormous respect he was paying to this child, who, with so very few weapons, was overcoming them all! Admitted that she was young, lovely, helpless . . . quiet and proud . . . need her stunned state be other than her very natural reply to the successive strokes of a business accidentally come upon her by her relationship to Drapier, the nearness of her home

to Devil's Tor? . . . No, he feared her, too. And because of herself;
not her fortuitous, if germane, rank in these affairs. A height in
her was loftier than any height in him—so that he was shrinking
from her: nearly as the unclean from the clean, or the brown-
skinned from the fair. It was not her quite surpassing beauty. . . .

But Saltfleet had maligned him. Always he had studiously
held back from that unimaginable picture of a mystic marriage.
Pride he possessed, or his career had been less lonely: he could
not willingly consent to the advancement of another man over his
head in a charge appropriated to him by the celestial. But he was
of a piece. Pride, always a modern virtue or vice, he had; but
monstrousness, an antique character, he had not. Never had his
faculty of image-forming cared to anticipate the scenic happening
of so frightful, so barbaric and satyr-like a case. Doubtless his
nervous modern hypersensibility was towards the feminine:
distasteful he found such an insane gloating. . . .

But altogether he was baffled by Saltfleet. He should be in-
fatuated, yet apparently was not. Since her entry into the room,
his manner towards this girl had retained its quiet control. His
obvious honouring of her seemed less like the homage of sex than
a troubled approval of some high quality in her soul. There were
no lingering intent regards, no stolen glances of a kind to mean
one thing only, no unnatural humilities, for the involuntary revelation of his illicit interest. . . . It was impossible he should be
fascinated by her physique. Yet out of his course she had dragged
him. Within a couple of days he had reconsidered his friendship,
withdrawn his alliance; in every way was acting eccentrically. . . .

Now Arsinal, with ghostliness all around him—upon the Tor,
and in this room, and on his very person—dared to contemplate
again that suggestion which during all their months in common
never once had occurred to him; but only to-day, when, with the
recollection of the dread splendour of his night, fire and pale
spirit vision still confusing his eyes beside the stream, he had said
to Saltfleet, yet so introspectively that he was unsure if the words
had been heard to be understood, *"You may be the man, after
all! . . ."* The fancy had faded since: but now it was come back

with the first new psychic wonder, and he was quieted by the return as by an inward shock.

For had there been the signs of a weak admiration between these two—Saltfleet and the girl—his mind, contemptuous of such a drifting together, so ignoble and unseasonable, could not be thus continuing to dwell upon the consequent defection as though a treachery. The absolute sin against friendship was not enormous. His colleague's mistakes and offences since arrival here were under fate, appearing indispensable at last: the result discharged his part in them. Nor had the intimacy ever risen quite to affectionateness, that his will to disservice (the disservice itself being resolved to its reverse) should wrench an emotional chord, humble a secret vanity. Nor was his decamping so late to represent an injury: there was little more to do, and that he (Arsinal) could do alone.

So his anger for the apostasy signified a deeper stab. . . . This man had been invited to service. The invitation he had accepted, the service he had professed, and in part fulfilled. But now suddenly, without declaration of war, he was transferring his allegiance to . . . *That* directly, which hitherto had employed them both . . . transferring it at once and unhesitatingly: with such a simple quietude that the notification was not intended to have been made to himself; only by the inevitable discovery of his acts. . . . Yet without a power in Saltfleet, this will was still nothing. He would perhaps have found himself ignoring it.

Thus his anger was on account of a challenge so swift; so formidable and bewildering. Within these hours Saltfleet had picked up some weapon, wherewith to fight a way to the predominant comprehension and last fruit of this ingliding tree of Night, throwing images and terrors before it. Magic should be such shadows cast by blackness on to the brightness of day! . . . A tree, a growth, of Night: merely to *know* which, without behaviour, should bring more fame to the soul than feats for human worship. . . . The weapon was the woman, here, however. . . .

Then for himself she should be as necromantic. Had he come a day too late upon her? The crudely-expressed thought could be called almost untrue, its core of truth was so much more mystical. *Too late*—therefore losing her: but how could a woman be lost to a man, whose beauty and spirit of love were perhaps for her defence; whose sex was . . . symbolic? To stop before her beauty of form, her music of voice, her very inward person and nature, was to be arrested by her womanhood. To pass through these to the . . . *beyond*, was to see her not as a woman, but as a sign, a door: neither to be lost nor won. For priority in that passage should lie outside time: "a day too late" could have no meaning. The mystical core of truth in his thought, however, seemed to consist in whether the mischance of his lateness in knowing her could be a prefiguration of his supernatural exclusion. . . .

Scarcely he knew how her sex could be interpreted as symbolic . . . yet, somehow, that "one bed" of the prophecy might itself be mystical. Back through all written history, and long ages before, *Her* phantasmal corpse had sought a seeming last bed beneath the top of Devil's Tor, that then had borne another name: and such might be the reference. If this girl, this woman, were symbolical of that mysterious living-on of an ancient dead One; if in that most real sense she were herself semblance only: *thus*, it might be, the miracle without animality could occur. . . .

Accordingly, his anger with Saltfleet—an anger debasing itself with the rough tongue of common jealousy—was on account of this woman. It appeared from another significance; he thought it did. The very quietness of his renewed shock for Saltfleet's abrupt emergence to individuality, surely it was because it was no true shock. His recesses had been lighted by the knowledge of that emergence ever since his friend's first eccentricities were joined in one conversation to his earliest reference to a strange and noble girl in the background. *Then* had sunk into his unsleeping wiser soul how the man had strode swiftly forward. The after-shocks for his consciousness, anticipated within, held no longer the initiatory terror that had found indirect other ways up. The threat to the whole spiritual scaffold of his life was staled.

Now was he ashamed of his so many vulgar and absurd fancies of the day, bearing on the two. How could it ever have been a shaft of eroticism so quickly, when Saltfleet, temperamentally cold to women, was without the requisite speed of eye and imagination, that came from habit: when *she* went preoccupied of heart? But an alien spirit was irresistibly drawing and troubling his associate, through this woman's immaterial person.

In the grossest fashion had he explained to himself that startling deflection for a character so essentially direct and forcible as his friend's. He had seen in it only such a sex ineptitude. Thence had sprung his false translation of an unearthlier emotion into terms of anger. For being assumed from sex, from pleasure, Saltfleet's jettison of his duties towards himself had appeared the detestable treason of a frivolous hollow nature, too long masquerading under a severe exterior.

The explanation was wrong: therefore, the anger. The explanation was wrong, because it was so manifest now that Saltfleet had become fast set in sternness, attending not at all to the woman's femininity. . . .

Nevertheless his own unconscious wisdom from the first concerning this man's personal advance to destiny, just as surely as it must have been accompanied and heightened by some subterranean emotion at least as vivid as anger (for it had been a shock at that deep level), so its derivative of duller surface-shock had been preceded by his anger, that was a derivative of that secret emotion, coming to consciousness more quickly, because an unorganised shapeless feeling should be finer and quicker than any thought. But anger the deeper feeling could not have been, since anger was unsustainable without the fastening upon a responsible cause. Thus a child, rather than forego its anger for a hurt, would retaliate on an inanimate post or table. A man's under-surface mine of intuitions, so much more delicate of wisdom as it was than the coarser upper working brain, could not in such an infantine way set up its bogeys in order to knock them down again. Saltfleet, acting in all these matters automatically, began to loom a figure of menace for his eyes: *underneath*, the menace might be showing as separate; lighting the man as well with its ghastly glare. Arsinal felt it was probably so.

These other supplanting shapes, then—this man in his new aspect, and this woman: seeming to betoken the rise of another curtain in so fearful a drama of the rent earthly envelope, for the displaying of another scene from which he himself should be at last absent . . . the picture's fancy might be both true and false. It need not be as a drama, exhibiting ranks and importances; relentlessly clearing the stage for the significant glory of the at one time unlikeliest: but rather, as an unrolling scroll of history, where phenomenal shapes should everlastingly appear and disappear, for the sake of *none* of whom would the tale be. . . .

Standing on this floor, in increasing dismay, from moment to moment expecting the hateful interruption of a voice, he knew himself incapable of consecutive thought, and lost his hold: but another image immediately came to him, that somehow struck him as very noteworthy and peculiar. All these reflections that had flitted through his head since the silence of the room had fallen, they were extraordinarily like those white vapour-clouds incessantly passing across the star-sprinkled black sky of the flint surface. He fancied that the similitude might be not fortuitous, but intended. Then these last thinkings of his should have been as real clouds; throwing no light on a permanence behind them, but, rather, concealing that permanence from him.

His debt was to be repaid, for instance. His uninstructed intellect could not conceive the manner of payment. But should he tear away his intellect with all its motions, in order to gaze upon the sky of reality beneath it . . . would not that be—*madness*? Could the state and resolutions of madness, then, conduct him to what he had to do? . . .

He kept glancing now at Ingrid. He found it just as remarkable how, during the last minutes, the entire drift of his ideas should imperceptibly have set in towards her. And truly, her simple existence having the power so (without her effort) to have transformed an inessential man, there should be in her this strong magic for the acting upon men and ideas. That her will seemed quite broken, must be a necessary part of all. It brought her away from women, like a fated one. For there was a difference between men and women in outlook. Men might see the world purely as object, but women must see it as subject-object: they themselves were the half of what they saw. Now, to contradict the law, this stricken girl was cast into so low a pit of apathy that she too should be forgetting her sex, her self, in . . . discovering herself, perhaps, still within a world. So, the female subjectiveness being the same with life itself, as some asserted, *she* should be near dead.

Out of her instinctive ordinary womanhood knowing no self-struggles, doubtless, had she within these few days slipped, wondering and wondering, into her unsexing dream. Impossible was it for him to conceive how she might ever return to her old naturalness. Such marks in her too easily-torn life must be ineffaceable.

She was so high, in her despair . . . so proudly shrinking from assistance; so content mutely to suffer: what could be upholding her? But the force that moved through her should be upholding her. Thus actually she was to be regarded as a phantom in the room. Her sex life had nearly vanished, she was hardly still a woman; her sustaining animation was one with the magnetic stream passing by way of her, between that invisible fount of all these extraordinarinesses and the persons susceptible to its hither end in time and space. If this stream failed her, she must no doubt suddenly collapse. Therefore her life was no longer anything in itself, but symbolic: stationary or falling with that of which it was the symbol. . . .

Through her window a spectral gleam was shining; and they three crass men had joined to shutter the window: but the shining which had found that window was over-strong for human obstruction: the ignorant proposal should be as foolish as the design to arrest the swing of a great sea tide. . . .

Accordingly had each in the studio with Ingrid (privately revolving his fancies, while guessing nothing of the fancies of the others, during the continuance of that queerest of long silences which a dubious phenomenon had begun and its mysteriousness for all their minds prolonged) come by a different strange road to something very like the forgetting of the girl's physical personality, in his surrender to her psychical place. And all their interminable talk for an hour or more past (each at last in his own way recognised) had been futile, even though their decision against to-morrow's Tor assembly should hold because of the obstinacy of a majority. An affair was inexorably shaping itself like the falling into place of plates of iron. Truly it was a moment of complication, when three or four moved in translating dreams, and each man believed that he alone was in one.

But Ingrid's thoughts were unimaginable. In the fading light she looked an ash-faced figure, clad in black; a still pillar of waiting tragedy. She saw nobody. She stood away from the others, sideways to them, and stared straight forward, as if heroically relaxed to whatever new shocks should befall her.

They perceived how, without any muscular hardening of her features or grimming of her eyes, she assumed under their regard the likeness of one still a woman, but a woman indescribably remote from all that in the world womanhood stood for; immeasurably unidentifiable with the frivolities, softnesses, universal modes of feeling, of women . . . just as though her sex, the half of humanity and all life—the clean-cut half—were itself, by this phenomenal illustration, suddenly demonstrated to be divisible into sub-sexes or halves: the feminine, and the *thing of sacrifice*; the nameless thing, pushing through the feminine in the hour of greatest need. . . . So with Ingrid too the feminine seemed to have dropped away like a cloak let fall. . . . Difficult was it for those seeing the case, to apprehend it.

They witnessed also how the paleness of her face appeared to grow whiter and brighter, until at length it shone out in the manner of a moonish lamp, while the dusk had come quickly on. But two of the three men watching knew to what direction that radiance should point, and the intuition of the third supplied his ignorance.

Thus they stood; and not a sound was uttered or a movement made before the room was lighter again; Ingrid's paleness as dull and ashy as at first. Her expression had never varied. If this contradictory change of her colour had been sign, then must it have been for the information of those seeing it, each thinking himself alone in the wonder. Clearly it had not been the outward manifestation of any internal sign to Ingrid, whose face could remain so unstartled.

XXIX

Peter's Surrender

Peter wished to end the silence: but, distrusting his control, he first lit a cigarette, to veil himself in its blue-white wreaths of smoke through which he looked away. Afterwards he said:

"Something must be done. We can't stand here all the evening like sculptures. This long wait can mean only one thing for every-body. . . ."

Saltfleet regarded him.

"What?"

"Why, perhaps you have been too hasty in improving on the idea of a meeting, and I too emphatic in inveighing against it. I have been reconsidering. . . . Miss Fleming's words were calcu-lated to a delayed effect . . . an unknowable influence as well should be in the room. I shall stand back."

"You are now suddenly agreeable again to Mrs. Fleming's arrangement?"

"I stand out of it."

"Still, if you do only half want it, after so vehemently protest-ing against its notion, I think we ought to be told why."

Another smoke-cloud floated and twisted between them, while Ingrid and Arsinal continued mute, apparently unheedful of the sprung-up dialogue.

"To speak the truth," said Peter, "my head at this moment is such a hell-pot of flights and emotions in dispersion, that I prefer to hold my tongue altogether, leaving Mrs. Fleming's direct answering to you.”

“Your indirect responsibility will be the same.”

“I feel this: that in handing the business to you, I hand it to fate.”

Saltfleet went on looking at him queerly:

“But then, if we see no reason to change our minds, the stone will be brought down to-day: a plain conclusion that hardly needs the invocation of a mystic fate.”

“Probably. Nevertheless you have had an offer and must reply to it: and I intend neither to help nor hinder you any more.”

“A greater candour in you would be our best help, Mr. Copping.”

Peter hesitated, drew at his cigarette, and was silent. Then:

“A man may find himself at a parting of roads, without known direction or a soul wiser than himself to consult. It should be a situation where the equivalent of the spin of a coin is as good an expedient as any other.”

“A counsel of impotence indeed!”

“You are as undecided, I judge. . . . Believe me, it really may not matter.”

Saltfleet shrugged.

“Let me hear you, Arsinal.”

Arsinal at that came into the talk: but his voice struck the others as curiously lowered and altered.

“I shall confess that I too feel the necessity of reviewing Mrs. Fleming’s proposal—in itself so inexplicable. Mr. Copping is in open doubt about it; you, Saltfleet, are too full of questions not to be at least hesitant; and I—I think I must be chiefly amazed at our earlier precipitancy. . . . Almost it is as if a sun had come into the sky, to twist our thoughts in its direction. The triple coincidence alone is past any ordinary explanation. Miss Fleming’s persuasions for each of us have perhaps borne fruit, but the case transcends that. Let us have the courage of our illumination, and dare in very great calmness to believe that within the last minutes we have been—*visited*. . . .

“Your parting of roads, Mr. Copping: you cannot mean that

you are pulled between yourself and another; but, rather, that that other's truer advantage hides itself from you. Neither shall I mention a name, nor shall I pretend ignorance. If she attends this meeting on the Tor, you see unpleasantnesses for her, and a possible danger: but if she remains away . . . you feel perhaps, that you will be depriving the business of a principal actor . . . you may even fear to incur some wrath—of the spirit governing. . . . So, since you know not what to do, you will do nothing: and I am willing. Yet I aver that you do know beforehand what my choice must be; that your neutrality accordingly is impure; and that your *responsibility*, accordingly, is equal with mine—with ours. . . ."

"Mr. Copping has no choice and no responsibility." . . . Ingrid's inscrutable, weary eyes rested on Arsinal from out of her face of endurance. But Peter let drop his cigarette, and crushed it with a heel.

"Why, if they want to involve me in your meeting, Ingrid, in God's name let them! If the general supernatural dictation is necessary to their assurance of your presence at it, let them have this dictation, and let each of us be cognisant of what the rest are thinking and feeling! I can arrange for you; they cannot: that is what Mr. Arsinal means."

"But I mean that I will attend no meeting for which you have a responsibility."

She had begun unconsciously to approach him; but stopped. Her eyes sought Arsinal again.

"Mr. Arsinal, I tried to disguise it, but your first ignoring of my mother's plan mystified me. You had a right to disdain it, it is so fantastic and dark, and you could not know her natural simplicity of good sense. But I, who do know her, understood that it never could have sprung from her own inspiration. So when Mr. Copping quietly announced that the plan was refused in favour of a better, all my thoughts seemed to die in my head. . . . Then I remembered a story in one of the northern sagas: of a timber log carved with magic runes, that makes its way across the sea, against tide and current. Could not it be the same with this meeting of my mother's? I waited to learn: now it is appearing I was right. A magic has worked. . . ."

"The statement is instructive, Miss Fleming; for I could not at all grasp the underlying idea of your mother's proposition before. Her mind being strange to me, I could not tell if the suggestion for a postponed and somewhat theatrical settlement were characteristic or uncharacteristic. Now that I am told it should be outside her habit, the fatality extends."

"I hadn't finished. I was going to add that it is my queer intuition of the meeting's certainty that has been stopping me from supporting my mother. I could so conclusively have supported her. I could simply have forbidden Mr. Saltfleet to remove the stone. . . . It was not to depend on me. It was like a wonderful and terrible play going on, that I have not been allowed to interrupt. . . . Considering these things, how could you, Peter, of all people, be called to account for a meeting to-morrow?"

"Yes, I fancy I see what you are arriving at."

"I am not dramatising it, I am only trying to say it as shortly as possible. The lives of some of us may be abruptly ended or fearfully transformed to-morrow on the Tor. I feel I might not come down as I should go up. A deeper darkness seems moving against me all the time . . . just like the temple of Nyx I have sometimes imagined: only this is moving to surround me, not I into it. When light returns and dreary normalness begins again—as it always must—if I am still alive indeed . . . I think my existence to the present may be . . . *gone.* How could you—supposing that you escape, as, of all of us, you and mother might, Peter—but how could you sustain that everlasting mountain of self-reproach? . . . Hugh was killed yesterday. His death, I say, was unpreventable. But if anyone had loved Hugh overmuch and had innocently contributed to his being on the Tor, could she ever forgive herself his death?"

"You are not to die," objected Peter suddenly.

"It hardly concerns the argument, what is to happen to me. If I am anyhow subjected while you go free, a dreadful self-poison must begin in you to-morrow night that may last with life itself and bring your art to nothing. So this must be settled first."

"You should have opposed us at once. To hold your hand as you did was rather too delicate and cunning a manoeuvre to lie in your nature."

"I conceive it thus," interposed Saltfleet. "Miss Fleming's mind has been double. Its conscious part has been very weary, humble, and aloof, desiring not to intervene: but, underneath, it was in a manner aware that to-morrow evening's assembly was already invisibly established in futurity; and that part of her mind has been spinning out the time, to get the thing arranged while we should be here together. . . . This may be the actual truth. Yet we may have been listening less to an exposition of the truth than to—a sacrifice."

"What sacrifice?" demanded Peter.

"Of her apathy. And if you cannot apprehend, Mr. Copping, how, the will in a matter once being believed permanently stilled, its unexpected sharp resuscitation may represent the acceptance of sordidness and horror again—why then, I fear that Miss Fleming's return to activity will have proved too high for you. . . ."

Ingrid faced Arsinal, who, very pale, put his arms behind his back in waiting. She said:

"If there is any responsibility at all in this room, Mr. Copping is sharing it, and I will not come to a meeting."

"We shall none of us have been able to help a meeting."

"Then I will speak to you afterwards, Peter." . . . She came back to Arsinal. "You will leave the stone meanwhile?"

"Yes, I promise that."

"And the time you know?"

"We were told nine."

Saltfleet was silent.

"And you . . . ?" Peter asked him suddenly.

"Yes, I am personally willing. . . ." He paused; then went on with a marked reluctance: "But I cannot let Miss Fleming's attitude pass without a warning—a remonstrance—what you like. . . ." He looked at Ingrid. "At this last of our conference, Miss Fleming, you are become so spiritually formidable to me—

but I will not say on what account—that I could only seek the deeper truth of whatever you should choose to assert: and still, I *would* seek that truth. I would seek it in my own way; and perhaps that way might have little ostensible connection with your words; and perhaps the underground connection, discovered by my instinct, might be the more real. . . .

"The absolute value to us of happiness I do not know, but I am not without experience of the world, and I have found this: that while some persons are most benefited by happiness, others improve, rather, under one form or another of suffering; but those who react most to the happiness seem to be the softer and ignobler class of persons. Happiness, besides, is good for a particular case, but the sea waits always to sweep in; pain cannot be kept out of our lives. In erecting a dam against a misery, we are doing doubtless a very instinctive and necessary work, but we must not imagine that happiness is any the more to be ours. . . . Therefore, the better gift to Mr. Copping, instead of this assurance of his peace of mind to come, which neither your action nor his acceptance can translate into a permanent general condition for him . . . I repeat, the better gift would be the indestructible recollection that in a great crisis of his life he conducted himself greatly. . . ."

"Now you have rebuked me!" said Ingrid, with a flitting faint smile. "You know, however, that I could not speak of this to you, or before you."

"Arsinal and I are immediately to be off, to leave you two alone."

Peter was staring at his own feet, and frowning. He glanced up to ask Saltfleet pointedly:

"What is your disturbing interest in my future well-being?"

"I saw how it went with Miss Fleming on the Tor this morning. These transcendental changes may hardly be endured without a following confusion in all the lower faculties: accordingly, she may easily be in want of a human adviser."

"A transcendental change?"

"I judged that you were nearly at your limit." He spoke to Ingrid; who answered him:

"Straight roads are the rarest, and before the limit is reached, another time, a quite different turn may be given to everything."

"It should have been like an inpouring."

"I could not wish to be filled only, in the manner of the saints, though the world should have my spillings. To come too soon there—to heaven, I mean—is certainly to come by the wrong way. The right way is the thwarting of instincts, a sunless mind, an evil conscience . . . dishonour, contumely, and the like. . . . The unfortunate know things that have the stamp of *first lessons*. If the radiance of another world is to kill, in filling, me, I almost hope it may. . . ."

"You want distress?" asked Saltfleet.

"It seems to be the one grandeur we can grasp."

"I cannot clearly see how far you are speaking from new insight, how far from race. Fineness, daring, giving; instead of the current virtues of getting and holding: the substitution may just as well be the distillation of ancestry."

"I think that ancientness is in many men and women that one here and there may be equipped with special qualities for certain deeds."

Saltfleet said no more. Then Ingrid's face relaxed to nerveless-ness again, as if her strength for talking were suddenly run out. But a moment afterwards she re-knit her brows to their previous half-sternness.

"It is getting late, and you were to go. But tell me first . . . is it that you are more *concerned* in these events than other persons? . . ."

"In the different senses that *you* are concerned, and Mr. Arsin-al, and Mr. Copping . . . and even Drapier *was* . . . no, I do not seem to be concerned at all. I should be the one outsider. . . . And still undoubtedly I must be, and am, concerned. . . . However, it is to-day we are putting our questions, and not till to-morrow will they be answered. I am unsure whether it is because I am more concerned, or less, that I am wishing you well, Miss Fleming; but I would have helped you through a time that must be considered perilous, if I could. . . ."

Ingrid gazed at him silently, clasping her forehead as in trouble and confusion. He bowed to her, and left the room. Arsinal, with a grave civility to the unheeding girl, followed him.

Thus Peter and Ingrid were left standing alone.

It was felt between them that neither was she to stay, and so he did not desire her to sit. But with an odd abstracted yet nervous playing of his eyes on and off her face, he waited for the slamming of the front door, then began at once what he had to say.

"Ingrid, the girl I spoke with in the garden two days ago has disappeared, and here in her place, talking to me, is an apparition. For that you are not to blame, but the consciousness annihilates my every opening: I have twenty explanations to demand, and I cannot demand them of a ghost. But what did Saltfleet mean before?"

"About my better gift to you?"

Peter nodded.

"I think he meant, Peter, that passive submission to . . . a change . . . is too low and negative a state for a man whose life is to achieve something . . . that an active surrender, rather, should help him to power, and be an undying source of power. So that I ought not to assist you to the feebler state, but to the fiercer and self-scorning and more vivid."

"To approximate to *his* nature, doubtless! Yet how may I surrender that which I no longer hold in keeping?"

"Until I am taken from you, I have not left you."

"But these are words, and I say that you have left me."

She remaining quiet, he added:

"Or unless Saltfleet thought so, why should he regard the precipitation of a doubtful disaster as my most helpful plan?"

"He is ignorant, fallible, as we all are. He cannot be understanding our relations. I haven't left you—of my will I couldn't leave you . . . but if you are able to look forward underneath tomorrow—if you can see something else there, Peter—then———"

"Words! words! . . . What! you are among the ignorant and fallible, and can take on the colour of heaven? Don't you know that your face grew bright? It was at the end of that last long silence, which must have been its preparation. No human face could be so bright without a divine informing. . . ."

Appearing startled to rigidness, Ingrid stared across the studio, while moments passed and Peter would not relieve the starkness of his statement. But when her eyes seemed about to seek him again, her pale lips staying closed, he asked:

"Or truly were you unaware of it?"

"I could not know that," she said, after a pause. . . . "It is awful. . . ."

"How otherwise you were altered, I can't describe. . . . And before—at the *beginning* of the silence—the same silence—a thing moved in the room that my eyes were too slow or too blind to catch. Is it any wonder that determinations have gone by the board?"

She turned, and began to drag her feet slowly from him, as though seeking escape in a dream.

"For who am I, to refuse out of the fullness of my vanity that others can have seen these portents with me? . . ." But when Peter glanced aside at that familiar shapely back, his thoughts flowed on in twin streams, one alone of which became speech. Inly he assured himself how the insensate womanish frame was now nearly everything his affections still retained of her territory. Her dim incomprehensible mythical features, her eyes like the quietude before an organ-noted storm of terror, when she should move round again—*they* were not of the past; not his. That other supernatural brightness had been but as a wave of the incoming tide higher than the rest: already she, as to the more spiritual of her parts and instruments, was marked with the mark of separation; only her body was a vestige. . . . "Saltfleet found you formidable, at least. He said so—he who can't tell a lie, and probably finds few *that*. Arsinal thought we had been visited. We have been visited."

Ingrid looked at him from where she stood.

"Therefore the meeting is meant."

"Yes, but it is also meant that you especially are claimed, and not for me any more."

"No one can say how it is to end."

"That woman of the Tor, whose funeral I witnessed and whose spirit appeared to you, I think this morning—*she* has been in the room."

"You can believe so on the ground of a strange change of colour in me?"

"Ingrid, I repeat—it was a pale brightness not of your skin but through your flesh—wholly outside nature; yet not illusion. Something was shining from behind your mind, to make you look like that. Whether it was a sign to us, watching you, or whether it was the inevitable effect of an alien divinity occupying your soul . . ."

"Her divinity is unproved . . . for you, at least."

"I won't snatch at the implication. The divinity is sufficiently probable even for me. I will not name her Ourania, daughter of Ouranos, or any other name; but it is the multifariousness of these cases that lifts them out of the common psychic order, to an upper one of heaven—or nearly heaven. Heaven should indifferently, and more or less simultaneously, make use of all phenomenal forms—sensible, emotional, volitional, and fatal. A tomb was hurled open by lightning and closed by earthquake; Drapier was killed by a rock; necessary persons have been assembled in the same half-week from over the world; ancient scenes come back in shadow-play; a spirit of the dead appears; the flesh of your face burns like a moon in this very ordinary room; supernatural hints and suggestions are everywhere; arrangements are made only to be unmade, and wills are as fluid as water; the loveliest engagements break easily across the middle. . . . Here, I say, are the marks of heaven. . . ."

"What do you want, Peter?"

He recollected himself.

"But because we are animals ourselves, it is the similitude of the human animal person that must most impress our imagination and convince our reason: and so I would—if it were still possible—see the ultimate visual phenomenon with my own eyes, daring the result . . . and *this* I want."

"To-morrow."

"If planetary art has ever stood for anything in the sight of our symbol for the highest, the grace should be conceded."

"I am not her priestess, Peter: nor if I were could I entreat her appearance, even in the name of the loneliest art. All such matters seem a universe removed from me."

"Yet, standing here not long ago, I thought this—that as many of us as are to find our account to-morrow on the Tor may know apotheosis in different modes, according to our characters and uses. . . ."

"Then it may be a presentiment. Indeed, if death has served Hugh Drapier, why might not illumination serve you? That his death has served him I know now: I begin to feel a great peace when I think of him. Perhaps I should feel an equal peace for your death in the eyes of the world. . . . Already I am much quieter about mother. She may not be required to go up at all. . . . No, she hasn't reconsidered," she answered Peter's raised brows, "but it is a last intuition of mine. What could she have to do at an unearthly tryst? How can she not conclude living out her simple straightforward life, either in monotony or sorrow? . . . However, this talk is nothing, Peter. Let me go home. . . ."

He stood uncertainly, glancing away from, then at her.

"You speak of peace, Ingrid—when some of us are to swim in black waters, and Drapier, for aught you know, may by this be tumbled into new troubles. Your peace, I fear, is like the bloom on mountains: it is due to intervening distance: you are travelling from us. So my removal may show me to you deathly, when actually the quiescence would be covering the whole war against grief, wrath and despair. With such a facility you have cast the old! . . . Still, it would be unjust to revile for a prime iniquity what is merely an issue. First and foremost in your soul, I suppose, is this constant horror of an approach that already causes the secondary disasters to others to appear like Buddhist blessednesses. . . . And we know that a drowning person will clutch at a straw; but you are scorning to consult me in anything. I must believe it is that my instinct you could have trusted has now for three days been obscured.”

“We are all in ignorance. I hoped you would spare me.”

“Then go. But this is not good-bye? I shan’t try to see you before to-morrow evening: when, if your mother does accompany us . . .” He ceased, and she came quietly closer to him.

“Because our friendship and love have stood for wonder, though now another wonder has power to forbid, you want the memory as a perfect thing . . . a quietly sprung-up long association, risen sharply at the last to a height, then ending in a sudden drop, like a cliff—but not vanishing into empty air, as if it had all been Hindoo magic with the concluding confessed trick. . . . Only, if the new displacing wonder were a new incorporeal space, and we were both in it, not as circling globes everlastingly facing one another with the same face, but as separate essences moving different ways; yet to one ultimate purpose, in one space . . . should not we, in that more faith-demanding sense, Peter, be still bound together—perhaps with the larger assurance that nothing any more could tear us apart? . . . Peter, it isn’t heartlessness that we can endure to see each other in real being, instead of against a background of emptiness. It still may not be; but if it is——”

“I very clearly understand that in your present mood you will love no one else; and with that I must be content! . . .”

He went on looking at her, twitched his shoulders, and gave an unsteady bitter little smile. Ingrid said no more. After a minute Peter lit a cigarette, then moved to the door, which he threw open.

“And yet,” he observed, “since the fiat has gone forth that everything in these mystic hours shall signify something else, it remains queer to my intelligence what our very brief embracing in time has stood for, and why it need have been. Certainly it cannot have been for itself. Then has it been necessary for my love to declare itself before I could find my way to the Tor with you others?”

“It may be that too.” She was with him at the door. . . . “I am sure that it is your support which has enabled me to face these men at all. . . .”

"So to-morrow, at or about eight, I shall call at the house for you and your mother, as the plan stands. *They* will meet us up there."

Ingrid returned an assenting answer. She desired him not to go with her downstairs: accordingly they parted on the room's threshold. But had she not slipped like a phantom past his irresolute hand, he still could not have dared to meet her flesh in farewell.

Moving slowly back to the nearer window overlooking the wasted garden at the rear, he stayed there for a time gazing out.

XXX

The Suicide at the Monument

From the top of Devil's Tor the sun was not long set. The vast sky was a weirdness of strange cloud-shapes and all the colours— vivid, sombre, delicate—from burning crimson to ambiguous green, with great expanses of still bright blue vault to show the tinted battlements and monsters interrupting them more grotesque and even portentous. In four days the weather, after painfully climbing to fineness again, was become tragic towards another storm. Ingrid and Peter stood alone on the edge of the hill farthest from the ruin, pondering in silence that unnatural splendour in the west. They were early. At the house they had settled that Ingrid should recover the flint before the others' arrival: now that it lay in the pocket of her knitted coat there were still minutes to pass. Like a living thing the sky went on changing visibly before them; the dark solidity of the away-stretching moorland was a floor to it; a wind, faint and fitful, whispered to their ears of the hour to come.

Coming up they had hardly spoken. He was sullen; she, fallen into another mysterious apathy, from whose retreat her own moving, breathing body seemed to her like an independent animation. In unearthing the stone but a few monosyllables had been exchanged. Now at last he faced her, to say:

"We had better get across. But perhaps you will explain to me first about your mother. I would like to know. At the inquest she was definitely in the same mind: then, in your hall, just before you came down dressed, she appeared quickly and quietly from nowhere and took my elbow—'I can't go with you—I am prevented. I trust you in everything'—and that was all. . . . I know you foretold it, but it is the queerest business to me that a mother can abandon her daughter, having every reason to imagine her in danger."

"I have seen little of her all day."

Ingrid had not attended the inquest, which had passed off without episode, and altogether had been dreamlike to more than one. The coroner had called no jury, the evidence was taken as in a plain, straightforward case unconcerned with neglect or the suspicion of foul play, and there were neither superfluous questions put to the witnesses nor stops for legal consultation. Nearly before persons were aware that the proceedings had actually terminated, they found themselves filing out of court again. In a curt and towards cursory voice the withered-looking coroner had pronounced his verdict of "Accidental death." Saltfleet, old Colborne, and Helga had stood in the witness-box; Peter and Arsinal had been present. Reporters carried back the story, and the dead man might now be buried. . . . Once or twice in coming out Peter had wondered if Mrs. Fleming's refusal to accompany them could be due to the curb she had put upon her tongue in the court. Because she had there spared Saltfleet, so might she all the more desire to avoid even the shadow of a new friendliness towards him.

He pursued, to Ingrid:

"You may have seen enough, though, to be able to satisfy me. Is it that she doesn't care to meet Saltfleet?"

"No; if it were the fear of him, she must have come."

"Have you no conception?"

"I think she has been praying."

Peter uttered a short laugh. "Praying! To Whom?"

"Isn't it a case for prayer? Or does the mode matter? Our words may well be misdirected, but a launched misery should steer itself. . . ."

"So this staying away is the answer?"

"Yesterday a marvellous plan came to her through her wretchedness on my account . . . and if it was wrong in a single particular, that only goes to prove that it presented itself suddenly and uninvited—she hadn't thought it out. Now, if she has been praying, the error has been corrected for her."

"It is possible. But has she been praying?"

"Don't you know what I mean? You may pray in words, or thoughts, or tears, or terrors. You may pray without the attitude of prayer—without being aware that you are praying."

"Then what is prayer? I may some time want to know."

"I think it is when all other help has gone, and the mind works no more."

So they debated and surmised. But it was no more than a few hours since that foreign reiterated utterance had kept sounding within Helga's head, that Ingrid was wiser, Ingrid was wiser— wiser and older—wiser because older, than she . . . old as the beginning of sex, when sex as yet was not, but women still were. For it was mystical, and not what the biologists taught—truly taught. On the famous biological ladder sex was long before humans. That was for earth. There was another instinct in women: men knew it not. So Ingrid, in the fierce immaculateness of her very ancient instinct, was protected against evil adventures of the heart, and had no need of kith or kin. . . .

And a little after had been her violent impulse (equally strange with that obeisance to her own child) of clinging to their low-set house when immediately to be required to quit it to attend a rendezvous of her personal suggesting. It was more than the deep dread of an unknown trial: it was a sort of prescient knowledge that she could never return to the house to find it the same. . . . Perhaps if over it she stood guard, the angel of death and change might glide ghostly back disconcerted, and take another time. . . .

Yesterday she had been possessed to put forth this proposal that in her—in her, unpossessed—had been mad. Already gleamed like an emerging signal her unworthiness to bear her part in it. She grew old in the way of women, understanding no new thoughts, reclining among friends, loving softness and fair words and respect . . . but on that lonely hill her daughter had faced a spirit, and Hugh had died. No less spectral, deathly, could be its other awaitings: while she—she had no resources, she could not so much as answer for her rigour of courage. She was surely to bring shame upon them all. . . .

That altitude of her interview with Ingrid was departed. The flight was over, and, stupefied, crushed, bleeding, her soul lay prone on its iron ground of reality, remembering but the fact of the exaltation. Her psychic passion had been true, Ingrid's transfiguration before her eyes had been true: her present fumes and confounding were not to take from the actuality of those prodigies, only she could not recover them. Therefore, although it was yet by no means too late to annul the meeting, substituting another arrangement, it was impossible, impossible, for it had been a doom. . . .

But out of a new prolonged chaos of distaste, aversion and terror—terror for her daughter, terror for all that sane settlement of which she herself was a living part—these things striving against another terror of the unseen if defied, striving also against the simple deadweight of a decision made and expected by other persons to be acted upon . . . out of that hour-long chaos, endured crouched or pacing in her room, or restlessly seeking indiscoverable relief throughout the house, Helga, by slow victories of perception, had at last been brought to see that the meeting could stand unvaried, yet she not go to it. . . . Ingrid, Peter, should go: the one because—she must; it was the meaning of all; but Peter, to shield her from—unworthinesses; and because it yet remained his duty. . . .

Then the front door had closed behind them: hearing which, Helga in her chamber went upon her knees. But in praying to a formless God she had somehow lost her thoughts; she had found herself instead beseeching her own mother in heaven. For a mystic minute a forgetfulness of her distress had overtaken her that was just the same as sweetness; yet whether it were a happiness come or an anguish gone, she hardly asked; but seemed, rather, to be recollecting a sensation of her childhood, as it were a curious unnamed perfume. And though soon this faded again from the stale, hard inscription-walls of her worn brain, its bare recalling afterwards was sometimes to be to her in hours of darkness an enchanted key where otherwise no door was. . . .

And now, as the ancient saga-men would say, Helga Fleming goes out of the story.

Peter and Ingrid returned very slowly to the great stones at the east side of the hill-top, which indeed had never been out of sight. She could walk again nearly without hindrance. They were in time to view the others just appearing by quick degrees over the height across the valley. Arsinal was in front. Saltfleet, curiously unlike his wont, seemed to lag.

So, while waiting, Ingrid sat down on her old seat by the hill's south edge; but feared to face the stairway ruin. Having it behind her, she gazed nervously across the low-lying country . . . yet too soon she discovered that neither would that succeed: the intrepidity failed her to continue sitting there in ignorance of what could be passing at her back. She rose impulsively, to move to a second weathered rock much farther off, from which she might hold the tomb-entrance with her eyes and still be secure from its immediate awfulness. Peter, who had not sat, now did so near-by, looking the same way.

They talked no more. The distance between them was unsuitable: neither could they have talked. The past was meaningless, the future unthinkable, the present unreal like a dream. Peter's heart ached, and he strove for stoicism. Within the hour—within the half-hour, Ingrid's lips murmured, everything must be resolved, whether for better or worse. She understood that one of three things was certain: the new life, or the old life, or death. . . .

Automatically her fingers felt for the flint in the pocket of her coat. . . . How dark the evening had grown!—how was she noticing it? Where was she? What was happening? . . . There Peter was sitting, but why was he so statue-like? . . . All the people! . . . And the Devil's monument, it was up again—but perpendicular now—and how extraordinarily clear were its outlines! . . .

Then she accepted her vision, as three men before her had accepted theirs.

All was grey and shadowy as in early dawn before the first colours of the day; or as in late evening dusk, after the last. Unless indeed this preternatural twilight resembled rather the hushed darkness of an eclipse of the sun. . . . Everything in it and of it was somehow primitive and gigantic—and miles upon miles away, surely she was beholding the flamy vapour-cap of a dim conical volcano! . . . This very Tor where she sat had changed character: it was ruggeder than moorland, it was a mountain. Another massive mountain, overtopping her, rose across the emptiness that was in the place of the familiar valley. She could not determine where to keep her eyes. . . .

The low thunderous roar of a torrent below deafened her to any other sounds in its constant alternation between the full fury of its energies and their re-gathering. The noise, though it seized her whole frame, stunning her delicacy while exciting her blood to fever, nevertheless seemed to pass comparatively so unnoticed, she could not remember when it had *not* been. . . . Faint stars sprinkled the sky.

Those animated shapes in skins, they were like ridiculous gnomes in their shadowy slinking about the base of the monument. But *it*, piercing the upper gloom, seemed a monstrous fungus. . . . Yes, at last she could be positive it was neither dawn nor nightfall, but an uncanny full day. Its duskiness was ominous and horrid. Some immense natural catastrophe impended. . . . They were brutes—but were they brutes? . . .

They were nearly brutes, at least. Their thick ungainly trunks, apish legs, and prehensile arms of quite disproportionate length, their mane-like hair, too, and the bestial crouch of their carriage, all declared that they should be sub-human. Yet, as in a nightmare, she also made out that these loathly phantom creatures were still adorned with beads, and clothed in pelts, and armed with savage weapons. . . .

The hoarse blare of a lung-blown horn shocked her: then torches appeared, with more shapes. But in the new yellow-red flaring she recognised them at last for humans. They should have speech, manipulation, laughter and fancy. The sexes were too obvious. Soon her eyes had separated a young female from the rest.

She, the single one, stood apart from the interwoven moving throng, seeming as if lost to her surroundings in melancholy musing. In her rudeness she could not pretend to beauty, and yet she might be on the path to the future beauty of women. Paler than the other females she was, more slender, more erect even, far more pensive . . . doubtless of a finer birth, if that discrimination was between them: having in the slightly sinister slant of her eyes a suggestion of some wild nomadic Asian origin. Not without grace she wore a bear's fur, shaped to her waist, leaving her limbs branching.

Next, a male, older than many and seeming to possess authority, advanced within the circle of Ingrid's vision. In daylight his beardless face might be yellow: his black hair descended to the shoulders. He was the thickest and strongest she saw—aggregated and buttressed quite out of resemblance to the fair human shape. But the network of deep lines impressed by years, anxiety, possibly grief as well, everywhere crossing the superior sagacity of his physiognomy, quickly restored him to manhood, emphasising him thereafter as the most awful to watch. So his chieftaincy grew clear. For she witnessed how a space became emptied about him almost of itself, of which he was the centre, the rest viewing him in fear, while he for his part continued as if oblivious of their attendance, brooding over thoughts. He lent no eye to anyone; but, standing bowed, rested his weight heavily on a spear.

And then, since nothing immediately was to alter in that weird picture, Ingrid let herself observe one more creature, who had posted himself midway between the chief and those expectant others: and he might be young, for his lithe restlessness. His glittering eyes were never still, as he perpetually played with a stone mace, tossing it from hand to hand, then twirling it, not once looking at it. But she was unable to understand whether his forwardness were born of impudence or privilege.

That one who could be thought a girl—were there not the beginnings of a likeness between her and the old chief, thick and unsightly though he was? Very well she might be his daughter or granddaughter. The hint of a loftiness invisible in the other creatures showed in them both . . . but her eyes were stranger than his, looking out from that unfitting face. Indeed their colour was indiscernible, yet Ingrid marvelled how they were so sad and distant, full of mystery. What could she be enduring—she, with her few thoughts, her heart ignorant of complexities? Who was she? What were these? What were all doing here, congregated beneath a granite pile that sparkled in the torchlight with new-ness?

Her memory of an ancient tomb in front of her slept. As if spontaneously come to her the apprehension that someone of supreme honour in this assembled tribe of man-like beings lay interred under that queer-shaped ponderous stack . . . that a barbaric ceremony about to begin concerned the new erection of such an emblem of reverence. Within a stone's-cast of her might be shed the blood of human victims. . . . Her limbs' paralysis from the sudden imagination forced her revulsion into channels of impotent passionateness. That atrocity, then, was perpetrable in despite of her alien protesting womanhood, and she must sit on as a spectator at an arena. So from shuddering she turned to angry horror and vain furious essays to break her spell. . . .

Desisting, she tried again to place herself within the case of that girl creature. Was she in sorrow for the dead? Surely she would then be moaning and rocking her frame—concealing with tight hands the sacred springs of her eyes . . . but she was quiet. . . . Nor was it her sex that caused her to stand there weaponless, for other females bore spear or spike, and life it seemed went dangerously: but it might be that, as chief's daughter, she should walk defended by every hand of her community . . . and yet Ingrid rather believed that she was not caring overmuch for safety. Perhaps some new quickness of her soul tortured her, for which she was unable to discover the expression. Then all the brutalities of these brutes would be to her horrible: and still she would not know why: and might not escape by flight—for it should be an outer world of enemies and blackness. Deep pity for her stole into Ingrid's heart. . . .

The monument, in light and shade, seemed farther set from the hill's edge than she could comprehend. Somehow she knew that its front was on the side away from her, overlooking the falling of the ground there; yet the old leaning head and neck of all her life till this week—the picture was not in her consciousness . . . and still she thought the edge should be nearer. She was incurious about the invisible face of this stalked bulbous grave-stone of more might than art. It was of savagery, but it was that appearing through the savagery which she expected—expected. . . . The old chief was moving.

She saw how his left hand was clenched over something in it. With the right he brought down the stout wooden shaft of his spear so forcibly on the rocky ground against its butt that the hollow sound separated itself from the noise of the torrent. Immediately everything changed.

Torches flitted. Countless thick shapes passed into and out of the illumination in seeming confusion, only to resolve themselves into a dreamlike formation. Four males, having instruments of the appearance of large twisted sea-shells slung around their necks, stepped mystically forward, to blow a blast of oddness—for long years it rang sometimes at dead of night in Ingrid's ears. The audacious half-chief—if such he was—stopped sporting with his mace, though his shifty eyes still roamed. The supposed chief's daughter seemed to shrink upon herself in helplessness.

Another male moved into prominence. He was anthropoid like the rest. His age was unguessable, but his face the grimmest there, yet without ferocity, without malice; while extraordinarily deep-sunken were his eyes. He flourished a great stone axe aloft; and those nearest to him fell away. . . .

Then Ingrid, gazing at him, was perplexed. She had somehow not conceived that all these beings could be so individual. And their unlikeness was not the unlikeness of *people*—for that seemed to belong to the past; as the number of human ancestors grew, so grew the differences . . . but these creatures, she felt more than thought, were unlike as to the future. Vigorous new natures were dawning. She understood in them a robust, straining blood, of another chemistry—not effete, orderly, obedient, cynical, like the blood of people. . . . Thus she might no longer condescend to these shades for their brutism and hideousness and unrisen souls: but knew herself instead venerating them on account of that mystical grandeur of very life. They advanced in wonder, the true sires of an immense rising, then ebbing, humanity, fated to flow fanwise from them through as many parted roads as here were persons. This strange quality in them she responded to as another person might respond to the invisible real movements of the universe of stars. The riddle was read by another sense in her: not fully grasped. . . .

But the grim one, of no prompting that she had remarked, took in head to commence an amazing dance forward, cutting rhythm with his air-sweeping axe, with all those phantoms following. First on his heels were the musicians, stepping the four abreast; periodically raising their instruments to wind in unison singular chords that were never twice alike. She never doubted but that those chords possessed a significance. After danced the whole company, first males, then females; and in their exaggerated agility she found nothing absurd; none could be laughing in heart, therefore neither could she smile. He of the mace might leap more extravagantly than the rest—she knew that not even he could as yet be infected by the deep poison of the comic, which later was to course resistlessly through the world, and kill souls. . . . She witnessed how next to the last walked downcast that chief's daughter: but the absolute last was he himself who should be her father, bowed, sullen, planting his feet.

Thrice the circuit of the monument was completed; but when

the procession was returned in place against Ingrid for the fourth time, the leader stopped, and all with him. Fronting his followers by a sudden wheeling spring with both feet in air, he made a sign that they understood: whereupon a great ragged horseshoe of creatures took form, the opening of which was as if closed by the monument, though it was still yards distant from those nearest to it. But whether they numbered hundreds or but scores she, seeing all through her coming and going mists of emotion, never thought to calculate. Alone the horn-blowers, with those other four to whom she had paid principal heed, assembled within the horseshoe's space. The torches lit them, so that they looked excrescent on the earth.

The male with the axe danced by himself towards the monument, throwing up his arms as though beseeching it: or perhaps he banned the hateful, the invaders of its sacredness. He should be declaiming or chanting, but the roar of the waters carried off his voice. Then, not pausing, he vanished into the dusk, round the pile and past it.

They waited; while time seemed to have no meaning. When he reappeared, it was in another quarter and his axe was gone. He was unbloody—Ingrid knew not what had happened. The old chief went forward to encounter him. They conferred apart.

Once more the chief stood alone, while the beings with seashells sounded a mad chord. He, as the other had done, lifted high both arms to the memorial; then, higher yet, to the overhead sky. . . . He thrust the broad spade-like point of his spear deep into a cranny of soft soil: instantly following the action in shocking surprise by casting himself headlong on the ground, face-downwards. His frame seemed to heave with terrible sobs. His daughter stood near, looking away, not weeping.

He rose awkwardly. The daughter and he of the mace approached at his beckoning. The chief gave her the thing he had held in his constantly-closed left hand. Her eyes shut as in pain while she received it. Afterwards Ingrid was to know what it had been, but now she saw it not.

A miracle came without warning. For gradually the female's

bare skin, wherever it showed, became suffused with a silvery brightness, that was like the light of a lamp, or moon, triumphing through the torchlight: and at the same time her countenance grew spiritually transfigured to a beauty of angelhood: yet the beauty was always moving, either in increasing or, immediately afterwards, fading. . . . Ingrid could not gain the full impression for her thoughts gathered round it. She was trying—dimly, unsuccessfully, not with her whole mind—to recall under what circumstances she had sometimes seen such a brightness and transcendence before. . . . But while she still conjured the past of another order of reality, the phantom filling her eyes shed that impossible glory, becoming, how swiftly! her earthy self again. . . .

The old chief gripped the wrist, the free wrist, of him with the mace, forcing down his hand to clasp his daughter's fore-arm. She seemed to shiver, yet offered no resistance. The old one, however, should be made aware of an aversion in her, for, heavily bending his great brows, he well-nigh set a pointing finger on a region of her body. Then Ingrid knew two things at once—that this young phantasm was to be a mother, and that her right protector was departed from her. . . .

Meanwhile the chief, scowling, had jerked the upright spear out of the ground. Obediently to his sign a male creature advanced, and their two mouths worked alternately in inaudibility. The superior seemed to command something that the other endeavoured to evade. Suddenly and abominably—yet as so unreal it swept past Ingrid's consciousness—the elder brought up his weapon with a curiously swift twist, ran hard and fast at that brute-man, and fairly broke through his chest with its frightful death-point, instantaneously loosing a fountain of dark blood. The victim gazed at him steadily, until abruptly he sank, to continue lying crumpled on the earth. . . .

The killer crooked his finger to another, who so reluctantly approached that the whole of a minute seemed to pass before they stood opposed. Then again the old one's mouth went uncouthly through the visible motions of speech: but the second stayed cowed and dumb. The chief glared at him, turned away, and swung back, to proffer his blood-wet spear by its shaft, which the inferior at last took. The cantor who had borne the axe joined them, seeming to make sounds of exhortation or ceremonial instruction. Thereupon the tribal creature stuffed the spear tightly under his armpit; then waited.

The old chief clasped his daughter. . . . And Ingrid had the surety that here was an eternal farewell—since better they could not dream of . . . yet where *now* were these two, who upon a time had so wept upon each other? . . . All the scene was true and false—half was it like life, half like the fearfullest of spectral plays. . . . The sea-shells blew again.

The commanded one gripped his spear in such a manner that the ugly, darkened breadth of its stone death lay right before him on the level of his breast, his hands being wide apart upon its shaft. With a wild, monstrous cry, that Ingrid heard, he announced his readiness, or valediction, or protesting grief and horror. The old chief, his head bent, strode from him towards the monument, between those ranks of unmoving shades that watched him. There, a dozen long paces from the other, he stopped and turned again to face him. So he stood stock-still awhile; but he with the spear now eyed him with a gloomy fixity. . . .

She saw a heavy body hurtle across the intervening space . . . towards that senseless waiting spear . . . oh, right upon it! . . .

But while the suicide, all bloody and still, lay unattended yet upon the ground, he who had been joined to the female tried suddenly to snatch from her closed hand the thing she had been given. And at the first her eyes flamed and it seemed she would have resisted; but whether she feared him, or realised that he was the stronger and must have his way, or thought the use to her of the object not worth the struggle for it, almost at once she allowed her fingers to be opened, and what was under them to be removed. Then Ingrid beheld a small, black stone, like the broken half of a rounded pebble. The appropriator, the excitement of quick victory on his face, was holding it up to a torch for examination. . . .

An appalling sound, as from the destruction of all Nature, out-thundered the roaring of the torrent. Ingrid shot a terrified eye across the emptiness that was the valley, in time to witness vast masses of precipice descending in smoke. The mountains were cracking . . . and simultaneously the dusk began to change to day. For this very cataclysm it had been waiting ominously. . . . The entire top of the height she was on swayed, as though it were a tidal stage. . . .

She, *that spirit*, came, standing as a moon among all those savage shapes of darkness, who seemed unaware of such a presence. Now was She remembered by Ingrid. She stood, a pillar, beside the female, facing, with indistinguishable eyes and low-crossed arms, the despoiler of her father's gift. Nearly at once the creature, moving with the mountain, staggered, regained his poise violently, again staggered, this time irrecoverably, and fell, crashing his skull against a ground protuberance of rock. He never rose.

The female, disregarding and disregarded by all those rushing, screaming shades, went to bend over him. Quickly she abandoned him, next to search, crouching, the ground around his lying form: and presently she appeared to find the stone. . . . The daylight strengthened until the torches had become pale and useless. Phantoms threw them down. A ghostly shower of rain descended, that could not wet Ingrid. The dust from the land destruction mingled with the heavy raindrops to create an atmosphere of grease and grime and smoke; while she alone, unsullied, need know no panic, as that mighty mountain opposite continued to lose its cliffs and prominences. . . .

The spirit was gone. . . . The face of the chief's daughter was ashen and drawn. She pressed her hand hard upon herself below the bosom, then slowly steered a way towards the hill's margin, remotest from that falling world. None stayed to notice her, nor did she seem to desire company for her journey, which perhaps was to be as long as the endurance of her hatred of these scenes. . . .

She was the last of Ingrid's vision. The grey daylight returned, as by the slow waving of a wand, to the weird clouds and colours of this hideous postponed evening of fate. . . . Dazed, shocked to her roots, she sat on within the two existences. She could not think. She understood that there would be no time for thinking. . . . Her heavy eyes, seeking an escape, fell startled on Saltfleet's erect form standing a little from her, while he no doubt awaited her emergence from her ended state.

XXXI

Sinai

The phantom woman had come to Peter Copping at once. Hardly had Ingrid taken the flint into her hand when the moonlike shape stood between himself and the torn bed of the ancient stack, in the full awfulness of her height and beauty, facing him, but a dozen yards away. He had not seen her before. . . .

Not till moments had passed did his heart stop. Even then was his horror of the flesh rather than the imagination. He was able to reason against unreason, assuring himself that such an illusion must have an adequate explanation in optical laws, or else be pure hallucination, in which case it *was not*. His flesh, of older wisdom, continued to know that this unnatural adversary was not of life, therefore must be of death: threatening the kingdom of death. . . . And no frowning, skilled contemplation of that shining could resolve for him whence it came, unless from a source of light unknown to painters. The sky colours were nearly obliterated by it—at least he saw them not, but only *her*.

That spectral funeral had been of another order: to it he could equalise himself. But this bright, still ghost was like the end of a beam from heaven . . . translated by his paucity of images into the presentment of a woman, because he was acquainted with nothing lovelier.

The notion, as still he dared to lower his lids at her, began to exalt him. So that she need not be a woman at all! For if she were one, then her face's curves and organs, her duplicated limbs, her milk-breasts, were a legacy from the first mammals, she had been framed to bear and nourish young, and never could her beauty exceed the bounds of her skeleton within. Moreover, if ever she had truly walked the earth, she should herself once have been a helpless sucking infant, and obeyed her childish vanities and passions through life; and died—the final act sealing the imperfection of her nature. . . . And *thus* her dreadful gleaming beauty could stand for no Platonic ideal; but she was merely here before him, the dim record of one who had been very beautiful. The better alternative, however, was that he was not seeing truly. It was in him that this face and form were but symbolic: that his eyes were beholding something very much nearer than shaped womankind to God. . . .

How could her lunar luminosity be unmeaning? It was of the colour of light reflected from a distance. So might not whatever in him projected her to his eyesight be as profound in his soul as, for instance, the moon was far from the sun? But his eyesight would represent the earth. . . .

Accordingly, while every revolted fibre of his physical nature shrank from the contiguity, his spiritual logic went on solidifying to the conviction that she, just as she appeared, could be no more and no less than the terminus of his mortal capacity for receiving a beauty greater than any of the world; a beauty prior to the world's faded examples of beauty put to use. . . . Thereupon overcame him a strange calm and careless blessedness during his agreement to such a limitation of his faculties, for the inaccessibility concerned only his wretched four-limbed self, whereas now the assurance could shine to his art that the Ideal was an entity: no mere high-sounding name for the giving and enjoying of the largest aesthetic pleasure.

And while this confrontation in its supernatural intensity could not last, nor the full exploration of its meanings come till too late to him by reason of the perpetual imminence of its vanishing, already he was informed that he was to emerge a metamorphosed man for its simple experience and memory. Ever more tranquil became his face as with open, glowing eyes he forgot boldness in absorbing what of her pale radiance might yet be permitted him. She was priming him with a grandeur to suffice him all his days. Even now a great general stir and whispering of vital ideas seemed to work in him like the awakening of irresistible spring. . . .

She drew closer, in a gliding that was unlike any woman's tread. The silver of her flesh burned with a peculiar fire, suggesting neither heat nor flaming: suggesting only his own crass ignorance of all matters outside his little house of the world. . . . Then, when her advance must have ceased, she appeared much distincter and tall beyond credence . . . yet his eyes were no higher raised to her, so that the distance was still unreal, still mystical, as it had always been. Her arms hung straight against her sides relaxed: her draperies should be appropriate to the dead.

Her eyes would not acknowledge the intension of his, yet so mildly she looked—not at him, not from him—in an undimensional direction impossible to determine or understand—that the involuntary shuddering of his frame as well subsided at last.

The inspiration that falsely he saw her as a woman—now it led quickly to another. Not without reason could that falsification be. The womanliness of the image must have a source. Rightly it was impossible she should be a woman: yet that which so presented itself to his sight must needs be of the womanly kind.

Her eyes—for thus mysteriously his could meet them without being met—were dark, swelling seas of feelings such as he had never felt. Their sense exceeded him. Only their chaining was bringing what occasionally in his life the quietly sympathetic eyes of the best, the purest women had brought—coolness, friendliness, repose, the perfect encounter, the cessation of all willing, that was like timeless heaven itself. On such occasions, when every factitious excitement of his spirit had been laid, its native soaring could begin. But never had any man so stilled him. Therefore this ghost was of women . . . of *women*: not of the one woman whose shape it feigned.

And still the quality of the quieting was different. He received the analogy that the sympathetic loving looks of women resembled the isolating yellow rays of feeble candles, to light his soul into beauty against an outside world of contrasted darkness: whereas from these miraculous eyes sprang an illustration nowise less than that of a sun, to cast the world itself into a flood of beauty. . . . In *this* serenity his egoism, that was the eternal enemy of beauty, might not exist.

His certainty of the womanliness was underived from her mammalian form, but was coming to him through her eyes. Yet there was a distinction felt by his intuition—he tried to clothe it in a thought. The emission from these eyes was not softly regarding like a woman's: it was soft and enriching . . . arriving from the vast and distant—passionate without the descent to persons . . . the definition failed. . . . Her womanliness was not in lack of sex: sex was a curtailment and limitation, and degradation. The emission was something of women, not men—softness, mercy, emotion—yet the instinctive lasciviousness and allurement even of good women, though in them repressed—their absence was like a presence of original essence, mighty past bonds and boundaries.

So he too came to conceive how femaleness could be before sex. Existing alone, needing no completing half, marvellously wise, solitary, ancient, awful, the *female* had in some unthinkable hour of cosmic tragedy fallen into sex, thereafter to become the slave and sport of its derivative. Thus the unnatural effeminacies of women, their animal voluptuousness and cowardly sheltering from the knocks of the world, their infantine love of dress, their intense interest in the interrelations of men and women, their passion to outvie other women in wealth, rank, influence, society, and beauty: all came from that fall to sex. But the heights of woman were original. In nobler purity she was once a whole nature. . . .

So many fancies now assailed him at once, that some were lost. His early portrait of Ingrid . . . Mary had two aspects: one as an anomaly in womankind because of her miracle; but the other as the presentation in a ruined world of that femaleness knowing not males. Well might she bear a god! . . . He thought of Ingrid, forgetting that she was on a hill with him. When he had so painted her, she too should have been without sex for him, a like presentation of the original of women: and indeed these years had passed during which he had not dared to propose marriage to her . . . but lately his intuitions must be coarsened and failing. . . . Yes, she too could be mother of a child having no father—so said her face and eyes, and life, and conversation, that were all of the prior nature. And this in the real world might not be: yet, in the symbolic sense, so it was. . . .

Then what of men?—who did exist in a place where existence was but too serious. . . . He also conceived that men might derive in part from that femaleness which was before the later feminine. For sure it was that mankind's spiritual advance owed itself in principal measure to the men with very much of women in them: and this through the instinct of childbearing. If women had little assisted, the failure had arisen from their natural channel for the instinct's relief: in men, however, such relief must filter slowly and laboriously through the brain; and great works, great children, ensue. But also it seemed to follow that no grandeur could be born of men save by the womanly dictations of the heart, impelling to sacrifice. . . .

So Peter came to know he had been blind. For the passionateness he had wished to bring to painting was but a term to express a desire for the absent. The passions were infinite according to the heart, they agreed only in a base of desire. How could desire be painted? But desire could paint, passionateness could paint. And thus it needed but that his heart should be so increased that through the obscene purgatory of the split sexes the heaven of the undivided soul should shine its images. . . .

But *she* throughout was standing up before him, compelling his forgetfulness of time and place and circumstance, while he remained lost in those effluxions that were her eyes, as in a slow flood of insights. He thought that he was being given these few minutes to change his whole life. . . .

Yet it was a point of terrestrial space, it was this hill, no other spot, she haunted. Here Ingrid too had seen her. Therefore she indeed was a ghost of the dead, she had been buried here; and once had been a living woman. Why then was he judging her his deceived perception of a shaft of splendour? Was it that that life as well had been unreal? Had she walked the earth a symbol? . . .

On what account could she have done so? . . . Or the softness always attacking him—a tidal softness of other life and loveliness, pouring out through her eyes as if through an emptiness—had its function and purpose in the past too been to withdraw from the idle, profane world those persons preferred for its encounter?

But most fearful of all was it that this wraith could persist upon its ancient ground even after the lapse of immense ages. For it made the duration of the planet to be nothing. An invisible force was fulfilling its will regardless of the inexorable beats of the clock governing the events of men: then its acts could have no applicability to the reason of men, no meaning. . . . Or if it were required that the great grey gap of years should occur between the first coming and the return, just as remote was a reason. A flouting of law, an imposition of hidden law, were equal. . . .

Out of a previous thought stole another. A woman's sex-love was a delight and an instinct not towards that delight. The delight was a delight in the person, but the instinct was towards the future child. Both, however, because they were constituent parts of that sex-love, belonged to the effeminacy of her fallen state; neither to the original femaleness. The instinct to a child lay through a receiving: an essence must only give; its nature was sacrifice. Then Ingrid—his willingness during years to renounce his happiness for hers, it surely meant that thereby he thought to serve by no means her sex, but altogether her soul. For that mystic *other* he had feared for her should be not to procure her a child of her body, but of her soul. . . . And therefore, though he had been willing to it, he had feared it. Indeed, he had not feared for his own mean happiness. But the fate, though still to the best, humanly was sinister. Naked she would come to the sacrifice of her earthly purity, where other women came to it clothed in the beautiful veils of love, such as the marriage customs symbolised. . . .

Then also it wrote itself in his mind that this confronting phantom should be for him as an angel of the Annunciation, to declare that of a soul once more most urgent it was that a child should be born. . . .

Now the strangest sensation swelled through him, which never afterwards could he bring back. It came to him that the whole of contentless past time for thousands upon thousands of years—the bare passage of time unconcerned with persons, things, states or happenings—was rushing upon him in one huge unceasing wave, that always passed over his head, while he seemed to know that always also he drew nearer and nearer to where he already was. The intangible illusion dazed him as if he stood on the crust of the globe spinning free, watching sun, moon, planets, stars, slipping frightfully by. One self was here, one self approached with that dreadful smooth onrush of the past: but when they should meet and coalesce, these selves, he thought the wave must surely still run on, to leave him *dead*. . . .

The contact arrived. Nothing had happened. The self that had come up with the past continued forward with the time-wave into the future: the other self looked after. Hardly, though, had he accustomed himself to his new security when the phenomenon abruptly and altogether ceased. He could fancy that the wave, too great for him, was gone on, discarding him stranded and sense-less. . . .

Half-night wrapped the hill, and the spirit had departed; but exactly in her place stood a faintly shining man. Very indistinct he was . . . nigh as tall as *she* had been, gigantically broader and stronger. His vast chest looked an iron arc, while his uncovered arms seemed fit to drag down trees. He was dressed as if for coldness and roughness. Through the deep dusk he loomed like one of those fabulous contenders with giants, monsters, trolls, of the northern tales: only it needed that he should bear an antique weapon; but his hands were empty.

What of his features could be discerned was stamped with such a hardiness that even were he not spectral he yet could not be of the modern world. His eyes were unjoking, his jaws grim and set. It was a problem that the face should be hairless. Thus he could be standing there the reappearance of no wild man of the old. Out of the past he had not come. Rather he seemed some vast dim gleaming shape cast back from the future. . . .

Then Peter kept thinking that it was Saltfleet. It was the odder since there could be no distant likeness between this unreal shape of mist and might, impossibly emerged from a world perhaps yet to be, and Saltfleet's recalled smaller, meaner actuality, son of facetiousness that he was, with every living man. And still, while he frowned on at the projection with the queerest screwing of his eyes, the notion unreasonably persisted that it should be Saltfleet himself, so singularly transformed.

The deceit sank only when the eyes of the apparition began in such a way to stand out that they became a bright animate focus for all the rest of the unchanged insubstantial form. Thereupon Peter believed that he was again to know that beam: but nearly at once it went differently. For in some special manner that his unskilled brain could not receive, these male eyes were representative of this male phantasm seeing by their means, and the whole frame was the intelligence, not the eyes alone were. And the illusion was willing—exerting its will—to appear from futurity: but closest to the will were the eyes, which therefore could press forward before the rest, and not only take on the semblance of life but be it—be life itself . . . while the far lower degree of intelligence of the enveloping body was causing it to stop still there in half-obscurity. . . . But neither was it quite so. The eyes and shape assuredly belonged, yet were of different worlds. They were two messages in one . . . that resulting one was apart from either—a third highest message. . . .

Most incredibly, the deep spiritual blue of those eyes always increasing in power and lustre was implanting another meaning in the grimness of the pale phantom face, making it appear as of divinity . . . a terrible constant-emotional engine for the adventuring singly through the black, whistling night of the Devil . . . to destroy his traps baited to the taste of all, with honey, or wine, or opium, or foulness—the lusts of life, the flight before pain and death. . . . But in itself the soul-light of the eyes was stern and incorrupt. And, away from that rocky face and enormous form, such must have been the vision's communication: but in the iron, giant setting, the eyes held war as well. They were Ingrid's. . . .

Often in her unconscious glancings had he seen her eyes thus, travelling past the eyes of others seeking her sympathy, past all her surroundings, as far as to an unseen heaven; but never once in all the hundreds of his acquaintance or millions of his chance encounter had he witnessed such journeys of the spirit at all: and so these eyes were Ingrid's . . . yet more resolute, more hateful, than hers. . . .

Nevertheless was it strange how that unparalleled soul of the fair fragile woman he had once been near to, which he had ever set so infinitely above the coarser souls of all other women and all men, should now seem to be surpassed as to its peculiar virtues by the created nature that quested past him from the ghostly orbits of a male whose time as yet was not—who was still to be born and live. . . . In Peter's art were the similitudes of all things. Sometimes a work would start from one inspiration, only to be arrested and changed by a second that made it as of another genius—richer, deeper, more amazing. Then would the original conception, in his later re-examination of its sketch, be rudiment-ary and ancient to him, bringing him pleasure by reason of its nigh incredible crudity. Not *crude* could Ingrid's soul be: but still he understood not how her eyes should be the same to him, from these. . . .

Thereafter again he found Saltfleet in this dusky glimmering figure. He reissued from the set of the mouth, the harsh patrician hollows of the cheeks. Now he confessed in thought what always he had seen and hated—yet loved too . . . that that man was a great natural lord . . . but how insignificant beside this mighty one! . . .

Or it was derangement, this discovery of resemblances in a nameless thing. Their persons were haunting him more than he knew—agitating him even in the awful presence of the powers of night. In artists was this visualising faculty to excess. . . . How far indeed reached it? Two persons appearing in one—each must change, dropping something of identity. Thus would follow the illusion of real change; an advance into the future. That could be this shade's character of futurity. . . . It was no reasoning in him, but the lightning skeleton of a scheme for escape. The scheme died in his invention's womb. The way was not one. Those blue phantom deeps were not from *him*. Deeper than his deepest soul, they reduced him, unstruggling, to the proportions of a dwarf. Neither was the grimness imaginable by him. Not for his lightness was it to envisage the world with that terrific energy of masculinity. . . .

The change of two to one, he knew, was *growth*.

A mystical union had brought two spirits to compactness in one frame . . . the elements were distinguishable, that the fact might be clear. The fact indeed was clear: but the meaning he deduced not—he *dared* not. . . .

Surely some monstrous malignity of world-existence was to be contemplated by these skyey eyes and encountered in death-grips by this shape of roughness. Inadequate was the thought that here miraculously stood one still unborn, whose life, when it should come, was to express no more than the mortal turmoil of his own few years. Like a father and founder of a new earth he shone forth so unequally. Pressing forward into their kingdom in infinite numbers from the inexhaustible procreative vigour of this menacer and his resembling sons, the freeborn men and women of a clean and high and holy race, it came to Peter, were in due season to bend the knee of awe before a Spirit, the beginnings of Whose right nature no smaller spirit of human creature had yet imagined. . . .

He recognised the coloured, broken sky—and yet the recognition must have been gradual. His vision was gone and not gone: it worked in him, and gave him no peace. But chiefly he understood that an essential thought contained in it remained to be grasped. . . .

In a little while he rose, to cross to Ingrid. She sat where she had done, her eyes persistently cast down on the ground, waiting for he knew not what. Those men were up. Saltfleet stood nearer than Arsinal to her, but both were watching her. He had no idea how long his trance had lasted.

Extraordinary was her skin's light. Through its bloodless pallor it was so luminous that for an instant he could fancy he was beholding a third apparition. . . . Yet it was the Ingrid of life. And as, avoiding Saltfleet, he came closer to her, his eyes could even detect the motion of her quiet breathing: only she did not look up to him. . . . But the amazing gleaming of her flesh failing to depart notwithstanding, he turned quickly to *them*, to learn how they seemed. His uneasiness leapt. Arsinal's colour was unaltered, while he stood there thoughtfully, his hands behind his back in the familiar manner: Saltfleet's visage, however, appeared illumined by the same preternatural splendour as Ingrid's. The same— though the emanation was less pure, less shining—his man's coarseness of ground intervened . . . or the explanation was elsewhere. . . .

Then from one to the other he kept glancing in that alarm . . . and suddenly an impropriety of their modern clothing struck him with an acuter terror. For his instinct was that they, being so dreadfully lighted, should have been garbed, the one in those shroud-draperies of the ancient past, the other in that grim war-dress of a dateless future. . . . And thus his thought, contained in the vision, that had waited to be released, must now be upon the very verge of delivery. It had been concerned with Ingrid—with Saltfleet as well . . . with both associated. . . . the most weird conjoining of their qualities in another *shape*—ah God! had it been in any way different from—a marriage? . . . Yet that he had known. This duplicate gleaming before his eyes, it was the mystic token of the union of these two, in another place not physical. . . .

Not a marriage: since under no conditions of reality could two persons become one. . . . But in a *child*. . . .

That was that thought.

He turned to gaze abroad over the darkened country. Then Ingrid came up behind him, and spoke—strange a voice sounded to him again. The others could not overhear. He was unsure whether her hand was touching or only feeling towards him.

"Now you are going down, Peter?"

"Yes."

"Have you seen Her?"

"You are so wise—you can hardly need to question others."

"But answer."

"Yes, I have seen Her. Your face is gleaming like Hers. Yesterday it was so too. . . . Therefore you are Hers—not mine . . . and I am going off the hill."

The phantom brightness of Ingrid's face, in fact, was like an inset in the rest of her person that grew indefinitely darker or reflected the colours of the west. She said:

"You call me wise, but I am very ignorant if your words mean that we are never to meet again."

"It is the end."

"Then how will you live?"

"Why, I shall always have this evening to remember. I beg you not to waste your pity on me at any time."

"Will you not say why you are leaving me?"

Peter smiled fearfully.

"By your very first question, you knew I was to go. . . . Reason enough is there I should go! . . . I saw your son—the son of your body . . . or perhaps he was more distant in time than your son . . . but at least he was not mine as well. . . ."

Understanding that she was to be silent, he pursued:

"So should we marry, this thing would be a grave sin in you. . . . Nor may we suppose that these illuminations and prefigurements are all deceits. . . . Accordingly the step is to be mine. I wish you not to break any word to me—because it would be a great everlasting pain to have to feel I had lost your love also. . . . It is implied, though; and my attitude has no sensible meaning. . . . Anyhow, now I am going back to the world. I beg you to write me in London. I want you to offer no commentary on the text of these events; but barely give the facts—what you are to do, what practically is to happen to you. This, I think, is my meed.”

“You wish that we shall never meet again?”

“I wish we may. It will be the sweetest and ghastliest reunion of all my life. . . . Earnestly I shall endeavour to keep out of your sight. Now give me your hand. I dare not kiss a spirit. . . .”

Ingrid slowly extended her hand as if she were a woman bewitched. It seemed to Peter that this elastic soft warm thing within his grasp presented the last of his selfish delights. Retaining it, he said:

“In the matter of your strength—are you able to undertake the business waiting for you?”

“I must.” But he could scarcely hear her.

“Where have *you* been, Ingrid, in this last time?”

“A long way away.”

“You don’t want me to stop to see it through?”

“No, you cannot. . . .”

His unearthly sensitiveness responded to the very secret alarms on his account contained in the inflexions of her voice, and he looked intently at her, while she took away her hand at last.

“Then already you have experienced some momentous matter too!”

“Peter, someone may die here this evening. It may be quite soon—before the appearance of the first star in this extraordinary sky.”

“Not you?” he questioned sharply.

“I have no feeling of death for myself, but I feel as if there were death near.”

Of smallest account seemed to him the menace: yet in the gloom his face showed grey, while his eyes, now stern, prepared to quit hers that still was palely lucent. His voice fell to quietness again.

“For all unkindnesses of mine in the past, Ingrid, I beg you to forgive me. . . .”

Thus they parted.

But to the two others, who courteously had been looking away while waiting, Peter said, crossing to them for the purpose:

"I am going down off the hill, gentlemen: and you will transact your business with Miss Fleming alone. Her mother, you see, is not here. She was unable to come."

Only Arsinal bowed in silence—and now a heedfulness in Peter's eye transmitted to his unheeding brain how this man's face as well was changed. Dull, thin, pinched, white and haggard to the very likeness of death, it seemed still attached to life by a sluggishness of careworn anxiety alone. He was as a stranger on the hill-top, that had these miracles for all, but they must be alive—of the future. . . . Then, more peculiarly, Peter glanced at the other, to perceive that he was faintly shining yet. . . .

Delaying no longer, he turned his back upon all three and started to walk towards the eastern homeward edge of the plateau. And for the few moments that his receding shape remained in sight, it was ennobled as a spectacle of solitude to the eyes gazing after by the mighty sky silhouetting it. Minute by minute the massing clouds, in form and colour, had grown more fantastic and savage and fearful. The earth was entering night.

Ingrid wondered why she felt so little emotion. Surely it should be sinful and detestable that she could let him go from her thus and know no impulse to recall him. But with deeper workings was her heart filled. Her mind, that was its echo and consequence, resembled a great swaying sensitive web of sombre thoughts, floating this way and that. Now immediately were all they that were left to go into bitter sacrifices. Now Peter was in safety—she could not have retained him. Suddenly she drew a long, wavering breath. Now she must prove her race, and it was time to have done with thought.

XXXII

The Rejoining

When Peter had quite disappeared, the evening of a sudden seemed to grow much darker, the inapprehensible discord of sky colours to die down in its different regions to a finer but even more disturbing intensity of sphinx-like depth, the great baneful crawling clouds to crouch closer to earth; a living tragedy now rapidly to approach, heralded by these insubstantial cyclopean portents. What stood for the human companionship of those three was all that remained to save them from a crushing sense of helplessness in the presence of fate about to strike. With that vanished fourth, somehow, was gone their last material link with the world, leaving them for want of his support cut off and exposed to the immaterial attack. In more or less distinctness was felt by them that his art should be an activity of the world, related to its other activities: therefore that he himself, notwithstanding these late experiences, had still been solid of the world.

But first one, then the other, of the men came up again to Ingrid, who awaited them quiet-faced and silent. And Arsinal perceived neither in her nor in Saltfleet anything of the gleaming that Peter had perceived but too well: because it was a spiritual light, not for the conceited simplicity of the eye of the brain thinking to construct everything from surfaces. Indeed, yesterday he had seen the shining in her, and otherwise understood what it should betoken: but now his impatience prevented him; an impatience in the service of a larger anxiety that was his will and life. . . . Saltfleet beheld Ingrid's exaltation of flesh so dimly that he fancied himself deceived. He spoke not to it, but to her human circumstances:

"Here is very much the eleventh hour, I am afraid; and yet important changes of mind have been made so late. I am not to pain you by referring to Mr. Copping. I know, and wish to know, neither the motive for his present conduct, nor your last relations.

But if you as well would rather put off the trial in front of us all to another time, we shall of course readily consider your natural feelings of a woman—remembering especially that you must just have been through another unpleasantness already. Mr. Arsinal will concur that we have certainly no wish to push matters beyond common humanity.”

Arsinal made no sign.

“Thank you: but I think we must do it now,” replied Ingrid, in a faint, resolute voice.

“There is an alternative proposition. It shall be done now, since you so desire; but perhaps there may be no need for you to participate actively. . . . Just now I saw your stone in your hand. . . .”

“Yes, I have it—it is in my pocket.”

“Please keep it there for a minute. My proposal is that Mr. Arsinal shall do the joining . . . while I stand by as immediate witness, and you remove yourself to a distance—staying in sight if you like, though my counsel is that you should walk right away. . . .”

“And can you engage that the danger to me will then be averted?”

“Unfortunately I cannot—so long as you are on the hill at all. But the risk should be less.”

“You know I have not come up here to avoid a risk.”

“I will be plain. You are no more than a girl, and I ask you to entrust your stone to me, and return home.”

“Nor have I come here only to go home again. The meeting was arranged between us for a purpose, and I am here for it.”

They looked at each other. Saltfleet’s face had no supernatural light for her, but somehow she saw it thinner, sterner, nobler. . . . He said:

“What was arranged was a general meeting; whereas Mr. Copping has deserted you, and your mother has not appeared at all.”

“Her staying away is to deprive you of nothing.”

“We do not know that. I shall still be very plain. You are a single young woman, on a hill remote from other persons, with night coming on, in the company of two men much older than yourself, nearly entire strangers. Another accident may happen within the next minutes—the hill may again become publicly notorious. Then I should not care to pronounce whose plight will be the more unenviable, yours or ours. Decent men must conform to the prejudices of society. . . . Do consider the point, for I am not distorting the probabilities in the very least."

"You are talking of the world. We have left the world behind us, down there. This place belongs to a spirit."

"You should also reflect that a girl living at home has duties towards her people. . . ."

"I am grateful for your reminders, but have seen too much here this evening already to have any thought of leaving before the work is finished."

"Why is this reapplication of the stones to each other necessarily to be witnessed by you?"

"Because there is no meaning else."

She turned upon Arsinal. "Cannot you satisfy Mr. Saltfleet that my undefendedness, and obligations, and social liabilities, all vanished from the moment I set a foot on the slopes of the Tor? He must know it too—but should be so used to looking from all sides. . . ."

"I do indeed consider, Saltfleet, that you are rendering Miss Fleming an exceedingly bad service by this belated pressure. She feels herself called, and is called. The same courage that has brought her here to meet us will enable her to go through the passage now waiting. You deliberately ignore that a high heart may more than cancel the disabilities of Nature—as also that we are assembled in the invisible presence of laws definitely more dreadful than those dictated by the mutual fears of persons forming society. But you yourself are here frivolously. . . ."

"Neither have *I* ever failed in audacity for the furtherance of my own ends."

"I will not be drawn into anger now."

"Nor will I leave Miss Fleming here alone with . . . a sacrificer. You want me to follow Copping, I know."

There was a pause.

"Stay, then," said Arsinal. "But to a sacrifice go knife, rope, altar, and victim, and I have none of them. I have no power to detain Miss Fleming against her will."

"You will not go down alone," Saltfleet put to Ingrid, "but will you go down with me?"

"No, I cannot."

"My insistence distresses you."

"I am distressed already. . . . You know how very near to me Peter Copping was. You saw how he left me so quietly. He is out of my life. Never have I honoured him so much. He could not have acted in any other way to keep my full esteem. . . . Well, he did not beg me to come away from this place."

Arsinal took a short step towards her.

"He was overtaken by a state of trance, during which he should have had a vision. Did he relate it to you?"

"He did not tell it all."

"Here, in this extraordinary hour, beneath this presaging sky, insolence must be far from my mind, Miss Fleming. Your statement, however, signifies that you are now free. Then doubtless Mr. Copping was shown in his vision how marriage to you would be . . . a great unrighteousness. . . ."

Moments passed before Ingrid answered him.

"Yes. . . . He thought we ought not to marry."

"Therefore you are dedicate."

As Peter had done, Ingrid turned to gaze over the low south country. It lay there extended, a steadily darkening dusk of insignificance and the picture of death, so shifted was all the presentness of the scene to the giant castles and cities and seas above. Those vast, torn, rounded, crowded clouds were less masses than depths: down through their chasms were other clouds, other chasms—and others again . . . until she wondered what that journey could be like. On fire were some of the surfaces. Surely the sky was obeying a powerful word. Its great transformations, gradual but perpetual, were no driving of a wind, but should be the slow convulsive movements of some held mythological prodigy, as broad as the heavens, towards its doom of metamorphosis. Night now approached fast. . . .

She replied to Arsinal:

"I am leaving it all to you: I wish only to look on. If anyone is dedicate, it will appear afterwards."

"Has no instinct spoken within you?"

"I think that what you have in mind to say will be better left unsaid."

Coming to him from the sky, she saw him as if he stood there against her a dark ghost, and his voice was correspondingly low and unreal.

"It concerns the manipulation."

"I will give you my stone, and you shall do with it what you will."

The wind stirred at last in a long sharp gust that came straight from the sea. Facing now the west, Ingrid became filled with unimaginable fancies on account of what her eyes beheld— fancies grown together in a single riddle of emotion, that was as a music to her deeper agitation. The immense cloud shapes had welled up from within, until they were filling nearly all this quarter of the heavens, only a blue abyss or so remaining to be hidden; while every sunset glory of but a few minutes ago was replaced by an inkiness as uniform and without comprehensible cause as the coming of misfortune. So low were the lowest clouds that the earth's surface appeared a mere horizontal crack for breathing. The dusk was as if all this underworld were sinking, like a stone through infinite fathoms of water, to the mystery and blackness of ultimate repose. Only in the vertical line of the sun's descent a lozenge of darkest, quietest crimson hung over the horizon, as it had been a goblin window. . . .

She said further to Arsinal:

"So it must be. But if, in spite of all, you imagine you retain any vestige of control, then I am afraid the misconception is a bad sign for you."

"Are you prophesying?"

"I do not think that pride will gain a prize. I think it may be punished."

He faced her, pale but perfectly calm.

"Have you the gift of psychic foresight?"

"I seem to have it sometimes . . . and before Hugh Drapier died, I thought of death for him."

"Am I to die?"

"I cannot say that."

"You may be raised to the knowledge, since no doubt we are all in states of abnormal excitation. . . . But so I shall have been used indeed! Painfully, through long years, to work my way to the very threshold, only there to be stopped like an alien and interloper! . . ."

"It is this temper in you. Surely here is no work for the impression of personalities."

"My spirit is not craven," said Arsinal, "but you, I have seen, are selfless—an aim to you could mean nothing. . . ."

He stayed silent for a moment, then added:

"Yet so it may be, and we are in the blackness of night. A few more minutes will decide. In case, then, I perish, while you live on . . . to you I bequeath my earnest and unsparing conduct of this great mystery . . . but to you, Saltfleet, the two records at Knossos and Aphrodisias, for what they may be worth to you."

"In life or in death you will have your way!" Saltfleet's impatience of word and movement was his anger's repression. "Nevertheless the longer we stand here in idle gossip, certainly the more it will degenerate to futility. Also it is getting rapidly darker, and, whoever is to pay a toll, the others or other must find the way home across a blind moor."

"So give me your stone, and I will join them myself," said Arsinal to Ingrid. He reached out his hand.

While her fingers were yet on her flint, however, came the amazing intervention. . . . Arsinal, having his left hand outstretched and his right in the act of procuring his own stone, was all at once visibly encompassed as to his whole form by a mistily-glowing blue nebula, that seemed an emanation from his body, causing him to appear as if burning with a strange astral fire. And at the same instant Ingrid was glorified by an equal radiance: but her fire, or mist, was whitest silver. Their two shapes, but a pace apart, were like those of celestials about to meet and merge. . . .

Swiftly Saltfleet stepped between them, to snatch from the girl's delicate fingers the thing they so lightly retained and with the force of a blow plant it inside Arsinal's free hand, that closed upon it instinctively. The twin splendours vanished. All the happening had not lasted seconds. . . .

Then Saltfleet drew Ingrid away.

Arsinal stumbled forward towards the tomb-entrance and the edge above the valley. He was gazing at the dim erectness and marvellous stature of Her . . . as yet She shone so faintly. In either hand he held a stone, knowing that they were to be joined.

Undirected his fingers fitted them, for his eyes were always on this Shape before him. The junctures fell at last together, yet no immediate change had come. . . .

Thus She was his boyhood's vision by night—since yesterday he had been aware that such was the identity. But in that phantom torrent scene She had been so distant. . . . His lips and heart prayed that a larger clearness might reward him. . . . This loveliness and awful calm, this deepest peace, so like a will-less eternity, that She both was, and was bringing. . . .

For now there could be no following work for him to essay: not again would it be needful for him to attempt the recovery of this majesty for the mean sake of a scoffing world. His frail existence on earth was no more to be prolonged. Its enthusiasm was risen to its last high flaring: then it and he must equally expire. Such death was not fear—not death. . . .

What proceeded interiorly was like the slow and dreadful emergence from concreted earth of a rare marble statue, long buried. He was being alarmed lest it should fail to come out perfectly. . . . It was *himself*, stripped of all the foul disfigurements of experienced life. Surely Her apparition was obstetric, and She was here to ensure him easy passage, by purification at the last. . . . He thought She saw him. . . .

"*Here is death, then!*"—he knew not if the words had been the hollow echo in some unknown empty gallery of his being—the echo of a comprehension too remote to be directly audible . . . or if She had said them. . . . He understood, however, that no blow of suddenness was meant, no sharp dividing line: but a movement slow—slow . . . in two modes: the gradual slipping away downwards from the life of will, and this other endless emergence. . . .

His folly clung on, endeavouring to know again some of the innumerable incidents and persons of his finishing phenomenal existence. He recalled Drapier, forgetting that he was passed before him: and found it singular that he should so inexplicably be absent from all these late scenes . . . but the scenes themselves he could not remember. . . .

And during minutes longer of earth-time his two movements continued uncompleted, joined for him in the mortal likeness and high gleaming, and in that heaven coming through Her eyes, of the One before him, that already was become as the Sea of all his baring soul.

Soon, however, his sensations belonged no more to the world: so cannot be recounted in a book of the world.

XXXIII

The Far Glimpse

Staring bewildered after Arsinal's diminishing shape through the gloom, the others saw how his hands were together before his body, no doubt for the purpose of fitting those counterparts. Then his right hand dropped to his side, and seemed to be shut over a dazzling blue light. The blue was shining through the cracks between the fingers: less brightly, it was gleaming through the substance of the hand itself.

It changed to silver, and almost simultaneously appeared to

burst within the hand, a flying hail of sparks, that were luminous white particles, escaping through the air towards all the cardinal points. They never went out, but became bigger, and, universally travelling upwards, at last were turned to fixed stars . . . in a sky that was pure night, and cloudless. . . .

Those stars grew to be magnificent gems, till the whole heaven before them was filled with great stabbing diamonds, rubies, emeralds, amethysts and sapphires, that were so much larger and fiercer than the stars of the common sky that they seemed as if alive. . . . And next, there *were* clouds again—huge separated masses, moving monstrously in endless procession across that lower vault of vision, alternately burying and restoring each field in turn of blazing orbs. . . . Thus they upgazing were in another world. Arsinal had disappeared.

Long afterwards they compared these outward happenings, and learned that they had been identical for each. During all their life together they had many such fearful talks. . . .

Now nothing of earth was visible except the lesser blackness of their immediate environment and the mind-supplemented perception of each other's shadowy column. So a strange comradeship sprang up between them, though no words were to pass and neither had the thought of seeking contact. The spoken symbols of another order were inadequate for this experience, as their bodies could express nothing of their personal nearness.

Saltfleet believed that he could make out—yes!—that the air's pure silence, as of a still and frosty midnight, was being very faintly troubled by some pulsation which was not from his blood. Heavier clouds came up, to blot out all the stars, and each watcher from the other, wrapping them in a solid blindness. Then, that pulsation remaining everything of their sensuous existence (for Ingrid caught it too), it promised to become music. The music should be from the buried stars. . . . The mighty cloud-drift was muting it, yet it grew distincter: so either they must be drawing nearer to the stars, or the stars were themselves descending. . . . Soon the rhythm and whole tone of the music, the direction of its sounding, dictated to their ears, which but a minute since with the utmost straining had failed to distinguish them. The harmony advanced from the entire sky ahead. It was like the ordered emotion of a far-distant orchestra numbering, not hundreds, and not thousands, but millions, it seemed, of instruments . . . that played otherwise than in groups, since each instrument, with its voice of unique *timbre*, should be proclaiming its own peculiar message. Thus the overruling thought was, as an organism, alive in all its parts.

But when the sounds grew—hardly louder any more, but clearer, vivider in definition—then they also became essentially mystical, because archetypal. They presented the music of humanity, without its associated mechanical noises. The forcing of air through narrow orifices, the scraping of resonant objects one against another, the striking of stretched elastic membranes, the vibrating of metals—all such impurities were absent—their familiar musical effect that was a second nature of the ear, it too was absent—from this music: and the remaining purity was hard to know. It was what a passion of the heart might be before the sympathetic arousing of the seconding will. Not even were the great sounds of the natural world brought to mind. . . . To Ingrid, each separate instrumental voice suggested the dropping of a new soul into existence from an ineffable ghostly Womb. . . .

And the theme bearing along these tones upon its back—its progress was not in *time*, but in some other incomprehensible mode of change from state to state. Its line of advancing was not between a full past and an empty future, carrying them listening upon its constant front: but they were carried by it—feeling, more than listening—towards another kind of future, already full, though this music was helping to fill it. Therefore the perpetual filling should be of intensity, not substance.

These individual tones—to Ingrid, like the dropping of souls—instead of running one upon the heels of another and vanishing at the moment of their sounding, were somehow joining themselves to and increasing the next tones following . . . wherefrom there was no light heartless stepping from corpse to corpse of sound until the last corpse should be reached and straightway forgotten, and all should be forgotten, as in the music of the world: but always there arrived, never again to depart, this grander and grander intensity of emotion, compounded of all the past. . . . Indeed, too little analogy there was between the dim stupendous astral communication and that other dull and simple music of humanity. . . .

But Ingrid conceived that if the tones were souls, and they were being born into life, then neither could they be so born for themselves, nor yet for the purpose of the creation of another world—another senseless work of art, expressive merely of a pre-existent reality: but perhaps they should be born for the ennoblement by sorrow of that great spectral Womb out of which, one by one, they marvellously issued. . . . So both end and beginning of this theme-progress must be in that Mother . . . for Whom, certainly, time could have no meaning. . . .

To Saltfleet, however, it occurred that he might be dead already. He found these experiences not to consort very well with what he had hitherto known of life. . . .

When, immediately, the most confounding leap of all for his senses began, and this very soul of music promised to forsake ear for eye, so destructive of the fabric of his human notions was the violence that, whether he were in death or only in its foretaste and resemblance, no longer might he suppose his state one for the exercise even of fundamental judgments. Reposings, or their quick series, were for the eye, actions were for the ear; from the gases and fluids of the atmosphere no living entity could be constructed: these things he knew, or had thought to know. But now the hereditary structure of his mind was declared by a new and last fact to be on wrong principles, and everything was to tumble about him. . . . For, from having beheld the translation of those bright sparks of the joined flints into stars of the sky, and then imaginably heard the same stars give forth a metaphysical music, now he was still to be marched along the road of impossibility by the return to vision . . . yet how different a category of vision from that elementary spectacle of stars! . . .

Nevertheless, because she was a woman, Ingrid was the more

greatly overcome. For her mental ways remaining always womanly, she was less than Saltfleet astounded by this latest eccentricity of heavenly changing for them both, yet in her depths could
be moved by the underlying spiritual significance to a degree and
in a manner that he might not share. Hardly of herself, little of the
world's women, was she reminded; only it was as if never before
in all her days had she stood even outside the door of such a new
conception of womanhood as now was distressing her spirit from
that mystic ambiguity in the sky. . . .

All the great continent of cloud had rolled by; the stars, that
should have been behind, were gone as well. The music was
receding. It was withdrawing into the galactic phosphorescence
occupying the heaven before them: and during the process was
losing its clarity that was instead of volume. The new conforma-
tion was as much more wonderful than the dying harmonies, as
they at their height had been than the blazing spheres that had
given them birth. A true passage it was. While the music departed,
so its diminution fed that increasing awful glow. . . .

Perhaps they swept not its length with their uneasy eyes at all,
perhaps neither had their ears ever heard—still were hearing—
right sounds; but a sensitiveness in their two souls sought an
organ, and found it not. Just as the vanishing had seemed more
and other than music to them, *this* appeared unlike shape—unlike
even light. It filled not all the sky, or must have been figureless;
its light was measured, or they must have dropped their gaze: yet
the black of the sky was but the negation of this strange holding
shine, that stopped not at pupil and retina, but went in and in. . . .

The music quite ceased, when there ensued a stillness as of a
world of graves. Far from conveying the cessation of life, it
brought the assurance of the presence of life undissipated by acts
of will and death.

Indeed, they saw Her not . . . but knew that She was there, as
if high before them; and lived. . . .

But it was revealed to Ingrid that without the dark solidity of
earth, so fearful a seeming adumbration could not have been . . .

that She behind it was born of this created world, as a mother is born of her child. It was her swift new insight, that was confusing all her nature.

Before the child, no mother: before the mother, no woman. For only by virtue of motherhood were women essentially other than men. Accordingly, not till the world, or the first of the worlds, was made, had its Maker likewise become made, as Mother. . . .

And Ingrid's soul, ever gazing up from its dungeon of night towards what should be a lowest rung of the ladder of heaven, went on to apply that the love of father for child, of youth for maiden, of wife for husband, of friend for friend, of saint for wretch, was of the richness of life indeed: but that the love of a mother for that isolated existence which had struggled within her was *mystical* . . . that its mystery lay in this—that she who knew such love was now of the very substance and essence of the All-Mother. . . .

There was a trinity: anguish, sacrifice, love. The ancient Ghost, living alone before the creation of the worlds, could not have possessed it; but with the coming into being of the first world, of necessity the Mother too had come into being: and that trinity was Her nature. And it had been, though incomprehensibly, better than the old nature of the solitary Ghost. . . .

Meanwhile Saltfleet, quelled as never yet in his life he had been by this strangeness seeming to possess the sky, still persevered in boldness, if not to seize it with his understanding, at least to find a means of living with it during the time he must. He knew that his sight presumed insolently. This that he saw as he had never seen other things, was neither as he saw it, nor so much as towards its true being: but rather was as an uncouth sign standing to his grossness for something else. Yet he felt too that he was surely in the presence of the same extraordinary sluice of invisible new life which lately—he knew not days, or hours—had chosen the abbreviated human mortal form for its disguise.

He remembered it had increased him: therefore this token should be auspicious. . . . Nevertheless, for increase to come as from a supernatural female ministry, certainly there must be a common bond between sex and sex, deriving from a date earlier than both, whether the date were terrestrial or celestial—earlier than the branching of the sexes. For supposing *spirit* itself to have been the undivided root, then in males it had just as much hardened, as in females softened. Perhaps, original *spirit* was without defences, as scorning to defend itself. The later male hardness represented that tough armour against fate that had been slowly forged through the ages. . . . Feeling this, he also scorned his manhood, that stood for defence. . . .

Such a bond between the sexes . . . he conceived that the primal Sublime, dwelling alone—before the issuing forth of Time, Space, worlds, angels, infernals, men and women—could still to this hour be so dwelling—still alone . . . while a female Demiurge, being detached from that Sublime to serve as fount and living principle of all creation, should present the archetype of animal maternity. . . . Whereby were explainable the two great instincts of mankind, that forever had been and must be at variance: on the one hand, the automatic gregarious life of the herd, speaking eloquently of kinship in a common Mother; on the other, the sporadic appearance among men of such stern recluses and austere visionaries as had ever been dubbed mad by the cheerful mob; *they* should be from that Ancient, dwelling alone. . . .

Yet no man could reach that Ancient except through the Demiurge, since She it was who created both bodies and souls: apart from Her, even souls had no existence. Accordingly, through and by Her was conceded the possibility of attaining to the Ancient. And because it was the highest of Her states, from the beginning She had willed this attainment. For this one purpose—namely, to carry created souls past and out of creation, as far as to the very throne of the Ancient—must the infinite flaming suns, and tortured worlds, and savage, horrible evil wills of the universes have been conceived within Her awful matrix. . . .

And with the continued stultifying of his indomitable eyes by that vast interception of the sky that not even named itself, Salt-fleet was inly conscious of the last disappearance of a conviction of all his intelligent years, the roots of which, interwoven in his brain with a thousand alien beliefs and habits, had grown even inconspicuous. The conviction was that the world's creation was from a God, not male indeed, but more properly to be associated with the male pronoun. Suddenly this was seeming as unreal to him as the flatness of the earth's surface, or the movement of the sun round the planet, or the impendence of hell-fire for sinners.

All the great elements of the world—the universal and all-powerful incentive of love, the enormous fact and cult of beauty, the endless production of children to supply the wastage by death, the seasonal mating of free animals and annual rebirth of vegetation, the orbits of planets and comets, the doubtless curved paths of the stars, the tides not only of the sea, the purely instinctive existences of all creatures save the moral among humans, and even of them . . . everything of this was so peculiarly of the female stamp—emotional, blind, repetitive—that it was as if he found himself in a house whose every room contained women's clothes, needlework, flowers, stuffs, silken draperies, fragile furniture, infants' toys and garments; and were asked and required to consent that the residence had been equipped for his own use by a man. . . .

But the indubitable male side—the wars, political cruelties and bloody hubbubs, the trade helotisings and plottings for self, self, and again self, the private lusts, appetites, buffooneries, vulgarities . . . evidently no character of any Creator, unless a Devil, could be represented by these: but if they were more than the accidental necessary incrustation of the metal in the melting-pot, then perhaps their function should be the secondary one of disgusting souls with life, in conjunction with the principal fundamental evils of disease, insecurity, need, bereavement, frustration of instincts, and death; thus serving to bring them before that remote throne of the Ancient.

Because a man was rootless, he was first free-moving, then competitive, then hard, merciless, and military: while because a woman was rooted in the Demiurge, she was first sedentary, then attractive, then soft, pacific, and compassionate. But though such a divergence of destinies was to render women practically the inferior creature, men were still for women, not women for men. The roots of women were for a purpose. The sedentariness was to procure ease for child-production. The production was in order that of the souls produced, some might return soon, some late, to the Ancient. . . . It was a mighty mystery. . . .

Well had the Prophet said that the created universe was no joke. Its Conceiver had not disunited from the Ancient by joke, or by accident. The Weaver into the world of the passions and emotions, the instincts of creatures and the ascending instinct of all life—that Weaver had woven from the knowledge.

And very positive it was that this frightful pain-journey, for one planet alone, from floating specks of colloid jelly to the visited and crucified ones, with all its infinity of slaughter, dispossession, insult, degradation, enforcement, denial, physical and mental torture of a terrific range, could not be fiend-invented. The savagery was too thorough not to have meaning. It was from the Ancient, dwelling alone before the Demiurge.

The soul could be no such simple, spotless entity, able to be kept clean and ripe for heaven by a few years of blameless living, as the holy innocents of all ages had presumed: but it must be a terrible piece of wrought work, needing for the fusing and refusing of its constituents the totality of these piled-up agonies. Of no other stuff than the Ancient were the worlds made. That Ancient was both torturer and tortured. Then how could there not be an original Necessity, more crushing than the combined weight of all the rushing spheres of all the universes? . . .

And this representation to himself of the whole of created existence as a sub-infinite groaning mountain-press for the formation of a grandeur obtainable no other way, made so profound an imprint upon Saltfleet's soul that never afterwards in his life could he quietly contemplate at leisure the chance actions of persons, creatures, or things without at the same time being reminded of what actually (in no sense metaphorically) they stood for. Whether it were the slow, glassy breaking of the ocean on a western shore, or the uneasy faces and shuffling steps of a city throng, or the rending of some still-alive bird or smaller beast by a cat having the face of Satan, or the focused glittering of light from polished forks and spoons against white napery, or the clanking of shunted railway trucks distantly heard in bed at dead of night, or the blue smoke rising straight as a spear from the chimney of a Norse wooden house perched on its pine-clothed mountain flank—always now he recognised that the identical invisible operation proceeded in each, to the identical end . . . to the formation by torture of *grandeur* . . . that to the Ancient at last might come that grandeur. . . .

He thought no more of being dead. The unseen woman beside him he had forgotten: his own mortal body he had as nearly forgotten as its chains permitted him, while seeming to inhabit it, in conscious meditation of all these things.

Yet perhaps, unguessed by him, Ingrid had suddenly moved. He turned about, to face sharply the opposite half of night.

Sky and earth were joined in an impenetrable blackness unrelieved. No longer above his eyes was the Emblem that they, as the last and most ambitious of his senses, had attempted. Now for him it would have been like blindness, but for a single queer hint of light ahead, a little lower than his level; that did not yet, but might, foretoken a slit in the night. . . . It grew more marked, but he could know neither what it was, nor whether near or distant. . . .

When, however, the long, horizontal cleft became ever more vivid, as it were blood welling within a latitudinal wound, then it would have begun to speak of daybreak behind serrated mountains incredibly far off; were it not that its colour was blue.

He was perplexed by this perpetual blue—the blue of the falling meteor, the blue of the joined flints in Arsinal's hand—yet could not be recalling those other cases . . . he understood not why he was perplexed. And so he made it metaphysical. It might be that blue should symbolise the earliest beginning of an advent. It was the hue of sacredness, freshness, mystery: it was compound of night and day; but night not yet dislodged, day still a land away. . . . Thus the world, with its red dawns, was false. . . .

Almost it was an impossible blue—a blue including phantom elements. He did not imagine but was passive to the impression of a far-distant spectral city, concealed from his emotion by mountain parapets, whose upper indentations alone were distinguishable. Between himself and that city lay an emptiness immeasurable by miles or millions of miles. . . .

The spectacle was only quickening his thoughts. He saw, as by playing lightning, that if all—the worlds and souls and agonies— were from the Ancient, then the very thoughts of man must be so also. Beggar, thief, clown, prostitute, in thinking at all, were thinking the living thoughts of the Ancient. . . . It was of the whole crucifixion, and mattered not. . . .

But likewise, the loves of the world—they could be but the *self-love* of the Ancient. . . . Wherein the incomparable majesty of the Ancient was declared. For the self-love of persons presented the basest of the world's states: this other self-love of the Ancient was that towards which the deepest and most sacrificing love in creatures dimly reached. Towards it the extraordinary mystic love in creatures for their unseen Maker likewise reached. . . .

Accordingly, the Christs had not passed through the worlds to effect peace and holiness among creatures, but had suddenly descended as apparitions without regard to history. For the initiated, such apparitions should be no other than the swift irresistible impulses of that self-love of the Ancient. They preached not reconciliation. After their vanishing, sprang up always hatred, wars, massacres, the stake, the rack, the scourge. . . .

He felt reborn.

Through to his generative force it went. The stamp of these awful truths possessed the quiet violence to pass outwards— inwards—he knew not how . . . right through his soul as far as his living physical reliquary, whose magic should raise the future. Those of his blood coming after him must no less partake of the penetration. . . .

But Ingrid, confronting the same strange vision of blue distant dawning, was as little as he diverted thereby from her fearful ponderings. Only by its agitating incomprehensibility were given a new branching, a lonelier depth, to her so dreaming soul.

Truly a mother was born of her child: and yet, in the world, the mystic love was too scarce. Native selfishness in the mother, a temperamental dislike of her child, or of all children . . . or a warm love made nothing for want of spiritual sympathy—a triviality of character depriving the love itself . . . or too many children—other passions—other needs and preoccupations . . . few indeed must be the mystical mothers. Of those women possessing the capacity, some might not marry; some might marry unwisely or unluckily. The children of these should not be rightly theirs: the love must lack something of the mystery.

So it might even be, that mystic mother-love was but the loveliest ideal, hardly to be attained ever. . . . Yes! so that each chronicled instance of the achievement had flamed forth like a beacon on earth. For to be the noble mother of heroes was not enough. There the mother had not needed to be born of her first-born: of full stature had she been before his coming. In order that a mother should be born of her child, must be the preliminary dissolution of her soul by its pre-natal pangs . . . darkness, chaos, sightless passion, the joy and anguish of dreadful presentiment: a black world of stirrings and longings. . . . So had Mary been born of Christ. . . .

Therefore, just as the fewest women possessed flawless beauty, though all women in their persons contained some hint of beauty, so perhaps all mothers might know the distant instinct towards mystical motherhood although but a single one in a planet's history should experience it in its human fullness. . . .

Yet being set against the embattled sweet affections of womankind that were the everlasting theme of song and story—the expected and honoured tendernesses of those in whom they were meet, as well as the other darker passions of the law-breaking—how wonderful in its selfless endurance seemed that journeying through the night of storm and pain, for no raptures, no thoughts of a haven at last. Should not it be the perfect justification to a woman of her womanhood? For indeed it was the sacrifice that every woman in her profoundest heart must be desiring. . . .

Verily, to be born like Mary of her child, a woman must make heavy sacrifices. The wild ascent to the stars before marriage, the dreamlike wandering hand-in-hand down an eternal forest path afterwards, towards hope, ever hope!—these must be renounced: and still, most fearful of all, she must marry. . . . And, against every light instinct of a girl, she must always have shunned the world, while remaining of it. She must have refused homage to her own body's beauty, though addressed to it by an unending stream of temptation. So must she have exposed herself to the scorn and amusement of other women, and to the wonder and defamation of men. . . . And must have hated dark damp churches, with their hypocritical priests . . . and have kept herself innocent from the arts, given over to worldliness: and not stupefied her spirit with much reading: and not destroyed it with sports and laughter. . . . She must have dwelt among the grand grey shapes and shades of the immemorial past. Her familiars must have been the mists, rains, winds, the secret moors or mountains: while always in her soul must have been that singular sense of something presently to befall her that should be like nothing that ever yet had happened to any. . . .

So Ingrid described herself, knowing that such a nature was impossible to be acquired, but either was or was not to a woman. And yet too certainly she was shutting her eyes to her dross. For no girl could grow to be a woman without having made a million surrenders—of dress, of agreeableness, of enjoyment; even of flattery. Small was the need to enumerate: had not she descended to common *love*? . . .

This far blue mountain daybreak perpetually before her eyes— it was like a liquid conflagration. But its wisdom was so slow, it was as if her ignorant mind were between, yielding elastically, but never bursting. . . . Oh, that her life might be one long wound!— passion! passion! . . . How frightful seemed to her suddenly the old craving to live at peace within her instincts! . . .

But if in shocking truth that passion could be for her, by what marks—by what signs . . . ? For *he*—that necessary man, who should present himself in the spirit of these unearthly moments . . . he must not stand out from others, there must be no attraction—not that treacherous deceitful downhill path to a fascination of sex. . . . Rather should they hate. For her he must be *nothing*: a man unmarked, unsignalised—indistinguishable. . . . Then should he bear a supernatural token. . . .

As from her sight, so from her mind were those two gone whom Peter had left behind with her upon this hill-top. Only at midnight, in her room at home, came to her that it had been intended she should thereafter through her life know the certainty that her choice had not been influenced. Had she recalled who should be standing beside her, doubtless for many years her doubts must have remained of the deathliest. . . .

But what should be his motive—his reward . . . that one who from her should receive nothing? Never might they grow familiar: not his were to be the awful raptures of that mystic bringing forth. Perhaps from the Ancient he would receive a gift of passion. . . .

Indeed, before that fearful Mother of all creation, had still been the Ancient. . . . Therefore of two passions must such a child be born: as other children, of two lusts. But here could be no sensuality, for their bodies, even in being used, were to be forgotten. . . . By his eyes she would know him, and they would be the sign. No adoration in them of her would there be; but the presence of an agony. . . . And the child should be from their two agonies, and not from themselves: not towards their joy. . . .

Yet he would be the nobler, for that he would be servant of a servant, and know no rank even in surrender. So must she revere him. For the like humility must Mary also have reverenced Joseph, though none other did. On account of his anguish in the Eternal, bringing him no mortal blessedness, must Mary have willed to join herself to him, understanding that from him alone could the Christ within her come.

Why went she so much back to Mary?

She felt not Mary's kindness for her fellow-creatures. She was not quick to see good. Sometimes she fancied that souls had long since died in the world: that loving-kindness was but an instinct of association, heroism the same, and nobility a fastidiousness of the educated mind. But all such deceits were real to those practising them and to the others admiring them—until the terrible temporary world of mud, blood and bubbles was become for everyone a palace of infinite glittering possibility, outside which was—nothing. And Mary, to have borne Christ, must have believed the corruption of hearts curable: but she herself no longer believed that.

She least of all women was like Mary. Yet always now was it seeming to her that Mary might best have counselled her in this dreadful time. For not only Christ had been crucified, but Mary too. The faith, the character, were little things. . . .

There was no need that she should be Mary. The teachings of her Son remained, and could not die, until nobler should be taught. But His teachings alone had not been enough. At His coming, the old peoples were dead: a new sweetness, a new cleanness, were preparing in the North, whose innocent giants of the snows and forests were to move southwards with their wholesome souls, high hearts, manhood, simplicity, and veneration of the invisible. Then, in a little while, had they found in Christ's words the lessons He had put there against their coming. . . . But now that race too was degenerate and irreligious. Another Christ could not raise a dead world from its tomb. He who should raise another race to receive the first Christ would be of more worth than a second Christ. . . .

Terrible was this prayer of her heart: that another race, possessing souls anew, should suddenly come! . . . For thus once more, in the name of the Ancient, destruction must float over the face of the earth, to wither all the happiness of decadence to its very roots, and fill the world with groans and curses, and the white-faced spectres of men and women, and sudden death.

She that should be permitted to offer her single self to the sacrifice truly would need to resemble the infinite Mother of all; Who likewise had been permitted, by the Ancient. But in Herself the Mother was nothing: only a living Pity for those born to terror within Her Womb. Not even was She Her own Pity; but She was the Pity of the Ancient on account of that forced into foulness and mortality, for a Purpose. . . . So she, a mortal woman, to whom it should fearfully be given to bear another annihilating race, she also must be nothing but a living sorrow for all the agonies born and to be born of her. For more than the men of a race must her womb contain. She must be mother, too, of horrors and madnesses, men shattered, women demented, children starved and orphaned, the skies never silent for the ascending sounds of the undone. . . . Her responsibility could be no less.

Unless her sorrow were so living that her heart also could be broken for the breaking of all those other hearts in their pain sprung directly out of her single existence on earth, how could she endure to be the instrument of the Ancient, though her intelligence should grope towards the shadow of a Design? How could she endure it for the mere human triumph of one race of men alone? Those others outside such a race—the dispossessed, the unworshipping; the merely suffering—they also were in creation. The torture of one soul in the Ancient, the emergence of another soul to the Ancient, they were a single operation. . . . Unless that mortal mother of nobler souls should shudder perpetually in heart for her deed to those destroyed ignobler ones—should weep always, and become as phantom as they . . . she was not of the infinite Mother. . . . It were better she had never been born. . . .

Upon the inky castellation defining that blue glare which crowned it, stepped a silver form . . . of a woman, draped. For a time she stood there like an unmoving flame.

She seemed as distant as a fainter star, so marvellously small she was to see: yet Ingrid was given to distinguish her clearly. It was the *spirit* who sometimes had been so close to her. Now she was as if across a sky of space.

Then she went out, also like a flame: but at once the weirdest sequence began instead. Saltfleet too saw it, and was confounded. No advancing source of light was ever visible; yet, from where the silver form had stood, a passage came towards them of successive blue-silvery glows, showing but at intervals; and as they did so—as the glows approached—they were bringing into fleeting view wonderful features of the intervening different regions of space . . . the nature of which was incomprehensible: while the space they had thought empty.

Otherwise all to their eyes was night: for when the silver shape had vanished, the far blue fire had vanished also. These glows might be the shape; the fire was no more for them.

But the regions in succession shone upon seemed neither void like air, nor as a flat landscape, but to possess the boundlessness of air or space, while containing, as though they floated free, the hints of great natural masses which should surely have demanded the solid core of a mineral world for base. There were, moreover, the strangest other existences in the regions, that also were never revealed, but merely suggested, by the dim uncertain radiance. Nearly the tops of mountains—not quite lakes—monstrous, passive forms that might or might not be of life—rushings-together of things, and violent pullings-apart . . . it was like a mythological world, heavy with dark, fabulous shapes and allegories, and personifications of primal nature. . . .

Yet invariably the thing so merging and disappearing as in a thought, beneath that glowing which never itself was caused, seemed nearer than the last to the watchers: and still all distance was incalculable, for time contradicted space. The completed passage should be of the breadth of the eye's whole universe, but while the chain of gleams remained so leisurely, the latest already was close upon them.

Then Ingrid believed that she was seeing the lowest of the heavens. She thought that certain wise men in the ancient past might have seen it too, and been divinely inspired. . . . Saltfleet, however, considered that the fecund night before his eyes might be to the half-mystic ether of modern science what that ether should be to the gross matter of the senses. If out of ether matter was formed, out of these unutterable suggestions of things the inter-stellar universe of invisible substance, named ether, might be formed. For it was incredible that the rich variety of the world's teeming life should have arisen from the simple mechanical action of electric whirls. . . . Thus this night was like a second step inwards from the life-ground of the body, where it played, worked, and wondered; while still there was no beginning of a simple origin—no approach to an explanatory unity. Then should not variety, perhaps, be stamped through and through creation, to express the fearful essence of the Ancient? . . .

But soon the light caught them, and bathed them, lingering but whilst they might know and remember each the other.

Neither exclaimed: only Ingrid beheld in her companion's face, illuminated by this pale silver shining, what in it she had never remarked before, though always it had been there—its scorn, not of men, but of the littleness of men, which had presented but the unconsciousness of his own worship of the Height. . . . And she understood that this was the sign she had been to await— that this was *he*. . . . But Saltfleet perceived in the drawn pain of those young, moonlike features the stern unearthliness which his swollen soul might best approve; discovering in them no beauty.

Then was restored to him his unspeakable sensation of being pierced throughout his nature, as far as to his very seed, by the white-hot finger of the angel that was his nearest wisdom to the Ancient . . . Whose claiming of him was as an exultation in him, because freely and contemptuously he was to cast away his worn life, in the remembrance of that awful Purpose. Neither to any other end was *she* here, with him. A child—a man, that should be a spirit, was to enter life, without whose coming all the past agonies of the world must have stood suspended in memory, a dream. But, for as long as this pain and this sternness should ward her approaches, he knew that never could he feast his imagination upon her loveliness, that other unwanted ones should enter, instead of that one. . . .

Their eyes avoided the other's. It was not from fearfulness, nor to conceal their souls: it was that the love appropriate between man and woman was never to go between them; and so there was no need for them to seek each other's eyes. Indeed, neither saw the other's person, but only as that counterpart instrument of a will. Their pulses were not hastened because he should be a man, and she a woman.

Their lunar light further took from their humanity. In after life they, though none else, were to see each other thus in the rarest hours, when their moods were most raised above common existence. Ever was it to be the most terrible of reminders. . . .

But now too quickly the glow left them; and they were again in night.

The sky was full of natural stars. They felt that they had dropped suddenly to vulgarity. . . . Obeying Saltfleet's swift movement of turning, Ingrid beheld with him, high in the sprinkled blackness, a star that was brighter and more fairly gleaming than the others, of a strange blue . . . plainly falling, but very slowly. It grew in beauty, and she saw its path to be a curve. She never doubted but that the star was the same with the moving glow she had seen across that other universe: only, now that it could no longer make gifts, it became itself. Perhaps in this simpler world its power should be different, and more, or less: and it descended, because the plane had changed. . . . Or it lighted no shapes in passing, because in this dead material world all shapes had sunk to the bottom, and were piled, one upon another.

The star vanished suddenly. A body tore past their ears in the darkness. . . . Saltfleet thought to have recalled a previous happening that had once astonished him: but his passion on another account was deep, his objective mind confused and careless. Then there had been more sights and sounds, but now it was finished; silent. The girl with him, who had become a woman, comprehended that she had witnessed the entering into body of that ancient Mother. She would have knelt had not all her soul been stunned by its own transfiguration.

But when she could think again, she supposed that she had been shown the manner of occurrence of this event in order that never afterwards might she be at the mercy of those more intellectual than herself, who might try to persuade her of her imagined folly. And yet it could not matter, and she cared nothing . . . she wished not to understand things, but only to keep alive the pure pain and grief of her surrender, whether in ignorance or otherwise. Indeed, she wished to have done with all those hideous reminiscent prides and curiosities of the old Ingrid Fleming, that could but drag her back into personal life. To her terrible election she hoped to be permitted to join, as a condition, that the rest of her days should pass inconspicuous and humble; that she should be without the cleverness and genius and distinction of other women. . . .

The blackness gave place to a dusky grey, through which the familiar features of the top of Devil's Tor began to show vaguely.

They saw the dark upright shape of Arsinal, swaying, between themselves and that part of the hill nearest to the valley. And while they went on impotently looking, in distress for this first intrusion upon them of the coarsenesses that must now be awaited from the world, he still did not fall, but appeared rather to sink to the ground as from some progressive failure of his supporting frame. . . . He continued lying there, a shadowy shape of repose, his down-turned face hidden upon a bended arm.

Thereupon Saltfleet's old human instincts began to move again within him, and, scarcely realising what he did, he took those steps—not many—to the senseless man. It grew lighter still. . . .

The phantom personality, then, of that infinitesimal part of the Ancient which men had termed "Stephen Arsinal" was truly dispersed. The mystic red stream of his channels, upon which his false life had floated, was suddenly arrested as at the magnetic command of a word across the times and spaces; and that ghost was stripped of its unreal substance. . . .

He fancied that Ingrid had called out to him by his two names, but at a future time she averred she had not done so. However, believing that he was so summoned, he turned . . . and perceived that the Spirit of that other dead One stood, at enormous height, directly between himself and Ingrid, whom he imagined to have called to him for the purpose of his seeing. . . . Never had Her flesh been so bright . . . but Her eyes, somehow, he looked not for. . . .

She retreated, still facing him—back—back, to Ingrid behind Her . . . with whom, incomprehensibly, She became incorporated—so departing. . . . But Ingrid at the same moment beheld that moonlike Shape—so diminished—so human—recede from her direction towards Saltfleet . . . to become a cloud of silver glory before She reached him . . . and so envelop him, and vanish. . . .

Again the desolate hill-top was in departing day. Again those weird tremendous clouds filled the four skies, while in the west the elf-window lingered. The wind came up in great abrupt gusts, that were like threats of the evils preparing for them in the world below.

They drew slowly together, regarding each other. And each saw how the other's countenance gleamed . . . with such a gleaming that for long they dared not speak, yet might not let fall their eyes.

Saltfleet stirred at last, breaking the spell of stupor.

"We must go. We cannot stay here."

But she responded only by a movement that spoke nothing.

"You know he is dead?"

"Yes."

"The stones are gone."

Then Ingrid, after another moment, said:

"I will not see him. I wish my last remembrance of this place to be of life."

"That I understand."

"For unless this hill has been of life, I would pray to be mercifully dead myself."

"Let us not talk of this now," he answered.

There was a longer pause.

"The joined stone," said Ingrid, "—you mean it has been withdrawn altogether?"

"Doubtless it has repassed into its elements."

"Then that is the last sign."

Saltfleet glanced towards Arsinal's lifeless form.

"There will be another inquest, which will be thought queer. But stranger things must be for us two."

She replied:

"I will go to live in the far North. I cannot breathe here."

"I have no wife, and I am clean of women."

"That had to be. . . . Yet give thanks that you are to break no living heart. For me are two I dare not think of. . . ."

And she added:

"I beg you always to forget such small beauty as I may have. . . . And I beg you to propose no vows—no ceremonies. I could not enter the church of a foreign God on a false pretence. I could not ask the sanction of society."

"Your word shall rule in everything."

"You are to gain no honour of me."

"A man born out of wedlock may well scorn opinion."

"Who, then, was your mother?" asked Ingrid, viewing him steadfastly.

"Rightly you assume her dead. She was the best of mortal women: and not of this land."

"You will tell me of her afterwards."

Saltfleet went across to cover the face of the dead. Then they departed from the Tor together, gleaming still as to their faces, leaving Arsinal there to be the quiet witness of those happenings.

But when they had descended to the stream, and had passed it, there sounded from the top of the hill they had quitted a long and low, yet mighty, roll of thunder, which they knew to be the first of a storm that was to make their homeward journey terrible.

About David Lindsay

David Lindsay (1876–1945) is best known for his first novel, *A Voyage to Arcturus*. Published in 1920, it has been called "the greatest imaginative work of the twentieth century" (Colin Wilson), "a stupendous ontological fable" (E H Visiak), "a masterpiece... an extraordinary work" (Clive Barker), "that shattering, intolerable, and irresistible work" (C S Lewis), and "less a novel than it is private kabbalah" (Alan Moore). John Grant, in *The Encyclopedia of Fantasy*, called it "a masterpiece of allegorical fantasy".

Lindsay himself said that as long as publishing existed he would have readers, however few, and has been proved right. *A Voyage to Arcturus*, and his subsequent novels *The Haunted Woman* (1922), *Sphinx* (1923), *The Adventures of Monsieur de Mailly* (1926) and *Devil's Tor* (1932), have found a growing audience of devotees, enabling his unpublished novels (*The Violet Apple* and the unfinished *The Witch*) to be brought out in the 1970s. He has been translated into French, German, Spanish, Dutch, Bulgarian, Russian, Japanese, Catalan, Romanian, Turkish, Icelandic, Finnish and Greek.

www.ingramcontent.com/pod-product-compliance
Lightning Source LLC
Chambersburg PA
CBHW071956190726
48293CB00001B/45